ROSE of NANCEMELLIN

Also by Malcolm Macdonald:

THE WORLD FROM ROUGH STONES
THE RICH ARE WITH YOU ALWAYS
SONS OF FORTUNE
ABIGAIL
GOLDENEYE
THE DUKES
FOR THEY SHALL INHERIT
TESSA D'ARBLAY
ON A FAR WILD SHORE
THE SILVER HIGHWAYS
HONOUR AND OBEY
A NOTORIOUS WOMAN
HIS FATHER'S SON
AN INNOCENT WOMAN
A WOMAN ALONE
HELL HATH NO FURY
THE CAPTAIN'S WIVES
A WOMAN SCORNED
A WOMAN POSSESSED
ALL DESIRES KNOWN
TO THE END OF HER DAYS
DANCING ON SNOWFLAKES
FOR I HAVE SINNED
KERNOW & DAUGHTER
THE TREVARTON INHERITANCE
TOMORROW'S TIDE
THE CARRINGTONS OF HELSTON
LIKE A DIAMOND
TAMSIN HARTE

Rose of Nancemellin

MALCOLM MACDONALD

St. Martin's Press New York

for
Craig Tenney
my Rock of Manhattan

For information, address St. Martin's Press, 175 Fifth Avenue, New York, N.Y. 10010.

www.stmartins.com

ISBN 0-312-27301-0

First U.S. Edition:April 2001

10 9 8 7 6 5 4 3 2 1

Part One

Stranger on the shore

1 Rose gave Fenella's hair a final pat and said, "There!" She picked up the small hand-mirror and held it behind her mistress's head. Fenella, who had watched the maid's every move in the large, dressing-table mirror, turned her head to the left and surveyed herself with dissatisfaction. The view did not improve when she turned to the right, either. "Hold the glass properly, you stupid girl!" she snapped. The fact that Rose was twenty-three, five years her senior, and that she, Fenella, had not been looking into the hand-mirror in any case, was neither here nor there. She had asked for her hair to be plaited and coiled in this way; the result was hateful; so she had to vent her annoyance on someone.

Pity it was Rose, though. One might as well shout insults at a wooden post. You could call her any name under the sun and she'd never react. And if you asked her an insulting question – like, 'What on earth induced you to mess my hair up like this?' – she'd always have some smart answer – like, 'I believe it is what you asked for, miss?' Which, of course, was true, so Fenella knew better than to give her the chance.

"Shall I redo it, miss?" Rose asked. "Put it back to the usual?"

"There isn't time now," Fenella said. "Anyway, that's why I wanted a change. The 'usual' is just horrid. The real trouble is you've got no imagination." After a pause she added, "You might venture an opinion, you know. You could at least tell me it's not so bad, really."

"Well, miss," Rose began, "the last time I ventured an opinion, I seem to remember that you ..."

"Yes-yes! But that was last time and this is now. Good heavens! One passes some trivial little comment and you immediately elevate it into ... I don't know – an Eleventh Commandment or something."

The real trouble is, Rose thought, *you are not one of nature's beauties and no amount of messing about with your hair is going to make the slightest difference. So, if you can't acquire – or even frame – a beautiful face, you could aim for a beautiful temperament, instead, ha ha.* "Many have admired the 'usual' arrangement, miss," she ventured. "However, there is one other possibility."

"What?" The girl was suddenly eager, her annoyance seemingly all forgotten.

Rose began to unplait the bun on Fenella's right side.

"What?" she asked again.

"I'll show you directly," Rose told her.

She combed the girl's hair into a long hank, brushed it, rolled it upward around the handle of the brush, and pinned the inner side of the roll above the girl's ear with a long, thin, tortoiseshell grip; the effect was as if a wave of hair were breaking upwards around the side of her head.

"Très soigné, hein?" Rose commented.

Fenella gave a little scream of delight. "Oh, Rose!" she exclaimed. "You absolute angel! You are quite utterly brilliant – as I'm sure I've told you many times. Go on! Do it all like that! I'll get out more grips for you."

Rose worked in silence – a small, personal oasis of silence in the vast desert of her young mistress's prattle.

"It's such a shame that Mama won't agree to take you and Mary along with us I shall miss our little chats you know and I'm sure the servants we'll hire in Egypt and the Holy Land will be quite quite horrid. I'm not really looking forward to it or not most of the time except that I suppose it will be quite fun to see all those sepulchres and pyramids and things. And the Sphynx! You're supposed to ask it a riddle I think. You must put your thinking cap on, Rose, and come up with a good one for me. I wonder if it speaks French? And another thing I thought of is my scrap book with all the college crests and family arms of the nobility. I've got all the dukes except Portland, stingy old thing. You could send him another letter. Sign it as my private secretary, perhaps that'll impress him. And I've got all the marquises so we could start on the earls next. You could go through *Burke's* and make a list, don't bother about foreign counts and countesses although they rank with earls, and we could start as soon as we get back. Don't forget the addresses of the country seats *and* their London clubs. Did I say Papa has decided to go to Damascus after all? We can hire a dragoman down on the coast and go up in a caravanserai, such romantic names! In Aleppo or somewhere, and go up by camel. Real camels. The book says that some of the houses in Aleppo are so close together they don't have any streets between them, not even pathways, and people walk across the roofs instead. Oh, dear, dear Rose – I do so wish you were coming. Ouch! Careful with that pin you clumsy imbecile!"

The gong rang for dinner and for Rose's release.

Her name was not, in fact, Rose; it was Lucinda-Ella – her mother's choice. 'Very American!' people said, because Ella-Mae, her mother, *was* American, being the daughter of a Cornish miner, one of the thousands of 'Cousin Jacks' who had gone over to try their luck as a Forty-Niner. She grew up there, in Nevada and Connecticut, and only came back because the man she wanted to marry, William Tremayne, had decided to return to *his* ancestral town, Falmouth, and take over the family greengrocery. But Lady Carclew had decreed that Lucinda-Ella was not a suitable name for a servant, not even for a lady's maid, and not even if it were contracted to Lucille; so she had commanded Lucinda-Ella to adopt the name of Rose, instead. However, to be quite honest, Rose herself was not too unhappy about the enforced change; her school chums had, of course, nicknamed her Cinderella and then shortened it to Cinders. And the name had followed her into the wider world, which was enough to make any girl miserable. After a few years as Rose – as many as she could stomach here with the Carclews at Nancemellin House – Cinders would fade from memory and she could seek another position as Lucille, the name she preferred above all.

The release offered by the dinner gong was not, of course, a release from her daily work. It was only half-past six and a whole evening of needlework, ironing, goffering, and invisible mending lay ahead of her still. For tomorrow they would begin packing the eight trunks and four travelling wardrobes that Sir Hector and Lady Carclew, together with Fenella and Noel, their daughter and son, would be taking on their two-month excursion to Egypt and the Holy Land.

She made her way to the back stair and so down to the servants' hall for supper. It was the same meal as the one the family called dinner (except that the servants' cuts were from the scrag end of the joint); the servants ate their dinner at noon, although, again, it was identical to the meal the family called luncheon – allowing for the same preferential servings of the best bits. Lady Carclew feared that servants who ate luncheon at noon and dinner at six-thirty would soon get other ideas above their station.

On this particular evening the four Carclews were dining *en famille*. So they needed no more than three servants – Mitchell, the footman, and Rogers and McCormick, two of the parlourmaids – to tend their needs. There were twenty-three servants in all – fourteen in the house, five in the gardens, three in the stables, and Rodda, the odd-job-man. The gardeners and stable 'boys' did not eat in the house, so a mere nine were assembled for supper in the servants' hall when Rose joined them. They stood behind their chairs in strict order of precedence, waiting to say grace. Tregembo, the butler, was at the head of the table, facing his wife, the housekeeper, at the farther end. To his right stood Mrs Browning, the cook; to his left, Mary Hind, her ladyship's maid. And so on down through Penvose, Sir Hector's valet, Dunne, the third parlourmaid, Perkins, the assistant cook, Barley, the laundress, and Pennycuik, the scullerymaid. The tension in the air was higher than usual that evening for this was the moment when they were all to learn their fate at last. The speculation had raged among them in whispers for weeks – ever since the Carclews had decided to go on their expedition; they had let it be known that they wouldn't be retaining the entire staff for the two months of their absence, so now an unlucky half-dozen or so were to be 'let go.'

"For what we are about to receive, Lord, make us truly thankful," Tregembo said.

"Mmmnnn," came the tenfold response, its tail end being drowned in a scraping of chairs on the flagstone floor.

All turned their eyes to the butler, who remained standing and pretended to be surprised at their scrutiny. He picked up the carving knife and whetted its edge on the steel. He tested it several times before he was satisfied, then he looked all around and said, "This is not a monastery or nunnery, you know. Conversation of a decorous nature is permitted."

There was a dutiful ripple of laughter before they resumed their breathless vigil of his lips.

"Very well!" he sighed, speaking now as he carved. "Seven among us are to be kept – the rest turned off."

"Seven!" exclaimed more than one among them – those who considered themselves indispensable. The tone was jovial for the pessimists had expected no more than five.

"Those to stay are myself and Mrs Tregembo, naturally, Mrs Browning and Pennycuik ..."

The scullerymaid let out a little scream at this; as the lowest of the low she had quite expected to be the first to be turned off.

Tregembo silenced her with a frown and continued: "Miss Hind, you will be kept on, too. Also Miss Tremayne and Mitchell – whom no one will inform before I get the chance."

Rose winked at Mary Hind. They had both suspected they would be kept on, because good lady's maids were snowdrops in June nowadays; all the same, it was a relief to have it confirmed.

"What – not even one of the parlourmaids?" asked Dunne, their sole representative at this gathering.

"You may not be too unhappy, maid, when you hear the rest of the news," the butler replied. "Those who remain are to be on board wages!"

"No!" Rose and Mrs Browning cried in unison.

"I *beg* your pardon?" The butler drew himself up to his full five-foot-ten-and-seven-eighths.

"What's board wages?" Pennycuik asked.

"The run of your teeth and pocket money," the cook answered in disgust.

"That's so unfair," Rose said. "I say they should pay us our full wage or let us go."

"And don't forget to add that the moon is made of cheese," Tregembo sneered.

"We could insist," Rose said. "Surely if we all stick together ..."

"Aherrm!" The butler cleared his throat. "There'll be no talk of mutiny on *this* ship," he warned. "Or we'll all be out on our ears – without a character – which is a lot worse than board wages." He turned again to Dunne. "You may yet end up better than those who stay on," he said. "I've made inquiries of butlers in other households and I already know of two places where they're looking for parlourmaids or soon will be. And there were two pages of situations-vacant in the last *Falmouth Packet,* so I see little cause for weeping and wailing and gnashing of teeth."

"How many were for lady's maids, Mister Tregembo?" Rose asked, expecting no better answer than a baleful glare, which was, indeed, all she got.

"You were trusting your luck a bit," Mary said when they were alone at last in the sewing room. "At supper tonight, I mean – cheeking old Tregembo like that."

Actually, her real name was Marietta but her ladyship had vetoed that for the by now familiar reasons.

"Cheeking?" Rose answered. "What's cheeky about standing up for our rights?"

"The manner of it," Mary replied.

"Anyway, how much do they save by putting us on board wages for two months? Have you thought about it?"

"All I can think about is two months without that young ... without Master Noel – I was going to say a rude word then – without him pestering me morning, noon, and night. To say nothing of two months free of her ladyship's tongue. You must have thought the same?"

"Bloody Noel – if that's what you were going to say – doesn't pester me."

"Only because you're too tall for him. You intimidate him. Anyway, that's not what I meant. Go on – do her! What did she come out with this evening?"

Rose glanced at the door, as if she could see through it to catch any eavesdropper. Then, flopping her head about in imitation of Fenella, she said, "Oh *dear* Wose, it's such a shame that Mama won't let me take you with us I shall sorely miss our darling chats you know and I'm sure the servants we'll have in Egypt and Palestine will be quite quite howwid. But I suppose it will be quite jolly to see all those pywamids and temples and things. And also the Sphynx! I'm going to ask it a widdle all on my own. You must set your bwain cogs whirwing, Wose, and think up with a good one for me. In Fwench, of course, because I do so wish to impwess ..."

"Stop!" Mary had laid aside her needle in self defence and was now pressing her ribs at each side. "Oh, help me loosen my stays, do! It hurts. It hurts." She caught her breath and pulled a punch on Rose's arm. "How d'you do that? Not just the voice but the way her head wobbles and everything. And the way she says 'howwid' and 'Fwench'! I wish you'd do it in the servants' hall just once ..."

"No!" Rose was alarmed. "And don't you ever dare suggest it, d'you hear! Someone would tattle and then I'd be for it. You're the only one who knows – you and Mom and Dad – so if word does get out, I'll know who to blame. Anyway – to get back to what I was saying – d'you know what they're saving by putting us on board wages for two months? Guess."

Mary shrugged.

Rose sighed. "It's important, my lover. It's a measure of their meanness. On each of us they save one month's wages – right? They pay us one month's wages instead of two."

"Oh yes!" The simplicity of the calculation had not struck Mary until then.

"You live in the clouds, you know." Rose shook her head sadly. Then, in an equally perfect imitation of Lady Carclew, she went on: "In the case of cook we save three pinds, fifteen shillings. Mitchell – three pinds, three shillings, end fawp'nce. Ouah two deah leedies' maids – four pinds, one shilling, end eightp'nce. End thet little creachah in the scullery, whatsername? Penny-something. On her we save a hundred and fifty pennies – or twilve end sixp'nce." Dropping back into her own voice she concluded, "Altogether that comes to ...?"

Mary dabbed her eyes and said she had no idea.

"Fifteen pounds, four shillings, and tuppence."

"You left out Mister and Mrs Tregembo."

Rose gave her a withering look.

Mary was shocked. "You mean you don't think they'll be on board wages, too?"

"What d'you think? He wouldn't have been as bright and breezy if he and Mrs T were treated like the rest of us."

"But he said ..."

"He very carefully *didn't* say – if you were listening. He said vague things like, 'It's the same for everybody' and 'We're all in the same boat' but he very carefully avoided saying that he and she were also getting a cut. The thing is, they're robbing five of us of a month's wages just to save fifteen-odd quid! *She's* spent twice that much on one hat. That's what the five of us are worth to them – half a hat!"

"Why d'you stick it, Rose? Why don't you look for a better place?"

"Because they're all the same. You find me a place where girls like us are appreciated …" She saw the door open a crack while she spoke these words.

Young Noel poked his face around the door. "I'll show you this much," he said. "If you like it, I'll show you the rest." He sauntered in. "A place where girls like you are appreciated, eh?"

"Whoy, bless moy soul but 'tis the Young Maister!" Rose curtsied low as she put on a fake Cornish accent, imitating some up-country mummers who had tried to ingratiate themselves with a Cornish audience at Helston Harvest Fair last fall.

"Very funny, Rose," Noel said irritably as he oozed fully into the sewing room. "Please rise from that ridiculous posture."

"Whoi, thank'ee, maister, thank'ee, thank'ee, thank'ee!"

He ignored her and turned to Mary. "Anything I can do for you?" he asked. "Just to show you *are* appreciated. Read you a story? Or I could read you bits of Baedeker about Egypt – kill two birds with one stone."

"You could kill *these* two birds with one *paragraph,*" Rose told him as she picked up her sewing again.

Mary crossed the room and shut the door again. "Why d'you bother?" she asked him as she returned to her place. "You know my feelings well enough by now. Why persist? You must surely be aware that it's fruitless."

His wide, alarmed eyes swivelled in Rose's direction while he tried to keep his face toward Mary.

"You think she doesn't know how you pester me?" Mary asked him. "We share a room, in case you've forgotten. D'you suppose she doesn't tell me how you badger her for advice on how to *go for* me? And d'you think I don't say a word to her about it, either?"

"How's a fellow to gain experience?" Noel sighed. "All the bucks at school talk of the fun they have with maidservants in the hols. What's wrong with …"

"You're too choosy," Rose told him. She gave Mary a surreptitious wink. "That's your trouble. How many have you tried? What about Sally? Or Flora? Or Heather? Surely one of them …"

"Who are they?" He frowned.

"They're the ones you call Rogers, McCormick, and Dunne."

"Oh, them!"

"Yes, them. They're not bad looking, you know – if the light's right. Quite adequate if all you want is experience."

"But I haven't lost my heart to them – not the way I have to Mary."

"I've told you not to call me that," Mary said angrily. "If your mother ever hears *you* call me Mary, she'll suspect something's up – and then I'll be out on my ear."

"I'd look after you," he assured her. "I shall be quite rich one day, you know."

"Yes, well, come back then."

"No, honestly. When I'm twenty-three I come into my inheritance from my godmother. Over a hundred thou', you know." He sniffed and gazed superciliously at his fingernails.

Both maids pricked up their ears at this, though from their outward demeanour he would never have guessed it. Disappointed at their lack of obvious response, he said, "That stopped the conversation, eh!"

Rose said, "We're both thinking that you won't be twenty-three for another four years."

"Three and and a half," he replied.

"Very well – three and a half," she repeated.

"I can borrow against it. Tyzack the pawnbroker has already said that if I need a little help … you know."

"I'll tell you what," Rose said. "You pay me four pounds, one shilling and eightpence and I'll let you kiss me as much as you want for five minutes."

"Eh?" He was both stunned and intrigued. Rose had never done anything but treat him with contempt, sneering at him and saying things to wound. It was wonderful what the mention of spondulicks could do!

"So will Miss Hind, I'm sure," Rose added.

"I will not!" Mary exploded.

"Anyway, why four pounds, one and eight?" Noel asked. "Why so precise?"

"I was hoping you'd ask," Rose said in a much harder tone.

"Rose, leave it!" Mary murmured.

"I will not leave it!" She laid down her sewing and stared the boy in the eye. "For your information, young master, four pounds, one and eight is what your mother pays me – and Miss Hind – per month. That's fifty pounds a year – to save you working it out. And it's what she's proposing to pay us for *two* months while you're away. Board wages. You may bet all Lombard Street to a china orange that we won't be working half time but we'll be paid as if we were. All I'm saying is that if just *one* member of the Carclew clan is prepared to show a little generosity, then so can I."

The young man's expression hardened. "You're not saying that at all, Miss Tremayne. You are calumniating my mother – and trying to inveigle me into joining you. Well, I shan't – so there!"

Gathering what was left of his dignity he turned on his heels and left the room.

"You do take risks," Mary said unhappily. "What if he blabs to her ladyship?"

"He won't. He wouldn't dare. He can't stand her, anyway. Besides, they could still send him to VPS camp while they go swanning off to the orient."

After a thoughtful silence, Mary went on, "Would you really do that – let him kiss you for five minutes for four quid and a bit?"

"Well … he's quite good looking," Rose replied. "It wouldn't be a fate worse than death." She laughed. "I'd make sure of that!"

2

The following morning the two lady's maids went up into the attic to select the trunks and travelling wardrobes. With them went Rogers and Dunne, to clean each item of the selected luggage before Mitchell and Rodda carried it down. The selection was a matter of moments but the cleaning and portering took longer, which left Rose and Mary time to wander around, pretending to search among a century of haphazard cast-offs for anything that might be useful in the subtropical regions for which the Carclews were destined. They did actually find a battered solar toupée, with neckshield, a canvas bed and washbasin, and a roll of torn mosquito netting – mementoes of Uncle Oswald, who tried to map the Mountains of the Moon in Central Africa, returned with some fatal sickness, frightened the life out of the maid who had had to empty a chamberpot full of black urine each morning, and died within months. The two maids passed onward with a shudder.

"Look at these," Mary cried, whipping a dust sheet off six chairs. "They're Chippendale, you know."

Rose looked at them more closely. "They're the same as the two in our bedroom, except that ours are hidden inside about a dozen coats of white paint. In fact, all the servants' rooms have these same chairs. They must have had a big set of them originally."

Mary consulted a mental picture of the chairs in their room and saw that Rose was right. Annoyed with herself for not spotting the similarity, she said, "Typical you! You only notice the outward form, whereas I notice the real substance. If ours hadn't been painted white, I should have spotted it at once."

"Oh dear!" Rose murmured. "I hear a certain young master's footsteps. You slip down the far stairs and I'll misdirect him."

Too late. Mary was still a few paces short of the stairhead when young Noel cried, "Ah, so there you are!" and joined Rose half way along the attic. When he stopped at her side she thought he must have missed sight of Mary; but his first words were, "I'm glad – for once – that she's vamoosed. I want to talk – in strictest confidence – about last night."

"What about last night?" She moved away and almost stumbled over a plaster cast, a life-sized human head on a square plinth.

"The bargain you suggested."

"I wasn't serious, sir." She bent over to see if there was a name on the plinth.

"Don't call me sir. You can call me Noel when there's no one else around."

'Henry Jarves,' it read. 'Hanged at Bodmin Assize for the stealing of sheep, 12 August 1847.'

"I could call you lots of things, come to that," she replied. "Pest, bane of our lives, affliction, gravel in the shoe ..."

There was another plaster head beside it. She moved an ancient bassinet. Several plaster heads, in fact.

"Careful!" he cried. "That was my carriage when I was a baby."

"I'll push you out for a walk in it later, then," she promised.
'Carver Lethbridge. Hanged at Plymouth for piracy, 14th November 1809.'
"I'll pay you four quid to let me kiss you for five minutes," he blurted out. There was a shivery edge to his voice ... of excitement? Or of fear? Either way, she did not really wish to know.
"Four pounds, one and eightpence," she reminded him.
'Thomas Jacob Carr. Hanged at Bodmin Assize for murder, 7th August 1856.'
Now that she looked more closely, she could see the marks of the rope around their necks. These were death masks, or, rather, casts of the whole head, made after death. She counted them – eight in all.
"Like this, you mean?" He opened his hand to reveal four gold sovereigns and a florin.
"That's fourpence too much," she said, her heart beginning to race. True, she had meant last night's offer as a joke, a rather bitter joke to show up his mother's meanness, but the sight of a whole month's wages there, and all of it hers just for the granting of five-minutes' worth of kissing – and him so young and harmless (and quite handsome, too) ... it was enough to quicken anyone's blood.
But was it the first step on a very slippery and depressingly well-known slope?
"That's for the little bit extra," he replied. He was now shivering quite violently.
"D'you know what these things are?" She rose, dusting her hands and giving the nearest cast a tap with her foot.
"Death masks of criminals hanged in the last century," he told her. "Before Uncle Oswald was bitten with the exploration bug – and *long* before he was bitten by the bilharzia bug – he was a keen phrenologist. I don't suppose you know the word?"
"He studied the bumps on people's heads."
"Sorry, I should have known better than to ask. Anyway, that's what he did. He was sure he could give the police a method of detecting murderers and other criminals, just from the bumps on their heads. So he bought some early nineteenth-century casts and then later got the prison authorities to cast some up-to-date ones specially for him. We've got about twenty of them here, somewhere."
"And did he succeed?" She wasn't really interested – but then she was even less keen to discover exactly how far she'd go for four pounds, two shillings. And what did he mean by 'a little bit extra'?
"He was convinced he did," Noel told her, waving a hand vaguely toward an old chest of drawers. "There's a pile of papers there somewhere, proving his point in seven different ways. But some unkind soul sent him a cast of the head of one of the deans of Truro Cathedral – after the fellow died, of course – saying it was a felon who died before he could be hanged and challenging him to identify the crime. And poor Uncle O came out with fraud,

embezzlement, fraud, forgery, and the criminal conversion of the affections of another man's wife. That's when he started taking an acute interest in the remoter corners of Africa."

Rose laughed despite herself. "You're making it up," she accused.

"Only slightly," he admitted. "You've got a beautiful laugh, Rose." He opened his fist to reveal the five coins, four of gold, one of silver, yet again. "What about it? Are you on?"

"What was that 'little bit extra,' then?" she asked warily.

"Ah, I'm glad you reminded me. Could we change the terms to four minutes of straight kissing followed by one minute of kissing *and* fondling?"

She took a step back and eyed him suspiciously. There was still a shiver in his voice but intuition told her it was born of suppressed mirth rather than of fear or ... the other thing.

"Fondling?"

Every shred of common sense was telling her to go, to turn on her heel and walk away; instead, she just stood there, staring at him, knowing that he was now in command of the occasion and dictating each turn in their conversation.

"Yes. Those soft swellings inside your blouse. I'd give my right hand to know what they feel like – and I'm sure my right hand feels the same way as me about it."

There must have been dozens of humiliating, cutting, devastating things she could have said but not one of them came to her rescue. She just stood there, appalled to discover that she was still actually considering it. Her moral sense was fighting everything else within her, and not exactly winning.

Seeing her hesitate he smiled more broadly still and continued, "And actually, Rose dear, that's still not quite all. I'd go as high as five guineas if you'd agree to a fondle and then lift up your skirts and let me just look ..."

At last she found the resolution to turn and walk away. She'd have slapped his face hard, too, if Rogers and Dunne hadn't been at the far end of the attic, washing the next trunk for the men to carry below.

"Just to look!" He called after her. "No touching – I promise. Just to see what it looks like."

She turned again and pointed an angry finger at his face. "You pester me once more," she hissed, "and you'll be spending the next two months at a camp for wayward toffs. And Mary will back me, so you just be careful!"

His unwavering grin lingered in her mind's eye long after she had gone down to help Mary with the packing. Yet, curiously enough, she was not nearly as angry as she ought to be, as she had every right to be, as she would have predicted if someone had put that conversation to her as a hypothetical case.

She had made a stupid offer last night – a joke, it was true, but a stupid joke for all that. And today he had come back and called her bluff. Whether by accident or insight he had shown her things within herself that she would rather not have discovered. Lord, but she hoped it was by accident; if he was capable of such insight at the age of almost-twenty, he was going to be a dangerous young man when he came of age.

3 The following day, Friday, four trunks and one travelling wardrobe were dispatched from Falmouth per luggage-in-advance to await the Carclews' arrival at Charing Cross Station, where, on Saturday, 12th March, they would catch the 9.00am Orient Express to Constantinople. Over the following days there were further consignments until all twelve items of 'impedimenta,' as Sir Hector called them, had gone. So the family, who were travelling entirely without servants for the first time in their lives, had nothing to fret about, at least until they and their luggage were reunited in London.

The reason they were travelling without servants was that the Orient Express was a first-class-only train and a single ticket all the way cost £18 4*s.* 1*d.* It wasn't that the Carclews could not afford the £72 16*s.* 4*d.* it would have cost to take one maid and one valet to Turkey and back – plus whatever other expenses their presence would necessitate during the two months of their wanderings – but they could not accept that the pair would be mingling in the first class for three days out and three days back. Heaven alone knew what dangerous ideas such an unavoidable privilege might put into their heads.

During their orgy of packing, unpacking, and repacking, Rose and Mary were hardly troubled by Noel; his mother and sister were too often in and out of the room for him to risk starting one of his usual conversations. But his triumphant smiles and knowing winks were enough to show Rose that he knew very well that he had called her bluff and won. It was his more-than-daily goad to her. His only chance of a conversation, though, came toward the end, when the two maids were sent upstairs to his room to pack his trunk – the last and least important of all. He opened the contest in his characteristic style.

"You'll miss me when I'm gone," he told them.

The maids glanced at each other and sighed. "He must be talking to you," Mary said, "for he cannot possibly mean *me.*"

Rose, who had been about to say the same, changed tack at once. "Oh, but he's quite right," she said.

"Really?" he asked in surprise.

"Desperately," she assured him.

"For instance?"

"For instance, I shall miss that sinking feeling I get when I see you approaching along a corridor. For instance …"

"All right, all right. You're only saying that."

"I could say a great deal more."

"You'll be sorry. If I get trampled to death by a camel or something – then you'll be sorry."

"What – that it wasn't an elephant or a steam roller? Yes, you're right again. I'll weep buckets. Oh, Young Master, you know me so well! D'you think you'll be wanting a cricket bat out there?" She brandished it. "Knock the fuzzy-wuzzies for six?"

"I suppose I might," he replied without thought. Really, he didn't care what they packed.

"You and they would be pretty evenly matched," she added. "Mentally, anyway."

Mary snatched the bat from Rose and put it back in the drawer. "You two!" she exclaimed. "If you could just hear yourselves. And I don't know what's come over *you.*" She nodded at Rose. "Ever since the other night."

"It would be hot enough for cricket," Noel mused aloud. "I never thought of that. Perhaps Rose is right – seriously."

They ignored him. "What other night?" Rose asked.

Mary pursed her lips and said nothing.

"There are bound to be other chaps out there for a knock-up game or two."

"What other night?"

"Come on! The sooner we're finished, the sooner we can be out of here."

"Two scratch teams ... five a side ... that sort of thing." He retrieved the bat from the drawer and handed it to Rose.

"What other night?" Rose insisted as she packed the bat without giving it a glance.

"You should oil that first." Mary handed it back to him. "It hasn't been touched since last season."

Rose grabbed it and put it back in the trunk. "Then all his clothes would reek of it. I'm sure they sell boiled linseed oil in Turkey." She looked daggers at Mary but did not repeat her question a fourth time.

It took half an hour to pack his trunk, every minute of it filled with similar innuendo and sarcasm. For once, Mary played the spectator to, rather than the recipient of, Noel's picayune challenges. It ended with his advising Rose to drink a glass of hot milk and honey last thing each night, for she certainly needed a great deal of sweetening. She responded that her last daily act was to say her prayers and that she would certainly be including one for him – that he, treading the ground where Three Wise Men once trod, would somehow acquire the very smallest pinch of wisdom for himself, for he certainly lacked it now.

He had the last laugh, though – in his terms, anyway. When the moment came for Mr Negus, the head stable lad, and Negus, his eldest son, to drive the family to Falmouth station, Noel caught her on the servants' stair and pounced. It was Lady Carclew's rule that when any female servant had to pass a male – servant or master – she had to turn and face the wall while he went by. This was to avoid any accidental contact, genuine or contrived, between any part of his body and those parts of a female that protrude beyond the rest. Rose ignored the rule on this occasion because ... well, because. And so Noel pounced. He gave her a bear hug in which she was, momentarily, too surprised to struggle, and pressed his lips firmly to hers.

Firmly at first, that is, then, when he met with no resistance, more gently.

She would have struggled except that something within her said why bother? He'd be gone for the next two months ... and, actually, it wasn't too unpleasant. There was little enough tenderness in her life and, as long as she wasn't struggling more than a token, to keep her self-respect, he was being quite tender.

Everything changed, though, the moment he put a hand to her bosom. Then she turned her face abruptly from him, got an elbow under his encircling arm, against his ribs, and gouged hard.

He sprang backward, laughing. "Dunnit!" he cried as he left her standing. "I said I would before I left – and so I did!"

Furious she ran after him, caught him by the elbow, and hissed, "And *I* was equally sure you'd never keep your word."

Stung, he paused. "In what way?"

She held out her hand. "Four pounds, one and eightpence!"

He swallowed hard and reached for his purse, only then recalling that it held a sovereign, a fiver, and some loose change. "I'll ... er ... damn! Tell you what – I'll wire it from Constantinople. Or Cairo or somewhere."

Laughing, she now left him standing. Only when she reached the far end of the corridor did he think of saying what he ought to have said at once: "It wasn't five minutes, anyway!"

"Really?" she asked in amazement, and without turning round. "Well, it certainly felt like it."

A few minutes later the remaining servants were all dutifully lined up beside the front portico, ready to wave farewell to their dear masters and mistresses.

"In maintaining you here at considerable expense while we are away," her ladyship told them before she mounted the carriage, "we repose a great trust in you all. I feel sure you will never-never let us down."

Miniature curtsies and murmurs of agreement that fell just short of actual words greeted this implicit command.

"We'll bring back something jolly for each of you from the orient," Fenella promised gaily – words that evoked wan smiles and silence.

Sir Hector cleared his throat, glanced up and down the line from beneath his bushy eyebrows, growled a few consonants and vowels, and joined his ladies in the carriage.

"Do not grieve, my dear, dear people!" Noel leaped on the running board and waved an heroic orator's arm at them. "We shall be gone but a season and, as the dragonfly ..."

Lady Carclew's umbrella handle hooked him round the neck and, like that much larger hook they use in the theatre, yanked him off his tiny stage.

"The funny thing is," Mary murmured as the carriage rumbled away along the drive, "I think I shall miss him."

Rose turned to her in amazement.

"I know!" Mary agreed. "'After all I've said, too. But he's like an infuriating little puppy dog, don't you think? He annoys you but you can't be too hard on him."

"Puppy dog," Rose repeated as they drifted indoors. "That's right. He only knows two levels of behaviour – play or indifference, which, in a puppy, is sleep. Even if you wanted to be serious for once, it's no good – he always forces you to descend to his level of childishness."

Now it was Mary's turn to look askance. "When would you want to be *serious?*" she asked. "With *that* one especially?"

"Not in *that* way!" Rose exclaimed. "Good heavens, that never even crossed my mind. I mean serious discussions about ... you know ... life and things."

But there she was not being entirely truthful. Her lips still tingled at the memory of his and, though one small part of her resented the fact that it had been *his* lips, by far the most of her was still slightly shocked to recall how pleasant it had been.

4

Apart from those irksome board wages, life at Nancemellin House became quite pleasant once the Carclews were well and truly gone. However, it took all that first weekend before their presence faded completely away, for long habit had accustomed the household servants to expect her ladyship's presence at every turn, not to mention her prying eye and her desire to control. Tregembo had often remarked that Lady Carclew would command more respect if she could only bring herself to command fewer activities. A mistress of the house, in his view, should consult her housekeeper at the start of each day and leave the details to her; his wife felt the same, only about ten times more strongly. Those morning consultations, she felt, should be for the mistress to learn, rather than to dictate – to learn, for instance, that today the box room would be turned out, or that a certain pair of sheets should now be turned sides-to-middle and sent to the servants' quarters, or that the china cabinet would be unlocked so that its contents could be dusted and rearranged. But whenever she tried it, Lady Carclew would say something like, "An excellent idea, Mrs Tregembo, but not today, I think. Today we shall ..." and out would trot some little task that had been suggested last week – and vetoed then in similar terms.

The housekeeper had grown used to suggesting next week's tasks this week, so that they could be vetoed now and then revived as if they were her ladyship's own ideas a few days later. The arrangement suited Lady Carclew pretty well, for it allowed her to seem in absolute control without the drudgery of planning every detail; or, indeed, *any* detail at all. But it annoyed Mrs Tregembo beyond words.

So these two blissful months were an opportunity for the butler and the housekeeper to put their own principles into practice. They gave each servant a general outline of what they expected him or her to have achieved by suppertime and they left them to get on with it, and with only the lightest supervision.

For most of that first delightful weekend – apart from divine service on Sunday morning – they 'put the house into mothballs,' as Tregembo expressed it, covering all the furniture and cabinets with dust sheets, putting ammonia and whiting on the silver and leaving it all chalky and caked, ready to be polished off in the week before the family returned. Ditto all the leather boots, leaving them matt with Cherry Blossom, ready for a good hard shine-up at the end of April.

Oddly enough, the class structure of the servants' hall underwent subtle changes once that unseen upper tier of master and mistress was removed. It did not, of course, degenerate into utter democracy but the two lady's maids combined with little Ann Pennycuik, the scullerymaid, to do parlourmaids' work, and the lady's maids, in turn, were not too proud to dry the odd glass or set of cutlery after the last meal of the evening. And any of them might be found rolling out pastry for Mrs Browning on a day when pasties were promised, for her pasties were a legend. But Mitchell, the footman, was left in no doubt that he had overstepped the mark when he offered to hold Mary by the ankles while she stood on the top platform of the stepladder and dismantled the crystals of the drawing-room chandelier for their annual washing; he was, instead, sent to change the water in the pail, which really should have been Pennycuik's task.

All the same, the days seemed curiously flat and lacklustre as they passed evenly by.

"Perhaps a picnic isn't a real picnic without ants and wasps," Rose said to Mary as they undressed for bed one night.

There was a frost outside – uncommon for the far west of Cornwall in March – and they had spent an hour on the foreshore that afternoon gathering driftwood, which they were allowed to burn in their bedroom fireplace since it cost the household nothing. To make the most of it they raced out of their clothes, washed quickly, and threw themselves into nightshifts and dressing gowns, so that they could stand with their backs to the blaze and, by lifting their garments, roast their blind cheeks and nether limbs before climbing into their icy beds, which a stone hot-water bottle did little to make more comfortable.

"My mum calls this ..." Mary began. "No, I can't say it."

"Go on! You can't just leave it there," Rose protested. "Your mum calls it what?"

Mary bit her lip, looked away, and mumbled, " 'Warming the old man's supper.' I shouldn't have said it. I'm sorry. What did you say about picnics?"

Rose laughed. "That's what my mom calls it, too. It must be what everyone says but never speaks about. The thing about picnics is that the ones you always remember are those where there was some disaster – when Tommy fell in the weir or Daisy tripped into the nettle patch or Dad spread the rugs on an ants' nest – that sort of thing."

"What made you think of that?"

Rose shrugged. "Just the way one day seems to follow another and even though we get through the work, it just feels ... I don't know. Flat. We should *do* something."

"What?"

"I don't know. If I did, I'd suggest it. Isn't this glorious? I think I'm hot enough to warm the whole bed."

"Not yet," Mary said. "Let the flames start to die. Then we can dowse the light and lie in our beds and look at the flickering patterns they make on the ceiling. I used to do that as a little girl, when I was sick and they put a fire in my room, didn't you?"

"Mmmh! That's one thing I miss out here in the country – street lights. When they shine through bare twigs and you can turn the shadows into almost anything you want ... islands with buried treasure ... faces ... patterns for colouring ... anything. I know! Maybe we could play charades in the servants' hall one evening? D'you think Mister and Mrs T would join in?"

Mary giggled. "We could do a wonderful charade on 'Carclew' – 'car' could be something about a ride in a jaunting car, and 'clew' could be like a clue in a murder, and you could do your imitation of her ladyship for the whole word."

"And get booted out on my ear? Thank you very much!"

"Well, it was just a thought."

"We could certainly try charades. I'm not saying no to that. Just not that one." She glanced sideways over her shoulder at Mary's derrière. "You're like a lobster," she said, turning round and exposing her front up to her waist.

Mary glanced at her and said, "And you're so white as crabmeat."

"Mom calls this 'warming the better half.' "

Mary chuckled. "I must tell my mum that one." After a pause she added, "What about your cousin, then?"

Rose's cousin was Frank Tresidder, who worked on his family farm, Trefusis, in Mylor parish, a mile away to the east – the very next property to the Nancemellin estate. In fact, he was her second cousin, for her father's father's mother was also Frank's great-grandmother; and to say that he 'worked on' the family farm was no more than a courtesy to his father, who had been ailing for years and who now left all the decisions, and the work, to Frank.

"What about him?" Rose asked.

"Why don't you ask him over to supper one night." Mary turned round to warm her better half, too. "I'll bet Mrs T wouldn't deny you the chance."

It was common gossip in the district that Frank and Rose were intended for each other, having played together since Rose was a toddler – for Frank was only two years older. She thought it was a fine idea and kicked herself for not hitting upon it. "I'll see if I can send Negus or Noy over there with a note tomorrow," she said, *"if* Mrs T agrees."

"I'll have him if you don't want him," Mary said. "I don't care about his reputation."

"What d'you mean – if I 'don't want him'? Of course I want him. The very ..."

"Well ..." Mary became awkward. "If you're not aware of it ... why should *I* say?"

"Say what?"

"It doesn't matter. Forget I spoke – I was only joking, anyway."

"You're doing it again – saying only half of what you mean."

"Oh, all right!" She hung her head lower with each word, then jerked up straight and, fixing her gaze on Rose, asked, "Don't you think it odd, me 'ansum, considering all those times you've grumbled about the long hours we work here and how you'll never get to see Frank ... isn't it odd that you've not once talked of asking him over? Or of going to Trefusis yourself to see him?"

"Not *talking* about something is different from not *thinking* about it," Rose pointed out.

"Oh well, that's all right, then." Mary was only too eager to drop the subject. But she could not resist adding, "It's just that you're never what one could call 'on fire' about that man."

"On fire?" Rose chuckled and let her nightgown fall again. "I will be if I stand here much longer." She tripped across the room to her bed and slipped between the cold sheets with a loud, shivery groan as her feet reached eagerly for the hot-water bottle.

"You forgot your prayers," Mary said.

"The rector says if it's frosty you can say them *after* getting into bed. As long as ..."

"When? I never heard him."

"Well, I'm sure he meant to say it and just forgot. Anyway – ssh! I'm saying them now."

She did the Lord's Prayer and Perils and Dangers of This Night and then the litany of people she wanted to be kept safe and well, ending, as always, with Frank Tresidder.

"It's different when you've grown up together," she told Mary when she'd whispered the final amen.

"Ssh!" the girl replied from between her sheets. "I'm saying mine now."

Rose reached for her *Golden Treasury* and read a poem – Herrick's *Gather ye rosebuds while ye may.* She liked to read at least one poem each night, to have something to think about until sleep laid claim to her. Tennyson was her favourite; her dad had given her *The Collected Works* for her twenty-first. You needed the eye of a needlewoman to read the fine print of it.

She had finished the Herrick and was just about to reach for it when Mary asked, "What's different?"

She put the book back and blew out the candle. "Getting all 'hot and hurrisome,' as they say. Anyway, I don't believe in all that stuff. Romantic love. Romeo and Juliet stuff. Going out of your mind and not being able to eat and ... yeurk! It's wonderful as poetry but in real life it's just stupid."

"If you say so." Mary yawned.

"I do say so. They never end up happy ever after if you notice. Romeo and Juliet. Helen of Troy and Paris." After a moment's thought she added, "Abélard and Héloïse ..."

"Who are all these people?" Mary asked petulantly. "I've never heard of them – except Romeo and Juliet."

"They're all people in plays."

"Oh!" Her tone was weary. "People in *plays!*"

"But they were real people once upon a time – I think. Why d'you say *'plays,'* like that? Don't you like going to the theatre?"

Mary's reply was barely intelligible, being spoken on one long yawn: "At the moment all I want is a nice, sweet dream. G'ni..."

"Anyway ..." Rose made one last stab. "What d'you mean about 'his reputation'?" She knew well enough, of course. What with all the gossip about Frank throughout the neighbourhood, she'd have to be both blind and deaf not to. But she wasn't going to let such a remark pass unchallenged.

Mary, not wanting to get drawn, said, "I thought you were going to read out a bit from that guide book each night – so we'd know what *they* were up to."

The Carclews had taken the latest *Baedeker* for Egypt, Syria, and the Holy Land but they had left behind an older edition for Palestine and Syria and the *Orient Line Guide* for 1890, which had a chapter on Egypt. She read aloud from this latter until she heard Mary's first gentle snore; then she read on silently to herself because it was quite fascinating – all about heiroglyphics and Gizeh and the Shepherd Pharaohs and cries for *bakhsheesh* and how dirty the mosques were in Suez and 'searchlights' on the Nile boats ... really, it was almost as good as being there.

When at last her eyelids drooped, she closed the book quietly and blew out the candle before snuggling an enveloping hollow into her feather mattress; then she pulled the covers down tight at the back and front of her neck, and soon was floating in a cocoon of warmth. Her thought fled home from the orient, from the Sphinx and the pyramids, back, of course, to Frank.

She *did* love him but it *was* different when you grew up together and had promised yourselves to each other for as long as you could remember. There was none of that aching and yearning and torment; just a great big warmth, through and through, like the warmth of this bed, something that just was and that wrapped itself all around you. It was much better than all that tragic stuff because it didn't interfere with your life. You could forget it most of the time. Or not forget it so much as ignore it. And it wouldn't take offence. It would just stay there patiently waiting for you to notice it once again and then it would wrap itself around you, as always, and be a great comfort. So there, Mary Hind – put that in your pipe and smoke it!

She moved her head a fraction, until the pillow touched her lips. It became his lips, Frank's lips, which were strong and firm and the best thing about him – except, perhaps, his eyes, which were deep-set and dark. Or his body, which was broad and stocky and strong, as it ought to be in any champion Cornish wrestler. But the pillow was, at this moment, his lips – his face – and she kissed it hungrily, silently, passionately, over and over again. She rubbed her cheekbone against it as a cat will do to a hand, a cushion, a chair leg, at the slightest encouragement. A few minutes later, when Mary's gentle snores had become genuine, she eased the pillow down beside her and hugged it tight to her, body to body. Actually, it was more a long sort of bolster than a pillow – long enough to be both head and body.

All these things she and Frank had done in reality, so this nightly ritual was more a feast of memory than a flight of fancy. Nor was it true that she never felt 'all hot and hurrisome' for her lover; these were passions she could rekindle at any time when she was truly alone – and safely out of reach of Frank himself. She was always more cautious when he was actually there, with his arms around her and his lips seeking hers.

Not that she believed *all* the talk about his 'reputation,' mind. She had suffered that way herself, being both good looking and – thanks to her American mother – more independent of mind than most Cornish maids of the same age; people had said many a hurtful thing about her, too. In fact, that was the main reason why Frank's family – mainly his mother – was against any possibility of marriage. But for that, they'd probably already be man and wife. And she'd be lying in a bed a mile east of here, and this bolster would really be him. And then – oh my! – they wouldn't need a toe-stubbing hot-water bottle to warm the bed! She shivered at the prospect and, burying her lips in the 'head' of the bolster, whispered her nightly promise: "Soon! Soon!" – which, alas, she had been making to it/him for more than a year now. 'Soon' turned out to be like the pot of gold at the end of a rainbow – it stepped back each time you stepped forward.

All the same, she had to admit that Mary had a point. It *did* strike her as odd – now – that she had not immediately seized upon the freedom of these days on board wages to invite Frank over – much less to go and see him, herself. Even this afternoon, when they were out there collecting driftwood along the seashore, it would have been so easy to come back a slightly longer way via Trefusis Farm; yet it hadn't even crossed her mind.

Despite all that, she must be in love with Frank – otherwise what was the meaning of this nightly orgy of hugs and kisses with him, here in the safety of her own fantasies? Surely it was love that set her heart beating so fast and made her feel all hollow inside, as if her innards were falling away for ever. And surely it was love for him and him alone, because no other name and no other mental image could provoke those same passions?

Yes, of course she was in love and of course it was he and he alone who stirred her heart to such turmoil. So that was that.

The clock over the stable yard struck eleven. She imagined the solemn chime rolling down over the Nancemellin parkland, crisp beneath its rime of frost, down to the moonlit foreshore and out over the sheltered waters of Carrick Roads and Falmouth harbour, and across the sleeping countryside, too, to Trefusis Farm. Frank would surely hear it on a still, fine night like this, and he would just as surely recall that his Rose was lying, thinking of him, not a hundred paces from that mournful bell.

Knowing that it was so, that it must be so, she closed her eyes tight and struggled to send him her thoughts, as if each clang were an invisible carrier: "Good night my love, my love, my love …"

Moments later, it seemed, that same bell tolled six times and she awoke with a groan from a dream in which the air above the entire Nancemellin parklands – all two hundred acres or more – had been buzzing with the largest bee-swarm the world had ever seen. And they were angry, too, which had made it impossible for her to run across to Trefusis Farm, which was all she had wanted to do to warn Frank about the swarm.

She sprang from the bed and ran shivering to the window. The air was crystal clear and utterly still. She could see the smoke rising from the Trefusis chimneys, as if an artist had dragged a fine brush, loaded with pale ochre, vertically upward across a cloudless azure sky. If a single bee were out there, flying around, it would be frozen stiff within minutes.

Rose knew it was absurd to feel relieved but she could not help it. Frank was safe out there – safe and a mile away.

5 Rose soon began to doubt her own cynical suggestion that the Tregembos had been left on full pay while the rest of them had to accept only half-wages. If the butler and his wife had been on full pay, she felt, their consciences would never have let them take a whole Fri-to-Mon off, only two weeks after the Carclews had departed. An afternoon, or even a day – yes; but not three. But when Mr Tregembo's brother, who ran a boarding house in Torquay – very quiet at that time of year, of course – had written suggesting they pay him a brief visit 'while the cat's away,' the temptation was too great and the wages obviously too small to detain them. Then Mitchell, seeing his chance, asked if he might go and visit his aunt, who lived at Paul, on the far side of Penzance. So the household of seven was suddenly reduced to just four: Mrs Browning, Pennycuik, Mary, and Rose. None of these who were left behind complained, especially as they had not been set tasks that the Tregembos expected to find completed upon their return; it was all part of an unspoken bargain in which none of these events would ever be mentioned when the Carclews returned from the orient.

"Now you can have Frank for breakfast, dinner, and supper!" Mary said as soon as they had waved the three deserters farewell.

Rose lifted her chin to supercilious heights. "Brikf'st, lunchin, ind dinnah, if you please, my gel."

"Eeoh yes, may lady!" Mary laughed. "I know – let's play at being her ladyship and Miss Fenella." They linked arms and went back indoors. "We could take some of the dust sheets off again and be At Home to Mrs Browning and little Pennycuik ... and Mister Tresidder, if you mind to?"

"I don't know," Rose replied cautiously, in her own voice again.

"Go on! Where's the risk? Word of it would never go higher than old Tregembo – and *he'd* not dare report us for it, not after what he's now doing."

"This afternoon, perhaps. But we could pass the morning dressing up in their clothes – how about that?"

And so they did, beginning with the most opulent of their respective mistresses' gowns, the ones they had not dared take to the orient for fear of seeing them ruined by incompetent native maids, venal innkeepers, sand, sun ... and all the other hazards of that region.

Fenella was due to come out that Season, almost immediately after their return, in fact, and so all her gowns were ready and waiting. One was an old-fashioned crinoline for the actual coming-out ball but the rest were up-to-date, with straight, slender skirts, almost tubular in shape, and no bustle at all. Bustles were quite definitely *out* this Season. There was one that Rose coveted in particular, a midnight-blue evening dress in velvet with a bodice of

Venetian point lace, cream-coloured over a body of cream chiffon. Mary had her eye on a black-beaded net dress over a black satin under-dress; it had a flesh-coloured bodice of pink net, which, from a distance and in a candle-lit room, gave the impression of a neckline that plunged daringly, all the way to the waist.

But they could not simply throw such exquisite gowns around themselves; it all had to be done properly, with the full assistance of a lady's maid. They tossed a coin and Rose won. With many a giggle and many an anxious glance out into the passage, in case Pennycuik should take it into her head to wander into the forbidden regions of the house, she stripped right down to the buff and put on a set of Fenella's nainsook camisoles and knickers, deep-cut to allow for the décolletage of the dress.

"Oh, Mary! I'm going to be rich-rich-rich one day," she said, stretching her arms high and shivering with pleasure at the gentle caress of the fine muslin. "Now the stockings – the blue silk." She giggled. "I'm going to be a rich bluestocking!"

"Talk like *her,*" Mary urged as she searched the hose drawer. "You're going to be wich-wich-wich – go on!"

Rose pulled a face. "Not if I've got to keep it up all day. I should just be fwightfully, fwightfully sick before it was halfway fwuh."

"Well at least talk posh – properly – or *I* shan't feel right, playing your maid."

"Eeoh yeas, ay cæn æt least do thæt. Neow the cawwset, gel!" She drew on the stockings and thrilled again as she ran her hands upward from her ankles, to smooth out the wrinkles. "And oh I shall sleep between sheets of silk – you'll see."

"Thass better, muy lady." Mary dropped into broad Cornish.

But their giggles and their rather febrile high spirits fell away as the dressing-up progressed and they saw what a change it wrought. First came an under-skirt and under-bodice of stiff, cream-coloured silk taffeta, crisp and lustrous. Surveying the effect in the two long mirrors on the outer doors of the wardrobe, which opened to face each other so that a woman could see herself front and back, Rose had the first intimation that she and Mary were here engaged in something much more than a cat's-away game; these gorgeous clothes were actually beginning to transform her in some subtle, as yet indefinable way.

Then came the bodice, fully boned and lined with figured white cotton; the fastening at the back was with hook and bar, which was rather fiddly. If Rose had still been playing Fenella, she would have snarled a few impatiently sarcastic comments. Instead, she just stood there, awestruck at the image that stared back at her from the mirror – equally lost in amazement. The rich cream lace over the cream chiffon body formed two pleated revers on either side, meeting in a vee below the bottom of her breastbone. As a result, their points hung clear of her bosoms, where the dappling of the lace created a pale shadow, a zone of half-glimpsed mystery before the firm line of the waistband established her contours once again.

She lifted the points gently forward and let them fall back. The effect was extraordinary. She had to tear her eyes away from the mirror and look down at herself – to be sure it really *was* herself. Even her arms looked different now. The cream chiffon sleeves ended in a narrow band of the midnight-blue velvet, an inch or two above her elbow, and was completed with a frill of lace that just covered the elbow itself. By some curious magic her bare forearm, which she had always thought looked distressingly muscular, now seemed elegantly slim and graceful, especially when she moved it languidly, this way and that.

Mary became aware of the change in her. "Don't get carried away now," she warned. "There's still your hair to see to – and what earrings are you going to choose?"

"It fits me better than it does Miss Fenella," she said.

"It suits you better, too."

But those were not the thoughts that this new vision sent tumbling through her mind; they were just something put out for public consumption. Deep inside herself she was beginning to realize that so many random ideas and feelings that she had experienced lately were all just beginning to come together.

It had started with ... well, with this very dress, among other things – with the preparations for Miss Fenella's coming-out. The girl had been noticeably more tetchy since their beginning. Several times she had made disparaging remarks about being 'in the ring at the Royal Show' or, more directly, the 'Society meat market.' Rose knew very well where such ideas came from, for Miss Fenella did not have the intellect or upbringing to have hit upon them all alone. They were in the ladies' journals she had to tidy up and in the more general magazines that came into the house, like *The Strand,* the *Spectator,* and *Twentieth Century.*

A working-class woman, ran their theme, was a *real* woman whereas her middle-and upper-class sister was no more than a pampered object, an item with a price; it was a bittersweet echo of that love of paradox which had beguiled the Nineties of the previous century. Incapable of independent existence, she was passed from the protection of her father to the protection of a husband, for whom she was a kind of living trophy, to be clad in such sumptuous garments as these. She was, in short, a display horse for his wealth.

So much they dared to express in print; but now, surveying herself once more in that faintly peach-tinted glass, Rose became aware of all those thoughts that public decency forbade them to advance. The display horse was also an object of *desire.* The contrast between the neat, modest, plainly dressed maid she had been half an hour ago, buttoned tight from neck to ankle, and this gorgeous butterfly, with her soft, clinging fabrics, her deep-cut neckline, her bare shoulders all set about with lacy frills, her swelling bosom, and her sinuous waist, almost shrieked it aloud.

Rose had never worn anything so magnificent in her life. And though, of course, she had often dressed her mistresses, past and present, in costumes of similar grandeur – and, just as naturally, had held their gowns to herself for brief moments before hanging them away again – nothing could have prepared her for the impact it would have upon her to be so clothed, not just superficially but from the innermost garments outward.

I am desirable! she thought, seeing herself as a man might see her, for every feature of this gown was delicately intended to draw a man's eyes to just those features that most distinguish a woman from himself, from the svelte grace of her arms to her suddenly ample bosom to her slender waist and curvaceous hips. It thrilled her, of course, but it frightened her, too. She was used to being valued for her skill; compliments on her looks, of which there had been plenty, were quite secondary – 'frosting on the cake,' as her mom often said. But now, to realize that she could so easily throw everything into the other pan of that delicate balance between inner merit and outward beauty was … well, more than frightening.

"I don't want to go on with this," she said suddenly, reaching behind herself to fiddle with the hook and bar between her shoulderblades.

"What?" Mary complained. "I haven't fixed the train on yet – and there's still your hair. Wait till you see what I'm going to do with that!"

"I don't need to. I don't want to."

"There's no danger – if that's what's worrying you. Shall I lock the doors?"

"It isn't that, it's …" Rose gestured at the object of desire in the mirror, the 'occasion of sin,' as the rector would say.

"You're spoiling it," Mary said bitterly.

"I'll dress you if you like," Rose said encouragingly, putting on a broad accent herself now. "You'll make some proper 'ansum lady in all they black beads."

"No!" Mary was not won over. "I want to see it when you're properly finished off. This is like snatching away a bit of embroidery when I'm only half done."

"All right!" Rose sighed heavily and sat down at the dressing-table. "Just throw a shawl or something over *that.*" She gestured at the mirror. "So's I can't see myself." The dress had deep, well concealed pleats in the back, which made sitting remarkably easy. *A dress for a wallflower!* she thought unkindly.

Mary fetched a mantilla from a drawer in the wardrobe. On her way back she passed a window and then, suddenly, halted and went back. "Oh my dear life!" she exclaimed.

"What?" Rose got unsteadily to her feet, because of the weight of the velvet.

"It looks like there's been an accident."

Rose caught the merest glimpse of the four groundsmen on the far side of the side lawn – Kitto, Chivers, Oates, and Pascoe. Between them they were carrying what looked like the body of a man – in fact, what could only have been the body of a man. Then Mary pushed her away in a kind of panic. "No!" she cried.

"What?" Rose asked, anxious now.

"I can't be sure ..." Mary stared hard at the men below, who were now approaching the front of the house across the lawn. She bit her lip hard and turned to Rose, eyes already large in sympathy. "I do believe 'tis Frank Tresidder. If 'tisn't, then he has a twin."

Rose dashed to the window and, for a moment, she, too, felt sure it was Frank who lay, pale, soaked to the skin, and apparently lifeless on the makeshift stretcher. Moments later, however, when the party passed below the window and his face started turning the right way round, she could see it was a stranger who lay there; in fact, the resemblance was no more than passing. Her fears had made it closer.

"Oh, I'm sorry!" Mary fanned her face as a token of embarrassment and gave Rose's arm a gentle squeeze.

Rose realized that the men were intending to take him through the stable yard to the kitchen door. "No!" she cried, throwing up the window. "Bring him to the front. I'm coming down."

Mary wondered if she realized she was talking in the tones of the upper class.

The train, which Mary had half-fixed while Rose was throwing her tantrum, had three lead weights to drag it out behind. They startled Rose as they went bang-bang-bang ... bang-bang-bang ... in triplets as she hastened down the stairs. She paused at the halfway landing and said, "Take this wretched train off, girl!"

Laughing, Mary complied. "You *are* playing the part," she said.

Rose did not share her amusement. "Work it out for yourself," she replied. "If this young fellow needs help, we can't *not* tend him. But if he then recovers and realizes what game we're playing ... well, *we'd* be game then – fair game for him. We'll see how bad he is and then I'll slip away first chance and change up again."

The stretcher party was already in the outer vestibule.

"He'm still breathin, Miss Rose," Kitto said, goggling at her.

"Us found'n on the shore, miss," Oates added. "Near drownded."

"Straight up to the master's bedroom," she said, stepping aside to let them pass. "And what's come over *you?*"

"Them glad rags, miss," he said over his shoulder as they clomped across the hall.

"How else d'you think we pin them and tuck them right?" she asked. "Especially when the one who's to wear them is two thousand miles away. Listen! Do I tell you your job – or gawp at you when you're doing it?" She winked at Mary behind their backs.

"Sorry, miss. And sorry about all this-yur mud, too."

"Never mind that. We have six weeks to clean it up."

When they reached the landing they were lost, of course, and Mary had to slip ahead and open the door to the master's bedroom. "On the couch, there," she said, passing beyond it to draw the curtains and cut down the light.

"How's he breathing?" Rose knelt at his side, oblivious to the mud beneath her knees.

Chivers and Pascoe pulled the withies from the arms of their jackets, which had formed the bed of the makeshift stretcher, and put them on again. Oates picked up the withies and stacked them out of the way.

The man's breath came in shallow pants, finishing in an unpleasant bubbling sound, both on breathing in and on letting it out again. *What do I do?* she wondered.

Pennycuik, drawn by the commotion, poked her head around the door. She was more surprised at the sight of Rose than at the man on the couch. "Kindle a fire, girl!" Rose commanded. "Quick as you can. Use some paraffin and get it roaring."

On a sudden inspiration – or, rather, not being able to think of anything else – she turned to Pascoe, the tallest and burliest of the groundsmen, and said, "See if you can hold him upside-down, by the ankles. Kitto, you help him. See if that'll help some of this water in his lungs to drain out again."

When the man's hair fell away from his brow, she saw he had cut his forehead rather badly, too. The moment he was upside down, water began oozing from his mouth and nose in long, glutinous skeins. He coughed violently and almost shook himself from Pascoe's and Kitto's combined grasp. His face was turning an alarming shade of purple.

"Lay him back down again," she said quickly.

Mary took a towel from the washstand and started mopping up.

The moment he was on his back he breathed more easily – more deeply, too, though there was still that unpleasant bubbling at the beginning and end of each breath.

She let him rest a minute while she felt for his pulse. It was there, all right – thin and thready and rather erratic, she thought, but there, all the same.

"Try it again," she said. "But put him back down as soon as some of the water has come away."

They lifted him, as before, and, once again, the water coughed and spluttered from his lungs.

Four times more they repeated the treatment, allowing him to rest and breathe in between. Each time he coughed up a little more and then bubbled a little less until, on the fifth attempt, no more water would drain. His lungs still bubbled but his breathing was now twice as deep as it had been at first.

By now, Pennycuik had kindled a merry blaze, so Mary told the men to lift the couch over to where it would warm him, for she had laid out several corpses in her life and this young man, breathing or no, felt as cold as any of them.

When the men had all gone, taking their muddy boots and the withies with them, Rose told Pennycuik to start cleaning the place up again, beginning at the portico. Alone at last, the two maids stared at the young man, at the fire, at his clothes, which were beginning to steam, and finally at each other.

It was Rose who had the courage to say, "We ought to get them off him, you know."

"I know."

Neither moved.

"He could catch pneumonia," Rose said.

"I know."

"Well, go and get the enamel bath. We'll put his wet things in that. I'll get a pair of the master's inexpressibles so we can get him decent again as soon as maybe."

As soon as maybe! she thought as she busied herself finding underpants and bath towels. *Now what does that mean, pray?*

She answered herself: *It means whatever you want it to mean – that's what.*

Mary returned with the bath, which was like a giant arum lily in brown enamel – brown on the outside, white on the in. "This should be big enough," she said, laying it down near his feet. "Well now!" She rubbed her hands awkwardly and stared down at the fellow. "Should we apologize in advance or what."

"Oh, come on!" Rose started unknotting the bandana he wore round his neck. "Pretend we're nurses. I'll bet they aren't so squeamish."

Mary started with his shoes, which were of the canvas type with rope soles, such as sailors wear. "D'you think he's a sailor?" she asked, pointing them out.

Rose turned one of his hands palm-out by way of an answer. "Not with those hands. A yachtsman, maybe."

His jacket, made of faded blue canvas, was quite a struggle to get off, being all wet and clinging. His socks, by contrast peeled off like loose skin. Then it was a question of shirt or trousers – possibly the only two garments left.

The thought put the girls n a quandary. Rose undid the buttons across his chest. "He's also got a vest," she said, trying to sound professional and to keep the relief out of her voice – not too successfully.

Mary peeped up his trouser leg. "Long combinations," she said. "Right ... well ... here goes!"

They unbuttoned everything in sight and, taking a trouser leg each, hauled them off him. He groaned and gave an involuntary kick when they had them only halfway.

"Lord!" Mary exclaimed. "What if he wakes up when he's completely ... you know!"

"We should get a big towel ready so we can cover him at once," Rose suggested.

"This'll do." Mary took the biggest of Sir Hector's bath towels and stretched it out over the fire guard, which she moved back, about six feet away from the flames.

He was wearing the all-in-one type of shirt, where the front and back aprons button between the thighs to form, in effect, short trousers. Rose glanced pointedly at the fire while she fiddled to undo them. Mary, the mere spectator, felt more at liberty to watch.

"I know I shouldn't ought to say it," she said, "but he's even better-looking than your Frank."

"I thought the same myself," Rose replied as she eased the shirt off his right arm. "And these are really good-quality clothes, you know. He's not short of a bob or two, as anyone can see."

"He's not short of a ... of a ... a lot of things." Mary's eye lingered pointedly on the bulge beneath his long comms.

"Come on, my girl! You take that other sleeve off and be quick about it!"

"Yass'm!" Mary laughed as she threw the clammy shirt upon the heap in the tin bath. "And now!"

"Yes ... and now." Rose stared down at him, wondering what sort of fellow he was – and realizing how little one could tell from a face in utter repose.

He *looked* like a thoroughly decent young chap – the sort of man that any girl would feel proud to be seen walking out with. In fact, if she weren't already promised ... more or less ...

No! She mustn't ... that is, there was no point in starting along that line of thought. None whatsoever. He was above her class and no good could come of it.

"Start at the top end," Mary said. "Go on."

"Why me?"

"Because you're nearest. Oh, for heaven's sake! I'll start then."

Rose just beat her to the top button. "You shall do the next one," she said.

While Mary complied they both counted the remaining buttons – tinker, tailor, soldier, sailor ... and Rose saw with dismay that she was destined to undo the last one of all, the one whose pale ivory disc sat upon that ... that mound like a single, baleful eye.

Well, at least it gave her time to prepare.

His chest was a mat of thick, dark hair, which thinned out to a line all down his firm, flat stomach.

"Let's leave it like that for the moment," Rose said when her turn finally came.

"Cowardy-cowardy custard!" Mary sang softly, gleefully. "Your bones are made of mustard!"

"Let's get the top part off him first, so he's exposed as briefly as possible. See if you can slip his arm out of that sleeve. Then I'll try to hold him up while you roll it down underneath him."

"Oh ... yes." Mary left off her banter and became serious again.

Rose stood beyond the arm of the couch, insinuated her hands beneath his armpits, and heaved upward with all her might. He still felt desperately cold to the touch; in fact, she could feel him starting to shiver. "We must get him dry and warm," she said.

Mary worked swiftly to roll the combinations down beneath him; she managed to get them as far as the small of his back before his weight defeated her. "If you could just manage the other side now ..." she suggested.

Between them they managed another couple of rolls, down beneath his buttocks.

"Well now it should be child's play," Rose said as her fingers reached nervously for that one remaining button. "I mean easy."

The woolen cloth sprang apart ... fell away.

"Well!" Mary exclaimed, now that the focus of all their fear – and curiosity – lay exposed. "My brother's was bigger than that when he was just fourteen!"

"Perhaps they shrink in water?" Rose suggested. "They've got curly hair there, too, just like us!"

They were both so absorbed in the spectacle that neither noticed Pennycuik entering the room, bearing a tray of hot broth.

"They do always do that," she said, giving them a fright as she set the tray down on an occasional table.

"And what do *you* know about it, pray?" Rose asked sharply.

"A lot!" The girl laughed. "More'n you two maids by the sound of it. Look – I'll show 'ee summat else."

And before they could stop her she had leaned over the back of the couch, pushed his unresisting thighs apart, and was raking one fingernail gently up the inner side of his left thigh. "See! See!" She giggled and pointed to his left testicle, which was climbing upward to the point where it was about to vanish inside his body.

"Well I never!" Rose knew she ought to reprimand the girl – and severely at that – but she was much too fascinated in this extraordinary phenomenon.

That's what it was – a phenomenon!

"Now the other one." Pennycuik repeated the trick on his right thigh – with the same amazing result. The left testicle had meanwhile descended again. "They'll only do that a couple of times," she told them, making the left ascend again even as the right one relaxed. "Then it's stand by for boarders!"

"How d'you know all this, Pennycuik?" Mary asked.

"Ha ha – that'd be tellin," the girl replied. Curiously enough, she spoke these words to Rose, as if she had asked the question.

"How's he faring?" Mrs Browning called out from the stairhead, where she paused to catch her breath.

Never was a man got into fresh warm underpants so swiftly, nor wrapped about the torso with a vast, luxuriously hot bathtowel in such record time.

6 They moved the couch nearer the fire until he turned pink and then, when he began to sweat, they carried him to the bed, still unconscious and still breathing as if through a hubble-bubble. The broth, meanwhile, went cold and was carried back to the kitchen. Mary bathed the cut on his forehead with salty water and Rose dabbed up to its edges with mercurichrome. She winced in sympathy for she knew how it could sting, but he hardly stirred. Mrs Browning sent Pennycuik into Flushing village for Doctor Perrin; she returned with the news that he was out on another call but his wife said he'd come as soon as he was free.

"You should go and change back into your proper clothes now," Mary said to Rose. "I'll stay by him."

"I can't manage the hooks and bar," Rose lied. "You go and get my things and bring them here."

"I can undo it now. See?" Mary started to work at the fastening of her bodice.

Rose twisted herself away. "Just do as you're told!" she snapped.

"Oh hoity-toity!" Mary cried. But she obeyed all the same – though there was a knowing smile on her lips as she left the room.

The young man gave a little moan and then inhaled with a strange, shivery awkwardness, pausing several times before snatching at yet more air, as if he still could not get enough. He held it a moment and then let it out explosively, ending with a most gruesome bubbling sound.

Or could it be called a *rattle?*

Rose began to panic. She had been present at two deaths – of her grandmother and of a man who had a fit and swallowed a clay pipe in King Charles's churchyard – but she had never actually heard the famous death rattle. Was it that curious bubbling sound?

"Oh please!" she cried, putting a hand on his chest and pushing hard. "Breathe! Please don't die now!"

She heard bubble-bubble-bubble but he did not start breathing again.

She put her ear to his open lips – his beautiful open lips – just in case he was breathing too gently for her to notice.

Nothing.

She felt for his pulse and found it still there – even feebler than before but, God be praised, not absent altogether.

Whether it was an unconscious memory of all those fairy tales in which sleepers are awakened with the magical power of a kiss, or whether it was a far more primal urge that moved her, she felt compelled to put her lips to his and try to breathe some life back into him.

All that happened was that her own breath came back through his nostrils and fanned her cheek. She pinched them off between finger and thumb and tried again. This time his chest swelled out beneath her resting arm; she eased its weight and found she could empty her own lungs completely into his.

If it had been a death rattle, a moment or so earlier, there was now the hope of a life rattle to match it as his-her breath rushed out again. Its warmth fanned her cheek. She waited for him to breathe spontaneously and, when he did not, she repeated the action. His lips moved like those of a suckling baby between one teat and the other. She was almost overwhelmed with an emotion she could not name, for she had never felt anything like it before. It was part maternal, to be sure; was she not, after all, giving him life? But it was more than that. The lifegiving breath he exhaled was her breath, too. It was as if their very lives had become fused together in that act of sharing.

Five times she filled his lungs from hers, and still he did not begin to breathe.

"Oh ... please-please-please!" she cried, putting her lips to his yet again.

But no sooner did they touch than she became aware that his eyes had suddenly opened. She froze. For a moment their eyes dwelled deep in each other's, though his were quite vacant; then he blinked rapidly, many times, and his eyes went crossed as he tried to focus on her. She released his nose and broke contact with a guilty haste. She patted and soothed his hair as if to suggest that that was what she had been doing all along. "Breathe!" she urged.

He tried to say something but his throat was full of phlegm. In attempting to clear it he began at last to breathe unaided – which swiftly turned into a coughing fit. She helped him to a semi-upright position and, reaching into the night commode beside the bed, produced Sir Hector's chamber pot.

"Dizzy!" he wheezed as he coughed it up. Then, "My head!"

The door opened and Mary came back, with Rose's clothes draped over both arms. She began to apologize for being gone such an age but her voice trailed off when she took in the scene. "Thank the Lord!" she exclaimed.

"Drop those things and give me a hand, here," Rose said. "Or no! Better still, go down and get that bowl of broth. We seem to be coping here."

Mary laid the clothes out on the back of the sofa and went.

"Lie back, now," Rose said as she returned the pot to the commode. "You've had a nasty knock on your head and you almost drowned."

He clenched his eyes and winced as he settled back against the pillows, which she plumped up behind him. He clearly had the king and queen of all headaches. "Falmouth," he murmured.

"Well, at least you remember where you are!" she said jovially. "Mary's bringing some warm broth and the doctor's coming and I'll get you some willow bark for your head. Is it very bad?"

"Where?" he asked.
"Inside your head."
"No ..." He waved a hand vaguely about him.
"Oh, I see. This is Nancemellin House. Falmouth is ... well, you'll be able to see it through that window when we draw back the curtain – which we won't do just yet, I think."
He nodded, but even that sent fresh paroxysms of pain through his head.
"Is there anyone we should tell?" she asked. "To let them know you're safe?"
He shook his head.
She wondered how that could be but she did not think it her place to press the question.
"Just lie still and don't talk," she urged. "I'm afraid you're going to be here for a day or two at least, so there'll be plenty of time for talking."
He had another fit of throat-clearing, which meant more business with the chamber pot. "Disgusting," he growled when it was over. "Forgive me."
"Don't be silly!" she replied. "And stop trying to talk."
"Your name," he said. "At least I should know your name. Mine is Redmile-Smith, Louis Redmile-Smith."
"Lucinda-Ella," she replied hastily, not really knowing why – or, rather, knowing only that 'Rose' was wrong. "But plain Lucinda will do."
"*Plain* Lucinda? Oh no!" He tried to laugh and succeeded only in coughing again, briefly this time. Then he whispered, "Lucinda-Ella? It sounds American." He found whispering easier than croaking through vocal cords still clogged with phlegm.
"My mother's American – from a Cornish family, though. Are you connected with the millers and brewers?" Her mother swore by Redmile's wholegrain self-raising flour and Smith's Pale Export was her father's Sunday-lunchtime treat.
"The same," he replied. "D'you mind?"
"Mind?" she echoed in surprise.
"Your mother then – will she mind when she learns that someone *in trade* is hogging what is obviously one of the best beds in the house?"
"It would never cross anybody's mind," she assured him. "Not under *this* roof." She hoped her tone of absolute confidence would let them sidestep all the awkward questions he might otherwise unwittingly pose.
"And where *is* your mother – if I may ask?"
"Why? Does it matter? She's not here, anyway."
"It's just that I feel awkward – being alone with you – without her knowledge."
"Who says it's without her knowledge?"
"Well – if she's away ..."

"Oh … I see … yes."

She couldn't see how to get out of that. *Tell him who you really are!* her common sense shouted at her. *Explain why you're dressed like this. He's a decent fellow. He'll understand. He won't give you away – and although it would give him a certain power over you, he's hardly in a state to take advantage of it. Go on – own up!*

"In fact," she said, "Sir Hector and Lady Carclew are away on a visit to the orient – so, if you wish to obtain their permission, you'll have to remain an invalid for the next six weeks or so."

"Can't do that, I'm 'fraid." He tried to chuckle but only winced again. "Got to be in France by Tuesday – or *my* mother will never speak to me again."

"You live in France?" she asked, wondering if he had sailed, or drifted, all the way across the Channel.

"No. I live wherever the family business takes me, just at the moment. I keep a little single-handed yacht at the Falmouth Yacht Club – I mean, I *kept* it there. I just came down from Plymouth for a weekend's sailing. I hadn't even found a hôtel – though it would have been the Prince of Wales as usual, I suppose. My suitcase was in the yacht. Davy Jones has it by now, I suppose." He frowned. "What day is it, by the way. How long have I …"

"It's still Friday. I don't know how long you were lying unconscious on the beach. Not long, I should think. But you've been up here about two hours. In fact, it's past time for luncheon. Where *is* that girl with your broth?"

She rose and went to the door; but the moment she opened it she heard Pennycuik and Mary arguing at the foot of the stair – "I'll take it up." "No, let me!" and so on.

"Quiet – both of you!" she called down. "Are you arguing over a bowl of broth?"

Silence.

"Mary! You bring it up," she went on. "And Pennycuik – you be about your business."

"When the cat's away, eh?" he wheezed from the bed.

It was the perfect prompt for her to confess, wipe the slate, and start again.

"If that's what they think, they'll soon learn I'm no kitten," she replied.

"Oops – sorry!"

She waited by the open door, hoping she might somehow signal to Mary that she was continuing the charade they had begun with the simple act of dressing-up. But she need not have bothered. Mary had already twigged and, like Mrs Browning and Pennycuik, thought it the greatest joke.

Rose realized it the moment she saw the tray, which was set out for two, precisely as she herself would have set it out if a mistress of hers had been tending an invalid and would take luncheon with him – right down to the little pomade jar of Cornish violets.

That's what had taken their time, of course. "Good for you," she whispered, coming out to meet her on the landing.

"What name?" Mary asked urgently.

"Lucinda."

Mary giggled.

'Lucinda' returned to the room and, taking up the tray-bridge on which Sir Hector liked to rest his wake-up cup of tea each morning, spanned it across Louis' legs.

"Thank you, Mary," she said. "You may like to know that our invalid guest is Mister Louis Redmile-Smith, of the wholesale brewing and milling family. I'm sure Cook will be interested, too. She swears by Redmile's flour, does she not?"

"She won't use none other, Miss Lucinda," the maid answered. She was relishing her descent, several rungs down the social ladder, just as much as Rose was enjoying her self-elevation – even more, in fact, for she had little to lose if her imposture were to be exposed.

"D'you happen to know where her ladyship keeps her willow bark?" Rose asked as she took up a soup spoon. "Poor Mister Redmile-Smith has a dreadful headache."

"She do 'ave some of that *aspiring* medicine, miss. She belong to say 'tis better far than that old willow bark."

"Aspirin, you mean." Rose struggled to keep a straight face as she tested the temperature of the broth. "Do bring it here, please." When Mary had gone, she asked, "Can you manage it yourself, Mister Redmile-Smith? It's not too hot."

"I think I can," he replied, wincing as he moved his arm.

She suspected he was putting it on. Not that she minded – in fact, she enjoyed the opportunity it gave her to study his face without rudeness ... to touch his lips, even if it was only with a napkin-swaddled finger when not all the spoonful went inside.

It was a good face, expressive and full of character – not what you'd call lopsided, but not quite even-sided, either. When he smiled, the right half of his lips stretched farther and made a deeper dimple than the left, and his right eyebrow went slightly down while the left one went up. His hair was all tousled still, so she could not even guess which side he parted it; she tried to imagine it and ended up concluding it would be best combed straight back. Or maybe forward, like Julius Cæsar's hair on the statue down in the hall? She wondered if he'd let her experiment with it in the days to come.

He, meanwhile, had obviously been doing some thinking.

"This nightshirt ..." he said. The broth was helping to clear his throat. His voice was pleasantly deep.

"It's the master's," she told him. "Sir Hector's, I mean. Dear me! Here I am talking to you as if to a servant!"

"He's your father?"

"No! He's my ... ward. I mean, I'm *his* ward."

"He's your guardian, then."
"That's the word, yes."
"Not one you use too often, it seems."
Rose said, "Eat more, talk less!"
Mary returned with a jar of aspirin tablets. " 'Er ladyship belong to take up to four, miss," she said.
Rose turned to Louis. "Have you had them before? How many do you usually take?"
"I've never had cause," he replied. "Let's try two to start with."
"Well, Doctor Perrin will know, but I don't suppose two can do much harm."
"Not more than this headache, anyway."
When the two tablets – and Mary – had gone, he returned to his earlier theme. "Forgive me if I trespass," he said, "but I should hate you to get into trouble with your guardian on my account. Will he take offence ... I mean, how will he respond when he learns of this situation?"
It was too good a chance to let pass by. "Need he ever know?" she asked. "You will be in France weeks before they will return."
"I see." He became thoughtful again. Then he shrugged – without wincing. "Do I have any choice?"
"I'm in your hands," she said.
He smiled. "Metaphorically speaking."
Their eyes met. She had just made him a conspirator in something much deeper than the ostensible subject of this conversation, just as she was offering him far more than her 'guardian's' unwitting hospitality. It emboldened him to continue: "My own clothes ...?" He left the question hanging.
"... are being washed and pressed," she assured him.
"And these ... this nightshirt and these ... undergarments?"
"... are Sir Hector's," she replied patiently, as to a confused child – though she knew well enough what was troubling him. Then, hoping to unruffle his fears, she added, "Four of the estate workers found you lying on the beach and brought you up here – Pascoe, Chivers, Oates, and Kitto. Which reminds me – someone had better clean up all this mud now that it has dried."
"Aha! I see!" He was relieved, believing she had tactfully answered his unaskable question.
She should have felt relieved, too, she realized. So whence this sense of disappointment? Something within her wanted him to *know* that she had seen him naked, had rubbed him dry with these hands, had caressed him tenderly through that towel from head to toe, had put her lips to his and breathed the life back into him when he had surely lost the ability to do it for himself ... why, gol'darn it, as her mother said, he practically *owed* his very life to her. He *was* hers!

7 Rose kept out of the way while Dr Perrin called. He was not too worried about the amount of fluid in Louis' lungs; the human body, he said, had amazing powers to absorb such things. He was more concerned with the cut on the young man's forehead, which he closed with three stitches fine enough to arouse Mary's envy.

"You'll have a bit of a scar there, I'm afraid," he told Louis. "Pretend you got it in a duel – impress the ladies, eh, Mary?"

She chuckled, to avoid making a choice between broad and refined Cornish.

"Not the ladies of *this* house, doctor," Louis replied dolefully. "They know the truth – that I'm just a bungling single-handed yachtsman. Besides, they've seen me at my most vulnerable."

This last statement prompted Mary into an unguarded response: "Oh, but we were quick to cover you up again, sir!"

For one brief moment he was baffled, then, even more briefly, shocked; a split-second later he was smiling. "Really?" he said. "Well, thankyou – that's good to know."

All three emotions passed over Mary's head. To her relief, the doctor was eager to get on to yet another call, so there was no chit-chat that might have led to uncomfortable revelations of Rose's part in the business, much less to talk of the mysterious Lucinda, a hitherto unsuspected ward of Sir Hector Carclew.

"Your bill, doctor!" Louis called out as the man reached the door. "Send it to my club – the Royal Automobile."

"My dear fellow – it's a pleasure to treat a *real* malady in this house!" The doctor waved the offer away and was gone. The fees he extracted from the semi-hypochondriac Carclews paid for his attendance on a dozen of the poor, anyway.

Rose waited until the front door banged – indeed, until she heard the scrinch of his dog-cart wheels on the gravel – before she dared show her face again. "Oh, has he gone already?" she asked in a disappointed tone as she returned to the sick room. "I wanted to ask him about the aspirin."

"All taken care of," Louis said cheerfully. "It is wonderful against headaches, I must say."

"You want to get out of that ballgown now, do 'ee, Miss Lucinda?" Mary asked pointedly. To Louis she added, "We was trying it on, see, when they boys brung you up along."

"I can trust you not to do anything silly, I suppose," Rose asked equally pointedly.

She realized it would seem distinctly odd for her to stay dressed in a magnificent ballgown after such an explanation.

"You do know me, miss!" Mary was doing a passable imitation of Pennycuik.

"Yes, indeed," Rose murmured as she left.

"Call of nature, I'm afraid, Mary," Louis said as soon as they were alone. "Could you kindly fish out the chamber pot and help me to my feet?"

"Oh, there's no need for you to stand up, sir. Just sit on the edge of the bed. I'll slip into the dressing room until you've done."

He did as she suggested and called her back when he'd finished. She carried the pot outside the door and rang for Pennycuik to come and take it.

"A bit pointless now, all that modesty," he said when she returned to his bedside. "What? Eh?"

Mary, who had had time to think over her outburst and now regretted it, said, "I shouldn't ought to of said nothing, sir. You won't go and tell Miss Lucinda, I 'ope?"

"Not if it would get you into trouble, no. But tell me, was she there when ... you know?"

Mary, safe now in his promise to say nothing, thought she might as well get a bit of fun out of the situation. "Lord, sir, she was the one what done it."

"Was she, by George!" He grinned. "What, you mean she actually ..." He mimed the pulling off of his combinations.

She shook her head. "I said enough already, sir. Too much, and that's a fack. But I'll just add this – I never seen she so frantic ... so *hurrisome,* if you take my meaning, over anything in all my life as what she was to save your life."

"Really?" His grin faded and he became thoughtful.

"The moment she clapped eyes on you ... why, she was a changed woman. None of us never seen she like that afore. She's a changed woman."

"Why? What is her usual temperament, then?"

"Cold! There – that's a-tellin' of 'ee. She'm what they do call a cold fish."

"Cold!" He couldn't believe it, of course.

" 'Es!" She spoke the word on an indrawn breath, as Cornish women often do for emphasis. "So cold as a quilkin in a cundard!"

"Whatever that is!" he murmured.

But she had no time to explain, for the cold fish herself returned at that moment, dressed now in one of Fenella's plainer day dresses. "What rubbish has she been prattling?" she asked as she crossed the room. "Never mind! Mary, I had a word with Doctor Perrin as he was leaving. He recommends fish – fresh fish and plenty of it." She smiled at Louis and added, "For the brain."

"I need that," he admitted. "Hot or cold." He winked at Mary.

Rose was kicking herself now. If she had had a word with the doctor 'as he was leaving,' why had she returned to this room, apparently surprised to discover he had left?

She must think of an answer to that one – quick!

She turned again to Mary. "See what cook has and if it's not absolutely fresh off the quayside this morning, send Pennycuik into Flushing for some fillets of hake or ray's wings or" – she looked at Louis – "what d'you like best?"

"Whiting, plain and simple," he replied. "I know – I'm a great disappointment to everyone."

"Make it whiting, then," she told Mary.

The maid curtsied and left.

"Why were you surprised to find that the doctor had gone?" he asked at once. "If you met him on the way out, I mean?"

"Because when I met him I thought he was going *up*stairs. It was only when I found he'd gone that I realized he must have been leaving. What is this? Are you a policeman?"

"No!" He laughed apologetically. "But I do have another question. What does 'so cold as a quilting in a custard? Cundard?' Something like that ... what's it mean?"

"So cold as a quilkin in a cundard!" She laughed. "Quilkin is Cornish for a frog and a cundard is a drain – cold as a frog in a drain. Why?" She became worried. "Are you cold? I'll ring for more coals."

"Not at all. I've never felt so comfortable, in fact. I hope you don't mind my saying this, but you should laugh more often, Lucinda. May I call you Lucinda?"

"Tomorrow – perhaps," she told him, simply working on the principle that a well-brought-up girl does not rush pell-mell into any stage of a developing intimacy – even though everything else within her was shouting, 'Yes! Yes! And kiss me, too, while you're about it!' To soften the rebuff she added, "I think we should be able to look back on at least one day of formality, don't you, Mister Redmile-Smith? Anyway, I believe I do laugh quite enough as it is – excessively, some would say."

"I'm sorry I spoke, then." He hung his head.

"I'll admit, however, that I didn't laugh all that often between the moment we saw the groundsmen carrying you across the lawn and the moment you opened your eyes and began breathing again on your own."

"Eh? What does that mean, pray – breathing on my own?"

She shrugged awkwardly. "Figure of speech."

"Dashed odd."

"Oh, all right! If you must know, there was a moment, after we got you into bed ... I mean, your breathing was always quite erratic, and bubbly ... much more than the noise you heard after you came to ... anyway, there was a moment when you stopped breathing. At least, I couldn't hear anything – nor feel anything when I put my cheek close to your mouth."

"And so?"

"So I ..." She swallowed hard. "I breathed *for* you."

"But how?" He gave a baffled laugh and, raising his hands, let them fall helpless to the counterpane. "It's not possible."

"D'you want me to show you?"

He sensed the sudden nervous tension in her and was seized with it, too. Something momentous – he knew not what – was about to happen. "All right," he said quietly.

"Lie back, then. And close your eyes. And breathe right out. And don't try to breathe in again."

He obeyed each instruction as she spoke it. He started slightly when she pinched his nose. He started more than slightly when she drew a deep breath and put her lips to his. And he gave an indrawn moan of amazement when he felt his lungs inflate with her breath.

"You did *that?*" he asked when she took her lips away.

Not too far, though, and not for long, either. She lowered her mouth again, this time for a kiss.

A kiss?

If all those previous moments in her life when her lips had met those of another were kisses, what word was left to describe an experience of *this* power, this intensity? It was a moment outside time and space, when the entire universe shrank to a cocoon for just him and her.

It lasted for ever and yet it was over too soon.

"There now," she whispered as she broke to draw breath.

"No!" He reached out to cradle her head between his hands and draw her back to him.

There was a knock at the door. Mary came into the room without waiting to be told she might. One look at Rose standing there, flustered, pulling her dress straight, told her all she needed to know. "Please Miss Lucinda," she said, "Oates is at the door, miss, to say as they've found Mister Redmile-Smith's boat washed up on the rocks."

"Damaged?" Louis sat up and smoothed the counterpane.

"The mast, sir. He says 'tis broke. And the rudder's all gone."

"Oh well …" He laughed awkwardly. "Could be worse."

"Thank you, Mary," Rose said coldly.

"There's other matters, miss." She looked awkwardly at Louis.

"Oh, very well," Rose answered tetchily. Then, to him, "You'll be all right for a moment?" She bent over and pretended to tuck him in so that he could speak without his words reaching Mary.

"I'll count the seconds," he murmured.

She blew him a clandestine kiss and flounced past Mary to stand belligerently, hands on hips, on the landing outside.

"Are you quite mad?" Mary hissed, dragging her away down the passage and beyond the green baize door to the servant's quarters. "This is where you belong, maid – just as he belongs on the other side there. What are you thinking of?"

"You don't understand," Rose said. Her lips still tingled with the memory of that kiss.

"I understand very well. You're playing with fire – and you will get burnt. You *will.* You know it."

"If I am, it's my business. All I know is …"

"Oh no it's not! It'll bring fire and retribution down on all of us, even Mister and Mrs Tregembo. What are you thinking of? What can you hope for? What's the very best you can hope for?"

"I don't know. I don't know." She closed her eyes and put her hands over her ears. "Just leave me be! All I know is I love him. I've never …"

"Don't say it! How can you? It can't be true, anyway. You never set eyes on him before today. It's ridiculous."

"I know! D'you think I haven't said all that to myself? I sat there, all that time before he came to, I sat there, knowing I'd fallen in love with him and sneering at myself for being such an idiot …"

"Then what happened to such good sense?"

Rose grinned and ran her tongue around her lips.

"God in heaven!" Mary exclaimed. "You catch one glimpse of the man naked, you get an eyeful of his family jewels, and …"

Rose lashed out with her hand and caught her a stinging slap across her cheek.

"Right you are!" Mary said grimly as she rubbed the spot. "If it's a fight you want, I'll give it you. Beginning now. I'm going straight back into that room to tell him the truth – about you, about me, about this whole situation."

She turned to go but Rose caught her by the arm. "I'm sorry. I'm sorry. But you shouldn't have said that – what you did say, about his family jewels. It's nothing to do with that. Oh Mary! I've never felt like this before. I never even believed such feelings were possible. I'm in such a turmoil … you can't imagine. But please don't spoil it for me. If you do, I'll kill myself – or you!" She laughed wanly to show she didn't mean it. "I *know* nothing can ever come of it. I know it's all going to fizzle away to nothing next week when he goes away. He has to go to France, he says – some promise he's made to his mother. So it *has* to end then. I know it. I know it's just an impossible little … fairy-tale … something. An idyll. But it'll be something I'll never forget. So just let's keep up the pretence for these few days. Please?"

Their eyes locked. Mary hesitated.

"Please?" Rose repeated.

She yielded, saying ruefully, "I don't like it. Everything in me is shouting no!"

Rose danced for joy. "And everything in *me* is singing yes!"

"Well, I'd never have guessed it!"

"Oh, you're an angel." Rose threw her arms around Mary and tried to make her join in the dance.

"I am no such thing." Mary thrust her away. "If anything, I'm the devil here. Maybe I put your darling Louis up to it."

Rose stopped her dance. "What d'you mean?"

She looked about her awkwardly. "I meant it as a joke. He as good as asked who undressed him and put the master's underclothes and nightshirt on him, and …"

"But I *told* him. Or not exactly told. I let him understand it was Oates and company."

"Yes, well, I wasn't to know that, was I! And I said it was you."

"No!" Rose hid her face in her hands.

"And I said you'd been hurrisome about him ever since you clapped eyes upon him. So of course – he's trying his luck with you now, isn't he! He must suppose Christmas has a later echo for him this year."

"It's not true, not true!" Rose, still hiding her face, shook her head violently.

"I wouldn't tell you if it was a lie. It's just to make you *careful,* my lover. That's all. Don't throw yourself at him. Were the pair of you kissing just now?"

Rose lowered her hands at last. "And if we were?" She smiled once again.

"And who started it? Did you kiss him or did he kiss you?"

She hesitated.

"There you are!" Mary cried. "That's what I mean." She grasped Rose by the shoulders and shook her in gentle exasperation. "Just go a little easier, eh? Just keep telling yourself that he *might* be no more than trifling with you – thanks to what I said."

Rose nodded. Tears were prickling her eyes.

"Promise?" Mary insisted.

"Promise." Her voice broke. She flung her arms around her friend and hugged her tight. "Sorry," she whispered. "Sorry I slapped you."

"It's all right." Mary patted and stroked up and down her back.

"I've never felt like this before about anyone, you see."

"That's why it's so dangerous, my lover."

8

Rose returned to the bedroom to find Louis out of bed, standing at the window and staring down into the garden.

"What's this, young fellow-my-lad?" she cried jovially. "Back to bed with you this minute!"

He did not respond.

When she reached his side she saw that he was watching the men drag a small sailing boat up the stone walk; it was perched on one of the garden trolleys and it was rather more badly damaged than Mary had led him to expect. When they realized he was watching, one of the men picked up a battered and sodden-looking suitcase and waved it triumphantly over his head.

"Thank God for that!" Louis waved back.

"Never mind your old boat," Rose went on. "You'll catch your death …"

He interrupted her. "I shall have to go, Miss Tremayne."

"No!" she cried.

He turned to face her. His eyes had lost all their sparkle. "I fear so. What happened just now was ..."

"Wonderful," she said.

"... unconscionable." He nodded to reinforce the word.

A dozen idiotic responses occurred to her all at once, from fatuous pleadings to even more pointless threats. In the end all she said was, "Shouldn't I be the judge of that?"

Whatever replies he might have prepared himself to hear, that was not one of them. He hesitated.

"You're shivering." She gripped his arm gently and tried to turn him back toward the bed.

"Not with cold," he told her.

"Then with fever. Whatever it is, you should get back into bed."

Her grip on his arm was gentle but unyielding.

He began to move.

"Then we can discuss it calmly and gently." She even steeled herself to add, "If you have good reason to go, then I shall not stand in your way." She crossed her fingers and added to herself, *I shall get Dr Perrin to do it for me.*

While he settled himself between the sheets once more she pulled her chair back a token but significant six inches and said, "There now!"

"I really ought to leave," he said at once. "I am already ... I mean, there is ... oh dear!"

"Another young lady?" she suggested.

He nodded and stared at his hands.

"You are formally engaged?"

Her heart leaped up when he shook his head. "It's just a sort of understanding. We grew up together, you see. It has always just been assumed."

She laughed.

Wounded, he looked up at her.

"I'm not mocking you," she said. "I'm in exactly the same boat." She laughed again, this time at her unconscious choice of metaphor. "And I have to confess that it's just about as smashed as that boat of yours down there. Frank Tresidder is a second-cousin to me. If you could stick your head out of that window and look east, you'd see his farm. It marches with Sir Hector's estate. We've been promised to each other since we were both in petticoats."

He nodded glumly, as if to say that their situations were pretty alike. "And now?" he asked.

She shrugged. "At least I know it's not love – and never has been love."

"How do you think he's going to respond?"

When she did not reply he said, "Eh?"

"You make me see how selfish I am," she said morosely. "The question had not even crossed my mind."

"Well, now that it has ...?"

"It's a funny thing, but I just don't know. We've never been tremendously … hurrisome, as they say round here. More like very good friends. The best of friends." She laughed bleakly. "Perhaps we'll stay the best of friends. What about you and …?"

"Augusta. I don't know. Without wishing to sound conceited, I think she might take it quite hard."

"Yes, well, I wouldn't blame her."

"Aaargh!" He closed his eyes tight and clenched his fist. He seemed to be about to strike himself on the forehead with it, forgetting his stitches.

"No!" She darted out a hand and grabbed him by the wrist.

He had, indeed, been about to beat his brow, so the effect was that he pulled her to him. And then their hunger for each other took over. Her lips sought his; his reached out for hers; and a moment later they were locked in an embrace even more passionate than before.

"Oh God!" he moaned when at last they broke for air. "There is no resisting it, is there. Poor Augusta! I feel awful. Even to be speaking her name to you, I feel …"

"Sssh!" She forced him back into the pillows and lay across him diagonally, resting her head beside his where she could kiss his cheek and neck and play with his curls. "If we could just mend that boat of yours," she murmured, "and sail away to an island somewhere and just be the only two people who mattered. We wouldn't even need names. Just thee and me."

"Mmmmnh!" He closed his eyes and relaxed utterly.

"I've never seen such beautiful ears."

"Have them! They're yours."

"Ooooh! Well … in that case … I've never seen such beautiful lips, either."

He turned and kissed her briefly. "They're yours already."

"Eyes!"

He opened them and peered into hers. "If I wanted to tear them away from you, I couldn't."

She kissed their lids and searched his face for something else to claim. "Adam's apple!" She giggled.

"I was saving that for your birthday – which is when? Mine's the twenty-third of August."

"August and Augusta," she pointed out.

"I never thought of that. When is your birthday?"

"It's just gone," she told him. "March the second."

"Pity. You'll simply have to wait for the old Adam's apple."

"The twenty-third is just into Virgo," she mused. "Pisces and Virgo – that's supposed to be one of the worst possible combinations, you know."

"It only goes to show how wrong they are, eh?"

"Are they? I wonder. I thought I detected a trace of the Virgo in you just now."

"I don't really know what it all means, all these crabs and goats and archers."

"Oh, well, Virgo is supposed to be all neat and tidy and completely disciplined and in control."

"And that's *me?*" He opened his eyes in amazement.

She kissed them shut again. "Didn't you want to go and draw your 'understanding' or whatever you call it – with Augusta – didn't you want to end it all neatly before coming back here and beginning all over again with me, free of that encumbrance?"

"Yes," he admitted freely. "And just see how tenaciously I stuck to it! Fifteen seconds? That's practically a Redmile-Smith record for tenacity. What's Pisces, anyway?"

"We're supposed to be vague and dreamy and artistic."

"And relentless? Singleminded? Un-deflectable?"

She kissed his cheeks. "Only when we meet Virgos. You bring out all that's best in us." She chuckled. "The funny thing is that, today, *you* were the fish – and a pretty wet fish, too."

"Oh!" He responded unthinkingly. "And I suppose that means you were ... no, never mind." When he swallowed, the Adam's apple he had promised her for next March bobbed up and down.

"What were you going to say?" she asked, grinning.

"Never mind."

"Some other time?"

"Maybe."

9 The idyll continued all that long weekend. Rose was hardly ever out of Louis' company. She knew it must inevitably end, that her impersonation would surely be unmasked if she were so foolish as to persist with it beyond his departure and into those weeks while he was away in France. So they took walks together in the Nancemellin parkland. They played bezique of an evening like an old married couple. He played the piano and they sang duets – *Plaisirs d'amour, The last rose of summer,* and so forth. The knowledge that she would all too soon be left 'blooming all alone,' with at least one 'lovely companion faded and gone,' brought tears to her eyes, which he wrongly believed he understood.

"I shall be back, my love," he promised when the days had dwindled down to mere hours. They were walking arm-in-arm down to the beach where the groundsmen had found him. "I shall spend one unavoidable month with mama at Cap Ferrat and I shall have to spend a further month attending to the business – but then, oh *then!* You shall be my first rose of this summer – and of many a summer to come."

"'And after many a summer dies the swan,'" she murmured.

"Tennyson!" he exclaimed. "My favourite. D'you like him?"

She told him of her twenty-first birthday present and promised she would read nothing else after he had gone.

"For my sake?" he asked. "Or do you like him for yourself?"

"Parts of him – where he can make you see how puny we are and how little we count in the vast bustle of ... things. History. Life. You know. If you're feeling sad or neglected or if you suspect you'll *never* get to achieve anything, he can assure you it doesn't really matter because even the greatest achievement doesn't count for much, anyway." She spoke the lines that preceded the one she had just quoted: "'The woods decay, the woods decay and fall. / The vapours weep their burden to the ground, / Man comes and tills the field and lies beneath, / And after many a summer dies the swan.' That sort of thing. And later, where he speaks of 'happy men that have the power to die ...'"

"'And grassy barrows of the happier dead,'" he concluded. "Oh, my darling!" He took her into his arms. "So elegiac all of a sudden! I'll be back. I promise. The hours will drag for both of us but I will be back."

Small wavelets lapped the sandy foreshore, like slow-motion applause; they gurgled among the low, weed-strewn rocks that bounded it to the east.

"Listen!" She clung to him, thinking *soon he will be gone. Soon these arms will be empty and you'll have to put all this romantic nonsense behind you and live your life as if this had never been. Don't spoil these last hours with sadness.*

"What now?" he asked.

"Just this. If anything should happen – I don't know what – but if life ... the gods ... circumstances – you know – if they should conspire to keep us apart, I just want you to know that these three days have been the happiest days of my entire life. Just remember that – the happiest *ever!*"

"Dear girl!" he began but she hugged him even more desperately and continued:

"I shall never regret them – nor forget them, either, not if I live to be a hundred."

"Which you will!" He forced a laugh. "I guarantee it – and I shall be there to pop the corks. So let's have no more of this dismal talk, eh?" He smothered her answer with a kiss. "Tell me, then - which bits of Tennyson do not meet with your approval? Maybe they are brighter?"

"Oh ..." She laughed and broke free of him. Picking up a flat, round pebble she made ducks-and-drakes with it – a respectable seven or eight bounces – out to sea. "Where he says things like 'Man for the field and woman for the hearth ...' You know? How does that go on?"

"'Man for the sword and for the needle she ...'"

"Oh yes, that's it! And 'Man with the head and woman with the heart ...'"

Grinning, he joined in and they completed the stanza together: "'Man to command and woman to obey; / All else confusion!'"

"You don't agree?" he asked as his pebble hit a small wave, soared upward, and fell back without a further bounce.

"'All her life she was a dab hand with her needle, duster, flatiron, and skillet' – it's not much of an epitaph, is it?" Her pebble bounced three times, ploughed a brief furrow, and sank.

"How's this, then: 'All his life he was a plaything of the market, the treasury, the shareholders, and the weather – and they did for him at last.' Not much better, I'd say. I often watch the maids at home, you know, and ..."

"Hold on!" she cried, putting her hands to her ears. "Are you sure you want to confess to this?"

"Not *that* way," he replied. "Though I have to admit we've had some fairly eyeable girls down the years. I have been tempted! Anyway, as I was about to say, I've often envied them their uncomplicated lives. Everything mapped out for them ... little achievements to take pride in at the end of each day."

"Mmm," she conceded. "It really makes one wonder why Tennyson didn't marry one of them. And what about you, Louis – could you marry one of *them?*"

No one watching her could have guessed how much hung on his reply – not just the next dozen words she would speak but the rest of their lives, perhaps.

He was about to throw another stone, for he had still not managed a respectable number of bounces, when something out to sea caught his eye. A four-masted clipper was rounding Pendennis Point, overtaking a little coastal steamer, even on this light breeze. "What a beautiful sight!" he exclaimed.

"The *Cutty Sark*, probably," she told him. "She puts in here quite often. The whole town smells of Indian tea. We can even smell it on this side sometimes."

The words 'Cutty Sark' were supposed to be the first she ever spoke, when she was little over a year and a half old.

He stood in admiring silence until the clipper entered Carrick Roads, where she struck all her sail and submitted to the indignity of three steam tugs.

"You didn't answer my question," she reminded him.

"I've been thinking about it, though," he replied. "It's not a simple yes or no, is it."

"Isn't it?" she asked. "I know I couldn't marry a footman – or a stable lad."

He was shocked. "Not *any* footman? Nor *any* stable lad? How can you be so sure? You don't know them all – which means you can't be talking about actual men. You must be talking about their stations in life."

Her heart leaped up. "And you're shocked?" she asked. "What if the boot were on the other foot? Suppose one of those pretty housemaids of yours had been as well-spoken as me and could hold a civil conversation and knew all about visiting cards and ..."

"Never mind that! Can she spout Tennyson by the yard?" He laughed and threw his stone at last. "Ten, eleven, twelve – rah! Beat that!"

"I'm serious, Louis. This is a serious question. Suppose you felt attracted to a maidservant who had everything it takes to pass herself off as a lady …"

"That's a big suppose."

"Never mind. It's not impossible. The question is – could you court and marry her?"

He picked up two stones this time. "Why d'you want to know?" He threw one in the air and, as it reached the top of its arc, hurled the other at it, missing by a mile. Both splashed down a few yards out to sea.

"I just do. It would tell me a lot about you."

"Golly! This is serious, eh?"

She nodded.

He picked up two more stones, one big, one small, and hefted them in his hands. "How deeply do I fall in love with her?"

"Head over heels, as they say. You can't stop thinking about her – day and night."

"So I love her as badly as I love you."

"Worse." She grinned.

"Then I probably do marry her – but with a heavy heart and deep foreboding." He threw the larger stone in the air and flung the smaller one at it. This time he hit it; the smaller stone smashed to pieces against its target. He stood dumbfounded. "That's the first time I've ever managed that in my life," he said. "Until now I didn't really believe it was possible."

"There's a first time for everything," she said. "Why would you have a heavy heart?"

He turned his back to the sea. "I ought to go, you know. I presume all my things are washed, desalted, and dried by now?"

"Yes, and all darns mended, and buttons sewn back on, and creases pressed."

"So the least I can do is pack them myself – I'm quite accustomed to that. I owe it all to Mary, I suppose. What d'you think I should tip her?"

"A guinea?"

"More than that, surely? She's been an absolute brick – not insisting on chaperoning us here, there, and everywhere. I'll give her five, I think."

Rose whistled. "In that case I think *I'll* apply for a place in your household, sir!"

He looked at her askance. "I hope you *will* have a place there one day, Lucinda – right at the top. And surely you know that, as soon as I'm free to offer it …"

"I'm sorry!" She blushed. "Oh dear – you must think I was prompting you to propose. How embarrassing!"

"What? You mean nothing was further from your mind?"

"Oh, Louis, my darling, darling Louis!" She linked arms with him and rested her head against his shoulder as they sauntered back up the hill toward the house. "Let's not bow to that dishonest old convention, eh? Nothing has been *nearer* my mind from the moment I set eyes on you."

"Really?"

"D'you doubt it?"

"No, of course not. In fact, I, too, knew straight away that you were the girl I've been waiting for all these years."

"Oh no, Louis! Not just waiting for. It's much deeper than that. It's *made for.* You're the one I was *made* for. I am yours, body, mind, and spirit." She heard the words pour out of her and frowned. "D'you think it's silly to talk like this – only days after we've met – when we know so little about each other? It *is* silly, isn't it – it must be."

He shook his head and kissed her brow. "Some things you just know. I can remember the first time I tasted strawberries – to go from the sublime to the ridiculous – but strawberries are my favourite ..."

"Mine too! Go on." She gave him a quick peck of a kiss on the side of his jaw.

"D'you remember the first one you ever tasted?" He kissed her in return, also briefly.

She giggled. "Yes." Another quick kiss.

"And did you need a second bite? Didn't you know at once?" Yet another kiss.

She halted, turned to him, and pressed her lips against his once more – to let them answer for her.

"D'you think there's some kind of spirit out there?" she asked as they resumed their homeward stroll. "Something that knows which two people are made for each other and makes sure they meet at the right moment?"

He chuckled. "Do you?"

"If there isn't, it's hard to explain what's happened here at Nancemellin this weekend. I mean – we *are* made for each other, aren't we? We both agree to that."

"It's impossible to deny."

"So how many times have you gone sailing, solo, out there in Carrick Roads?"

"It was my first time across this side. I thought I'd try going up the Fal. I usually head directly for the open sea. I wasn't aware how the winds could funnel down these valleys and ..."

"And how many times has Sir Hector gone away for two months – taking the whole family with him except me? Never! Or never before this. So I think it's pretty amazing that two unique events should happen at the same time like that – and, as a result, that two people who have never met before should discover that they are made for each other. There *must* be someone or something out there – some power that makes such things happen."

"The Romans called him Cupid," he said.

She wrinkled her nose. "A fat little baby with wings who flies around with a stupid grin on his chubby little face, shooting darts at people? No! It's not that. It's something that's also quite frightening, something that stirs in the dark, and tramples over ... other things. Old loyalties. Promises given in good faith. It's ruthless." She glanced over the fields toward Trefusis Farm as she spoke these words. A shiver of apprehension ran up her spine.

"Yes," he agreed. "We're back to that."

"Back to what?"

"The ruthlessness of it – of a love as strong as this. It's why I'd marry you, even if you were a servant girl. That's what you were really asking, isn't it?"

Half of her screamed that she'd never get a better moment to confess her deception; the other half warned her that men are prone to give such answers when they are absolutely sure the question is hypothetical. 'I'd swim a thousand oceans, crawl across a million miles of desert ...' That sort of thing.

"You didn't explain why you'd do so with a heavy heart, though," she reminded him.

"Oh, I should have thought that was pretty obvious. Surely you know how cruel people of our class are to what they call jumped-up working class parvenus? No matter if your imaginary maidservant could mimic one of us to perfection – and, after all, there are several who do it on the stage for a living, perfectly – can't you imagine how all the middle-class matriarchs in our circle would behave once the truth got out? And it always does get out. We could move from Cornwall to John o' Groats and the truth would follow us and that many-headed beast called 'polite society' would turn our life to misery."

When he said 'we' he was referring to himself and her hypothetical maidservant; she, however, knew that, by that very same token, he meant him and her. "So what would you do?" she asked bleakly.

"Selfishly? For my own happiness? We'd go and live in exile – in France, probably. But honourably – to spare her all those years amid the alien corn? I'd go away and never see her again – throw myself night and day into the business – which could certainly do with a bit of attention, anyway – and leave her free to find real happiness with someone else."

She realized she had been a fool ever to ask such a question – and an even greater fool to imagine he could give any other reply than that.

10

There was one way in which Rose could not – or would not – imitate a female of the upper-middle class. Fenella, like every other young lady of her circle, would have wept many a gallon at the departure of her love for two unimaginably long months – to say nothing of the moping, the refusal of food, the neurasthænia, the tantrums that would have punctuated each hour while Nature replenished those bodily cisterns where tears are stored. A maidservant, by contrast, is trained, long before she actually enters service, to hide her feelings, no matter what they may be nor how great the provocation.

The master makes a joke that splits the family's sides? The maid smiles at the risk of the butler's reprimand. The mistress At Home tells her friends that servants are getting lazier by the day? Not a flicker of the maid's weary eyes, not a tremor of the rage that seethes in her exhausted body, must betray her reaction. A child in a temper scalds her with soup? She must apologize if her screams give madam a headache. The whole family stays out until three at the Yacht Club ball? She must be there, even at that hour, to help her lady undress and to see her comfortably to bed, and she must be up betimes in the morning though the lady may slumber on until noon.

So Rose showed no *extraordinary* strength of character when she hid the pain that racked her from the moment the taxi carried her darling Louis up the drive and out of sight – and out of her life for ever. She stood there waving until even the sound of the taxi had dwindled away; then she turned to Mary, whose eyes were ready to weep with her, and said, "Well, that was fun!"

And so she continued all that day while they prepared for the return of the Tregembos and Mitchell. And in the days and weeks that followed, the Tregembos themselves unwittingly helped in her efforts to hide her sorrow, for they had returned to Nancemellin House with sorely troubled consciences and a list of things to do that would keep them all busy for the next five weeks – until the last hour of the last day of their time on board wages.

Of course, being on half pay, they could not require the servants to work into the evenings as well, so Rose took to going on long solitary walks about the lanes and through the woods that adorned the estate. The darkling day, the vast skies, the overpowering sunsets, the mighty seas – all these played to her mood, which Louis had so aptly called elegiac. It was over; she knew that. Dead and gone. Lost in death's dateless night. Her sighs and tears, when she was sure she was not observed, were, indeed, its elegy. And yet those words she had spoken to him, assuring him that she would treasure those three precious days for ever, and never for one moment regret a single word or act between them, remained the truth behind the sorrow.

In the earliest days of her loss she avoided Trefusis Farm, suspecting that the self-discipline which helped her conceal her feelings from her fellow servants would break down if Frank were to take her in his arms and do those things that Louis had done. And yet, as the days drew on and the family's return came closer, she realized that her chances for an evening stroll would diminish. And she did feel the lack of a comforting embrace and a friendly kiss, no matter how feeble it might be in comparison with those she had enjoyed in Louis' arms.

One fine evening toward the end of April she decided she could not forever put off seeing her cousin, so she dressed in her best, pulled on her galoshes, and set off across the fields. What was she going to tell Frank? How to explain her long absence when she had not even the excuse of a demanding Fenella or an oppressive Lady Carclew to detain her?

Tell the truth? Or gild it, rather? Say it was a bit of a lark but it was all over and done with now?

Or look surprised if he even mentioned it? After all, her mom was forever saying that a girl never found happiness by throwing herself at a man, always being there when he wanted her, and apologizing when that wasn't possible. 'Never say sorry unless you have to, and never explain yourself, even *if* you have to' – that was her motto.

Yes! She would behave as if *he* were to blame for not coming to see *her,* even though he knew the Carclews were away. And, come to think of it, he *was* to blame! He didn't even have the excuse of a muddy mile-and-a-bit to walk; he could have saddled any one of half a dozen horses and ridden over to see her without a fleck on his boots.

There was no one about in the farmyard so, instead of opening the lower gate, she took off her gloves, climbed onto the bottom rail, bent forward, grabbed the second rail on the inside, and flung her heels high into the air, swinging over the top bar in a gymnastic arc and landing with an easy spring.

"Whew!" she said aloud. It felt good to be so fit. She longed for the summer, when she could go down to the sea and swim to exhaustion or do watery acrobatics out of her depth.

"Frank?" she called out as she drew on her gloves again.

The only response was an excited grunt from Buzza the boar's pen; his ears covered his eyes most of the time so he lived in hope that any activity out there in the yard meant that someone was driving a sow or a gilt for him to serve.

She paused as she passed the sties. Two sows had been brought in for farrowing – and were close to their time by the grunts they were making. She recalled a day, in the summer of '08, when just such a pair had farrowed out in the bracken near the shore. She had come across Frank, standing nearby, cursing the labourer who had failed to bring them into the yard but also amazed to see that the two sows were lying in such a way that the piglets from one were born directly onto the other sow's teats, and vice-versa. It was even more amazing to see that a piglet who was only half-born, with his hind quarters still inside the sow, was nonetheless so alert that he could suckle from the other sow and even fight off his siblings. It was all over in ten minutes, during which time the two sows had completely swapped litters.

"No fear of that today," she told them, each in her own pen, as she reached across with a stick and scratched their backs in turn. They seemed to enjoy it. She was more circumspect when it came to scratching Buzza for, as Frank had warned her, those massive jaws could bite off a man's arm as quick as any crocodile. And those tusks could rip you open without his even meaning to, just with a toss of his head. Frank said you could commit the perfect murder with a couple of really hungry boars for they wouldn't leave so much as a fingernail behind.

"Well, Buzza, are you docile today?" she asked, holding her arm high, out of his reach, while she scratched the back of his neck with her stick. "Have you earned your keep with the ladies?"

He accepted her attention with porcine eagerness, straining his neck this way and that for full coverage. He was always more biddable after a couple of servings. Frank said a maid could learn a lot from Buzza about how to keep a man content.

"Frank?" she called again when her arm grew tired.

Still there was no reply. She leaned the stick back against the outside wall of the sties and made her way across the yard to the farmhouse, where she went round to the front door. She pulled the bell-chain and, while its jangling died in the corridor inside, she wiped her galoshes on the grass. She was in the act of taking them off when Mrs Tresidder answered the ring in person.

"Oh, it's you," she said, staring at the mud and dung on the grass. "Lucinda-Ella!"

That was typical of her, Rose thought. There was nothing wrong with wiping her galoshes on the grass – coarse, rough old stuff that it was. No one could call it a lawn. The woman just wanted to make visitors – particularly *this* visitor – feel uncomfortable. "It'll grow a bit extra-green there now," Rose said cheerfully as she put a spotless shoe to the threshold. "Is Frank in?"

"He's about," she replied, stepping aside reluctantly.

"Not in the yard. I called his name twice."

"Maybe he didn't think 'twas you – or he's forgotten what your voice do sound like."

They drifted vaguely down the long stone passage, which had the front door at one end and the back door at the other – a characteristically unimaginative piece of design.

"I'm not interrupting anything, I hope?" Rose asked.

"I was just buttering the eggs for market."

"Oh, let me help. Four hands are better than two."

Mrs Tresidder's usual response to any offer of help from Rose was to hint that she was too delicate, or that the work was too dirty for such a refined young maid. She ran an unrelenting campaign to persuade her son that this particular cousin was quite the wrong material for a farmer's wife; she deeply resented it that Lucinda-Ella (she never called her by any other name) could play the piano, do fine needlework, speak passable French, quote poetry, and 'talk posh.' "What good is all that when it comes to delivering a stuck calf in a full gale at two o'clock in the morning?" she liked to ask. Her attitude was all the more odd in that, of the pair of them, she was by far the more frail and delicate-looking. Rose's mom had once compared her head to a skull – 'a darn neat, pretty li'l skull but a skull for all that.' Any farmer who needed an assistant to help him push an arm and a noose up into a cow's womb to help drag out a stuck calf, would have chosen Rose rather than her, without a second glance.

However, since the old woman could hardly say that rubbing butter into eggshells was no work for dainty hands, she was forced to allow, grudgingly, that two pairs of hands would, indeed, speed the work.

They had just arrived at the entrance to the kitchen when the back door flew open and Frank's stocky frame was silhouetted against the crimson of the evening sky. 'Yard Bull,' was his nickname and, seeing him standing there like that, panting as if he had just run half a mile, Rose could well understand why.

"Lucinda!" He advanced to greet her with outstretched arms – though, thanks to his mother's presence, his hug was brief and conventional. "You're quite the stranger."

Over his shoulder, Rose saw a movement deep in the shadow of the haybarn, which was on the far side of the mowie, almost two hundred yards away. At that distance, and in such a darkling light, she could be sure of nothing, not even when a wicket gate opened in the back door to the haybarn and a pale figure was briefly framed against the dark of a hedge beyond; but that figure was either a labourer in a very long apron or smock (of a kind that few would wear these days) – or it was a woman.

He returned to the door and kicked it shut.

Rose had absolutely no reason to suppose it had been a woman, much less to connect her departure (by the barn's back door and into a lane that led nowhere, except down to the shore or across the fields to Mylor) with Frank's sudden, breathless appearance at the farm – and all this only minutes after she herself had walked past the mowie wall and loudly called his name. But, thanks to his reputation, the connection made itself.

"Are you going to help us butter the eggs?" Mrs Tresidder asked her son.

"I do only break them," he explained.

"Of a purpose," his mother murmured.

"But I'll sit and have a bit chat," he added. "And I daresay I can make a pot o' tay and cut a slice o' fuggan so well as any woman."

He busied himself with these chores while the two women settled at the farmhouse table and started buttering the remaining eggs. The coating of fat was said to improve their keeping qualities. Whether or not that was true, it certainly added to the price – three farthings a dozen, which was a halfpenny more than the cost of the butter.

"Sad about old King Edward," Mrs Tresidder remarked. "Still, he had a good innings as Prince of Wales."

Frank sniggered. "Many a good innings with many a fine woman!"

She ignored him. "Wonder what the new feller's like? Speaks English like a Prussian, so they do say."

"News travels fast these days," Rose said. "The day after he died – when was it?"

Mrs Tresidder glanced at the farm calendar. "He died on the night of the seventh. 'Twas in all the Sunday papers on the eighth. How d'you ask?"

"Well, the next day, the Monday, we got a telegram from the Carclews in Jerusalem to say, if the Season wasn't cancelled – because there was talk of no Ascot, remember? – we were to look out gowns in black and purple and to get black ribbon to trim the other dresses. So they must have heard it just about the same time as us."

"What *other* news from the big house?" Frank asked. "Any more drowned mariners to keep Sir Hector's bed warm while he's away?"

"You heard about that, did you?" she asked without looking up.

"Eventually, yes."

"What's that?" his mother asked.

So Frank had heard of the event but his mother had not. Interesting.

"Apparently," Frank said, grinning all the while at Rose, "this young Greek god came walking across the water, looming out the morning mist, when ..."

"All right, honey!" Rose laughed. He was good fun, really – when he wanted to be. She could imagine quite a tolerable life with him, even if the finer points of love would pass them by. "I'll tell it the way it really was. When did you hear about it, by the way?"

"This very evening, since you ask."

"From whom?"

"Whooom!" Mrs Tresidder aped her speech, shaking her head and refusing to look up.

"Aha – that'd be telling," he replied, winking and sticking out the very tip of his tongue.

"Someone from Flushing? Or Mylor? I just want to know how wide it has spread."

"Get on with the story!" Mrs Tresidder cried.

"Well, it's very simple. A young man, Louis Redmile-Smith by name, connected with the Redmile flour mills and Smith's ales, was out sailing, solo, in Carrick Roads, when some kind of squall must have hit his sails and the boom cracked him on the head and knocked him overboard. That's what we think, anyway. Nobody saw it but the groundsmen found him down on the beach, half drowned. The first we knew of it in the house was when we saw them carrying him up on a stretcher. We lit a fire, got him warm and dry, gave him some of Mrs Browning's Scotch broth ... Doctor Perrin stitched the cut on his forehead ... and three days later he drove away in a taxi, right as rain." She grinned. "Not much of a story, really."

"Not when you tell it that way, no," Frank said, putting a mug of tea and a slice of fuggan down before her and his mother.

"Oh, Frank!" the old woman cried. "'Tis the best chiney for Lucinda-Ella – not these old cloam mugs."

The two younger people were so accustomed to such jibes that they merely exchanged glances and smiled. "What way did *you* hear it told, then?" Rose challenged him, wondering, even as she did so, whether it was wise.

"I heard that three spinster-giglets couldn't wait to pull the wet clothes off the poor sleeping feller – and when they did, they had a high old time with him until he woke."

Unseen by his mother, he winked at Rose and ran a fingertip once up and once down the inside of his thigh. She, aware that Mrs Tresidder was looking at her, waiting for her to deny it, did not react – or not outwardly, at least. But her mind was racing. Mary would never have told him such a thing, not even if she had had the opportunity. The only other maid present had been Pennycuik – so when had *she* found the opportunity?

"You never!" the old woman prompted her at last.

"Of course not," she replied quietly, not taking her eyes off Frank. "I'm just wondering how such a travesty of the truth could have winged its way over the fields to this house. Or perhaps it never got as far as the house. Perhaps it stopped when it got inside the haybarn? What d'you think, Frank?"

"I'd hate to say 'tis impossible, Lucinda," he replied evenly.

His mother looked daggers at him. "You're a fool, boy!" she shouted. "You just can't keep that trap of yourn shut, can 'ee! You got to lay a scent like a fox."

By now Rose and Frank were locked in some kind of eye-wrestling game – she aghast, he smiling truculently, but a touch uncomfortably, too.

"Pennycuik?" she asked in disbelief. "Our little pot-scourer over to Nancemellin? With her hands all cracked by soda? Has she been carrying tales here?"

"She's more'n some little old scullery maid," he said defensively.

"That she is!" his mother chimed in. "She's a farmer's daughter."

Rose laughed, for what would a farmer's daughter be doing, working as a scullerymaid at Nancemellin House? "Her father is a riveter in Falmouth docks."

"Is that what she told 'ee? Well, let me put 'ee right, maid. Her father is John Pennycuik, who do farm Pednavounder, dreckly across the Fal from here. If we knew the tricks of Moses, we could part the waters and walk across in a half-hour. So there!"

"Well!" Rose now knew what a farmer's daughter would be doing, working as a scullerymaid at Nancemellin House. She put down her slip of greaseproof paper, which had not really lived up to its name, and wiped her fingers on a napkin, left behind after supper. "That does rather change the situation, doesn't it! I think I should be getting back to Nancemellin." She had come over here, half prepared to tell a sorrowing Frank that it was all over between them – if the occasion arose. This made it all so much easier.

"You haven't drunk your tea," Frank said. From his general demeanour no one would have guessed that the Pennycuik revelations had the slightest connection with him.

She gulped it down without pausing for breath.

"And I'll eat the fuggan on the way," she said, wrapping it in a clean strip of greaseproof.

"I'll see you to the gate," he said, gulping his mug down, too.

"To the gate!" his mother echoed, like a warning. "*We* still got two more trays to butter!"

It was almost dark by now but the moon, which had been full a few days earlier, was already risen, casting a pale, silver-gilt light over the rooftops and the hedges around the garden. Frank's lips looked as if he had been drinking purple wine. And away to the southwest, over the ridge of land between there and Nancemellin, the last dying of the sunset vied with the upcast light from Falmouth to underpaint the clouds either crimson or grey.

"It's no idea of mine," he said at once, taking her by the arm.

"I'm not blind," she said, shaking him off. "Not in any sense of the word. She was here tonight, wasn't she. That's who I saw. Out there in the haybarn – and you with her. I shan't bother to ask what you were doing!"

"I'll tell you nonetheless," he replied. "I was being very careful. If she thinks she can trap me into marriage *that* way, well, the smile is on my face, not hers."

"At least you don't deny it!"

"Why should I? She doesn't mean no more to me than a pretty heifer I'd drive into market. If a giglet like she do lift her petticoats and say help yourself, why should I say no thanks?"

"Ecurgh!" She shivered and drew away from him as soon as they gained the wider spaces of the field. "To think of you and that ... that *creature!* Like a pair of animals."

"That's it," he said, matter-of-factly. "You got it, maid. Animals – that's all 'tis. Just like animals. Like Buzza after ... when he's done his business with a dainty young gilt. His business and ourn. Forgotten already."

It was hard to stir up an argument with someone who cheerfully agreed with every word you said. She tried again: "And if we were to get married, you and I, would you expect to continue with these animal couplings in haylofts and hedgerows – and would you expect me to be as understanding about it as you obviously expect me to be now?"

"I don't see why not. I do love you, Lucinda – you do know that, surely? Love and respect you. But I'd have more love for half a cold pasty than for any woman who'd go with me like that."

"I see. Perhaps we should have had this conversation years ago. What about me?"

"What about you?"

"Would I enjoy the same tender and philanthropic understanding as I'm expected to extend to you?"

"'Course not!" he exclaimed angrily. "A woman can't be careful. She's got to trust a man to be careful. The cases aren't the same at all. Besides, 'tis different for a woman. She's got choice. A man's got no choice. He's driven to it."

She came to a halt and turned to him. "I think I know my way from here, Frank," she said. "You go back and help your mother."

"She thinks Pennycuik would make a better wife for me than you," he said.

"Really? I'd never have guessed it." In the dark his features became fluid. She found it easy to imagine him in middle age – a romeo without the charm of youth, a philanderer who had made the same excuses so often that they no longer even shocked, much less amused. "How long has the girl been coming over to ... how can I put it? To 'lift her petticoats' for you?"

He shrugged. "How long has she been at Nancemellin, then?"

"Four months?"

"Four months," he said.

"So there must have been occasions when you have gone straight from my arms to hers – or from hers to mine?"

"No!" he objected.

"Never?" she pressed him. "D'you have some system for avoiding a clash – like a signalman on a single-track railway?"

"It isn't the same. Like I said – she's for the animal doings and you're for real love. Love and respect. What else would you have me do? Take the ferry to Falmouth and throw money away in they sailor houses up Vernon Place?"

She turned and walked away, taking him by surprise. She bade him goodnight without looking back.

But he ran after her. "Not even a kiss?" he asked.

"Not now I know where those lips have been tonight."

11 After that evening, Ann Pennycuik seemed an entirely different person to Rose. In social rank, which was just as important below stairs as above, she remained the lowest of the lowly; but, woman to woman, Rose could not help feeling herself the inferior. Pennycuik had Been There, as they say. She had Done It. She knew things about men that would even astonish most married women – like that trick she had shown them with the unconscious Louis – and she was not ashamed of it, either. Perhaps anyone, man or woman, who grew up on a farm and who stood around making jokes while Buzza and his like earned their keep, would have a different attitude from townsfolk, who took their guidance from the pulpit, the sunday school, and the public posture of important ladies and gentlemen.

Outwardly, if Rose had been pushed to make a judgement on Pennycuik, she would have conformed to those public postures and condemned the girl; but secretly she could not help feeling a tinge of admiration, not to say envy. Throughout that wonderful weekend with Louis, the image of his naked body had haunted her. Time and again she had wanted to tell him what had happened, or at least to give him some hint; and yet she had always shied away at the last moment. And it had been on his mind, too – she was sure of it. After Mary let it slip inadvertently. He, too, had come within an ace of opening that vast Pandora's Box of a subject but, like her, had fought shy at the last. Why? Because they were of their class, of course, him by upbringing, her by artifice (though it had felt less and less of a pretence as the weekend progressed). They had that public posture to maintain.

Yet some were free of those constraints. The aristocracy, for instance, who paraded their mistresses in fine carriages in Hyde Park every afternoon, for all the world to see and envy; and (it would seem) the scullerymaids, who could wander into the nearest haybarn, lift their petticoats, and say, 'Help yourself!'

One of that tribe could, anyway. How curious that the two groups stood at the opposite ends of respectable society, at odds with all who jostled in between!

And what of Frank – where did he fit in? He was closer to Pennycuik in attitude than he was to her. Perhaps the pair of them deserved each other. She herself had always pooh-poohed talk of his 'reputation' whenever her friends, particularly Mary, brought it up, even though she knew it was well enough deserved. Indeed, there were times when she had secretly hoped that even the wilder rumours were true – because he had never taken the slightest liberty with her. She had accepted it as proof that he set her on a higher plane than all those women who conspired with him to give him his dubious fame. But now that she had truly fallen in love at last – though not with him – she began to doubt that it was such a compliment after all. Love was so complete. It should long to take those same liberties.

She knew that her yearning at least to *talk* about forbidden things with Louis was a mere prelude to some kind of exploration, however shy and tentative, of the forbidden things themselves. The way their hands had cruised each other's bodies proved it, caressing oh-so-close to places that everyone knew were out of bounds. So in that sense she, at twenty-three, was a mere child to Pennycuik's mature and experienced dame of eighteen.

Her shyness with Louis, and his with her, contrasted strongly with Frank's ... well, *frankness!* How was it that he and she could talk so easily – as they had last night. True, that talk had provoked her to anger ... jealousy ... disgust. No, not disgust, curiously enough, but to anger and envy, certainly. And yet it had been easy ... natural. Could it be that he and Pennycuik had the right idea, after all? Were she and Louis the fools – fumbling together in tongue-tied excitement, each willing the other to be bolder than he or she was prepared to be? The more she thought about Frank and Pennycuik, the angrier she became – and the more she wished she could be like them!

It was even possible that the scullery-maid knew what a turmoil she was causing. The knowing look she gave Rose at breakfast the following morning was the strongest hint of it, anyway. Next thing, when the fun of private glances wore off, it would be some sly remark. Then open taunts. Rose's instinct was to keep out of her way, except on those occasions when Tregembo's presence would inhibit the girl and keep her desire for triumph in check. Instead – on the theory that if a horse is about to kick, and you can't run away, you get as close to that lethal hoof as possible – she took the first opportunity to be alone with the scullery-maid.

It came when Pennycuik carried out yesterday's scraps to feed to the chickens, who were penned in the long orchard, beside the walled garden. It was not an orchard in the usual sense – wide acres full of fruit trees. In fact, it was a long, narrow enclosure of brick, about fifteen foot wide, running the full length of the garden's south-facing outer wall, against which fruits of every kind were trained in fans – figs, nectarines, peaches, medlars, damsons, as well as many varieties of apple and pear. The chickens kept down the creepy-crawlies responsible for so many diseases of fruit-trees, without harming the bees that fertilized them.

Rose found a few scraps that had evaded Mrs Browning's trawl and went out after the girl.

Pennycuik was not deceived, however. "We got nothing to talk about," she said at once.

Rose's heart sank. "There's no need to adopt that tone," she replied, throwing the scraps directly to the birds.

"D'you love him, then?" the girl asked pugnaciously.

"I didn't come out here to discuss *me.*"

" 'Es! I knew you'd be frighted to answer. Well, that's one thing I aren't. I do love him and I do mean to get him. So there!"

"And you'd deserve him, Ann." This use of her Christian name surprised the girl. Rose took advantage of the silence to add, "You seem to have the same opinion of yourself as he does, so you'd probably get on pretty well."

Pennycuik stared at her, certain she'd heard no compliment but unable to detect an insult, either. "Fat lot you know!" was all she said at last.

"Believe me, Ann, since last night I've been made only too aware of my *lack* of knowledge – in certain directions, anyway."

"He never discussed me with you," she said, more to herself than to Rose.

"Not specifically you, no," Rose replied. "We were discussing that whole band of females, young and old, who … let me see if I can recall his exact words – who 'lift their petticoats to him and say help yourself!' I'm sure that's how he described you all. He assured me he valued the lot of you rather less than a heifer he might drive into market. However, that's not what I came out here to say to you, either. I wanted to discover whether you, like Frank, thought of it as just a bit of idle fun – in which case, I'd have said good luck to you while it lasts and no harm done when it's over – or whether you imagined it could be anything serious."

The girl raised her chin belligerently and thrust one shoulder forward. "He've promised to marry I – that's how serious he is!"

Her air of confidence shook Rose, though she hoped she did not show it. "I wouldn't spread word of it too wide, Ann," she countered. "Not until he's put the offer in writing. Or repeated it with witnesses. Or given you a ring. I don't suppose he's been careless enough to do any of those things, eh?"

Cornered finally, the girl lashed out with the only weapon she had. "A ring, is it?" She sniggered. "I've given he a *ring,* all right – many and many a time! And mighty spronsey he is to see how snug a fit it do give!"

"Yes, well, we've already covered *that* ground – rather more literally in your case than mine."

"I don't see no ring on your finger, neither," Pennycuik added, realizing it was what she should have said in the first place.

"There's only one other thing I want to tell you," Rose said wearily, "and it's this: If you and he should ever marry, it will be because I have released him from a lifelong obligation that needs no ring, *of any kind,* to secure it." She walked a few paces away before turning to add, "Just think it over – I cannot make him marry you, nor am I claiming that I can, but I do most emphatically claim that I could stop him. So if you really do want him, you'd best stay on the right side of me!"

12 The Carclews were due to return late in the afternoon of Monday, the sixth of June. The Tregembos, as arranged, spent much of the previous ten days in scouring the employment agencies in Falmouth, Truro, Redruth, and farther afield, seeking replacements for the servants who had been let go two months earlier. By mid-day on the Friday they had managed to line up one possible chambermaid and a doubtful valet. Not one of the original seven wanted to come back; all had found new positions within a couple of weeks. Even in Cornwall, where the three main industries of farming, mining, and fishing were notoriously uncertain, and secure indoor labour in a comfortable household ought therefore to have been oversubscribed, it was a seller's market.

"I even let them understand we should not be too nice when it came to scrutinizing references from past employers," Tregembo said, "but it made no difference."

Sir Hector and her ladyship were not going to be too pleased; in fact, Tregembo predicted, she would fly off the handle, call him an incompetent, say she'd manage the business herself – and be forced at last to realize what pennypinching fools they had been to let so many go.

"And what did they save?" Rose asked. "The two months' wages for the six they let go amounted to twenty pounds odd. The amount they saved by putting the rest of us on board wages was maybe another twenty." Here she diplomatically swallowed her remaining doubts that the Tregembos had taken a cut, too. "Forty quid they saved! Forty quid. Sir Hector can lose three times that much on one single horse."

"Well, that's enough of that sort of talk," Tregembo said awkwardly. The news that the dismissed servants had all found places so quickly was clearly encouraging a mutinous tendency. And things could only get worse when this skeleton staff of nine (including his two doubtfuls) realized they were being required to do the work of the original fourteen – without any extra pay to sweeten it.

The seven who had been kept on realized as much, well before the family's return, of course. There was plenty of furtive discussion about handing in their notice and looking elsewhere themselves. The drawback was that, if they all did it at once, they would look like a combination of blackmailing troublemakers, after which, shortage or no shortage, no one would employ them.

However, Mary and Mrs Browning thought that Rose should hand in her notice as soon after the family's return as practicable, for it was doubtful her ladyship would write her a good character if she were ever to learn what had happened with Louis Redmile-Smith. Rose knew they were right. It was, beyond doubt, the only sensible thing to do. But some stubborn streak prevented her. Nancemellin was where she and Louis had met. To Nancemellin he would return. Here, if anywhere, she would confess her deception, beg his forgiveness, hope for reconciliation, and talk him out of running away to France. Here she would stay, come hell, come high water.

Yet the advice was good; she could not deny that, either. And if Louis really loved her, he would come to wherever she was working. And if he really-*really* loved her, he'd take her away from it all and ... no. Daydreams could only push the bounds of realism so far.

On the last Sunday of freedom, or relative freedom, still uncertain as to what she should do, she decided to lay her troubles upon her mother, across the water in Falmouth. She took the noonday steam ferry from Flushing over to the Prince of Wales Pier in the heart of the town. Her parents' greengrocery shop lay half a mile away as the crow flies, just beyond the Custom House in Arwennack Street. She started off in their direction but then realized that the direct route along Market, Church, and Arwennack streets, which together made up a single commercial artery, would be rather depressing on the sabbath. All the shops would be closed, with black blinds drawn down over most of the windows. And, in any case, she was in too much of a turmoil to face her mom and dad just yet. Every time she settled her mind on precisely what she would tell them (and what she would withhold), new suggestions came barging in, upsetting everything. She was afraid it would happen, too, just as she began unburdening herself – and then, in a panic, she might tell them everything.

She wanted to tell them just those things that would make her mom say, 'Love is the most important thing in anybody's life, honey. It doesn't just laugh at locksmiths, you know – it laughs at everything that stands in its way, and that includes class and social convention. You see a gap – you go for it!' Anything else she didn't wish to hear.

She turned aside then and chose a more roundabout walk, giving herself the chance to settle her thoughts yet again. Unfortunately for a young woman gnawed by hunger and looking forward to the Sunday roast, every path except the direct one involved a steep climb at the outset and a steep descent at the end.

For Falmouth is a curiously hilly town. If those same hills had been on the bank of a river – instead of lying beside one of the largest deepwater harbours in the west of England – no one in their right mind would have built a single shop or house there. The long, sinuous hill that fringes the southwestern shore of the Fal estuary is something between a precipitous rise and a sheer cliff; had it not been for that, the town might have grown as large as Plymouth or Bristol. As it was, Falmouth town became, essentially, a single narrow street snaking lazily along the foot of that precipitous hill – corseted between the deepwater that gave it birth and the land that stifled its expansion.

To Rose, Falmouth-born and Falmouth-reared, it was more of a village than a town. She knew and loved every little alley that wriggled along the side of the hill, above that main street, and all the narrow granite-stepped passages between them. She once worked it out that she had the choice of twenty different paths between her school on Smithick Hill and home, which was only a quarter of a mile away. As a schoolgirl it had been her habit never to go directly between one point and another whenever she had to cross the town.

So, on this particular Sunday, she chose one of the most difficult, though not the most roundabout, routes of all, climbing more than a hundred feet from down near sea level to the highest point in town. From there she would have to drop back down again, for the shop was practically at sea level, too. She reckoned it would allow her to arrive just as the Sunday roast came out of the oven – so there would be no time for mom-and-daughter chats while they were both hungry. *Those* chats always led to arguments.

She turned inland to the Moor, which is not a moor at all but the broad, flat bottom of a giant scoop cut out of the long hill on which the town stands. It served as a market place on Saturdays and a playground for children to bowl their hoops and play hopscotch, tops, and marbles during the rest of the week – except, of course on Sunday, when even the children's swings in the park were chained up and padlocked. Rose paused awhile beside the Town Hall, where Market Strand opens out into the Moor. She thought of the many carefree hours she had spent here, not just at outdoor amusements but indoors, as well – in the Passmore-Edwards Free Library away to her right; she had been one of its most voracious patrons. Today, of course, it, too, was closed. Behind it reared the tall clock-tower of Trevethan School, where she had spent her final year, before her parents said they could no longer afford it and she had to go into service. That year had been a happy time, too.

But even back then she had not been free of the emotions that racked her now. What about Maggie Royston? She had been one of the senior girls at Trevethan, captain of hockey and a prefect, too. Rose, like many other little girls in first year, had nursed the most dreadful, wonderful 'pash' for her. She had spent hours writing her notes that she never sent, had copied her walk, her way of talking, her hair style ... had hung about the corner of Gyllyng Street, where Maggie lived, just in the hope of seeing her. And then, later, there was Tony Trevean, who used to stare at her soulfully from under his beautiful long eyelashes, who filled her waking hours with longing, made her tummy go all hollow, made her heart beat faster just at the thought of him. Where was it all now? She ran across both of them from time to time – Maggie was in the library and Tony was a clerk in Angove & Snell, the solicitors in Arwennack Street – and all she could think was, *What did I ever see in you?*

Would the same ever happen with Louis?

No. Impossible. Louis was utterly different.

She turned from her survey of the Moor and all its memories and began the long, steep climb to the top of the hill. To her left, dominating every other building around the Moor – especially the modest little Anglican Mission Hall – was one of the largest Methodist chapels in Cornwall. And beside it was Jacob's Ladder – one hundred and fourteen granite steps rising almost ninety feet to the hilltop road that overlooks the town and its harbour.

In her schooldays she had taken pride in running the full height of Jacob's Ladder without resting at any of several small landings that punctuated its ascent, especially in competition with the boys. Like her mother she was long in the leg and could cover many of the steps two at a time. She would arrive at the top, panting furiously, feeling as if iron bands had clamped themselves around her ribs, and with the world reeling and threatening to dissolve in flying clouds of blackness all about her, but she had the satisfaction of beating every boy of her own age as well as many who were senior. The best was when they raced ahead, shouting 'Nyah-nyeah!' over their shoulders, only to conk out at the topmost landing and watch her fly past 'leaping like a gazelle' – as one old gentleman spectator had put it when he gave her a penny prize.

If she were still allowed to wear short skirts – and tuck them into her bloomers for a race like that – she could probably still manage to run all the way. She certainly felt fit enough to try a stiff walk without a pause. She overtook one old woman, who called after her, "You wait, my lover! Enjoy they knees while yet 'ee can." And she passed a middle-aged man, coming down, who paused to admire her and cried, "Whew – the Cornish Flier!" as she trudged on up with grim determination. She took it as a compliment of some kind.

She felt somewhat less confident of her fitness by the time she arrived at the top. Her calves and the backs of her thighs were shrieking with pain and no matter how deep she gulped she could not seem to get enough air. Fortunately there was a stiff easterly breeze up there at the top and her brow and neck did not drench in perspiration – though she could feel it tickling her as it made its way down the small of her back, inside her stays.

As she paused to regain her breath she faced a choice between Vernon Place, to her left, and Wodehouse Terrace, to her right – where all the posh houses were. Now that she came to think of it, that was another good reason for taking this route, of course – to see if any of them had POSITION OFFERED notices in their windows. They were the grandest houses in Falmouth, together with those in Wood Lane, but they would still consider it something of a catch to get a lady's maid from Lady Carclew.

Vernon Place would lead her a little way down the hill – which she would have to descend at some time, in any case – and past her first school; the nostalgia it offered was tempting. But Vernon

Place was also full of those houses where the only position offered to a maid would be of the horizontal kind; she could see two or three of them now, in fact – tall, narrow, neglected houses with their shutters all closed or curtains drawn, at half past noon. Falmouth being an international port, they were kept busy all year round, and especially on a Saturday night. She shuddered and turned toward Wodehouse Terrace. Thank God she'd never have to sink to *that* sort of degrading work to keep body and soul together! It gave her the creeps to think of what went on behind those blinded windowpanes; what Pennycuik did was bad enough, but at least she *chose* her man freely and didn't ask for money.

What a contrast, though – just one street away! Here in Wodehouse Terrace was a world of white stucco, neat little gardens with palms and well-clipped shrubbery, polished doorknobs, and lace curtains. She heard strains of hymns and other sacred music, played on pianos and harmoniums, muffled behind the windows; upstairs in the nurseries, no doubt, the children were allowed to play with the animals from a toy Noah's Ark, because it was biblical, but forbidden to touch the sometimes identical animals from their toy farm, because it was not.

Several of the houses had discreet POSITION OFFERED notices in their windows. It was a sign of desperation that they were left on show during the sabbath; ten years ago, in the old queen's day, they would all have been turned face down from Saturday night to Monday morning – even though many servants would have part of Sunday off, making it the best day to advertise.

Actually, she wondered, was Pennycuik really doing anything different from the women in those immoral houses back there? She'd made it pretty plain that the prize for 'catching' Frank was a ring on her finger and a wife's stake in Trefusis Farm; wasn't that the same trade, bodily favours for material reward? Frank, for his part, had seemed in no doubt – with all his talk of 'being careful.' What was that if not a boast that he'd thwart her cunning schemes in the end and get It for free?

A great weariness overcame her. She did not care which of them beat the other; she did not want any part of him – she knew it for certain, now – so they were welcome to each other. And, looking up at those fussy, lacy, chintzy windows, she did not want a respectable place behind any of them, either. The thought of traipsing from house to house, showing her needlework sampler and her reference from Lady Carclew, asking about hours, haggling over wages, uniforms, days off ... she couldn't go through all that again. Not when Louis was out there somewhere, feeling as lost without her as she was without him. Or so she fervently hoped.

But even as her mind veered toward that hourly daydream she took a grip of herself and returned to the world of practical, attainable ambitions, even though, when it came to specifics, her mind was blank. There must be *some* alternative out there that did not involve an endless round of sewing, ironing, mothballing, mending, goffering, in between pampering, powdering, combing, and generally fawning over an immature puffhead like Fenella or a shrewish termagant like her mother.

Her mind remained a blank.

The daydream beckoned once again. As she walked along Wodehouse Terrace, vaguely noting the houses that had positions to offer, she pictured herself somehow waylaying Louis on his return to Nancemellin House – catching him as he stepped off the ferry at Flushing while she was there on some petty errand. And he would see her in her servant's dress, and she would explain and beg his forgiveness and throw herself on his mercy and he'd take her in his arms and tell her she was a silly for imagining her class could ever come between them and he was a fool for saying those things about having to go and hide themselves in France and he couldn't live without her and, in fact, he had a special licence in his pocket, so, if she'd just go back and pack a few things, they could be off on their honeymoon that very evening.

Aiee!

Reality reclaimed her. And yet, between the enchantment of that improbable future and the dreariness of the one that almost certainly was to be her lot, there *must* be something just a little more inspiring.

13

The greengrocery had a single-front window with an entrance off a side passage that served the houses on either side. The 'front' door to her parents' home was at the end of this passage and opened directly into a stairway that led up to the accommodation, which occupied the two floors above the shop and storeroom.

"Only me!" she called up as she let herself in.

She paused and breathed in deeply through her nose. Every house has its own aroma. Nancemellin's was of damp books, floor polish, and some African wood they were very proud of. Her parental home smelled of linoleum and sarsaparilla, her mom's favourite drink; she pronounced it 'sarsprilla' and said it was really birch oil and sassafras – which left most people none the wiser.

The linoleum was on the stairs. It was getting pretty worn but, she guessed, there were more important calls on their money – like simply keeping a roof over their heads.

"Why, land sakes, Miss Lucinda-Ella – ef'n you ain't quite the stranger!" Her mom looked up from mashing the potatoes and did her Black Mammy imitation.

Rose laughed as she skipped across the tiny kitchen and threw her arms about her for a hug. "Last day of freedom," she said. "The Carclews come back tomorrow. Where's Pop?"

"Mixing some putty in the back room upstairs," she replied.

"One of the windowpanes in your room rattles, so he's fixing to fix it. You can haul out the roast and give it one final baste."

She took off her bonnet and gloves and did as she was asked. She liked the way they still called it *her* room.

"And lay a place for yourself," her mom added.

But when Rose went through to the parlour, she found the table already set for three – and her own napkin ring there, too, so it wasn't set for a friend.

"Ha ha," she said as she came back to the kitchen.

Mom winked. "Knew you'd be coming."

"How has business been?"

"So so. We've had worse months. The maincrops are all coming in now, so, between that and the summer visitors, we should end up the year quite well. You'll be glad to get back on full wages."

"I have some savings, you know – ten pounds odd. You can call on them anytime – I keep telling you."

She heard her l-sounds darken, getting closer to her mother's American. It always happened within minutes of their being together. Her dad, who had lost all trace of his American accent, replacing it completely with the ancestral Cornish he had heard his father speak in childhood, never failed to notice it. 'My fair chameleon,' he called her.

Mom squeezed her arm. "It's good of you, honey, but you know we'd never do that. They say the bookings are up in all the boarding houses, so we'll do all right. We still have beef on Sunday!"

"And still make it serve four more meals in the week?"

"Good meals, too. We ain't complaining. 'Sides, you'll need those savings one day, to fill your bottom drawer." She took the plates from the warming oven – there were three there, too – and gave them to her daughter to carry to the table. "Talking of which," she added, "how's Frank? I guess you're seeing quite a bit of him while …"

"Don't ask!"

"Oh?"

They went back to bring in the roast.

"That's over and done with – if it ever began. He's … he's just too …" Words failed her.

"Yes, well, you know what my opinion of that young man has always been – or not *always,* maybe. He was charming in his teens. It's since he turned into a bobbydazzler." She smiled at her daughter as they set the roast, the carving knife, the fork, and the steel just so. "Dare I ask – is there any *other* young man in sight yet?" She raised her voice as she went out to the foot of the stairs. "Pop! Come an' git it!"

Rose followed her. "I'll tell you after," she promised as a little squirt of fear upended her already rattling stomach.

"My-oh-my!" Mom said admiringly. "It must be good if it'll keep that long."

Pop hugged her on his way to wash off the linseed oil. That was the 'linoleum' smell, too, of course. "Th'ole woman said as you'd come today," he remarked.

After saying grace, mother and daughter sat down and looked expectantly at Pop, who sharpened the carving knife on the steel with a ritual flourish before addressing the joint. He cut a paper-thin slice off the end – 'the scrumpy bit' he called it as he offered it to Rose. That was also a ritual.

"Oh no, Pop," she said. "That's your privilege – besides, I prefer the redder bits, near the middle."

He cut several more semi-transparent slices and served her the reddest two; then Mom; then himself.

"Lucinda-Ella has a new prospect, honey. Not Frank," Mom said. The vegetables, being unsold (and now unsaleable) stock, were as generous in portion as the beef was sparing.

"I didn't exactly say that," Rose complained. "I said we could talk about it later."

"This is later."

Rose sighed; there was no evading it now. "It happened five or six weeks ago," she said, "when the Tregembos took leg bail from Fri-to-Mon. I was trying on one of Miss Fenella's gowns, getting ready for the season, because we're about the same size and I wasn't happy with the hemline. Anyway – in the middle of this, the groundsmen bring up a man they found half-drowned on the shore. So we get him inside, light a fire, get him out of his wet things, et cetera ..."

"Who did that?" Pop asked. "Not you, I do hope."

"We all did. It wasn't a time for finesse. We didn't even know if he'd live."

"Hush now!" Mom told Pop before turning eagerly once more to her daughter. "And?"

"This is good beef!"

"Never mind that – get on with it!"

"Well, he did live. He came round quite smartly, and" – she drew a deep breath – "this is the awkward bit. You see, I was still wearing Miss Fenella's gown, and so he ... naturally ... oh dear!"

"He assumed you were a daughter of the household?" Mom was greatly amused. "What's his name? Who is he?"

Rose told them. Pop raised his Sunday tipple – a glass of Smith's Pale Export – and said, "Here's health to him, then!" Mom clapped her hands with delight. "And you fooled a man of the world like that – that you had as much blue blood as he!"

Rose lowered her eyes and said, "You see, Mamah deah, I gave the poor gentleman no cause to think otherwise."

Pop cackled proudly and slapped his thigh. "My fair chameleon," he said. Mom chuckled.

"It's not funny," Rose said bleakly, back in her own voice.

Her mother cottoned on to her meaning at once. "Oh no!"

"No, what?" her father asked, looking from one to the other.
"She fell in love with him – that's what!" Mom said.
"Worse." Rose spoke without looking up.
"Not ...?" Pop was horrified. "You don't mean ...?"
"He fell in love with me, too."
"But you didn't ... you and he ..."
"Pop!" her mother exploded. "Butt out! She's a grown woman. We gave her a proper raising – what she does with it is her affair. You didn't, did you, honey?"
Rose shook her head.
"See!" Mom cried triumphantly. "Fancy asking such a thing! So what *did* you and this Louis do?"
"Talked and talked ... and went for walks together ..."
"And cuddled some?"
"Of course. He left before the Tregembos came back. He had to join his mother's summer party in France somewhere."
"And all the time he thought you were some high-quarter maid?" Pop asked.
She nodded and pulled a rueful face.
"Did you tell him your real name, honey?"
"Lucinda, I said. Lucinda Tremayne. I pretended to be Sir Hector's ward."
"Close enough! He'll find you."
"That's the trouble, Mom. He'll find me all right. He'll come directly to Nancemellin on his return and then he'll discover how I deceived him and ..." Her lips trembled. She swallowed hard. "I don't want it to happen *there.* Every morning I wake up feeling so happy. And then there's a moment when I can't think why. And then I remember. And then I also remember he's going to return to Nancemellin to thank the Carclews for what their nonexistent ward did. And ... oh, it's just going to be so *awful!*"
"Hand in your notice as soon as they come back," Pop said. "Tomorrow, is it?"
She shook her head. "It ain't that simple, Pop. I'll hand in my notice. Her ladyship will give me a good reference. I'll get another position. Louis will turn up at Nancemellin. The truth will out. Her ladyship will write a furious letter to my new mistress – she may even put an announcement in the *Falmouth Packet* – and bang goes my new position."
"Write him!" Mom suggested. "At the Redmile-Smith head office. They must be able to get to him – mark it *Personal and Private,* of course. That'd keep him away from Nancemellin."
"It might also keep him away from me – and I couldn't bear that. I want to tell him myself – even if he calls me every name under the sun and slaps my face. Suppose I wrote this letter, and he didn't come to Nancemellin, didn't reply, didn't say a word, didn't come near me again. I'd be living in hell."
Her mother nodded sadly.

"Go Penzance, then," Pop suggested. "Go Plymouth. Who do read the *Packet* there? That's far enough away, I'd say."

"Not when her ladyship's got her dander up. You've no idea how vindictive she can be. She'd find out, no matter where I went. Scotland ... Ireland ... she'd hunt me down."

"Besides ..." Mom said.

Rose nodded her agreement.

"What?" Pop asked. "Besides what, dammit?"

His wife gave him a pitying glance. "There's another reason she wants to be there when Mister Redmile-Smith comes back – don't you see? It's her one chance."

"Don't put it like that, Mom!" Rose complained. "It's bad, but it's not like a death sentence."

"If he still loves you, though – in spite of everything – then you can shake the dust of Nancemellin off your feet. And every other grand house like it. Isn't that what you're hoping?"

"Sure."

"I guess you really love him, huh?"

"Oh, Mom!" She reached across the table for her mother's hand. "I can't stop thinking about him, day or night. It's like a fever. I honestly think I'm running a temperature! I have to bite my tongue to stop talking about him. Mary calls me a hopeless case. I talk to her about him, after lights out, until she snores – and even that doesn't stop me."

Her mother squeezed her hand; their eyes dwelled in each other's a long moment. Pop cleared his throat, drew a deep breath ... and then thought better of whatever he had been going to say. For a while the only sound was their breathing and the ticking of the clock.

"I guess you've got to do ... just whatever you've got to do," her mother said at last.

14

The day of the Carclews' return was overcast and muggy. The clouds were dark enough to threaten rain, which would, in fact, have been a welcome damper on the warm, fitful breeze; but it never came. Then, about four in the afternoon, it was as if some celestial giant had cut the clouds with a knife. A great arc of clear blue sky rose to the southeast, over Roseland, and grew, and grew, until it covered half the sky. Every servant in the house, including Peggy Trussell, the new chambermaid and the sole new addition to the staff, went out to witness it – a sky that was uniformly dark and grey to the northwest and just as uniformly blue to the southeast, and a line you could draw with a ruler to separate them. The breeze dropped, too, and the air grew dry and warm.

They watched until three-quarters of the sky was blue. Then, just as Tregembo was about to shoo them all back inside, the carriage bringing the Carclews home from Penryn station came into view at the far end of the long drive.

"We might just so well stop out here, then," the butler said. "Stand up straight now, everybody, and put a brave face on it."

"I'd swap grey skies for *this,* anyday," Mary remarked as the carriage drew nearer.

The others giggled. Tregembo said, "Get a hold on yourselves!"

"What a smiling welcome!" Lady Carclew cried as she stepped out of the carriage, assisted by Paddy Negus, the head stable lad's favourite son. "There was no need for this, Tregembo, though it's much appreciated." Her eye swept up and down the line as she spoke. Her smile vanished. "*One* new maid, I see." She went up to Trussell, who curtsied and introduced herself, adding, "I'm here on trial for a month, my lady."

Her ladyship was about to tell her, in no uncertain tones, that, indeed, she was, when the maid added, "To see if you suit me."

Lady Carclew bridled and turned to Tregembo, who shrugged and nodded unhappily. "It's the time of year, my lady. Everyone who's going up to Lunnon for the Season is hiring servants down here to take up with them – servants up there being impossible to find and not worth the double wages they demand while the Season lasts."

"Well!" Her ladyship choked back the angry words she had been going to utter. "We shall just have to see about this. How many have you hired to replace the four we let go?"

"The *seven* you let go, my lady. We've found just the one – Trussell here."

"On a month's approval," Trussell insisted again.

Lady Carclew rounded on her and raised a furiously trembling gloved finger. "Now listen!" she began.

Tregembo cleared his throat loudly.

The finger went on trembling, and so did the lips, but the words were stifled behind them.

Meanwhile the rest of the family had lurched and faltered out of the carriage, stretching and yawning after a long, tedious, and servantless train journey from London.

"What a bore it all sounds!" Fenella cried. "Come on, Rose – I can't wait to get out of these things."

"Miss Rose will stay where she is!" her mother snapped. "If our household is reduced to but one housemaid, then the work must be shared out between the remainder. Tregembo – I see Sir Hector has no valet ..."

"What? What?" An outraged Sir Hector stared at the line of servants for the first time. "Where's whatsit – Penvose?"

"... so *you,*" her ladyship continued speaking to the butler, "will be butler-valet until the deficiency is remedied. The two lady's maids will share ordinary household duties with Trussell and Mitchell. Poor Mrs Browning has no assistant, I see. Well, you will just have to train up little Pennycuik, who can divide her time between kitchen and scullery."

Pennycuik dropped a curtsy and smiled at the cook, who raised her eyes to heaven but said not a word.

Lady Carclew's gaze swept imperiously up and down the line, where looks were growing distinctly mutinous. "Yes!" she crowed. "Nobody likes it, eh? Good! Now we'll see how long this alleged shortage of servants will last! Come, Sir Hector! Come children!" And with that she flounced indoors.

"I'm a different man, Rose," Noel managed to murmur in her ear as he passed. "I'm fed up with this family. I'm going to strike out on my own."

"Good for you," she replied wearily. "You still owe me four pounds, sixteen shillings."

He'd clearly forgotten it.

"Noel!" his mother yapped.

Mitchell ran belatedly to hold the door – and held it open long enough for them to hear her add, "That'll teach them! They'll find new staff soon enough now."

Tregembo's hands were already raised against the brewing mutiny. "Let us remember," he said, "that the family has had a long, tiring journey. Everything may look very different after a good night's sleep. So let us do nothing – and say nothing – to hinder that restorative process."

"It had better look different, Mister Tregembo," Trussell said. "Else I'll tell you now – I shan't even last the month."

He nodded gravely at her but said nothing either way.

Sir Hector went to his study to sort through the pile of letters that had accumulated during their long absence. Noel, seeing the entire harbour and estuary bathed in bright sunlight, changed into his swimming trunks and dressing gown inside two minutes and ran down the long, sweeping lawns to the shore. Lady Carclew, despite her earlier reassignment of Mary's duties, took her maid upstairs to help her change out of her travelling clothes.

Fenella looked inquiringly at Rose and said, "We might as well do the same, Rose."

Did any of them even notice how bright the window panes were? Rose wondered. How all the woodwork gleamed? How every inch of wallpaper had been sponged and brightened? How springy was the pile on every new-beaten rug and carpet?

"I'll bet you're glad we're back at long last," Fenella prattled on. Noel might be a new man but his sister was the same old child as ever. "Now you can all get back to doing the things you do the best. But, oh! The time we had of it – I can't begin to tell you ..."

That didn't stop her, though. From the luxurious appointments of the Orient Express to the tedium of the homeward journey from Paddington to Truro, Rose must hear it all: the unbelievably elegant food, the darling ferry down the Black Sea from Constanza, the first sight of Constantinople's palaces, hareems, minarets, and bazaars as dawn painted the sky pink above them ... the pyramids ... breathtaking ... made out of *real* stones, you know ... and there was a sultan of Constantinople who got tired of his two-hundred and fifty wives all bickering so he tied them up in sacks, weighted with stones, and threw them live into the Bosphorus ... and the Dead Sea, which is where the Jordan just evaporates away into thin air, because it never flows out into the sea, you know, one never realized that before, you float on the surface without hardly even sinking, so it's maybe where Our Lord walked on the water ... and the tomb where the Magdalene found He was risen ... and the wall where all the Jews kick up a dreadful racket which was enough to give anyone a headache ... and Jericho, where they won't let anyone play the trumpet (that was a joke, by the way) ...

On and on it went. Rose combed and brushed Fenella's hair and gazed out of the window at Noel, swimming around where Louis had almost drowned. And she thought how wonderful it would be to be rich – or not even rich, just comfortable enough to live in a little cottage somewhere in a forest glade – but also near the sea – it would have to be near the sea – and just dabble in water colours or something – and swim whenever you wanted. Perhaps, if she got away in time this evening, she'd go over to Trefusis and swim off their bit of foreshore. The Carclews would never let any servant take a dip off their precious four-hundred yards of strand. And even with people of their own class they could be pretty short – as a Falmouth yachtsman had discovered last February when he moored at their jetty to make some minor running repair within screaming distance of her ladyship.

But, of course, the sun had long set by the time she, or any of the servants achieved their liberation for the day. In two weeks' time the whole family would be setting off to London for the Season – to find a suitable match for Fenella. And, thanks to Tregembo's timely warning, her ladyship decided, on that same evening of their return, to take everyone except the Tregembos, the cook, and the scullerymaid with them. They had already rented a house in St James's and had engaged a genuine French maid, at ruinous expense; the prospect of hiring London servants at double rates, when they had a whole gang of them down here, eating their heads off in blissful idleness, was just too-too ghastly. So they would come, too. But a mere fortnight was barely long enough in which to organize such a prodigious transhumation from one social-grazing pasture to another.

With very little exercise of her imagination, Rose could picture how her life would run over the next two weeks. She would be on tenterhooks every waking hour, looking out of windows, straining her ears for the sound of an arriving motor or gig – and it was a moot point how much sleep she'd enjoy between those waking hours. At the very least, she realized, she'd have to confess her crime to Tregembo. He'd have more opportunity than anyone to intercept Louis on his arrival and explain matters to him so that he wouldn't blurt out anything too damaging – unless, of course, her deception roused him, Louis, to such anger that he'd go directly to her ladyship and demand her instant dismissal – which, of course, she would grant at once.

She waited until she knew Mrs T had retired for the night – when Tregembo would be sipping his nightly whisky and going through the form for tomorrow's races – before she knocked timidly at his door.

Her confession followed almost exactly the same form as the one to her parents. He was a little more sceptical than they had been when she explained about trying on the dress merely in order to adjust the hemline but he did not dwell on it; he was experienced enough to guess that something far more serious was coming.

When she had told him all, he, too, asked who had taken off Louis' wet clothes and dried him and dressed him in new ones.

"I did," she replied, not wishing to implicate Mary and Pennycuik.

"And the other maids?"

"They said to fetch in one of the gardeners to do it. But I thought it more important to get him warm as soon as possible. Was I wrong? We thought he was near to death, see?"

"Hmmm." He scratched his chin, where tomorrow's shaving stubble had already sprouted. "That depends. Did he learn who did it?"

She nodded and lowered her gaze.

"So here's a gentleman – a so-called gentleman – who falls in love – or so you claim – with a maid who's forward enough to strip him naked and who talks as good Cornish as you do – refined talk I grant you – but Cornish for all that – and he's so besotted that he doesn't even notice these departures from the standards any *true* lady would obey without even thinking? I don't think so, Rose! I don't doubt you're in love with him, maid – alas for you! But these old and ugly bones tell me he was chancing his luck – stringing you along in the hope of a bit of you know what." He smiled reassuringly. "No harm done, fortunately. But I don't think Mister Redmile-Smith's sudden arrival at our gates is going to trouble this household in the next fortnight. Nor never."

He returned to the racing page.

"Now there, Mister Tregembo, I'm afraid you delude yourself," she said in her perfect upper-class voice.

The man dropped his paper and sat bolt upright, almost knocking his whisky over. "Eh?" He gulped.

"Neither in speech nor in demeanour did I give Mister Redmile-Smith the slightest reason for supposing I was anything other than Sir Hector's ward. He *will* be back."

"We-el!" The butler picked up his glass, drained it in one gulp, and poured himself a refill. "Justified, I think," he said heavily.

"'Fraid so," she said glumly, back in her own voice.
"Do that again," he said, smiling despite himself.
"What? Talk like that?"
He nodded. Relieved that his fascination was stronger than his sense of outrage, she filled her mouth with imaginary pebbles and recited: "Round the rugged rocks the ragged rascal ran."
He put a hand to his mouth to stifle his laughter.
"Or if you prefer it," she felt emboldened enough to add, "Wound the wugged wocks the wagged wascal wan."
"Hush!" He reached across the whatnot to grip her arm. "Never let them hear you speak like that! It's too accurate – too 'cwewell'!"
"Mister Tregembo!" she exclaimed, once again in her own voice. "I must say I never expected you to respond like this."
He nodded. "On any other day but this you'd be right, maid. But that disgraceful scene on the front steps, when the family returned – it's quite disconcerted me, I don't mind telling you. I came as close to handing in my notice – there and then, in the spot, in front of you all – as ever in my life. Not a word of this to the others, mind! See – we each have a secret to keep now."
To say nothing of your weekend in Torquay, she thought, though she said nothing. He'd be thinking it, anyway.
"So, of course," she concluded. "I'll go on keeping both eyes and ears peeled for Mister Redmile-Smith. But, seeing as you'll probably get to him first, you could prepare yourself to explain matters?"
He nodded. "That would be best all round."
"And tell him ..." she hesitated.
"Yes?"
"Oh, just that my feelings were the only genuine thing about me – and *they* haven't changed, and ..."
"Yes?"
She shrugged. "That I hope he may forgive me in time – and not judge me too harshly."

15

Noel came into the maids' sewing room, pulled up a chair, and sat on it the wrong way round. He leaned his chin against its back and stared at Rose with great, soulful eyes.
"Go away," she said wearily. She was sitting near the open window, keeping her eyes and ears peeled, as always. "Where's the four pound, sixteen shillings you promised me?"
He ignored her rebuff. "I've thought of that. When we get to London ..." He paused.
She jumped in: "Which will be never, if you don't leave me alone to get on with this. I don't know what you think you can gain by badgering me every chance you get. If you were just a few years younger, I'd bend you over a chair and spank you."
"Go on then!" he exclaimed, leaping up dramatically. He looked about the room, spotted an old rattan carpet beater that had been

brought up for repair last November and then forgotten, and ran to get it. "Here! He thrust it into her hands and bent himself over the back of his chair. "Go on! Hard as you like – I'll bet you're too scared to do it hard."

It was a tempting challenge. Nine out of ten muscles in her body reached automatically to comply with the request. But there, too, was the reason for the caution in the remaining tenth – his words had sounded much more like an eager request than a hasty, picayune challenge. In fact, he was so sure she'd do it that he just stood there, bent almost double, eyes closed, grinning, and trembling all over.

"Noel! What are you doing in that ridiculous posture? Stand up this minute!"

Her imitation of Lady Carclew was so chillingly close that he sent the chair flying in his eagerness to obey. He stared at her open-mouthed, looked beyond her, craning his neck to spy behind the curtain, then looked back at her. "You?" he asked, still unable to believe it.

"What about me?" she asked, all innocence.

"It must have been you – imitating my mother. Whew!" He picked up the chair and resumed his *other* ridiculous posture. "Don't you *ever* do that to me again."

"There's one way to make sure I don't," she told him.

He giggled. "Can you do Fenella, too? Howwible, howwid girl?"

She hesitated, tempted, and then said, "No, of course not."

"I'll bet you can," he said. "Can you do a posh accent – not imitating anybody – just a posh accent in your own voice?"

She could see no harm in that, so she obliged, reciting Wordsworth's *Daffodils* in her best upper-class tones.

"God! You should be on the stage, Rose!" he said. "I mean it. All you need is some good patter – life below stairs and life above stairs – and you doing all the accents. You'd be a star! Actually, that's what I was going to say – about when we all go up to London on Monday – only I didn't know you could do all this sort of thing then. But what I *was* going to say is that the mater will be so busy mating young Fenella – that's why she's called 'mater,' you know! She'll be so busy that I'll be less under her thumb than usual. And the pater will find somewhere to snore the afternoons away in his club, I'm sure."

"That's very nice for you," Rose told him, making her needle fly almost as fast as any machine's.

"It could be nice for you, too, Rose. I don't want to do the usual things, you know – play cards, lose a fortune, stand around braying haw-haw-haw in Rotten Row, pick up some diseased totty off a Mayfair pavement ... all that. Instead we could go to the music halls, you and me. You could see how they do it – the professional comediennes."

"And then?" she sneered.

"I know what you're thinking," he told her, "but it's not that. I like you, Rose. Really I do. You're different from every other housemaid or lady's maid I ever knew – not that I've known very many, but still. You are different. Of course, there can never be anything serious between us. We both know that. But it doesn't mean we can't be friends – real friends, does it?"

She looked up from her work, gave him an exasperated smile, and said, "You're bloody impossible, you know that?"

But he was staring out of the window, only half attending to her now. " 'Ullo-ullo," he murmured. "Who are *you,* fine sir?"

Since he was facing her, and since she had seated herself to be able to watch the drive, this stranger was obviously approaching from the opposite direction – from the shore.

Of course!

She did not doubt for a moment that it was Louis. But why had it not even crossed her mind that he might come *that* way, rather than by road? Because she was in such a sweat about his coming at all that she just didn't think – that was why. Well, she'd better make up for it now!

She pushed Noel aside, threw wide the casement, and saw that it was, indeed, Louis out there. She was just about to call to him when she noticed that Sir Hector was standing on the path immediately below her – not just standing there, either, but relieving himself on the flower bed.

Noel saw it, too. "Dear Pater!" he said. "He has all the attributes of an aristocrat. Pity he's only two generations away from the counting house!"

"Listen!" Rose said hastily. "I'll do anything you want, Noel – anything – honestly – if you'll just do exactly as I tell you now."

"Done!" he answered at once.

"It's not a joke – this is the most serious moment in my life. Literally the whole of my life depends on it."

"Promise." He caught on to her seriousness.

"That man's name is Louis Redmile-Smith. When ..."

"Of the ..."

"Yes of the brewing and baking family. When he gets to the corner there, call out his name."

"What?"

"Just *do* it!"

"Fine, fine! And then what?"

"I'll tell you. He's there now. Go on!"

"Ahoy! Mister Redmile-Smith!" Noel called out.

"I love you, Noel, I really do! Now introduce yourself."

"Noel Carclew!" He waved.

"Glad to meet you, Mister Carclew." Louis had noticed the imperturbable Sir Hector, who was now giving himself a prodigious shake before, as the notices in gentlemen's lavatories put it, 'adjusting his dress.' Glad of this rescue from his embarrassment,

Louis walked a wide circle onto the front lawn until he was able to look into the upstairs window directly.

Rose, hanging back in the room, said, "Now introduce me as *Rose* Tremayne, your sister's lady's maid. Stress the *Rose*. I'll come to the window as you do it."

God love the boy, he didn't hesitate over this astonishing request, though it must have mystified him completely. "Although we have only just met, Mister Redmile-Smith," he called out, "allow me to present you to Miss Rose Tremayne – my sister's lady's maid."

"What the devil?" Sir Hector roared up at his son. "How dare you! And you, sir" – to Louis – "who are you?"

But Louis' eyes were fixed on the window, where Rose was now standing, her hands held in an attitude of prayer. For a moment he just stood there open mouthed. Then he shouted, "Really?"

She nodded.

"Understood," he said. "Rose."

He was smiling! She hoped that was a good omen. Before she withdrew from the window she mimed the tearing out of her own heart and blowing it, like a kiss, in his direction.

"Same here!" he shouted.

"Sir! I must insist!" Sir Hector ranted.

Rose turned made to run for the door but Noel gripped her by the wrist and said, "What the hell was all that?"

"Come down with me," she replied. "Tell you on the way."

She felt so relieved she wanted to descend the stairs in cartwheels, or by sliding down the banisters. All that worry had been for nothing! In less than ten seconds he had understood all – and forgiven all. And he still loved her. But how could she ever have doubted him? Now all she needed to do was to show the Carclews that she and he had maintained a proper master-servant distance during his convalescence.

"Well?" Noel grabbed her arm to slow her down.

"Oh – yes. I suppose I owe it to you. What happened was this. Mister Redmile-Smith was nearly drowned – out in the estuary – one Friday morning, shortly after you left. They brought him up here, where I was playing dressing-up in some of Fenella's clothes and when he came round he assumed I was the daughter of the household. He stayed three more days and I did nothing to disabuse him. Now you know."

"And the Tregembos permitted it?"

"That's one question too many, Noel. Just be satisfied with what I've told you."

"Ha! So the Tregembos slipped away for a crafty weekend, eh!"

They were approaching the drawing-room door by now.

"You'll cut yourself if you're not careful," she told him.

"I'm on your side in this," he replied.

They went into the drawing room, where, as she had expected, Louis had entered by the french windows, having given some sort of hastily revised explanation to Sir Hector. He, in turn, was just introducing their unexpected visitor to his wife. Noel, for some reason, slipped away again.

"Ah!" Louis smiled in her direction. "And here is the young lady to whom I think I owe my life."

"Young what?" Lady Carclew turned in bewilderment. "You mean Miss Rose?"

"I do, indeed," he said. "I was washed up on your shore, half drowned – more than half drowned. It was Miss Rose who nursed me back to the land of the living."

"Miss Rose?" her ladyship turned upon her maidservant.

Rose said, "I was wondering if I should bring in some tea, my lady?" In the corner of her eye she could see that her natural accent was causing Louis some amusement; she hoped he would conceal it before others noticed it, too.

"Why have we heard nothing of this since our return, two weeks ago?" Lady Carclew asked.

"I assumed you *had* heard of it, my lady, and did not wish to speak of it."

"From whom?" she snapped.

Rose shrugged and said nothing. The obvious people to inform her and Sir Hector were the Tregembos, but she didn't want to say as much.

"My fault, I'm afraid," Louis said suddenly. They all turned to him. "I asked them to leave it all to me ..."

Tregembo, rather breathless, entered the drawing room, with Noel grinning at his heels. He interrupted Louis. "Ah, Mister Redmile-Smith, sir," he cried. "How good to see you again – and looking so well. You possibly don't recall me? Tregembo, the butler?"

"I remember you very well, Tregembo. It's good to see you again – I want to thank you, too."

"Oh, sir! We all know who it was who nursed *you* back to life!" He smirked at Rose.

"I still don't understand," her ladyship said.

"Rose – bring some tea." Tregembo said.

"I'll give the orders, if you don't mind," his mistress said tartly. Then, turning to Louis, "You were saying, Mister Redmile-Smith, you asked my servants to say nothing of these extraordinary events?"

"I'm afraid so, Lady Carclew." He smiled. "As the one who is so profoundly indebted to you for your unwitting hospitality, I thought it best that the explanation and thanks should come from me – and immediately upon your return home. That was my intention – but I muddled the dates, I fear. It's unpardonable, I know – and I am deeply sorry. And here I am to say it."

Lady Carclew smiled. Rose relaxed. Louis' charm had completely won her over. Now, surely, nothing could go wrong.

16

Louis thanked Rose yet again and insisted on shaking her by the hand – which Lady Carclew considered a scandal. She said nothing but Rose knew what those twitches of her lips implied. She gave Louis an imperceptible (she hoped) tilt of her head in the direction of his boat. He responded with a nod that would mean nothing to those who had not seen her signal first.

She ran outdoors and waited just inside the brick-arched entrance to the stable yard. She knew that Louis would have to pass by on the way back to his boat. He certainly took his time about it, but at last she heard the crunch of … not two but four feet. She risked a quick peep and saw with dismay that Noel was with him. What was Louis thinking of? Surely he had understood her gesture? She just stood there, grinding her teeth and plotting all sorts of torments for Noel.

And then, through the mists of her anger, she heard Louis saying, "… keep this to yourself, old chap – I'm only telling you because I know you'll be a friend to her and she'll certainly need a friend if things go wrong – but the trouble is, the family business is in a spot of bother just at the moment and I'll be struggling every hour God sends to get things back on an even keel."

She could actually feel the blood draining from her face. She sidled round into the stable yard and let them pass. When they were half way across the opening they could have turned and seen her, but neither did.

Noel was saying, "But you do love her? And you do mean to marry her – come what may?" He gave a short, staccato laugh. "Here am I talking like a brother – which, actually, is pretty much how I feel."

"If the firm goes smash," Louis replied gravely, "life will no longer be a bed of …" He completed the saying in his mind and laughed. "You know what I mean. I'd be bankrupt. No discharge for years. Could I ask her to share such poverty?"

Ask me! Rose shrieked in the silence of her mind. But she had already heard enough. Risking all, she ran out into the open and shouted, "Hi, wait!" She feigned breathlessness. "Didn't you understand I'd be waiting for you outside?"

Louis pointed vaguely ahead. "Thought you'd be farther off."

She laughed bitterly. "Believe me, nowhere is far enough." She gave Noel's arm a little squeeze. "Only this man makes it bearable. Noel, you've been an ebsolute and utter brick today. I take back every murderous thought I've ever hed about you."

"It's uncanny." Noel laughed and looked at Louis. "I had no idea she could talk like this."

But Louis had eyes only for his Lucinda. "Where can we go?" he asked. "There's so much to discuss."

"London?" she offered. "I'm ready-packed."

He exchanged a brief, awkward glance with Noel. "Could you leave us to talk this over, old boy?"

Noel dipped his head. "Of course," he replied and turned to go.

"And I hope you're mature enough to respect a confidence," Louis called after him. He responded with a wave of his hand but did not turn round again. "Where's best?" Louis looked all about.

"Here," Rose said. "Anywhere. It doesn't matter now. I don't care if her ladyship herself is watching every move."

They stayed on the path that led down to the water.

"She won't dismiss you?" he asked.

Rose chuckled. "She's learned her lesson there, I think. Forget her – let's talk about us. Oh darling, darling, darling Louis! I've been so afraid of today, and yet you were ..."

"Afraid of Lady Carclew?" he asked scornfully.

"No! Afraid of *you.* I don't give a fig for her – not now. I was afraid you'd hate me for deceiving you like that. I didn't mean to – honestly. It's just that when you came to and saw me dressed in Miss Fenella's gown ... mmnmnmh ..."

In the full light of day, in full view of every window on that side of the house, out there in the open parkland, he took her in his arms and crushed her words with his lips.

After that, nothing mattered. She loved him and he loved her. Forgiveness was not even mentioned for he saw nothing to forgive.

"So?" she asked when their kisses and embraces were exhausted. "Shall I even bother to go back for my bags? We could always just send for them."

"Well now, darling," he said, slipping her arm through his and resuming their gentle downhill stroll, "that's something I want to discuss. While I was in France, you see ... well, it was a case of when the cat's away. Certain decisions were taken – in the business, I mean – I'm talking about the business – certain decisions were taken by people who were not authorized or competent. We face a very angry shareholders' meeting, which is due next month ..."

"I can do anything," she said eagerly. "Sums ... adding up – I'm good at that ..."

He patted her hand. "I'm afraid it's a little beyond ..."

"Read correspondence ... make précis for you ... answer the telephone ... address envelopes ... Don't shut me out, Louis. 'Wheresoever thou goest ...' you know. That's me. Ruth amid the alien corn."

"Ruth ... Rose ... Lucinda ... you'll make me dizzy, love."

"You see," Rose said glumly, "you do resent my deceiving you, really – or you wouldn't say a thing like that."

"It was a *joke,* darling. Anyway ..."

"I'll even sweep floors and make you cups of tea. There must be something I can do?"

He laughed, trying to cajole her into a more optimistic frame of mind. "It's not that sort of crisis – truly. It can all be put right. It *will* all be put right. And then ..."

"How long?"

He hesitated. "Six weeks." She realized he meant double that, if not even longer. Plans flashed through her mind to go to his offices, wherever they were, and squat; but all she said was, "If it must be, well, then it must be, I guess."

"It'll flash by, you'll see. We've survived six weeks already with our love undimmed – on my part, anyway." He paused.

"Are you doubting me!" she said. "When I go to bed at night, when I wake in the morning, every hour of the day – I think of you. Only of you. It's like a fever. And it's going to be worse now I know you're not angry. There was always that little warning to hold me back, saying not to fall too deeply in love in case you turn me away. Tell me again that you won't!"

"I won't. Not now. Not ever"

"You ought to. I would, in your shoes. How can you marry a servant girl and move in Society?"

Another laugh, this one more heartfelt. "That's simple. I don't 'move in Society.' Mother does, but I hate it. Take her ladyship back there – she's friendly enough and, on a personal level, I think she quite likes me."

"You had her eating out of your hand."

"That's as maybe. She still despises my class because I'm 'in trade.' Granted it's wholesale, not retail. And granted that if the Carclews went smash tomorrow, she'd very soon forget such scruples. But at this moment she despises me for it. Am I right?"

Rose leaned her head against his shoulder and nodded. She was happy at last – or as happy as she could be in these circumstances. He had laid her last remaining fear to rest – that when the high fever of their love started to cool, as it inevitably would, the difference in their class would, by keeping him out of Society, make him dislike her.

"So that's why I avoid the lot of 'em," he concluded.

"And all those things you said about having to go and live abroad?" she asked.

He hesitated. She guessed he had forgotten saying such things during that weekend; he was thinking about his conversation with Noel just half an hour ago – and wondering if she could have overheard.

"To avoid social disgrace," she added. "You said it that weekend, about marrying a maidservant, when you didn't know I was one."

"Oh yes!" He laughed with relief. "Well ... let's just say you weren't the only one who was putting on a bit of class during those three days!"

They arrived at the jetty.

"You'll enjoy London," he said.

"Do you have offices there?"

"No – Plymouth and Bristol. Plymouth's the main office. Don't you actually *want* to go up for the Season? You don't have to, you know. I could send you some money to tide you over, till we meet again. You could live independently. I'll send a hundred guineas if you'll let me know the address."

"No!" she protested, thinking of what he had told Noel about possible bankruptcy. She could not imagine a smash so great that a mere hundred guineas was neither here nor there. "I'm looking forward to London and the Season. I'll be fine!"

"Yes. You'll go to all the balls and meet all the other lady's maids and pick up such gossip – you'll be quite the insider by the time it's all over. And there'll be time off, too, and so much to do and see – the museums, the National Gallery, changing the guard ..."

"Louis?"

"What?"

"Just kiss me and say goodbye."

"Not goodbye," he murmured as his lips closed on hers. "Just au revoir."

They kissed until they ached – until he said, "'No more, dear love, for at a touch I yield; / Ask me no more.'"

She smiled, recognizing the quotation, and would have kissed again if she had not steeled herself to push him onto the jetty. "Go!" she urged. "I'll survive somehow. And I'll be waiting for you here, right here, the day after we return. And every day thereafter – promise."

"I'll be here already," he promised, "God willing." He untied the painter and pushed the dinghy out into the rippled water, where the breeze strengthened to a fair wind. There he hoisted his single sail, waved to her, and was away. Rose waved after him until he passed out of sight behind a belt of young trees. Then she turned and hastened up the hill to find a point where she could see him once again, over the tops of those trees.

To her surprise she saw Lady Carclew almost running down the path toward her; even more improbably, she was carrying a small suitcase, which jerked and swung against her legs as she walked-trotted-walked-trotted downhill.

Had Louis left something behind?

No – impossible. He had been carrying nothing when he arrived.

A moment later she realized with a shock that the suitcase was her own – a battered cardboard thing she had treasured since her schooldays because Tony Trevean had written *I love you – TT* inside the lid.

When her ladyship realized that Rose had spotted her, she stopped dead and stood there, breathing heavily.

Rose ran up to her but her ladyship got in first. "Take this and go, you wretched, ungrateful creature!" she almost screamed. She was shivering with rage.

"I beg your pardon?" Rose asked, outraged but calm.

"You heard me well enough, I think. You are never to set foot inside my house again. Here are your nightclothes and toiletries. We shall send the rest to your parents' shop in Falmouth."

"Don't you think you owe me an explanation, Lady Carclew?" She was damned if she'd call her 'my lady' now, after this. "You certainly owe me two weeks wages in lieu of notice."

"Hah! You may whistle for that! And do stop speaking in that ridiculous accent. It may have deceived a semi-gentleman in trade but it certainly doesn't deceive me."

The full implication of her dismissal hit her now, belatedly. She turned and shouted across the lower parkland, out across the water: "Looo-eeee!"

He heard her, for he turned and waved.

She waved more frantically.

He waved again.

She jumped up and down, still waving.

He waved once more, one last time, just before the red sails of his dinghy passed out of sight beyond the headland.

17

Rose picked up her suitcase and ran after Lady Carclew. "Who told you?" she called out when she was still several paces off. Her ladyship hesitated and then walked on, but Rose soon caught up. "Doesn't it occur to you that you might have been told a pack of lies?" she asked. "You've dismissed me without even hearing my side of the case."

"As long as you persist with that ridiculous accent, I shall not even listen," was the reply.

" 'Oo did tell 'ee, then?" Rose asked. " 'Ow can 'ee turn I off an' not yur moy soyde."

Lady Carclew tossed her had angrily. "That's just going to the other extreme – and it will meet with the same response." It occurred to Rose that she had never seen the woman out of doors before without a hat. She must have been furious beyond all bearing to do such a thing.

Then, without another word from Rose, she said, "You think I don't have eyes in my head? I saw it all."

"And what exactly have I done wrong?" Rose asked in her everyday voice.

"That's better. What have you done wrong? What have you done *right!* That man was making sheep's eyes at you from the moment you entered the room. It was quite clear that something more than gratitude had moved him to return. I didn't need your disgraceful display down there on the jetty just now to confirm it. I shudder to think what you and Mister Redmile-Smith may have got up to while we were away." Hearing Rose draw breath she held up her hand. "But pray don't enlighten me! I have not the slightest desire to know. My sole concern is that you should not be around to contaminate my children. I hope you don't imagine you'll get any kind of character from me?"

"You think that's a terrible threat, don't you," Rose sneered – even as a small, reasonable voice within told her to shut up. "You should take a short drive around Wood Lane, Alma Terrace, Wodehouse Terrace ... and count the positions-offered notices in dozens of windows there. They even keep them showing on Sundays – which shows how desperate they are."

Lady Carclew stopped, turned slowly toward her, and smiled a most contemptuous smile. "You think that, do you?" she said icily. "Then I promise you this. If any lady in Falmouth – no, I go further – if any lady in Cornwall is importunate enough to offer you a position, *I* shall get to hear of it. I shall make it my business to hear of it. You will not last anywhere above two weeks. I'll teach you to sneer at me."

Both women were shivering with rage by now – cold, controlled rage. Rose threw off the last vestiges of caution and said, "You are a vindictive, evil snob, but if it's promises you want, I'll promise you this. I don't know where, I don't know when, I don't know how – but one day I shall make you eat those words. No! I *do* know *where* at least – here!" She stamped her heel into the soft turf beside the gravel walk. "On this very spot!"

Their eyes held each other's a long, silent moment. Rose felt a strange exhilaration such as she had never experienced before, and some intuition told her that Lady Carclew felt the same way, too. The thought flashed through her mind that, given different circumstances, the two of them could actually be as close in friendship as they were now in sworn enmity. But it did not last. It was too ridiculous.

To Rose's surprise, it was her ladyship who batted her eyes first. "Dear me, Tremayne, you are even more stupid than I had supposed," she said as she resumed her homeward way.

Smiling to herself, Rose turned aside and started to march, head high, across the grass, heading directly for Flushing. She might still be in time to catch up with Louis at the yacht club.

18

The steward at the yacht club told her to go to the tradesman's entrance. He kept her waiting there a good five minutes, to let the lesson sink in, and then he told her what he could have said from the beginning – that Mr Redmile-Smith had left the premises fifteen minutes before her arrival.

"Thanks," she said, leaving the same route, "you've been a real pal. I'll be certain to let Mister Redmile-Smith hear of it."

My day for threats! she thought as she set off up Greenbank toward the High Street. Already the exhilaration of her clash with Lady Carclew was fading. If it had not been for her reunion with Louis, and his assurance that he did not care whether she was a lady or a servant, she would have been down in the dumps long before she reached home.

Down the High Street she went, into Market Place, along Market Street and Church Street into Arwennack Street – it was all one single street, really, but with five different names, in less than a mile. In America, Mom said, some streets had numbers up into the thousands. Everything was bigger there, she said. "Including the loony bins," Pop would murmur. Thinking of her parents, Rose was looking forward to being at home again, no matter how brief her stay. To be alone at a time like this would be awful.

She knew many of the people she passed along the way. She nodded, waved, stopped for a chat, depending on how well their acquaintance had worn in the nine years since she had left school.

"Not goin' up Lunnon, then?" Ann Tiddy asked from the door of her father's fish and chip shop. She gave a nod toward Rose's battered suitcase. She would be guessing that the Carclews were going up for the Season; many families, even those who did not have the excuse of an oriental journey, had delayed their departure until June because of the king's death and funeral in May.

Everyone would notice her suitcase, Rose realized. And some, unlike Ann, would actually know that the Carclews were London-bound. She ought to have prepared a good story instead of wasting her time on fantasies of revenge against her ladyship. "Country life doesn't suit me," she replied, waving in the direction of Nancemellin – the best answer she could think of on the spur of the moment. "I miss the city lights of good old Falmouth."

"There's scats of positions going," Ann reassured her.

"I know. I was up Wodehouse Terrace last Sunday. I saw. That's what made up my mind."

"Good luck, then. See 'ee 'gin!"

"See 'ee 'gin!"

And that brief conversation became the template for several further encounters before she arrived home at last.

"Where's Pop?" she asked as she walked through the shop door. She sniffed deeply on aromas of cabbage and leek, oranges and tomatoes, and said, "Aaaah!" Her mother was going through a box of new apples, picking out the doubtfuls. Her eye, too, fell on the suitcase and she said, "Oh no!"

"Oh yes," Rose assured her. "And I've never been more glad to shake off the dust of any other house in my life."

"Have you a character?"

"I won't need one, honestly. Is Pop out the back?"

"He's delivering." She crossed her fingers. "The Gyllyngdune Hôtel – they've given us a one-month contract, on trial."

"Out of little acorns ..." Rose said.

"We hope! D'you want an apple? They're Beauty of Bath. This one's not too bad."

Rose accepted it and took a large bite of its crisp, juicy flesh. A moment later she pushed it genteelly out with her tongue into the palm of her hand. The entire core was black-rotten. "I hope that's not an omen of my life to come!" She showed it to her mother, who took a knife from the till drawer and passed it over.

"That'll cut out easy," she said. "The rest is good." After a pause she added, "I guess Lady Snooty cottoned on to what happened back in May?"

"I don't think so. Not all of it. Not that it matters, anyway." And she went on to describe that afternoon's events.

Her mother passed no comment, not even after she had finished her tale.

"Well?" Rose prompted.

"Gee, I don't know, honey. That bit you overheard – what if he does ... I mean, assume the worst."

"If he does go bankrupt?"

"Right. I don't even know if they'd *let* him marry. I mean, they take over your entire life, you know. And even if you did marry him – he's right about the sort of hole-and-corner life you'd lead. If you could call it a life."

Rose took a deep breath and said, "I've thought about that – and you're right. I wouldn't marry him, not if he went bankrupt."

Her mother stared at her in open amazement. "That is so *unlike* you!" she exclaimed. "I mean it's so *sensible!*"

Rose did not laugh. "I'd only be a burden round his neck."

"Would you?" Her mother turned all defensive. "Pardon me but I don't think so. You can earn good money – not as a living-in lady's maid, I grant you – but with your knowledge of fashion and your skill with the needle ..."

"Good money?" Rose gave a hollow laugh. "Mom! How many women d'you know who eke out a living sewing kid gloves in garrets? You know what they're driven to do sometimes!"

"Fashion Advisor!" Her mother's hands created an imaginary shingle. "Miss Lucinda-Ella Tremayne, former lady's maid to the gentry, will advise the ladies of Falmouth – no, West Cornwall – on all the latest modes as seen in London and Paris. Modes! That's the word. Not fashion advisor – *modiste!* Miss Lucinda-Ella Tremayne, modiste! And you could do it, honey. You've got the nerve to carry it off."

"I like the bit about the gentry," Rose said. "But one of them – you know who – is the fly in the ointment. She'd make sure I had no custom. She's already threatened she'd get me sacked from any house that gave me a place. I guess over the next few weeks I'm going to discover how real a threat that is."

Later, when they repeated the gist of this conversation to her father, he said she might try a new family, recently moved down from Plymouth – the de Vivians. "They've one daughter left unwed," he said, "and from what I heard tell, they only got one lady's maid – and her likely to give in her notice before too long."

"What have you heard tell, then?" his wife asked. "Who is the maid in question?"

"Very much in question!" He turned to Rose. "You recall a pair of red-headed twins who were in first form when you were in fifth at Smithick Hill?"

"Yes!" She closed her eyes tight. "Pengilly? Penhaligon? Pen-something."

"Penhallow," he said. "That's them."

"Not Ruby Penhallow?" Mom looked at him, slightly shocked.

"She was one," he said evenly. "Gemma was the other."

"But Ruby ... didn't she go to the bad?"

"She certainly went to the *bed!*" he replied with a laugh. "Roger Deveril's bed."

"Now, now – nothing coarse, please!"

"It's okay," Rose assured them. "Word of the scandal spread as far as Nancemellin, you know. In fact, Tregembo made sure we all heard of it – a cautionary tale. She had a baby by the young master of the house, Roger Deveril, and her name was never mentioned again. What about her, anyway?"

"Not her, the sister – Gemma Penhallow. It do seem as history is repeating itself with her and another young master – Peter de Vivian."

"Where did you hear this?" Rose asked.

"Their cook, Miss Eddy, buys her vegetables here sometimes," Mom explained.

"Well, I heard it off of Jimmy Walker, the butler," he said. "Anyway, it do seem as if Miss Gemma is not eager to follow her twin sister into perdition. They're up Lunnon for the Season now, but he do say she'll hand in her notice the day they come back."

"But that'll be another month – at least," Rose protested.

"Well, it could have happened already. Master Peter went up Lunnon with them. The house is only up the hill from here – Number One, Alma Terrace. No harm in looking in."

"You think they might offer me a place because they're new? Because they wouldn't know about the Carclews and the influence they have?"

"No!" He gave a cunning smile. "They're the de Vivians of the de Vivian Bank. I shouldn't think there's much love lost between them and the Carclews, would you?"

Rose laughed. This prospect was just beginning to sound hopeful, for the Carclews were big shareholders in the arch-rival Lemon Bank. And, knowing the ways of upper-class ladies as well as she did by now, she thought it more than likely that Mrs de Vivian would leap at the chance to show up her ladyship as the sort of woman who'd cut off her nose to spite her face.

"I'll make it my first port of call tomorrow," she said. "No – I mean Monday."

END OF PART ONE

Part Two

Up and Down

19 Rose called on the de Vivian household in Alma Terrace, as early as seemed proper on the following Monday morning – the day on which the Carclews were due to leave for London. Since the de Vivian family had gone up to London some weeks earlier, she was interviewed by Mr Walker, the butler, who thought it highly likely there would be a place going begging when they returned from London, which would probably be around the middle of next month. But he thought it even more likely that Rose would find a dozen other places eager to take her long before that. When she told him something of the circumstances in which she had left Nancemellin House, he reduced his estimate to half a dozen – which was still encouraging, especially as it still included his own establishment. Then, taking a liking to her for her frankness, he added that the Roanokes, who lived in Wodehouse Terrace, would also have little affection for the Carclews. Not too long ago – back in February, in fact – Henry Roanoke, the master of the household and a keen yachtsman, had tied up at the Nancemellin jetty to free a stuck keelson and her ladyship had given him 'a good helping of tongue pie'; so an ill word from the Carclews would be something of a recommendation to the Roanokes. Unfortunately, Mrs Roanoke had accompanied the de Vivians to London for the season, so she, too, would not be back for a month yet.

Since Mr Roanoke, a yachting fanatic, had not gone with her, Rose thought it might be worth a call, anyway, if only to have a look at the place and gauge its atmosphere. They lived, she discovered, in one of the larger houses toward the middle of the Terrace, commanding a superb view over the whole of the harbour and estuary. It made her revise her specification for the cottage of her dreams. It would still have to be in a sylvan glade in the middle of the forest but now it would have to be not just 'near the sea' it would have to look out over just such a prospect as this. There was NO POSITION OFFERED notice in the windows.

Nothing daunted, she knocked at the side door and was soon admitted by one of the maids, a flustered young woman who cut Rose's explanation short with, "You'd best come to the servant's hall and talk to Mrs Dyer."

"The housekeeper?"

" 'Es. I'll fetch her."

Mrs Dyer was a small, neat, and round. "Well, Miss Tremayne," she said when Rose had spoken her piece, "I'm sorry to say that Mrs Roanoke already has a lady's maid – Sally Kelynack."

"Oh, but I know her," Rose exclaimed. "She was in the form above me at Smithwick Hill. I'm sorry to have troubled you. You don't know anywhere else that might ..."

"However," the woman interjected, "I was about to say – would you consider a parlourmaid's position – even temporarily? I'm sure I could persuade Mister Roanoke to pay your former wage – as long as you kept word of it it to yourself, of course. Poor Lizzie's rushed off her feet with the entertaining the master does while the mistress is away."

Rose was tempted. She could live at home, which would mean she'd be paid at the higher, living-out rate, and it would be so satisfying when Lady Carclew got to hear that she had secured a place within twenty-four hours, allowing for the intervention of the sabbath. An idea occurred to her – two ideas in fact.

"Has Mister Roanoke a valet just at this moment?" she asked.

Mrs Dyer shook her head; she saw Rose's drift at once but, just to reinforce the point, Rose added, "A good lady's maid can do a valet's work with one hand tied behind her back."

"As you say, Miss Tremayne, she could. It would be most unconventional – but then, this is not a conventional household, even at the best of times. Hmmm! It occurs to me that someone who could do a valet's work with one hand tied behind her back would therefore have time to turn round and use both hands to help Lizzie with the housework, eh? What d'you say?"

Rose laughed. "I walked straight into that one, didn't I! Yes, all right, I'm sure I'm not too proud to do that – as long as I'm put down as lady's maid and get a character as such." She was so eager to poke Lady Carclew in the eye that she accepted the place – subject to Mr Roanoke's approval, of course.

And the other idea? She kept that to herself for the moment.

To help win her new master's approval she asked the housekeeper if she might be shown his wardrobe. And once there, of course, she found half a dozen faults that needed attending to immediately – a frayed buttonhole, a stained turnup, an ill-pressed seam, a hat whose nap had turned to shine, and so forth. Enough to show off her versatility. Roanoke himself was out sailing, today as every day, but Mrs Dyer said he would be delighted when he returned that evening with all his crew – or with the gentlemen among them, anyway. She was sure he'd agree to the arrangement.

"On a matter of some delicacy, Mrs Dyer," Rose concluded, "what with the lady of the house being absent, he's not the sort of master to take advantage of a girl. The position of valet is even more ..."

The housekeeper's laugh cut her short. "As a matter of some delicacy," she replied, "and you never heard me say it, Mister Roanoke is not the sort of man to take advantage of any *female*."

"Holy Moses!" Rose was shocked into exclaiming.

"I wouldn't answer for his crew, though," she went on. "They are idle young men with more money than sense – and we all know what that means. However, you look like the sort who can take care of herself."

To show extra-willing, and to pile up what Mom called brownie points with Lizzie, Rose spent the lunch hour helping her to polish all the silver cups and trophies Mr Roanoke had won down the years. At two o'clock, since she was not yet officially employed, she felt able to excuse herself, saying she had to go home and run a few errands. This was her other idea.

The Carclews would be taking the two-forty train from Penryn to Truro, where they'd catch the afternoon express to London. Since the branch-line train started from Falmouth, she went down to the station to catch it there. Penryn was three winding miles away. She travelled first class, of course – which cost fourpence halfpenny instead of threepence – and could hardly contain her excitement as it trundled out along the cutting, through Spernenwyn, out on to the embankment overlooking Swanpool, and on through open country, hugging the contours to the top end of Penryn.

And there they all were: Sir Hector and Lady C., Fenella and Mary, now the solo lady's maid until the French maid joined them in London, and Noel, looking bored already. Also, at the farther end of the platform, Mr Negus and his favourite son. They were there just to help load the boxes and trunks, of course.

"You!" cried an astonished Lady Carclew as Rose opened the carriage door. The sight of her dismissed servant flustered her so much that she looked up and down the train, under the impression that she must have misread the '1st' on the door Rose had opened. "What are you doing here?" she snapped when she discovered she had not been mistaken.

"Now there, Lady Carclew, I can safely say – for the first time in two years – and without a trace of impertinence, I do assure you – that it is none of your business."

"Ha!" her ladyship gasped. "Not a trace of impertinence, indeed!"

"My dear," Sir Hector murmured. "Pay her no attention. She is clearly unhinged."

"No, I mean it is quite literally none of *your* business – it is actually my *new* master's business."

"Oh, I see," she responded frostily, clearly torn between heeding her husband's advice and trying to discover who this new master might be. Her curiosity won. "He has a name, I suppose?"

"Cheer up, Noel!" Rose cried. "The Season doesn't last for ever." Noel, who had actually been grinning his head off, laughed out loud. "She's bluffing," Sir Hector said. "We must get aboard. The chappie's waggling his flag."

Rose held the door open for them, wishing Mary good luck as the maid headed for the second class. Her ladyship breezed into the compartment without a word. So did Sir Hector. Fenella whispered, "Miss you!" as she passed. "Good luck!" Rose replied. Noel, more brazen, promised to look her up the minute he was home again.

"Oh, but you can write to me before then if you like. Send me you-know what." Rose replied – for he had still not paid her the four pounds sixteen, shillings. "Miss *Lucinda* Tremayne, care of Mister and Mrs Henry Roanoke in Wodehouse Terrace. Lady Carclew knows him."

"Do I, indeed?" she responded coldly.

"Yes – surely? You exchanged a few words with him down by the jetty one afternoon last February. You can't have forgotten it? He certainly hasn't!" She slammed the door and set off up the platform to talk Negus into carrying her out to Nancemellin to collect her trunk.

"Oh, Mister Negus!" she exclaimed. "Prize-money to the seaman. To the soldier – pillage. But sweet to a woman is revenge!"

"If you do say so, Miss Rose," the man replied. "Want a ride out Nancemellin, do 'ee?"

20

Rose's trunk was already packed and waiting inside the back corridor; Mary had packed it, so Rose knew nothing would be missing. Tregembo told her that Lady Carclew had said there was no particular urgency to get it across to Falmouth but he had intended sending Mr Negus with it that same evening. She told him not to bother because Frank Tresidder would bring it – and her – home.

"Are you going over there this moment?" Tregembo asked.

She was puzzled. "How else can I get him to bring me home?"

The butler was curiously hesitant, uncommunicative even. She did not understand why until she arrived at Trefusis, where she found Frank leaning morosely over the gate to Buzza's pen, scratching the massive boar with a stick.

"Well, one of you is happy enough," she called out as she drew near. He turned, gazed at her, and looked away again. "Glad I am to see you, too," she went on.

"Ha!" he replied.

"All right – I'm not glad. But I would appreciate a bit of help in getting my trunk back home. And it's been quite a while since they saw you over there."

"You're a bit late," he said, giving the boar a playful whack on his spine.

She squinted at the sun. "It's mid-afternoon only."

"I don't mean that." He gave a morose laugh. "Actually it's Ann who's 'a bit late' – three months, she do say."

"Well, well, well."

Buzza arched his back and luxuriated in the new movement of the stick, up and down his backbone. They were two of a kind, she thought – living for food and sensual pleasure. She could not suppress a further thought, much less comfortable: that life with such an elemental man might not be as bad as you'd think. She herself had a strong sensual appetite, too; she only had to close her eyes and think of Louis to know that – though she was far less certain of him. Sometimes, in the heat of their passionate embraces, she had wished he would be slightly less of a gentleman and slightly more ... well, like Frank – of the earth earthy. Frank would certainly satisfy her in all those ways, and as for the rest, he was easy-going and tolerant. He wasn't one of those farmers who'd pull a book out of her hands and tell her there were cows to milk, turnips to hoe, anemones to bunch, or croust to carry out to the hungry men in the fields.

Of course, all this was in the abstract – an appraisal of old possibilities that had vanished the moment the tides beached Louis upon Nancemellin strand.

"Sympathy from you's like blood from granite," he said.

She laughed. "Frank – just listen to yourself, will you? You put Ann Pennycuik on her back as often as she'll let you – and any other maid west of Truro. And now you've made new feet for baby's boots with her, and you want *sympathy?*"

"You should have come over here more often. 'Twould never have happened then."

"Oh, don't deceive yourself, Frank. You're like this fellow here." She took the stick from him and started tickling the boar down near his working parts. The creature stood rigid, trembling.

Frank looked at her in amazement and then snatched the stick back. "Don't torment him. There's no sow or gilt coming in troublesome for days."

"Troublesome!" She echoed with a laugh. "Yes – that puts us women firmly in our places, doesn't it! We're not 'passionate.' We're not 'loving.' Not 'warm-blooded.' Just *troublesome!*"

" 'Tis only a word," he grumbled. "When they do want service from a bull or a boar, they'll break out of fields, smash gates, push through hedges – what else would 'ee call it?"

"I'll bet you didn't call Ann Pennycuik 'troublesome' when she broke out of Nancemellin, crossed the fields, and pushed open that barn door. Where is she now, by the way?"

He tilted his head toward the farmhouse.

"Here?"

"Making arrangements with th'ole woman."

"She'll be happy, anyway – 'th'ole woman.' She was never in favour of you and me. Oh, cheer up, Frank! Ann will make a much better farmer's wife than ever I would. She's eyeable enough when she's scrubbed clean. She's a hard worker – with no dainty hands to fret her. With those gurt hips she'll have no trouble over childbearing – you'll have a football team before you know it. And when she comes into that farm across the Fal there, you'll be like two pigs in clover. Learn to sail and you can farm them both from here."

He nodded glumly, unable to deny it.

"You're just all crabby because your days of sniffing out the *troublesome* girls of six parishes are over. I wouldn't like to be in your skin if she ever catches you dancing the horizontal jig with any of them again."

He nodded even more glumly, unable to deny that, either.

"Meanwhile," she continued, "will you help me get my trunk back to Falmouth? If we leave now, you'll be back before dark."

He was about to agree when a shriek of "No!" came from the kitchen door of the farmhouse.

They turned to see Ann, with her skirts hitched up to her knees, rushing toward them. Lumps of semidry clay went flying from her heels at each pace.

"What are you doing here?" she yelled at Rose as she drew near.

Rose waited for her to join them, at which she repeated her question, panting and staring furiously.

"Calm yourself, cousin Ann," Rose said.

The girl's jaw dropped, "Eh?"

"We will soon be cousins, I understand?" Rose continued. "By marriage? Let me be the first to congratulate you!"

This violation of the polite convention whereby one never congratulates a girl upon her catch was entirely lost on both of them. "Frank?" Ann said. "Is that what you told she?" He shrugged. "It don't seem as I got much choice."

"Choice is an illusion at the best of times," Rose told him. "You may think you've got a dozen choices, but you can only pick one of them, and then the others vanish."

"What's your game?" Ann asked suspiciously.

"That's my business," Rose told her. "All you need know is that it doesn't concern Frank, nor you, nor – most important of all, I should think – Trefusis Farm. I hope you'll both be very happy. And prosperous. Honestly and truly." She spoke these last words to Frank but Ann came between them, gripped Rose by both wrists, and stared into her eyes. "You do mean it," she said quietly.

"You know I do," Rose answered her. "You know my heart is engaged elsewhere."

The idea that love had much to do with marriage, farmland, dynasties ... was clearly a hard one for her to grasp. Rose would have laughed aloud at the life Frank would be living once that little gold ring was on Ann's finger. If rings were being handed out, he might as well have one put through his nose at the same ceremony.

"And now that we've settled our differences," Rose said, "you surely won't grudge me a couple of hours of my cousin's time while he helps me bring my things from Nancemellin back to Falmouth. He can break the good news to my parents in person. My mother will be delighted, for she was every bit as keen for me to marry Frank as was your future mother-in-law."

Arm in arm, the two women walked up to the farmhouse, to explain these developments to Mrs Tresidder while Frank harnessed the horse to the gig.

He spoke but little as they wound their way through the lanes between Trefusis and Nancemellin, but once the trunk was loaded and they were Falmouth-bound, he became more talkative.

"Next time I enter that house," she said, looking back down the long drive, "it will be through the front door." She had no idea why she said such a thing, except as a general statement of defiance against the Carclews and all they stood for, but it left her with a satisfied feeling.

It opened up Frank's thoughts, too. "Mebbe 'tis for the best after all," he said as he clicked the horse to a trot. "You always had your eyes set higher'n Trefusis."

"Not always," she demurred.

"Always," he insisted. " 'Twas no more'n dreams till that Louis Redmile-Thing came along. Now you can see the hare. You reckon he's got a good edge to'n, do 'ee?"

"He's the crop of the bunch, Frank."

"And the business?"

She was alert at once. "Why d'you ask?"

He tilted his head nonchalantly, this way and that. "There was talk over to Perranarworthal last Friday night – the last night of my freedom!" He sighed dramatically and grinned at her.

"The Norway Inn?" she asked. "There's always talk at the Norway. Every farmer and business in the county has been bankrupt twice if you went by what you'd hear there." She was putting a brave face on it, of course; if he really had heard rumours about the Redmile-Smith companies there, it must be serious. "Anyway," she went on, hoping to change the subject, "what's all this about your 'last night of freedom'? Do you really prefer sniffing around field girls and servant maids for the one in twenty who's willing to air her heels? In a month or two you'll be able to tuck into a nice warm bed with a nice warm wife and have a nice warm time together before you go to sleep. Isn't that a million times better?"

"S'pose so," he mumbled.

She persisted: "I mean, if you were hungry and someone showed you twenty trees and said there was a slice of cake you could have at the top of one of them – all you had to do was climb up and find it – or, on the other hand, you could step through this wide open door and you'd find a whole banquet spread out ready for you – which are you going to choose?"

He laughed reluctantly and said, "A man can get used to climbing trees, 'specially if it makes the cake taste richer."

She flapped a hand at him. "Then there's no hope for you."

"She *tricked* I – that's what do stick in my throat."

"*She* tricked *you,* eh? I'm trying hard to imagine that, Frank. Did it go like this. She sidles up to you, all grins and winks, slips an arm about you, and says, 'Come on, big boy – how about it?' And you say, 'Take your hands off of me, maid – I'm a respectable lad, I am.' And she says, 'Go on! You know you do enjoy it so much as what I do!' And you say, 'Well, all right but only a bit cuddle – nothing more!' Was that the way it went between you and Ann?"

He was staring at the road, pinching his lips not to laugh. When he gave up the unequal struggle he said, "Not then. That's not when she tricked I. 'Twas ... well ... later."

"Well, spare me the details. It doesn't require much imagination. You still don't understand, though, do you?"

"Understand what?"

"She didn't trick you. She let you trick yourself. She didn't come to Nancemellin House by accident, you know. If you'd farmed up beyond Mylor, she'd have found a place at Killiganoon. If you'd been the far side of Restronguet, she'd have worked at Trelissick. You were in her sights long before she was in yours. You wanted her for ten minutes. She wanted you for life. You were on the losing side from the beginning."

"How did I trick myself, then?"

She shivered suddenly.

He noticed it for once. "What now?" he asked.

"Imagination," she told him. "I know it's not real. I mean, I don't believe in ghosts but I always get a creepy-crawly feeling when I pass here. I'd never come this way after dark, I know that."

"Oh!" He slumped demonstratively. "You had me worried a mo." He followed her gaze up across the fields. "Is that the barn where it happened? I often wondered."

She nodded, not taking her eyes off it. "That's what the Penryn people say. You know the story?"

"They killed their own son, didn't they?"

She was glad of the chance to laugh. "You not only know the story, you know how to kill it stone dead! His name was Randal Wilmot and he left home very young and travelled to many lands and had many adventures – this was back in James the First's time, the beginning of the seventeenth century and he came home a rich man. And the first member of his family he met was his sister, who lived in Penryn – only she didn't recognize him. So when she was convinced he was who he said he was, she said why don't they play a trick on the old folks, who were down on their luck out on the farm here and who would be delighted to welcome their rich son back home – only he wouldn't reveal himself until the following morning. He'd pretend to be a sailor, home from sea and looking for a night's lodging. But it all went wrong when the son couldn't help bragging about his money and showing them some of his gold – still pretending he was a sailor. So the old folks gave him lodging in the barn for the night. Then, when he was fast asleep, they crept in and murdered him. And stole the gold. And then, when the daughter turned up next day and asked after the sailor who'd slept the previous night there, they denied they'd ever seen him. But she persisted and eventually she let the cat out of the bag. And old Agnes – the mother – when she realized she and Old Wilmot had butchered their own son, she went mad." She looked back at the barn, which was well behind them by now. "I can just imagine her running about the fields there, tearing out her hair and scratching the flesh off her bones."

Frank looked at her askance.

She laughed. "And then I snuggle down between the sheets and thank the Lord for a good roof overhead and well fitting windows and nice warm blankets."

At Penryn they had to wait for the swing bridge to close again, having let a topsail schooner through into the inner basin by Fox-Stanton's sawmills.

"You never explained how I tricked myself," he said.

She had to think back. That conversation – in her own mind – had closed down some while ago. "Oh yes – I said you wanted her for ten minutes and she wanted you for life. That's when you tricked yourself – when you put on those ancient blinkers so you could concentrate on nothing but those ten minutes – you lost sight of what was really going on around you – the rest of the picture."

"So 'twas a baited trap," he grumbled.

"If a mouse sees the bait but not the trap, no one can blame it. No one ever mentioned traps to it before. But if a *man* sees the bait but not the trap, there's no one to blame but himself."

It struck her there was a common theme here with the story of the murder in the barn – people who kept secrets, who hid their motives from one another, who assumed that others would behave as they themselves would behave in the same circumstances. But it was both too fleeting and too complex to share with Frank

And, in any case, she immediately began to wonder if that same insight did not have lessons for herself and her love for Louis.

21 Henry Roanoke was pleased enough with the work she had done on his wardrobe to offer her a week's trial. In any case, he added, the position would be only temporary. Rose could have told him that, though. He seemed amused at the unorthodox arrangement, for a female valet, or 'valette,' as he called her, was quite unheard-of. And understandably so, since she would be in and out of his dressing room during his morning ablutions, she would be the one to shave him (though she had never held a cutthroat razor in her life), and hers would be the fingers that tied, hooked, or buttoned his outer garments at least. At first, Rose feared that the intimacy involved in these situations was what attracted him most, especially as his wife was away in London, but her first morning in her new role was enough to reassure her on that score.

Mr Roanoke showed not the slightest interest in her – of an unchaste nature, anyway. A woman can always tell such things. A man may engage her in conversations of the highest moral character but his eyes, his voice, his pauses, his other bodily language will give him away if his true purpose is *not* of that same high character. Henry Roanoke exhibited no trace of those telltale symptoms. In fact, he was so lacking in that direction that Rose felt ever so slightly insulted ... disappointed, even. He was an extremely handsome man in his early fifties – twenty years older than his wife, according to the other servants – though no one would believe it to look at him. He hardly seemed a day over forty and he moved with all the lithe grace of an athlete. Down at the yacht club – his home from home, Mrs Dyer said – he was surrounded by young men half his age, who all seemed to revere him. They had good reason, of course. He was quite rich. He had one of the finest racing yachts in the West – a Yarmouth yawl built by Hastings of Yarmouth themselves – and he was liberal with his hospitality. It would have been a marvel if such a man was *not* surrounded by a court of high spirited young bloods. His 'Jolly Roger crew' he called them; they called him Skipper. Rose looked forward to meeting them. She felt sure they would reveal the customary interest in her that such young men are expected to take. She needed such reassurance after experiencing this total blank from Mr Roanoke.

He was, however, interested in her in every other way. His toilette and dressing on that first morning lasted over an hour while he quizzed her on her parents, her life, her previous masters and mistresses ... everything, in short, except her erstwhile love for Frank and her present devotion to Louis. She told him about Louis, of course, for she felt sure that Lady Carclew would try to poison his ears with her version of those events just as soon as she could put pen to paper. She said nothing about being in love with him, though; she did not consider that was anybody else's business. She said it was a simple case of mistaken identity which she had allowed to continue until the young man left. The story amused him even more than had the notion of employing a valette.

"I happen to know the young fellow, as a matter of fact," he said.

"I suppose he's not a very good yachtsman?" she fished.

"Oh he's not bad," was the reply. "Better than he is at business, anyway – from what I've been hearing lately."

Now she could have kicked herself for not being more honest with him. "Really?" was all she felt she could say – and hope she did not sound too concerned.

"Well, keep it under your hat, Miss Tremayne, but he warned me he may be forced to resign before the summer is out. He wouldn't say why but I gather it has to do with the family businesses. I took the hint and got rid of my shares – and not before time, too. I see they have just about halved in the past month. If they go much lower, he'll have to call in administrators."

"What does that mean, sir?" she asked.

"It's the end of the diving board, lassie," he replied. "One more step and ..." He whistled on a descending note and made his hand dive until it crumpled dramatically on his dressing table. The relish in his action made Rose wince.

"And where" – she swallowed hard – "would you find out about the shares – how they rise and fall?"

He looked at her askance. "In the City pages of the newspapers. Why? Thinking of a little flutter yourself, are you? Shipbuilding is strong at the moment – and tipped to rise. Because of this race against Germany."

She laughed and the subject was dropped.

Still intrigued by her tale, though, he asked her to 'speak posh.'

Some imp of mischief prompted her to adapt a text she had once learned at Sunday school: "A woman's physical weakness, her feminine trials, her inability to face alone the menaces of this cruel world – these all prompt her to an implicit willingness to lean upon the stronger arm of a man. Such trust is a woman's enduring strength and her chiefest jewel."

The words, the sentiment behind them, passed him by completely; the mimicry of accent was all that interested him. He began listening with amusement, he ended in open amazement. "It is quite extraordinary," he said, gazing deep into her eyes, first one, then the other, as if trying to discern what lay behind them. "Your mimicry is so faultless, in every little nuance, that I have to take your word for it that you are who you say you are, and that you do, indeed, come from those humble origins you claim are yours. In fact, if Mrs Dyer had not already assured me she knows your parents and their shop so well, I should have to challenge you to prove your story to me."

Rose did not know how to reply, being unused to compliments

that stretched beyond a few perfunctory words. "Mister Roanoke!" she protested. "It's as well that my position here is only temporary. I must make sure to leave while my head is still small enough to pass through the doorway!"

"Well, don't *drown* in modesty," he replied. "A wee dram of it is all you need if you want to advance in life. The really amazing thing is ... do it again. Say something ... anything."

She recited from *The Lotus Eaters* – by Tennyson, of course: " 'Surely, surely, slumber is more sweet than toil, the shore / Than labour in the deep mid-ocean, wind and wave and oar; / Oh rest ye, brother mariners, we will not wander more.' "

"Yes!" he cried excitedly. "You see! You do not simply speak a servant's words and thoughts in the voice of her mistress. You choose words that could hardly be more apt. It is as if you become a different person." He peered deep into her eyes again. "Do you? Can a mere change in pronunciation create a different *being?*"

As soon as he had gone, she rushed for that morning's *Times* and turned to the City pages. She was hunting among the small print for the share price when a paragraph on the facing page caught her eye: 'Small rally for Redmile-Smith,' she read. The text beneath informed her that shares in the company rallied a halfpenny yesterday and that the firm's chairman, Mr Louis Redmile-Smith, had assured 'your correspondent' that the recent adverse tide had turned. She sang through her work all that morning, and after lunch she was so helpful to Lizzie that the girl managed to get an hour's free time, her first in weeks.

Mr Roanoke came home quite late, having dined at the yacht club. This surprised all the servants for it was the first night since his wife had gone away that he did *not* invite the gentlemen members of his crew up to dine and carouse the night away here at his home. Often the revelry went on so late that one or more of the young men had to sleep over. Mr Roanoke was very protective of them all; sometimes, if one of them got very drunk, he'd even insist on letting the boy sleep beside him in his own bed, so that he wouldn't vomit and then choke on it in his stupor.

He had also insisted on Rose's sleeping at Wodehouse Terrace, rather than going home each evening. She had wondered why at the time and she hoped his late-night summons – calling her from her bed to assist him in undressing – had nothing to do with it. She obeyed of course, but not before she had buttoned her dressing gown from ankle to chin. On the other hand, she reflected, she could hardly complain at the summons itself since she had been the one to ask for the position, and this particular duty was undoubtedly part of it.

His only interest in her, however, was the question he had posed on parting that morning. "D'you know what would be quite amusing, Miss Tremayne?" he said. "In fact, more than amusing – I think it would hold a mirror up before us. And, I might add, it would show us in a none-too-flattering light. What if I were to give a little dinner party here, to introduce you into local Society? We could pretend you were my niece ... newly come home from India, Africa ... somewhere like that. You could do it – I have no qualms on that score. And ..."

"But what would it tell us, sir?" Rose asked. "That your sort of people will treat a young lady differently from the way they'd treat a servant? That won't sell many newspapers, as my mother says."

"Wait – I've not finished. I'll invite some local people who like to consider themselves among the leaders of Falmouth's untitled aristocracy and unlanded gentry; but I'll also bring a sprinkling of my Jolly Roger crew, eh? And then, the very next evening, we'll have a bachelors-only dinner for the *same* young gentlemen from my crew – only this time you'll be in servant's homespun, dishing out the soup. We'll see first of all if even one of them recognizes you – which'll be interesting in itself. If they don't, we'll spill the beans and then, even more interesting, I think, we'll see how their treatment of you changes. I'd quite understand if you turned the whole suggestion down but" – here he eyed her shrewdly – "I think you'd be as curious as I am to discover if you could pull it off. Also to see how gentlemanly the young gentlemen will be once they know the truth."

He knew damn well it was a challenge she could not refuse.

22

The 'snobs' dinner' was arranged for the following Tuesday, a week after Rose's engagement as valette began. The other servants were delighted becuase it meant he could not spoil the surprise by inviting any of his young men home before that day. Rose, however, started getting cold feet the moment it was settled – too late, though. The bets were laid.

All that week the rally in the Redmile-Smith share price continued. Admittedly the rises were small – a halfpenny one day, a farthing the next – but they were all in the right direction. Rose began to lose her fears that she would one day, and soon, have to make good her quasi-promise to her mother that she would not marry a bankrupt Louis and become the millstone round his neck.

Then came the bombshell – not in Louis' life but in hers. Three local papers, the *Falmouth Packet,* the *West Briton,* and the *Cornishman,* all carried an identical announcement:

To All Masters and Mistresses
Sir Hector and Lady Carclew of Nancemellin House, Flushing
desire to inform prospective employers of one
Lucinda-Ella Tremayne, posing as 'Rose' Tremayne,
was lately dismissed in scandalous circumstances
which her ladyship will be pleased to furnish
to *bona-fide* inquirers who enclose s.a.e.

It was the talk of Falmouth, of course. The milkman was the first to bear the news to Wodehouse Terrace. It sent Mrs Dyer scurrying to retrieve the *Packet* from the master's breakfast tray. Her first impulse was to rip out the page and say nothing, but, realizing that would merely postpone the evil hour, she went up to the master's dressing room (he being still asleep in his bed next door) and took Rose well out of earshot before handing over the offensive thing.

Rose read it and burst into tears – but there was more anger than rage in it and she was soon mistress of herself again. *"Posing* as Rose!" she fumed. "It was Lady Carclew herself who insisted on giving me that name. God, if she were here now ...!"

Grim faced, she thanked the housekeeper and, tucking the paper under her arm, returned to the kitchen with the woman, to collect the master's tray of early-morning tea.

"It's another fifteen minutes, yet," Mrs Dyer warned her.

"I think he may want to see this scurrilous announcement immediately," Rose replied.

At first he was annoyed at being woken early but when he had read the thing for the second time he told her she had been right to rouse him at once. "The bloody woman!" he fumed. "Can't even write a literate sentence. Pardon my French. Bring me pen and paper. We'll see about this. No! You write while I dictate. My hand's shaking much too much."

"My dear Lady Carclew," he said, "I write as one whose personal life has been singularly unfurnished (underline 'unfurnished') with scandalous circumstances recently. I confess I was on the point of despair when my eye fell upon a curious announcement in today's papers – to the effect that you are willing to furnish any inquirer in my position with the said scandalous circumstances, and for nothing more than the price of a stamp. If I may be so bold as to point your thoughts in certain directions, I would prefer you to furnish my life with scandalous circumstances of a financial nature rather than of an amorous one – financial scandals being so much more fashionable this year, don't you think? Paragraph.

"However, when it comes to scandalous circumstances of all kinds, I have to acknowledge that you are the virtuoso and I the mere beginner; so I leave the choice entirely to you. Having had personal experience of your generosity, I know you will not let me down. Yours etcetera. D'you think that's gilding the lily a bit?"

Rose, who had been chuckling from the moment she caught his drift, said, "She won't get the point, you know. But that's even better – because she'll know you're getting at her for *something* and she won't know what!"

By breakfast time she had made a fair copy of the letter, which he signed before going off, as always, to the yacht club.

Her cheerful spirits fell, though, as soon as she set her nose outside, on her way to post the thing. She could feel the eyes of the world upon her – *posing* as Rose. True, she liked the name itself but when she recalled how deeply she resented the reason Lady Carclew gave for insisting on her taking it, that word 'posing' was especially wounding. As she walked along Wodehouse Terrrace she saw chintz curtains quiver; pale faces moved back, swallowed into dark interiors; people strolling toward her along the footpath turned in at gates as she approached; dogs lifted their legs against lampposts but they looked at her in such a sharp way that she knew they understood all about her disgrace, too. *I could just hide myself away for the next twenty years,* she thought. *Then it might be safe to emerge again.*

Or she could face them down now.

But how? She couldn't walk up to every stranger who knew her by sight or who had her name whispered in his ear and say, 'It's all a pack of lies, you know. For a start – *she* forced the name Rose on me ...'

Plaster the entire town with handbills saying LADY CARCLEW IS A LIAR?

It was about then, when she had run the gauntlet of Wodehouse Terrrace and was approaching the top of Jacob's Ladder, that the most obvious idea of all came to her. "Sauce for the goose is sauce for the gander," she said aloud. She, too, would put an announcement in the papers – or at least in the *Packet,* if she couldn't afford all three. She tripped down the hundred and fourteen steps as blithely as she had at the age of nine, crossed the Moor giving out a cheery 'good morning!' to anyone she vaguely recognized, and hastened homeward once again.

She was so eager to get back that she nearly passed out while mounting the last dozen steps of the Ladder. She had to stop just four steps short of the summit and cling to the hand-polished railing for fear of swooning and falling all the way to the bottom. The old woman she had overtaken last time – she felt sure it was the same one – now passed her, going down. "Oh 'ess, my lover," she said in a tone curiously compounded of sympathy and triumph. "That's 'ow it do start."

Rose was too winded even to look up and smile.

A moment later another voice, vaguely familiar, said, "Lucy-Ella? It is, surely?"

She looked up to find Sally Winnen, once her bestest-bestest friend at Smithick Hill National – looking on top of the world, too. In fact, of all her friends from those days, it could only have been Sally; all the others would still have called her 'Cinders.' Rose laughed with pleasure and, still gulping for air, threw her arms about her and gave her a hug. "I heard tell you were in London," she said. Then, looking at her more closely, "My! Aren't you the fashion plate!"

Sally, dismayed, peered down at herself. "Not too much, I hope?" There was still a trace of Falmouth in her speech but the accent was greatly refined – or *refeened,* perhaps, Rose thought unkindly, for the vowels were borrowed rather than acquired. "Not in the least," she assured her friend. "You're the very picture of quiet good taste." Boldly she reached out and fingered the material of her sleeve, a mauve moiré silk, set off by black handmade lace at the cuff. "You didn't find stuff like *this* anywhere here in Falmouth."

"You'd not find it west of Plymouth," Sally assured her. "If there, even. You got time for a coffee, have you? And a little Kunzle cake?"

"Coffee?" Rose hesitated.

"My treat," Sally assured her, thinking that was the stumbling block. "The Gardenia Tearooms down in Market Street. D'you know what they're like? I've only just come back to Falmouth so I've not been there myself but they look nice and clean from outside." Rose said that she, too, had only seen the place from outside. "Come on, then!" Sally took her by the arm and steered her back down the Ladder toward the Moor. She sang a snatch of 'The grand old Duke of York' – about marching up to the top of the hill and marching down again – before dissolving in laughter. "Remember when we used to beat Graham Rosevear and Billy White up these steps?" she said. "They weren't too bad, really, those days, were they."

"I heard you went up London," Rose said again.

"London ... the world," she replied vaguely.

"And did pretty well by the look of you."

"I'll tell you when we're comfy. Oh, Lucy! I'm so glad I bumped into you – on my first morning back in Falmouth, too!"

"Really? Didn't your Mum and Dad move away?"

"Only up Truro. I stayed along of – I mean *with* them all last week. But dear old Falmouth's the place for me. I was just up top there, taking rooms in Wodehouse Terrrace."

Rose laughed with delight and then explained. "So we'll see a lot of each other."

"Maybe," Sally replied cautiously. "Though I hope to be quite busy – finding suitable premises ... opening up shop."

"Shop?"

They had reached the Moor by now. Sally paused a moment to look all about. "Nothing changes," she murmured. Then, as if Rose had only just asked, she added, "Yes – shop. Something in the fashion line."

They sauntered toward Market Street.

"Hats?" Rose suggested. "Millinery?"

Sally shrugged. "I don't know yet. I'll first see what sort of competition there might be in Truro, Camborne, Redruth ... Penzance, even. Find out what the cream of Falmouth have to go to Plymouth to buy – or send away to London. Ask around among the lady's maids. There should be several by now who went to school with us ..."

"You're walking arm-in-arm with one now."

"Really?" Sally leaned forward and looked at her, almost as if she couldn't believe it.

"Don't you think I was good enough?" Rose was slightly miffed.

"*Too* good, I'd have said. You were always with your books and poetry and things. I'd have thought you'd have taught yourself up to be a governess by now."

Rose was about to protest that for a poor girl who left school at fourteen to rise to being lady's maid at Nancemellin House was no mean achievement – when she realized there was more than a grain of truth in what Sally had said. She could have studied more. There had been opportunities. The Workers' Educational Association held evening classes in every town. And there was the Polytechnic, too. She could have studied, taken her Cities and Guilds, and become a teacher or a governess. It wasn't talent she lacked, nor ambition. It was drive. "I suppose so," she replied with a sigh. "Maybe that's what I'll have to do next."

And she went on to explain about her 'disgrace' at Nancemellin, her loss-that-was-no-loss of Frank, and her temporary home with Mr Roanoke, ending with the bombshell in that morning's papers. By then they had reached the door to the stairway that led up to the Gardenia Tearooms, which were on the first floor, over a newsagent-tobacconist's. What Sally had meant by 'looking nice on the outside' was that they had neat curtains and huge bouquets of artificial silk gardenias in all three of the windows that overlooked the street.

The stairs were narrow so Rose raced ahead, pausing at the first landing to let Sally catch up; she, for her part, was ascending demurely, swinging her hips slightly more than her anatomy would strictly require. She saw Rose's eyes upon her, laughed as if she'd been caught out in something childish or secret, and walked the last few steps more naturally. "Old habits!" she said as they ascended the remaining half-flight. "Remember how we used to tease the boys when the grown-up bits of us arrived?"

Rose remembered Sally doing all the teasing, but she made no comment now.

They gave their order and settled at a table by the window. "What are you going to do about her ladyship's announcement?" Sally asked. "These flower arrangements are clever because you can see out through them without people looking in – not that there's much to look in on at the moment! We can be ladies of leisure for half an hour."

"I thought if she can defame me in the papers, I can surely insert a reply?"

"D'you suppose they'll let you?"

"I can try."

"Anyway, what good would it do? The lord chief justice of England could announce your innocence on the front page of every paper in the land – you still wouldn't find anyone to employ you." Rose didn't want that to be true – so she ignored the point. "I'd still have the satisfaction."

"How much could you borrow on the strength of it, though? How much bread would it put on the table? You're taking your eye off the goal, pet."

Rose began to feel hopelessly inadequate. Sally had always had that effect on her, even when they were just a pair of giglets. She always knew what to do in any circumstances, whether it was getting caught in someone's orchard with an apron full of stolen apples, or seeing off a boy when the teasing had gone a bit too far. Her savoir-faire had done her no harm, either. She had obviously come up in the world, but more than that, she had acquired even more self-confidence and savvy along the way. *Listen to her,* she told herself.

"What d'you suggest?" she asked,

Sally eyed her up and down shrewdly before replying. "Start from where you're at now, my pet. You've made yourself unemployable as a lady's maid – so you've got to accept that. No use crying. Even old Roanoke knows it in his bones. You're for the push when his old lady returns."

The waitress brought their coffee and a whole plate of mouth-watering, chocolate-drooling Kunzle cakes.

This is the life! Rose thought as she topped her coffee with cream. "She's not so old," she said. "She's twenty years younger than him, in fact."

"There you are then! She's not going to have a flaming-haired beauty posing as her hubby's valet, is she! No, your best hope is that Mister Redmile-Smith is going to weather the storm and sweep you off to ... wherever. Somewhere a gentleman can live when he's married to a servant maid. So what you really need is an emergency plan in case he fails. You sure you wouldn't marry him if he was bankrupt?"

"Oh, Sal!" She spoke around a mouthful of dark chocolate and liqueur-soaked cake. "I'd marry him even if he was condemned to death! It's stupid to be so certain, I know when I've only known him three days – and him thinking of me as something else all that time. Somebody much ..."

"But you said he told you it didn't make a hap'orth of difference to him! Lady or servant, you're one and the same to him. Personally, I think you'd be a fool not to marry him, floating or sinking. Still, that's only my opinion."

"I couldn't saddle him with the responsibility. What about when the babies started arriving?"

Sally leaned toward her and lowered her voice. "There are ways of stopping that, you know. And I don't mean knitting needles or gin and hot baths. Queen Victoria is long dead." Rose noticed for the first time that she was quite heavily made up – expertly, too.

"He'd marry me, I know," she said. "Or I'm pretty sure he would. But we both know what poverty does to marriages. That would break my heart. If only I could bring something … I mean, it's not fair, is it. There's Fenella Carclew going up to London to snare a husband and Sir Hector will settle fifty thousand on her the moment the knot is tied – and she'll probably marry a man worth ten times that much anyway."

"Yeah, but you know why, don't you," Sally interrupted. "It's to give her a bit of independence. That sort of marriage usually ends up as a sort of armed truce. The women breed and the men stray – but they won't stray too far or too badly if they know she could up-sticks and live quite comfortably off of their marriage settlement. You wouldn't like that sort of marriage, would you!"

"I wouldn't mind the settlement, though," Rose replied. "Five thousand crinkly ones would do me, never mind fifty." She sipped her coffee and asked as casually as she could, "What's the secret, my lover? How did you do it?"

"You didn't read it in the papers?" Sally asked in surprise. "The law suit? The fight to disinherit me? I thought everyone knew."

Rose shook her head.

"It was the scandal of London last Season, anyway." Sally settled gleefully to tell a story she obviously relished but which she had supposed was already stale news to everyone in Falmouth.

After a number of places in various London households she had ended up as lady's maid to a Mrs Boyce of Peckham. When the lady died, Mr Boyce had moved into an apartment at the top of his house and let the lower floors; Sally had become his housekeeper and the caretaker of the letting. On Boyce's death, four years later, he had left her the entire house and two thousand pounds. His nephew and two nieces had contested the will but without success. That had been the scandal of the 1909 Season – she said. "I managed the house as a boarding house for a year, built up the goodwill and the income, sold it as a going concern last month … and bob's your uncle – here I am! I could live on consols in quiet despair for the rest of my natural, if I liked. But I don't like. I prefer to *do* something with it."

Rose sighed. She was happy for Sally, of course, but could hardly expect such luck for herself.

"Cheer up, my lover," Sally said, helping herself to another cake. "I'm going to get fat and it doesn't matter any more! And I'm sure your Louis will survive and prosper. He'll come after you with a ring in his pocket before the summer's out. And if he doesn't – if the worst comes to the worst – ask me again and I may have thought of something else for you by then." She winked.

"Like what?"

Sally shook her head. "There's no sense in going off at all sorts of tangents just yet," was all she'd say.

23

Roanoke was sure they would all come on time, or pretty close to it. It was something that Falmouth's *crême-de-la-crême* hardly ever condescended to do, preferring to arrive 'fashionably late.' But he and his wife so rarely gave a dinner at home, always preferring the professional services of the yacht club, and *he* never entertained at all when she was away – except for carousing with his Jolly Roger crew. So curiosity alone would bring them hotfoot. And then there were those young men, of course – half a dozen bachelors, all idle, all rich, all eligible. In short, it was one of those occasions when those who did not arrive on time would probably miss something interesting or important.

Roanoke had picked his guests well. All had nubile daughters who would soon be in the market for a husband. Naturally, none of the girls themselves had been invited – they never were to these preliminary appraisals, for they were sadly capable of making the most unsuitable choices. As for the six young men, only two were local; three others were from Plymouth, the remaining one from Cowes – and all, of course, fanatical yachtsmen and, therefore, not short of one, at least, of the ingredients of a successful marriage.

Rose had elected to call herself Lucille Marteyne, a condensation of her Christian name and an anagram of Tremayne; and, rather than just having returned from India or Africa, as Roanoke had suggested, she decided on America – specifically Connecticut – where she'd have her mother's reminiscences to fall back on.

The servants were all party to the practical joke, of course – as, indeed, they had to be. Rose asked Mrs Dyer if she wasn't scandalized. She replied that of course she was, but, on the other hand, nothing that involved Mr Roanoke could surprise her any more. Why, only last year the master and his Jolly Rogers had been shown all over HMS Agamemnon, one of the navy's finest battleships, posing as the Maharajah of Sqwat and his entourage, their faces stained with gravy browning that had started to run in the heat of the galleys.

She added a word of warning, too – that one of those Jolly Rogers should have a special eye kept on him, name of Roger Deveril. It rang a bell with Rose; in fact, she knew she had heard the name very recently somewhere. A moment later it struck her – "Ruby Penhallow!" she said.

"That's the feller. He got her belly-up. He's been sent to more VPS camps and mountaineering camps and I-don't-know-what camps than you've had new pinafores – and all for tormenting poor servant maids. 'Course, he may be different with high-quarter girls – he must be, else he'd never be invited out anywhere twice. But you watch him, all the same."

Rose dressed herself in one of Mrs Roanoke's evening gowns – a swishing, swooshing creation in chrome-yellow watered silk. She combed her hair back and up, the way she had suggested to Fenella that evening. For jewelry she chose two small garnet earrings in a diamante setting and a choker of freshwater pearls with a large garnet at the throat. Lizzie helped with her stays and with buttoning up the dress at the back; otherwise Rose managed everything herself – which showed just how much a lady's maid was *really* needed most of the time.

Roanoke met her on the half-landing; she descended from his wife's boudoir, he from his dressing room – where he, too, had somehow managed to dress himself unaided. He was extremely natty, in full evening dress, of course, but with a vividly coloured floral waistcoat in art silk; he also sported a white gardenia – not made of paper – in his buttonhole. He offered her his arm, without a trace of parody or condescension, and escorted her the rest of the way.

"Nervous?" he asked.

"Beyond that!" she replied.

"Try and hold out for ten minutes. If you really feel you're not up to it, plead a migraine and you'll be excused."

"Oh, I've 'been excused' ten times in the past hour already."

He choked and then giggled. "For God's sake don't come out with things like that! Aha! I hear the click of the front gate. The fun begins! It is *fun,* Lucy. Just hold on to that."

"Lucille."

He bowed his head, accepting her pedantic correction. "Lucille it shall be. And don't forget I'm Uncle Harry. Now you're my hostess. Come and stand by me in the drawing room."

"It's when we ladies retire here, leaving you men at the table, that I'm dreading," she said.

The front door bell rang. Rose instinctively tensed herself to answer it. Roanoke said, "Steady the buffs!" and they both chuckled. She was glad of her long cotton gloves; without them the sweat would be dripping off her fingertips.

"Mister and Mrs Lanyon," Lizzie announced.

She entered the room 'with the eyes of a travelling rat,' as Rose's father said of ultra-inquisitive people. Her mother had a gentler but no less apt description: 'She could value an entire room for auction at a glance.' She was a short, skinny woman in her forties, with a marked forward stoop. She had frizzy brown hair, losing its colour, and a husband about ten years her senior, whose personality probably never had much colour anyway – a tall, languid man who positively radiated detachment. He drawled something like 'awfly goodovu,' a couple of times but otherwise contributed nothing intelligible.

"You don't sound American to me, Miss Marteyne," Mrs Lanyon said after they had exchanged a few empty pleasantries.

Rose had a ready answer to that – ever since she and 'Uncle Harry' had discussed whether she should have any trace of her mother's accent. "My mom would be delighted to hear you say so, Mrs Lanyon," she replied. "She spent enough on elocution lessons for me."

"Really?" she trilled. "I'd like to shake her by the hand. We've known some awfly nice Americans but their speech does grate so."

"The American accent is very close to the Cornish, I often think," Roanoke put in.

"Exactly so," she said. "They all sound like one's servants. It's disconcerting – isn't it, Lanyon." She nudged her husband with her chisel-like elbow.

"Awfly," he said.

Roanoke touched Rose's elbow – her cue to offer a small glass of sherry. But instead of the pre-rehearsed phrases she said, "I was going to offer you a small sherry, Mrs Lanyon – but if you wish me to prove my transatlantic credentials" – and here she broke into her mother's accent and lilt – "I can fix a pretty mean highball."

The woman laughed shrilly – and nervously, too, as if she had just been made to realize that she had insulted a living, breathing member of that nation.

Rose had expected a much stronger squeeze at her elbow, warning her to go easy; but one glance at Roanoke was enough to tell her he approved heartily. She understood then that risk was his intoxicant; she could skate on the thinnest ice this evening and he would approve – as long as that ice held, of course. More than that, however, she realized that she, too, was more than a little intoxicated with the risk they were taking. She hadn't felt so alive since ... well, since the last time she kissed Louis.

"Goodness me!" Mrs Lanyon was saying, "I don't even know what a highball is."

"It's a small measure of any kind of liquor or wine and a lot of soda water. Uncle Harry has a splendid white rum. Would you like to try just one?" It delighted her to be offering them the favourite tipple of the common sailor. "Uncle Harry and I will join you."

Lanyon glanced at Lanyon and she said she supposed it might be amusing. Poor Lizzie was meanwhile signalling frantically with her eyes that she hadn't the faintest idea how to mix such a cocktail. Rose tipped her a wink and said, "Now this is something that, back home, a hostess must do in person." She rubbed her gloved hands together and was glad to feel how dry they were. The ice was broken – the social ice, of course, not the thin stuff on which Roanoke was encouraging her to skate – and she was away.

Roanoke accompanied her to the buffet to find the white rum. "Not too mean," he murmured as, heads together, they searched in the cupboard.

"You betcha!" she mumbled back. "I'll spike her guns for her!"

She poured each of them a stiff three fingers. For Roanoke and herself, she tipped out a bare one – and a little finger at that. The rum being white, the difference did not show when all four glasses were topped to the same level with soda water. "Your health, sir!" A glass thrust into the hand seemed to galvanize Lanyon to life. "And you, Miss ... er, young lady."

"Here's mud in your eye!" Rose replied.

"Eh? Begyapardon?"

"A toast among the petroleum fraternity, Mister Lanyon," she told him. "When a drill strikes oil, the first thing that comes gushing up is mud. So it's like wishing you good fortune."

Mrs Lanyon took a sip and murmured, "Barbaric."

She actually meant the expression but it wasn't a bad description of the highball, either.

The doorbell rang. Lizzie went to answer it.

"Lucille, my dear girl!" Roanoke exclaimed. "This is pure nectar! I shall drink nothing else for the rest of my days!"

"Well, I shall not be here to mix it for you, Uncle, dear. You do remember that I am going to London next week?"

"For the Season?" Mrs Lanyon asked.

"Mister and Mrs Dean," Lizzie announced.

They were younger, both in their late thirties. Rose recognized them at once for, although they were not the sort of people the Carclews would have invited indoors, they had been to several garden parties at Nancemellin. The garden party is an essential feature of English social life in that it allows the upper classes to entertain their inferiors in the middle classes, and be terribly gracious to them, but without granting them the slightest degree of domestic intimacy. The big question now was, would the Deans remember her?

From the moment of their introductions it seemed clear that they did not. Nothing is more invisible than a maidservant in full view, and nothing is less like her than a confident young lady with her hair up, wearing expensive jewelry and a costly gown, and speaking with a refined accent.

"Miss Marteyne has just mixed us a curious concoction called a hayball," Mrs Lanyon said.

"Hay *bale,*" her husband murmured. "Hay comes in bales."

"No, dear – *this!*" She nudged his hand, pushing his glass to the centre of his field of vision.

"Awfly good," he said.

Mrs Dean did not touch spirituous liquors so she had a grenadilla and soda; her husband said he was game.

"Miss Marteyne," Mrs Lanyon said. "You were telling us of your visit to London – for the Season, one presumes?"

A mischievous imp whispered in Rose's ear and, before she could think better of it, she heard herself saying, "As a matter of fact, Mrs Lanyon, I'm hoping to renew my acquaintance with Sir Hector and Lady Carclew, whom I met recently in Egypt."

A more sober interior voice warned her she was storing up trouble for later – when the ladies would have her all to themselves.

Why was she giving so many hostages to fortune, she wondered? Partly to please Roanoke, of course – once she realized how much he enjoyed the risk; but also to satisfy something within herself, something new, something that had blossomed since her meeting with Sally last week. She always been brighter than Sally at school, had always read more – well, that wouldn't be too hard since Sally never opened a book from one year to the next – and had always known more about the big wide world, the world that neither of them had then experienced. And yet Sally had some sort of energy or will-power that she, Rose, seemed to lack. Or perhaps it wasn't a simple matter of energy; perhaps it was a willingness not to conform – to say, 'You may require this and this of me ... you may think this is all I'm fit for ... you may assign me this particular place on Society's great ladder ... but, sorry, I have my own ideas.' It wasn't a refusal to conform merely for the sake of rebellion; it was because she had goals she set herself – and had the will to go for them. In a way it *was* energy, of course, but that was its source. Without those goals in the first place, mere energy would be self-destructive. And ever since meeting with Sally, and thinking about her, she had been consumed with the possibility of doing something similar with her own life. Tonight's harmless little charade was like a rehearsal for a more serious assault on the futile conformity of her life so far.

Also Louis, of course; if she could carry off her imposture this evening, she'd feel that much more confident of being able to play the lifelong role of Mrs Louis Redmile-Smith. And the harder she made it for herself, the greater her ultimate confidence would be. So yes, of course she had met the Carclews in Egypt. And thank heavens for the *Orient Line Guide* – and for a good memory, at least for those things that interested her!

"I heard they were in the orient recently," Mrs Dean said. "But I thought it was the Holy Land?"

"They went on there after Egypt," Rose said.

"And you?"

"I came to England on the *Ormuz.*" That was the liner most fully described in the 1890 *Guide*. She just had to hope it was still in service. "She's a bit long in the tooth now but still very comfortable. Her coffee room is on the upper deck, you know – which allows much more space on the hurricane deck for first-class staterooms. And since the galley is immediately behind the buffet, one can more or less dictate one's own times for taking breakfast, luncheon, and dinner."

One way to stop people from asking questions, she had noticed, was to show that you were prepared to answer them *very* fully.

"And talking of dinner," she concluded, "where are all your young men, Uncle Harry?"

He consulted his fob watch and said, "They should be here any minute now, my dear."

"And talking of young men ...?" Mr Dean simpered at her, leaving the question hanging.

The women stared daggers at him. That topic was reserved to *them,* when the ladies retired from the table.

The doorbell jangled again and the Jolly Rogers arrived in a bunch, together with Mr and Mrs 'we-don't-imbibe' Faull, the last of the married-couple guests. It worried Rose that at least three of the company would be staying stone-cold sober throughout the evening – a possibility that had not occurred to her when she and Roanoke were drawing up the list.

The young men looked like making up for it, though. Roger Deveril made a beeline for the buffet, saying, "What? No butler, Skipper? You should have asked me to come early." He grinned at Rose, to imply that she was the true cause of his wish. Without asking any of his fellow crewmen he sloshed out glasses of whisky-sodas, gin-and-bitters, and so forth for each one.

"Miss Marteyne was telling us she came from Egypt on the *Oruba,"* Mrs Lanyon told the Faulls.

"Orient Line," Mr Faull said. "I know her well. Which cabin did you have?"

Had Mrs L made a genuine mistake, or was she testing? "It was the *Ormuz,* actually," Rose replied. "But they're sister ships, practically identical, I believe."

"Know her, too," Faull said. "She put in here for a quick repair a couple of years ago. She has a painting of Falmouth in the saloon."

"By R. Napier Henry," Rose said. "I thought it a bit romantic. My favourite was 'The Old Squire' by Pettie ..." She started to bore for America on the subject of the brushwork and chiaroscuro until 'Uncle Harry' halted her with a discreet cough.

"Do you habitually travel alone, Miss Marteyne," Deveril asked.

The Jolly Rogers were showing the sort of interest in her that might be expected – ranging from shy to bold but nowhere shading off into indifference.

In for a penny ... she thought. "I prefer it," she replied. "Mister Deveril, isn't it? Yes, I find that if one travels with an older female, it is her wishes that get attended to."

"And if with a male protector?" he asked.

"Oh, then I seem to vanish altogether!"

To her surprise, mesdames Dean and Faull actually laughed at this reply; she had obviously touched some nerve with them. They only stopped when they caught sight of what they thought was Mrs Lanyon's disapproving frown (which was actually Mrs Lanyon trying to discipline her eyes). Rose wondered if she had been right to ply the woman with so much rum; it might make her more belligerent than fuddled.

"Did you come directly to England, Miss Marteyne," asked Mrs Faull. Rose, realizing that the woman's husband was something of an expert in maritime affairs, did not wish to risk her memory of the Orient Line's routes – which was, in any case, twenty years out of date. "Oh, you know us Americans," she replied with a laugh. "We think you can 'do' the whole of 'Yurrup' inside thirty days – and we go back home reeling with confused impressions that don't add up."

Whew!

"You don't sound American," said Mrs Dean.

She dealt with that one again, and then dinner was served.

The lady guests, being outnumbered three-to-one, were spread thinly around the table, mesdames Lanyon and Faull on one side, Mrs Dean on the other; the bachelors were clustered around them, leaving Mr Faull and Roger Deveril to Rose's left and right and messrs Lanyon and Wells, one of the Jolly Rogers, on either hand of Roanoke.

Conversation was organized in pairs – rightward or leftward but not across the table. The system was that when Rose spoke with Faull, to her left, then Dean, to his left, spoke with Jolly Roger Twigg, to his left, and then – continuing around the table – Mrs Dean with JR Cox, Lanyon with Roanoke, JR Wells with JR Philp, Mrs Faull with JR Howe, and Mrs Lanyon with Roger Deveril, the last remaining Jolly Roger. However, when Rose turned to speak with Deveril, to her right, then Mrs Lanyon broke off her conversation with him and turned at once to JR Howe, to *her* right, at which Mrs Faull spoke with JR Philp, JR Wells with Roanoke, Lanyon with JR Cox, Mrs Dean with JR Twigg, and Dean with Faull. It was Rose's duty to switch from one side to the other every ten minutes or so. Naturally, when conversations are conducted on such a formal plan, it would be bad form to embark upon any topic of absorbing interest to either party – since one might be forced to turn away when the other was in mid-flow.

So they spoke of the recent weather; a building that collapsed in Penzance, harming none; the slightly less recent weather; the efficacy of salt water in curing colds; the weather last winter; a novel called *The History of Mr. Polly,* which none had read, and Elgar's violin concerto, which none had heard, and another tale – *Howard's End,* which Mrs Faull was in the middle of reading; and the prospects for the weather over the rest of the summer. Not discussed were: Charles Parsons' speed-reducing gear for turbines (of keen interest to Mr Faull); Albert Schweitzer's new book, *In Quest of the Historical Jesus* (Mrs Lanyon's latest hobbyhorse); Pius X's latest encyclical, which had the German protestants foaming at the mouth (Mrs Dean was a Roman Catholic); and the latest Act of Parliament, curbing the powers of the Lords (enmities going back to the days of Roundheads and Cavaliers could still surface around Cornish dinner tables and so topics that might trigger their release were best avoided).

Of the fourteen seated round that table, Rose had the most interesting – or, at least the most varied – conversations. Her heart sank when she first opened the conversation with Mr Faull, who at once asked her to tell him more about her voyage on the *Ormuz.* However, it soon transpired that he merely sought an excuse to tell her about *his* experiences in the shipping business. He was a forward agent for several cargo lines, which either called at Falmouth or sent their coastal tramps there 'for orders.' Lady Carclew, in one of her rare genial moments, had shown Rose how to suppress a yawn by clenching your jaws, lowering your head slightly, and breathing in through flared nostrils; Rose was never more glad of the information than during her ten-minute spells with him.

"Why, Mister Faull," she said toward the end of the meal, "you ought to write a book about all your maritime adventures."

"I am engaged in that very project, Miss Marteyne," he assured her. "It is to be titled *My Fifty Years in Shipping.*" He waited for her to remark that he didn't look a day over thirty-nine – at which she dutifully obliged him – whereupon he added, "I shall be by the time I finish it – going at my present rate!"

Joke!

Her conversations with Roger Deveril could not have been more different. She could have wished, however, that Mrs Dyer had not cautioned him quite so fiercely about the young man's reputation, for, as she now discovered, such a warning, especially when applied to a tall, dark, and handsome young man, has the contrary effect to that which was intended.

In the abstract, without seeing him, she could easily think of him as an evil villain – the sort who was portrayed in the melodramas that travelling theatre troupes toured around Cornwall several times a year, and which she never missed if she could help it. (In fact, there was one down on the Moor that very evening.) His eyes would be cruel; his lips would curl in a permanent sneer; and his behaviour would be so grossly overbearing and boastful that the housemaids he had ruined would only have themselves to blame for letting him have his dastardly way with them.

In the flesh, however – the all-too-enticing flesh – he seemed warm, sympathetic, engaging. It helped that his eyes were deepset and dark, that his thick locks of hair curled in a most endearing way around his ears and just tickled the fronts of his lobes with their tips, and that his voice was deep and resonant, and that his lips were strongly modelled, full of passion with just the merest hint of heartlessness behind it. It helped most of all that those enticing eyes were never still. They explored her face like a caress. She could almost swear she felt a physical pressure, a sort of tingle, wherever they alighted. And when they strayed to her neck, her shoulders, her uplifted bosom … and his pupils went larger still, darker still, glistening in the candlelight, it was more than a tingle, more than a caress, it was like an actual embrace.

And yet what did they talk about?

The sea and its many moods – he knew just how she had felt while crossing Biscay in a storm. The trampling of wine in Burgundy – he was assiduous in making sure her glass was never empty. The pleasures and pitfalls of travel – he was sure she'd had many adventures, not all of them suitable for repeating to one who had led such a sheltered life as he, himself, had done.

He did nothing to dent, much less diminish, her love for Louis, of course. However, since one could not be miserable and forlorn for all twenty-four hours of each day, he was just the man to raise her spirits and make her feel like a somebody. By the time the dinner drew to a close, she had actually forgotten she was 'just' a maidservant under false colours; and she felt that Roger Deveril would be a friend even after midnight, when the gilded coach turned back into a pumpkin and the glittering ballgown became a drab housemaid's uniform again.

"Well, ladies, shall we leave the gentlemen to clear up this mess?" she asked, rising to her feet. There was a moment of dizziness but she was steady enough as long as both hands could touch the table.

She had meant to say 'leave the gentlemen to their cigars,' which was the conventional phrase, but the other words just popped out. However, she had presided with commendable aplomb over an immaculate meal, without a trace of awkwardness, and for that they were willing to forgive her much – even what they assumed was some sort of crude colonial humour from across the Atlantic; so they laughed moderately as Rose led the ladies out to the drawing room, where liqueurs, bonbons, marshmallows, and hot, strong coffee awaited them.

Mrs Lanyon thought a small crême de menthe would do no harm. Mesdames Faull and Dean chose coffee at once, of course.

"As black as that bourne from which no travellers return," Rose said as she poured for them. "As hot as those realms we pray to avoid. And as sweet as that which we most desire. There you have the formula for good coffee."

"Goodness, Miss Marteyne, you make it sound like a new religion!" exclaimed Mrs Dean.

"But," Mrs Lanyon put in, holding up a portentous, if slightly unsteady, finger, "what is 'that which we most desire,' eh?"

"Such conviviality as this?" Mrs Faull suggested tactfully.

"Feeble!" Mrs Lanyon snapped.

"Well! I'm sure I ..." Mrs Faull floundered as she caught Mrs Dean's eye, which was giving her a Significant Glance. "Ah!"

Rose remembered that young Deveril had been just as assiduous in keeping Mrs Lanyon's glass full; that, together with the liberal shot of white rum in her highball, had probably carried her beyond her limit. If not, then the crême de menthe certainly would. The hostess within her took command – though she wished she could feel just a little less dizzy herself. "What I most desire?" she said.

"A light breeze, a hot sun, a shady bower, the waft of lavender, the distant lapping of waves, two attentive admirers with their tongues cut out, and that story by whatsizname Forster ..." She waggled loose fingers toward Mrs Faull. "I overheard you telling Mister Howe about it. What's it called?"

"Howard's End."

"Do tell us more about it, dear Mrs Faull. I'm sure we're all dying to read it for ourselves so don't spoil the ending – but what's it about?"

Mrs Lanyon was disgruntled. She wanted to loosen her tongue on the topic of what was sweetest to her but she was not sufficiently in thrall to the demon drink to ignore her manners entirely. So she sat and fumed while *dear* Mrs Faull started trying to summarize the plot of the first half of *Howard's End.*

"It seems to be about the futility of helping the lower classes," she said. "There are these two frightfully well-intentioned, young ladies – of *our* sort, you know – very modern and suffragettist and so on ..."

"I have no sympathy with the suffraggeum ... suffring ... I mean the votes-for-women people," Mrs Lanyon said. Then, turning to Rose: "Are you, my dear? Being American, I suppose you are. That would be sweetest of all to you. Whereas to me ..."

"Well, it's not about the suffrage or anything like that," Mrs Faull insisted. "So it's of no consequence. It's about how every well-meaning attempt they make to help these poor people only makes things worse. It even threatens the equilibrium of the two families of decent people. So I think it's saying that assistance to the poor should be left to those who understand them – professionally – and who know what they're doing. All attempts by nice people like us, nice but woefully ignorant, can only make things worse. It's a very moral and instructive book despite the lax behaviour of some of the characters."

"Ah!" cried Mrs Dean, turning to Rose and once again thwarting Mrs Lanyon. "Talking of lax characters, what did you make of the neighbour to your right, tonight?"

"He showed a lamentable ignorance of steam turbines." She smiled at Mrs Faull, who smiled back and said, "That's probably the kindest thing anyone has ever said about Master Deveril. I hope someone warned you about him?"

"Too much, perhaps," Rose told her. "There is a little bit of Pandora in all of us, I'm afraid."

"I rather took to him, I must say," Mrs Lanyon put in. "I, too, had heard the most intriguing tales ... well, perhaps 'intriguing' isn't the word."

"I'm adding both Cox and Twigg to my list," said Mrs Dean. "Cox is in land. Twigg is in wholesale jewelry – or his family is, rather." Mesdames Lanyon and Faull took out notebooks with small ivory propelling pencils and scribbled some notes. In looking to see whether Mrs Lanyon might be ready for coffee, Rose managed to read, 'Today he smiled at me in Church and I smiled back!!!' on the page facing the one where the woman was scribbling. Suddenly her own life did not seem so desperately small and bleak any more.

The ladies spent the rest of the time before the gentlemen joined them in comparing notes on the Jolly Rogers – just as Roanoke had guessed they would. They decided that all were 'in' except Roger Deveril, whose reputation had ruled him out before they even met.

"I shall put him in but with a query," Mrs Lanyon said. "The Rake's Progress is not always as Hogarth depicted it. And infidelity is ..." She suddenly realized what she had started to say, and swiftly added, "just a word."

24

When the guests had gone, 'Uncle Harry' and Rose enjoyed a mint julep nightcap and an orgy of mutual congratulation.

"But tomorrow night will be the real test," he said. "I'll bet none of them will even recognize you when you stand dutifully beside Lizzie Moyle, ready to pass out the soup. Dear God! What a comment, eh – on our *liberal* and *humanist* and allegedly *Christian* civilization!"

"Why did Mister Deveril not rejoin us with the others?" she asked offhandedly.

He smiled knowingly. "Disappointed?"

She shrugged. "I just wondered. He doesn't strike me as deserving the reputation people give him."

"Well ... let's just say the port decanter lodged with him a little too frequently." Roanoke, too, was speaking rather nonchalantly, she noticed. "He's upstairs at the moment, as a matter of fact, sleeping it off. I wonder if you'll find him so congenial at breakfast time tomorrow!"

On her way back to her servant's garret (which was actually quite a comfortable, well-furnished, unshared room in the attic), Rose cautiously opened the door to the spare bedroom, only to find it uninhabited. The same was true of Mrs Roanoke's room, where she slipped out of her gown and jewelry and put on her old dressing gown to go up to her own room in the attic. So, unless Deveril was occupying Roanoke's bed, he was *not* 'sleeping it off upstairs' at all. She wondered why the man would lie about something so inconsequential as that.

But she was too tired to ponder the matter further; she realized that the preprandial highball, however weak, reinforced by Roger Deveril's diligent attention to the level of burgundy in her glass, and topped off with the goodnight julep were all still affecting her – especially now that there were no other distractions. The foot of her bed kept on jerking up and up and up until it seemed to be rising forever. Sleep, which soon claimed her, was a merciful refuge from that vertigo.

It was, however, a less than merciful refuge from Roger Deveril, who managed to get between her sheets and clamp his hand over her lips before she realized what was happening. "Don't scream," he said quietly. "I only want to talk. I promise I'm not going to do anything unless you consent to it. D'you understand?"

She nodded fiercely. Her mouth was dry with fear – and, she realized, she was desperate to use the chamber pot. Also, she didn't believe he would 'only want to talk.' His body was pressed tight against hers from behind and she could feel that hard *thing* of his nudging against her b-t-m.

"And you won't cry out?"

She shook her head.

He took his hand away, a mere quarter of an inch at first, then altogether, when all she did was breathe as if she'd sprinted a mile.

"Please go, Mister Deveril," she said. "What you are doing is criminal. If you leave at once, I shall say nothing about it. But if you persist ..."

"Criminal!" He gave a hollow laugh. "You think *this* is criminal! I tell you – I need a woman, just to assure myself that I'm not ..."

"If all you need is a woman, there are certain houses – you can actually see them from this window. I'll point them out ..."

He interrupted her again. "Why are you sleeping up here in the servants' quarters?"

"Because Uncle Harry told me you were sleeping off a drunken stupor – obviously you haven't quite succeeded yet. That at least is the charitable explanation I shall assume ..."

"So you thought I was in the spare room? But why did you not then sleep in Mrs Roanoke's bed?"

"I don't have to answer to you, you know. But if you really want to know, I like a firm mattress. Mrs Roanoke seems to prefer a cream puff. Now will you go!"

"A firm mattress, eh?" He chuckled. "And anything firm to go with it? Something I might supply?"

The odd thing was that at least half of her was lying doggo inside her brain, listening to the other half saying and doing all the right and proper things in this dangerous and unpredictable situation, and it was whispering: *Actually, would it be so terrible? You know you're more than slightly attracted to him. And you know it's a purely physical attraction, too – you don't actually feel much emotion for him at all, so you wouldn't be too worried about pleasing* him *or being good for* him, *et cetera, as you certainly would be with Louis. You could just suit yourself and treat him like a nobody – the way he treats the girls he's ruined.*

He misread her hesitation and started to fondle her body. She dug her nails into his hands and said, "I need to use the chamber pot. Please go!"

To her surprise he leaped from the bed and crossed the narrow room to the door. "And have you lock me out?" he whispered as he removed the key. "Oh no." And, to make doubly sure, he kept the door a few inches open by inserting his foot in the gap.

She was tempted to charge the door with her shoulder, but the certainty that his scream would wake the entire household deterred her, what with the all-round embarrassment, the explanations, the lingering suspicions ... Mud sticks, and she could ill afford another fleck of it after Lady Carclew's announcement in the papers.

He waited until he heard the rustle of bedsprings before he put the key back in the door and returned to her bedside; he was quite unabashed at the way his nightshirt bulged before him. Indeed, he made a show of it as he returned to her bed. The moon was waning but was still bright enough in the room to show every detail clearly.

"May I?" he asked, lifting the bedclothes an inch or two.

"Only if you put that thing away," she replied. "I can tell you now – it'll get no exercise tonight."

He grinned. "But you don't mind talking, eh?"

"Do I have a choice? You might as well put a pistol to my head."

He climbed back in but this time lay as far apart from her as the narrow mattress permitted. "How loud can we talk?" he asked. "Where are the other servants?"

"What d'you mean *other* servants?" she snapped. But she was also worried. Had he been trying to test her? If so he must have his suspicions. Or had Roanoke let something slip? If he thought for one moment that she was a mere servant, he'd be a great deal more brusque and overbearing.

"Sorry! I'm so used to asking the question in these surroundings!"

"Yes," she sneered. "I've been warned all about that."

"All about what?"

"About you and a maidservant called Ruby Pen-something, for a start."

"Penhallow. Ruby Penhallow. You've been told *all* about her? So you know where she is now? And what she's doing?"

"I can guess."

"Try."

"This is silly. It's a pointless conversation. What can I say that will make you go?"

"Ruby Penhallow lives with her own lady's maid, cook, and man-of-all-work in a charming little villa in Maida Vale. That, in case you don't know, is a fashionable little village on the edge of London, much in vogue with the aristocracy. She has her own carriage and rides daily in the park, wearing finery that would put the gown you wore tonight to shame. I'm sorry to be so blunt but you did ask for it. She puts as much money in the bank each month as she previously earned in a year when she was a servant in our household. Were you told all this? Did they tell you that her protector is John Thynne, the Sixth Baron Carteret – and that I arranged it all for her – seeing her comfortably settled, I mean – *after* she thought she could trap me with a baby?"

"Ah!" Rose clutched at this last straw. "So at least you don't deny the baby!"

"She wrote me a note recently thanking me for everything – saying it was the best thing that ever happened to her. She wouldn't go back and change a single moment."

"But she did have a baby?"

"It was stillborn."

"I don't mean that. I mean you. Your part in it. You did ... *get* her in child."

"She got herself in child. She promised me it was the safe time when, in fact, it was quite the reverse – and she knew it. She did it deliberately."

"Well," Rose said lamely, "I only have your word for that."

"What can I say?"

"Try 'goodbye'? Try 'sorry' ..."

"Try saying that wholeheartedly, Lucille."

"I did not give you permission for such familiarity, *Mister* Deveril. What d'you mean, anyway?"

"I mean I can read eyes as well as lips – and I *know* that part of you does not want me to go. Or not just yet."

"You really have the most ..."

"No – listen! Just listen. I mean it when I say I will do nothing unless you consent to it. But just hear me out. I make no secret about this. I enjoy pocketing the red ... the horizontal waltz ... whatever you want to call it. It *is* the supreme pleasure in life."

"For you!"

"For girls, too. If you don't know it, then I think that's sad. It is the sweetest joy for both sexes – and it's not at all difficult to achieve. I have enjoyed it with more girls – and women, and ladies – than I can remember. I don't think there's a street in Falmouth where I haven't done it at least once. And what's more – though again you'll say you only have my word for it – but those females have rejoiced in it, too. Maybe not in the beginning, when I was just *dizzy* with rapture and went at it like any farmyard beast. But the married women took care of that! Bit by bit, one by one, they've showed me all the little tricks that please a woman most and help her experience ... well, when a woman reaches the peak of her ecstasy, let me tell you, it is awe-inspiring. It leaves a mere man speechless and consumed with envy."

"And that's what you think I ..." Rose could not finish her question. She was shivering all over and it affected her voice – which she didn't want him to hear. Also she ran out of breath after only three words.

"Yes," he replied. "It's what I'm hoping you'll consent to. You above all, Lucille, because, I must confess, you have affected me in the strangest way."

"Oh?" She was both curious and alarmed.

"Indeed. I don't think I've ever met another woman quite like you. I've known hostesses twice your age who would have been in tears at that ghastly dinner party this evening, but you carried it off with such grace, such aplomb. But that's only a tiny part of it. There's something about you that's ... very *special.* Different from every other woman I've ever met."

"Are you ..." She swallowed heavily. "You're not ... I mean, this isn't ... love or ..."

"I have no wish to fall in love. I'm much too young to die. But ..."

"So you want to do this to me – to make me like all the other women you've ever ..."

"Not *to* you – *with* you. Yes, of course! That's partly it, anyway. But – again I come back to this – what *I* want isn't really the issue. I will *always* want to do it, and with just about every presentable woman between sixteen and sixty. It's what *you* want that counts here. You've never done it before – that's pretty obvious. So d'you even want to see what it's like? D'you want to know what is so ecstatic about it that they have to threaten hellfire and eternal damnation to warn you off it? Just say yes – or no – and we'll take it from there." He found her hand, raised it to his lips, and kissed her with a passion that set her trembling all over again.

"And there's no ... risk or ..." She heard a voice quite unlike her own saying faintly.

"I promise."

"And if I ask you to stop?"

"At any time."

She just lay there, breathing in shivers, not saying yes but knowing she wouldn't say no, not once he started. *Start!* she shrieked at him in the silence behind her eyes.

His hand stole across the flannel of her nightdress, pinched a fold of it, and tugged it gently this way and that, making it the caresser of her body rather than him. She felt peeled all over, raw to every new sensation.

For a long while he did nothing but caress her through the material of her nightdress. He caressed her all over, lingering nowhere but making her wish he *would* linger in certain places. As the shock of unfamiliarity wore off, she felt herself relaxing – or, rather, the nervous tension, the half-readiness to push him away and leap from the bed and flee, vanished, only to be replaced by a tension of a different and far more pleasant kind. A strange, melting sensation weighed on her limbs, making them feel heavy and unwilling to stir. She breathed in long, deep, even breaths, which she exhaled (or so she thought) like whispered sighs. And the feeling of collapse that accompanied it was very like an impulse to yield.

"For heaven's sake – sshhh!" he whispered urgently.

"What?" she asked.

But it was too late. There was a noise in the passageway outside. They froze. Through a chink in the ill-fitting door they could see the light of a guttering candle.

"Roger?" It was Roanoke's voice, soft but urgent.

"Get out!" Rose whispered in a panic. "Hide! Get in the wardrobe – or slip out on the roof. Go on!"

"Worry not! He can't hurt us. You're his niece – he won't want a public disgrace."

"You don't know. You don't understand. Just please, please, please do as I ask!"

But it was too late. The door swung open and there stood Roanoke, candlestick in hand, staring at Deveril in horror. Yes – at Deveril, not at her.

"I had to, Skipper," he said, stepping out of bed – and still stiff down there! In fact, he flaunted it at his host. "See!" he crowed. "That proves it, eh – you sad old deviant! I had to do it." He slipped back into his nightshirt and held Rose's convenient for her.

The candlestick tilted. Wax fell to the threadbare carpet.

"Have a care!" Rose shouted as she emerged through the neckhole of her nightdress.

"You can take that off again, Miss Traitress," he said with quiet menace, though he continued to stare at Roger. "And put on your clothes and pack your pathetic little suitcase and leave my house. I give you fifteen minutes. I do not wish to see you ever again."

"But nothing happened," she told him. Roger looked from one to the other in bewilderment. "What's this?"

"I don't know you," Roanoke told him.

"Not for want of trying!" Roger taunted him. But he was talking to a dying footfall on the stair.

Rose ran to the door and called after him: "You could at least let me explain. You're being very unfair."

Without turning round he replied, "Now nobody will employ you, no matter what they think of her ladyship."

"What's he talking about?" Roger asked as Rose came back into her room. He was fiddling with the vestas, intending to light her bedside candle.

"Why did he only look at *you?"* she asked.

"Ladies first."

"Yes, well, that's the whole point, in a way. I'm not a lady, I'm a maidservant – a lady's maid. This evening was one of …"

"Sorry, old girl, you'll have to try another one. I simply don't believe you."

She rose from her bed, which was no longer her bed, and started dressing in her everyday clothes. And as she did so, she reverted to her everyday accent to tell him the truth of what had happened. She had to slip back into her upper-class voice – and then leap over to her American voice – before he was finally convinced.

"But that's utterly fantastic," he said. "You don't simply change the accent and go on saying the same words. You change everything – even the way you stand. Are you even aware of it?"

She laughed, despite her plight. "You mean Americans *stand* differently from the English?"

"I don't know about Americans, but *you* do. When you talk American, your shoulders go back a little and your chin goes up."

Rose pictured it in her mind's eye and realized it was how her mother stood. So she did pick up more than just the accent – something she had not realized before. Not that it was of any practical use, mind.

Mind! Her mind was numb. She knew something dreadful had just happened to her – and right on top of something utterly wonderful, too. So it was all just too much. She'd go out and walk around until dawn – right round Pendennis Head, perhaps. Something might occur to her on the way.

There was a soft thud on the landing outside – Roger's evening dress, all wrapped round his shoes.

"How d'you do it?" he asked as he went out to gather them up.

She shrugged. She was fully dressed by now and she went to help him. His thing was flaccid and smaller than one of her fingers.

"How are the mighty fallen!" he said, following her eyes.

She reached out and touched it, fascinated to see it give a little kick and grow by half an inch. "Shall we try again?" he asked. "What can that old pervert do now? We could lock the door."

She laughed and held his shirt for him to slip into. "You understand women so well, sir – so you'll know what fickle creatures we are. The mood has to be right." As he wriggled into his shirt she answered his earlier question. "I've been mimicking people since before I can remember. Sally Winnen and I – she was my best friend at school – we used to follow behind the foreign sailors and I used to copy all their lingo. Sometimes they heard and it would amuse them. They'd say things and I'd repeat it, just like a parrot, and they'd laugh and sometimes they'd give us a penny or two. So it was just a trick that grew and grew."

"It grew and grew into an evening-long impersonation. You weren't just parroting someone else this evening, you *were* someone else. I can still hardly believe it. You ought to be on the stage ... though, actually ..."

She laughed. "You're the second person to tell me that. Maybe I'll have to consider it now."

"There is another possibility," he said casually as he struggled to knot his white tie. "Damn! Can you do this?"

She suspected he could do it very well for himself; he just wanted to see her face while he said: "Would you consider becoming my mistress, Lucille? Or what is your name?"

"Lucille will do." She drew a deep breath and held it.

"I'm moving to London. Somehow I've gone off sailing! Remember the conditions I described for Ruby Penhallow? You can assume the same for yourself. And your only duty would be ..." He tilted his head in the direction of the bed.

"How often?" she asked, thinking *Are you mad?*

He chuckled. "Dear me – did my clumsy fumblings frighten you so much?"

"No!" She butted him with her head. "You know they didn't. It was everything you promised, as far as it went. I don't know why I asked that question."

"But?"

"But what?"

"You tell me – I could hear a 'but' coming."

She sighed. "There's a man who ... he wants to marry me."

"Rich enough to do so? Or still saving? He needn't know about me. I can arrange the most respectable reference ..."

"It's not that. He may be rich enough – or he may be bankrupt. Everything's in the balance just now."

"May I ask his name?"

"Don't you believe me?"

"It's not that. But I have this well-paid hobby – speculating in shares. I have lots of insider information."

She took a chance. "His name is Louis Redmile-Smith."

Even in the candlelight she could see he had turned pale. "I think you should sit down," he said, clearing her Tennyson off her bedside chair. "You didn't see the evening papers?"

She shook her head but did not take the proferred seat. "Go on. It can't be worse than my nightmares."

"I wouldn't be too sure about that. He's gone smash, all right – one of the biggest smashes this century. His mother tried to commit suicide. He's at her bedside now – otherwise the vultures would have the shirt off his back. Oh, Lucille, I am so sorry. So very sorry." After a pause, during which she just felt utterly numb, he added, "I won't press my offer now, but do think it over, eh?"

25

By the time they reached the street they discovered it had started to rain – gently but it ruled out a walk around Pendennis Point.

"I don't feel happy leaving you like this," Roger said. "I'll put you up in a hôtel if you like?" He read her face by the street lamp and added, "Single room. I feel responsible."

She smiled wanly and told him he *was* responsible but not to worry as she had a friend who lived nearby.

He gave her his card – just in case she decided to accept his offer. Then, after a brief, awkward hug, they parted. It was four o'clock, an hour before sunrise; the eastern horizon, across the estuary, was already beginning to pale.

Fortunately Sally's apartment was on the ground floor. Rose selected a small handful of pebbles from the gravel drive and started shying them gently against her windowpane. She opened it after the fifth.

"Lucy?" Her voice was gravelly, her tone incredulous.

"I've been sacked."

"At this hour? What time is it?"

"Can I come in? It's raining."

"Yes, 'course you can, my lover. I'm sorry."

She was wearing silk pyjamas in a bright floral pattern – oriental poppies about six inches across. Her rooms were filled with the pleasant, minty aroma of patchouli. "Cuppa tea?" she suggested.

"Not really. All I want is oblivion – or just to get back to sleep."

"Well ... you'd best tell me *something* about it, or *I* shan't get back to sleep."

Rose started to tell her story in outline; then, realizing it hardly made sense, she told her everything – except that she could not quite bring herself to admit that she and Deveril had not actually crossed the Rubicon.

"And you'd never done it before?" was Sally's first, incredulous question. Rose was taken aback. "Does that matter now? The main thing is that one of the few people in Falmouth who was willing to employ me – probably the only one after tonight's little charade – now won't even talk to me. I'm finished here. Washed up. I haven't even got a character. And as for Louis ..." She burst into tears – inconsolable tears that would not stop.

Sally held her in her arms, patting and stroking her back and saying, "There, there, now!" and similar words of comfort. "You're certainly not finished or washed up – take it from me!"

"You mean ... Roger Deveril's offer. You think I should accept?"

Sally hesitated. "It's certainly a possibility, my lover. Not to be sneezed at. But it's not the only one. Listen!" She glanced at her mantelpiece clock. "Tell you what. I've got to spend the morning with two rich ladies who may be willing to put a little money into my shop. They want me to think a little grander than the poky little one-floor-up establishment I had in mind. But the afternoon is my own. I'm yours from about three o'clock. So why don't you take a draught of laudanum now and sleep right round till after noon? Things'll look very different after a good deep sleep – take it from a specialist in that department!"

It was a measure of Rose's dejection that she did not balk at the offer. But something within her must have stayed undrugged, alert for the sound of Sally's key in the door, for she was wide awake by the time her friend came into the bedroom.

"Feeling better?" was her first question.

"Feeling rested, anyway. How were your two rich ladies?"

"Generous ... but shrewd. They really put me through it but we've come to a mutually satisfactory arrangement. The only question now is should we open up shop in Falmouth or Truro? But that's for another day."

While she spoke they went through to her poky little kitchen, where she discarded her gloves and set about making scrambled eggs and bacon. "You look after the toast," she told Rose. "Sit on the stool and keep an eye on the grill."

She chattered away about her plans for her new 'fashion emporium' while she stirred the eggs and turned the rashers in the pan. "But wasn't it lucky I had so much capital of my own to add to the pot!" she said. "Else I'd be working eighteen hours a day just to make those two a little richer than they already are."

She said it several times in different ways.

But when they carried the makeshift meal back to her sitting-dining room, as she called it, she ceased talking about herself and turned all her attention to Rose. "The first thing to settle, my lover," she said, "is Mister Redmile-Smith. Do you ..."

"Oh but that's over," Rose said. "It has to be. Because ..."

"You don't love him any more?"

"Desperately!" Her voice broke. "That's why I feel so awful about Roger Deveril last night – doing that with him ... even though it was ... nice."

"Nice!"

"Very well." Rose laughed reluctantly. "It was ... wonderful." She lingered on the word. "But that only makes it worse. I don't *feel* anything for Roger Deveril. I mean, I can look at him and say to myself, 'all right – you're a handsome devil ...' "

"And he knows how to light a fire?"

"He certainly does! But there's no actual feeling" – she spread a hand across her heart – "here. I mean, I only need to whisper Louis' name and I know the difference."

"So why can't you go to him now – to Louis? If things are like what you say, he's never going to need you more desperately than he does right at this moment."

Rose closed her eyes and shook her head. "I just couldn't do it. That's all."

Sally heaved a sigh. "You must have your reasons, I suppose."

"How could I ever be sure ... I mean, he made a promise to me when he thought he was going to rescue the company and restore it to, well, what we all thought it was anyway. He was absolutely sure he'd manage it. But how can I treat those promises as binding now that everything else is just topsy turvy. He's got nothing left."

"That's why you don't want him any more?"

Rose knew that Sally was being deliberately provocative but it did not prevent her flaring up. "Of course I want him! The moment Roger told me what had happened, I had this wild idea that I'd go to him at once and tell him it didn't matter and I still want to be his wife. But don't you see? If he said yes – and he probably would say yes – how could I ever be sure he wasn't just saying it to honour his earlier promise, which, as I say, was made in circumstances that no longer apply?"

"You'd know that within a day," Sally protested. "A man can't hide a thing like that. They can hide the things they *do* from you – their actions – they can hide them better than a squirrel with his nuts. But not their thoughts and feelings – except from women who want to delude themselves, anyway. So, if you still feel like this about Louis, why didn't you just say no to Roger Deveril?"

"I tried. I mean I'm still talking about Louis now – I tried to tell him I didn't mind – when he told me about the troubles in the business. I told him I'd come with him. I'd lick stamps and address envelopes ... cook for him ... sweep floors. I'd even have been his mistress, though I didn't say so, of course. But he knew I was offering *everything,* just to be with him."

"And?"

"And he said no. He'd manage on his own. I think he was telling me that he didn't want me around if he failed."

"So – I return to my question – why didn't you tell Roger Deveril to take a long walk off a short pier?"

"Well ..." She swallowed heavily. "His offer is something I might seriously consider. I mean, it's one way of earning quite a lot of money quite quickly. I know it's immoral, strictly speaking, but it's *almost* like getting married, isn't it? I mean, lots of women *do* get married just because the man can offer them money and security – not for love."

"Go on." Sally's face had become an unreadable mask.

"What more can I say? I don't love Roger but I do quite like him." She laughed awkwardly. "And I certainly like what we did last night!"

"And? What about the money?"

She shrugged. "He didn't say anything specific but he did say that Ruby Penhallow could put a year's wages into the bank every single week."

Sally snorted.

"I mean every month."

"Yes, that's more like it – though it still sounds high to me. What would she earn as a domestic? Thirty ... thirty-five a year – something like that?"

"Something like that." Rose stacked their plates.

"Let's be generous and say it's thirty-five. That's four hundred and twenty quid a year – plus little tips and Christmas boxes and birthdays ... say, four-fifty. All right ... I suppose that's about fair. Does that tempt you?"

Rose laughed. "Twelve years' wages in one! Does it *tempt* me?"

"What if I told you you could earn ..." she paused, eyeing her friend speculatively.

"What?"

She rummaged in her handbag, saying, "What if you could earn *a whole lifetime* of wages in a year? More than two and a half thou'? I'm not joking."

Even so, Rose laughed in disbelief.

Sally pulled a piece of paper from her bag and placed it on the table – with, Rose noticed, a slightly trembling hand.

"What's that?" Rose asked.

"Read it."

"I've read it. It's an address in Paris."

"It's the address of a house where you could earn eight quid or more every night."

Rose stared at it and felt the blood draining from her face. "But how do you ...? No! I couldn't do that – never! Eight quid? In one night? Two months' wages in a single night? No! I couldn't be one of *them*. The girls who do that sort of thing are ..." Her lip curled in a sneer as she sought for an appropriately contemptuous word.

Then her eyes caught Sally's and she saw the pain already welling in them ... and at last she understood. "But ... but ..." she stammered. "You said ... Mrs Boyce of Peckham."

"And you believed me?"

"Yes!"

"And I thought you were just being the perfect little actress you always was – were! You honestly *believed* me?"

"Of course I did."

Sally laughed. "There's hope for me yet. Now what were you going to call girls like me? You who were quite willing to spread your legs for a man you don't love, so he could pop it in – as long as he also pops a measly four hundred and fifty quid a year into your bank book?"

Rose darted a hand across the table and caught her arm. "I didn't think. I'm sorry – honestly. I just gave the conventional response. Also you look so *healthy!*"

"What, you mean no pox? No disappearing nose? No rotten teeth ... hair falling out ... no madness?" She patted the scrap of paper. "Believe me – in a house like that you get better medical care than any royalty. And why wouldn't they? For every quid you earn, they get a quid, too. Though it's francs, really. One pound is twenty-five francs. So your *client,* as they call him, pays fifty francs and you split it with the house – twenty-five, twenty-five. So if they've got fifteen girls in the salon each night – you work it out."

"Three thousand francs a night ... a hundred and twenty quid!"

"Out of which, admittedly, they would feed us, provide all the linen, the rooms, the light, the heating – and medical costs, including inspections. But even so, it still leaves a tidy sum over, believe you me."

"And ... you know – babies? What about accidents like that?"

Sally shook her head. "Very rare, love. You let half a dozen men a day leave their visiting cards and they cancel each other out. You've seen boys in school playgrounds – they fight as soon as set eyes on each other. They must do something like that down there, too. Besides, there's lozenges and douches and things."

"Six men a day!" Rose pulled a face – not too disgusted in case she insulted Sally again.

"It's not *day,* really. It's evening. You work from six to one in the morning – plus two afternoons a week. That's on a rota. Did you ever sew six buttonholes in an evening?"

"Of course."

"And when you got to buttonhole number five, didn't you never look back at one or two of the earlier ones and think, 'I don't remember doing you!' Haven't you never done that?"

Rose nodded ruefully. "Often. You sort of go like an automaton. Or no – your mind drifts off onto other paths while your fingers keep going."

"Perfect!" Sally laughed again. "I couldn't have put it better myself. And I'll bet you never had to unpick those buttonholes you stitched while your mind was a million miles away? I'll bet they were every bit as perfect and professional as any you stitched while your mind was on the job?"

Rose nodded.

"That's how it is with *clients,* my lover – after the first couple of weeks, anyway. But listen! I'm not trying to persuade you into it. There's lots of girls try to do that. They feel degraded, see? They think their friends look down on them – so they try to get them into the game, too, just to stop their sneering. But I don't feel an ounce of shame" – she patted her breastbone – "not in here. Mind you, I'm not going to go up on the roof with a megaphone, either. In fact, you're probably the only person I'm ever going to admit this to. So if word does get about, I'll know who's eyes to scratch out!"

"Of course I won't breathe a word, Sally. Who would I tell, anyway? Even if I ..."

"I know you won't, love. All I'm saying is I'm not saying you should and I'm not saying you shouldn't. It's what I chose to do and, like in any other job, I had good times and bad. I met men I admired and was glad to please – and men I wanted to kill, but I managed to please even so."

"And the other girls?"

"Friendship you mean? It's more *camaraderie* than friendship. Strong while you're together but like smoke once you've parted. I still write to one or two but I don't know how long it will last. But, like I said, it's there if you want it. And if you decide you do want it, I'll help you write your letter of application and I'll cover it with a letter of my own to Madame. You'll have no difficulty getting in – I can promise you that."

Rose pulled a face. "I'm not particularly beautiful."

"You are – but, anyway, that's not the important thing. There were girls there as plain as a burned saucepan but it didn't matter because they had character. Personality. That's the important thing – and you've got it running out of your ears!"

Rose, who had been fidgetty for some time past, stood up suddenly and began pacing about. "I can't believe I'm taking this seriously," she said. "And discussing it so matter-of-factly."

Sally nodded sympathetically. "I remember feeling like that."

"When did it change, then? When did it not seem extraordinary at all?"

Sally closed her eyes tight and scratched her head. "I think it was before I started. I went there on a Thursday ... Thursday, the sixteenth of June, nineteen-oh-four ... and ..."

"When you were seventeen!"

"Yep! I told them I was twenty-one. The law says you have to be twenty-one but they don't fuss if you look right. Anyway, Thursday's a good day to arrive because you're not allowed into the salon until after the weekly medical – which is on Tuesday in that house. So I had five days to talk to the other girls – the *filles-de-joie!*"

Hearing her immaculate pronunciation of *clients* earlier, and now of *filles-de-joie,* Rose asked, *"Mais – alors – tu parles français, n'est-ce pas?"*

"Of course!" Sally chuckled. "But you're never going to hear me doing it. What a giveaway that'd be!"

"Why?" Rose frowned.

"Well – where's a common giglet like me going to learn to speak French, eh?"

"Same place as I did – from books. And from making friends with French sailors in the port. And the onion men."

"Yes, well, that's you and this is me! I never opened a book for study in my life, and everyone knows it. Anyway, I was saying – I had five days to watch through the one-way mirrors and talk with the other girls and ... you know – just absorb the atmosphere. And it was something Madame said that made me think it wasn't extraordinary at all. It certainly helped over the first few days."

"What was that?" Rose sat down again and leaned attentively across the table.

"I can't remember the exact figures but it went something like this. There were twenty-thousand *prostituées* working in Paris every night. That includes everyone, from the high-class *filles-de-joie* like us to disgusting *putains* who didn't dare show what was left of their faces outside of the darkest *impasses.* Half a million of us in France as a whole. A million in Germany. A million in England ... I mean, the numbers stopped meaning anything. But if you reckon that they each cop half a dozen *clients* a night – that's three million Frogs, six million Sourcrouts, and six million Johnny Bulls."

The figures seemed to overwhelm her for she closed her eyes and shook her head, as if to clear it, saying, "How did it go next? Oh yes, I remember. If you reckon on ten minutes per *client* – I mean, we had to spin it out to a minimum of thirty minutes and we got fined if we came down with a *client* before that. But some *putains* get it over in four minutes. So say ten, right?"

She paused again and said, "No, I've gone wrong somewhere. Anyway, the point she was making was that when the door to your boudoir closes and you're alone with a *client,* especially in those first few days, you think it's something very ... unique. I mean, it's never happened to you before and your feelings are the most important things in the world to you, right? So what she was saying was just remember – there are ... I don't know ... so many *hundred* other girls, even just in Paris, doing *exactly* what you're doing – no matter when you're doing it! It's as common as walking dogs, buying newspapers, hopping on a bus."

Rose got a scrap of paper from the kitchen and scribbled a few calculations. "From the figures you gave me," she said, "just for Paris – forget the rest – there would be four hundred and seventy-six girls doing it at any given moment between six and one in the morning. And if you want to expand it to Germany, France, and England, it means ..." She turned pale. "It means nearly six *thousand* girls. No!" She stared incredulously at her friend. "It seems impossible. Now – at this very moment, maybe – there are anything up to *six thousand girls* selling that favour for money! Right now, while we sit here! And all the rest of the time!" She closed her eyes and shook her head, just as Sally had done earlier.

"But it makes you realize what a very ordinary, everyday step it is for a girl to take," Sally said. "Right?"

26

When their conversation began to circle around the same three possibilities – Louis Redmile-Smith, Roger Deveril, and a certain big-number house in Paris – for the third time, Sally realized that Rose could talk around them forever. A couple more circuits and she'd become so utterly paralyzed that she'd end up doing nothing ... just drifting ... helping out in her parents' shop until they pointed out that it could not support three. And then what? No shop would take her – not after that announcement in the papers. And Roanoke sounded vindictive enough to make life difficult for her everywhere else. Barmaid was about the best she could hope for.

She should go to Louis, of course. No question. But as long as she thought she was being noble and self-sacrificing by staying away from him, there was no talking her into it.

There were times, Sally knew, when it was kind to be cruel. A little bit of a shock might just light a fire under Miss Lucinda-Ella Tremayne and put some steam in her boiler. *So here goes,* she thought. *When all else fails, the truth is not a bad last resort.*

"I don't know how to say this, my lover," she said, "but when you're in business – especially if you're a woman and even more especially if you're just starting out with the support of two very proper and respectable ladies ... d'you see what I'm trying to say?"

"You can't afford a breath of scandal?" Rose guessed.

"Bless you!"

"But ... I don't understand. I've already promised I won't breathe a word."

Sally's face fell. "Not that, pet. I know my secret's safe enough with you. But I can't afford to be associated with scandal." She smiled ruefully. "Can I, now."

"You want *me* to go," Rose said bleakly. "I'm the scandal. Yes, of course."

"It's not what I *want,* my lover. It's the way the world goes. Besides, don't you think your mother will want to know?"

"About Roger's offer? About Paris?" She gave a hollow laugh. "But you're right. I'll go." She looked around for her suitcase. When she found it she showed Sally the inscription inside the lid: *I love you Lucinda-Ella – TT*. "Tony Trevean," she said. "He works for Angove and Snell. Maybe he can get me in there." There wasn't a chance of it, of course, but she felt she had to leave on a hopeful note and that was the best she could improvise.

It was half-past seven by the time she went. She couldn't face going back along Wodehouse Terrace, nor along any of the streets behind, all of which were filled with smug, respectable houses where she would never be welcome again, not even as a scullery maid. That left her the choice of going down Jacob's Ladder and along the main streets – or past Vernon Place and down Smithick Hill, where she would pass the old school playground. Perhaps there she would meet the shade of the little girl she once was. Oh, if only that were possible! she thought as she set off. What things she would have to tell her!

'Stick by Sally, little one. Stick like a leech. Whatever she does, you do, too. Go to Paris with her when you're seventeen. Why? Never you mind. Just do it – because I can promise you, by the time you're twenty-three, you'll be rich enough to run to a man called Louis Redmile-Smith – don't forget that name now – engrave it on your heart because that's where it belongs – and then you can take him away beyond the reach of his creditors and live with him happy ever after.'

She hesitated at the top of Jacob's Ladder. She knew why she thought of going down along Smithick Hill – because it would take her past *those* houses in Vernon Place. She remembered how she and Sally used to lurk in doorways near the end of Wellington Terrace, just where it opens into Vernon Place; and they'd giggle as they watched the matelots going in, and giggle again when they saw them coming out, until someone spotted them and shooed them away. One ancient lady used to bring out a huntsman's whip and try to sting them with it. "Off with ye, little bitterweeds!" she'd cry. "Or ye'll end up inside one of they places – and it's no more giggling then!"

Was that where Sally got the idea? While she, Rose, could only shudder at the thought of lying naked on a straw paliasse in a room with bare boards (such were the playground legends) and having those dirty foreign sailors come shambling through the door and letting them … yuk! – while all that was going through her mind, was Sally already thinking along quite different lines … counting the men going in, counting them out again, noting the time they took, calculating it into so much copper and silver, and making the coldest of cold-blooded choices about the shortest line between leaving school and opening a fashion emporium?

By now her feet had made the choice for her; they were leading her along Wellington Terrace, past those same doorways, toward those same houses. The sun was well down in the west by now, shining almost horizontally and throwing her shadow far ahead of her. By the time she realized it, the image of her head and shoulders was cast upon the steps leading up to one of the houses. If she continued further, she'd be there from the knees up.

An omen?

Trapped in a house like that – no legs below the knees – can't run – can't escape – once in, no way out?

Was this her guardian angel talking to her?

Had Sally truly escaped, come to think of it? All those men – seven to eight thousand, she had guessed. *Guessed!* Most of them French, of course, but quite a few from England. Someone must recognize her sometime. Does she wake every morning thinking *this could be the day?*

Not Sally. *But I would,* Rose thought. *It's not for me.*

Too much of a scaredy-cat. But you could read the omen another way. No matter how close to that house she walked, the shadow of her legs below the knees would never fall on the steps – not unless she crossed the street and actually went up to them. And she certainly wasn't going to do that.

While she stood there, taunting herself with all these possibilities, the door opened and … at first she could not believe her eyes – but, yes, it was, indeed, Noel Carclew standing there. He was actually half in her shadow. He stood, blinking at the sun, looking right and left, and adopting the pose of a man in front of a fire – tails up, warming his bum.

He saw her, standing there across the street, but, with the sun directly behind her, did not recognize her. He started across the roadway, walking directly at her, and as he drew closer he said, jovially, "Thinking it over, eh? They'll take *you* like a shot, I can promise you."

"And you haven't even seen my face, Noel!" She laughed.

"Rose?" He was not in the least embarrassed. He looked at her, looked at the house, then back at her. "Surely not!"

"I should slap your face for that," she replied.

"Oh!" He threw up his hands in comic despair. "Why tell me *now?* For free? If you'd told me twenty-five minutes ago, you'd have saved me five bob." He rubbed the seat of his pants and added, “Whew! But she was good!” He laughed again. “You haven’t the foggiest notion of what I’m talking about, have you! Come on! I’m feeling on top of the world. Let me treat you to the theatre.” He turned her round, grabbed her little suitcase, and linked his arm through hers.

“Theatre?” Her eyes lit up. “Oh, yes – the travelling troupe down on the Moor. I’d clean forgotten. What’s on tonight?”

“*Leah the Forsaken.* All the world’s passion in the confines of the village green.”

“Oh, goody! I know it.”

“Oh – well – shall we see if there’s a dance on at the drill hall?”

“No! I love the play. I’ve seen it six times – not by this company. I’d love to see it again – as long as you’re paying!”

He hugged her arm tight to him. “Oh, Rose! You are jolly good fun, you know.”

“Should I ask what you’re doing back in Cornwall? I thought you were staying in London for the whole Season.”

“I disgraced myself. I was tricked into mounting the stage at the Holborn Empire, where I sang ‘She was poor but she was honest’ to the great delight of *hoi polloi.* And word of it somehow got back to the old mater. Not by way of the pater, however – even though he happened to be in the stalls at the time!”

They started down the Ladder, going sedately.

Rose laughed. “Your father? Sir Hector? Going to a music hall? I don’t *believe* it!”

“With a pair of chorus girls! He gave me ten guineas to keep mum – or, as he put it, to prove I’m a man of the world.”

Rose didn’t know why she laughed so heartily. Sir Hector was party to her dismissal for ‘conduct unbecoming’ and his wife had put that scurrilous announcement in the papers. And yet it was funny. “You know the trouble with me,” she said as her laughter died. “I can’t hate – or not for long.”

“You’re not talking about me, I hope?”

“No, your people. You saw the notice your mother put in the papers, did you?”

“Yes – silly old bat! People will just laugh, surely?”

“I’m afraid not, Noel. It’s left me in rather a spot.”

“Well!” He gave her a reassuring hug. “You can tell them all to kiss your … heels. Just hang on until Louis comes back for you.”

She stopped dead. He went on a step, which swung him round and brought them face to face. “You haven’t heard?” she asked. “You didn’t read the papers yesterday?”

He shook his head.

She told him.

“Oh Lor, Rose,” he murmured, reaching up and stroking her cheek. “What are you going to do?”

She shrugged – and grinned at him. “Go to the theatre – and let tomorrow take care of itself!”

27 *Leah, the Forsaken* was not presented quite as its author, one Augustin Daly, had seen it on its First Night, which had taken place at the Howard Athanæum, Boston, on December 9th, 1862. For one thing, the casting called for nine actors, seven actresses, and A Child; Lord Gordon Fitzroy's Players had A Child, right enough – eleven-year-old Petronella Fitzroy, Lord Gordon's very own Infant Prodigy – but there were only three actresses and five actors. So the Baker had to double with the Village Priest, the Country Youth with the Tailor, the Barber-Surgeon with (appropriately enough) the Butcher ... and so forth. This, in turn, entailed a certain amount of cutting, rewriting, and redistribution of parts – to say nothing of frantic quick changes in the wings. But, as the play could be 'represented free-of-charge' in England, Lord Gordon assumed the same literary *droit de seignieur* over the text as the Henry Irvings and Beerbohm Trees of his profession assumed over Shakespeare – to say nothing of the Thomas Bowdlers. Five acts and eleven scenes were shaved to three and eight respectively, reducing its length from two hours and a half to just under two – *without* an interval. Previous experience in Cornwall had taught the Players that any interval tended to remind audiences of the rival attractions of the dance hall and the public bar.

For those unfamiliar with the story, it is a triangle of love set in An Austrian Village in the early eighteenth century – a time and place when antisemitism was particularly virulent. The villagers have always assumed that Rudolf, the magistrate's son, will one day marry Madalena, the niece of the Village Priest. But tragedy looms when he meets and instantly falls in love with Leah, the daughter of some wandering Jews on their way to Bohemia, where they will be welcome. The doomed lovers decide to elope to America, land of the free. Enter the villain – Schoolmaster Carl, a virulent antisemite because he is, in fact, Nathan, a Jew masquerading as a Christian. He tells Rudolf that Leah will renounce her love for a purse of gold and suggests a test. Rudolf consents because he is sure she will spurn the offer. Carl gives the purse to Leah's parents, pretending it is a gift from himself; but the old man recognizes him as Nathan the Apostate Jew. Carl kills him and ascribes the death to a thunderbolt from God. He tells Rudolf that Leah accepted the gold. Rudolf will have no more to do with her and marries Madalena, his childhood sweetheart. Stricken with remorse, for he still loves Leah, Rudolf wanders alone in the churchyard on his wedding night. There Leah, her heart now hardened against him, lays on him a curse so awesome that it usually has the audience groaning in horror. In the final act, five years later, Rudolf, Madalena, and their four-year-old daughter (called Leah) are happy and prosperous farmers. Rudolf has become a Good Samaritan to all the world yet he still fears that the curse of Leah, the Forsaken, will one day strike him. As the curtain rises, he is away in Vienna, petitioning the Emperor to repeal all the country's anti-Jewish laws. Leah, ill and faint but not dying, arrives in the village, part of a large band of Jews on their way to freedom in America. She calls in at Rudolf's farm to see how well her curse is progressing and is astonished to find everyone cheerful and affluent. She soon learns it is because they are all so good and charitable. There is much hiding and reappearing as Carl, heading a band of Peasants, all out for Jewish blood, roam through the village. They catch Leah and are about to drown her when Rudolf returns with the Emperor's decree abolishing all anti-Jewish laws and granting them equal status with Christians. Leah recognizes Carl as the Apostate Nathan who murdered her father and she unmasks him. While he kneels in chains, she whips out a dagger and goes to cut his head off – as Judith did to Holofernes. But she cannot manage it in her enfeebled condition. The curtain falls with her deciding to leave vengeance to God and to think of life, liberty, and the pursuit of happiness in America, instead.

Such, at least, was the story as poor Augustin Daly intended it. On Falmouth Moor that night, however, his purpose was not simply compromised by the merging of several parts and the reduction of Angry Band of Peasants to Angry Peasant (played by the company's odd-job man) it was actually subverted by the fact that Mrs Ivy Fitzroy, Lord Gordon's wife, was very evidently about to produce a little brother or sister to young Petronella – which made her an odd choice for Mr Daly's chaste and virginal Leah. She had to be rewritten as Rudolf's lover of at least nine month's standing – which introduced an almost Ibsenesque complexity into the plot. Unfortunately, a character of Ibsenesque depth was quite beyond Lord Gordon Fitzroy's acting range, so he, at the age of fifty-four, continued to play the twenty-five-year-old Rudolf as the stock young lover of every other melodrama in which he had ever appeared.

None of this mattered a jot to Rose. She had, as she said to Noel, seen the play many times before, but never until this particular evening had she observed so many parallels between its story and her own – the expectation that childhood sweethearts should marry, the rejection of Leah for a crime of which she was innocent, the issuing of curses and threats that were futile even at the moment of their uttering, to name but three. And, tenuous though some of the connections were (she would *not* be marrying her childhood sweetheart, for instance), the unjust manner in which Leah became the Forsaken, cast out of 'decent' society and left to wander alone in a friendless world, was so powerfully reminiscent of her own wrongful treatment, first by Lady Carclew and now by Mr Roanoke, that she could not help identifying herself and Leah completely. She wept when Old Abraham, Leah's father, says to her: 'From the points of thy fingers stream floods of light. When thou are near, the stars rise in my firmament.' They were surely Louis' sentiments toward her, as well. And Leah's terrible cry of 'Rudolf! Rudolf!' at the end of the scene in which he accuses her of accepting gold in place of his love and then slams the door in her face was the most heartrending thing she had ever seen; and the poor, crumpled body left alone and sobbing in a single limelight upon a darkened stage was surely a harbinger of the life that now awaited her.

Noel watched her responses in amazement. He was even beginning to think she was, after all, just an ordinary servant girl, with all the standard responses to cheap and shallow emotional manipulations such as these. At last, unable to bear it any longer, he murmured, "It's her own fault," you know. "She shouldn't have gone off picking wildflowers while Schoolmaster Carl was strangling her father. And she should surely have asked for her accuser to confront her. She'd have recognized him at once then and we'd be spared ..."

"Oh, shuttup, shuttup, shuttup!" Rose hissed, and continued to cry at every fresh twist of Leah's cruel fate.

But when it was over – when a tottering and exhausted Leah, having failed to cut off Carl/Nathan's head, says, to a final, demi-slow curtain: 'Thine, thine is the vengeance – vengeance, madness, and folly. To Him above, and not to me, even as He said it. Alas, alas! Who embraces me? Who dares to ... oh, Rudolf! You! But I must not remain. I must now away with my People, for this night I shall wander into the far-off – to the promised land!' – Rose stretched, gave a happy sigh, dabbed her cheeks dry, and, grabbing Noel's arm passionately, said, "Wasn't that just *marvellous!* Thank you, thank you, darling Noel!" And she followed it up with a kiss that was just as fervent, adding, "I'll let you off the four pounds, sixteen shillings for this."

"No, no!" he assured her. "This is just outstanding interest – and so is a slap-up dinner now awaiting us at the Prince of Wales. And then I shall pay you in full."

"You overwhelm me! But let's first go and see the actors, eh, and tell them how splendid they all were?"

As they made their way out by the marquee's only exit she caught him staring at her with a somewhat puzzled expression. "What now?" she asked.

"Women," he replied. "The sheer, utter impossibility of understanding you."

"Why? What don't you understand?"

"But really, I suppose, it's not important. We don't need to understand. All we need to know is what works with you and what doesn't. It's technique that counts, not science."

"Well, I'm sure you know what you're talking about," she said, being too happy to get involved in any deep philosophy.

As they drew near what passed for the green room, however, they heard a furious argument in progress between Rudolf and Leah – or, rather, between Lord Gordon Fitzroy and his wife. Rose gripped Noel's arm and put a finger to her lips.

"I said it wouldn't work," she was telling him. "It just makes a mockery of your character – that he's knocking off my character in the forest for nine months ... that old Abraham and Sara don't notice she's got a belly like a football ... that his father and the priest don't mind him never going to church 'cos he's too busy pocketing the red with Leah ... I mean, you're supposed to be a *noble* character who gets distracted for just a *moment* – a week or two – by a wild and beautiful young girl. You can't spin it out over the best part of a *year!*"

"Can I have a bag of niceys now?" asked the Child Leah, or Miss Petronella Fitzroy.

"No, you'll get fat," her parents said in what was probably their only moment of accord all evening. They continued over her screams. "The solution, my dear – as I' have said more than once – is for you to play Dame Gertrude and let Miss Moore play Leah. Then we can revert to the original ..."

"What? And let Hortensia Skerret play young Madalena? Yes, it's time we did a new comedy – although, come to think of it, she can still give *you* a good sixteen years! Besides, I am *not* playing old dames just yet, thank you very much. It's the start of the slippery slope to oblivion."

"I have the answer," Rose whispered to Noel.

"Don't tell me," he replied, giving her a push toward the tent-flap opening.

She stood there blinking in the light of the naphtha flare by which the rest of the cast were removing their makeup.

"Ah!" Lord Gordon gave a bow that was probably not intended ironically. "Our dear public, my precious!"

Rose, abashed, began stammering her appreciation of their performance that evening. But Noel cut her short, saying, "She has an answer to your present difficulty."

"What? Eh? What difficulty, pray?"

Husband and wife exchanged glances of incomprehension.

"Forgive me," Rose stammered, "but we couldn't help overhearing your slight contretemps as we ..."

"Just tell them the solution," Noel said.

"I'll kill you when I've done," she snapped before turning apologetically to Mrs Fitzroy to explain. "It just occurred to me while we were watching the play tonight ... I mean ... oh dear! It's just that there was a slight sort of titter when you first appeared ... because of ... you know." She nodded at what the woman herself had called a belly like a football.

"And?" the woman demanded imperiously – though she did not deny Rose's account of what had happened on her entrance.

"Well, it just occurred to me that with quite a simple alteration to your dress … I mean, you play it in the fashion of the *early* eighteenth century, but if you reset it to the Regency period … look!" And, greatly daring, she took the lady's mantilla and draped it in a triangle from a point halfway down her ample cleavage. "See! They all looked *enceinte* in that period."

A silent Mrs Fitzroy pinned it there with a single imperious finger and turned to examine herself in a half-length glass. "Drat it, Fitzroy, if the gel ain't right," she said.

Her husband tugged at his beard, à la Brabantio in *Othello.* His silence was agreement.

"If we can postpone tomorrow's performances," she went on, "I could remake the costume."

"Postpone?" he roared.

Noel cleared his throat to speak, but Rose, knowing what he was about to say, forestalled him; later she assured herself she would have done so anyway. "I'm as good a needlewoman as you'll find anywhere in Cornwall," she began.

"In England," Noel said.

"Shut *up!*" she told him. "I'll do it for a quid. And I'll patch this burn mark … and you need a gusset in here …"

"Done!" Lord Gordon said grandly.

"You could have waited till she'd finished saying all what she was doing for a quid," his wife chided.

"You may commence upon the instant!" He waved expansively toward a rickety bentwood chair and a card table."

"I prefer to work by daylight, thanks all the same," Rose replied. "Don't worry, it'll be ready in time for the matinée. I'll be here just after dawn."

"Dawn?" He stared at her aghast. "D'you mean there really *is* such a moment in each day's round?"

"Dawn," she said. "I'll bring my own sewing things. Just leave the entire costume out on that table. I'll be here."

"You should have asked for more than you did," Noel said as they walked away.

"Oh but I shall!" she said, amused.

"What?" He frowned at her. "Leave it late and hold them to ransom? No, Rose, that's not …"

"Oh, I'll do *this* job for a quid, but not the rest. Didn't you notice the other costumes? They're threadbare most of them. There's not one of them there can use a needle properly. I reckon there's ten days' work just on the costumes they used tonight – and lord alone knows what horrors they've got stuffed away in baskets."

"But they leave Falmouth in two days. They're playing in Helston all next week."

She chuckled. "Then I shall just have to go along with them – won't I!"

28

They did not go directly to the Prince of Wales for dinner. Rose went home first, partly to give her parents a brief and heavily edited summary of recent events but mainly to ask them to leave out the key as she'd need her old bed for the night. She said nothing of Louis' bankruptcy just then.

Dinner was every bit as slap up as Noel had promised – oysters, game soup, tournedos Rossini, mangoes in lemon water-ice, rounded off with Turkish delight and coffee. Rose pondered the irony of two grand dinners on two consecutive nights – for a girl with no secure position and very few prospects.

Noel had not heard of Louis' smash but he was in no doubt that she should go to him at once, wherever he might be, and support him in his climb back to prosperity. "I only met the fellow for a few minutes," he said, "but if you ask me to put my penny on the drum – *he's* not going to stay down for very long. Unless," he added, watching her closely for her response, "he fritters away his time hunting for you!"

"He knows where to find me," she replied uncomfortably, and repeated the argument she had made to Sally – that even if Louis accepted her and married her, she could never be certain that he had not acted out of a sense of duty, honouring a pledge he had made in quite different circumstances. It had sounded quite convincing the first time. Now it seemed less so, which perhaps had something to do with the way Noel just kept on looking at her, saying nothing.

"He would never be sure, either," she added.

He just shrugged and said, "Very well. If that's what you truly feel, Rose."

"You think I'm lying," she challenged.

"I think you could be deceiving yourself."

After an uncomfortable silence she said, "You'll have to explain that, I'm afraid."

"No I don't." He grinned. "But here's something I *do* have to do." He assembled a pile of four sovereigns, four half-crowns, and three florins upon the tablecloth, pushing them across to her as croupiers move piles of chips at casinos.

She saw their waiter raise his eyebrows and then have a word with the head man, at which both of them watched their table with a suspicious eye. She realized what sort of transaction they thought they were witnessing – rich young swell and servant girl – their only surprise was that it was done so blatantly. She folded her menu and pushed it back with a smile, saying, "Give it to me later – somewhere where the eyes of the evil-minded are not able to witness it."

"Thoughtless of me!" He blushed. "It never crossed my mind."

Hoping he now felt vulnerable, she said, "Even if you don't *have to* explain, you might do it as a favour to me. How might I be deceiving myself?"

He picked the coins up one by one, slowly and lazily, dropping them back into his pocket with a *clink!* each time. "D'you believe in destiny, Rose?" he asked. "I do. I don't think I was really *destined* to be one of the idle rich – not that I'm rich at the moment, mind, but I will be in a couple of years. I tell you – when I walked up onto the stage of the Empire that night it was like ..." His eyes raked the ornate ceiling of the hotel dining room. "It was like coming home. To my real home, I mean. Standing up there on the stage ..."

"I thought you were going to tell me about *me?*" she interjected.

"I'm getting round to it – honest. I'm talking about destiny. I felt that was my destiny. Standing up there, on stage – I mean, they only get the desperate amateurs up there so's they can mock them, you realize? I was almost taking my life in my hands. And there I was, facing a barrage of hostile eyes and sneering faces – as much as I could see, which was only half a dozen rows – but knowing there were hundreds more in the dark behind them – and then I started to sing." He sang softly there, at the table. *"She was poor but she was honest, / Victim of the squire's whim. / First he loved her, then he left her, / And she lost her maiden name!"* He gave an embarrassed laugh but she was enthralled by now, for he did, indeed, have a fine voice – which she had never even suspected.

How could two people live under the same roof for two years and one of them not know such a thing about the other? Easy if one was a servant and the other high-quarter!

"Et cetera – all ten verses," he continued. "They were a bit rowdy at first, especially up in the gods, and I thought I was going to be lucky to escape with my life. But I was determined to go on with it. I sang it in my toff's voice, of course, because I can't do accents 'loike wot yoo can'!"

She winced at his attempt. "I see what you mean."

"But the toff's accent surprised them – the ones in front who could hear me over the boos and hisses. And then I began to hear them shushing each other – starting down there in the front stalls but soon spreading back right across the pit. And then it spread to the gallery, and the upper gallery, and then the gods. And *then* you could hear a pin drop. Oh, Rose! That moment! That moment when you know you've got two thousand people eating out of your hand – I tell you, there's nothing like it."

His eyes gleamed and she saw he was shivering all over. She reached across and grasped his arm. "Oh, Noel! What are you going to do?"

"I don't know." He shook his head. "It's like a drug, you know. Even just sitting here, telling you about it ... I can feel the craving coming on again."

"Is that why you went to the theatre tonight?"

"Tonight?" He laughed and flapped a hand at her. "No! That was just to remind myself of where I'd have to begin. Nobody walks straight into top billing at the Holborn Empire, believe you me! I'd have to spend years in smoking concerts at the head of Southend Pier or music halls down in the East End. And I don't know I'd have the patience for that – not if I had all those lovely spondulicks wilting away in the bank."

"So what's your destiny, then?"

"I don't know – something to do with the theatre, even if I haven't the patience – or guts – or whatever it takes to be a performer. But what I was *really* going to say was that we're in the same boat, you and me. We've both been born into the wrong ... what can I call it? The wrong life-story. You're a bloody good lady's maid – pardon the French – but it's not what you were born for. Don't you feel that?"

She laughed grimly. "I should think three quarters of the lady's maids in the country fondly imagine they were born for something better. Three quarters of *any* group of people, come to that. I'll bet three quarters of all the dukes think they'd make a better king than this one!"

"Well, anyway," he said cheerfully. "You've taken the first step. The most important one."

"What? Sewing a few costumes for a group of strolling players?"

"No, you goose. Much more important than that."

"What, then?"

"You've burned all your bridges behind you! You've nowhere else to turn."

"Oh, that! Yeah – thanks so much for reminding me."

Rose did not get home until gone midnight. She let herself in as quietly as possible, only to find her mother waiting up. Her first words were, "You don't have to do this, honey – going off with these fit-ups. There's a place here at home for you – always – you know that. Certainly until Louis Redmile-Smith comes back to claim you as his bride!"

Rose explained about Louis and gave her by now tired-sounding reasons for not rushing to his side. Like everyone else, her mother told her she was being just too darn fastidious. Though Rose had slept all morning and half the afternoon, she was, by now, too tired to argue. "Thanks, Mom," she yawned, "but that's the way it is with me. And anyway, you know the business won't support three."

"Well, we could each do some part-time work. They're building a new canteen down at ..."

"No, Mom – honestly. I know this work with Lord Gordon's Players isn't going to last out the month but I hope by that time that they'll consider me indispensable."

"How?"

"I don't know yet. I'll just keep my eyes open. I'll find something. But wardrobe mistress will only be part of it."

"Well ... hon ... as long as that's the *only* kind of mistress this Lord Gordon will expect you to be!"

"Mom!" She gave an embarrassed laugh.

"Sshh! You'll wake your Paw."

"Although ..." Rose said hesitantly.

"What?"

Curious to see how her mother would react, she said, "You've heard of Roger Deveril – you remember Dad talking about him when I came for Sunday dinner? Well ... you know how people say he ruined Ruby Penhallow? But d'you know what really happened? She tricked him into giving her that baby and even so ..."

"Honey – every seducer who ever lived will say that as soon as the paternity summons drops on the mat!"

"No, listen! Ruby Penhallow is now living in London – in a charming little villa in Maida Vale, with her own lady's maid and cook and coachman – and her own phæton, in which she rides in Hyde Park every afternoon ..."

"Oh – one of them!"

"Yes, one of *them.* With beautiful clothes and jewelry and things. And four hundred pounds a year – four hundred and fifty with tips and presents and things."

"And Roger Deveril is the one paying for all this? Is that what he told you, too?"

"No. Her protector – that's what he called him – is John Thynne, the Sixth Baron Carteret. But ..." She hesitated.

"Go on," her mother said.

"Promise you won't scream or explode or anything?"

"I'll do my best not to." She shifted nervously.

Rose produced Deveril's card and passed it over. "He made me a similar offer. He asked me to think it over and let him know."

She held her breath.

Her mother's face was completely unreadable as she scanned the card, turned it over, and over, and scanned it again. "So," she said at length. "What's all this about going off with Lord Gordon's Players? The raggle-taggle gypsies-oh!"

For a moment Rose could see no connection. Then it dawned on her that Mom expected her to have accepted Roger's offer – otherwise the question made no sense at all. She was dumbstruck.

She handed back the card, adding. "You mean you're only filling in time while you string him out?"

Rose gulped. "You think I should say yes?"

"I don't know the man, of course, but from the way you were talking ... well, I didn't get the feeling he was some kind of *ogre.*"

"No! He's very handsome and witty and ... just good fun. No one could blame Ruby. He's very ... well, let's just say he knows how to treat a woman."

Her mother caught the insinuation in her tone and said, "Oh?"
It was all Rose needed to spur her into a full account of her peremptory dismissal last night, and the events that preceded it.
When she had finished her mother said, "So he left you wanting more, huh? Smart man!"
"You're not shocked?"
"Oh, listen honey – in an ideal world this proposed arrangement is about number fifty on the list of desirable outcomes. But you can tell how far off that ideal you are by the fact that, until you mentioned this Deveril's offer, I was thinking how lucky you were to earn a pound and maybe more patching up some old theater costumes! So we're not talking about the forty-nine choices that come before number fifty – because they jess ain't thar!"
"You think I ought to say yes, then?"
"That's up to you, honey. I just don't think a downright no is anyways too smart right now – that's all." She licked her lower lip and, eyeing Rose shrewdly, said, "You wouldn't find the ... how shall I put it? The *work* side of the bargain too unpleasant?"
Rose looked down at her hands, sure her ears were going scarlet. "I don't think so."
"And what about Louis?"
"Oh, Roger promised me he need never find out."
Her mother laughed loudly before clapping a hand to her mouth and listening fearfully for sounds of her husband's stirring. Reassured, she continued, "That ain't exactly what I meant, honey – but I guess it answers the question, in its own way."
She continued staring at her daughter until the girl felt compelled to ask, "What now?"
"I've often thought it," she replied. "As you moved up the domestics' ladder to lady's maid, I often used to hope you wouldn't get *too* good at it – because it would only trap you there. I never thought you were meant to be in service. Not all your life."
"That's funny – you're the second person to tell me that in as many hours." She explained about Noel. Then she cried, "Oh damn! I'm *never* going to get that four-pound-sixteen!" She had to explain that, too.
Her mother said, "You're gonna jump down my throat when I say this – I know – but I kinda think your real reason for not running to Louis, even in his hour of need, is ..."
"He needs *money* – hundreds of thousands – not me!"
"Just hear me out. I think there's something inside you that has always known you weren't cut out to be in service for ever. And that same something also tells you that running from lady's maid to wife is like leaping out of the skillet onto the coals. Right at this moment you want independence even more than you want Louis – which doesn't mean you don't love him. It just means you've got to be *you* – fully yourself – before you can think of being you-and-him. Tell me I'm crazy!"

Every word her mother spoke fell on Rose's ears like a truth they had been hungering to hear. Out of all the hithering-thithering confused thinking and talking of the past two days – or weeks, or whatever – this was the truth around which her mind had wheeled and circled without ever being able to see it clearly. "Yes!" she cried ecstatically, even as a further thought struck her. "And – you know what? – *that's* why I'm going to say no to Roger. It's not because it's immoral. Nor because, God knows, I couldn't do with the money. Nor because I wouldn't enjoy keeping my side of the bargain in bed with him – to say nothing of beautiful clothes and the carriage and things. It's what you just said. I've got to be myself first. Not this man's something or that man's something else but my own *me.*" She laughed and clapped her hands. "Or, to put it another way, 'This night I shall wander into the far-off – the promised land!'"

29

Rose had Leah's costume changed from earliest Georgian to Regency by noon, well in time for the Saturday matinée at two. Mrs Fitzroy was delighted with the effect, not least because it meant they could all go back to – or, at least, get *closer* to – the original script, in which Rudolf and Leah had fallen in love a mere week or ten days before curtain-up, and chastely in love at that. Other members of the cast watched her plying the needle with the same fascination as Rose felt in watching them at their trade.

Mr Dudley Dennison, the magistrate and Rudolf's father, who was sixty if he was a day, sought her opinion on the correct placing of his kerchief if the time of the whole play were to be transposed to the end of the eighteenth century. Rose, who had no real knowledge of the subject, nonetheless spoke her opinion with complete confidence: He should wear it tucked into the left sleeve rather than the right. He went away practising a number of new flourishes. Although they were nothing alike to look at, there was something about the old fellow that reminded her of Roanoke. Both had the same tasteful courtesy – and the same lacklustre eyes when they looked at her. In passing she found several defects in his costume, which she promised to remedy if Lord Gordon would consent to it.

Mr Ralph (pronounced 'Rayfe') Lamb, the Barber-Doctor-Butcher *et al,* who was no more than twenty-two, was quite the opposite. His eyes sparkled as they looked her up and down. His costumes were immaculately cleaned and pressed but she still managed to find several defects in the material itself, which she said she could remedy if Lord Gordon would consent to it.

Miss Titania Moore, Madalena and Old Sara, was even younger – no more than twenty, Rose guessed. She was blonde, and pretty enough when made up, but was still awkward with her movements upon the stage. She was patronizing in her behaviour toward Rose, whom she treated as a near-Unfortunate – until Rose discovered that her costumes had been cut down and cut up and cut across from costumes made for actresses long departed, actresses with shapes quite different from hers. She said she could remedy every single one of these faults – if Lord Gordon would consent to it.

Mr Walter Rendle, Schoolmaster Carl, alias Nathan the Apostate Jew, and other small parts, was thirty-five, though he behaved as though he were ten years younger. Miss Moore said it was because he always played the parts of elderly men – so, off-stage, he tried to compensate by acting younger all the time. His costumes were in fairly good condition but the padding he wore to simulate the gravitas of age was lumpy and unconvincing. Rose said she could rework it to fit both the clothes and his own elegantly slim contours – if Fitzroy would consent to it.

Mrs Hortensia Skerrett, Dame Gertrude, Mother Groschen, and Old Peasant Woman at Spinning Wheel, was a fat, jolly, character actress admitting to thirty-eight. Of all the cast she had managed to keep her costumes in the best condition; but her corsets, which she had not renewed for some years, when she was many pounds lighter, were killing her. They were of the finest whalebone and had cost a small fortune, so she was reluctant to discard them just yet. But, oh, the laces did cut into her spine somethink crewel! Rose thought that she could unpick the seams and let in a panel on each side, which would go some way to alleviating her distress – if Lord Gordon would consent to it. (And, she added silently, if we may have them laundered first.)

And finally came Mr Brian Swindlehurst, Father Herman, Tailor, and Baker, who was in his early forties. He had watched Rose at work, not simply upon Mrs Fitzroy's costume but on the vanity and fears of the rest of the cast as well. "I think you'll find no fault with mine, my dear," he said with a wink. "But if it will help, I can easily manufacture an insignificant cut or rip here and there."

She looked up into his eyes and saw it was pointless to pretend. "Was it so obvious?" she asked.

"Only to one not *utterly* consumed by vanity – or, in Mister Lamb's case, by the charming flutter of your eyelashes. I must say that of all the ruses that young men and women pick to join a theatre company, yours is among the best. I tell you what – you keep my street clothes neatly sponged and pressed, and I'll put in a good word for you with old Fitzroy. Is that fair?"

Rose considered the matter briefly and said she thought it pretty fair – if he was also willing to throw in the odd bit of advice. "For instance, how much d'you think I should ask per week to stay on and do all this work on the general wardrobe?"

"Twenty-five bob plus board and lodging – which is bed, breakfast, and evening meal," he said. "Be prepared to drop to a quid but then remember to ask for an early review – after you've been with us a month, say."

"A month!" She was pleasantly surprised. "D'you think there's as much work as all that?"

"Not on the costumes – at least, not if you keep up your present astonishing rate. But once you're on the road with us, you'll find other things to occupy you, I'm sure. I'll wager you're a wizard at painting scenery. And you can handle papier mâché like a baker his dough. And you'll be able to tidy up the props basket so that nothing will ever go astray again. How's your eyesight? Magnificent enough, I'm sure, to read prompt by candlelight. And tomorrow evening, when we strike the tent, you could gather up the pegs – they *always* go missing. Oh, a resourceful girl like you will surely become indispensable well within a month! And then you'll be able to insist on twenty-five bob. Shall I bring you my trousers for pressing now?"

Taking this hint, Rose stood in the wings during that matinée, holding the new script – the one that did not need to take account of Mrs Fitzroy's condition – and following the action with it. There were two 'dries,' as she later learned to call them – one by Brian Swindlehurst (which Rose did not think was entirely genuine, bless him) and one by the great Lord Gordon himself. She rescued them both with a prompt that did not even carry to the first row.

When he came off at the end of the scene, Lord Gordon gave her the oddest look and, after thanking her, said, "Just one thing, my precious. The prompt must speak the missing words in the flattest possible diction."

"Why?" she asked. "What did I do?"

"You *acted* the words – like the troupe in Elsinore, lassie. Just remember what Hamlet had to say to them!"

He was pleased, though, because the new version was going down much better with the audience.

After that, she was both prompt and needlewoman.

Between the matinée and the evening performance, several members of the cast showed him the defects she had spotted and they suggested, as if it were entirely their own idea, that the new needlewoman should take care of the problem. He said he would consider it.

Word of the improvements in the production had obviously gone around the town, for the evening show was a sell-out and there were plenty of advance bookings for the final two performances on the morrow. It put Lord Gordon in such a good mood that, before the make-up was off that night, he had consented to keeping Rose on for a month – at a pound a week plus board and lodging. Her title was wardrobe mistress and assistant stage manager. She asked who the stage manager was and he said they didn't need one now they had her. The cast had digs up in Killigrew Road. She and Miss Moore would share.

The cast went off for pasties and something to wet their whistles. Rose went home to tell her parents and collect her things. Her father said it was a big come-down from being lady's maid to titled gentry but if it was what she really wanted, she should do it. Her mother said that most people would consider a strolling actress little better than "you know what, honey – the things we were discussing earlier."

In reply, Rose protested she was not going to be an actress but wardrobe mistress and stage manager (she decided to promote herself to the ever-vacant post).

Her mother's eye was coldly sceptical but she said nothing, preferring to change the subject. "And what do we tell Louis Redmile-Smith?" she asked. "He's sure to come looking for you here the minute he's able."

She had already thought of that. "I'll write him a note tonight. I won't post it. I'll leave it with you to give to him. He may not come at all. It depends on whether his mother lives or dies – and, if she lives, how well she is."

Tears sprouted suddenly behind her eyelids and a lump in her throat made talking difficult. Ashamed of her weakness, she went to the front window, which overlooked the docks. It was shrouded in darkness now, but the occasional brilliance of an arc lamp, here and there, created startling vignettes of toy ships and antlike men, set in a warm, velvety blackness.

Her memory supplied every detail the shrouded moon could not reveal, for she had gazed out at this scene from her earliest childhood. And not just gazed at, but loved – from this window, from other windows in the town, where she had been in service, and from Nancemellin across the water there. She could just make out the lights in a couple of its windows, though if she moved her head, the sailor's home blotted them out.

And it suddenly struck her that she was about to leave all this behind her – possibly for ever! How could she not have thought of it before? Tomorrow, Falmouth and all its dear little alleys and passages, all the people she grew up with, the ones who called out her name and stopped to pass the time of day, the ones who just smiled, waved, nodded – even the ones who remembered ancient hurts and looked the other way – she was leaving it all behind. That whole, rich reticule of loving, liking, disdaining, hating, of memories shared – she was wrenching herself out of it. And for what? For one anonymous, interchangeable town after another, places where no one knew her and she knew no one, where the eyes of women would judge her for her fashions and assumed pretensions – and the eyes of men? For her availability.

Panic seized her. She suddenly felt she was about to make the most monumental mistake of her life. Surely *any* kind of position, no matter how menial, would be preferable to that – if only she could stay in Falmouth? A scullerymaid, even, as long as she could still roam these beloved streets at will and feast her eyes on these cherished scenes?

The tears streamed down her face and hung cold at the angle of her jaw; when she swallowed she displaced them and they ran down her neck to soak into her collar. Her mother put her arms around her and hugged in wordless comfort. Her father came and touched her neck, stroking it gently with loving, calloused fingers.

"You can still say no," her mother said at last. "After all, it's not your only choice."

But it was. Standing in the prompt corner that evening, watching the tawdry magic of the play work its nightly miracle on an audience of which she was no longer part, she had suddenly realized that she would not consider Deveril's offer now, not even for ten times the money. Her mother's words, by sparking that memory, were a more effective rescue from her panic than any others she might have spoken. There *was* a magic – tawdry or not – in front of the footlights. And, at least while the play was on, there was a camaraderie more intense than anything she had ever known. You could sense it from the moment the curtain rose. And it was now her privilege to become a part of that bright company. Actually, there was nothing so very wonderful about Falmouth, with its grubby little alleys, filled with people who knew half your history (the discreditable half, of course) and made up the rest to match. No, a few anonymous towns, where no one knew her from Eve and she could become anything she wanted, were just what her life needed right now.

The tears vanished, her cheeks dried, and a genuine smile brought back the colour. "Just a moment when it all seemed too much," she said apologetically. "It'll be better tomorrow – and I'll come and say a proper goodbye before we leave for Helston."

"Helston!" her mother exclaimed. "Why, that's only a shilling return by bus."

Precisely what relevance the observation might have was unclear to Rose, for they all knew that her mother would never find the time, much less squander the money on such a journey, merely to see a daughter who'd left home a week ago. And yet its hollow comfort was oddly comforting.

Her father took her large suitcase and laid it on newspaper in the cart they used for deliveries and for hauling vegetables from the station. He harnessed the horse and took her to her night's lodgings in Killigrew Road, which was halfway up the hill leading out of the southern corner of the Moor. They drove the first furlong in silence, as far as the Custom House, where Rose said, "Are you cudgelling your brains for something wise to tell me?"

He laughed awkwardly. "Something like that. But I daresay if we didn't rear our nestle-bird aright till she were fourteen, and life didn't fill out the holidays since, then whatever I could say now would be neither gick nor gack."

"Funny," she replied. "I always thought I was a bit kitey – that if I wasn't in service but had the run of myself, I should do edjack things. I thought the discipline of service was needful – to stop me going all, you know ..."

"Betwattled?" he suggested.

"The very word! But I've been free of it, well ... more'n a week, really – and the temptations I've had to 'go all betwattled' you wouldn't believe! But I turned my face from them – and that's a strength to me now." She patted her father's hand. "So you rest easy o' nights, you hear? I'll not shame you and Mom."

He carried her suitcase into Mrs Montmorency's, the company's lodgings, and hastened back out into the relative dark of the gaslit street. There they hugged in silence, kissed, and parted, pretending not to notice the tears on each other's cheeks.

Mrs M offered her 'a dish o' tay and a bit chat' when she realized Rose was from Falmouth, too. The 'bit chat' lasted an hour, which, for Rose, was like packing away her memories, one by one. But as soon as they heard the company returning, she shut the door to her parlour and cleared the tray away to where it could not be seen by someone who merely poked his head in at the door – which Lord Gordon did only moments later.

"On our way up the wooden hill to Bedfordshire, dear lady," he said. Then, noticing Rose through his beery stupor. "Ah! Our neophyte! Our acolyte! Our ingénue!" His wife plucked him back into the corridor in mid-flourish.

Rose was horrified to discover that she was expected to share not just a room but a bed as well with Miss Titania Moore, who had clearly not taken a bath for – at a charitable estimate – at least a week. She herself had no bath at home, of course, but she had strip-washed from head to foot each morning, as always.

"Will you bath first?" she asked, "or shall I?"

"Oh, God!" Miss Moore said wearily. "You're one of the fussy ones, are you. It costs tuppence for the geyser, you know. It's not free." Her breath was gin-laden but she did not appear drunk, or even tipsy.

"I think I could just about stretch to that," Rose said.

"Oh well, in that case, I'll go first." But when she reached the bathroom door she turned back. "On second thoughts, I'm not going to nod off and then have you waking me up. We'll bath together – it's big enough."

It was, too – a cast-iron giant in crazed, once-white enamel standing on four silver feet that looked as if they'd been hacked from a metallic crocodile. The geyser resembled the funnel of a substantial ship and its flames were like a forest of sailmaker's needles, six inches tall. But the water came out piping hot and at a satisfactory rate.

Rose stripped off and then, not wishing to gawp at Miss Moore, who was making a pile of her jewelry, turned to read an Important

Announcement in poetic form on the wall. *Please remember,* it ran, *don't forget / Never leave the bathroom wet. / Nor leave the soap still in the water. / That's a thing you never 'orter'! / Nor keep the bath an hour or more / When other folks are wanting one. / Just don't forget – it isn't done!* There was more.

"Funny woman," she murmured.

"Who? Mrs Monty-thingy? That poem's in every boarding house in England, I should think. Some have drawings by Kate Greenaway. Give us a hand with these corsets, there's an angel."

While Rose's fingers worked at the knot, Miss Moore went on, "Ever done It, have you, darling?"

"What?" Rose started. "You mean ...?"

"Yes. With a man."

"I think that's a private matter, really, don't you?"

"Oh, well – suit yourself. I was just wondering if you could tell me if it's worth the bother?"

"I'm afraid I wouldn't know."

"See! You could have said that in the first place."

"No – I mean whether it's worth *your* bother. Only you can judge that, surely?"

"Oooh! Sharp!"

"What's it mean when the flames go up and down?"

"It means the meter's running out. Never mind. There's oodles of lovely hot water here. We'll have to put in some cold."

The geyser died as she opened the cold tap. She bent over the bath to swirl the water round – showing everything. Rose stared in amazement, never having seen such a display before, then joined her guiltily and swirled the water round, too. Servant girls were usually very prudish with each other. She'd shared many a room – and bed – with other girls but Mary was the only one she had ever seen in a state of nature, and never in such an exhibitionist pose as that.

Miss Moore leaped into the end away from the taps and soaped herself vigorously. "Heavens, but you were right, Miss Tremayne," she said as the loofah picked up rolls of rubbed-off skin. "See!"

"Yes." Rose suppressed a shudder and climbed in beside her. "Where's the soap? Don't leave it in the water."

"That's a thing you never orter!"

They both giggled. While Rose soaped her upper half, Miss Moore lay back, threw her legs in the air and wriggled like an eel to wash off the soap.

I could have behaved like this when I was eleven, Rose thought, wondering how old the girl really was.

They both stood up and lathered their legs. "You're right," Miss Moore said. "I really-really needed this. I think you're going to be good for me, Miss Tremayne. Perhaps you can help me sort out my life, too?"

"Matthew fifteen, fourteen," Rose replied with a laugh.

"The Bible?" she guessed.

"Where it says: 'If the blind lead the blind, both shall fall into the ditch.' Yes."

"Oh God – you're not religious, are you?"

"Not more than most." Rose lay down discreetly on her front and rolled her body from side to side in the water. "Scrub each other's backs now?"

Miss Moore started on hers. "Blind leading the blind, eh," she mused. "So is your life in a bit of a mess, too?"

"Whose isn't?" Rose replied defensively. "Once you get beneath the surface."

"Ha! You needn't go very far beneath the surface of mine to see the mess. Is that nice?"

Rose arched her back into the pressure of the loofah. "Just below the shoulderblades ... yes! Oooaah!" She shivered with pleasure. "I'll listen if you like, but I'll warn you – I'm not one, myself, to wear my heart on my sleeve. That's enough – you could sponge it off now."

While she scrubbed Miss Moore's back, the girl said, "I'm from a very good family – as you can probably hear. I mean, Mumsie is absolutely *appalled* at my going on the stage. Even I can still hardly believe it."

"How long have you ..."

"Donkey's years! Six months."

"And your father?"

"Oh, Daddy's chief accountant at a bank. Need I say more? He washed his hands of me ten years ago ..."

"When you were ...?"

"Ten, of course. Didn't I tell you I was still a minor? Really they could snatch me back and it wouldn't be kidnapping. But they know I'd only run away again. That's lovely – you can do that for ever and ever!"

"When you say 'run away' – is that as in 'run away *to'* something or 'run away *from'* something?"

"To. I never wanted to do anything but act, you see – even though I'm not very good at it yet."

"You will be when you have a properly fitting costume!"

"Eh? Oh, yes – of course!" She laughed but was soon serious again. "The thing is, can an actress ever be any good unless she had known suffering? I mean – playing Madalena, now ... she's such a little goody-goody, don't you think? Being so good and kind toward Leah even when she knows the little Jewess is stealing her lifelong sweetheart. She's either a fool or a long-suffering saint – and I haven't known enough suffering to play her like that. See what I mean? What d'you think I ought to do? How can I experience suffering without it hurting too much?"

Rose cleared her throat delicately. "Is *this* the mess you mean – when you say your life's in a mess?"

Miss Moore looked back over her shoulder in surprise. "Of course – what else? Madalena *is* my life just at the moment. What can I do?"

Rose sponged the soap off the girl's back, thinking furiously.

"Eh?" she prompted after a long silence.

"Well, Miss Moore, I'm afraid the only truthful answer is: Try to persuade Lord Gordon to put on a more subtle drama. The characters in *Leah, the Forsaken* all run by clockwork. You wind the Villain up and he plays the Villain; you wind the Hero up and he plays the Hero. There's only one really wild, genuine, human moment in the whole drama – which is when Leah utters her great curse, alone in the churchyard."

"Yes!" Miss Moore turned to face her, eyes sparkling.

"However!" She held up a finger of warning. "You must have noticed how uneasy it makes the audience? They wouldn't pay to see it if the whole play were like that. *Then* you'd be able to suffer for the sake of your art!" She laughed and the girl joined in.

They rolled this way and that, dipping their colder parts into the hot water until it was no longer hot. Then they got out and started to dry off.

"You going to be long in there?" Mr Lamb shouted from outside the door. Rose could see the yellow of his dressing gown as it recoloured the mock stained glass in the door panels.

Miss Moore ran to the door and pulled her own dressing gown to the left, draping its lower part over the doorknob. "One can see through that bit where the transfer has scraped off," she whispered to Rose. "It's not real stained glass, you know. It's only a transfer."

Rose asked how she knew one could see through that bit.

She giggled and said, "Because I've done it! And I'm sure Mister Lamb does, too. He keeps trying to persuade me I'll never play a love scene properly until I've let a man – he means *him,* of course – make a woman of me. D'you think he's right? That's why I asked if you'd done It. What should I tell him?"

"I think that depends on what *you* want." Rose hunted for her toothbrush and dentifrice in her sponge bag. Miss Moore must have had a conscience somewhere, she thought, for she was now cleaning out a rather disgusting bath with white scouring powder.

"I don't think I want to, to be honest."

"Then tell him about the Knights of King Arthur's Round Table – how their valour and chivalry increased along with their dedication to chastity. Now – is there anything else you'd like to know before we return to our room. I have a letter to write – but I promise not to disturb you when I come to bed at last."

30

My dearest darling darling darling Louis,

How I wish I could be whispering those words, those loveliest of all words, into your ear, instead of sitting here in this cheerless boarding house, past midnight, with nothing but drunkards and cats astir, committing them to paper for you. If you are reading them, then it means you have come looking for me – to honour your promise, I am sure. Already you must have asked yourself why I am not there, waiting for you? Why have I not sought you out? Why did I not race to your side the moment I heard the dreadful news?

Believe me, there was nothing I desired more than to do that. Hour by hour I thought of you, and only you, sitting at your poor mother's side with the rest of your world collapsing around you, and every nerve within me urging me to join you there, to share the worst as I would happily have shared the best. And I still must fight that urge. But why? If you ask it, you are not the only one. I have shared our secret completely with just three people – my parents and my oldest friend from school. All of them tell me I am mad, wrong, sinful even, not to be with you at this hour. I suspect you are of their mind, too. I can only answer that I would not be a burden to you. I mean I would not <u>want</u> to be a burden to you.

You made your vows to me at a time when you were sure you could overcome whatever difficulties you and the company faced. You promised you would return to 'claim' me, prosperous once more and ready to cock a snook at Society and its narrow-minded ways. And now it must seem to you that, since <u>for the moment</u> our difficulties endure (though I am sure it is temporary), I am no longer interested in you. I forgive you utterly for the suspicion, unless you persist in it. The truth is – and you must surely acknowledge this – that a business-man down on his luck is one thing. He may still fight his way back to a new prosperity. But if you, a business-man, and I, a servant girl, choose to marry at the very pit of our fortunes, we must turn ourselves into some kind of laughing stock among the very people you will need to help restore your position in the world.

"He has obviously given up," they will say of you. "How can we invite him to this dinner, this club, those functions, when he has <u>that</u> wife?"

I will not become such a millstone for your neck.

I had thought I might overcome those objections. My parents will tell you I worked for a week as valet (yes, <u>valet!</u>) to a rich Falmouth eccentric called Henry Roanoke, who, for a hoax, persuaded me to play the part of his niece and act as his hostess at a dinner for some of Falmouth's high and mighty ones. And, amazingly, we carried it off! Not one of them suspected I was not as high-born as they. So I have no doubt but that, taking one day with another, I could satisfy your most suspicious acquaintances of my high-quarter credentials. But sooner or later the truth would out. You know, from your life on your side of the green baize door (and I certainly know it from life on my side of it!) that such attempts at a life-long deception will always fail. Someone would recognize me. A servant would see my birth certificate alongside our marriage lines. My photograph from when I won the Falmouth Packet essay competition two years ago would stare up at someone out of the drawer lined with that particular issue. Who knows? But out it would surely come!

And then you would not simply be the fool who married a servant-maid; you would be the liar who tried to brazen it out all these years. I cannot risk tarring you with that brush merely because I ache with every fibre of my being to lie in your arms and whisper, "Husband!" So do everything you must, my darling, to restore yourself to fortune. Then, when you can once again thumb your nose at the silly folk we must presently live among, if you still want me, I am yours. At least, I shall never be anyone's else while you remain unspoken for.

And I, meanwhile? What shall I be doing? Well, our behaviour that wondrous afternoon – Saturday, the 18th June, 1910, as I shall never forget – ensured my instantaneous dismissal by her ladyship, followed up, as a boxer's right hand is followed by his left, by a scurrilous announcement in the papers. That and my lack of character from her ensured I could never again obtain a place in Cornwall. And I am sure she would have harried me to John o' Groats had I applied for a position up there. Besides, even a lady's maid cannot put aside more than £30 a year for her bottom drawer. So I have embarked upon a career that may (I only say may) hold out the promise of a great deal more.

Calme toi, chérie! It is quite respectable, so I have no qualms in admitting it at once: I hope to become an actress! At the moment I am but an humble wardrobe mistress and principal stage manager to a troupe of strolling players – Lord Gordon Fitzroy's Players, to be precise – but I see it as no more than my foot upon the first rung of the ladder. I have a Plan – but I shall not divulge it here in case it should fall into the wrong hands. (I am having to write this while the rest of the company snores – not least my room-mate, Miss Titania Moore.)

And who put this absurd idea into my head? Why you! And Noel Carclew. And Mr Roanoke. But chiefly you.

I must close now, gadzooks, for I must be up betimes!

Seriously, I cannot give you our forwarding address because, as I said, we stroll from town to town, or, rather, travel in a rickety looking 'cherry-bang' and a furniture lorry that has seen many better days – and furnishings. But you may always write to me c/o my parents, and I shall endeavour to collect from them as frequently as possible. If you will let them know your directions, they can let me know and I shall write directly to you from thenceforward.

Be brave, my dearest Louis – as I know you are. Be strong. Be clever. Many an engagement is cruelly prolonged by the need for the two lovers to be able to afford the burdens of a household. We are in no different a situation from those many. We simply have a bigger hole to climb out of, that is all. Meanwhile you must know that not an hour passes but I think of you – and sigh for you, even though I alone can hear it. Every laugh I give to others seems a betrayal of you, but I masquerade as well as I can, as far as I must. Think of me each day at noon and you shall feel your ears burn with the passion of my thinking toward you. I love you I love you I love you I love you I love you I love you I love you I love you I love you I love you ...

For all eternity,
Lucinda-Ella

O that 'twere possible
After long grief and pain
To find the arms of my true love
Round me once again!
– Alfred Lord You-know-who

END OF PART TWO

Part Three

Overture and Beginners

31 Lord Gordon Fitzroy's Players had a standard handbill, which ran: 'Due to overwhelming popular demand from the discriminating playgoing public of [blank for town], Lord Gordon Fitzroy and his Players will be returning to [blank for venue] to present a short season of inspiring dramas, new and old. They will begin with [blank for title] on [blank for date] ... etc.' There followed the cast list, or *Dramatis Personæ,* for the play in question, which was set out in a descriptive rather than tabular mode. That is, not:
MADALENA ... ... (Niece of Father Herman) ... ... Miss Moore.
but: *The part of MADALENA, the chaste and angelic niece of Father Herman, will be played by the ravishingly beautiful Miss Titania Moore.* And so forth.

The blank for the title occupied almost half the bill because it had to allow for an electrotype illustration of a scene from the drama, usually pirated from the title-page of the *Dick's Standard Plays* version of the drama.

Rose learned that one of the most important tasks of the assistant stage manager was to get some local printer to overprint the blanks and then visit the next town, a week ahead of the Players, and offer the bills to shopkeepers, business premises, churches ... even private householders in important locations, for display; in return they would receive one free ticket for each bill. Lord Gordon had already distributed the ones for Helston, of course, but, he now suggested, she could slip over there on the bus and do a surprise inspection of the shops, business premises, and so on, to see that they were sticking to their side of the bargain. And while she was at it, she could have another go at these and these people – he gave her a list – who had refused the offer first time round. Perhaps she might find some way to persuade them where he, Lord Gordon, had failed? Oh, and another thing – he had been unable to find lodging for the entire company in one house; here was a list of three landladies who had agreed to take them in ones or twos but he was still short of lodgings for Mr Dennison and Mr Swindlehurst. Could she take care of that? And finally, he, Lord Gordon, was extremely fond of a brand of Cuban cigars called *Angelos;* could she be an angel, ha ha, and slip into Bassett's, the tobacconist, and see if he'd part with four of them for a pair of free tickets? Be careful not to crush them on the way back!

How had they ever managed without her, she wondered?

She had little under half an hour before Blight's Omnibus set off for Helston at nine. She just made it to her parents and back in time – to leave her letter for Louis and say a last farewell. She boarded the bus, panting for breath, clutching a carpetbag filled with playbills, free tickets, and a packed lunch from Mrs Montmorency; in her purse she had a pound float – Players' money for which she would have to account.

As the bus was about to depart, Mr Swindlehurst came running across the Moor, just in time to tell her that he was *not* willing to share a room, much less a bed, with 'that greenery-yallery Dennison cove.' Completely separate digs would suit him best of all, but he understood she was no miracle worker.

"Says who?" she asked with a confidence she did not really feel.

She wondered why the seat with the best view, right up in front beside the driver, was not taken. Moments later, after she had taken it herself, she discovered one possible reason – it was also beside the engine, which lay between her and the driver, vibrated alarmingly, deafened her, and emitted wisps of burned oil around its ill-fitting cowling from time to time. As they shuddered and roared up the High Street to Greenbank, she considered moving back to an empty seat near the rear; but two things dissuaded her. One was the view, the other was the fact that the driver had already opened a conversation with her.

"G… … m… far, ar'ee?" he asked.

"Helston," she guessed. But he already knew that, for he had sold her the ticket.

"No," he said. "… the … … further?"

"Coming back this evening," she shouted.

He stopped to pick up two more at the top of the hill, for Penryn and Mabe Burnthouse turn. Rose gazed down over the roof of the steam laundry to the yacht club; was it really less than a month ago that she had been sent round to the tradesmen's entrance by that stuck-up steward? She ought to have told Louis about his behaviour in her letter – except, what could the poor man do about it now!

Oh, Louis ...!

No – save it for bedtime tonight, when the ravishingly beautiful Miss Titania Moore has gin-tippled herself into slumber. Have a comforting weep at the ineffable sadness of things then. Oh yes – she could be flippant about it now, all right; but the sharpness of the pain when she was alone in the dark with her loss was real enough. Perhaps it was only by being flippant by day that she could get through the waking hours at all.

"..., eh?" asked the driver as the vibrations, the racket, and the wisps of oil fumes picked up where they had left off.

"Sorry?" she shouted back.

"I said ... first ... ..., eh?"

"There's a first time for everything," she bellowed.

The conversation continued in that vein all the way up the bank of the Penryn River to Penryn itself, with Rose catching one word in ten and responding with the first cliché it brought to mind. This was the road along which Frank had driven her into Falmouth that day. Were he and little Pennycuik married yet? They'd just about have had time to read the banns, so it was possible. She really ought to make a habit of reading the papers. Then she wouldn't have had to learn of the Redmile-Smith crash from Roger Deveril. And she wouldn't be wondering about Frank and Pennycuik now.

A funny thing – the Pennycuiks' farm was in the parish of Come-to-Good. Penny quick ... come to good – do such names govern our destinies? Tremayne, they said, came from Old Cornish *Tre,* a farmstead, and *maen,* a standing stone or cairn. And Falmouth was, well, the mouth of the Fal river, obviously. Pretty meaningless. Except, come to think of it, the *original* name for Falmouth was Penny-Come-Quick! Could it be an omen that she, Lucinda-Ella Tremayne (the rock that stands proud through every storm) from Penny-Come-Quick, was on her way to a fortune? Maybe there was something in it after all.

They were approaching Penryn now and there across the river was the barn where, exactly three centuries ago, Old Wilmot and his wife Agnes unwittingly murdered their own son Randall for *his* fortune. So much for fortunes and omens, then!

The swing bridge was in their favour but from here onward, the next two or three miles were all uphill, winding at first through the town and then, past the railway station, along a bendy road through wooded hills. Here the roar and vibrations were so violent that even the driver gave up his attempts to converse. Rose sat and watched the needle on the thermometer, which stuck up out of the engine cowling, climb steadily into the red portion; it had an elegantly scalloped arrowhead and a tail like an earwig's. She noticed the driver kept an anxious eye upon it, too. They had just made it to the top of the steepest slope, to the Mabe Burnthouse turn, when the relief valve opened and the bus did a creditable imitation of a steam lorry, standing there on skirts of white. The more nervous passengers dismounted hurriedly and walked a little distance away, ahead of the bus. The driver waited until the hiss dwindled to an occasional whoosh of steam before he took off the cowling and, after wrapping the radiator cap in a rag, unscrewed it. He fished out a billycan of water from under his seat and tipped it in, producing some pleasantly musical pings and another whoosh of steam. He refilled it at a nearby stream, which drained some old quarry workings a little farther up the hill, which was here but a gentle slope compared with what had gone before. Six refills later and it overflowed.

A minute later still, they were all back in the bus and on their way again. The driver, who had been mute all this while, resumed his conversation, saying, "Well! I ... ... every time."

"One can get used to anything in the end, I suppose," she yelled back at him.

She wondered if he were now so used to the racket that he could only speak while the motor was roaring away beside him.

Up to Longdowns they went, with the needle well below the red; then across rolling, almost treeless country, past Dead Man's Corner. "Man killed here last week," the driver told her in one of his few intelligible sentences, spoken while the bus coasted downhill. On through Rame, they groaned and whined, past the Halfway House inn, Laity Moor, Retanna Hill, and up to Manhay. There she saw Wheal Lovell, a scattering of gaunt stone engine houses belching smoke and steam as they sent miners below and pumped water up to the adit level or brought the ores of copper and tin up to grass. Rose could see the bal maidens – big, burly women in coarse-spun dresses – sorting the ores onto conveyor belts for the crushers and vanning tables. Beyond them the calciner was pouring out yellow, sulphurous fumes that caught her throat with their tang, even inside the bus.

Several passengers began coughing.

"Ha ha! .... cure ... ... asthma!" He pointed directly down at the ground to make his meaning clear.

"The final cure for all life's ills!" Rose agreed. It was getting easier to reply to the man if not to hear him.

At Treloquithack a donkey lying in the road refused to rise. The driver seemed quite used to this for he left the motor ticking over while he leaped down with a bundle of newspapers in his hand. He crumpled it sheet by sheet and stuffed it all around the creature's belly, while it watched impassively. But the moment he produced a box of matches – even before he struck a single one of them – it lumbered arthritically to its feet and wandered off into the farmyard. The driver scuffed the paper to the verge and set it alight anyway, which scattered the hens, who had also constituted a minor obstacle to the bus's progress.

"If old donkey only *tasted* a little better ...!" the driver said as he climbed back on board.

There was a final anxious moment with the thermometer as they climbed up out of the dip at Trewennack and then they were out onto a gentler slope to the crest of that hill on whose long, southern slope the town of Helston is built.

"Gwealmayowe!" The driver pointed to the fields on their left.

It was the name of the venue on her handbills for the town. It looked fair enough on a fine July morning but she could imagine it bleak and windswept in a November gale; if they returned here then – and if she were still with the company – she hoped they would find a more sheltered spot lower in the town.

The bus shuddered on its brakes and gears down the steep slope of Wendron Street and just managed to judder to a halt among the other, mainly horse-drawn, buses outside the Angel Hôtel. The wheels came to a rest within inches of the miniature Helston River, which flows at quite a rate in treacherous stone kennels between each foot-pavement and the roadway, a trap for many a drunken or unwary carter or automobilist.

This particular driver both stood on the footbrake and hauled on the handbrake with both hands to achieve his precarious halt. Then he thanked Rose for some of the most interesting conversation he'd enjoyed in weeks and vanished into the public bar to 'lubricate the old voice box.'

Standing on the footpath outside the Angel, carpetbag clutched tight to her, looking up and down Coinagehall Street, Rose suddenly felt very small, alone, and incompetent. Where to begin? Helston seemed so large, so unknown.

She had visited the town only once before, eleven years ago when her teacher, Mr Trebilcock, had organized a class outing to Helston Furry Day. That was when people danced through houses and gardens and streets in the wake of a little shall-I band. The churches were trying to stamp it out as a pagan custom, and modern freethinkers were also opposed to it for its associated superstitions. So, old Trebilcock had said, it was important for all true Cornish people to rally round and defend it. As a result, she and Sally – and forty-two other Falmouth children – had enjoyed a splendid day, dancing through people's houses and being given enough niceys to make a camel sick by other true Cornish people.

But there would be no dancing in the streets today – not for her, anyway. Perhaps the best way to begin was with a cup of tea in the Cober Tea Rooms, to wash away the oil fumes and the lingering tang of sulphur. She could also study the list of shops that had agreed to display the handbill and work out the shortest walk to take in them all.

It was a wise decision. Not only did the tea wash all trace of sulphur from her throat but Mrs Laity, the proprietress, agreed to place a handbill in her window, in return for a free ticket, of course.

"I never took to that Lord Gordon feller," she confided in Rose. "Too many *actions* with un, if you do know what I mean."

Rose did, indeed, know what she meant – the man was affected in his manners. She was careful to be crisp and businesslike, as unaffected as possible, in her approaches to those shopkeepers who did not already display a handbill, and in that way she managed to win over a few of them – about one in three, she reckoned. She was also pleased to discover that every shop that had made the bargain had also stuck to it. In the only shop that appeared to have reneged, they discovered it had been blown down behind a display of Carter's Little Liver Pills; the man was most apologetic. The nonconformist conscience was alive and well in Helston, anyway.

For her lunch she went down to the bowling green behind the Grylls Memorial at the foot of Coinagehall Street, where she could enjoy the sunshine, and a godlike view of the cattle market and gasworks in the valley of the River Cober, below. An interesting building beyond the gasworks – it looked like an agricultural merchant's of some kind – had a large sign saying, Kernow & Daughter; you didn't see too many of them! If she tore up her letter and went to join Louis at once – and created a new business with him – could they call it Redmile-Smith & Wife? You didn't see *any* of them!

She ate the heart of Mrs Montmorency's doorstep-sandwiches and as much of their crusts as conscience pricked her to swallow. The rest she threw for the seagulls to catch on the wing, which they did with amazing accuracy. *Carpe diem* – seize the day. What was the Latin for crust? Anyway, if you were looking for omens, there was one: Snatch the prize and win.

She called in at the Blue Anchor on her way back up the town, hoping to help the rather dry bread down with a swift half pint. At first the landlord tried to bar her way, as single females were not allowed in the bars; but when she showed him her handbills and made the standard offer, he treated her as a commercial and directed her to the private bar, the only one where business was, by custom, permitted. He was one of those who, having refused the bargain from Lord Gordon, changed his mind and accepted it from her. He went on to accept Mr Dennison as a one-week boarder, and at a slightly cheaper rate than a landlady would charge – so Mr D would be pleased. He even treated her to a half pint, brewed on the premises, to seal both deals.

It must have been stronger than it looked, or tasted. She had no other explanation for what she did next. She settled Mr Swindlehurst as a private lodger of Mrs Laity, of the Cober Tea Rooms, who took in occasional lodgers, short-term only. She managed to get four *Angelos* cigars from Mr Bassett, the tobacconist, in exchange for *three* free tickets – which she didn't think Lord Gordon would mind. And then, having ninety minutes to spare before the departure of the bus back to Falmouth, she hired some wallpapering materials from Gilbert's, the ironmongers in Meneage Street, and went about the town pasting up all her remaining handbills at every likely spot that caught her eye – lamp posts, telegraph poles, litter bins, the fire-station door, the Methodist Church notice board ... and she managed to cover the entire window of a boarded-up shop with the last twenty in her bag.

She crossed the street to admire it and was joined almost immediately by a constable, who stood at her side, going up and down on his toes in a rather ominous way.

"And what's all this-yur, then?" he asked.

"My job," she replied. "I'm the advance party for the company. We're opening up at Gwealmayowe next Monday. I can sell you a couple of tickets now if you like. They'll be going like hot cakes, you know."

"I shouldn't wonder if they do," he said. "The way you've been a-carrying on. I've had my eye on you all the way up the town. And if it's *parties* we'm talking about, young madam, I should like to invite *you* to a party upalong at the station."

"Oh, but I have to catch a bus ..." she began.

"Now! The bus do go past the station so if you step lively and give no trouble, you'll catch 'un easy." He gripped her firmly just above the elbow and propelled her across the road, round the corner, and up Wendron Street to the police station near the top. They dropped the hired material in at Gilbert's as they passed. Over the first fifty yards or so he asked her name and address, occupation, and so on; they had to keep stopping while he wrote it all down in his notebook.

"What am I supposed to have done wrong?" she asked after he had tucked the thing away in his breast pocket – though by now she could guess the answer well enough.

As if he read her mind he replied, "Just 'cos there aren't no signs up saying as fly-posters will be prosecuted, it don't mean there won't be none up in court."

Her heart fell to her boots. "What's the fine?" she asked.

"Two shilling per offence." He tapped the breast-pocket. "I got you down for forty – so that's eighty shilling you and your Lord Gordon Stuck-up Fitzroy is gonna have to find."

So there was a personal feud of some kind going on here, she realized. And if anything could act to clear her mind and sharpen all her faculties it was the thought of involving her employer – the new master of her universe – in this wretched business.

She said nothing more until they came to the station, where the constable, a PC Hind, handed her over to the sergeant to fill out the charge sheet. He read all the details out of his notebook.

Rose waited for him to finish and then she said "Tell me, sergeant," in a steely, upper-class voice that stiffened the PC and quite changed the sergeant's attitude toward her. "If you find a man drunk and disorderly in Church Street, follow him up the hill into Coinagehall Street, and thence into Wendron Street and finally Penrose Road – where you arrest him – would that amount to *four* charges of drunk and disorderly in four different places? I only ask for information."

Sergeant and constable exchanged glances, for they could both see where her argument was leading. Eventually, the sergeant had to admit it would amount to only one charge.

"And yet the offence was undoubtedly committed in all four places," she mused aloud. "How interesting. But I'm sorry – I'm wasting your valuable time, I'm sure. You were about to say ...?"

No matter what he had been about to say, what he now actually did say was, "Lucinda-Ella Tremayne, I am cautioning you that you will be reported for one or more offences of illegal flyposting" – he read all the details of times and places from the constable's notebook – "and you are bailed in the sum of five shillings in your own recognizance to appear before the justices at Helston police court on Monday next at ten o'clock in the morning, where you may or may not face charges. Sign here if you please, miss."

32

In all his talk of not finding enough digs for his cast – and could Rose find a couple more? – Lord Gordon completely forgot Rose herself. *Don't worry,* she thought when he broke the news to her an hour after they had erected the marquee at Gwealmayowe, *I shall probably have lodgings provided at his majesty's pleasure soon enough.* It was then midday on Sunday – not the best day to go seeking rooms in strictly sabbatarian Cornwall.

She toyed with the thought of splashing out on a room at the Angel – since it might well be her last night of freedom – but, in the end, it was Mrs Laity who saved the day. She suggested that, as Mr Swindlehurst's room had two comfortable single beds, they could tack a pair of large sheets together and hang them on stout blind cord across the room. And tomorrow she could go looking for proper digs.

It worked well enough. Their night-time preparations went forward with perfect propriety, except that Rose saw him undressing in a sort of shadow play on the makeshift partition and so was alerted to place her own candle where it would cast her shadow on one of the walls, instead. They bade each other goodnight and settled to sleep.

Half an hour later, Mr S asked softly, "Can you not sleep, lady?"

"Sorry," she replied, speaking equally gently, "is it so obvious?"

"You were tossing and turning like a condemned man."

"Not a bad comparison!" she said – and went on to confess the entire episode with the fly posters and PC Hind.

When he had done laughing he congratulated her on the quick thinking that led to her question about the drunk and the number of offences. In telling him the story, though, she had merely described herself as speaking in an upper-class accent – she had not dared repeat her words in the accent itself, in case his professional ear should catch nuances that rang as false to him as Sally's attempts at 'posh' had sounded to her.

Now, however, he insisted.

With her heart in her mouth she repeated her words to the sergeant as closely as she could remember them. When she finished, there was complete silence.

"Well?" she asked nervously.

"Again," he commanded.

This time she spoke some lines from *Maud* – as in 'Come into the garden, Maud ...'

"U n c a n n y!" he exclaimed, drawing the word out dramatically. "What else?"

"What d'you mean – what else?"

"Can you do a Scotch accent ... Welsh ... Yorkshire ... Cockney?"

"We get a lot of Scots engineers on the ships that put in, but I can't understand a word they say. You think they're just clearing their throats, getting ready to speak – and then you suddenly realize that *was* them speaking." She gave an example along the lines of: "Huts hoots a'wee agin turrn ea bu the toon aneet!"

Swindlehurst laughed into his pillow to avoid waking the house.

Rose, emboldened by this reception, said, "There's French as well." And she gave him a sentence or two from a piece of French she had learned for the oral part of a Polytechnic course she had enrolled in once – and, as usual, had never completed. *"Le courage! C'est de dominer ses propres fautes, d'en souffrir mais non pas être accablé et de continuer son chemin."*

"Courage!" he said, vain enough to wish her to know he had understood. "It is to conquer one's own faults, to suffer because of them without being crushed and to continue upon one's way. How true! Oh, how very true! And, I think, Miss Tremayne, rather apt in your case, no? But – *alors!* – you speak like a native Breton!"

"Do I? I suppose it's because so many Breton fishermen come over here – and a lot of the onion men, too. Listen, Mister S, I'm glad this entertains you – especially as I'm butting into *your* room tonight, not to mention ruining your beauty sleep ..."

"Oh, please!" He made dismissive noises. "Only too delighted, lady – especially to hear this astonishing versatility of your tongue. But you are right. This isn't helping you in court tomorrow."

"I didn't say that."

"No, but you were about to. It so happens that I have an idea that may help."

The following morning he accompanied her to court, which, on that day, was held in the dining room of the Angel, since the regular courthouse was being fumigated for bats that week. The little creatures' habit of defecating in flight had spoiled several portraits of past magistrates, mayors, and other worthies, giving them a poxed appearance.

The change of location suited the two Players' purpose well, for there were several alcoves where they could sit and pretend not to notice a nearby member of the Cornwall Constabulary, preferably of high rank. Rose fluttered her lashes at a young solicitor and asked if he could kindly tell her who the various policemen were, standing in groups around the temporary court.

"Be careful what you say," he warned her. "They spread themselves out, you know, and try to eavesdrop."

"On what, pray?" she asked innocently.

"Well, people like to bring along a friend or two and naturally they run through a last-minute rehearsal of their defence. Are you a witness?"

"I *may* be accused of illegal flyposting – that's what I'm here to find out."

He shrugged. "A pretty clear-cut offence, I'd say. Are you represented?"

"I'll wait to see if I'm charged first."

"Well ... I'll be here most of the day, I expect. Meanwhile, you want to know who's who ..."

He got no farther than "Inspector Lang, officer-in-charge of the local cop-shop" before she thanked him and gave the nod to Mr Swindlehurst.

Lang was sitting just outside one of the alcoves and, thank heavens, its only other occupant was a middle-aged lady; she was rather fat but there was still enough room for Rose and Mr S.

"What really annoys me about that PC Hind," Rose said as they passed the inspector and took their seats on the alcove bench, "... sorry – are these seats taken?" This last to the fat woman.

"They are now, my lover!" she cackled, looking Rose up and down as a farmer might eye livestock in the auction ring. "Which of 'ee is up today, then?"

"Me, I'm afraid," Rose told her. And then, in case the woman should divert the planned conversation, she added quickly, "But I was just telling my friend here that what really annoys me is that the copper who nabbed me – PC Hind – actually watched me commit the offence *forty* times. *Forty times!* Before he stepped in to arrest me."

The script had inevitably changed, thanks to the woman's intervention, but Swindlehurst recognized his cue. "I think you have a point there, Miss Tremayne – a very good point. I'd put it to the magistrates like this. Suppose this PC Hind had seen a street bully kicking an old lady in the shins down in Church Street – where, by his own admission, he first saw you sticking up a flybill – and did nothing. Then he followed the brute into Coinagehall Street and calmly watched him kick ten more old ladies in the shins – and again did nothing except record it in his little notebook. And so on and so forth until forty old ladies were lying in agony on the pavements of Helston – and only *then* did he step in and arrest the evil perpetrator of these forty dastardly crimes ..."

"What would the justices say!" Rose cut in as if finishing his rhetorical question for him.

"Never mind the justices," Swindlehurst came back. "What would his own *superior officer* say? Such a constable would hardly add much lustre to his station's reputation. In my sober opinion, you have a strong case to put to the magistrates there." He turned to the woman. "You are no doubt a witness, madam," he said. "May one inquire ...?"

"Witness!" She hooted with laughter. "I'm the accused in the case," she said, turning angry. At least, her tone was angry, her words were angry, but her eyes danced with a secret mirth. "Me," she continued, "as never done nothing but kindly acts to weary travellers! Me – as showed more charity to three poor lil' lacemaker orpheling maids than every church in Cornwall!"

"Disorderly house," Swindlehurst murmured to Rose.

The woman heard him and grew angrier yet. "That's what *they* do call it. But what happened, see, is I was sleeping all my might, last Friday night this was, about two o'clock, when I heard this feller outside the door, dagging for a fight, I thought. Hooting like a steamer, he was, and knocking at my door like the drummer of Helston band. So I throws up me winder and says – all polite, like – I never raised my voice to un – I says, 'Is that Reverend Coulter from up Breage?' 'Cos 'twouldn't be the first time, see? So when he says no, he wasn't Reverend Coulter from up Breage, I thought I got you now, my boyo – I reconnize that voice right enough! 'That's Mister Blewitt, innit – magistrate from over Redruth!' 'Cos he's come battering at my door often enough at that hour for me to know him in a coal cellar. But 'tweren't he, neither. These old ears are fading fast. So then I has me last shot, 'cos I'm sure as duck-eggs I do know that voice. 'Why!' I says. 'That's Colonel Dancey! *Now* I got you!' 'Cos he's what I do call 'my regular soldier,' he is!"

"And was it the colonel?" Swindlehurst asked with a straight face, for he had realized some time back that the woman's purpose was the same as their own.

"No!" she replied scornfully. " 'Twas some old police informer sent to trap me by imitating three of the finest, most upstanding members of the community who just happen to enjoy keeping a bit company of my three poor orpheling lacemaker maids – and where's the harm in that?"

The three of them had time to enjoy a cup of coffee and a sustaining slice of heavicake before Rose's case was called. Half a dozen routine drunk-and-disorderlies came and went. There were two paternity summonses, uncontested. A breach of the peace – bound over. The theft of a plough – sent to the next assize. And then the inspector, the sergeant, and the PC could be seen shuffling papers and glancing in Rose's direction from time to time.

"Well, inspector?" the clerk asked peremptorily. "I have you versus Tremayne down here?"
"Er ... the police have decided to withdraw the charge, your worships. It seems there was a misunderstanding. The defendant will be let off with a caution."
"Was an offence committed or not?" the clerk snapped.
"Er ... no, sir," was the reluctant reply.
"Then Miss Tremayne is no longer 'the defendant.' Is she perchance in court?"
Rose stood and came out of the alcove.
"You're free to go, Miss Tremayne," he said.
"And all the papers in the case, sir?" she asked.
The clerk glanced at the senior magistrate, who said, "I suppose Constable Hind's children may enjoy scribbling on the backs of them, young lady."
There was general laughter, which, Rose and Swindlehurst assumed, referred to some previous answer to a query about abandoned papers.
"In that case," the clerk said, "we have time for one more before we adjourn for luncheon. Put up Mrs Harvey!"
The fat woman was only half-way out of the alcove when the unhappy Inspector Lang had to admit that the case against her, too, had been withdrawn. Mrs Harvey left the court without waiting for the clerk to tell her she, too, was free to go; with immense dignity, and never a glance in the direction of the police, she went out to the bar and ordered a pasty and a pint of Smith's Best Export.
Rose and Swindlehurst joined her, somewhat perplexed. They understood very well why the inspector had decided to drop that flyposting charge – but keeping a disorderly house? Surely that was much more serious? And surely she'd never have dared make those scurrilous suggestions in open court? In fact, that was the first question Rose put to her – would she have dared?
" 'Course I would, my lover," she cackled. "Anything said from the witness box, by the accused or by a witness – no matter – is privileged. You can't be had up for slander nor nothing. Say what you will! And all the newspapers are free to report it, too, as long as 'tis word-for-word. That's a handy thing to know, that is." She winked and took a third of the pasty in a single bite.
"Well," Rose exclaimed. "We may be poor but we do see life!"
They had their own lunch in the bar, too, and, before they left, Rose asked the barman if his Smith's ales were old stock or was the firm still going?
"Still going," he told her, "but under new management. You heard about the crash then, did 'ee?"
"I read about it somewhere," she replied offhandedly.
But one look into Swindlehurst's eyes as they left told her he had not been deceived by her casual – perhaps too-casual – tone.

33

Lord Gordon was also in town that morning. He was, of course, horrified to see his handbills stuck up illegally all over the place – indeed, even a racing-car driver flying through the town at a hundred miles an hour could not have failed to notice them. He returned at once to Gwealmayowe and waited for the inevitable summons from the local police, busying himself meanwhile with the speech in which he would tell Rose how much of her pay he would be docking for the next year or two. But then Roberts, the company's odd-job man, came back from town with the news that all charges against Rose had been dropped – not even dismissed, just dropped.

"How the hell did she do that – as the drunkard said when the two nuns parted to walk one each side of him?" Lord Gordon exclaimed. "Is she some kind of witch?" Until then he had not even known she was up before the beaks.

But when Rose and Swindlehurst returned, he said not a word about it. Instead, while Rose got on with her promised sewing marathon, he summoned the whole company to a rehearsal of the play they were to perform in the second half of the week, *The Mysterious Family,* by Mr G. Herbert Rodwell, a farcical comedy in two acts, first performed at the Adelphi on November 13th, 1843 – "and still going strong," as Lord Gordon said. It ran for only an hour but, in conjunction with a program of dramatic monologues by messrs Dennison and Lamb, acrobatics and juggling by the Child Prodigy assisted by her father, a bouquet of romantic songs by Miss Moore accompanied at the piano by Mr Rendle, and a few conjuring tricks from Mr Swindlehurst ably assisted by Mrs Skerrett, it would pad out to a full value-for-money evening for the paying customers.

The first Monday's performance in any new town was usually pretty sparsely attended but on that particular opening night in Helston the Players managed to sell all but twenty seats. A full house is always livelier than a half-empty one and the company responded eagerly, playing better than they had at any performance during the previous week in Falmouth. There was no doubt but that Rose's action in plastering handbills all over the town had swelled the audience. Even then, though, Lord Gordon said nothing directly to her.

"Tell me, lassie," he said, more or less in passing as he went to take off his makeup, "if you had been fined this morning, er, how much would it have amounted to?"

"I wasn't even charged, sir," she replied.

"I know that. But if you had been?"

"It's a maximum of forty shillings per offence ..."

He winced.

"I hadn't finished," she said, and went on to explain how she had managed to get up to four dozen individual offences treated as a single one. But she did not explain how she managed to get even that one dropped.

He became thoughtful again. "So we could have flyposted four dozen playbills for a maximum of forty bob, eh?"

"They hardly ever apply the *maximum* fine," she pointed out. "The constable said two bob is more usual."

"Quite," he said.

"I was thinking of looking up the Penzance byelaws on flyposting when I go there tomorrow, sir. I presume I *do* go there tomorrow?"

He tugged at his beard.

"Sir?" she prompted.

"There are two things that frighten me, lassie," he said. "One is underlings who cannot think for themselves. And the other is underlings who can."

"And so?" she asked.

"And so I don't know which is the more frightening – that's all. But yes, you do go to Penzance tomorrow."

"One more thing, sir?" she called after him. "I was wondering – would a PC Hind have any cause to resent you or this company or anything like that?"

"Doesn't ring a bell," he replied vaguely. "Ah – the bells! The bells!" He ambled off under the smokescreen of a passable Henry-Irving imitation.

She was fairly sure it *was* a smokescreen, too.

She ought to have gone about the town to find other digs that afternoon but Swindlehurst said he saw no real harm in their present arrangement, and he did enjoy their little chats before dropping off to sleep ... so why not leave things as they were, eh?

And, since she shared his sentiments, she agreed – fully expecting him to ask her why she had been so interested in Smith's Ales at the Angel that day. But he seemed to have forgotten about it and they spoke, instead, of poetry and particularly of Tennyson, whom he also admired. He suggested she might run her eye over Dryden, too, as his stately mockery of all human vanities was a good counterweight to Alfred Lord's more cosmic disdain.

She was sorry he didn't ask about Smith's because she would have welcomed his opinion.

The following morning her first call in Penzance was to the library in Morrab Road, where, she discovered that the town's byelaws on flyposting had not been amended since 1807; the maximum fine was still set at eighteen pence. Like those ancient fines of a halfpenny for whistling on the sabbath, it would be worth neither prosecuting nor collecting.

In fact, her stroll through the town had already suggested something of the kind; she must have been about the hundred-and-fiftieth would-be fly-poster to have realized how worthwhile it would be to break the law and pay the fine, if it were ever demanded. Taverns, pieshops, strolling photographers, auctioneers, concert parties, charity balls – anyone with anything to sell, it seemed, had but a single thought: to rush to the printer and leave with an armful of paper with which to decorate any blank surface in the town that happened to be around head height. She enjoyed a busy day there and yet managed to return to Helston with not a single handbill distributed, much less flyposted anywhere.

"But I have something that could be worth a great deal more," she protested when Lord Gordon started to roar his displeasure.

He groaned at the news. "I cringe at those conditionals, lassie," he warned. "When you say *'could* be worth a great deal more' you also imply *'could* be worth a great deal less.'"

"It's just an idea," she said. "There's a firm of photographers there – Collett and Trevarton. They have these photographers strolling up and down the beaches and promenades, taking snaps of all and sundry and handing out these little leaflets to people, telling them where they can pick up their 'snaps,' as they call them, and the prices and so on." She showed him one. "They're blank on the back, see?" she went on. "So what I thought is this: Why don't we make an arrangement with Mister Collett or Mister Trevarton, or both, to print a little announcement on the back ..."

"Which, no doubt, you have already composed?" he asked.

"It's funny you should say that," she replied, showing him a neatly pencilled layout of the wording she had composed on the bus coming back. "It'd mean that for the rest of this week – and all next week, too – *their* people would be all over town and the beaches and the promenade, handing out *our* publicity to all the holiday-makers. About two hundred a day, I'm told."

"Told? By whooommm, pray?" he asked magisterially.

"By Mrs Collett, actually. A very charming lady who was once a lady's maid herself. We got on very well."

"Tell me, lassie," he said, sitting down at last, "do you ever have a dream in which you enter a room by a certain door – in fact, the only door – but when you turn round ... it's gone! Pffft! Vanished! And you find you're left in a room from which there is no possible way out?"

Rose shook her head impatiently. "Anyway," she went on, "Mrs Collett said she had never thought of placing advertisements on the back of their leaflets – though now she could kick herself for it. I would, too, if I were her – but I didn't tell her so, of course. But in future, she said, it would pay all their printing bills. And because of that she was inclined to persuade her husband and his partner to let us 'have a free ride on their backs,' as she put it, until the end of next week."

He smiled broadly but, before it grew too broad, she added, "All we have to do, you see, is pay for the reprinting on the backs of their existing stock."

"All!" he grumbled.

"Two thousand leaflets, we reckoned."

His jaw dropped but no words emerged.

"And then we'd have four men walking up and down the town all day – for twelve days – passing them out, and all at no further cost to us."

" 'No further cost,' she says! And what will it have cost us already to print two *thousand* leaflets – even tichy ones like that?" He stared at her carefully lettered mock-up. "I don't think I've ever *seen* my name printed so small!"

"Well, I did manage to have a quick word with their printer – who ..."

"Why am I not overwhelmed with surprise at this point?" he asked a high-flying seagull.

"Mrs Collett says he's extremely reasonable. He assured me he could do them at a pound a thousand – seeing as the stock already exists. We don't pay for that."

"Stock?"

"It must be what they call paper for printing on."

He licked his lips and stared away into the distance. "Two quid, eh? Two crisp ones."

"That's what the man said, sir."

"Well, lassie," he said at last. "I can safely say you're going to learn a great deal while you're part of my little company – of that there is no doubt. My only sorrow is that very little of it will have been taught to you by me!"

"So I go back to Penzance tomorrow?"

"Of course! On the very first bus."

"The two pounds will be in advance, he said."

Lord Gordon sighed. "They always do, my dear. Now don't let me keep you from your needle and thread a second longer!"

That night, after a little celebration for playing to yet another almost packed house, Rose and Swindlehurst tiptoed to their room, undressed under the same decorous arrangements as the previous two nights, and sank into their beds.

He surprised her, as always. "Did you have shares in Smith's Ales, then?" he asked.

She needed no further prompting to tell him the full story as far as it concerned herself and Louis, though she said nothing of Frank and Pennycuik nor of herself and Roanoke, Deveril, and Sally. All she wanted was his opinion about herself and Louis – so why muddy the waters with all that? "And I still can't decide if I'm doing right or wrong in not being at his side at a time like this," she concluded. "Sometimes I think we working class folk worry more about class and class differences than the middle classes do – and certainly more than the upper-middles, like the Redmile-Smiths. I'm staying away from him for the best of reasons, honestly. The noblest reasons. But I'd hate him to think me just ..."

"You!" he said.

It sounded like a judgment. She wondered what condemnation was about to follow.

"Are doing absolutely the right thing," he added.

"You think so?"

"Why? Were you hoping I'd say the opposite?"

"Maybe if enough people told me I was being foolish ... well, I'd go to him like a shot. It's where I want to be more than anything else in all the world – selfishly, I mean."

"You make me wonder if I'm right, then," he said after a thoughtful silence.

"You were very certain just now."

"Indeed, I was. What I had in mind was that ... well, you've fallen right on your feet here – don't you think? You've taken to this strange way of life of ours like a duck to water."

"D'you think so?"

"Come on! Whence this show of modesty? You know you have. All right – the flyposting in Helston was a bit of a lark – an accident – but what you did in Penzance today – all off your own bat – it surely tells you that this sort of life and you were made for each other?"

She felt too embarrassed to reply at once.

"No?" he prompted.

"I must admit," she replied reluctantly, "that when I was doing it – noticing that those leaflets had one blank side – getting the idea – going to see Mrs Collett – chatting with her – then going on to see the printer – I didn't feel a single doubt from start to finish. Not until I got on the bus on the way home. Then I thought ohmigawd – what 'ave I bin and gawn an' done, nah!"

"Cockney!" he crowed. "I knew you could!"

"We had a cockney parlourmaid at a house where I worked once. Anyway, what's the significance in the fact that this job and me are made for one another?"

"Because, by the time your Mister Redmile-Smith has picked himself up again and got back on an even keel, you're going to be ten times the woman you are now. At the moment you have youth and bravado – which is a nice enough dowry for any man. But give it four or five years, lady – half a dozen, say, to round it off – and you'll have traded those for experience and poise, which is a better dowry by far."

"It did help a bit – knowing something of Mrs Collett's story," she said. "I mean, it made me less afraid of her."

"Blackmail?" he asked, surprised.

"No! Nothing like that. I was thinking about it on the bus home, too ..."

"See! You call it home already!"

"I was thinking how all this class business wrecks so many lives. Why are we so stupid?"

"Did it wreck Mrs Collett's life, then?"

"In a way it did – but before she was born. Her mother was very high-quarter – one of the Trevartons of Swanpool. And she fell in love with the coachman – eloped with him. I knew his name once but I've ... Moore! That's funny – I wonder if he's related to our dear Titania? Anyway, they eloped. Not very far. Here in Helston, I think, where he started a haulage business, and did quite well until he took to drink."

"Then he probably *is* related to our dear Titania."

"Miaow! The mother died of tuberculosis and the father, Mister Moore, of drink, both in the same week. And the powers-that-be split up the family – except they reckoned without Mrs Collett, or Miss Moore as she then was. She vowed she'd get them all back together again – and so she did. There were three boys and two other girls – something like that. They were scattered to homes and orphanages all over England, but she gathered them all back. I think the little girl even got sent out to India, but she got her back, too. You've got to admire a woman like that, don't you think? I just sat there, looking at her while we were talking, and I thought, 'You're the sort of woman I want to be like when I'm your age.'"

"Which is ...?"

"She must be about thirty-five now. She couldn't have been more than eighteen then."

"So how do you know all about it? Sorry – silly question. This is Cornwall, isn't it!"

"I know about it because that cockney maid I told you about – she's a cousin to Susan Trevarton, the wife of Mister Collet's partner, Mister Mark Trevarton. And Mister Mark, according to *some,* is Mrs Collett's cousin."

"And according to others?"

"Her uncle, even though they're both about the same age!" Rose laughed. "This *is* Cornwall, as you say."

34

One particular scene in *The Mysterious Family* relied on a risky piece of business. Without going into a plot of Byzantine complexity, it is enough to know that a woman is hiding in a wardrobe (second hand, courtesy of Oliver's Furniture Emporium, Meneage Street), a man (in fact, her husband though none of the other characters knows that) is hiding under the bed (ditto), while another man slithers into the room seeking the woman; if she is discovered there in those seemingly compromising circumstances, lives and careers will be ruined. The man tiptoes to the wardrobe and opens the door.

At this point, some of the more enraptured members of the audience can usually be relied upon to exclaim, 'No!' in their excitement. What is then supposed to happen is that the searcher starts in guilty surprise at this 'unexpected' interruption, comes down to the footlights, and stares out into the dark beyond them.

The audience laughs, which puzzles him even more. The woman seizes the chance to make good her escape while he is thus distracted. But what happens if no one gets excited enough to cry out that essential 'No!'?

That was how Rose acquired her first acting part. Just before that scene, she was to slip quietly in among the audience, right at the back, and make sure of the cry.

"You're not just a dumb Citizen or Spear Carrier, lassie," Lord Gordon said as he detailed her off for the task. "You leap straight into a speaking part! There's few of us can say as much of our own avocations upon these hallowed boards."

The first time she did it, she was filled with a curious mixture of excitement and terror. There was the excitement of knowing she was about to deceive the honest paying customers around her as she slipped quietly among them in the back row – which, if you think of it, *is* the true excitement of all drama from the actor's point of view; and then there was the terror of bungling it, of losing her voice at the crucial moment, or just croaking something utterly unintelligible through phlegmy vocal cords, or ... well, those were nightmares enough.

It was so stupid, she told herself. All she had to do was shout a single word and then act slightly embarrassed for the benefit of those nearby – and, come to think of it, the embarrassment would be genuine enough. And yet she stood there among the clerks and farm boys and maids and shop girls, shaking all over and trying to clear her throat without making a sound.

The moment approached. The clandestine husband and wife – Mr Walter Rendle and Miss Titania Moore – hoping to enjoy some clandestine connubials, were startled by a sound offstage. They panicked. He rushed for the wardrobe, she for the darkness under the bed. Each realized the futility of his or her chosen hiding place and emerged again, staring wildly at the other. They milked the laughter thus for as long as it lasted. Then, to fresh guffaws, she chose the wardrobe and he the under-bed. The wardrobe door was barely closed when, with impeccable timing, the searcher – Lord Gordon himself – made his entry.

Some idiotic woman near the front cried, "Oh, my gidge! Look who's 'ere now!"

The audience roared with laughter but Lord Gordon ignored them – which would have been a perfectly conventional thing to do in any drama ... except what was poor Rose to do now? Instinct told her that the joke wouldn't work if Lord Gordon ignored such a monstrous interruption from the front but then reacted to a single cry of 'No!' from the back. She'd have to improvise something even more spectacular – but what?

Quick! He was halfway there already.

But what was this? He wasn't making the usual beeline from door to wardrobe ... he was hunting this way and that, instead.

Giving her time, of course. Signalling to her that, because *he* was doing it differently, so must she. Think, think!

The world started to swim around her. Her mind remained a blank. For God's sake, she shouted in her mind, don't faint now!

His hand went to the wardrobe door, and still she felt paralyzed. Her glorious acting career – smashed before it even started!

Suddenly she felt a sharp, painful pinch – right in the middle of her left buttock. She let out a scream that pierced the night. Part surprise, part pain, part anger, it brought everything to a halt. Audience and Lord Gordon turned to face her; even Walter Rendle dared to lift the concealing bedspread to see who might have been murdered out there.

"The window!" Rose shouted. "She jumped out the window!"

There was a loud male guffaw from behind her, where it was too dark to make out anything, or anyone. But someone was there, on the grass below the raised tier on which she was seated. His laugh was quickly taken up by the spectators nearby and then it spread throughout the audience. The moment was saved.

Lord Gordon ran to the window and tried desperately to open it. Being painted, it would not budge, of course. The audience went into hysterics at his foolish antics. And Miss Moore, at last, made good her escape.

Rose slipped off her bench and dropped to the grass below. She ran backstage again where the first person she bumped into was Mr Swindlehurst.

"Well done, lady!" he exclaimed, slightly out of breath.

"That was you, wasn't it," she said.

"What was me?" he responded, all innocence.

She just gave him a hug and went back to her prompt corner; of course, it would be most embarrassing between them if either openly acknowledged that he had pinched her in such an intimate place – no matter how good the intention. 'Everything for the sake of my art!' was a fine slogan but a poor motto.

When the final curtain calls were done, Lord Gordon himself sought out Rose and congratulated her on managing to augment her part by no less than seven hundred percent – that is, from one word to seven. "You have all the right instincts, lassie," he said. She decided not to tell him that an increase from one to seven is, in fact, only six hundred percent – thus adding further weight to his concluding remark.

And that bit of impromptu business went so well that, the following night, Miss Petronella Fitzroy slipped into the front seats and cried, "Oh my garters, look who's here now!" while Rose repeated her show-stopping cry from the back – this time without the need for external stimulus. After all, she was by then something of an old trouper.

35

Whenever they played Penzance the company had regular theatrical digs in Mrs Wilkie's boarding house on Chyandour Cliff at the eastern end of the town; it was within walking distance of Penzance Green, where the marquee was erected. Chyandour Cliff may once have been an actual cliff; now, however, it was the main road into and out of the town from the east, overlooking a deep one-sided cutting for the terminus of the Great Western Railway, beyond whose protective wall stretched the wide, bright waters of Mount's Bay.

Rose was once again obliged to share quarters with Titania Moore, thankfully in separate beds this time; but the girl was still as fond as ever of a nip of gin and Rose feared that even breathing the same air might make her tipsy. She knew Titania's technique by now for, while standing in the prompt corner, she'd had every chance to study her behaviour minutely. When waiting to go on she would pretend to sniff at a bouquet or pot pourri, which, considering her dislike of soap and hot water, was not a bad idea in itself; but, in fact, the garland, or whatever it might be, concealed a small medicine bottle of gin, a sip of which vanished down her gullet at each and every sniff.

Rose's habit of taking a bath once a week and strip-washing from head to toe each morning fascinated the girl. "Aren't you afraid your skin will go all cracked and wrinkled prematurely?" she asked on the Monday morning, their first in these new lodgings. "Soap is *terribly* bad for you, you know. It leaches out all the natural oils that keep skin young and supple."

Rose pinched up a fold of skin on her own forearm and then one on Titania's. "Where's the difference?" she asked.

Titania ignored the question. "Why d'you bother, anyway?" she asked in return.

If it was to be question for question, Rose decided to respond with one of her own. "What d'you think of young Mister Lamb?" she asked.

She herself actually had little or no interest in the young man but her chance to observe Titania and him at close quarters over the past week and more had persuaded her that, notwithstanding Titania's offhanded dismissal of him on that first occasion, back in Falmouth, she was more interested in him than he in her; she was also sure that most of Lamb's aversion was because of her refusal to wash or bath.

Titania stiffened. "Mister Lamb?"

"Our juvenile lead – our *only* juvenile lead, though don't ever tell Mister Rendle I said so."

"I know very well *who* he is!" Titania snapped. "What has he to do with ... whatever we were talking about? What was it, anyway?"

"Washing. Taking baths. He takes one every day, you know. In fact, this morning he's going swimming – or so he told me. I rather think he hoped I'd keep him company."

"Swimming!" Titania echoed thoughtfully. "I say – have you got a bathing costume?"

"I left mine at home in Falmouth, but I'm sure one can buy them in the town. Maybe even hire."

She shuddered at the thought but Titania was by now so eager that she went and asked Mrs Wilkie if she had a costume to lend. She had, indeed, and so, a few minutes later, the two of them went down to the eastern beach, across the railway lines, to see if Mr Lamb was true to his word. Titania wore the borrowed costume beneath her ankle-length dressing gown; on their walk back to the digs, that same dressing gown would become her towel. Young Mr Lamb was there – and rather disappointed that Rose was not coming in but nonetheless glad of any sort of company. He had a bar of salt-water soap, such as they use on ships. With it he lathered himself all over, through the thin material of his costume. Intrigued, Titania asked if she might try it, and he, misunderstanding her, started lathering her arms. She protested, of course, but feebly and briefly. She snatched it from him, however, before he could lather portions nearer her heart. However, when she had lathered her front and nether portions herself, she actually asked him to soap her back. Later still she returned him the favour.

Rose, who liked to count paving stones, railings, and steps up or down when she had nothing better to do, counted the number of times the young man glanced toward her during these little frolics. He started off at a rate of some ten glances a minute but during the final five minutes he looked her way only twice. It bore out one of her mom's sayings: 'A shapely figure's as good as any glue.'

"That was glorious," Titania enthused when they returned to Mrs Wilkie's. "I shall go for a swim every day we're here. You are a goose not to go in yourself."

Rose told her (which was true) that it was the wrong time of the month for her.

"What d'you mean?" the girl asked.

"You know! My little friend? The cardinal?" In desperation, when each of these euphemisms met with a blank stare, she said, "The monthlies! The curse! Bleeding! Down there!"

"Oh yes!" Titania responded at last, but as if at some ancient memory. "D'you know – that sometimes happens to me, too. What's it mean? It's horrid."

Rose stared into her eyes to see if this were some kind of legpull – only to realize that it clearly was not. "You really don't know?" she asked.

"No. Why? It stopped after a while, so I didn't bother."

"After a while? You mean after several days."

"No. Just a few hours."

"And how often does it happen?"
Titania shrugged. "Once or twice a year. How often with you?"
"They're called 'the monthlies,' my lover – and that's for a very good reason."
"Monthly?" She was aghast. "That must be awful."
Rose was aghast, too – though in not quite the same sense. "You've never talked about this with anyone? Your mother?"
"We never talked about much of *anything.*"
"At school, then?"
"I didn't go to school."
"Well, your governess, perhaps?"
Titania just laughed at that.
Rose, feeling quite out of her depth – also that she had already trespassed too intimately – said, "Well, it would take more time to explain than we have before us now. Tonight, maybe."
That afternoon she and Mr Swindlehurst went for a walk through the town and out along the Esplanade. They were, on the face of it, an oddly matched couple – a reserved bachelor (one assumed) in his early forties, dapper and introverted, and an outgoing, inquisitive young woman who was enjoying the first real taste of freedom and responsibility in her life. Yet each found a rare ease in the other's company – and they both knew it was because they had shared a bedroom for a week, talking softly into the small hours, without either of them feeling that unspoken desires lay behind the mutual pleasure it had given them.
"I feel I've had such a narrow escape, Mister Swindlehurst," she said as they set off up Market Jew Street.
"You mean your postponed engagement to Mister Redmile-Smith?" he asked.
"My postponed *marriage* to him. I do consider myself engaged. D'you mind my prattling on about it forever?"
He chuckled. "Would it make a hap'orth of difference if I did?"
"Probably not. Anyway, I know it sounds dreadful to talk of *not* marrying Louis as a lucky escape, but what you said the other night was quite true. I will be a much better wife for him after a few years of this sort of experience. And, on the negative side, if I'd never done this foolish, madcap thing – I mean, never run off with you raggle-taggle gipsies-oh – I'd think about it and regret it until the day I died. I am doing the right thing, aren't I!"
"You'll know the answer to that question, lady, when you no longer feel the need to ask it."
"Mrs Fitzroy will be having her baby soon, I suppose," she continued casually.
"Y e s ," he said, drawing the word out as if he had been expecting the remark for some time past.
"D'you think Miss Moore will be given the part of Leah then?"
"Mrs F may have the baby in the afternoon and go back on stage that evening."

"Oh." Rose had not even considered that possibility.
"She did with Petronella."
"Really." She was disappointed.
"Mind you, that was more than eleven years ago."
"That's true. Let's just suppose she doesn't feel quite so heroic this time – d'you think Miss Moore would take over the part?"
"Who was Sir Humphry Davy?" he asked, looking at the statue as they sauntered past it.
"A Cornish hero, born and reared here in Penzance. He invented the safety lamp for miners – that's what he's holding. D'you think she will?"
"I think Lord Gordon will offer her the part and she will turn it down. Why? D'you want to take over Madalena?"
"Me?" Her cry turned several nearby heads.
"It's what you're really asking, isn't it – 'where will I fit in when the company is one lead short'?"
A street photographer from Collett and Trevarton snapped them and handed them his leaflet – which was, of course, already half theirs, too.
Swindlehurst read the text. "Did you write this?"
She shrugged modestly. "Someone had to."
"It's not bad. The answer to the question you really want to ask is – I believe you should prepare to play the part of Leah."
It stopped her in her tracks. She had dreamed of such a thing, of course – years ago – in the way that half of any theatre audience dreams of being on the other side of the footlights (and of making a better fist of it than the clowns who are performing at that moment). But to hear someone else suggest it ... and not just any old someone but a pro with more than two decades on the stage behind him ...! "The others would be absolutely furious," she said.
He laughed.
"They will!" she insisted.
"Of course they will." He took her arm and resumed their stroll toward the western beaches. "But that's the first thing you'll have to become accustomed to if you really want to make something of yourself in this business – the steady, undeserved hostility of those you've passed on the ladder to fame. You'll find that the applause makes it astonishingly easy to ignore. Unless, mind you, there is no applause. Then you slip back down the ladder and the problem vanishes. Everyone backstage loves the Spear Carrier."
"Were you ever famous, Mister Swindlehurst?" she asked, adding hastily, "I mean *more* famous than now?"
"Well done, lady!" He patted her arm. "You're what we call a quick study – apropos which, I daresay you already know Leah's part by heart?"
"I think I know every part by now. I should do – I've prompted enough performances."
"Half a dozen? Enough? Well, well!"

They had to go in indian file through a narrow passage leading into Morrab Road, which, in turn, led down to the Esplanade. When they emerged at the farther end he said, "The reason I asked if you wrote this little handbill all on your ownio is that you might consider writing some material for yourself, now."

She frowned. "For what?"

"Well, if you become one of the Players, you'll have to do a solo turn on our smoking-concert evenings, when we do *The Mysterious Family*. Just something to think about."

She felt her stomach already beginning to turn over inside. "I could sing 'She was poor but she was honest'," she offered.

"That *would* be original!"

"All right! I'll think about it," she said huffily, then, feeling she had been a bit sharp, "And thanks for the warning."

"All part of the bargain," he replied. "I feel quite the flâneur in these togs – The Man Who Broke The Bank In Monte Carlo. My wardrobe has never been so well tended."

That Monday evening's performance had one rather frantic moment, halfway through the first act, where Leah is dragged into the village by the peasantry (or, in the case of Lord Gordon Fitzroy's Players, a peasant) Mrs Fitzroy had a contraction and had to limp on stage on the arm of the peasant instead. It passed, however, and the rest of the play went well.

And, once again, it was gratifyingly well supported. No one could be certain that it had anything to do with the lavish dispersal of announcements on the backs of Collett & Trevarton's handbills, but Lord Gordon, having indorsed the scheme to the tune of £2, chose to think it had. He told her to go to St Ives, which was to be the following week's venue, the very next morning – adding that he was confident she would hit upon some equally ingenious method of publicity, uniquely suited to that little haven of artists and discerning holidaymakers.

"What d'you think we'll do if Mrs Fitzroy has a baby?" Titania asked as soon as Rose blew out their candle that night. Then, answering her own question, "You'd better be ready to read her part, I think."

"*Read* it?" Rose wondered if this were some actor's term for stepping into the breach.

"Yes. It's what happens when there aren't any understudies and someone dies."

"She's not going to *die!*"

"We all hope not, of course. I mean dies or falls seriously ill. Things like that."

"Or is too drunk to go on?"

Titania sniffed at that. "Anyway, what usually happens is that some member of the backstage crew goes on with the book and reads the part. The audience is very understanding. That'll be you – seeing you're the prompt."

"Not to mention being the only member of the backstage crew, as well – the only one who can read, anyway."

"Just be ready – a word to the wise."

Nothing was said about that morning's conversation, for which Rose was grateful. And the following morning, when it was no longer the wrong time of the month for her, she donned the swimming costume she had bought on her return stroll with Mr Swindlehurst yesterday and joined the other two for a swim. Unfortunately, Mr Lamb started trying to lather her with his salt-water soap, to the neglect of Titania. So she, who had swum on Falmouth's old harbour almost from the time she could walk, swam well out of depth, leaving the two of them inshore to deepen their budding acquaintance.

After breakfast she took the mainline train to St Erth, where she changed onto the branch line to St Ives, a town she had never seen before. It made her realize how little she knew of the world. She had lived in Falmouth all her life, had grown up among sailors who spoke of Hong Kong, Valparaiso, Panama, Perth, the Cape, the Horn ... Zanzibar, and yet she had visited Helston only once before joining the Players, Penzance once, Truro half a dozen times, Camborne-Redruth, twice, Newquay and St Ives never. *So, Lord Gordon,* she thought. *How do I walk into this utterly strange town, this 'little haven of artists and discerning holidaymakers,' and, in the space of a single morning – which is all you've allowed me – discover your 'equally ingenious method of publicity'?*

Certainly her first sight of the place – an oval amphitheatre of small houses, cheek by jowl, focused around an oval harbour, sheltering behind the long arm of a breakwater-jetty – provided no inspiration. Nor did her first stroll into the town, from the station down to the inner wall of the harbour. Nor did her walk through the central streets, which seemed to have been designed – and indeed built – entirely by romantic artists. She could just imagine them laying it out, encouraging each other. 'Narrower!' one would say, and, 'Yes, narrower!' the others would all agree. 'And much more wiggly.' 'Oh yes, a *lot* more wiggly.' 'And no two houses on the same building line.' 'Certainly not! Every house must jut forward or shrink back from its neighbour ... and some must have outside staircases ... and all the roofs must be of different heights and angles ... and then we'll make some of the streets even *less* accessible by closing them off with these utterly sweet little arches ...'

Ladies and gentlemen – St Ives!

Artists adored it. Trippers flocked to it. The Players *ought* to do very well here, too – but where in all this visual chaos could they let people know they were in town at all?

What a relief it was to get out on the harbour wall, which had a roadway wide enough for a donkey and cart, to carry away the catch from those fishing boats that moored on that side of the harbour. She was not the only one of that mind, either, for several small parties of holidaymakers were out there, taking their constitutional. They were easily distinguishable in that they were not dressed in the traditional Cornish colours of black and dark grey, as worn at all festivities.

She walked to the far end of the jetty, which she might not otherwise have done had she not spied an artist sitting there, painting the harbour scene. He was a young man with a wild shock of dark, unruly hair and a Vandyke beard. He wore canvas trousers and a fisherman's smock, which looked as if he used it at the end of each day to wipe his palette clean.

Quite apart from his handsome appearance, the intensity with which he was working combined with her natural curiosity to make her want to see how well he was managing. And there, too, she was not the only one.

As she moved past and behind him, trying to disturb him as little as possible, he took down his canvas and put up another – which struck her as odd, for both of them were of the identical portion of the harbour. And, now that she came to study his little set-up more closely, she saw two more resting among the legs of his easel, also of the identical scene.

She watched him at work for ten minutes, feeling guilty at the waste of time. And she was still unable to resolve the riddle of the four identical canvases.

She was just about to go when he laid down his palette and brushes and took out a bottle of squash, which he poured into a glass and sipped with obvious relish. Seeing her chance, she approached him and cleared her throat politely.

"You stood it longer than most, young lady," he said, turning to her with a smile.

"Most what?" she asked.

"Most other trippers. They watch for only two or three minutes before they go. Are you a painter yourself?"

"Theatre scenery – if that counts. D'you get a lot of trippers coming out here to see what you're doing?"

"Not *a* lot – *the* lot. Everyone who comes to Saint Ives, I should think. There's something about this jetty – they have to walk on it and they have to walk to the very end. Which theatre?"

"A travelling group called ..."

"Lord Gordon Fitzroy's Players?" He laughed when he saw he was right. "Be so good as to give the old scoundrel my compliments – I'm Napier Henry."

The name rang a bell but it was a moment or two before she remembered where she had seen it before. "You didn't do the painting of Falmouth that hangs in the deck saloon of the Orient Lines steamer *Ormuz,* did you?"

"No, that was R. Napier Henry, my uncle. Fancy you knowing that! You've seen it?"

"I'm from Falmouth," she replied, avoiding the question. "I'm Miss Lucinda Tremayne, by the way." She closed the small gap between them and they shook hands. "Why the four identical canvases?" she asked at last.

He turned them all the right way up and rested them side by side against whatever was to hand – his leg in the case of the fourth. And then she saw that, although the scene was identical, the shadows were not. "Ah! It's morning, noon, afternoon, and evening," she said.

"That's it." He began stacking them against his easel legs again.

"They're very powerful," she told him. "You give it just three dabs of the brush – like that bit there – and yet when you stand back it turns into two boats and a flash of sunlight on the water. I don't know how you do it."

"Nor yet do I," he said. "Talking of water – have some cordial." He tipped the rest of the glass down his throat, wiped it all round on his sleeve, and refilled it for her.

She hesitated.

"Fear not," he said. "The artistic bacillus is not infectious. Anyway, there's antiseptic enough in that glass to kill it."

"How encouraging!" she cried, but she took a sip, nonetheless – and then saw what he meant, for the 'antiseptic' in question was gin. "I know one artist – or artiste, perhaps – who's in danger of dying of it at this moment. Are you going to sell all four paintings as a single unit?"

He took out a sandwich. Immediately a small flock of gulls gathered at the jetty's edge, mewing and screaming. "Are you interested in buying?" he asked cautiously.

"It'll be a great day when I can afford to say yes," she replied.

"Thirty bob each," he offered. "Four quid gets you the lot. Can't say fairer than that."

A dapper little man in a dark suit and grey spats, who had been standing nearby, seemingly interested only in the manoeuvrings of a fishing trawler putting out to sea, said, "Five – when you've finished the last one."

"Six!" Rose said without even thinking.

"Ten," the man said. "I warn you, I shan't go higher."

"You won't need to," Rose said disconsolately.

The man handed the painter a crisp white fiver and his card, saying, "I'll part with the other five when you bring the paintings to me. I'm staying at the Tregenna Castle." It was the poshest hôtel in St Ives – maybe in the whole of west Cornwall.

"Certainly, Mister ... er, Sir James. Good heavens – *Sir James!*"

He nodded. "I collected your uncle in his day. We may come to an arrangement, young man. We'll talk about it when you deliver these four." He walked away a dozen yards or so and then added, "One more thing – if you sell any more paintings from your stock this week, ten pounds is your rock-bottom price. Understood?"

"Perfectly, Sir James." He laughed. And when the man had gone he turned to her and said, "Thank *you,* Miss Tremayne."

"For what?"

"For driving him up to ten."

"I don't know why I did that, but thank God he did step in. I really wanted them but I could never have afforded six quid."

"Oh, well," he said, lazily running his eye up and down her figure. "We could have come to *some* arrangement."

"Oh no we couldn't!" She grinned and handed him back her glass of gin and something rather pleasant-tasting, which was still three-quarters full. She knew she ought to be affronted by his impertinence, but she actually felt flattered and quite pleased. "But I've been thinking. My employer, Lord Gordon Fitzroy – as you know – could run to a couple of quid – and you wouldn't have to part with a single canvas, either ..."

She went on to describe her scheme, which he accepted eagerly.

"You did *what?"* Lord Gordon asked immediately after she had repeated the tale to him.

"It'll work," she insisted. "You'll see. Absolutely *everybody* who visits Saint Ives has to go to the end of the jetty ..."

"It's a bye-law? What are you saying?"

"It's much stronger than a bye-law." She patted her breastbone. "It comes from in here. They get attacks of claustrophobia in the town and they walk it off on the jetty."

"And what if they don't go to the end? It's wasted then."

"But they all do. Everyone loves watching an artist at work – especially an artist like Napier Henry, who handles paint with such ease and fluidity. And even more especially when, from a distance, he seems to be trying to paint on the back of a poster. And they're almost bursting with curiosity when they get close enough to read it and they discover it's nothing to do with art – it's all about a dramatic presentation on Saint Ives Island."

"Nothing to do with *art?"* he roared.

"You know what I mean – with painting. It'll work – I can promise you. And anyway, I distributed twenty handbills in the usual way, all over the town. And, since you can leave the place behind you inside five minutes, no matter where you start from inside it, no one living there and no one visiting there can have the slightest excuse for not knowing that Lord Gordon Fitzroy is there on the Island all week."

"We shall see," he said darkly.

But he had other worries just then, for his wife had been having fresh contractions most of that morning.

36 The following morning, Wednesday, July 13th, Mrs Fitzroy was delivered of a bawling, prunefaced, adorable baby boy, a son for her husband, a brother for Petronella, and – when she refused to rise from her childbed for that afternoon's matinée – a headache for the Players. They met in a mood of controlled panic just before lunchtime, two and a half hours before curtain-up. Petronella volunteered to take on the now vacant part of Leah; she filled out her blouse with two oranges to show how it might be possible. Their predicament was so dire that her father even considered the offer seriously. But her spirited rendering of Leah's opening lines, 'I am here! What do you want with me?' dissuaded him. The part included many forceful, declamatory speeches for which a piping treble is not entirely appropriate. In a softer register, however, that same youthful voice could portray Madalena's gentler, sweeter character.

Besides, as Mr Dennison pointed out ... father and daughter playing passionate lovers? It would expose them to ribaldry from the pit.

"You – Miss Moore," he cried, turning upon the startled Titania, who had considered her tenure of Madalena to be unshakable. "You can take over Leah, surely?"

The poor girl could barely stammer out her reluctance, especially as the better half of her spirit lay tightly stoppered in a garland in the marquee half a mile away.

But Mr Swindlehurst came to her rescue – in passing, as it were, since his principal aim was to further his friend Rose's cause. "A moving speech from the curtain, sir, delivered as only *you* can deliver it – about this morning's joyous event, coupled with the unswerving dedication of your Players not to disappoint the public whom we cherish so dearly, blah-blah-blah, would sufficiently engage their sympathies so that they would accept the appearance on stage of our esteemed assistant stage manager with the script in her hand. Why, their hearts would swell with goodwill toward all!" And when he saw he almost had them, he added, "It would give us several hours before the evening performance to work out a satisfactory redistribution of the parts – to say nothing of the necessary rehearsal."

Murmurs of objections from several quarters were stifled at once when Lord Gordon said, "Precisely what I was thinking myself, Mister Swindlehurst! Miss Tremayne – you will, I trust, have no objection to standing upon the stage and reading the part? You normally stand in the wings and read it anyway."

Rose gave Swindlehurst a bitter glance and agreed that she would not object. But she took her friend aside as they dispersed for lunch and asked him why he had now gone back on the plan they had discussed a couple of days ago.

"Because, lady," he replied, "our lord and master would never have agreed to your leaping into the lead like that. It's up to you now. If you go on stage in costume, fully made up, with no book in your hand, they're not going to ring down the curtain, are they! The grand old tradition that raises it on Act One will keep it raised even if you fall flat on your face."

She hung her head and apologized for ever doubting him. "Though I'm not to sure I like your talk of falling flat on my face," she added.

"Theatrical honesty," he murmured. "Never wish another actor good luck. Also, while we're about it, never name the Scottish Play and never whistle backstage."

"Could you be an utter angel and bring me a lettuce leaf," she said. "I don't think I could keep down anything more substantial."

"Get used to it," he advised. "If you ever lose that fear of going on, it's you that's going off."

She managed the lettuce leaf, which put her in the mood for a couple of slices of ham and a tomato as well; also a small portion of bread-and-butter pudding. But as for getting used to the terrors that now possessed her – that she thought she would never do.

"Wait a mo and I'll accompany you to the field," Swindlehurst called out when he saw her setting off.

"I'll be all right – honestly," she assured him, meaning she was beyond all comfort and advice by now. It was, as he had said, entirely up to her.

It was no use telling herself it was only an absurd, out of date melodrama, performed by actors who had either seen or never would see better days, in a tent that certainly had, in a cow-pasture, in one of the most obscure corners of the kingdom ... in fifty-seven minutes' time she would be standing on stage, with all the limelight upon her, pretending to be a Bohemian Jewess deeply, passionately in love with old Lord Gordon Fitzroy, who would be pretending to be a young peasant farmer in An Austrian Village, two hundred years ago. She – who had never appeared in anything other than the school Nativity and a few dumb crambos on jolly evenings in the servants' hall.

Was she mad? She must be mad. How different was the dream from the reality! In all those happy fantasies where some leading actress fell ill on stage and she had leaped into the breach (knowing the part by heart, of course) and saved the day she had never once felt the slightest twinge of fear. How could she have failed to imagine that the reality would be such a torture as this?

Forty-eight minutes! She should change and start making up.

She walked through the unreal gates and over the unreal grass. How wonderful to be a real cow, though – with nothing to do but eat all day and let someone relieve you of your milk, morning and evening. Come to think of it, she could at this very moment have been sitting in her boudoir in Maida Vale, making up her face like fine porcelain, adorning herself in costly silks and jewels, before driving down to Hyde Park, the wonder and envy of other, less favoured women. She must have been mad that day she turned it down for *this!*

She sidled into the ladies' dressing-room tent and hunted for Leah's costume in Mrs Fitzroy's trunk.

"What are you doing?" Titania was watching her in the mirror.

"Oh, I just thought it would look a little less odd if I were at least dressed for the part," Rose replied. She was amazed to hear that her voice did not tremble, though it was the only part of her that was firm. She hoped it was a good augury.

"I suppose so," she replied dubiously. "What d'you think, Mrs Skerrett?"

"It's not usual," the lady agreed, "but I suppose there's no *harm* in it. You don't need spectacles to read by, do you, precious?"

"No, thank heaven," Rose replied from deep in the folds of Leah's dress – the one she had adapted (how many years ago?) to hide Mrs Fitzroy's *enceinture.*

"That would have looked a bit odd," the woman concluded.

Rose's trembling fingers could not manage the hooks at the back. Nor could Titania's alcoholic ones, but Mrs Skerrett obliged, saying, "My dear soul! You're shaking like a withy, child! No one expects any miracles from you. All it is is reading aloud. Just speak a bit higher than you think you need to. Try it now – say something."

Rose drew breath. "I am here! What do you want of me?"

"A bit louder."

"I seek ... no one."

"No. Drop your voice on 'no one' – you're disappointed, see."

"I know that. But you told me to speak louder."

"Well, not all the time or it would be monotonous. Say it again."

"I seek ... no one."

"Perfect!" The older woman looked toward Titania. "What d'you think, pet?"

It was quite clear what Titania was thinking, for instead of replying, she spoke the next lines in the play, which happened to be hers, as Madalena: "You seek bread?"

Rose, grinning now, continued: "No! I did not come to beg." She searched the tent anxiously. "Not here – ah me! He is not here."

Titania laughed and clapped her hands. "You're going to *act* it, aren't you! That's why you're dressing and making up."

"D'you think it's stupid?" Rose asked anxiously.

"I don't care," she replied. "That's your funeral. I'm in favour of anything that stops Lord Gordon forcing *me* to take the part."

"What d'you think of her Cornish accent?" Mrs Skellett asked.

The girl shrugged. "It's not *too* strong, I suppose. It should go down all right."

"Mrs Fitzroy played her with a slight lisp," Rose said. "D'you think ... I mean ..." She showed what she meant, imitating Mrs F's delivery of her next lines in the play: "Welcome O Night! In the mistherable hut over yonder vine-hillsth sthleep the mother and child, and on the threshold cowersth Abraham ..." Her voice trailed off as she saw the other two staring at her in amazement. "What?" she asked.

"For God's sake don't do *that!*" Titania cried in a curious mixture of horror and mirth.

"Old Fitzroy would have you out on your ear," Mrs Skerrett agreed. "But how d'you *do* that?" She glanced anxiously toward the entrance flap and added, "Do a bit more!"

They both huddled near Rose so that she wouldn't need to raise her voice while she obliged with, "Sthleep on! You need me not. Innocthencthe ith guarded by the angelsth, and the wingsth of the Eternal Majesthty sheltersth itsth head!"

They collapsed in a giggling tripod of heads, bathed in the reek of gin.

"Why does she lisp the part like that?" Rose asked.

"Theatrical convention, child," Mrs S explained. "Always a lisp and a slight stoop for a Jew or Jewess. It saves a lot of make-up with putty noses."

"Can you imitate little Wondrous Child?" Titania asked.

"No time for that, now," Mrs S chided. "We've got to make her up. And as for you, Miss Tremayne – stick to your Cornish."

Twenty minutes later, while Rose was making her second needless visit to the latrine tent, Lord Gordon stood before the curtain, speaking to the tiers of satisfyingly filled benches, exhausted and panting as if he had just played Lear. It was his habit to overplay his age on such occasions, so that when he later underplayed it as the romantic lead, his amazed public would marvel all the more at his youthful sprightliness. So, clutching its folds for support he wheezed, "My dear, *dear* public. You see before you – even before our little drama opens for your delectation – a happy but exhausted man! [Murmurs.] Happy in my good fortune this day and happy to share it with you, dear people. For at that very moment when the hands of the clock *scissored* the day in two, my dear lady wife, my childhood sweetheart and the bosom companion of all my days, presented me with as bonny, as bouncing, as bright a baby boy who ever drew breath to add 'bawling' to that list of attributes beginning with 'b' – and who, I daresay, will add at least one more we can think of over the coming nights and days! [Laughter and applause; cries of 'Well done' and 'We *knew* she had it in her!'] Yes, thank you, that man! Very droll. Happy I said. And exhausted I said. Exhausted in my efforts to patch the enormous gash left in our presentation for you by my dear lady wife's inability to play the title role. God willing, she will be well enough to perform this evening, but for this afternoon we humbly crave your indulgence while the part on stage is read by our most able assistant stage manager, Miss Lucinda-Ella Tremayne. I know you will treat her with indulgence for she is one of you – a comely maiden from Falmouth who has never appeared on a public stage before. [Cries of 'Oh! The dear!' and other noises of sympathy.] However, should anyone object to this temporary arrangement and prefer to exchange his or her ticket for one later in the week when, as I say, my dear lady wife will once again present the title part, I shall understand perfectly – and Mister Roberts will accommodate you at the door."

An eye whose ferocity was honed as Bluebeard, The Ripper, and Squire Corder, the Red Barn murderer quartered the assembly like a hawk's; not a soul dared move – indeed, they hardly dared to breathe.

It was done! The production – or at least the income it generated – was saved.

Rose stayed out of sight until the moment of her entrance drew near – just in case Lord Gordon should tell her to wipe that stuff off her face and get back into her everyday clothes. Perhaps because everyone was on the edge of their nerves, the opening scenes went wonderfully well – which only added to her trepidation, since it gave her an even greater height from which to bring the whole thing down again.

Slowly, slowly – and yet much too fast – the drama unfolded for the ... *oh, my God!* she thought. *For the thirteenth time* since she had joined the company! And when was that? Not years. Not even months. *Thirteen days* ago! And what was today's date – Wednesday, the *thirteenth* of July!

So it was bound to fail. Why had she not realized it before?

But wait a moment, she argued back with herself. *You're not superstitious. You don't believe in any of that old cant.*

Try telling that to me now! her other half countered.

But it was too late to worry. Nathan was already stirring up the Angry Peasant – and his offstage companions – to hunt down the Jewess. Any moment now he would come to drag her on stage.

"Goodness gracious!" That was Mother Groschen. "Where is my baby, my little Frank? Perhaps the Jewess has already killed him for their Passover feast!"

"The Jewess! The Jewess!" they all cried – while Rose stood trembling as if she really were Leah and the threat were real, too.

"Friends! Children! Hear me!" That was Father Herman – dear Mr Swindlehurst, seeking to calm their fury.

"Your miserable priest is a Freethinker!" Wicked Nathan, the secret Jew, in an aside to the peasantry.

"What! Who dared utter that word?" Father Herman again. Less than half a minute to go ...

"Away friends!" Nathan again. "Seek the accursed witch! Drag her here!"

And they will! They will! Any moment now ...

Angry Peasant and Nathan came offstage toward her, saw, in the gloom, what seemed to be Mrs Fitzroy ... certainly someone wearing her costume ... someone made up. A moment later they realized who it was.

"Are you mad?" Mr Rendle asked.

"Almost certainly," she replied glumly.

"Lord Gordon'll skin you alive," Roberts gloated.

"No time now. Come on!" They grabbed an arm each and pulled her toward the light, the merciless light.

She wished they would grip more firmly but the weeks they had spent in dragging the heavily expectant Mrs Fitzroy on stage had conditioned them otherwise.

In the meanwhile Madalena and Father Herman had been doing their handwringing best to calm the anger and bloodlust of the offstage peasantry. At least they both knew what to expect so there would be no confusion at the actual moment she was dragged blinking into that light.

"Down with her! Stone her!" The Angry Peasant's cry was augmented by the barber-doctor, the baker, and the rest of the company, on and off stage.

Something happened inside Rose at that moment. It wasn't so much that she forgot the audience – how could she, with every eye now fixed upon her! But, by some peculiar alchemy of that moment, *they* became the fantasy and the fiction in which she was now immersed became real. Indeed, more than real, for it suddenly acquired a heightened, almost ecstatic inner force – something she had occasionally glimpsed as a spectator in the wings but had never fully experienced until now.

"I'm here!" whispered an anxious Mr Swindlehurst, with his back to the audience.

She did not immediately recognize it as her prompt. When she did, she realized she must have been standing there quite a while, panting hard and staring round in wild-eyed terror. The audience, too, must have been on the edges of their seats, for there was not a sound out there, not a sigh, not a rustle.

"I am here!" She shook off her captors' feeble clutch as if their fists had been vices of steel and drew herself up. "What do you want with me?"

"What seek you here?" Nathan asked, his voice tinged with an amazement that was not demanded by his part. "Daughter of an accursed race!"

"I seek ..." She peered all about the stage and then, instead of murmuring the concluding "no one" in a dejected tone, she tossed her head and spoke the two words defiantly.

That particular interpretation did not entirely come to her out of the blue. It was one that had occurred to her among several others, and all merely as a matter of interest, while she had been reading prompt. She had tried them all on as she might have tried on hats in a hat shop. And this one had suddenly come back to her and just popped out.

There was a slight commotion in the audience – a little frisson of surprise mingled with curiosity. Was this the simple, comely Falmouth maid who, Lord Gordon had promised, would merely read the part? She did not even *sound* Cornish – more like a grand dame or a queen. The way she tossed her head like that, flashing defiance from her eyes ... it was very regal.

Rose heard the dying echo of her words in her mind and only then did she realize she was speaking the part in her best upper-class accent. Apart from Mr Swindlehurst, she had not dared speak to any other member of the cast in that voice, for fear they should imagine she was giving herself airs – or, conversely, that she was a real high-quarter maid come slumming among them. Well, there was nothing for it now but to play Leah that way to the closing speech.

"No!" she exclaimed in answer to Madalena's question. "I did not come here to beg. Not here! He is not here!"

Lord Gordon, who had run to the proscenium peephole the moment he heard her open her mouth, studied the responses of the audience and then gave her the Roman thumbs-up. Though relieved, she still could not relax, for she was having to improvise actions to fit words she could have spoken in her sleep. She was on tenterhooks from first to last and after each of her scenes she came off drenched in sweat.

Just before the scene in which she and Rudolf, played by Lord Gordon himself, had to exchange a passionate kiss, Mr Swindlehurst sidled up to her and whispered, "Open your mouth and shut your eyes and see what the king has brought you."

Trusting him, she did as he said. She felt him place something between her teeth and then he placed his palm beneath her jaw shut it quite firmly. A moment later she spat the thing out in disgust, for it was a clove of garlic.

"Good for the voice," he told her. "A sovereign defence against bacilli and *other primitive life forms* which try to invade that way."

She did not understand him until it came to Lord Gordon's kiss, when the man tried to stick his tongue right down her throat. He only did it once – and not for very long at that.

When she considered how every minute before curtain-up had dragged, she could not believe that the subsequent minutes went by so fast. In no time at all, it seemed, she stood, a forlorn and tragic figure in the spotlight, crying, "Thine, thine is the vengeance. Vengeance, madness and folly!" and so forth, all the way to her final lines, the last of the play: "Tonight I shall wander into the far-off, the promised land!"

The audience went wild. The cast took four curtain calls, she and Lord Gordon got three more. They had never had so many in the thirteen days since she had joined them. Lucky thirteen! She would have it on her dressing-room door when she became a big London star!

"Now, young lady," Lord Gordon said sternly as the curtain fell for the last time. "Kindly explain ..."

She knew what was coming and had her excuses ready. "Honestly, sir!" She was back in her Cornish voice again. "I forgot that kiss was coming up, sir. Clean forgot! And I've always eaten raw garlic for ..."

"Not that!" He cried.

"My parents own a greengrocery, you see. And ..."

"No, no, no! I'd stop your mouth with another kiss if I dared! Just tell me what little game you're playing here?"

"Game, sir? No game."

"And you can drop your mock-Cornish accent from now on. It always did sound a little too educated to me. Who are you really? Out with it!"

"Sir! I am who I say I am. Upon my honour."

He grasped her roughly by the arm and dragged her to the front of the stage, just behind the curtain. There, looking cautiously all around, he lowered his voice and said, "You were not sent to spy on us by ... a certain person, were you?" His eyes seemed to bore into her as he asked his question.

"I haven't the first idea what you're talking about, sir – truly."

"Because if you were ... well, the gaff is well and truly blown now, isn't it! And if you are what I suspect, you can tell that certain person that when Lord Gordon gives his word, he keeps it."

"I almost wish I were this spy you accuse me of being," she told him. "Then at least your *suspicions* would be over and done with and all I'd have to worry about would be finding ground glass in my porage or something."

He laughed, somewhat reluctantly. "Well, you're an odd cove, Miss Tremayne. I give you that. I never saw the like. Maybe you speak the truth. If so ..."

"I do, sir. I've always been able to imitate different accents, though – and people." Taking her heart in her hands she said, "Welcome O Night! In the mistherable hut over yonder vine-hillsth sthleep the mother and child, and on the threshold cowersth Abraham, the sthentinel."

His jaw dropped and he gaped at her in a strange mixture of horror and fascination. "How on earth ...?" he asked, clapping a hand over her lips when he had heard enough. "It's uncanny."

"Not really. It's just something I've been able to do as long as I can remember."

"Well!" He threw up his hands in a gesture of accepting the unbelievable. "This – together with today's performance ..."

"It was all right, then, was it, sir?"

He waved grandly toward the auditorium half of the marquee. "There was your reply, my lady – the only one that matters. As I was saying – this calls for some fresh thinking. You may remain in the role all this week at least. I was never happy with the thought that my dear lady wife would be back in harness so soon. As for next week ... we shall see."

"Sir?" she said as he made his customary royal progress off the stage. "A leading lady earns more than an assistant stage manager."

He turned and stared at her. Roberts turned the spotlight out at that moment but she needed no light to know exactly what he was thinking: *If she's the novice she claims to be, then I could pull the wool over her eyes with some fancy talk about being on probation. On the other hand, we'll be playing Plymouth sometime just before Christmas – where she'll meet and mingle with other theatre people, who will tell her the truth. Better, then, to get it directly from me.*

"Five pounds this week," he said. "Nine for a full week."

"And the ASM's job? Do I get those wages as well if I continue to do the work?"

This time he did not turn round. Laughing, he said, "You wouldn't care to dash off a few plays for us to add to the repertoire, would you?"

37

For Rose the last word, and the only one that counted, was Mr Swindlehurst's. She waited for him to catch up with her by the gate to the field and fell in at his side as they strolled back to their digs. "It is, of course, quite absurd," he said, as if they had already been speaking for some time, "to play an early eighteenth century Bohemian Jewess in the voice of the English county squirearchy ..."

"Oh dear," she said.

But he had not quite finished. "... and yet you were quite right to do so. No ear is more attuned to fine nuances of accent than those of the English lower classes – unless it is the ears of the English middle classes – and, now that I think of it, even they may be outdone by the English upper classes. All of them can tell the genuine from the fake inside three syllables. Did you *hear,* did you *feel* that nervous thrill which ran through the audience this afternoon when they heard you utter your first lines? 'I am here. What do you want with me?' You stick with it, lady!" He grinned at her. "And the trick with the garlic."

Rose, Titania, and Mrs Skerrett were privileged with an invitation to inspect and coo over little Romulus, as his doting parents had decided to call the new baby. Mrs S did most of the cooing; the two younger women were less impressed with the shivering, tight-swaddled little bundle of wants, terrors, and tics that lay at his mother's breast. But, being professionals in the art – both of them now – they acted their delight convincingly enough. They all agreed he had his father's looks, and privately wondered that anyone could take it as a compliment to the father.

"Miss Tremayne," the mother said, "I'd like a word with you, if you wouldn't mind staying behind?"

When the others had gone, she said, "I hear you carried the day before you this afternoon."

Rose made a few embarrassed noises and said, "I think people are just surprised I didn't fall flat on my face. Me too, actually. I was utterly *terrified!*"

For a long time after that Mrs Fitzroy busied herself with settling the baby, paying Rose no heed at all.

"Was that it, then?" Rose asked.

"I suppose so," she replied. Then, as Rose reached the door, "You have proved to be an excellent wardrobe mistress and ASM."

Rose thanked her and left, wondering what on earth it had all been about.

That night, after an equally successful second house, Titania asked her where she had learned to speak like that. "Half the company thinks you're top drawer," she said. "The other half thinks you just have a perfect ear for it."

"And which side do you favour?" Rose asked.

"I don't know. Every time I side with the perfect-ear people, the top-drawer theory sounds more convincing ... and vice versa. Which is it? I won't tell."

Rose laughed. "I don't in the least mind if you tell. I don't know about *perfect* ear, but I'm certainly not top-drawer."

"You could pass for it, you know."

"Perhaps. But it would be about as restful as performing on stage for twenty-four hours a day. So, no thank you." After a pause she added, "Do people mind?"

"Mind what?"

"You know – me going from a sort of glorified needlewoman to playing the second main female part in one leap?"

"Second main? It's *the* main part."

"Oh, no – that's your part, surely. You have many more lines than me."

"But they're just business lines. You have all the drama. Honestly – when you utter that curse in the moonlit churchyard ... well, it gave me gooseflesh all over."

Rose said nothing. The strange interview with Mrs Fitzroy had unsettled her, though she didn't wish to discuss it – certainly not with Titania.

"You don't seem too happy?" the girl prompted.

"And *you* don't realize how little I know. I've watched Mrs Fitzroy play the part thirteen times and I've seen the play, by other companies, on four or five other occasions in the past. So I've had lots of chances to get to know the part and develop my own feelings about it. But as for any *other* play – I'd be lost. Take Sheridan's *The Critic,* which I've never seen on stage ..."

"Funny you should pick that. We've got it in the repertory."

"It's not funny at all, you goose! That's *why* I picked it – I've seen the acting copies among the books."

"We sometimes perform it when we get nearer Plymouth – it's a more cosmopolitan, refined sort of audience up there."

"Anyway, the point I'm making is that I wouldn't have the foggiest notion how to play any of those parts. What's the female lead's name – the one who goes mad?"

"Tilburina. She's the daughter of the governor of Tilbury Fort. Mrs Fitzroy plays her and I play the confidante. She goes mad in white satin. I go mad in white linen – that's the rule."

"You see! there you go again. I don't know any of these rules. I wouldn't even know ..."

"It's a *joke,* darling. Sheridan's little joke!"

"Anyway, I wouldn't know how to start, or even *where* to start. Everyone has got a completely wrong impression of my capabilities. So I'd be very grateful, Titania, dear, if you'd let everyone understand that I actually know *nothing* about this business. Will you do that little thing for me? Please?"

"No."

"Why not?"

"No one would believe me for a start – no one who saw you utterly dominating the stage this afternoon and this evening. You know – you really should have more confidence in yourself, Lucy. More belief."

After a short, tense silence, Rose risked saying, "Talk about the pot calling the kettle black!"

She could almost feel the tension radiating through the dark toward her.

"What d'you mean?" Titania asked coldly.

"I think you know."

"I think I do not!"

"Confidence in oneself? You mean the ability to go onstage without a crutch."

"I don't need a crutch."

"A crutch of *any* kind? Specifically of the liquid kind?"

"Mind your own bloody business, Miss Hoity-toity."

Rose made no reply.

"Why?" Titania asked after a brief silence. "Has anyone been talking to you about it?"

"No. Nor I to anyone else. But we all have eyes in our heads. And we haven't lost the sense of smell, either. Why d'you do it?"

"I've always done it."

"Not as a child, surely?"

"That's when it started – gin on the handkerchief to dull the pain of teething. Never stopped. Never looked back. And it's my affair and no one else's." She turned over demonstratively and pretended to snore.

Rose played Leah for the rest of that week – and all the following week in St Ives. It was not, to say the least, a profound sort of character; there were no hidden depths to be teased out in different nuances of voice or timing, so she was able to repeat her earlier rendering each time, word for word (of course), pause for pause, inflection for inflection. And that, in turn, allowed her to detach part of her mind to study the wider scene – not just the play as it unfolded in the pool of light upon the stage but the mysterious communion between that intensely lighted world and the great pool of darkness beyond.

The more deeply she observed it, the greater the mystery became. Titania had talked of dominating the stage. Rose soon realized that each of the actors achieved that domination in their turn, passing it from one to the other like a game of pass-the-parcel, except that the parcel was invisible. At least, that was when it worked best. When one of them hogged the parcel to himself, which Lord Gordon was especially prone to do, that same mysterious communion seemed to weaken. It occurred to her then that the play itself was something much bigger than the plot and the words, the characters and the scenery; without that invisible passing of the 'parcel' it withered and could ultimately die.

"It's an interesting notion," Swindlehurst said when she tried to explain it to him. "You're saying there's a *platonic* play somewhere, an Ideal Play of which all actual plays are mere shadows. You could be right, lady. I've often wondered why some dramas work and others don't. If you're right, it's because, despite brilliant writing and wonderful characters, they don't 'pass the parcel' around dramatically." He patted her on the back and added, "How long before you outgrow our little compass, eh? Not long is my guess."

But if she was in danger of getting swollen headed with her success as Leah, it all came crashing down with a thump on the Thursday evening in St Ives, when they switched to *The Mysterious Family* and individual party pieces. Mrs Fitzroy had decided to return to the stage that night, since the play ran for only an hour; so Rose had no part in it – only in the smoking-concert section. She decided to do a comic patter she had written herself – a composite of Cornish tall tales and jokes she had heard most of her life. Most of them were her father's jokes, about a character called Zacky Polkinghorne, upon whose simpleton head and shoulders all the stories were laid.

Zacky was a farm labourer who slept in an old henhouse on the farm, but he left that farmer and went to another 'coz they 'ad a better 'en'ouse.'

Zacky was nailing up a fence one day, holding the nails between his lips, as nailer-uppers often do. Some had the heads sticking out, some had the sharp points. His fellow-workers noticed that Zacky threw half of them away and asked why; Zacky told them they'd got the heads on the wrong end. He felt hurt when everyone laughed but later he worked it out for hisself – they weren't on the wrong end at all ... those were the nails for *the other side!*

When Zacky was a manservant, he got sent down to the undertaker to tell them his master had died in the night and could they come and collect the corpse from the house, which was called Bougainvillæa Lodge, in Tywarnhayle Avenue. "How d'you spell those names, now?" asks the clerk. Zacky thinks it over for a minute and then says, "You give I a lend of your handcart, boy, and I'll bring un down to 'ee."

Zacky explaining the Theory of Compensation to a fellow labourer: "You seen a feller with one short leg, surely? Well, the other leg is always made a bit longer, see? That's called compensation, that is!"

She had a dozen more in a similar vein, for all Cornish jokes are about stupid people and the idiotic things they do or say.

Rose went out on stage, full of the confidence born of her success as Leah. She knew it wasn't going too well right from the start, when the expected guffaws emerged as mere titters. She knew it was going seriously wrong when a woman in the front row said to her neighbour, "You can get those sandals she's wearing in that shoeshop on the harbour front." She knew it was a disaster when the hum of conversation began to rise from several parts of the audience. But she stuck it to the end, smiling bravely.

"Why didn't you come on and rescue me?" she hissed at Lord Gordon, who was about to go on for his turn.

"That's how you learn, lassie," he replied evenly.

From the barely concealed smiles of the others she realized that her humiliation was not entirely unwelcome among them.

She did not start crying until she was a good furlong from the marquee, down on the edge of Porthmeor beach, where the Atlantic breakers drowned her sobs.

"That didn't go down too well," said a voice behind her – a half-familiar voice, too.

She turned to see Napier Henry, the artist on the jetty, standing a little way off, barely discernible in the last of the twilight. "May I join you – or would you prefer the company of the waves?"

"I'd rather be under them, the way I feel," she replied through the hiccups that always follow weeping. But she swept her skirts to her by way of invitation.

"Well, *I* thought they were funny stories," he assured her.

"Oh God! Don't say you were *there!*"

"I had to use my free ticket sometime." He sat beside her, actually touching, and put an arm around her.

She knew she ought to object – in case he got the wrong idea – but she was so bereft of comfort at that moment that she hadn't the heart to turn the smallest crumb of it away. Instead, she laid her head upon his shoulder and said, "Why didn't it work, Mister Henry? I've heard people laugh at those stories all my life."

"That could be it – they've heard them all before. But," he added quickly, "I don't think so."

"Why, then?" It really was very comforting to feel another human being beside her – all right, a *man!*

"More than half of them – perhaps three-fourths of them – would have come to see *Leah* in the first half of the week."

"So?" And to rest her head on his shoulder.

"So they are all convinced you're a young, high-quarter lady. Not an actress *playing* a high-quarter lady but the other way round. So when you tell jokes about this stupid Cornishman, you're not one of us telling jokes about one of us – you're one of *them* poking fun at one of us. I don't suppose they worked it out in so many words, but that was the feeling I got, sitting among them."

And feeling his arm around her. "There's nothing I can do about it, then," she said glumly.

"You could try something different."

"Like what?" The night was warm enough but she seemed to positively glow all down the side nearest him.

"I don't know. I don't know anything about you. Are you from a theatrical family?"

"My parents are greengrocers in Falmouth. I went into service at fourteen. Was a lady's maid to Lady Carclew until a month ago. Joined the theatre then. Make something interesting out of that!"

He didn't even need to think it over. "There you are!" he exclaimed. "You can not only imitate the upper classes, you've had a ringside seat into their lives. You know how they feel and think. What about a page from her ladyship's diary, then a page from her maid's diary – both describing *exactly* the same events! You could work in some cruelly funny contrasts, no?"

The hair at the back of her neck tingled. He was absolutely right, of course; everything in her leaped at the suggestion. She wanted to rush back to the digs and start drafting it at once.

And, as if to encourage her, a roar of laughter carried to them over the steadier roar of the waves. She suddenly realized that, but for her, he would still be sitting there, among them. "And you came outside, here, just to ..."

"I thought you wouldn't exactly be skipping and singing for joy," he said.

"You are good!" She turned her face upward and kissed him on the cheek. The moon, which was full that night, peeped over the roofs of the houses overlooking the beach, riming his silhouette with an edge of silver.

His free hand came up and held her there. His lips nuzzled hers and then pressed eagerly. She lay back in the sand and closed her eyes. His hand found her breast. Her knees came apart without her even willing it; the one nearest him slipped under his thigh. She heard her heart beating like a water-hammer just behind her ears.

"Mmmm?" he asked.

"Yes! Yes!" she whispered, edging her whole body beneath him.

38

After St Ives the company played Camborne-Redruth, during what turned out to be one of the hottest weeks of that summer. Hours before the first performance, conditions inside the marquee became impossible and they moved hastily to an outdoor arena nearby – an amphitheatre built into an ancient sunken mine-working near Tuckingmill, on the lower slopes of Carn Brea. John Wesley had preached there more than once, a century and a half earlier, but people still spoke of it as yesterday. "Thespis' loss was God's gain," was Mr Swindlehurst's gloss on it.

Rose once again played Leah, since Mrs Fitzroy did not feel up to the dramatic strain of the part; she was, however, well able to sit in the audience and watch, which Rose found impossible to ignore in daylight. Titania said her nervousness did not show; but the fact that she felt nervous throughout the performance was the real worry, whether or not it showed.

Between performances she was still looking after the costumes and props. And she was also acting as prompt in the scenes when she was offstage. And, too, she helped paint or repaint the scenery between performances – but then so did every other member of the cast except Mr Dennison, who claimed to be colourblind, and painted skies green to prove it. And on the Tuesday, when there was no matinée, she was given the day off until six that evening – but only in order to do her by now customary advance-scouting business in Truro, the next town on their itinerary.

Lord Gordon claimed it took him the best part of six hours to induce or bribe a satisfactory number of shopkeepers to display his handbills. He defined a satisfactory number as 'close to a third of the shops in and around the centre.' She never let him know she could usually manage to sign up that many inside two hours – which might or might not have had something to do with her eyelashes and her smile. Anyway, on that particular day it gave her all the time she needed to take the train to Falmouth, spend the afternoon at home, and be back in time for the performance that evening. She was eager to see her folks, of course, but her main purpose was to discover whether Louis had called or written. She had devoured the commercial reports in the press at every possible chance, but, though there had been plenty of coverage of the bankruptcy, it had all been highly technical, with Louis featuring more often as 'the Chairman' than as Mr Redmile-Smith. And no mention at all of his mother.

She arrived on the two-o'clock train and found her father already on the platform, waiting to unload some tomatoes and grapefruit, sent down from Plymouth. "Here's a bit of luck, maid," he said. "Put them two crates up, will 'ee? You might just so well sit on one."

"How's Mom?"
"Good as new." It was what he always said.
"Well?"
"Well what?" He was all innocence.
She climbed aboard the pony cart and they set off homeward. "You know very well."
"If I'd have known you were coming, I'd have brung his letter."
"Did he call? Or just write? He must be up to his eyes in it."
"He called. Back end o' last week. Thursday."
"And I was only in Saint Ives – aaargh!"
"How's the wardrobe-mistress job going on, then?"
She told him about her metamorphosis into an actress. He did not seem at all surprised. "Well, your mom said that's what you always wanted."
"Always? I never even thought about it until that night at the end of last month. Outside the realms of daydreams, anyway."
"I daresay you can want a thing without knowing it," he replied.
"D'you want tickets to come and see me when we get to Truro next week?"
"Wouldn't be a bad idea," he said. "We shall have to consult our diary though." He flinched and laughed as she punched his arm. When they got home, he took over the shop while she went in back with Mom.
And Mom, of course, was much more effusive in her welcome, hugging her daughter hard ... holding her at arm's length ... hugging her all over again. And when Rose told her about going on stage, she said, "Well, honey, just make sure you don't stick with that fleabitten little summer-stock outfit too long. You get a glimpse of open prairie, you go for it – you hear me now?"
"I hear you now! Except I don't think you realize how much there is to learn still – and how valuable it is to be in a company that's small enough to let me learn just about everything."
All the while she spoke, her eyes hunted this way and that about the room.
Her mother let her fret long enough and then, opening a drawer in the bureau, said, "I presume this is what's pre-empting your conversation."
"What's it say?" she asked, her heart thumping double to catch up on the beat it just dropped.
"How would I know? We didn't open it." Seeing her daughter's surprise she added, "*That* was when you were seventeen and we were entitled. You're your own woman now, hon."
She wondered if she'd tell her about Napier Henry, not now but later. She should plan these things more, she thought.
"I've got work to do," her mother said as she went through to the kitchen to put on the kettle.
Rose slit open the envelope, which certainly showed no sign of tampering, and read:

My dearest darlingest Lucinda,
I cannot deny I was bitterly disappointed when, having snatched half a day out of purgatory, I found you had gone. I had already missed you in London, when I called upon the Carclews, feeling sure you'd be with them. Needless to say, I was not received, but your friend Mary told me what had happened – including her ladyship's scandalous announcements in the press, which I had not seen. One day we shall make sure a suitable fate befalls that woman. Start planning it now because it must be a good one.

Oh, Lucinda, you are so strong. Everything you say in your letter is correct. The chances that we will ultimately enjoy a prosperous life together will, indeed, be greatly increased if we follow the path you advocate. And yet I ache to be with you, or to have you be with me. With your strength added to whatever commercial skills I retain, I feel we could make it to that promised land just as quickly – and far more enjoyably. But then that d–l conscience tells me I am just being selfish, seeking today's gratification at the expense of tomorrow, and I end up not knowing what to think.

In any case, my advisers suggest that I should seek fresh capital in America. An American banker, they say, will look at a bankrupt and say, 'Well, now he knows what to avoid next time,' and they'll at least consider a loan. English bankers look at me and say, 'If he's gone down once, he can do it again – and he's not pulling me down with him.' I have to find fresh capital somewhere, of course. The only work open to me is as a clerk, and I've employed enough of them to know that it's not the path to even modest wealth and security – pretty much as you've reached the same decision about domestic service. Great minds think alike!

Your mother thinks you will not remain a theatrical needlewoman for long, and I agree. So are we now engaged in some kind of race? Which of us will get there first, I wonder? With your gift for mimicry, you should go far on the stage. And with your beauty, I can easily imagine you as a kinema 'star.' In either case there are fortunes to be made. And if that should happen while I am still struggling, will it be my fate to worship you only upon the silver screen, like a million others?

Rose grew uneasy as she read these words. Suppose it were the other way about – that he rebuilt his fortune while she failed. Would he have the slightest hesitation in offering her marriage? She thought not. So why, if he were poor and she rich, would he feel compelled to worship her only from afar? He was, she decided, in need of a little education. She read on:

I shall know soon enough if I am to try my luck in the land of your birth. Or was it? Of your mother's birth, anyway. (I am writing this at her bureau and should add that I like both your parents immensely and will feel honoured to call them parents-in-law one day.) I shall write again as soon as I know, so, if this is the only letter awaiting you here, it will mean I am still uncertain. Much depends on my mother's health, which is greatly improved, I'm happy to say. Friends have rallied round wonderfully – and believe me, one discovers one's true friends unerringly at a time like this! By their grace and favour, she will be set up in a smallish apartment in South Audley Street, Mayfair – a moderately good address – and will be given a monthly allowance that is pretty generous in the circs. It goes without saying that, should my fortunes recover, it will be my first obligation to lift that modest financial burden from their shoulders. At least she is spared the indignity of a Home for Distressed Gentlefolk.

My other news you will probably have gleaned from the papers. Managing the bankruptcy is now my sole occupation. *Managing* a bankruptcy may seem an odd expression, but it is something that can be done either well or badly, curiously enough. A senior accountant told me the other day that, whereas we were originally set to pay back at a shilling in the pound, already, thanks mainly to my efforts, we have raised it to half-a-crown – and it could go higher yet. He added that if I could manage to get it to five shillings in the pound, the City banks and big shareholders would be so grateful they might give me a second chance – this time in a business of *my* choice. That would make a trip to America unnecessary. So that is where all my efforts are going at the moment – day and night.

Reading that back, it does look rather boastful. Never mind. If it encourages you to boast a little, too, I shall be happy. I long to hear that you are now a leading lady and that audiences gasp and weep and pass through every emotion known to man at all of your performances. I think of you day and night. You haunt me with your beauty. Your burning eyes regard me from behind every wretched column of figures. The sweet strength of your voice accompanies me through the dark labyrinths of London. While you are out there somewhere, even though we must now be apart, for as long as you are minded for me, for so long am I a blissful stranger to despair.

I have so many kisses stored up for you but here are some to be going on with:

There followed three rows of exes, neatly arranged as in a ledger, and his signature. In a postscript he gave her the address of the receivers, where letters would always find him quickest – 'Until it's time to do a midnight flit,' he concluded.

She sniffed saltily and looked up to see her mother gazing fondly down from the kitchen doorway. "Tea?" she asked.

"He is a good man," Rose said.

"He surely is. D'you want to write him a reply right now?"

She shook her head. "I'll sleep on it."

"He said he might go to America. I gave him some addresses in New Haven, though God knows if those people are still there – or if they'll remember me."

"He says that in the letter. You can read it if you like. I'll pour the tea. Pop! Tea!"

She returned from the kitchen just as her father came through from the shop.

"He likes us," Mom said, passing the letter over to him.

He checked with Rose and then settled to read it.

"They'd like him in America," Mom said. "What they don't like is snobs – English snobs, anyway. They've got enough of their own. And he's no snob in anyone's language."

"I hope he doesn't go to America," Rose said. Then, seeing her mother's surprise, she explained. "It would mean he'd managed the bankruptcy so well for the creditors that he was able to raise fresh capital in London."

Mom grinned. "And you'd get to see him more!"

"That, too," she conceded.

At the end of the visit her mother walked her back to the station.

"It hasn't been one long success," Rose confessed as they set out. "You know Pop's jokes about the man with the nails in his mouth ... and the meaning of compensation ... and not wanting to spell bougainvillæa to the undertaker's clerk? Well I cobbled them together into a sort of comic monologue – at least, *I* thought it was comic. But I was an audience of one. You could have heard a pin drop – until they started talking among themselves. It was ghastly. How I got off the stage I don't know."

"Not in tears, I hope? Oh, honey!"

"Save it! It's good for me. You only learn from doing things wrong. The tears didn't come until I was well away from the stage, down on the beach."

"The beach? You weren't thinking of drowning yourself?"

"Only in tears. But then a man I knew, a young artist who lives there, he'd been in the audience and watched me die, he came out to comfort me."

She felt her mother's arm stiffen. "'Comfort's' an ambiguous word, honey."

"He told me why the jokes hadn't worked ..."

"*I* could tell you that! They're a man's jokes. Women don't tell jokes like that."

"Yes, that's more or less what he said. But he gave me ideas for things I *could* do. The diary of an upper-class lady sort of interwoven with the diary of her maid – both describing the same events."

"Hey! That's good! I like that. And you could do *both* accents."

"That's the idea. I've started on it already."

"So tell me more about this artist – he sounds useful." When Rose did not reply she added, "Hon?" Now she could feel her daughter's arm grow tense.

"You know that ambiguous word – comfort?"
"You didn't!"
"I did. We did. I was so wretched and he was so kind. Hell, no! That's not the reason. I just thought, *Why not? Why not now?* So ... I didn't say no."
"I hope you were careful?"
"He was. And he was no beginner!"
"And?"
"And nothing. That was it. Nothing more. We'll probably never see each other again."
"D'you want to?"
"I don't *want* to and I don't *not* want to."
"And what about what you *did?*"
She shrugged. "It has taken the edge off my curiosity."
"That's all?"
"Oh – okay! It was pleasant enough. Not as bad as I thought. But I wouldn't go out of my way to do it again. Like I said – we only learn by doing things wrong."

39

Now that Rose knew their itinerary for at least eight weeks ahead, she wrote to Louis giving him a list of post offices where he could write to her poste restante; she also hoped it might encourage him to come and see her at one or other of the places, all of which were in Cornwall. The general pattern was that they began in the far west – Falmouth Penzance, St Ives, etc – and worked ever-closer to Plymouth, where they would arrive around the beginning of December, in time to put on their grand Christmas pantomime.

To replace her disastrous 'Zacky Polkinghorne' patter she wrote a sketch in which 'Lady Augusta Vane-Trumpington' describes amusing incidents arising out of her charitable work – which involves carrying a thin but perfectly nourishing gruel and religious tracts to the poor cottagers on her husband's estate. Each paragraph was interlarded with eavesdroppings on the gossip among the same cottagers' wives, regaling each other with details of her ladyship's visit.

It was a success from the first, mainly because her production of upper-class and Cornish voices was so accurate, not merely in her choice of words but in the accents in which she delivered them. 'Lady Augusta' was, of course, Lady Carclew to the last vowel and consonant. Perhaps for that reason, Rose was never entirely satisfied with her satire. She felt it was like a little tableau in a stuffed-animals museum – accurate, fascinating, and dead. Show by show she sharpened and refined it until, in its final arrangement, it was devoted entirely to a single, toe-curling visit to a poor, half-witted gamekeeper who had his leg taken off in one of his own mantraps, set by himself to catch poachers. His wife's comments, interleaved with her ladyship's, made it clear that he was half-witted from the pain; before the 'accident' he had been one of the brightest of men. She also revealed that it was 'his lordship' who moved the mantrap and forgot to tell his gamekeeper. The wife's inane comments – ''Er ladyship do smell nice, though' and ''Er ladyship do mean well, you got to give 'er that' and 'We must look up to our betters else the whole world 'ud fall abroad in bits' – would bring the house down and earn her a standing ovation as often as not.

During those months Mrs Fitzroy made several attempts to return to the part of Leah, though she never managed more than one or two performances in any particular week. The sturdy female trouper who had gone back on stage within four hours of bringing Petronella into the world was now a dozen years older – years in which constant travel, endless financial crises, rushed meals, and the demands of drunken, drugged, and lunatic actors had all taken their toll.

So Rose still bore the main burden of the part. However, if she had doubts about her long-term position with the company, they were put to rest one evening in October when they were playing Liskeard. By then, Louis had raised the repayment on the Redmile-Smith bankruptcy to five shillings in the pound; the delighted bankers, having proffered the carrot, put it back in their ample pockets and refused him any further capital; and so he had gone to America – to Trenton, New Jersey – to discuss a partnership in a new brewery aimed at 'breaking the Milwaukie stranglehold,' whatever that was. Louis would bring the knowhow, his partner, whose name was for the moment secret, would provide the cash.

It was on the first evening of their week in Liskeard – a Monday, of course – that Rose overheard a conversation that was to change her outlook on her new career. Mrs Fitzroy had decided to play Leah that night and, as usual, it had left her tired and irritable. When the stage had cleared, Lord Gordon, also as usual, had taken her to the front of the stage, down near the curtain, to soothe and calm her. They had been at it a little while when Rose, waiting to make a last-minute check among the benches for lost property, saw Mr Swindlehurst beckoning her from the front row; he put a finger to his lips as she started toward him.

As she tiptoed closer she heard Mrs F say, "I don't care how good she is, she could be another Sarah Bernhardt for all I care ..."

"She is," Lord Gordon interrupted. "She doesn't know it – and I shall make it my business to keep the knowledge from her as long as possible. But ..."

"Ssshh! Where is she now?"

Fortunately, both Rose and Swindlehurst had ducked down behind the lip of the stage apron, so that, when Lord Gordon parted the curtain and peered out, he was able to report, "Gone. She was quick!"

"Quick at everything," his wife said bitterly. "My point is that she unbalances everything. She shows the rest of us up every time she opens her mouth."

"She 'lies like lumps of marl upon a barren moor – encumbring what she cannot fertilize'!" Lord Gordon chuckled.

"Sheridan," Swindlehurst whispered.

"The Critic. I know," Rose whispered back, having already memorized the part of Tilburina in anticipation of taking over from Mrs F. That lady, meanwhile, was saying, "It's not funny, Mister Fitzroy. She's a duck out of water with us and she's got to go. If you don't let her go, there'll be trouble with the others, you mark my words."

"My dear!" The two eavesdroppers could just picture him throwing up his chin, pointing his beard like a pistol at his wife. "So far am I from 'letting her go,' as you put it – an elegant euphuism for booting her out, if I mistake me not – that I am considering offering her a contract."

"A... a..." She obviously could not bring herself even to say the word. "You *what?* Are you out of your mind?"

"I think not. In fact I believe I am the only sane one of us – at least I am not blinded by jealousy!"

"All the world knows that!" she replied scornfully. "All the world knows just what you *are* blinded by! How old are you? You ought to be ashamed of yourself."

"Can we stick to the point, please? Which is – the girl is a jewel in our crown. When we get to Plymouth, old Blaisdell or the egregious Mister de Witt will come to sneer at our humble offering – as usual – and they'll see *her!*"

"And then? If she's under contract to us?"

Like a magician explaining his tricks to an acolyte he said, "They will just have to buy her out of it ... won't they!"

There was a taut silence before his wife giggled. "Oh, Mister Fitzroy! How did I ever doubt you! You've been meaning to sell her all along!"

"From the moment she spoke her first lines in Penzance, my dear," he replied complacently.

He was obviously leaving the stage, speaking over his shoulder, because her next words were: "But soft you! A word or two before you go! What if the wench will not sign?"

"I am prepared for that," he assured her. "I have a scheme to keep her off the stage entirely, all the while we are in Plymouth. This year, next year ... we'll sell her in the end."

Rose and Swindlehurst waited until the Fitzroys were safely back in the dressing-room tent before they stood up, stretched, and made their way to the exit.

"You should sign this contract, I think," Swindlehurst said as he raised his umbrella to shelter the pair of them from the fine October drizzle.

"And let them pocket the profit?" she protested.
"Fair's fair – they deserve it for giving you the chance ..."
"And they've worked me to a starveling ever since!"
He pinched the flesh on the back of her upper arm and said, "Put the wheels back on the old one – it ran better. The real point here is not what the Fitzroy may or may not be entitled to get. It's what the other party has to pay to release you – and the higher the fee the better it is for you."
"Eh?"
"Of course! People don't value anything they get for free – look what they do with public parks and libraries and drinking fountains! If 'old Blaisdell or the egregious Mister de Witt' have to pay through the nose to secure you, they'll value you all the more. Their native language has an alphabet of just three letters: L for the pounds, S for the shillings, and D for the pence. That's why you should ..."
"But doesn't that mean there'll be less left over for me? I mean ... if these gentlemen have to pay a small fortune to ..."
He cut her short with a laugh. "It doesn't work like that, lady. It's not like the weekly housekeeping – blow it on beer and the geegees and there's nothing left for meat and the rent. If it were, the greatest stars would all be in the cheapest productions. Money pulls more money in its wake. Your hope must be that the wily Lord Gordon screws them to a small fortune to lift this particular jewel out of his crown."
"You see," Rose said glumly. "There's just so much I still don't know." She hugged his arm tight against her. "And you, dear Mister Swindlehurst, are so good to keep on enlightening me. What can I do in return? Pressing and sponging your things seems so inadequate. It is I who am *sponging* off you!"
"Ha ha! Don't ever use that one on stage! What *you* can do, lady, is remember me when you arrive on Mount Olympus. Then just dig a hole and pull me through."

40

Lord Gordon waited until after the second house on Saturday, when, he probably assumed, Rose would be exhausted by the week's performances and therefore at her lowest ebb. No sooner had they taken their final curtain calls than he invited her to join him in his tent-dressing-room. There he exploded a carbonating 'bomb' into a soda siphon filled with a white *vin ordinaire,* gave it a good shake, and squirted her a large glassful of the foaming concoction.
"Good as champagne, I always say," he declared as he handed it to her.
"To what do I owe this honour?" she asked, though she already had more than a faint idea of his answer.

"What I'm about to tell you, lassie, must not go beyond these four walls. Sub Rosa - ha-ha! But your word upon that or I'll say drink up and goodnight."

Since the nearest *walls* were those surrounding the field – and since Mr Swindlehurst was still within them – she gave her parole happily enough.

"You're not blind," he went on. "You're not deaf. You heard that applause tonight – and every other night. You've seen their faces light up. Ecstatic, they are. And it's all because of you ..."

"Or because we are all such a good team," Rose objected.

"Team! That's it! We *are* a team. And that's why I ask you not to breathe a word of this to the others, because what I'm about to offer you – and only you – is something I could not possibly afford to offer to all and sundry."

"More money, you mean?" she asked.

"It could be," he replied cagily. "It very well could be. But really it's something much more highly prized in our profession. Can you guess what, I wonder?"

"A pension?"

"Better," he said, trying not to wince.

"A share of the gross ticket takings?"

He closed his eyes tight and shuddered. "Better," he said again, and even less convincingly. Asking her to guess had been a bad mistake. "Look – what's the worst thing about this blighted profession of ours?"

"Having to work when everyone else is out on the razzle?"

She was doing it again. He must stop asking questions – or he must answer them himself before she got a chance. "I'll tell you," he said. "It's insecurity. I don't blame you, lassie, for not guessing it because you've not experienced it yet. Insecurity, I mean. But just ask Mister Swindlehurst, Mister Dennison, or Mrs Skerrett – they'll tell you. It's insecurity every time – working this week, starving the next, and never knowing when or if your luck's going to turn. So what's the answer, eh? I'll tell ..."

"Form your own theatre company?" she guessed.

"I'll tell you. It's a *contract!*" He produced a legal-looking document from a drawer in his travelling wardrobe. "A *contract!*" he repeated, placing it reverently into her grasp.

It looked very like the parchment rolls in the props basket, labelled *The Critic: Magistrate's Scene*. She tugged at the red tape that bound it and unfurled ... yes, a sheet of blank parchment.

"A question for the Mad Hatter," she said. "If I say, 'it's not worth the paper it's written on,' is it the same as, 'it *is* worth the paper it's *not* written on'?"

He laughed and pointed a jokingly accusing finger at her. "Sharp, lassie! We shall have to keep our wits about us when dealing with you – I can see that. Of course it's blank at the moment. It's for you and me to talk about what we want to pour into that empty vessel before we take it to the sharks and weasels and get them to cook it and serve it up in legal Latin. There's no sense in paying them if you're going to say no from the start, is there, now?"

"I think I will be saying no," she warned him. She was, of course, eager to discover what his alternative plan was – to keep her off the stage all the while they were in Plymouth.

"Of course you will!" He grinned. "I'd start from the same place if I was in your shoes."

"Oh, but I don't mean it as a trick to make you offer more, Mister Fitzroy. I mean that the thing I most enjoy about belonging to your company is – as I said – that we *are* a team, all of us. All in it together. I couldn't keep such a secret as this from them. It wouldn't feel right."

That had him rattled. Bargaining over cash and favours he could cope with. But ethics and honour were foreign countries. "We'll see," was all he could say in reply.

And for the next half hour they talked terms – or, rather, she talked terms while he hemmed and hawed and, eventually, said yes. Yes to three years. Yes to a percentage of the ticket office – *after* her first year. Yes to her own room at every digs – *after* the first six months. In short, as she soon discovered, he'd say yes to anything as long as he didn't have to pay it until after Christmas – in some cases, well after. Between now and then there would be nothing for her beyond a measly half-a-crown extra per week. It could only mean that he was utterly confident of selling her on to some impresario in Plymouth that December. And the point about postponing all the big-money items into the following year was that the more onerous the contract, the more costly it would be for them to buy her out.

The moment this struck her she changed tack, for this was a game that all could play. She let the financial demands stand as they were, for they would be bargaining points, to be whittled away in any discussion she might have with the lucky impresario who bought out the contract. The ones she would insist on inserting *unchanged* in any new contract were those she now negotiated with Lord Gordon. They included the number of hours of public performance she would be guaranteed in any week (or a swingeing triple-pay clause in lieu) ... the relative size of her name on any future playbill ... its invariable positioning above the title ... her control of any statement made about her to the press or public ... and so on.

Thanks to dear Mr Swindlehurst, she had had the best part of the week to consider such things. She had intended putting them into any subsequent contract with an impresario; not until this moment did she realize it would strengthen her hand if they were also in her contract with Lord Gordon.

She had one further trump card to play against him – her youth and stamina. The week had been just as exhausting for him as it had been for her; he, too, was at his lowest ebb right now. She waited until everything was agreed, agreed, agreed before she said, "But there's no hurry, is there? This is the Chinese Year of the Monkey, you know, and I'd be very reluctant to sign any long-term contract until it's over."

In fact, she didn't really believe there was such a thing as the Chinese Year of the Monkey; she thought it was a joke a Chinese matelot had tried to tease her with once, when she was ten. She could always tell him later that the Chinese years ended in November, so they could sign before the panto opened. Meanwhile, she'd find out what his alternative plan to keep her off the stage might be.

They parted grumpily and, over the following week, he tried everything in his power and every trick in the book to get her to sign up right away. At last, however, he yielded. It was a week to the very hour – once again after the second house on Saturday, when they had finished playing their week in Launceston – that he once again asked her to his tent.

"I can see that I have to accept your primitive and superstitious approach to life, Miss Tremayne ..."

"A bit like Macbeth, eh?" she commented brightly.

He stared at her in horror before leaping to his feet, shouting, "Damn you, Lucinda Tremayne!" three times while he turned three circles and threw two grease sticks and a powder puff from his dressing table over his shoulder.

"You were saying about *superstitions?*" she prompted as he resumed his seat.

"Theatrical tradition," he mumbled. "Different matter altogether. Anyway – as I was about to say – it may be for the best if we postpone drawing up a contract ..."

"Oh no! You may go ahead and draw it up. We just won't sign it until then."

"As you wish. The thing is – I have another idea, which I hope you will find congenial."

The plan he unfolded was for her to write a new version of *The Murder in the Red Barn,* a melodrama celebrating an allegedly true event in which a wicked squire, John Corder, gets an innocent country maid with child, murders her (in a red barn), buries her on the spot, is unmasked, and finally gets carried off, foaming at the mouth and cursing God and all His angels. The version favoured by the public was not yet stamped 'Free of Charge' in the English acting editions. So, if she could produce something *like* it ...? For which the company would not have to pay a royalty ...? Would she think it over? Everyone was so impressed with the little sketches she had written for the smoking-concert evenings – especially the way she had revised and revised and revised them, making each new version even better than the last. Would she please consider it? She could have the whole month of December off. Lovely though it would be to have her in the panto, she wasn't really necessary. She could go back home to Falmouth, if she wished – if it was easier to work there. He'd pay her the month in advance ...

"So there you have it," she said when she relayed the news to Mr Swindlehurst. "Pay in advance. Return fare home paid. And write my own part. I'm *almost* tempted."

"He would own the rights in the play," Swindlehurst warned.

She frowned. "Why?"

"Because he'd be paying you a salary, as an employee, and you'd be doing it to his direction."

"But that's not fair!"

"Oh, lady! That's a word you must try to forget in all these dealings – *fair.* Fair has nothing to do with it when you come to the legal arrangements between employers and employees."

"I wasn't going to write the Red Barn thing, anyway. We had a very juicy murder in Cornwall, only three hundred years ago. I was going to write that."

It was his turn to frown in bewilderment. "You mean you were seriously thinking of accepting this offer – instead of signing the contract? Surely not?"

"Oh!" She was momentarily nonplussed. "That's right. It was just a ploy to find out how he'd keep me off the stage in Plymouth, wasn't it! Oh, I do get carried away, Mister Swindlehurst. Thank God you're here to keep my feet on the ground! So! I'll let him stew for another week and then I can tell him the Year of the Monkey is actually over already and we're safe to sign."

"Yes!" he replied solemnly. "And this is Launceston, which is in Cornwall, England. And it's the twenty-second of October, nineteen-ten. And tomorrow's Sunday, when we're moving to Tavistock – which you have positively *plastered* with playbills. Now tell me – do you remember your name?"

All this while she had hung her head and teetered before him like an errant schoolchild. But the mention of *name* jolted her to attention again.

"That's right!" she exclaimed, hitting her brow with the heel of her hand. "My new name! 'Miss L-E. Tremayne' looks a bit coy, and more than a bit old-fashioned in the programmes. I thought 'Lucille,' which is a kind of compound of Lucinda and Ella, and 'Marteyne,' which is a ... what d'you call it when you muddle the letters – anagram! It's an anagram of Tremayne, see? Lucille Marteyne – doesn't that have a certain ring to it? 'Mister Hugo de Witt is proud to present Miss Lucille Marteyne in *She Stoops to Conquer* by Oliver Goldsmith. Other members of the cast include Miss Sarah Bernhardt, Miss Ellen Terry, Mrs Patrick Campbell, Mister Herbert Beerbohm Tree, Sir Henry ...' Oh no – he's playing Heaven now. But d'you like it? Lucille Marteyne. I do."

"Well, I'd never have guessed it," he said.

41 c/o Mrs Kelly, at the Saracen's Head, Fore Street, Plymouth Weds 23 Nov

Dear Mom and Pop,
Actually, this is mostly for Mom because I know that you, Pop, have taken root well enough in the Old World soil to understand what I'm going to describe, viz: the Great British pantomime. But you, mom, as a stubborn Hoosier-Yankee, are going to need some guidance. Think of it as a huge national in-joke. The British die laughing while foreigners – even Americans, who share the same language and theatre traditions – die of boredom or bewilderment. To start with, instead of a hero there is a principal boy, who is, naturally, a girl. That's my part in Lord Gordon's panto this year, which is Cinderella! You must have had some premonition when you christened me, though, as principal 'boy,' I play Prince Charming. My clothes don't exaggerate the upper storey, but my nether limbs, in sheer silk stockings, are undeniably female. Do I mean unashamedly female? Yes! I mean unashamedly female, because this is a fantastic 2½ hour romp and no harm in it.

There's no disguising my voice and face, either. No attempt to lower the pitch and no moustachioes in burnt cork. As principal boy I am obliged to be passionately in love with Cinderella. She's played by Titania Moore, who is around the same age as me and we enjoy, or at least enact, several love scenes and even go in for some rather perfunctory kissing, which brings oohs and ahs from the house always.

In all pantos the principal boy's mother is played by a man – the hairier and uglier and bawdier the better. But in Cinders her place is supplied by the three Ugly Sisters – all three of whom are men: Lord Gordon, Mr Dennison, who is 60, and my great friend Mr Swindlehurst whom I must have mentioned in every letter, I think. Of course, they make no attempt to disguise their masculinity. Even the pillows that form their ample bosoms are very blatantly pillows. Every now and then they take them out and plump them up! And on the several occasions when the plot, for want of a better word, requires them to lift their skirts, the underwear they reveal is comically masculine. Lord Gordon is courted by a Mr Rendle, playing the Vizier, a man so confused and short-sighted that he does not notice the Ugly Sister's deep voice, hairy arms, and beard. Lord Gordon acting coy when the Vizier attempts to kiss him-her is a theatrical gem.

You simply must come and see this show – that's what the enclosed PO is for – your train fares and overnight lodgings here at the Saracen's Head. But if you can't manage it, buy the biggest goose in Falmouth instead. What follows is just to whet your appetite – for the panto, not, I hope, the goose.

Most of the scenes have nothing whatever to do with the plot. This is because the plot is thin to the point of exhaustion. That, however, is an advantage for us performers since we can work in scenes peculiarly suited to our especial talents. For instance, we have a scene in which Mr Swindlehurst, now a citizen after a quick change in the wings, walks past a fishmonger's stall bearing a sign FRESH FISH SOLD HERE. (The fishmonger is Lord Gordon, also after a quick change.) He tells the fishmonger that it's the stupidest sign he's ever seen.

"Nobody's going to buy *stale* fish, are they!" he taunts.

And so, after some comic argy-bargy, Lord Gordon agrees to reduce the sign to FISH SOLD HERE. It's written on a slate, so he just rubs out the FRESH with one of the fish!

"And it must be obvious to an idiot that you're *selling* it," Swindlehurst continues. "There isn't a fishmonger in the world who gives it away."

So, after more patter, it becomes FISH HERE.

"What d'you need the HERE for?" is Swindlehurst's next question. "Even a fool can see the fish are where the notice is."

The notice is reduced to FISH.

Swindlehurst looks at the fish and holds his nose. Swindlehurst looks at Lord Gordon. Lord Gordon looks at the fish. They look at each other. Both hold their noses and nod. Slowly, wearily, Lord Gordon effaces the FISH.

Swindlehurst flourishes his hand at the empty slate, says, "Now *that's* what I call a sensible notice!" and walks off while the house rocks with laughter and applause.

What it has to do with the plot of *Cinderella* is anybody's guess but it always brings the house down. And the fact that Lord Gordon and Mr Swindlehurst appear in the very next scene in their chief characters as Ugly Sisters does nothing to break the magic spell.

They call little tacked-on scenes like this 'vignettes' and our production has fifty of them, not all of which get used in any given performance. It all depends on the audience we have in on the day. That's the other great feature of every panto: The audience is actually part of the performance. If someone doesn't roar out, "Oh no it doesn't!" when Lord Gordon declares that the glass slipper fits his foot, the show is a flop. But someone always does shout it, of course. What then follows is that Lord G comes down to the footlights and engages in an 'Oh yes it does – Oh no it doesn't' argument with the entire audience, all of them at the tops of their voices. This is usually enough to drive the few remaining foreigners and Americans from the auditorium, but I'm counting on your maternal pride to make you stay, Mom.

Oh, I should also say that we are in a bona-fide *theatre* with stone walls and balconies and a slate roof and everything – and I have one of the principal dressing rooms all to myself! That is stipulated in a contract I have recently signed with Lord G. The theatre is the Gaiety in Edgcumbe Street, which is the western end of Union Street. Our marquee and assorted tents have gone to some sailmakers in Mevagissey for their annual repairs, which they badly needed, I can tell you.

But to get back to audience participation. It doesn't end there. In our production there's a point at the end of the first act where the entire cast agree that we have utterly lost The Plot. There are suggestions that most of it is hiding behind the Lord Chancellor's blue pencil. You know about the Lord Chancellor? Believe it or not, every line of this farrago of nonsense has to be read by that solemn gentleman (wearing court dress and a full-bottomed wig, I have no doubt) so he can strike out any political, blasphemous, or salacious references. Anyway, wherever The Plot may be hiding, the Ugly Sisters send Buttons and Cinders to go find it and bring it back on stage. Then there's a (not too) long, awkward silence while the Sisters look at each other and agree that nothing can happen on stage without The Plot. Then, when they have milked the embarrassed titters from the audience up to full-scale roars of laughter, they divide the auditorium into three teams and pit each of them in a singing contest against the other two.

We also have some parodies of popular songs, such as Up in a Baboon, Boys! (I don't know how that slipped past the Chancellor – unless it was his wig that slipped) or The Man who Broke the Tank at Monty's Parlour. Monty, by the way, is a fashionable Plymouth hairdresser in George Street, famous for his aquarium tank 'for the delectation and education of my customers.' Local and topical references are a must in every panto. The more the merrier. Do come and see us if you can, though I know Christmas is as busy for you as it is for us. I shan't have a single day off until the end of January, except, of course, Xmas Day itself, which is a Sunday. So I'll come home then. Meanwhile, the above will be my address (or, as Lady Carclew always insisted, my directions) for the next two months.

So, did I say I'm having the time of my life? Do I need to?

I've had one letter from Louis since he landed in NY. He says things are progressing satisfactorily though there's no money on the table yet. That was Nov 1st. Nothing since then, so I hope no news really is good news.

That's all my news. Some big theatrical impresarios and agents often send their scouts round little companies like ours when we play the larger cities. So keep your fingers crossed and don't walk under ladders. This could be my big chance for this year. But if not this year, then next. And if not next, then the year after. Even old Mr Dennison never says never.

All my love and lots of hugs and kisses,

Lucinda-Ella

42

The railways ran a normal timetable over the holidays so Rose was able to catch the milk train from Plymouth, which reached Truro at 7:30am on Christmas morning. The connecting train to Falmouth would get her home by 8:15, in time, she hoped, to take her parents an early morning cup of tea. But when she arrived at Truro, who should she see boarding the train ahead of her – in the first class, of course – but Noel Carclew. He was still in evening dress, which, like him, looked decidedly the worse for wear. She waited until she saw the guard about to blow his whistle and wave his little green flag and then she hopped into the same compartment. It was a non-corridor train, so, what with its being Christmas Day, she thought she might get away with travelling there on her second-class ticket.

He glanced up briefly, groaned, and sank his head in his hands again. "I've no time for visions," he whined.

She laughed and took her seat beside him; they were alone in the compartment. He let himself fall sideways, slumping into her lap. His top hat fell to the floor, where it spontaneously collapsed. "That's how I feel, too," he sighed as he reached fruitlessly after it.

Rose picked it up and laid it on the seat beside her. She took off her gloves and began to massage his neck, where the two strings felt as taut as a drumhead. He stretched his neck toward those angel-of-mercy hands and sighed a luxuriant sigh. "Where did you learn to do that!"

"There's a young actress in Lord Gordon's Players who overdoes things from time to time," she told him. "This usually works the trick for her."

He made no comment, which struck her as odd. Did he already know she was still with Lord G after all these months? For the next few minutes he lay still, making contented noises while she worked away. The train was so short that each thrust of the piston produced a minute lurch in the carriage; soon they were rocking gently to its staccatto rhythm.

When they left the main line and roared into the deep cutting by Nansavallan Wood, he sat up with delicate stealth, as though he feared the imps of pain would ambush him once more if they noticed his movement. "How *can* you be so bright and full of vigour at this hour of the night?" he asked.

"*Your* night," she said scornfully. "Anyway, what have you been doing with yourself since last we met?"

"Oh, they forgave me and let me come back to London, so I was there for the last month of the Season. Met your friend Deveril."

"Alone and inconsolable, I hope?"

"Not quite. In fact, in the consoling line he seemed to be doing rather well for himself." He grinned at her. "Jealous?"

"Not a bit!"

"Is life with Lord Gordon so wonderful?"

So he had heard all about it, or something about it, anyway. "It is at the moment."

"And you've never once regretted turning Deveril down?"

"Once. We were playing Newquay and it was raining six-inch nails. The water came through the canvas like it was mosquito netting. We had an audience of fifteen. I played the whole thing in a sodden costume. The lights failed twice. I fell in a ditch up to my waist in the dark on the way back to the digs. And it did just cross my mind for a few seconds that a nice warm bed between silken sheets in Maida Vale wouldn't make a bad swap just at that moment. Otherwise the answer to your question is no. The Season ended months ago."

"Yes, well, I've just been hanging round since then."

"Hanging round here or up there? And hanging round what? Or whom?"

He chuckled. "Imitate Fenella again!"

"Are you trying to avoid the question?"

He sighed once more and moved a few inches apart from her, as if to say, 'Very well – if you want to be serious.' He took up his hat and punched it tall again. "Hanging around stage doors – but before the performances rather than after them."

"And?"

He stared out of the window awhile. "I'm good," he murmured. "But not quite good enough. And 'not quite good enough' is the same as 'no good at all' in this game." He turned sharply to look at her and then winced. "That's the difference between me and you, Rose – or is it Lucille now?"

She stiffened. "What do you know about Lucille?"

He grinned slyly. "I've heard the name. And, what's more, I'm not the only one. Lucille Marteyne, isn't it? Not bad!"

Her heart pounded. She went to sit opposite him and, gripping his knee, said, "Stop talking in riddles, Noel. What have you heard? Who from? And who else knows?"

"You've heard of an impresario called Hugo de Witt?"

She gave a contemptuous laugh. "*Heard* of him, yes. That's about all I have done. What do you know of him?"

"Well, when I realized I was never going to be good enough to play anything beyond the end of the pier – unless it was bait for the sharks – I thought the next best thing would be in the management side. So for the past month or so – actually almost two months now – I've been unpaid runner and chief bottle washer to Mister de Witt. 'Learning the ropes,' he calls it but it's more like learning the trick knots – the ones that tie *you* down permanently while H-d-W can undo them with one tweak of his little finger."

"And he's mentioned my name?" She was sitting so far forward on her seat that she started to slide off and had to wriggle back.

"Your name has been mentioned to him, yes."
"By whom? God, it's like getting blood out of a stone! Was it Lord Gordon?"
Noel laughed, and winced again. "He's not that big a fool. No. He must have mentioned you to Will Sanger and ..."
"Hang on!" Rose frowned. "Will Sanger is a deadly rival – or so Lord Gordon always claims."
"He is – that's the point. Sanger is also a bit simply furnished in the attic storey. He wouldn't realize he was being used. So Lord G tells him he's got this absolutely fantastic leading lady and, tee-hee, he's just got her nicely tied down on a three year contract but don't tell a soul. So, of course, the first thing Sanger does is go running to H-d-W. Why? Because if anyone can afford to buy out your contract, it's him."
"But that would put a lot of money into Lord G's coffers."
"True, but he also loses you – which is what Sanger's really interested in. Then he and Lord G will be back on even terms." He laughed again. "And I'll bet you thought that acting is just about you, a spotlight, and a packed house!"
She smiled dutifully and then sat, thinking furiously and combing her fingers through her hair. "N o - e l ?" she said at last.
"L u - c i - l l e ?"
"Were you thinking of spending the day in the bosom of your family at Nancemellin?"
"I was – but that was when no other bosoms were on offer."
"Well then, what about the bosom of *my* family instead? I'm sure they have one of the fattest and most succulent geese in Falmouth. And when I say 'I'm sure,' I mean I made sure."
He held his breath, eyeing her expectantly.
"Well?" she prompted.
"Oh, sorry! I was waiting to see if that was the end of the bosoms-on-offer list."
She formed her hand into a pistol and shot him.
"Good!" He relaxed with a laugh and chanted, "I like the girls who will. I like the girls who won't. But I hate the girls who say they will – and then you find they ... *here!* Here's another one! Take your teeth out, missus, if you're going to laugh like that."
"Yes!" she sighed. "I'm afraid you were quite right to set your sights elsewhere!"

43

It must have been the biggest, fattest goose in Falmouth. When they had demolished it – and pulled the Christmas crackers and put on the party hats and read the jokes (with more deliberatingly excruciating deliveries from Noel) and lit the brandy around the pudding and found the lucky sixpence (which Mom made sure went to Rose) and polished off the mince pies, to boot – when all this was done, Rose turned to Noel and said,

"You know that bit in the Gospel of Luke, where it says Jesus went down from Jerusalem and was subject to his parents?"

"Yes – vaguely?" He eyed her warily.

"D'you know what it means?" Before he could answer she added, "It means he helped with the washing up."

"Oh." He sighed. "Yes, I see. Be with you in half a jiff."

While he went across the backyard to use the jakes, Pop settled on the sofa for a snooze and Mom helped Rose carry the debris of the meal out to the kitchen.

"He's a very nice young man," Mom said.

"Very," Rose agreed. "He's talking about a contract with Hugo de Witt – *the* Hugo de Witt! One of London's ..."

"No, I mean a *very* nice young man."

Rose laughed. "It's nothing like that, Mom – honestly."

"Why not? Don't you think he'd be far more suitable for you than Louis?"

She shrugged. "Probably. But it doesn't work like that. I thought you liked Louis, anyway."

"I did. I do. But ... you know."

"What?"

"Well ... he's a long way off, honey. And, as you just told us, he's mighty sparing with his news – which doesn't look too good."

"Mom! He's been there four months! What d'you expect? Milwaukie-on-the-Delaware already? Give the man a chance! Besides, I love him."

"And Noel? Why did you bring him home then, if ..."

"Because he works for Hugo de Witt. No! That's just being smart. I brought him here because he's a friend. He's good company. The best. Yes, he's wonderful company – but that's all. Besides, he's not interested in me, either – not that way."

"How d'you know?"

"I just do."

"Aha! So you've tried!"

"We have not tried. We're more like brother and sister. That's it! If I'd had a brother, I'd have felt ... never mind. Talk about something else. He's coming back. You go and rest now. You've earned it."

"What about you? If anyone has earned a rest it's you, honey. Talking of which, *I'll* do the washing up. Noel can wipe."

Rose, knowing exactly what her mother was up to, said, "And then I'll take him for a walk and learn exactly what you've been telling him."

Noel overheard these words as he came back into the kitchen. "Take *him* for a *walk?*" he asked in horrified tones. "I trust you mean your father? Or a pet lobster or something?"

She handed him soap and a towel and pointed at the handbasin at the end of the passage. "We'll need to work up an appetite for tea," she said.

When he returned, she steered him toward the kitchen and settled herself to read the *Falmouth Packet*.

Mom shut the door behind him and then wasted no time. "What do people say about my Lucinda-Ella?" she asked.

"That she will go far," he replied.

"Really?" She stared hard, to see if he were being facetious.

"Oh, yes. Talent in the theatre is a funny thing. If you have it – and she most certainly has – all it needs is scope. If you haven't got it, all the training in the world is never going to make you more than a competent journeyman – which is all right, because not everyone can be a star."

"But she can be?"

"She will be. You'd better prepare for it, in fact."

Mom laughed.

"I mean it," he said.

"Sure. I was just thinking that we aren't the only ones who need to prepare. I *never* thought she'd be a servant all her life. I thought she'd work in some household where the young master" – here she winked at Noel – "would see her true worth and marry her. I even hoped that young master would be you, Mister Carclew! But I never thought you'd see her true worth in *this* way. If you'd stuck to *my* original script and plighted your troth, I'd be telling you a little cautionary tale right now, and leaving you to draw your own conclusions." She eyed him speculatively. "I guess I'll tell you anyway, because I suspect you and that Mister de Witt don't know what you'll be taking on."

"Suddenly I'm all ears," he told her.

"You don't need to dry those. They go in the plate rack. Anyway – you may see nothing in this tale, but I think the whole of Lucinda-Ella's character is there. It's about the time she first learned to ride a bicycle. She was around fifteen, I guess – just after the turn of the century. Her legs had just grown long enough for my bike – because, of course, we couldn't afford a small one for her. So she mastered it pretty quickly, and then – and this is the cautionary bit – she got too warm for her jacket so she took it off – *while she was riding!* She's only ridden the machine a few hundred wobbly yards and already she's trying something *I* wouldn't attempt even after years of riding. Everyone's yelling at her to stop, put one foot on the ground, et cetera. But no – she shucks her jacket off *and* folds it up *and* puts it in the basket all while she carries on wobbling. We've all got our hearts in our mouths but she gives us such a look of contemptuous triumph! I tell you, Mister Carclew – I've never forgotten it. That combination of ambition and arrogance ... she's grown quite good at hiding it but she's never lost it. In fact, I think that hiding it has only made it stronger. If your Mister de Witt enters into a contract with her, that's also what he's taking on."

"I think we're up to it," Noel told her. "What you've just described would apply to quite a few actors and actresses – not all of them, alas, as talented as your daughter. But thank you for telling me. It *is* a fascinating little insight."

"If your Mister de Witt thinks any contract is going to constrain her once she gets the smell of open prairie, he's wrong. I know her. She'll sign anything to get to London, but once she's there she'll start trying to whittle it away."

He chuckled. "Not a bad portrait of H-d-W himself, you know. As long as both parties know who bakes the bread – and which side it's buttered on – there won't be too much harm done."

"And who will remind them? You?"

He bowed ironically. "It's my trade, Mrs Tremayne."

She smiled, and then paused before adding, "What about my original notion? Her and the young master plighting their troth?"

He shook his head. "I think she would consider it a retrograde step. A cliché."

"Those might be her feelings. What about yours?"

"I don't think they count."

She realized she'd get no more out of him so she asked next, "And her infatuation, or love or whatever you want to call it, with Mister Redmile-Smith?"

He sidestepped the question with one of his own. "Do you think it's just infatuation?"

"It was all so hasty. Don't get me wrong. I *like* the man. But you have to face the fact that when he had to rebuild his life he also had the chance to do it with Lucinda-Ella at his side or to go it alone. And he chose to go it alone. One day *she* is going to have to face that fact. What do *you* think?"

He shrugged. "Who can say? She's going to meet a lot of new people – a lot of rich bachelors, many of them with titles. Who can say?"

When they had finished the washing up, Rose put on her coat and fur-lined boots and gave Noel her father's greatcoat and cloth cap. "No one will recognize you," she said.

"Suits me." He triced himself into the wind as they stepped out into the road, manfully taking the brunt of it and putting her in the lee. "No one will carry tales across the water there."

They paused a moment to stare at Nancemellin House, a dark granite cube made darker still by a light powdering of snow over the parkland all around. Beyond the ridge she could see smoke rising from Trefusis farmhouse. Had they married? Had little Pennycuik had her baby yet? Did she care one way or the other?

"I can't remember snow at Christmas before," he said.

"It happened once. When I was a little gel." She assumed a quavery old voice. "Long before you were born, young man."

He stared at her. "It's unnatural," he said. "One listens to a great tenor or a coloratura soprano singing one of those twiddly arias by Handel and you're just lost in amazement at how they do it. But I think the things you can do with your voice are just as fantastic."

"Thank you kind sir." She bobbed a curtsy. "Can we get going again, before my boots freeze to the pavement?"

As they moved along he jerked his head back toward Nancemellin. "Can you believe we were both living over there once? Doesn't it seem like a bad, boring dream now?"

She thought it over a while and said, "It is as though it all happened to someone else. Last summer was as if a guillotine came down on my life."

"But it didn't chop your head off."

"It chopped my lady's maid's head off – but then, just like in a panto – like in *Little Red Riding Hood* – where they chop the wolf's head off and out pops Old Grannie … out *I* popped. *This* is what I was meant for, you know – the theatre."

"I know."

"You're just saying that."

"Oh no I'm not."

"Oh yes you are!"

They laughed. "As a matter of fact," he went on cautiously, "I'm not just saying it. I've seen your Prince Charming and I think it's pretty good."

"When?" She was delighted, of course.

He sniffed. "Last night. But don't you …"

"You silly goose – you should have come backstage after!"

"Oh no I shouldn't! That's what I was about to say. Hugo de Witt is never to hear of it – that I've admitted to you that I was there. I'm supposed to report back to him and keep it all secret."

She hugged herself tight to his side and put her lips close to his ear. "Daaarling?" she whispered. Then a new thought struck her and she drew away again. "Oh, but you should also have seen me in *Leah.* That was much …"

"I did."

She stopped dead. "When?"

"When you played Saint Austell."

"Oh, but I was *dreadful* there. You should have seen me when I played in Truro."

"I did – there, too."

"Oh." She pondered that for a moment and then, walking and smiling once more, returned her lips to the neighbourhood of his ear and repeated: "Daaarling?"

"H-d-W won't buy you out of a current production," Noel said. "But I wouldn't plan anything for February if I were you. And, by God, I wish I *were* you!"

She went rigid at his side, still walking, but slowly and stiffly.

"Not happy?" he asked.

"Petrified," she replied. "You must coach me in how to deal with him."

He shook his head. "He'd smell a rat. You don't need coaching, anyay. He's not the type who responds only to one sort of actor or actress. Some are surly, some are arrogant ... self-deprecating ... shy ... lost in some other world ... it doesn't matter. As long as they're genuine – and brilliant – he accepts them all. Look – see that cottage up there?"

They had gone under the railway arch by now and were turning east along the road that leads round the Pendennis Peninsula, which guards the entrance to the estuary and harbour. The cottage he pointed out was one of a row, just below the artillery battery. "What of it?" she asked.

"That's where another bourgeois black sheep lives."

"Who's the first – oh, *you* of course. Sorry. Who is this one?"

"His name's Peter de Vivian."

She laughed. "Not from Alma Terrace!"

"That's the one."

"I went looking for a place there while they were in London. The butler there put me on to old Roanoke. Wasn't there something about Peter pestering Gemma Penhallow, Ruby's sister?"

"Yes. Don't look too closely but that's her now, throwing crusts at the seagulls. It looks as if she's eating for two."

Rose stared at the young woman in amazement. "That's Gemma?" she asked. "I was at school with her. I'd never have recognized her."

"Is she plainer or prettier?"

"Much pretier."

"Ah, well, you see, that's the effect of living with the upper classes. There's hope for you yet!" He was already running away, hampered by his heavy lunch.

But she was no more agile. They soon stopped, in a panting sort of truce.

Rose was still scandalized, though. "She's just living with him?"

"No, she's married to him. And he's working as a woodcarver – which is all he's ever wanted to be. But that's not all. Twin-sister Ruby's back in Falmouth, too – bold as brass. She came back with a friend from London – Miss Jennifer Divett, who is said to be the daughter of the rural dean of Durham, but if you ask me, she's had a pretty chequered sort of history, too. Anyway, the pair of them have teamed up with your friend Sally ... Winter? Winner? What's her name?"

"Sally Winnen."

"Yes. They've bought a big double-bay-window shop in Church Street and they're calling it the Falmouth Fashion Emporium. It's going to open in January."

"Oh, I must get back for that! But when I last saw her, Sally was having talks with two highly *respectable* ladies – she can't have meant Ruby Penhallow and this chequered dean's daughter?"

"No. I gather that the two respectable ladies had ideas about 'moral undergarments' which Miss Winnen found hard to reconcile with running a profitable enterprise."

At last she came out with the question she had been dying to ask ever since they started on this stroll: "What was my mother telling you back there?"

"Oh," he replied off-handedly. "Some tale about you learning to ride a bike."

"That!" she exclaimed wearily. "Did she also tell you how I always chose clothes too big – hoping it would encourage me to grow bigger, faster?"

"No. Did you?"

"And about taking *The Philosophy of Fine Art* by Hegel out of the library when I was only twelve?"

Again he shook his head. "Is it true?"

"Every word. I just liked the title. *Fine* art! It sounded … well, *fine!* Was that all?"

He hesitated and then said, "She also wondered if you were really in love with Louis Redmile-Smith."

"And what did you say? You told her yes, I hope? Emphatically."

"She didn't really ask my opinion. She did, however, point out that when he had the chance to rebuild his life with you or without you, he chose to do it without you."

"Ha! That's all *she* knows! We write to each other constantly. We are never *without* each other."

"That's all right, then."

She looked at him crossly. "You seem to think that doesn't count for much?"

"If *you* think it does, then what does my opinion matter? Let's talk about something else."

"Please do!" she answered, still cross.

As they continued their slow, relaxed progress round Pendennis Point, he chatted on about other Falmouth people, some of whom she knew only as names, of course, since they had not always moved in the same circles. And listening to him she forgot her annoyance as it dawned on her that, just as she now knew her natural home was the stage, so, too, was his the backstage. He had an ear for gossip, a memory for detail, and a tongue to spice it up in the serving. She could imagine that, wherever he went, he would light up the company; groups would open to let him in; people would hang upon his words. And if they wanted to know something, they'd say, 'I must ask darling Noel – he'll be sure to know the inside story.' And he'd make sure to get some little morsel out of them in return, even if they didn't realize they were giving it him. How valuable a friend he was going to be to her in London!

It was as well she made these discoveries in time, for his next words, when he had seemingly run out of Falmouth news, were, "So tell me all about life with dear Lord Gordon, then?"

How could she refuse?

44

Rose had imagined a tall, portly man, bearded and imperious, wearing jeweled rings like knuckledusters, and dressed in a camelhair overcoat with acres of astrakhan collar, greyed with the ash of chain-smoked cigars. Hugo de Witt was tall, but there the likeness ended. He was clean-shaven and almost deferential in manner – though Rose soon learned that this was deceptive. His only jewelry was a diamond cravat pin and his only concession to colour was a paisley-pattern cravat. It was ready-tied and slipped round his neck on a steel spring – something to make the editress of every lady's magazine reach for the extra-strong smelling salts. Though rumoured to be worth a million pounds, he bought his clothes off the peg at departmental stores, preferably in one of their periodic sales. He had been known to stand outside their doors from before dawn to be sure of being first through them to bag his prize. That was before Gordon Selfridge, whose store in Oxford Street was just over a year old, had realized the publicity value of having one of the world's great impresarios dressed in his sale goods and so created special opportunities for de Witt to exploit. And when it came to exploitation, the man needed little encouragement or instruction. 'Unto him that hath shall it be given,' was his favourite saying.

He said it to Rose at their first meeting, which was in a dim corner of the taproom at the Saracen's Head. "Unto her that hath shall it be given, Miss Marteyne," he said. "So let's just see what this young lady hath, eh? Stand up, if you'd be so kind, and show me your legs."

"Eh?" Rose was shocked.

"You show them to an audience of hundreds every night," he pointed out.

She wanted to tell him that was different and that if he wanted to see her legs so desperately, he could join that audience any night of the week. But he spiked the argument while she was still telling herself she'd be a fool to utter it.

"Would you prefer to go down the street to the theatre now?" he asked. "And we'll conduct this interview with you on the stage and me shouting at you from the stalls?"

The question was rhetorical, of course. Looking into his eyes, which were great, dark pools of interest and concern, she wondered how he did it. Here was a man with four productions in London – correction, four in the West End and possibly a further eight in London, and heaven knows how many in the provinces, and all those actors and actresses and backstage people to juggle with and worry about ... and yet he somehow managed to imply that she was the only one who truly interested him. Had he not come down all the way from London *just* to see her? Well, no, he almost certainly hadn't but he gave her the feeling that he had.

In that moment she would have done anything for him. What she actually did was lean down, clasp the hem of her skirt, and raise it. The moment she was committed to the action her shyness evaporated and she did it with a flourish worthy of any flamenco dancer, pointing her left leg in one of the ballet gestures Titania had shown her.

He ran a critical eye up and down her body, from head to foot, several times. "I ask you to show me your legs and you show me everything," he commented at last.

For a wild moment she thought he was obliquely asking her to strip. For an even wilder half-moment she realized she would do it, too. Then she realized he was commenting on the fact that she had put the whole of herself into the simple act of lifting her skirt hem.

"You can do it," he said, gesturing to her to let her skirt fall again. "What they say about you is true – you have everything that cannot be taught. All you lack are those things that can be taught. Beginning with arrogance. Sit down here, please." He rose and placed a chair for her, facing him. "What will you drink?"

Was it a trap? She didn't care. Talking with an upper-class accent all the time from now on was going to be strain enough without pretending to be Band of Hope and a plaster saint as well. "A half of Smith's export, please," she replied.

"Smith's!" He seemed pleased. "I'll join you. If there were more like you in the land, Miss Marteyne, I shouldn't have lost such a wad. You know they went smash?"

"I had heard of it, yes."

He smiled and she knew he was aware of her connection with Louis. Darling Noel, of course! Still, he seemed pleased. Probably because she could keep her private misfortunes from showing in her face and voice. He called out the order to Mrs Kelly, who pulled the two half-pints and brought them over at once.

"Lord Gordon's account," he told the landlady. Then, to Rose: "Your health!"

"Here's mud in your eye!"

"You were once a lady's maid," he said, taking out a small notebook and pencil, bound in blue leather. "That would have knocked the arrogance out of you – that arrogance we have somehow to put back."

"I went into service at fourteen and worked up to it."

"Not speaking in those tones!"

She repeated her reply in her true accent: "I went into service at fourteen and worked up to it."

"Excellent." He ticked off something in the book; he was holding it at too sharp an angle for her to see the page. "Give me something in American."

She gave him an American sailor from Galveston, an American sailor from New York, and an American sailor from Boston.

"Only sailors?" he asked, amused.

"They're the only ones I've met – except for my mother, who's sort of half-Hoosier, half-Yankee." She gave him a sample.

"Show me a curtsy," he said.

Then, "A pirouette."

Then, "Walk like a nun going in to vespers."

The only nun she'd ever seen was a cross little tar-barrel of a woman haranguing a crocodile of orphans on their way to a swimming treat on Swanpool Beach; but she did her best.

Then, "A lady of the town, walking up and down her little beat. Cold night ... rain pouring down."

No difficulty there! Even without her memories from Falmouth, she'd seen – and studied – plenty of such 'ladies,' who nightly paraded in their hundreds along almost the entire length of Union Street. And, of course, in the upper galleries of the theatre.

Then, "Take up that broom the maid left by the door and dance the waltz with it." Then, "You love your partner to absolute distraction – but he doesn't yet realize it." Then, "Turn it round – your partner is besotted with you but you don't reciprocate in the least."

"This is fun!" she cried, executing a couple of reverse glides to cure her dizziness.

There were several more impromptu tests – a mime of waking up; of walking down the street and suddenly remembering she'd left the gas on – with the penny about to die in the meter; of eating a chocolate and finding something bitter at its heart; of standing absolutely still for a full minute; and so on. The last was the most bizarre, when she had to mime the act of sewing her fingertips together with a cobbler's needle and thread. Her screams of pain brought people running from all over the inn. When they realized what was happening, they stayed to watch, both fascinated and appalled. Several swore they could actually see a needle and thread in her hand. Two chambermaids had to sit down; a third hid her eyes but could not resist peeping. When Rose had finished there was spontaneous applause. She looked around in a daze. The sweat was pouring down her back and, most curious of all, she could not make her sewn-together fingers part again!

"Here! Use my scissors," de Witt called out, handing her an imaginary pair.

It was so ridiculous she had to laugh – and yet, until she had cut that nonexistent thread, her fingers remained welded together.

"Well," he said as she settled in her chair again and took a grateful gulp from her glass, "you can speak, you can move, and you can mime. Excellent! Now all you need learn is how to do all three at once."

"And then?"

"And then, Miss Marteyne? Why, then you will be able to *act!*"

END OF PART THREE

Part Four

The name of the rose

45 Twenty pounds a week! Rose still couldn't believe it. Enough to provide for eight families – food, clothing, rent, beer, gaspers, the lot! It was even better than Sally's earnings in Paris – better in every possible way. In eight weeks, if she didn't spend a penny of it, she could buy a brand new 'wee but wonderful' Humber motor car. Or in twenty weeks she'd be able to afford a Farman biplane, including a *written guarantee* that it would lift off the ground; then she could do a matinée in Glasgow, an evening show in Manchester, and still be home by midnight. Home would be London, of course – to which this express train was presently whisking her. Twenty quid a week and she was still travelling second class, because she still couldn't believe it. And because she was going to save all she could, as well. For her and Louis. If Hugo de Witt could rise before dawn and stand for hours outside a shuttered store, just to get a half-price suit, she'd feel no shame in saving every penny she could – and in shaving every one she couldn't, as well.

Still, it was fun imagining what she could do with such a weekly fortune. For twenty quid you could get a Monarch Senior gramophone with the special 'Morning Glory' horn *plus* two dozen records – or only eight if they were by Melba or Caruso or Patti... people like that. Still, a gramophone would be nice. Or, more practical, a Low Vacuum Portable Dust Extractor; that could actually save money by doing away with the wages of a servant. Or so the advertisements said.

Servants! Wouldn't she be expected to have at least a maid? That would cost a pound a week – half for her wages and the rest for uniforms and keep. She probably would have to have a maid – which, in turn, would mean renting rooms in the servant-keeping areas of London. On the other hand, no one would know *what* she was once she'd slipped out by the stage door. She could be any little chorus girl then. That would be good. Then she could get a top-class bed-and-breakfast, with laundry, baths, and a rice pud in the evenings for the same twenty shillings a week. Noel would know what to advise; she had sent him a cable and she had his address in Bedford Street, so that's where she'd go first.

And then – reverting to the money question – there was the income tax, which she had never paid before. Lord Gordon had told her it would be around sixty quid a year! That was where it really became unbelievable – she would now be paying almost one and a half times more in tax than she had previously earned in total! Still, her magnificent twenty quid a week was already eroded down to seventeen-odd.

What about smoking? Titania had said that all the actresses on the London stage smoked Turkish cigarettes. Not being a smoker herself, Rose had looked them up – and discovered to her horror that even the cheapest were three shillings and sixpence for a hundred. And everyone would know they were cheap by the smell. The most expensive were thirteen shillings.

So there she was, reduced to seventeen quid already. And she really ought to send a *little* money home each week. A pound, say, it would make all the difference to them and it really wouldn't hurt her. Down to sixteen pounds. That was *less* than Sally had been putting away in the bank each week – though why she should make that her pacemaker, she couldn't really say. And still she had made no allowances for clothes or meals or books or gloves or taxis or magazines or chocolates or postage stamps ...?

It was only amazing how quickly the princely sum of twenty pounds a week could get whittled down to starvation wages!

And then, to set against all these cheeseparing dreams, was the advice dear Mr Swindlehurst had given when he treated her to a slap-up farewell dinner:

"Don't let the sum go to your head, lady. You are worth that much to the de Witt empire at the moment partly because of your talent and verve but mainly because of your pretty face and youthful figure. If you want to continue earning at that rate and more – a great deal more – when those charms have faded somewhat, you'll have to develop the talent and become like the Ellen Terrys and the Mrs Patrick Campbells of our profession. Don't let that man put you into too many frothy musical comedies and light operas. He'll try it on so as to get his money back quickly. And don't *you* be afraid to spend good money on dramatic coaching – there won't be time for it when someone taps you on the shoulder and says, 'You're playing Ophelia next week, Miss Marteyne.' And finally, make as many friends and acquaintances as you can while you may still coast along on your youth and good looks. Cultivate the theatre sets. Be seen dining at the Café Royal and the Grillion and Chez Crébillon. Never miss Henley or Ascot. Wangle invitations to the Eton-Harrow match. Keep in touch with all the scandal. Learn who's in, who's out. Sharpen your tongue. There's nothing that metropolitan Society loves more than a cutting observation at someone else's expense ... What else? Oh yes – get a thick skin for yourself and an amenable conscience to hide inside it."

Dear Mr Swindlehurst! He was sad and a little bitter to see her go, of course. But she would keep in touch and, if it were ever in her power to do him a bit of good, she'd certainly do it.

One tricky thing, though – she couldn't 'be seen dining at the Café Royal' etc alone. It would have to be with a man, or, better yet, with a string of men. They would pay for her, of course, so it wasn't a question of expense, more a matter of what they would expect in return.

Mr Swindlehurst seemed to think a smile would be all they could reasonably hope for, plus the distinction of being seen as the escort of London's latest 'star,' that rising young actress, Lucille Marteyne. Rose's previous experience of idle rich young men and their expectations led her to doubt it would ever be quite that simple; she was already quite certain there was no such thing as an absolutely free dinner.

What it boiled down to was a choice between saving every penny now, which would mean doing none of the things he recommended – and therefore, possibly, seeing her career shrink and wither along with her youth – or following his advice and ending up with very little saved, despite all the 'free' dinners. It would all depend on how quickly Louis could restore his fortunes.

These thoughts and dreams, interspersed with bouts of nodding off, reading, and dining in the restaurant car, occupied her all the way to London.

London! Long before their arrival at Paddington, she realized it was as unimaginably vast as her new salary. Even before the train reached its outer edges there were neighbouring villages or small towns like Ealing and Haynes, and the countryside in between was already so spattered with houses that you could easily imagine London reaching out to enclose them, too, before very long; it wasn't real countryside at all, just crowds of market gardens for feeding the Great Wen. Then, at a great junction of lines called Willesden, all semblance of countryside ended, drowned beneath the advancing tide of bricks and tarmacadam. And they were still two miles from Paddington – and Paddington itself was another two miles from the centre of the city! Imagine a city so big it would take you the best part of a day to cross it on foot – and in all that way the only green you'd see would be behind iron railings or garden walls, and the only trees would be where they took up a flagstone and planted one! All the rest would be houses, shops, factories, offices, hotels, restaurants ... and, of course, *theatres!*

She knew exactly how many there were because she had bought a guide book to the city by Ward Lock & Co – the 1*s.* 6*d.* edition because she'd hardly be needing the plans of Hampstead and Denmark Hill in the 2*s.* 6*d.* edition, nor the gold edges. And it listed thirty-one West End theatres, nine West End variety theatres and music halls, as well as twenty-one suburban theatres. And as for suburban music halls, well, it just said it was impossible to list them all; instead it gave a sample list of twenty-seven to be going on with! So altogether there must be more than a hundred theatrical establishments of one kind or another.

Her thoughts reeled to contemplate the number of actors and actresses who worked in them – never mind the orchestras, the people backstage, and those who worked 'out front.' Just actors and actresses. There must be at least a thousand, because some of the big West End places would have a cast of fifty and even a small suburban theatre would have ten or so doing repertory. So it could easily be fifteen hundred. And then, if what Mr S had said was true – that there were a dozen seeking work for every one on stage each night – the total number would be well over ten *thousand!*

She felt her stomach fall away inside her as she realized she was just the latest addition to that privileged thousand. And how incredibly lucky she was to be already among the top quarter of them in terms of salary. Was she mad even to dream of rising higher still, to be among the top fifty or so? Probably. And yet, without the dream, there wasn't a hope; only the nightmare of slipping down and out of that privileged thousand or more, down among the ten thousand knocking at stage doors every day and being taken on *just* often enough to keep the flame of hope flickering. How did they eke out those meagre earnings meanwhile? She shuddered to think of it. This nightmare would be there whether she liked it or not, for it was the underlying reality of her chosen profession. If there was madness anywhere, it was in her choice. So it might be as well to pursue the dream, if only as a counter to all that gloom.

Come and see me wherever I am, all you lovely people! She tried to project the thought at all those grim houses on either side of the line as the train slowed down through Kensal Green, Westbourne Park, and Royal Oak, from where it just crawled into the huge glass tunnel-shed of the terminus.

"I owe you twenty quid," Noel panted as he finally caught up with her on the platform. "I was waiting for you at the first class." He slipped an arm around her shoulder and gave her a hug. "How does it feel, eh?"

"I didn't mean you to go to the trouble of *meeting* me. Anyway, it was only four quid."

"I seem to remember it was a week's wages."

"Never mind. You've repaid it in other ways long ago. I haven't mentioned it for ages. I've got some luggage in the van."

"And I've got a porter – where is the fellow. Ah!" He saw the man and pointed a finger toward the luggage van.

As they went to join the scrum around it he repeated his question: "How does it feel, eh?"

"Frightening."

His face fell. "Someone's already told you!"

"What?" She didn't think her stomach had any farther to fall – but it had. "Told me what?"

He smiled with relief. "Two weeks from today you open in a one-act curtain-raiser at the Kingsway Theatre, Great Queen Street, just off Drury Lane."

She stopped and gaped at him.

"*Now* are you frightened?" he asked.

She shook her head. "Funnily enough – no. Not exactly frightened. Excited and ... trepidacious, if that's a word. What's the part? Is it a play I might know?"

"Hardly. The scribbler's still scribbling it. It's called *Twin Sisters.* The idea is that you play both parts. You can manage a Scotch accent, I seem to recall?"

The porter barked, "Wot nime, Miss?"

She pointed out her trunk and her suitcase and then turned back to Noel. "Tell me this is a legpull."

"Not a bit. You'll love it – and the public will love you in it, which is the main idea." To the porter: "I have a cab waiting in Praed Street."

"What's it about? I play twin sisters? Obviously not on stage at the same time!"

"It's not at all obvious, darling. In fact, you appear in both parts simultaneously in the final scene." He laughed at her bewilderment. "We have an actress of your height and build – and colouring. The make-up will take care of the rest. All you have to do is throw your voice like a ventriloquist and she'll move her lips in time with the words. How's your ventriloquism, by the way?"

"If it can be taught inside two weeks, I'll learn it – don't worry about that."

The cab was not the hansom or growler she had expected but a shuddering little red Renault, which looked as if it would break in two when the porter and driver loaded her trunk aboard. They were on their way 'up West' when Rose returned to this most exciting news. "The programme must make it quite clear," she said, "that I play both parts except in the final scene. Also that I *speak* both parts, even then."

Seated beside her, he leaned forward and peered up into her face. "How d'you *do* that?" he asked.

"Do what?"

"Think like a prima donna when you haven't even appeared once on the London stage? I suppose it's the same way cats know how to fall on their feet without the slightest training."

Titania would have said the same, she thought. *So would Mr S. So would everyone in the Players.* But she accepted the compliment – if that was what it had been. "What's the general story?" she asked.

"They're twins, separated at birth and brought up in very different circumstances – one, called Morag, in a Glasgow slum, the other, called Penelope, as the daughter of landed gentry. Imagine Ibsen writing *Little Lord Fauntleroy* and you'll get the general hang of it. The drama begins when Morag starts work as scullerymaid in Penelope's house. It's a split stage with an upstairs and a basement – and you're going to learn all the tricks of the quick-change artiste in getting between the two scenes. Are you still not terrified?"

She shook her head. "The more you tell me, the more exciting it sounds. Besides, I have one great advantage over a regular West End actress."

"Namely?"

"Seven months with Lord Gordon Fitzroy's Players – who do not know the meaning of the word 'impossible.' So I have no idea how difficult *Twin Sisters* really ought to be."

46

The taxi took them through a maze of streets, avoiding the congestion of such great thoroughfares as the Marylebone Road and Oxford Street; the driver was of the opinion that the sooner horse-drawn traffic was done away with, the sooner London would start moving about at a decent pace. As they wove a path across the Edgware Road they almost knocked a lamplighter down. He was weaving a different path among the traffic, hampered by the long pole, which he had to balance vertically as he rode his bicycle from lamp to lamp. Edgware Road was equipped with the new lamps that had a constantly burning pilot light, so all he had to do was hook his pole over the lever and turn the main gas supply on. Even so he was late, for the sun had set at ten to five and it was now almost six.

"Blame Paddington Council," the cabbie told his two passengers as the man cursed him. "Won't pay for an extra fifteen minutes of gas so's 'e can start in good time – oh no! How can 'e do 'is round in traffic like this? Honest, it gets worse every day."

He was still playing the same record as they darted dangerously across Marylebone High Street, which was clogged with carriages, vans, and drays, mostly horse-drawn. "How can we compete with the Tube when we've got to fight our way through this?" he complained. "I'd of tooken you through the park only it's banned to commercial vehicles. The *royal* parks!" he sneered. "Can't sully his majesty's lily-white hands with *commerce,* oh no!"

"You're not too keen on the royalties then?" Noel remarked.

"Me? I'd put them against a wall and shoot them – the lot."

"Well! You are clearly a man of high ideals," Rose said with apparent admiration.

"This is where all the posh doctors hang out," Noel cut in, mainly to stifle their laughter.

But a London cabbie is not so easily mocked nor so swiftly silenced. "New to Lunnon, are yer, miss?" he asked.

"Only temporarily," she replied.

"See that hôtel?" He jerked a thumb at the gloomy gothic pile of the Langham and simultaneously yelled, "Wotchit!" at a carter trying to control a frisky horse. "That was the site of Lord Mansfield's country 'ome once. *Country* 'ome, eh! He come out 'ere to avoid the stink of the city. Couldja b'lieve it? Got burned dahn in the Gordon Riots."

As the Queen's Hall passed out of view Noel just had time to say. "They put on good concerts there"

"And this is where the Duke of Clarence used to come for 'is bit of fun," the cabbie continued unstoppably as they bowled down Mortimer Street. "He was Jack the Ripper, you know – that's why they never caught 'im. Queen Victoria's grandson."

And so it went on, a two-man contest of inane snippets as they threaded their way among great cliffs of dimly lighted buildings, four or five storeys high and all cheek-by-jowl with no chink of light in between them. Their top floors, rising beyond the reach of the street lamps, were gaunt black silhouettes against a slightly paler sky. Occasionally a garret window, picked out by the light of a guttering candle, gave a hint of the building's true form. The tang of burnt coal, laden with sulphur, was everywhere, mingled, as always, with fresh horse dung.

Rose had already experienced the alien-ness of strange towns and cities during her travels with the Players. In Falmouth there wasn't a single street in which she could not name at least one householder or occupier. But places like Penzance, Newquay, and Plymouth – especially Plymouth – had introduced her to the tantalizing unknowability of alien streets. And now London was the crowning of it all. The buildings were taller, the streets longer, and there was just so much more of both; it seemed to go on for ever – all those intense little lives stacked side by side and one on top of the other.

"I'll never get to know it all," she said. "It goes on and on. There's just too much of it."

"And it never stops changing, neither," the cabby said. They were now past St Giles Circus, going south. "This part 'ere, before they pushed New Oxford Street through it – and Shaftesbury Avenue dahn there – before then it was a right rookery. The rozzers wouldn't even go in in pairs. And now you could walk dahn any street at any hour of the day or night."

"I'm glad to hear it," Noel said as they crossed Shaftesbury Avenue. He turned to Rose with the most innocent look on his face and explained: "Because our lodgings are just a couple of streets away now."

She wanted to say *'our* lodgings?' but didn't wish to start a squabble in front of the cabbie.

In fact, the lodgings proved to be a *pair* of furnished two-room apartments, so-called 'bed-sitters' because they consisted of a bedroom and a sitting room. Several houses in Bedford Street had been converted so as to provide this popular new form of lodging in the city.

"Now," Noel said when he and the driver had hauled Rose's trunk up to the first floor, "you may choose between the one at the front, overlooking the street, which is noisy but interesting, or the quieter one at the side, offering a superb view of a blank brick wall six feet away."

She hesitated. The sensible choice would be the quiet room, but the other one offered more liveliness. "The front one," she said.

He opened the door to the room with no view. "I knew you'd say that," he crowed. "See? I've already moved in here."

They deposited her trunk in the centre of the sitting room and then Noel said to the cabby, "Time to sully your lily-white hands with a bit of commercial silver."

He paid him off in the passageway outside. Rose's sharp ears heard the man murmur, "These was all knockin' shops when I was a nipper. If these walls could talk, eh! Caaw-er!"

"What's it cost?" she asked when Noel rejoined her. "The rooms, I mean."

"Ten bob a week plus two bob for service. There's a slot meter for the gas. And you've got a gas fire, as you can see, so there's no messing about with coals. "

"What's 'service'?"

"Clean your rooms, empty the waste paper, change the sheets once a week, make sure the gas mantles aren't broken ... that sort of thing. You can make arrangements with them for personal laundry, too."

"I could do all that myself."

"Of course you could, but you won't want to. There's a gas ring in that alcove, so you can make a pot of tea anytime. But we eat all our meals out. There's lots of good cheap cafes round and about because Covent Garden's only a hop, skip, and a jump away – the fruit and veg market. Also the opera, of course. D'you want to leave the unpacking and go for a walk? The Kingsway Theatre's less than half a mile away. We could walk up there, I'll show you backstage, then a bite of dinner up at the Holborn Restaurant, and home James for an early night. You've got a busy day tomorrow – costumes, and a read-through of whatever young Norris has managed to finish by then.

"The scribbler?"

"John Norris, yes. He's a lightning-fast worker – which, alas, means he leaves everything to the last minute. But he may even have it finished."

"What do we do for baths, etcetera?" she asked as they prepared to go out. "I could just have a quick wash and change."

He agreed reluctantly to a quick wash but he vetoed the quick change on the grounds that there was no such thing where females were concerned. More seriously he pointed out that time was short if she wanted to see the Kingsway before it got busy.

She unpacked as far as her towel – and a fresh blouse, which she wrapped inside the towel when he wasn't looking.

He pointed out the two bathroom doors at the end of the passage, where it turned to lead downstairs. "You take your pick – whichever one's empty, if you're in luck. It's a penny in the meter for the gas. If you wait till after midnight, there's usually enough unused therms piled up to heat one bath for free. Those are the WCS." He indicated two other doors, one each side of the twin bathrooms.

He waited in his rooms until he heard her return to hers. He noticed the fresh blouse but merely wagged a finger at her. She, meanwhile was busy writing a postcard. "Have you a threepenny stamp?" she asked.

"Threepence?" He was surprised.

"It's to America. I want to let Louis know this address." She filled the blank space with kisses while he hunted in his wallet.

He peeked at the address while she fixed the stamp. "Still living at the YMCA then?" he commented.

"If you know a better way to save, tell me." She popped it in her bag and took his arm.

"Unfortunately," he said as they left to go out, "there are quite a few theatre people in this house, so we all tend to want baths at the same hours. Signor Vignelli and Madame Devigny" – he lowered his voice and murmured – "both from darkest Whitechapel, if you ask me ... they like to take both bathrooms at the same time and sing duets from Verdi, Offenbach, etcetera. It's quite amusing for the first week. Their *Là'ci darem la mano* from Mozart is especially touching."

A thin mist drifted along the canyon of the street, visible only when it approached or moved on past a street light. Litter trembled in the breeze, which was not strong enough, however, to move it along. A scrawny black cat flattened itself on a window sill and hissed at them as they approached.

"Wait!" Rose plucked at Noel's arm and held him back.

They stared at the cat, which grew nervous, leaped down, and fled across the road.

"Good!" She urged him on again. "That's a good omen."

"You're superstitious!" he accused her with surprise.

"Only about the theatre. What's this street? Isn't it all dirty!"

"Henrietta Street. That's where Dickens's publishers used to be in his day. Just think – Charles Dickens's feet probably trod on this very paving stone!"

"It's funny he never wrote plays," she remarked. "Especially when you think how dramatic his readings were always supposed to be. They say it took ten years off his life, those dramatic readings."

"*A Christmas Carol* is almost a play. We tried a version of it in Leeds this season, instead of a panto. It went down quite well."

"*I've* written a play," she said casually, as if it hadn't been on her mind ever since Paddington.

He chuckled. "Go on then. This is Covent Garden market, by the way."

It was all closed and shuttered by now, of course, and would remain so until three o'clock that night – as Rose would all too soon discover. Holborn council workers were clearing away the last of the previous market's litter.

"What's it about?" he asked.

"Lord Gordon asked me to write it but I never had enough time to finish it before I left. Panto is much more exhausting than melodrama. Anyway, it's something on the lines of *Murder in the Red Barn* except that it's based on that sensational murder in Penryn about three centuries ago. When old man Wilmot and his wife Agnes murdered their own son, believing he was just a common sailor. Did you ever hear of it?"

She thought he must be racking his brains for the memory but he was silent too long for that.

"Did you?" she repeated.

"I don't know how to break this any more gently," he said, "but it has already been done."

"Oh!" She was crestfallen. "Well, there you see the advantages of a board school education! Who beat me to it?"

"A man called George Lillo. This is the Covent Garden Opera on our left, by the way. Bow Street police station over there – home of the celebrated Runners."

"More important," she said, "there's a pillar box. Hang on."

She darted across the road and posted her card to Louis.

Noel followed her. "Actually, Lucille ..." he said. "By the way, I'm going to call you that always now, even between ourselves, if that's all right? What I was about to say is that, actually, your bitter little dig at the *advantages* of board-school education may not be too wide of the mark. George Lillo died sometime around seventeen forty and, although he's credited with being the first English playwright to make dramas exclusively around the lives of common people, his language isn't all that inspiring. So if yours is in modern-day speech ... say, if you set it sometime in the eighteen eighties ... you might have something worth performing, you know."

"How amazing!" Her eyes gleamed in the bright electrical lighting pouring out of the theatre. "That's just what I have done!"

Notwithstanding the light, he couldn't have seen her crossing her fingers as she spoke, for that hand was well hidden from him. It wouldn't take much effort to modernize the language, anyway.

When they reached the corner of Great Queen Street, he said, "Look down at the pavement now. And don't raise your eyes until I say so."

They walked most of the length of the street, on the south side, as far as the Kingsway Hall. "Right," he said. "In years to come, whenever you find yourself in this part of London, you'll stop at this spot and say, '*There* is where it all began'!"

On 'there' he took her by the shoulders, from behind, and turned her to face across the street.

Disappointment was hardly the word. Without the name, The Kingsway Theatre, *painted* on the entablature between the ground and first floor, it could have been a public house, a saleroom, a lending library, or an art gallery. Its three-storey façade was dwarfed by the building to its left, a haberdashery with three domestic storeys above it.

Noel must have been expecting a lukewarm response for he added, "Seats six hundred, you know."

She looked at him in disbelief; she would have guessed a hundred at most.

"It seated a thousand when it was first built," he added. "But six hundred is much more comfortable. Come and see."

"Why does it say 'Novelty' at the top?" she asked.

"That was its original name. It's had rather a chequered history and several changes of names. The first night of Ibsen's *A Doll's House* was staged here, back in eighty-nine. And then in ninety-six – *you* might just remember it though I don't – an actor was accidentally stabbed on stage, a man called Temple Crozier. I can't recall the name of the actor who stabbed him but they say he used a jeweled dagger his aunt had given him – a real dagger – instead of the prop ..."

"Where the blade pushes back into the handle."

"Yep. He probably thought it would bring him luck! And then maybe he forgot it wasn't a prop. The play was called *Sins of the Night,* which was certainly apt that night! *Et voilà!*" He held the street door open and ushered her through.

Her faith in the size of the theatre was restored the moment she entered, for the three-storey façade was a disguise behind which stood a magnificent vestibule, running all the way up to a stained-glass roof. The decor was rich, with swags, cartouches, and heavily carved mouldings on every surface – gilt against a background of royal blue alternating with deep orange.

"The largest vestibule in any London theatre," Noel said. "By the way, the place has been almost completely rebuilt inside since the *Sins of the Night* tragedy, especially the stage area – just in case you were worried."

The only people around at that time of the evening were cleaners. They gave the two visitors a brief, incurious nod as they went about their work, leaving Rose with the feeling that they were the permanent fixtures of the place while she and Noel were mere transients; farce, tragedy, opera comique, burlesque, amateur nights, darkened stages … all could come and go but the cleaners and ushers were there to stay.

"It was also the first London theatre to number each seat and row," Noel said as he led the way into the auditorium. "So people could book an exact position in advance. The first with electric lighting *and* gas emergency lights. But its proudest first, I think, will be that it was here that Miss Lucille Marteyne first trod the metropolitan boards."

She gave him a grateful smile but shivered nonetheless. "I wish you wouldn't say things like that, Noel. It's like a ton weight on me." She sat down in one of the seats in the pit.

"What now?" he asked in surprise.

She stared at the fire drop, which was khaki green with a strange white oblong in the centre. "I just feel it will help if I can see what it looks like from here. It'll help me picture myself when I'm up there. What's the white rectangle?"

"Ah! There's an epidiascope up in the first balcony and we use it to project coloured advertisements onto that bit of the curtain whenever it has to come down. H-d-W is never short of ideas for raising another penny or two. This row, full, pays your weekly wage, by the way." He ran back ten rows from where she sat. "And when you have a name that can be guaranteed to fill the place every night of the run, you'll be able to ask for the takings from all of these as well. It always helps to remember where the money comes from. Let's go backstage."

She could smell the powder the moment they went from gilded plaster to bare, dirty brick. To her it was, by now, the odour of fear and of excitement. Already she could feel her heart quicken and her stomach beginning to fall, as if she were on tonight. Indeed, she wished she were. Two weeks of rehearsals would be two weeks of ever-tightening nerves.

"This'll be your dressing room," he said.

Members of the cast were already beginning to arrive but this particular room was not yet occupied. Noel merely waved at them but did not introduce her.

She looked for a number on the door as she entered but there was none. "I suppose they used up all the numbers when they did the auditorium."

"How amazing!" He grinned. "You're by no means the first actress, or actor, to notice that."

There were three places in this particular room. She sat at the one in the middle, switched on the lights, and stared at herself. *You could be in a nice warm sewing room right now,* she told her image. *Chatting with the other maids, looking forward to supper in the servants' hall … a few parlour games … an hour or so with a good book … and no butterflies in the tummy …*

The pointless homily faded away. Thoughts of life in the servants' hall made her realize how differently she regarded her image in a mirror these days. People talked of her good looks but she had never been satisfied with what she saw. Her eyebrows were too ragged, her nostrils too thin, her dimples too deep, and the flesh beneath her chin always seemed to need pushing up out of the way. So her self-inspections had always been cool and practical.

"Anything wrong?" Noel cut across her reverie.

"I was just thinking – at Nancemellin I'd be looking to see if anything about me would displease your mother. Incidentally, I forgot to ask ..."

"Don't!" He laughed. "And what are you looking to see now? To see if anything would displease the public, I suppose. Same difference in the end."

She shook her head. "It's more complicated than that. I used to have to look to see if I was hiding myself, me – Lucinda-Ella Tremayne – sufficiently. Now the question is am I revealing enough of a different me – Lucille Marteyne – sufficiently. I'm a stage property now. I survey myself as a commodity."

"And which is the better feeling?" he asked.

She grinned. "I'm here, aren't I – not there."

47

James Swaffer, that fine and perceptive drama critic, wrote in the *Telegraph:* 'The stage at the unlucky Kingsway Theatre has witnessed its share of real-life outrage and unscripted tragedy. One need only recall the first night of *A Doll's House* and the accidental stabbing of Mr. Temple E. Crozier by Mr. Wilfrid Moritz Franks as testimony to the assertion. And so it is an especial pleasure to report that last night's lucky audience was privileged to witness the appearance on that same stage of one among the brightest talents to arrive in the West End for many a year. The ghosts of tragedy and outrage were surely laid by Miss Lucille Marteyne's performance in *Twin Sisters,* which had us all on the edges of our seats.

'It was an audacious and at times even reckless performance, for Miss Marteyne plays both parts and there are several scenes in which the twin sisters are on stage at the same moment. I reveal no secrets (for it is plainly implied in the programme) that this is achieved by having a mute actress of the same build and appearance play the other twin and silently mouth the words that are actually spoken by Miss Marteyne! It cannot be easy but Miss Gertrude Scott manages all with her customary aplomb.

The story, by Mr. John Norris, is light enough, which is a mercy, for the weight of a heavy drama added to the suspense of waiting for Miss Marteyne to put a foot wrong, and so break that magical thread of make-believe, would have shredded the strongest nerves. The twin sisters of the title, Aggie and Annie, have been brought up in vastly differing circumstances, Aggie in a lower-class Caledonian slum, Annie in upper-middle-class affluence. Improbable as it may seem, this dichotomy is deftly explained. After two brief scenes to establish the sisters in their own respective milieux, the drama proper begins when Aggie, who speaks in a most authentic Scotch accent, becomes a scullery-maid in Annie's foster-parents' household. Annie, naturally, speaks in the polished tones of a refined young Belgravia lady ...

'The climax, when the sisters actually meet and embrace and talk rapidly and excitedly – ofttimes, you would swear, *over* each other – each in her own dialect, is a veritable tour de force by Miss Marteyne. If you have half a guinea to spare, you will not regret 'blowing' it on a seat in the stalls – much less a humble shilling in the gallery. And remember, the Kingsway is one of only two 'legitimate' theatres in London where all seats may be booked in advance (the other being the Playhouse).'

By contrast, that smug, self-satisfied nincompoop Laurence Barker, who preens himself as a drama critic, wrote in *The Nation:* 'One had supposed that London's 'great' impresarios could not possibly descend lower in their campaign to substitute flashy trickery for genuine drama, but *Twin Sisters,* which opened at the Kingsway last night, shows just how optimistic that supposition was. That cherished and revered stage on which *A Doll's House* first seized the London bourgeoisie by the throat and shook a few grains of social awareness into its smug and empty noodles now groans under such a farrago of contrived poppycock that one wonders it does not collapse in sheer embarrassment. How are the mighty fallen!

'Aggie and Annie, the eponymous twins, have, we are invited to believe (or, rather, to suspend our misbelief) been reared at opposite ends of the social spectrum, Aggie in a Gorbals tenement, Annie in Sloane Square. The mechanical trickery of the plot is to engineer them beneath one roof so as to contrive a 'discovery scene' of truly mawkish horror; the trickery of the production is that both parts are played by a newcomer to the London stage, Miss Lucille Marteyne – and that both are sometimes simultaneously 'on.' The mute part is admirably mimed by Miss Gertrude Scott while Miss Marteyne somehow contrives to throw her voice so that it seems to come from Miss Scott's moving lips, even while her own appear immobile. Such a splendid actress as poor Miss Scott deserves better than to be thus wasted.

'I would say "poor Miss Marteyne," as well, for, newcomer though she may be, she is clearly an actress of formidable talent and one who will go far. I would commiserate with her for having this inane drivel forced upon her at her debut. I wish I could, but she appears to enjoy every moment. I did not think there was an actress left in the metropolis who could deliver the cliché "I'm a good girl, I am" with a straight face, but Miss Marteyne not only manages it, she does so with a perfect Glaswegian inflection: "Ah'm a guid gerrul, so ah'm." In short, she plays her parts with a verve she would be better advised to reserve for a role with more depth and realism. The producer of Mr. G. B. Shaw's next entertainment would be wise to consider her for some part in it.'

Rose was not aware of any reviews until she turned up at the theatre the following morning. There she could only stand and stare, for the boards outside already proclaimed in letters that could be read from across the street:

"[Miss Marteyne is] one of the brightest talents to arrive in the West End for many a year. [The play] had us all on the edges of our seats." – James Swaffer, *Daily Telegraph*

[Miss Marteyne is] clearly an actress of formidable talent and one who will go far ... I urge you – enjoy every moment! – Laurence Barker, *The Nation*

Noel, who had gone ahead of her to get these particular quotations on display as early in the day as possible, was waiting at the door. "Bravoh!" he cried, waving handfuls of newsprint at her. "Not a bad one among 'em." When she drew near he added at a more conversational level, "Quite a lot of them slate the play but you come through unscathed."

"Does that mean I can put in for a rise?"

He just laughed and led the way to the manager's office, which was empty.

Rose read the lot – five in all. As Noel had said, few of them liked the play but all were complimentary about her.

"I hope this 'tour de force' doesn't mean I'll be forced to tour," she said. "Except to America, of course."

"America? What's the ... oh, yes. I see. 'Nuff said." He pointed at the review pages. "Cut them out, if you want," he said. "It's rare enough we get the chance to quote Laurence Barker."

"Why?"

"He fancies himself as a scribbler of plays – or, as he would say, a dramaturge. H-d-W has turned down several of his scribbles. But even so, the fellow balked at slating you."

"Those billboards outside ..."

"Yes?"

"I think you should add: *Miss Gertrude Scott ... such a talented actress* from *The Nation* or" – she searched through the papers – "this: *I have rarely seen Miss Gertrude Scott play* dot-dot-dot *better* dot-dot-dot by Cato in *The Times."*

"Eh? I don't believe it." He took the paper from her. "The fellow can't stand poor Gertie. She cut him dead at the Café Monico once and he's never for one moment let her forget it – vindictive old pansy!"

He laughed to see what 'Cato' had actually written: 'I have rarely seen Miss Gertrude Scott play well but at last she has found a piece in which her talents are put to better use than is usual.'

"You've got the idea, Lucille," he said. "Long live the dot-dot-dot! But why d'you want to puff little Gertie? This is your triumph, not hers."

He had his mother's habit of using the word 'little' to describe someone who was not paid much.

"Because," Rose said, "of something Mister Swindlehurst told me in Plymouth. 'Attend to others as your star yet rises that they may attend to you as it falls.' He gave me lots of good advice."

"The dear man!" Noel exclaimed. "How I wish that were true!"

"Isn't it?"

He shook his head. "Nothing is more chilling to the rest of the profession than the look of haunted desperation in the eyes of those whose star is waning. They might as well be forced to ring a handbell and shout 'Unclean!' for all the welcome they get. Failure is a kind of leprosy – desperately sorry and all that rot but don't come near me!"

Rose shivered. "He was very good to me, though, Mister S. Could we find him a part somewhere? He's never been on the West End stage. It would mean so much."

Noel pulled a dubious face. "Perhaps in the season before he retires. Before that it wouldn't really be a kindness, you know."

"Why ever not?"

"Because he'd get one part and then languish for weeks or months and then get another part ... and so on. He'd find it very dispiriting at his age, especially after a lifetime of steady work. That's why I say save it until his final season. Then he could retire to some actors' benevolent home and bore everyone stiff with reminiscences of the Garrick, the Lyceum, the Scala, etcetera. What does that look mean?"

"It's impossible to believe you're the same person as that giddy ass who plagued the life out of us girls at Nancemellin, only a year ago. One would think you grew up with the theatre in your blood."

"Look who's talking!" He chuckled and pulled up a chair, not quite facing and not quite beside her. Taking her hand he said, "We're two of a kind, Lucille. You were born to do what you did last night, just as I was born to be a sort of theatrical quidnunc and a mock-Maecenas to second-hand authors."

"Ha!" She recognized the quotation. "*The Critic!* That would be fun to do one day."

"Well!" He became serious again. "It's not a bad idea. As far as I know it's not been done this century yet. You'd play Tilburina?"

"Or Mrs Dangle."

"Tilburina's a much bigger part – and meatier."

"Yes, but Mrs Dangle's finished once the first act is over. She's not needed again until the curtain call – unless she doubles as the magistrate's wife. Which brings me to something I've been wanting to ask. You know my contract says I will not appear in any other drama while I'm in *Twin Sisters?*"

"Yes – of course. That's to stop you from slipping away and..."

"I know that, but what if – just supposing – I were to slip across to the Holborn Empire after I'm finished here each evening and do my comic turn for one of the houses? Would that count?"

"Comic turn?"

"Lady Augusta Vane-Trumpington and her little acts of charity."

"You want to keep that up?"

"Well, I'm not sure I'm really a *dramatic* actress, you know. I've called on a couple of self-styled drama coaches but they're all retired old histrios who want to teach me how to speak in quavering roars and saw the air and so on."

"Good God!" He stared at her, amazed. "But you needn't bother about all that rubbish! Your drama is so natural. It comes from here." He patted his breastbone.

"Actually, it comes from *here!*" She wiped imaginary sweat from her brow and flicked it at him so convincingly that he could not help ducking. "I've decided to take singing lessons instead, because that's something that *can* be taught. But I'd also like to keep my hand in at comedy. So ... may I?"

He thought it over before saying, "It would be best if you never asked me. I can't say yes, and I'm pretty sure H-d-W would say no – if only to conserve your energy for *Twins.*"

"But it's only a ten-minute act."

"It's still best you don't ask me. And if you get caught, you can always say you didn't realize it was breaking your contract – not the one on paper but the implied one, which says you're heart and soul for H-d-W." After a pause he added, "It's a pity Collins's Music Hall is so far away – up in Islington. That's one of ours. He wouldn't feel any betrayal if you were caught working there." He cleared his throat and eyed her speculatively. "There is one other thing I should mention."

"What?"

"Shall we just pop out somewhere for a coffee? I haven't woken up properly yet."

She hesitated. "I wanted to work out some slightly different movements for our discovery scene. There's one moment where I have to walk six paces stage-left, then forward to the footlights, then back to where I started – and you can actually feel the tension flag. We've got to shorten it somehow."

But he was already putting on his hat and coat – the one with the astrakhan collar only half as wide as H-d-W's. "There'll still be time for that. Come on."

The clouds that had earlier threatened rain were gone and the sky was now that bleached, smoky blue you get in a mid-February calm over London. It was cloudless as far as they could see in the narrow overhead strip between the buildings.

"I wish I'd been here ten years ago," Noel said as they went out into Kingsway. "Or fifteen. This was a cramped quarter of narrow old streets, straight out of Dickens. In fact, the Old Curiosity Shop is still going, just round the corner down there."

"Dahn theyah!" she echoed in cockney.

"Another colour for your vocal palette!" he said. "Mind you, the building of Kingsway and the Aldwych was what saved the Kingsway Theatre – or the Novelty, as it then was. People could actually *find* it at last. This is quite a good place."

The coffee house was small at the front but opened out at the back to something the size of half a tennis court. For a while after the waitress took their order they played the game of guessing what the other patrons did for a living – clerks, barristers, foreign visitors, and so on. Then Rose reminded him, "You wanted to discuss something else?"

"Oh, yes." He stared at the table and swallowed hard. "It's a matter of some delicacy, really."

"Oh dear! That usually means a matter of considerable *in*delicacy. Do go on."

"It's to do with the fact that our bed-sitters are adjacent."

"People think we're sleeping together?"

He laughed. "Well – since you put it like that – yes!"

"D'you want to?" she asked next.

He let out his breath as if she'd poked him in the stomach. "It sounds ungallànt," he murmured, "but ..."

"Not at all," she said. "I feel just the same. It would spoil everything if we did."

"Tricky thing to talk about, what?"

The waitress brought their coffees and a tray of little cakes.

"I don't know many other people I could talk about it with," she admitted. "Not like this, anyway. Certainly no other man. Except for ..." She hesitated.

"Roger Deveril?" he suggested.

She nodded and took a bite of the chocolate square.

"You and he ...? Did you ...?"

She smiled. "I think we started to. But then old Roanoke caught us and slung us out."

"And apart from that you've never ... you know."

"Never."

"So you're still ..."

"Yes. Still."

"Is it a burden?"

"Sometimes. Not very much, though. It helps to know that there are a dozen gallànts outside the stage door every night, any one of whom would gladly 'cure my night starvation,' as Vesta Vicky says – as long as I wasn't too particular. A certain young lady member of the company manages it most nights."

"Mi-aow! How d'you make them go away."

"I say, 'Ah'm a guid gerrul, ah'm!' No, actually I just tell them my lover would beat them to a pulp."

"You're lucky," he said. "The day will come when you'd give anything to have the choice of six young bucks. Anyway, the thing I was going to say is, d'you want me to move? There's a place coming vacant on the floor above, in two weeks' time."

She thought it over and then said, "I wouldn't mind it all that much if people thought we were sleeping together. All those actors who wouldn't want to cross you – it would stop them from making sheep's eyes at me."

He laughed. "You're a cool customer, Lucille." Then, serious again, he added, "The only problem is Louis. I'd hate it if he got to hear of it – the rumour, I mean."

"But he's three thousand miles away. God, my stomach goes all hollow every time I think of it."

"And is that often?"

"Every morning. Every afternoon. Every evening. Every night."

"Lucky man. Even in dreams?"

"No." Her shrug was almost apologetic. "There must be something inside me that knows it would be just too-too cruel. My dreams are bad enough as it is. I keep getting this one in which I'm walking naked among crowds of fully dressed people. Normal crowds. Somewhere in London. I don't know where but I do know it's London. And the really horrid thing is – nobody pays me the slightest attention. I'm mortified and yet everyone's ignoring me."

"Are you mortified *because* they're ignoring you or because you have no clothes."

"Because I'm naked. I think." She laughed to show she didn't take it seriously.

"To get back to Louis," he said. "Actors and actresses go from here to America all the time. And vice versa. It's not impossible that a company from here would tour, including to Trenton. And it would be very natural for Louis to ..."

"All right! It's possible he'd get to hear of it – despite the distance ..."

"So could you see yourself finding some ever-so-tactful way to mention these rumours? And to tell him why we're doing nothing to quell them?"

She nodded. "In my very next letter." She reached across the table and stroked his arm with one gloved finger. "About actresses going to America ..." she said.

48

Lady Augusta Vane-Trumpington took twelve minutes to describe her charitable soup round and her visit to the careless (and now legless) gamekeeper her husband had been forced to dismiss. Her make-up took twenty minutes to apply and ten to remove. From the Kingsway's stage door in Parker Street to the stage door of the Holborn Empire in Whetstone Sreet was just under two hundred yards. The journey – or mad dash – took no more than a minute or two, depending on the amount of traffic her ladyship had to dodge while crossing Kingsway. It could all be managed well inside an hour, so Rose was able to cover her absences by 'just slipping out for a coffee.' She appeared on the Empire's bill as 'Lucy Tremayne.'

She was pleased to discover that the London audiences found her little satire against the landed gentry just as funny as had her rural audiences in Cornwall, even though most of them had never seen a gamekeeper outside the pages of *Comic Cuts* or *Ally Sloper's Half-Holiday*. And for her dozen minutes of glory she would earn 4*s*. 6*d*. With two afternoon matinées, it added thirty-six shillings to her weekly income, which was nothing to sneeze at, for it not only recouped the pound she sent to her parents, it also paid for all her meals.

The 'turns' who worked in variety theatres – comedians, singers, jugglers, trick-cyclists, acrobats, magicians, sword-swallowers, and so on – would be booked in at several 'palaces of varieties' every night. A typical evening for one artiste might start out at Collins's Music Hall in Islington, then, after some furious bicycling, to the Euston in Euston Road, on to the Middlesex in Drury Lane, across to the Holborn Empire in High Holborn, to finish up at the Oxford by St Giles's Circus. Another might start out at the Hippodrome in Leicester Square, run to the Palace at Cambridge Circus, on to the Oxford, the Holborn Empire, and then back again for the second house at each of those theatres.

So when Charley 'the Sozzler' Knox asked Rose one evening where she was going on to next, and she replied 'nowhere,' he didn't believe her. "A smart gel like you!" he exclaimed. "Living off of thirty-six bob a week? Start again!"

Charley was big in every way. He had perfected a twenty-minute drunk act, which was no surprise to anyone who saw him; he could hardly have done anything else. He looked as if he had been put together lump by lump, at different times and places and by several creators with conflicting ideas about the final result. Even his lumps had lumps; there was, for instance, a huge wart near the tip of his nose, large enough to hold the hook of his broken umbrella at various points during his act. He started with his hands so shaky he couldn't hold the glass steady enough to drink from and he ended by disappearing into a road drain in search of the front-door keys he dropped there; his imaginary journey between pub and home included a long monologue with a lamppost that he mistook for an uncommunicative policeman.

But those were mere landmarks of the act – the beginning, middle, and end, as it were. His public greeted them as old friends but it was the bits in between that drew them to one or other of his theatres, night after night. He rarely said the same thing twice. His monologue was one long outpouring of random thoughts; some were bitter, some plainly absurd, and some – the ones that usually got the biggest laughs – were wry comments on the events and personalities of the day. For instance, when the news reached London that assassins had attempted to do away with Aristide Briant actually inside the French chamber of deputies, Sozzler Knox tried to solicit subscriptions from the audience so as to pay the villains, or heroes as he called them, to come and perform the same service in London; to show he was serious, he produced plans of the Houses of Parliament, which had appeared in the *Illustrated London News,* and explained just how it could be done.

His act alone filled half the theatre, which easily justified his pound-a-time fee – so he would be making fifty a week. That was more than almost any 'legitimate' actor or actress in London. Small wonder that he swept from theatre to theatre in the back seat of a magnificent black-and-maroon Rolls-Royce Silver Ghost. He earned the price of it in under three months. When Rose first saw it, she realized just how modest her daydream of owning a 'wee but wonderful' Humber had been. Two months went by before he even noticed her enough to ask her that question about where she was playing next.

His disbelief that she could exist on thirty-six bob a week showed in the way he ran his eyes over her figure; he clearly thought she must be supplementing her income in rather obvious ways offstage. It stung her into confessing the truth, though she had vowed to keep her two lives, in variety and in 'legit,' as far apart as possible.

The explanation intrigued him. "So you're doing high drama at the Kingsway and low comedy 'ere – is that the size of it?"

"Length, breadth, and height," she assured him.

"And which d'yer like best?"

"Well, when I did both, down in Plymouth – the comedy and the drama – I never saw much difference. But that was because both of them were done to a script. I treated Lady Augusta like a dramatic character, speaking the same part every night."

"But now?"

"Well ... the audience does make a difference, doesn't it." She pulled an apologetic face in case what she was about to say were *lèse majesté.* "Since I saw how you vary your act every night, I've been trying a bit of that, too. And now I think I like the low comedy the better of the two, especially when it works. Mind you, when it falls flat ..." She pulled a face.

He had to leave then, for even a Rolls-Royce takes a finite amount of time to get from A to B. But as he left he asked her to bring her press cuttings to the Empire the following night.

He cut his act by two minutes, which no one noticed, just so that he'd have longer to look through her cuttings and talk with her. She suspected it was no casual interest on his part, for, although comedians with his length of service were bound to develop an air of inscrutability, she could not imagine him being *idly* curious about anything.

"Bloody marvellous," was his only comment as he handed her back the scrapbook. "So what does the great Hugo de Witt say about this caper? Tickled pink, eh? I don't think."

"He doesn't know about it. And you're the only one I've told."

" 'E's bound to find out sooner or later. 'Specially as Lucy Tremayne's not a million miles off of Lucille Marteyne."

"I've managed it for two months so far. If he does find out, well, I shall just have to throw myself on his mercy."

"His *mercy?* Throw a feather on it first, love – just to see it don't snap. Eh?" He laughed uproariously. "Seriously, though – if he finds out, you'll be done up like a kipper." He scratched his chin. "You wouldn't think of hoppin' over the fence for good? You could make a lot more. Granted it's not so steady. You're only so good as your last house thought you was. You flop in London and it's another year on tour."

"To America? Do English variety artistes go there much?"

His laugh suggested it was something he'd never considered. "Why bother? 'Specially in your case. I mean – for a gel what can write 'er own material and 'as got a gift for the old drama ... well, there ain't what you'd call a boatload of competition. Gawd's truth, there ain't. Vesta ... Marie ... that's it."

"I'd need a lot more experience, Mister Knox."

"Sozzler, my lady! There's plenty with a pile of experience this 'igh" – he held his hand above his head – "what'll never get above so 'igh." He dropped it to his knees. "Experience is important, I grant you. But talent is worth ten times as much. And nerve."

"I'd need more of that, too."

"What – talent?"

"No. Nerve."

"Gotcha!" He laughed again. "So you don't doubt the talent, then? Good for you! Play to your strengths always. Can yer sing?"

"I'm taking lessons but I can't produce the volume yet. I couldn't get to the back of the stalls."

"Well, that'll come, I daresay. Gissa snatch of summink – anyfink yer like."

With her heart in her mouth she sang a ditty she'd been composing in her mind over the last few days, after hearing Jenny Valmore singing her well known song, *So her sister says:*

There's a gel I know what's lately moved into our neighbourhood,
And she would have us all believe that she is very good.
She don't get up till two o'clock and then she's off up West,
Performing works of charity for them as ain't so blest.

At least that's what she tells us and she swears that this is true.
But my! It's only marvellous what charity can do.
Forget your education – all that Greek and Latin,
'Cos charity can dress you well, in coloured silks and satin!

Sozzler listened solemnly and offered no criticism when she was done, which she took to mean a pass-mark of some kind.

She said, "And then there'll be a chorus on the lines of: *So it's charity, charity, charity, morning, noon, and night. For there's nothink else what pays the rent for a gel whose heels is light!* Something like that. It's a long way from Tennyson," she added apologetically.

He frowned. "Old Tommy Tennison? Used to play the New Bedford, Camden Town? 'E only ever sang patriotic-and-sentimental when I knew 'im. But don't tell me," he said, pointing an accusing finger at her. "Lemme guess – Whitechapel?"

"It doesn matter where the song's supposed to be set ..."

"No! Where *you* come from. Whitechapel – I'd lay a quid."

"You'd lose it, then, I'm afraid. I must ask Gordon Curtis if he's from there, though."

"'Oo's 'e?"

"He supervises all the bed-sitters in Bedford Street. I've been picking up the accent from him."

"And that song," he said. "It's a bit like the one Harrington and Brunn wrote for Jenny Valmore."

"Yes, I've heard her do it."

"Yours is better – more modern, anyway. But you couldn't do it on the same bill as 'ers."

"I wouldn't dream of it."

A dreamy expression came over him. "I was there, you know – first time ever she sung it. Palace of Varieties, Leeds, it was. About the time of the Jameson Raid. Ancient 'istory to you!" He pulled out his watch, a gold monster inscribed to him by the management of the Gaiety – the old one that had stood at the end of Wellington St. "Gotta go," he said. "Till tomorrah!"

This encounter left Rose feeling uneasy. She re-enacted it several times in her mind on the way home after the final curtain calls at the Kingsway. Sozzler's curiosity had obviously not been idle, yet where had it led him? Or her, come to that? More to the point, where *might* it lead her? She knew she was playing with fire as far as H-d-W was concerned – leading the double life of Lucy Tremayne and Lucille Marteyne. Everyone warned her – not in connection with her double life, of course, for no one but Noel knew of it – but they warned her in general that the man might seem absurdly indulgent to those in his favour but he could turn on a sixpence and lash out like a tiger. And then, regardless of how much money he'd sunk into advancing a person's career – actor, actress, playwright ... no matter – he'd drop them like a box and heater and never mention their names again.

True, there were a few stars who'd been at the savage end of his treatment and who had still made it to the top, despite all his attempts to block and ruin them; but there were many more who hadn't made it and who might have done so but for his disfavour. All in all, then, wouldn't it be better if, instead of waiting for the inevitable discovery, she went straight to the man and told him what she'd been doing?

Noel had developed a touch of hayfever and had gone to bed early with a basin of boiling water and menthol. "Cub id!" he answered wearily to her knock. So it hadn't worked very well.

"Good house?" he asked when he saw it was her.

"Not bad. About eighty percent. Half the audience had the same sniffles as you, though, so it's definitely something in the air."

She boiled up some more water to make him a fresh bowl. While the kettle pinged and sang she got him to lie flat so that she could rub oil of wintergreen all over his bare chest.

"Just think! If Louis came upod us dow!" he remarked.

"Men!" she said in a jaded tone.

"What?"

"If I felt like you look – and sounded like you sound – that's the *last* thought that would cross my mind."

He shot her a look of disbelief but said nothing.

The kettle boiled and she made up a fresh bowl for him to inhale. When he'd finished, she handed him a hot whisky toddy. She had made one for herself as well.

"Where did you get the Scotch?" he asked.

She smiled. "You think I don't know where you hide things? The whisky is behind *The History of the Rod* which is behind the book on Dan Leno by J. Hickory Wood. D'you think that can possibly be his real name, poor man? I suppose there are some parents like that. Cheers!"

She burbled on because she saw that her mention of the *Rod* book had made him blush. She gave a little laugh and said, "I thought it was about fishing when I first saw it."

He sniffed through a clear pair of nostrils. "That's a lot better," he said.

"What is this fascination with birching and whipping and things?"

He gave her a baleful stare and said, "It's a damn sight less perverse than what your friend Roger Deveril and that old satyr Roanoke got up to – or didn't you know?"

She dipped her head, conceding the point. "I didn't know – not then. But I could hardly have been in the theatre for ten months without finally copping on. And incidentally, I don't think Roger was that way inclined at all. I think – looking back and remembering certain things he said – I think he felt he *had to* come to my bed and prove it. To himself." She smiled wanly. "Funny – I thought he'd be one of the first people I'd find waiting for me outside the stage door."

"Such is hope!" Noel was glad to have steered her away from his own obsessions.

"So why are you so deadly fascinated by floggings and things?" she repeated.

He slumped again.

'Sorry," she said. "Some other time, eh?"

"Oh God – if you're going to go on and on ..." He closed his eyes and breathed deeply several times, like an athlete about to attempt a record. "It was something my nanny did. Used to do. When I was five or six. Nanny Constance was her name. If I'd been naughty – or sometimes if she just got bored – she'd sit down in a chair and make me lean forward in her lap, pressing my body between her thighs and pushing my face down ... well, you can picture it. And then she'd ease my britches off very slowly, murmuring, 'Poor little botty! Little botty's got to suffer pain now because of naughty little Noel.' And then she'd swish me with her bare hand, all the while pushing my face down and gripping my body between her thighs."

"Lord almighty!" Rose exclaimed. "How old was she?"

"Twenty? Something like that. And very pretty, too. I think the mater suspected something because she didn't last more than eighteen months."

"Long enough to ... well, to ..."

"*Warp* my mind?" He laughed. "Very likely. She did other things to me, too. In the bath and so on."

"Oh, Noel! I'm so sorry. It must be awful?"

"Not really." He put on a brave smile.

"So when you go to those houses – you know – like when I saw you coming out of that one in Vernon Place in Falmouth ... is that what you get them to do?"

He nodded. "She has to dress up as a nanny. They've got as many costumes and props as Lord Gordon, I should think. And she has to beat me just like Nanny Constance used to. Once a month is enough. I feel on top of the world after." His laughter was tinged with surprise. "I've never told this to a single living soul, you know. D'you wish you hadn't asked?"

"No! I'm glad I know. And I'm even more glad you trust me – and you honestly can."

"How about another whisky?"

While she reboiled the water he continued, "You can trust me, too – about your little sideline at the Holborn Empire. But I still warn you – you're playing with fire. H-d-W is bound to hear of it. I'm surprised he hasn't already."

"I was talking with Charley Knox this evening – or he was talking with me. I think he wants me to leave the legit theatre and go over entirely to variety."

Noel thought it over and said, "If you did, you'd probably make more money."

"That's what he said. It made me realize that it's *not* what I'm really after. I mean, I started out with money as my only aim – to pay my way, you know, and not be a drain ..."

"... on Louis, I know. And now?"

She didn't reply.

"You've found a career," he said. "You've *really* found a career."

She nodded. "And I don't think it's in drama. It's hard to describe, but when I'm in *Twins,* I feel like I'm in a glass bottle and the people outside, the audience, are looking in. I act and they watch. But when I'm on stage at the Holborn Empire, if I tried doing that, I'd die. I'd be wading off through knee-high tomatoes and cabbages."

He frowned. "So what d'you do instead?"

"Like tonight. I spotted this lady with an impossibly fussy hat in the third row. It must have cost a small fortune but it was awful. So when Lady Augusta came out with one of her ghastly opinions about 'the lowah ordahs,' I broke off and said, still in character, 'Theah's a lady in the third row heah who understends me perfectly, deon't you, deah!' And the whole house just roared. And then I realized – it's not money that drives me any longer, it's *that.* The roar. Playing the crowd. I love crowds. Over at the Empire I really feel I've got a couple of thousand pals out there, whereas at the Kingsway, on a good night, I've got six hundred well-wishers. It's not the same. D'you think, if I explained this to H-d-W, he'd possibly understand?"

"No." He gave an apologetic shrug.

"Well, that's just his hard luck, I'm afraid, because I'm going to have to try, anyway."

49

Time and again over the following days, Rose screwed her courage to the sticking place and set out to tackle Hugo de Witt at his offices beside the New Theatre in St Martin's Lane; but always her courage failed her at the last moment. Siren voices told her to leave well alone, suggested that as she had got away with it for two months, there was no reason for her luck not to continue for another two ... and another two, and so on. Once, when she saw him coming out into the street, she started toward him, thinking *Now or never!* But a moment later she saw he was leading a group of important-looking men and, again, she lost heart. He noticed her, however, and, full of pride at his discovery, called her over so that he might present the other gentlemen to her.

"An anarchist's bomb at that moment would have left every important theatre in London ownerless," she later told Sozzler.

When the introductions were over, H-d-W asked her if she had wanted to see him about anything.

"No," she replied airily. "Dolly Sturton opened at the Duke of York's last night. I just wanted to see what they've put on the billboards."

And another time, when she actually got inside the building, the doorkeeper told her that H-d-W wasn't in too good a mood that day; so she said it wasn't important and would just as easily keep to another time.

In the end her chance to speak with him came in the least expected way. She worshipped each Sunday morning at St Paul's, Covent Garden, which, being entirely classical in design, seemed more like a theatre to her than a church. It was, in any case, popularly known as 'The Actors' Church.' It even had balcony, rather like a dress circle. She usually sat in the main body of the church – the stalls, as it were – near the south wall and just in front of the balcony; and on that particular Sunday, the last in April, she happened to look up, to see what sort of 'house' today's preacher was drawing, and there, in the front row of the balcony, over against the northern wall, she saw the great man himself.

She glanced his way several times during the service but he appeared not to have noticed her. When it was over, she hung back until she saw him descending the balcony staircase and then made her own exit to coincide with his. He saw her then, outside in the piazza – and his opening words made it clear he had known of her presence all along: "I thought, 'If the mountain won't come to Mahomet …' "

"You knew!" she cried as they shook hands. "I was *so* tempted to stand up and sing *The man I love is up in the gallery!*"

"Well, well!" he replied calmly. "That *would* have given the game away! So it's to be no beating about the bush, eh. Let's take a turn around the churchyard – or have you an appointment?"

"None so important as this, I think."

He clearly knew all and had come here with the express purpose of sorting it out. Best thing, really. No time to panic or get in a flutter. She slipped her arm through his. "D'you mind?"

"That's rather your style, isn't it," he said as they entered King Street. "Act first, and only later think to ask if I mind."

"How long have you known?"

"Since last Wednesday. A friend of yours told me."

She almost blurted out Noel's name; just in time she realized that was what he wanted. She drew breath to speak but then let it out again.

"You were about to name him," he said.

She wondered why he was still being so calm. It was not what everyone had led her to expect. Was it because they had just come from the church, or were just about to enter the churchyard behind it? Somehow she didn't think so.

"Well?" he prompted.

"It can only have been one person, can't it."

"Your friend and mine," he replied.

"Quite." She looked around the churchyard, which, being entirely hedged in by tall buildings, is a dark little oasis of quiet amid the bustle of Covent Garden. "Some interesting people are buried here," she said. "Heaps of actors."

"Yes, he said. "It's known as 'The Actors' Church' because so many died here."

"Got buried here, anyway. Wycherley's over there. You should consider reviving *The Gentleman Dancing Master,* you know – it's a wonderful comedy."

She waited for him to speak but he merely nodded.

"And here's Doctor Arne, who wrote *Rule Britannia.* And Charles Macklin, who ended up as manager of the Drury Lane."

"Much more important than that," he said, "Macklin was the actor who rescued the part of Shylock from low comedians ... turned him into a tragic, dignified figure. It's what we have to guard against all the time – we in the legitimate theatre – the invasion of low comedians. I don't think I would revive the Wycherley play – or *any* Wycherley play. They're all too vulgar and bawdy. It's taken a hundred years to purge the theatre of all that. We can now make money with serious plays. You're too young to understand what that means. We can put on Pinero, Ibsen, Shaw ... *and make money!* It would have been impossible twenty years ago. In fact, I can date it from one particular production – Mrs Patrick Campbell in Pinero's *The Second Mrs Tanqueray* at the Saint James's in 1893, in George Alexander's time. She was unknown then. That play made her the talk of London. And what's it about? Who's the heroine? A high-class woman of easy virtue – not quite a harlot but certainly no saint. On the London stage! With Victoria still on the throne! It opened the door to serious theatre – serious *commercial* theatre – and I'm not going to be known as the one to close it again."

"I didn't know that about Wycherley," she said.

"There's so much else you don't know," he snapped. "Like who *really* told me about your whoring after strange gods at the Holborn Empire every night."

So he still wanted her to name Noel – which most likely meant it had been someone else. Otherwise, knowing the sort of man he was, he'd be crowing about it, to show her that even her closest friend in the business knew which side his bread was buttered. So, with nothing to lose, she picked the name of her only other close friend in the business – and a man whose back was broad enough to take it.

"It can only have been Charley Knox," she said bleakly.

She felt him stiffen at her side. Through clenched teeth he said, "So he told you!"

My God – it *had* been the Sozzler!

But why? To get her slung out of H-d-W's charmed circle? To force her into variety? It seemed far-fetched. Why should he take that much interest in her?

Well, there was one possible way to find out. "I suspected it," she said. "But I couldn't be sure. I knew it couldn't be Noel ..."

"Oh did you! How?"

"Because he doesn't know about it. Also, I'd like to think he'd have given me some warning. He'd have told me to stop the moment he got to hear of it. Aren't you interested in *why* I do it?"

He countered with another question: "Aren't you interested in why old Knox spilled the beans to me?"

So he seemed to accept that Noel had known nothing about it.

"I can have a jolly good guess. Oh look – Grinling Gibbons's grave. He was famous for something or other, wasn't he?"

"Woodcarving. What is your 'jolly good guess'?"

"He says London's dead for variety in summer. He's going to Blackpool with his own show and he wants me to go along. So, are you going to kick me out on my ear, Mister de Witt? Because that's obviously what he's hoping for."

He gave a short, unamused laugh, more like a bark.

"Is that an answer?" she asked. "Or am I completely wrong?"

"Worse than that," he said. "You're half right. He does, indeed, want to provoke me into washing my hands of you – so that you'll have no choice but to go with him. What he doesn't know – and which I'm going to trust you not to tell him – is that, for various reasons, I don't want to antagonize him just now. He's a powerful man over there on his side of the fence. Let me tell you something about him. He's the absolute despair of managements for the risks he takes. They send deputation after deputation to him when he mounts these summer shows, begging him to tone down the language and the innuendo and he always has the same answer."

"What's that?"

"'Buy a ticket to the show – *if you can'!*" De Witt's laugh was a blend of admiration and dejection. "And it's true."

"Four kings beats a full house, though," she remarked.

"You mean the four men I was with last week – in Saint Martin's Lane? I doubt even we could prevail against a comedian as universally popular – and loved – as Charley Knox. And, as I say, for various reasons I don't wish to antagonize him – not just at the moment."

Her stomach rumbled loudly with hunger. "Music to the chef!" she remarked.

He laughed reluctantly. "You're a cool one, Miss Marteyne," he said. "I'll give you that. You know your value. And you have absolutely no respect for authority or ..."

"Oh! Respect for authority, is it! Well, let me tell you – I respected authority for the first twenty-four years of my life. It was yes-m'lady, no-m'lady, three-bags-full-m'lady, day and night with me. And where did it get me? To a servant's garret. And what did it get me? Four pounds, one shilling, and eightpence a month."

This speech more or less made itself, leaving her mind free to race. H-d-W was beginning to sound as if he wanted to work round to some kind of bargain with her, rather than the angry 'never-darken-my-doors-again' sort of dismissal she had been led to expect. Maybe Sozzler knew more about this business than de Witt gave him credit for. Maybe he even knew that de Witt wouldn't want to upset him by punishing her, which was why he risked spilling the beans like that.

Softening her tone after her outburst, she gave his arm an encouraging little hug and said, "I know! Why don't you take me to a nice, leisurely lunch at the Trocadero – it's the only decent place hereabouts on a Sunday – and we can discuss careers and money? And mutual advantage."

They left the churchyard by the opposite entrance – a little alley into Henrietta Street – and went down to the Strand, where they took a cab up to the corner of Shaftesbury Avenue and Windmill Street. Their conversation was all theatre gossip – who was in what; who was replacing whom in what; which plays were touring well, pre-London; which were about to be closed ... the usual. At the restaurant he chose an alcove. There were several theatre people there – Edward Terry, who had turned his theatre in the Strand into a motion-picture palace the previous autumn ... Robert Courtneidge, who had transformed the Shaftesbury into a theatre for musicals, beginning with *The Arcadians,* a couple of years ago.

"Over eight hundred performances!" de Witt murmured to Rose when he pointed the man out. "And he looks set to repeat the trick with *The Mousmé* this season."

"I'm taking singing lessons," Rose told him.

He nodded glumly. "I'm not in the least surprised to hear it. I have no doubt but that by the time you are forty you will be a colossus of the theatre and, like the one at Rhodes, you will straddle both camps – variety and legitimate."

"Can it be done?" Rose asked excitedly.

"No!" He sighed. "But you surely won't let a little thing like that stop you, will you?"

She pouted. "Well, I think it *can* be done. A comedian like Sozzler is an actor – a great actor, I think. If ever you do *A Midsummer Night's Dream,* get him to play Bottom and you'll see what I mean."

De Witt just sat there shaking his head sadly until she dried. "You're missing the point, my dear," he said then. "Knox is not a comedian who can act. He's an actor who excels at comedy. And so are you."

She grew suddenly tense. "You've seen me!"

"Last night – second house. You cut it fine for the curtain call at the Kingsway."

She grinned. "It was good, wasn't it!"

The waiter came for their order. They both went for the table d'hôte – mulligatawny soup and roast beef carved off the trolley.

"The point," de Witt said when the man had gone, "is that you were an actress doing comedy. A proper variety comedian stands there and tells stories about 'an Englishman, an Irishman, and a Scotchman' or 'these two old Jews' and then he does 'a little song called *Never kiss a baby 'til you're sure it's the right way up.'* But that's never going to be your game."

From then on, through the first two courses, their conversation – on the nature of comedy and the character of comediennes – became more and more remote from Rose's transgression and all that might now follow. For pudding he chose a spotted dick and custard while she asked for lemon sorbet. Then, unable to bear the suspense any longer, she said, "So what is my punishment to be, Mister de Witt? Sozzler Knox says you'd cut off your nose to spite your face."

"And you believed him?"

"He gave several examples – actors and actresses you've ruined because they went against your wishes."

"And still you went on!"

"Well ... to be fair, he did also name several who've prospered despite your displeasure."

De Witt laughed. "And that's what kept you going, I'll be bound! The cunning old b–."

The waiter brought their puddings.

"Well," de Witt went on as they tucked in, "next time you see him, you can tell him I'm not going to play his little game."

"Aren't you ever so slightly forgetting it's a three-sided contest?" she asked.

"Certainly not," he replied. "I'm going to take *Twins* off at the end of next week ..."

"Oh? But it's still playing to packed ..."

"I know. Please allow me to know *something* about my own business, darling Miss Marteyne! I want to revive it in a couple of years' time. We'll both get more out of it that way. It's always easier to revive a play that closed with good houses than one where the audience just fizzled out."

"I'm sorry," Rose said. "Too many people have warned me about how vindictive you can be. I shouldn't have paid them so much attention."

"Too many? Did all of them know about your alter ego at the Holborn Empire?"

"No! Just talking about you in general. We talk about you all the time – surely you know that?" She laughed. "Anyway, if *Twins* is to close, what's next?"

"A gamble, as always. D'you know the play *Trelawny of the 'Wells'?* Another of Arthur Pinero's, incidentally."

She shook her head. "What's it about?"

"About? It's just about the most difficult play for any young actress to take on – that's all. The heroine is called Rose Trelawny, an actress at the Wells, who is engaged to be married to one Arthur Gower, the grandson of Sir William Gower, who is Vice-Chancellor of ... something or other. It's not important. The main thing is he's a domestic tyrant – a real upper-class bully. Rose goes to stay at his house in Cavendish Square 'on approval,' as it were. And Sir William decidedly does *not* approve of her. He makes her life hell. It all climaxes one night after the household has gone to bed and some of Rose's theatrical friends call. She invites them in for an impromptu party. They kick up rather a racket and it ends with Sir William chucking them all out, Rose along with them. She resumes her acting career but – and this is the fiendishly difficult bit for any actress to convey – her terrible experiences in Cavendish Square have taken away every last shred of her self-confidence. In short, she can no longer act!"

"Whew!" Rose fanned her face. "What a challenge!"

"Wait! We're not done yet! Sir William is no sleepwalking part, either. Having been so beastly to Rose in acts one and two, he now comes to her in somewhat contrite mood. She tells him her career is over and she shows him some relics of Edmund Kean that she's collected. This starts him off on a string of reminiscences – so that the bullying tyrant of the first half turns into someone much more sympathetic, you see. The upshot of it is that he agrees to finance a new production of a play with her in it. She gets back all her old confidence. And he's reconciled to her marriage with his grandson. Handkerchiefs out in all parts of the house. I want to put it on at the Saint James's, starting the first week in June, with you as Rose Trelawny ..."

"I already feel I'm halfway into the part!" Rose said.

"I didn't finish. Conrad Laughton will play Sir William. Go and see him in *The Twelve Pound Look* by Barrie – the curtain raiser at the Duke of York's."

"With Dolly Sturton."

He smiled. "Yes. The friend whose notices you were so solicitous to examine. We'll let the *Trelawny* play run to the end of July and take it off for August. Knox is right. London just dies then. We'll open again in September if it did well. Otherwise *Twins*. Meanwhile, you're free to enjoy Blackpool – assuming that the town's watch committee will allow him open there!"

Tears were prickling at the backs of her eyelids, but she was afraid to show this sudden weakness. "Why?" she asked.

"I'm hoping you'll come back somewhat less enamoured of life on the variety stage and somewhat more reconciled to my treadmill."

He escorted her back to Bedford Street and, as she was stepping out of the cab, he said, "By the way, if *Trelawny's* a success, we might take it to America next January. Charley Knox would never take you there."

She laughed. "So Noel did tell you *something* after all."

"He'd be no use to me if he didn't, my dear. And if you're fond of him, you might just bear that in mind."

50

Lady Augusta Vane-Trumpington did her usual turn at the Holborn Empire the following night. Hugo de Witt's talk of 'all that innuendo' – by which he meant salacious innuendo, of course – made Rose realize that it was the one thing her turn lacked. There was plenty of innuendo but it was of the dramatic kind, which allowed the audience to see her ladyship as a vain, uncomprehending booby – entirely through her own self-congratulatory words. So now she worked in a few lines about 'almond rock,' which was Marie Lloyd's wink-wink rhyming slang for you-know-what (or you-can-surely-guess), as popularized in her song of that name: 'I shall say to a young man gay, / If he treads upon my frock, / Randy-pandy, sugary candy, / Give me some almond rock!' So when Rose had Lady Augusta say, in all her wide-eyed innocence, that the legless gamekeeper had offered her, in return for her nourishing broth, a bit of *almond rock,* the house erupted in laughter that went on for a full minute, while her ladyship stared at them in affronted dignity, which only provoked their mirth to new heights. And then, when she informed them that she had declined the offer because *she didn't know where it had been,* it rekindled their laughter and stoked it up to the point where they were begging her to stop.

It put poor Rose on the spot, for the rest of her material could not possibly live up to that bit of impromptu. However, she was near the end of her piece, and the laughter had already pushed it beyond her normal twelve minutes, so, on a sudden inspiration, she just looked deeply insulted (in the character of Lady Augusta, of course) and left the stage, saying, "Well! I can't for the life of me see whay you awl faynd thet so verreh-verreh funneh. I can see I shell just have to come beck tomorrow and hope to faynd you good humble people in a more sensible mood."

It brought her six curtain calls – the most she had ever earned.

"What put that bit of business in your head?" Sozzler asked her when he came off.

"Not what," she replied. "Who! It was Hugo de Witt, if you want to know. He took me to lunch at the Troc yesterday. He knew all about me and Lady Augusta. What made you tell him?"

He grinned. "Do I sleep in the coalhouse tonight?"

"No!" She butted his arm playfully with her forehead. "But I'd still like to know."

"I knew he'd never give you the push – not once he realized *I* want you. I just thought I'd let 'im know that of all the indoocement 'e might offer me, *you* was the jewel in the crown."

"That's all very flattering, Sozzler," she told him, "but I had already worked that out for myself."

"What?" He was astonished. "He never told you?"

"Of course not. He's giving me August off, so's I can join you up North in Blackpool."

He cleared his throat diffidently. "Morecambe," he said.
"That's a quick change!"
"The Blackpool watch committee and me don't izzactly see eye-to-eye. Still, I'll take my revenge on them once we're up there. Ever flown in a hairyplane, 'ave yer?"
She shook her head, wondering what an aeroplane had to do with taking revenge on a committee of the Blackpool corporation.
"I'll save it till yer come, then." He pulled out his watch and said, "Crikey! I'll just tell yer this. Your pal and mine, Mister Hugo de Witt, has tooken a ninety-nine year lease off of the Bedford estate on that vacant ground at the top end of Drury Lane – 'im an' a few uvvers."
Rose suddenly realized she could probably name them, but she didn't want to interrupt his account.
"Leastways, it *was* a vacant lot 'til three weeks back. Now yer can already see the outlines of a theatre there. It's gonna be a palace of varieties – the Frivoli, they're gonna call it – for revue, see? Not for music-'all turns. Summink classy. So is 'e gonna kick yer aht for doin' twelve minutes a night 'ere? Yeah, I don't fink! An' you're the bait for me, see – 'coz I let 'im know as how I wanted you for my summer show up north. Big fleas 'ave little fleas – d'yer get me? Wiv me top of the bill an' you not too far down, the Frivoli's a guaranteed runner."
"He was saying something about an American tour early next year," Rose told him.
"Course 'e was!" Sozzler guffawed. "That's to keep you nicely out the way of 'is three partners – 'oo might 'ave uvver ideas about your future, see. Oh, 'e's the Lamb of God, all right – ain't no flies on 'im! Jesus! I gotta go now. That's the bleedin' trouble with a Rolls-Royce, you can't never say it broke dahn. Pip-pip!"
"Where are you on next?"
"The Coliseum, why?"
"I'll come with you. I want to ask you about Noel."
"In them clothes?"
"It doesn't matter now, does it."
They piled into the back of his Silver Ghost, which set off at a purr, straight across Kingsway and into Great Queen Street, right past the front of the Kingsway Theatre.
"The advantage of a haristocratic motor," he said grandly. "It does for traffic what Moses done to the Red Sea."
He was right, she noticed. All the traffic stopped to let them cross – but she suspected it was because they all recognized the owner rather than the car.
"About Noel," she said. "Can I let him know that *you* know what H-d-W is up to?"
"Why?"
"Because de Witt suspects he knew all about Lady Augusta's act and didn't tell him. He suspect's Noel's loyalty where I'm concerned.

It would help if I told him in confidence and then told him he could pass it on. How did you find out about the Frivoli scheme, anyway? Who put you on to it?"

He rocked with mirth. "You did, my lady!" he said at last.

"Me?"

"When yer said an anarchist's bomb would of left most of London's theatres rudderless, I made it my business to find out *their* business – which, I may say, was not too difficult. 'Ow many new theatres are they puttin' up in Lunnon just at this minute. So you tell your Noel to say as 'ow I spied them all climbing into a growler in Saint Martin's Lane an' I dodged them all the way up to the Frivoli."

"And it won't hurt your interests?"

They had travelled the full length of Long Acre by now and were turning into St Martin's Lane for the Coliseum.

"My darlin'," he replied, "it wouldn't even hurt the skin on my rice puddin'. Which reminds me. That extra bit of patter you shoved in tonight – abaht the 'almond rock'?"

She grinned. "What of it?"

"What you said was right – just right. About 'ow you didn't know where it 'ad been. Perfick! I was afraid you was goin' to say summink like it was all covered in fluff so yer did'n wanna suck it – which is what *I* would of said. And it would be right for me but dead wrong for you. So it's like what I said to you before – you got the right instinks. You can always trust them."

She didn't really work out what he'd been saying until she was halfway home. Then she went straight in and took a twopenny bath, full to the brim.

51

On the morning that *Twins* closed – at the end of the first week in May – Noel, flushed with excitement, came knocking at Rose's door while she was still in bed. Although it was only nine in the morning, she was not asleep; in fact, she had been lying awake for the past hour, obsessed with the problem of playing a good actress who somehow loses the knack.

"What d'you want?" she asked.

"To come in, of course."

"Well, come in backwards. My dressing gown's hanging on the door ..." She did not need to complete the instructions for he was already unhooking it and throwing it over his shoulder toward her.

"All right," she said when she had struggled into it. "What's all the fuss?"

"This!" He turned and brandished that day's issue of *Twentieth Century Theatre*. "When they print a carefully retouched photo of you and a few respectful lines of letterpress, it means I've done *my* job. But when they print a caricature by the great Orlando, without the slightest prompting from me, it means you've done *yours.*" He opened the paper out at its centre spread, saying, "Pom tiddley-om-pom, pom *pom!*" On the final 'pom' he thrust it toward her.

The caricature was mainly of Hugo de Witt, looking machiavellian as he stuffed a much smaller Lucille Marteyne into a cake box; she was clutching a ribbon with the legend TWIN SISTERS. The box was in the form of the Kingsway Theatre, of course; and around it seethed a hungry public, holding up empty plates as if they were begging bowls. The caption below ran:

MISS MARTEYNE: *Ah'm a guid gerrul, ah am!*

THE PUBLIC: *The best! The best! More! More! &c.*

H-d-W: *You sha'n't have it, my dear children. A little of what you fancy may do you good but didn't Nanny tell you: Too much of a good thing is bad for you. Perhaps you shall have some more in the autumn. But you must be very good meanwhile!*

"How many copies did you get?" Rose asked.

"You're holding it," he replied.

"For heaven's sake! Go out and get another half dozen, immediately! I need one for my parents, one for Louis, one for Mister Swindlehurst, and … never mind. There are bound to be more. My hair isn't really that frizzy, is it?"

He laughed and sat on the bed beside her. "This is what they call *arriving,* you know. With an Orlando cartoon you have *arrived* in the West End. Well done! Not that anyone close to you has ever doubted it, mind."

She reached out and squeezed his hand. "I owe most of it to you, Noel. You and Mister Swindlehurst. I won't ever forget it."

He winked. "Not while I'm here to remind you, anyway." He patted her shoulder and rose to go, saying, "It's going to be an emotional last night, I fear. The matinée and evening houses are both booked out. People are offering me up to five guineas for a ticket anywhere in the theatre!" At the door he turned and added, "By the way, would you care for a trip into the country tomorrow – out to Hertfordshire?"

"Why?"

"There's something I want to show you. I think you'll like it."

"All right. I hope it's something amusing?"

"It has its amusing aspects, yes." He left, refusing to say any more than that.

That night, after the last of her eight curtain calls, she came off, knee-deep in flowers.

H-d-W himself waiting for her in the wings. "Supper at the Café Royal," he said.

"Only if Gertrude is also invited," she insisted. "She's been absolutely brilliant – with a much harder part than me."

He hesitated before saying "Very well. I suppose you're off to the Holborn Empire now?" She slumped. "I was just wondering about that. I'm exhausted. D'you think ..." He cut her short. "That's why you must go. The two most important things in your life are your public and yourself – in that order. The moment you reverse the order, you're on the slippery slope. Off you go now."

"Is my hair frizzy?" she asked. "Would you call it frizzy?"

De Witt shook his head. "He always draws hair that way."

It was the first question she asked Sozzler when he came offstage and congratulated her on appearing in the cartoon.

"I didn't think I'd find *you* 'ere tonight," he commented without answering her. "Ain't yer off celebratin' somewhere?"

"Later," she replied. "Supper with you-can-guess-who at the Café Royal."

"Best o' luck! I can recommend the steak tartar, and they do a good cream brooley for pud."

"I almost didn't come tonight," she said. "But I've found the cure for nervous exhaustion. Forget your French and German spas! Just stand on stage while the curtain rises on two thousand expectant, happy faces. They give off something, don't they – audiences. Something doctors can't measure. And we soak it up. We're the only people who *can* measure it. You didn't answer my question, Sozzler. Does that mean you think my hair *is* frizzy?"

"Naah! Nor you don't neither. Did you never meet 'im face-to-face – the old Orlando?"

She shook her head. "I'm not sure I want to, either."

"Mark Lush is 'is real monicker – and *lush* is 'is character, and all. A bottle-a-day man is our Orlando. So when 'e comes to draw a lady's hair – which is what? A load o' twisty, curly lines all one beside the other ..."

"Parallel."

"The very word. Oh, the advantages of a board-school eddycation! Anyway, 'e can't do them. The old hand ..." He made his own quiver, as it did at the start of his act. "So all hair is either solid black with bits of white scraped out ... or ..." He left the conclusion to her.

"Frizzy," she said.

"We're a good double act, Lucille. Don'tchyer think?"

It was the first time he had called her anything other than an ironic 'my lady' or Miss Marteyne. "I've been wondering about that," she replied. "In Blackpool ... I mean, Morcambe?"

"I'm going up next Friday. We open in June."

"That's when I open in *Trelawny of the 'Wells'*." She grimaced and ducked like a boxer avoiding a punch.

"So we should 'ave a little get-together somewhere next week."

They settled on the following Tuesday afternoon, when he had no matinée obligations. "Stay sober," were his parting words.

* * *

Noel's opening words, the following morning, were, "It was a mistake to insist on taking Miss Scott along last night."

They were on their way to the Horseshoe in Tottenham Court Road for what was either a late breakfast or an early luncheon before strolling onward to King's Cross, where they would catch a train to Hertfordshire, specifically, to Welwyn, about twenty miles north of London.

"I don't think so," she replied.

"H-d-W wanted to discuss plans for your future with us – beyond the *Trelawny* play. It would hardly have been courteous to do that with Miss Scott sitting there, thinking, 'What about me?' all the time."

"But that's exactly why I did it. Or no, it's *one* of the reasons. The other was she bloody well deserved it."

"Your language has become coarse since you started associating with the riffraff of our profession!"

They laughed but he was still annoyed with her for spoiling last night, as he saw it.

"Listen," she said. "I know very well what his plan was. First he insisted on my going on to the Empire, though he knew I was dead on my feet – though actually that turned out quite well."

"Good house?"

"Yep!"

"It always works."

"And then the Café Royal – soft lights, carpets up to the ankles, good food, a little wine – just enough to get me slightly tipsy – and then the honeyed words. If he'd had his way, then he'd have nailed me to the rock by now. He'd be catching my shrieks in cups of gold."

He looked at her askance.

"William Blake," she said. "Instead, as it turned out, he accepted the situation with good grace and entertained us with some wonderful stories. And look!" She stretched out her hands and arms. "No nails!"

"I don't know," he sighed when they were at lunch. "Just about every actor and actress in London would give five years off their lives to be taken to supper at the Café Royal by H-d-W and have him explain his plans for their future."

"I know," she replied. "I don't know why he puts up with me."

Noel laughed grimly. "You know very well why he puts up with you. But one day you'll push him too far. And then it'll be like Cinderella after midnight strikes."

They returned to the subject when they were in the train, heading out of town. "I suspect I may end my own career long before my waywardness provokes H-d-W into doing it for me," she said gloomily. "It's the scene in *Trelawny* where Rose has to ... how can I put it?"

"Act badly?"

"No, that's the whole point. I don't think anyone who's ever been a good actress – which the script tells us she was – could ever switch to acting *badly*. She'd act like a good actress who had lost ... something. How can I explain it? Last night I had *poulet à la forestière* at the Café Royal. Superb! But if the chef had left out the rosemary, it wouldn't be a *bad* dish. It would still be a superb one that somehow lacked something. It wouldn't be half of some old boiling fowl, tarted up with mixed herbs and served on a silver-plated tin platter – which is the equivalent of *bad* acting. D'you see the difference?"

He nodded thoughtfully. "I never realized there *was* such a distinction, but you're quite right. The question is, what skill are you going to lose if you're going to remain a good-but-incomplete actress, rather than just turning into a bad one?"

She gave a hollow laugh. "The question, darling Noel, is what skill am I going to *find* first – in order to lose it. I am not one of your self-examining actresses. I have no idea how some of the things I do on stage happen to work with the audience. I just know they do work, and so I keep on doing them. It's a game of blind-woman's-buff."

"Or bluff!"

"That, too. Never mind!" She sat up and rubbed her hands and made herself seem cheerful. "It will come. The theatre fairy will wave a magic wand and it will come."

They alighted at Welwyn station, at the northern end of the massive Welwyn Viaduct, still one of the wonders of early railway engineering. A bus bound for Hertford was waiting in the station forecourt and most of their fellow passengers boarded it; but Noel suggested a gentle walk since the afternoon was fine and the thing he wanted to show her was just a little way up the hill.

The road was a tunnel of new-sprouted green beneath over-arching elms. The sunlight, filtering through their leaves, made shimmering patterns of lacy light on the dusty highway. Beneath the elms grew banks of rhododendrons, which were just coming into the peak of their flowering. Luminescent sprays of pink and orange, scarlet and mauve sang out of the deep shade on either side. It would have been beautiful if their song had not been of wealth and exclusion.

"Lady Vane-Trumpington country," Rose commented. "Every leaf says 'Trespassers will be prosecuted.' I'll bet there are mantraps set behind those walls."

"They're illegal," Noel pointed out.

"The bet stands," she insisted.

Near the brow of the hill the woodland gave way to open fields and the rolling Hertfordshire countryside. Here there was birdsong everywhere – which had been noticeably absent in the woods below. Thrushes darted from branch to branch with beaks full of old, dry grass and twigs; robins and sparrows twitted unseen; and, high above all, skylarks were holding crazy, early-summer auctions of lands they had owned long before there were title deeds to any of it.

"How can people *own* trees?" Rose wondered aloud.

"This is where we're going," he said, turning in at a gate.

The house was mostly obscured by a pergola, grossly overladen with clematis and wistaria, but when they had passed beneath it Rose saw a large house in red brick, with steeply sloping roofs. A country rectory, she guessed.

"Have you bought it?" she asked.

"That would be the ultimate irony," he replied.

As they walked up the final length of the path, the front door was opened by a tall, good-looking woman in her mid-forties.

"Nanny Constance!" Noel called out.

"Master Noel!" she replied.

It was a moment or two before Rose recalled the name of the nanny who had warped (his own word) her friend. Her heart sank and she stopped dead. "Do I really, really want to go on?" she asked the air.

Noel ignored her. "How is our patient today?" he called out.

"The same as usual, sir," was the reply. "He hardly ever changes."

"Come on, Rose!" He turned back to her. "You're about to get the surprise of your life – a pleasant one, I hope."

It intrigued her, of course, but still she was filled with foreboding. "Why can't I believe you?" she asked, looking from him to the woman and back again.

He returned to her, so that he could speak without Nanny Constance hearing. "It's nothing to do with all that. It was over and done with years ago. And she hasn't the faintest idea of the effect it had on me so don't breathe a word."

"Is this a rectory?"

He turned and looked at the house. "It was. Come on."

Nanny Constance curtseyed when Noel presented her – calling her Mrs Weighell. Normally Rose would have shaken hands but this time she found herself incapable of it. "Did you say 'patient'?" she asked Noel.

"Come and see!" Excited, he led the way along a dark, uneven passage to a garden room at the far end of the house. The sun, half way down the western sky by now, flooded much of the room, throwing the rest into comparative darkness – which was why Rose did not recognize the patient at once. Even when she did, she could not believe her eyes. He sat, or lay almost to attention, in a rattan chair with a glass of brandy and soda half sunk into a holder in its broad, flat arm. Pipe tobacco was spilled all down his front and his clothes had the look of all clothes that are dressed and buttoned up by other fingers than the wearer's.

"Sir Hector!" she cried in horror, cramming almost all of her gloved hand into her mouth.

"Eh?" He stared at her in confusion, having some difficulty focussing. "Fenella?"

"Miss Tremayne," she replied, shivering now in reaction to her shock. "Rose. Miss Fenella's lady's maid."

"Fenella!" He nodded and turned his eyes toward Noel. "And bless me – Charles!"

"Can you believe that?" Noel asked bitterly, not taking his eyes off the old man. "I never knew I had a younger brother called Charles until this old fool went gaga! He died in childhood."

"Noel!" She gripped his arm in both hands and shook him violently. "Noel!"

"What?" he asked testily.

"Why did you bring me here?"

"Why? Isn't it obvious? I thought you'd be pleased."

"Oh!" She could think of nothing to say – not that he seemed to be listening much, anyway. The room began to whirl around her and, fearing she might faint, she turned and stumbled toward the window. There she rested her knuckles on the sill and stared out into the garden. Two youngsters, a boy of about twelve and a slightly younger girl, were playing croquet. Beyond them a man lay asleep in a hammock, his panama hat over his face. Rose clung to this happy scene as a drowning woman might cling to a straw.

"Give me a hug, pater," Noel was saying behind her. "Give your son Charley a hug."

Giggling, Sir Hector rose to his feet and threw his arms around his son. "Charley! Charley!" He gurgled.

"That's it!" Noel cried exultantly. "A good hard hug! It's more than that little bastard Noel ever got out of you, what? What?" His laugh bordered on the hysterical.

"Noel!" Rose said in a placatory tone, not daring to turn round.

"It's all right," Noel replied. "He no longer understands much. Do you, you sad old creature!"

Sir Hector laughed.

"See – what did I tell you. The awful thing is he could have been like this for years – and how would anyone ever have known?"

Rose threw open the french windows and went out onto the croquet lawn. "Is this a private fight, as the Irishman said," she asked the youngsters, "or can anyone join in?"

They were delighted to have someone else to torment – and there is no more vicious game on earth than croquet – so they let her drop a ball one hoop ahead of them and then set about sending her to the four corners of the universe.

"Rose?" Noel was standing the other side of the low-pruned viburnum to which they had exiled her ball.

"I'm sorry, darling," she replied. "I can see it's something you just have to do. But don't involve me."

"Good God!" he exclaimed. "Don't tell me you actually *liked* the old ... liked him?"

"I had no feelings of any kind, for or against him. He might as well have been a leather armchair or something. But he was your father – didn't *you* like him?"

"What was there to like?"

She sighed. "Well, there at least we may be agreed. But not on anything else. Let me know when you've finished tormenting him and we'll go back to town." She turned to the children and cried, "Right! You've asked for it and now you're going to get it!"

Brave words, but the two brats beat her hollow.

"Did you win?" Noel asked as they walked back down the hill to the station.

"They thrashed me into the ground," she replied. "Thrashing is obviously in their blood – I take it they *are* Mrs Weighell's."

"Indeed."

"And that she discovered the cure for all her frustrations in Mister Weighell – the recumbent figure who never stirred from the hammock?"

"The same."

"And that his exhaustion today is not unconnected with that discovery?"

He laughed at last. "At least you're not angry."

"Of course I'm not angry – just desperately sorry for you. And for the old boy, of course."

"Funnily enough," he said. "Since confessing my deep-dark secret to you, the urge to go and get skinned alive by some unfortunate in nanny's clothing has weakened considerably."

"There's hope yet, then," she told him.

They sat in silence on the train, mostly staring out of the window as the countryside grew patchier and patchier – and ever dirtier. At one point she glanced at him and saw a tear roll down his cheek. She returned her gaze to the great outdoors and pretended not to have noticed.

52

Sozzler arranged to meet her at the Zoological Gardens in Regent's Park. It struck her as an odd choice of venue for him; she could hardly imagine him in daylight, much less in the open air. He seemed so much a creature of the footlights, the dressing room, and the gaslit streets of central London. They met at what was called the 'south' entrance, though it stands on the eastern edge of the zoo enclosure. Though still a large figure, he looked much smaller than he appeared on stage – where, of course, he wore a fair bit of padding. He paid two shillings for the pair of them, saying, "Pity we couldn't have made it yesterday. Mondays are half price."

"Come to that," she said, "if only I'd have thought to bring my step-ladder ..."

"You can do a lot wiv a good set of steps," he agreed.

"What? Like win dancing competitions, you mean?"
"Yes. No! I mean like cleaning winders."
"Oh! You mean you can *see* a lot with a good set of steps." She mimed a nice girl's response to something scandalous.
"Except on a yacht. Now a stepladder is the *second* most useless thing on the deck of a yacht."
"The *second* most useless thing, eh? Kindly tell me – what's the *most* useless thing, then?"
"A naval hofficer! Drum-roll and cymbal crash!" He laughed at last. "We can do it, gel! We can definitely do it." They were strolling slowly past the deer and cattle house. A bored red-deer stag stretched its neck toward them and barked. "Glad you agree, young man," Sozzler said.
"But I don't think we can just go out there on stage and speak ad lib," she objected.
"Don't you? I do. We just did. And with an audience to egg us on ... enough said."
They veered south of the duckponds toward the lion house; already the air was heavy with the stink of the big cats, which was both repellent and yet, she thought, curiously attractive, too.
"I think we should have some sort of structure – a loose one, but something underneath it all the time. We should play to our strengths – now who said that?"
"Go on," he chuckled.
"My strength is mocking the upper classes. Yours is ... I don't know what. Anarchy."
"Drunkenness."
"Yes, well, drunkenness is just one kind of anarchy. There are others. Suppose we set up a situation in which I'm an upper-class lady who's lost almost all her money but none of her attitudes. So I'm living in a big house without any servants and it's falling down around my ears. Or perhaps there's just one servant, but she's always off stage and I just shout to her. And you play the parts of the plumber, the carpenter, the glazier, the paperhanger, the ... oh! Look at him – the King of the Beasts! Don't you love those golden flecks in their eyes!"
The lion rolled over, away from their admiring gaze. She was amazed at how slim its hips were.
"It's only the second lion I've seen in my life," she said. "The other was in Plymouth zoo, but it's much mangier than this one."
They admired the whole pride awhile and then moved on toward the wolves and foxes, behind the lion house.
"What you were saying," he remarked, "I think that could work. Let's say you was this upper-class lady and you've got no water – well, we can milk that line for a start! Got no water!"
"No water in the *house!*"
"Yeah – well, we get there in the end. So you, being upper-class, don't know nuffink about plumbing and that. And me, not

bein' a plumber at all but a common, workin'-class idler takin' a chance ... I don't know a ball-cock from a hydraulic ram." He clapped his hands in delight. *"Ball!* And *cock!* And hydraulic *ram!* Blimey – we'll 'ave 'em rollin' in the aisles before we're one quarter done. Anyway, like I said, I don't know nuffink about plumbin' but what I do know is 'ow to pull your leg – oops! There goes another one!"

"Say it!" Rose told him. "Say, 'I don't want to pull your leg, lady' or something like that." She faced up to him, as if they were on stage. He obeyed: "I don't want to pull your leg, lady, but ..."

"Oh!" She looked him up and down with sudden interest. "I don't think you should entirely rule out ... Oh, I *see!"* She fanned her face with embarrassment but still eyed him coyly. "No – of course you don't. I'm sorry. I misunderstood."

"That's good," he said. "The best part of any joke is the bit yer leave aht! You've been thinkin' a lot about this, eh?"

"I'm afraid so." She pulled a face.

"Afraid?"

"I've been doing it to avoid having to think about a more immediate problem, Sozzler ..." And she went on to tell him about her difficulties with the Rose Trelawny part. They were outside the wolf pens now. The creatures sat around like so many dogs, scratching, sniffing, snoozing ... and utterly oblivious of the humans all around. Even the antelopes in their paddock next door did not rouse their interest. One grey-maned old male seemed to stare right through her, giving her the shivers. "They've got eyes like opals," she said. *"Cold!"*

"Talkin' of cold," he said, "the times when my act falters is when I've got a cold comin' on. Once the cold's there, I'm right as rain again. It's when it's comin' on me. I can feel the audience ain't wiv me like what it usually is. I mean, they don't boo nor nuffink. It's not so obvious as that. But most nights – you know yourself – most nights you've got them *there!"* He held an imaginary orb in the palm of his hand. "Right there. But wiv a cold on the way, they're *there* instead." He pointed to an imaginary crowd beyond equally imaginary footlights.

"And what's the difference in your performance?" she asked.

He shook his head. "I can't see it, myself. But others say they can. I get the timin' wrong or I fluff a word, an important word. You know, the difference between good and perfick is ..." He held thumb and forefinger an eighth of an inch apart. "Just *that* much. So maybe you're trying too 'ard to work it all out now – which surprises me, I must say."

They moved on toward the antelopes.

"I think you've solved my problem for me, Sozzler," she said thoughtfully. "The reason I'm working so hard at it now is ... well, I've never rehearsed things much in my mind before I get to the actual rehearsals. Even learning the part, I'd learn it like a bored schoolgirl rattling off a poem she was given for homework." She gave an example in a flat and hasty monotone: "'At-Flores-in-the-Azores-Sir-Richard-Grenville-lay-and-a-pinnace-like-a-fluttered-bird-came-flying-from-far-away …' That's only a slight exaggeration of how I learn a part."

He laughed. "I can feel another little sketch comin' on! 'Ow about there's this mechanic or watchmaker 'oo makes lifelike mechanical girls for … well, we'll think of a reason. But the only trouble is, they all talk like what you just done. Or, I know! When God first made Eve, *she* talked like that to Adam. No! Even Morecambe watch committee would never let that through."

"Why did Blackpool ban you?" she asked.

"Stupid!" he grumbled. "Still, I've plotted my revenge – which will be sweet. What's next? Storks and ostriches. Oh! Stand by for stork jokes on the starboard quarter! And ostrich jokes to port!"

She said, "Shall I stop asking why Blackpool blackballed you?"

"Black balls?" he echoed thoughtfully. Then, brisk again. "No – my idea's better. The reason they said I wasn't to come back – now you're not gonna believe this but it's true. We 'ad this drop, see, back of the stage, wiv a big mermaid painted on it. Very artistic." His hands sculpted the mermaid's breasts in the air – just in case she didn't understand 'artistic.' "And there was this moment when I stumble against her, see?"

"Being drunk."

"That's right. Well, the point where 'er 'uman form …"

"Her *artistic* human form!"

"You got the idea, gel! The point where it turned into 'er fish's tail was the same level as my nose. See?"

"I can picture it perfectly, Sozzler. There's no need to be more specific. I suppose you didn't exactly *spring* back in horror!"

"No. Being what they call 'hearty' with the drink, I took my time to hextricate my face from 'er … 'er …"

"Tail?"

He stabbed a finger at her and winked. "I took my time, I agree. But while I was stuck there I'll swear I did not say a word. Not. One. Little. Dicky-bird. Escaped my lips, so 'elp me Gawd. A grunt and a groan and a *hwoarrh!* – maybe. But not a word. I moved six feet … *ten* feet away before I spoke. And then *all* I said was, 'That reminds me …' I took out a pencil and licked it and wrote it down on my cuff. 'That reminds me,' I said. 'Fish and chips for supper tonight!' Now I ask you – where's the 'arm in that?"

Smiling, she stared into the eyes of an eland female, which was swaying deliberately from side to side as if engaged in some ritual.

"Wotchyer thinkin'?" he asked.

"I'm thinking I'm rather glad Morecambe is so far from Falmouth – if you must know. They can shut the shop for a few days and nip up to London to see me in *Trelawny*. But Morecambe's just too far away."

53 The Tremaynes decided to close their shop for a week – a bold move for people who did not belong to the holiday-taking classes; but it was not every Cornish greengrocery whose owners had a daughter in a title role on the West End stage. Noel moved into other lodgings for a week so that they could have rooms right next to her. There was, in fact, no need for him to do so, for there were several other vacant bedsits in the four buildings that made up the row, but Rose accepted the offer because she knew he wanted to atone in some way for that ghastly, misconceived visit to his father.

During the taxi-ride from Paddington they pumped her with questions, often simultaneously. Pop would keep asking, "What's that building ... where are we now ... do we pass Buckingham Palace ...?" while Mom wanted to know who she'd met that they might have read about ... was she eating enough ... sleeping enough ... she looked rather pale ... how much had that dress cost, or was it a theatre costume ... and so forth?

Pop's questions made her realize how little of London she knew. She had once glimpsed Buckingham Palace from the far end of the Mall. She had never so much as seen the Houses of Parliament, Westminster Abbey, the Tower of London, or St Paul's Cathedral. *Her* London was Theatreland and they all lay outside its unseen walls. She only knew the British Museum because she and Noel had passed it on their stroll from the Horseshoe to King's Cross. She had never travelled on the Tube. And she hadn't really taken in much at the zoo, either.

When she tried to explain all this to her parents, they found it hard to understand. "But what have you been *doing* with your time?" Mom asked.

"Theatre-theatre, eat-eat, sleep-sleep," she replied. "Besides, how long have you lived in Cornwall? When did you last go to the Lizard? Or Land's End? Or watch the Helston Furry Dance? Or even visit Pendennis Castle, which is just a mile away? Yet most visitors see them all in the first week."

They exchanged glances. "Guess she has a point there, honey," Mom said.

"If I was being cute," Rose went on, "I'd have said I've been saving all those places until the three of us could enjoy them. Anyway, I promise you we'll see them all during the course of this week. I'm rehearsing mornings but otherwise the day is ours. We can 'do' the sights in the afternoons and the theatres in the evenings. Until Saturday, of course. Saturday we open – which gives us Sunday to take care of disasters-revealed before we open again on Monday. The royal box is already reserved for you and you can ..."

"The *royal* box!" Mom exclaimed.

"Yep. We asked the king and queen did they want it but they said no, you're more important. Your host will be Hugo de Witt, who *is* more important than all the kings and queens in history."

"But we don't have anything to wear," Mom complained.

"You will have by then," Rose assured them. "You'll have something by tomorrow, in fact."

Mom continued: "Your Pop would like to see one of those shows they don't have in Cornwall – you know, where the girls kick up their legs."

"I would *not!*" he protested. Then, to Rose, "Are there any like that on at the moment?"

But nothing could top their delight at discovering that Covent Garden was right at the end of the street opposite their lodgings.

"There go the last threads of your apron strings," Rose said. "When you hear the name Covent Garden, *you* see the fruit and vegetable market while the only picture in *my* mind is the theatre."

When they learned that their rooms were Noel's it reminded Mom of something she had meant to tell Rose the moment they met. "You heard what happened to Sir Hector?" she said.

"Didn't he go off his rocker? Noel said something about it. I've been wondering how they could tell."

"And did he mention what Lady Carclew has been up to since?"

She shook her head. "'Fraid not. Noel has cut himself off from both of them."

"Well!" Mom's eye danced. "She's dismissed all the female domestics – not her lady's maid, but the parlormaids ... chambermaids ... whatever you want to call them."

"So who does all the housework?"

"Footmen! It's the talk of Falmouth. They have to be under thirty, tall and handsome, and she dresses them in old, eighteenth-century livery – you know – thighs and calves in white silk hose, and doublets and ... what do they call those short, puffy little pantaloons? Tabards? Lombards?"

"I don't know, but I know what you mean. I haven't done any costume dramas yet. Well, well, well! Embroidered codpieces, too – dare one ask?"

Mom hooted with laughter and covered her mouth.

"And what of little Fenella?" Rose asked. "Noel never mentions her so I don't ask."

"She got engaged to some Scotch baron. She's gone to live with his parents, sort-of on approval."

"Just like my character in *Trelawny* – you'll see. I hope she fares better. She was an infuriating little child but you also couldn't help feeling for her – with parents like that."

"They sent her away round about the time Sir Hector went doolally. D'you want to know about Frank Tresidder and Ann? You never said a word at Christmas. They had a baby boy last fall – one of those amazing ten-pounders born only five months into the marriage. They called him George. The dead spit of Frank, which is a mercy for him and his mommy. He dotes on them both and – so they say – hasn't lifted another skirt in all the seven parishes he used to haunt. Oh, honey, you had such an escape there! You haven't missed a thing."

Rose's remark about apron strings and the two meanings of Covent Garden had another aspect, which did not reveal itself until the small hours of her parents' first night in London. From around half-past two in the morning all the streets around the vegetable market came alive with carts and barrows, drays and lorries, all converging on the piazza and the surrounding auction houses. The rumble of iron tyres on stone setts and the cheery nightly greetings and chaff among familiars added up to quite a racket. On her own first night in town, Rose had risen and watched the bustle from her window; on her second night she had considered asking Noel if he'd swap; on her third night – and every night since – she had slept right through it. And so she did, too, on the night of her Mom and Pop's arrival. And yet, even though the amount of noise reaching over the roofs and down into the narrow area between the buildings, and finally penetrating through the windows into Noel's rooms would have been the merest whisper by comparison, it woke them all the same.

More, it excited them into rising, dressing, and making their way downstairs to join the tide of greengrocers, florists, and carriers below, all heading for the market.

"Oh! We were treated like *royalty!*" Mom said as they ate the second breakfast of their day with Rose next morning. "All those wholesalers and auctioneers we've dealt with down the years ... people who were just names to us. And I guess we were just names to them, too. So it was wonderful to meet with them in person after all this time."

"I had tea coming out me ears," Pop said. "The best thing is that everyone you meet, everyone that's up and about at that hour, is all in the one business."

Mom sniffed.

" 'Tis true," he insisted.

"Well, there were several girls there who weren't in *our* trade, thanks very much!"

"You get *them* everywhere," he said. "But you do know what I'm a-saying. For two or three hours, London was *us.* Just us."

"That's true," Mom agreed with a yawn.

They caught up on their sleep while Rose went off for rehearsals.

She had discovered the elusive trick of remaining a basically good actress while losing that indefinable 'something.' It had come to her shortly after the meeting with Sozzler at the zoo. She was, as she had told him, an instinctual actress who could not explain why she did certain things ... gave certain words an unnatural but nonetheless effective stress ... paused here ... trod upon the end of another's lines there ... and so on. She just knew it worked – and that if she tried to analyze it while she was actually on the stage, then it began to fail. Which is not to say that she acted heedlessly; some small part of her mind was always aloof, always watching ... herself, the rest of the cast, the audience, though as far as the audience was concerned, it was more a question of feeling than of watching, since most of them were invisible to her. It was that small, detached censor who controlled her acting over the long term, by noting what worked and what didn't and so nudging her performance continually toward improvement.

The trick she had discovered – though she preferred to call it a technique – was to give that modest little censor a larger role at just those moments when 'Rose Trelawny' needed to demonstrate the loss of that essential spark which can rivet the attention of a thousand pairs of eyes upon one lone, limelit individual on an otherwise empty stage.

The day she discovered it, which came at the end of the week prior to her parents' arrival, Marcus Turpin, the play's producer, slammed his famous 'little notebook' shut and hammered it on the back of the seat in front of him. "I knew you'd do it in the end, Miss Marteyne," he called out to her, for he had watched her try every other trick she could think of to convey Pinero's intentions. "Go on! Don't lose it now."

Later, when they were dissecting the scene, he told her that the part was considered a young actress's graveyard. "What most of them do," he said, "is to act *badly* – which is something a good actress simply cannot do. All they achieve is a sort of unconvincing burlesque. They become an actress having some self-indulgent fun, which nobody else finds in the least bit funny. And the audience loses all belief in any character who finally turns back into an actress again before their very eyes."

She didn't think it wise to tell him she'd already worked that much out for herself, thank you very much. Mrs Patrick Campbell would have done so, of course, but six good months on the London stage hadn't elevated her, Rose, quite that high yet. Instead she asked him why he hadn't told her these things much earlier, mentally adding, *You've torn just about everything else I've done to shreds – in the most constructive possible way, of course.*

"Because it's so fundamental," he replied. "If you ask a centipede how it manages all hundred legs, it trips over at once. It's like that."

"Marcus Turpin belongs to the new school of producers," Noel said. "Their model is the practical joker who taps you on the farther shoulder and then looks away and whistles."

However, from that moment on, all her terrors about *Trelawny* evaporated. Had her parents not been there, Saturday's opening night could not have come soon enough.

"Aintcha skeered?" Mom asked on their second night, when, after an exhausting tour of the Tower, she took them to dinner at the Café d'Italie in Old Compton Street – low-wattage lights all around, perfumed candles on every table, screens to create intimacy – and make the waiters' lives hell. Half-a-crown for the table d'hôte. They had their evening dress by then, of course, for no one could dine out in the West End without it.

"Skeered of what?" she asked.

"Everything! You, li'l ole Lucinda-Ella from Smithick Hill National, nine years in service, now going out on the London stage before the cream of the cream ... I still gotta pinch myself when I think of it. You must be scared – just a little?"

"I get butterflies in my tummy – of course. But that's excitement more than fear. If you don't get the butterflies, Charley Knox says, your act goes flat. It may still be champagne, but it's flat champagne."

She introduced Sozzler's name to see if they reacted; in her letters home she had not yet got round to mentioning her other life in variety.

"Who's Charley Knox?" asked Mom, who never missed a thing.

"I may be going to do a sort of play with him up in Lancashire in August, when *Trelawny* gets rested. Oh! And the other thing ..."

"Ho-back!" Pop cried. "What is a 'sort-of' play." He didn't miss much, either.

"A revue. That's spelled with a yew-ee at the end, not eye-ee-doubleyou. Revue."

"Vaudeville!" Mom said.

"Not quite. Vaudeville and burlesque are called variety and music hall here. They overlap a lot. But revue is a kind-of cross between musical comedy and variety. It has lots of comic sketches and songs. It's acting. Not standing up and telling jokes. And Charley Knox is one of the biggest names in the business. He seems to have taken a liking to me, so I'm very lucky to be working when everyone else in *Trelawny* will be looking around for something to do. 'Resting,' as they say. Also ..." She lowered her voice and leaned toward them. "It will make it easier for me to say this to you. About money ..."

"Oh, honey! The money you've been sending us has made *such* a difference – I can't begin to tell you. We have a girl to help in the shop now. And your father can take time off to go fishing. And I have a laundry woman every week. It's just transformed ..."

"I know all that," Rose interrupted her. "But wouldn't you like to move to a bigger shop? Mister Watts must surely retire soon and there's no one to follow him ..."

She could tell from the way they looked at each other that they were interested. Mr Watts had an italian warehouse farther along Arwennack Street, nearer the centre of town. Mom had often said that if there were room for two businesses of that kind, Tremaynes' would be the second one. She would just love to deal in fine foods like spaghetti and olives and German sausages and Bath chaps and French cheeses and wine vinegar ...

"No, honey, we're doing fine," Mom said. "That money's to help Louis – him and you both. Was that a letter I saw from him this morning, by the way? I saw the bald-eagle stamp."

She nodded. "You'll see one most mornings – well, three or four times a week."

"And you write him, too?"

"Only two or three times a week. Usually only twice. *But!* My letters are much longer. I tell him everything, just to set his mind at rest, because, you know, he could get jealous if he imagines it's all glamour and being kissed by handsome men on the stage and chased by the idle rich at the stage door after the show. So I tell him everything, like I say. But he doesn't. He seems leery of telling me anything. So I really have no idea how well or badly he's doing with this New Jersey brewery. He just says vague things like how different American tastes are and how they have different distribution systems. He says their beer is so tasteless they have to chill it to deaden the taste buds – things like that. I suppose he thinks I'd find details of the actual business too boring, compared with my own *fabulous* life!"

"Well now," Mom said. "Aunt Gwen has moved to New Hope, Pennsylvania, which is just across the Delaware from Lambertville, New Jersey. It's only twenty-thirty minutes on the train from there to Trenton. D'you want she should look him up for you, check him out, see how he's doing?"

Rose grinned. "The thing I was going to say earlier was that Mister de Witt may be going to take *Trelawny* to America next January – with the present cast! It would continue on here at the Saint James's with a new cast. But I'm not going to tell Louis until it's certain. Maybe not even then. It would be nice to surprise him. We'd play Boston, New Haven, and New York, but I could whiz down to Trenton easily."

She returned to the subject of Mr Watts's italian warehouse several times more that week, because she really did feel guilty at the contrast between her new life and theirs – not that she spent lavishly – quite the contrary – but the amount of money she was putting away in the bank was just unimaginable. In the nineteen weeks since she had gone on H-d-W's payroll, she had earned £380 – which, with the £20-odd she had earned at the Holborn Empire, made a grand, a very grand, total of £400. And £350 of it lay in the post office savings bank, earning her a further £12-odd each year.

She had never actually seen as much as £350 all at once. When she said so to Noel one evening, he made a pile of notes and coins to that amount from the theatre takings and led her into his office blindfolded. When he whipped the mask off, she gasped at the sight – and then could only stand and stare at it. It was both thrilling and embarrassing. Also oddly unreal.

"One day you'll earn this much in less than a month," he prophesied. "You'll see."

"And will I be able to give it up then?" she wondered aloud.
"Give it up?" He was appalled at the very thought.
"Well, I'm only doing it to be able to help Frank – I mean *Louis*. Oh God! Don't look at me like that – it's only because Mom and Dad have been talking about Frank. I'm doing it to help Louis. *Louis!* LOUIS! So as not to be a drag on him."
Noel just looked at the ceiling and said, "Yes. Quite so."
Finally, the only way she could cope with the sight of all that cash was to do a melodrama-style parody of a miser, combing her fingers through it, lifting it by the handful and letting it fall back to the table with eldritch cries of "Mine! All mine! Har-har-haaar!"
"You inhabit a plasticine world, don't you," he remarked with a curious mixture of censure and admiration. "Anything you don't like or can't cope with you transform into a tiny drama and act it out of existence."

54

'Miss Lucille Marteyne adds fresh lustre to her reputation among the more discerning theatregoers of London as the most promising new "star" to grace the stage for many a long year,' wrote James Swaffer in the Sunday edition of the *Telegraph*. "Her latest performance, in *Trelawny of the 'Wells'*, that notorious Waterloo of young actresses, is a triumph. The St James's Theatre, which gave us *Lady Windermere's Fan, The Importance of Being Earnest, The Second Mrs. Tanqueray,* and *The Prisoner of Zenda,* is a fitting location for such an outstanding accomplishment.'
'Poor Miss Marteyne!' wrote Laurence Barker in *The Nation*. 'Mr Pinero's embarrassing effusion *Trelawny of the 'Wells'*, masquerading as a play, needed an actress of Mrs Patrick Campbell's stature to make its creaking implausibilities work at all when it was launched upon an unsuspecting public shortly after the end of the last Ice Age. But, as several good actresses have proved since then, it is a hopeless concatenation of nonsense from start to finish. And now, when we had all hoped this mish-mash had been decently laid to rest, along comes Miss Lucille Marteyne, a worthy successor to Mrs P. C. if ever there was one, to persuade us it is a play after all and to put it back in the canon.
'The central character, Rose Trelawny, is one of those hopelessly divided personalities who have no real existence outside the minds of alienists and avant-garde novelists. It requires an actress of consummate artistry to catch up the ravelled threads of such a character and weave them into a persuasive whole. The general run of the acting profession will curse Miss Marteyne for doing precisely that; she has led where few, if any, can follow ...'
WELL DONE KIDDY BUT DONT THINK OF A PAY RISE IN MORECAMBE, ran Sozzler's unsigned cable, just fitting inside the twelve-word limit.
"Well – there'll be no need for *you* to come in tomorrow, darling," said Marcus Turpin.

For Rose it was the best accolade of all. Apart from anything else, it meant she could see her parents off again at Paddington. They still hadn't quite agreed to let her help them buy out Mr Watts's italian warehouse if and when he retired; the most they would agree to was to think over her suggestion that she would become a sleeping partner in the venture, taking a proper share of the profits.

London shrank again the moment they had gone. Westminster, the City, the royal palaces, the zoo, the museums and parks ... all were repacked in a box marked NOT WANTED ON VOYAGE. And what a voyage her life was turning out to be! The St James's Theatre was in the very heart of the West End – and at the upper-class end of it, too, aloof from the vulgarities of the Haymarket and Leicester Square. The area around was peppered with gentlemen's clubs, those homes-from-home to the aristocracy, the plutocracy, and their adult sons. And it was those adult sons who now flocked to the stage door in Angel Court, hoping to catch her eye. Since she was on stage in almost every scene of *Trelawny,* she had no time to whip out and do a quick turn at a variety theatre – not even at the nearest, which was the Pavilion at Picadilly Circus. So it was as a serious dramatic actress that she received those invitations to dine.

She came to realize that there were as many class differences among the 'stage-door johnnies,' as they were called, as there were in any other walk of life. At the Kingsway they had tended to be those *boulevardiers* who had earlier tried their luck for a chorus girl at the Gaiety, in Aldwych, or the Tivoli, in the Strand. Chorus girls were the favourite 'cop,' since, being poorly paid, they did not always refuse an invitation to dine in a *chambre privée* in order to supplement their income. There was little hope of making such an arrangement with a dramatic actress, ever since Irving and Bernhardt had made the theatre respectable for the first time in several hundred years. And, as it was no longer a social outrage for small parties of young, unmarried ladies to dine out with parties of young, well-connected bachelors, there was nothing disreputable for Rose in accepting an invitation to dine in such a mixed group at any of the more fashionable West End restaurants; the lucky young man who squired her for the evening could expect nothing more than the kudos of being seen with her and of boasting about it for weeks after. The respectable theatre had *glamour* and Rose did a gentleman – even a lord – a favour in letting him shine in its reflection for an hour or three after the performance.

She dined at the Blenheim in New Bond Street with Dudley, Viscount Sandon, heir to the earldom of Harrowby; at the Comedy in Panton Street with the Hon. George St Vincent, son of Lord Harris; at the Criterion in Picadilly Circus with the Hon. William Ormesby-Gore, son of Lord Harlech; at Frascati's in Oxford Street with the Hon. George Baillie-Hamilton, heir presumptive to the earldom of Haddington; and at Gatti's in the Strand with Rupert Nevill, a grandson of the Marquis of Abergavenny ... by which time they had all become fairly interchangeable in her memory. One who stood out, however, was Roger Deveril, untitled and heir to nothing but a million pounds in railway, mineral, rubber, and tea shares, which – since he had already come into his inheritance – made him part-owner of the world.

He stood well back from the usual crowd in Angel Court, looking slightly forlorn, as if he knew he hadn't a chance against all those titles and feudal estates; this was around the middle of July, when *Trelawny* had been running six weeks – or some fifty-odd performances – and the interchangeability of the johnnies was becoming tedious.

"Roger!" she called out over the heads of the hopefuls.

Roger? Roger who? Half a dozen pairs of frank, blue, unseeing eyes quizzed one another as their lordly owners parted in disappointment to let her through.

"Deveril!" One of the crowd at least recognized him. "Deveril, you unspeakably lucky cad!"

"Sorry you bounders," he called over his shoulder as she took his arm and propelled him toward King Street.

"Before you get too cocky," she told him as she raised her fan to a waiting cab, "we are *not* taking up where we left off thirteen months ago! Lord, has it really been thirteen months?"

"You never spoke a truer word," he replied as he helped her into the hansom. "Where to?"

"Let's try Ye Old White Horse Cellars." She named one of the most expensive West End restaurants, which was only three streets away, in Picadilly.

"Hatchett's," he told the driver. "Are you referring to my offer?" he asked as he settled beside her. "It wouldn't even have crossed my ..."

"No I'm referring to events that took place about an hour *before* you made the offer."

"Oh ... that!" He grinned.

"Yes, that. And don't try telling me it wouldn't even have crossed your mind."

He grinned. "Believe me, it wouldn't have crossed my mind to *speak* of it, Lucille."

"Did you see the show yet?"

"Quite a few times, actually."

"You idiot! Why didn't you come backstage? If you'd handed your card to old Benjy, I'd certainly have let you through to my dressing room."

He shrugged uncomfortably.

"Why?" she insisted.

"To be quite candid – I didn't think you'd want to meet anyone from the old days."

It was such a blatant play for sympathy that all she could do was laugh. "What d'you think of the play?" she asked. "I'm inclined to agree with Laurence Barker. Did you read his piece in *The Nation*? where he said the character's a nonsense?"

He shook his head. "I didn't. But he's wrong, anyway. You can't lift a character out of the play like that, like a cog in a machine. The way you and Conrad Laughton work together is ... is spellbinding."

She laughed.

They had arrived at Hackett's already. He took her to Ye Old White Horse Cellar foyer before returning to pay off the cabbie.

"Why the laughter?" he asked as the major domo led them to their table. It wasn't a *chambre privée,* but it was the next best thing – an alcove with curtains. Roger, however, was not so gauche as to offer to draw them.

She chose whitebait followed by stuffed quails; he joined her in the whitebait but followed it with jugged hare. When he asked her preference in wine she chose a Tavel rosé.

"I laugh," she said, answering his earlier question, "because your comment about Conrad Laughton and me working together is such a hoot. When he saw my reviews his face went black as thunder. And I don't blame him, really, because he should have got even better reviews than me. And we both know it. However, he's a brilliant enough actor to work *with* me for the sake of the production. I've learned so much from him – I can't tell you. So, as far as the audience is concerned, he and I work together in perfect harmony ..."

"Certainly."

"But wait! If you were on stage beside us, you'd see quite a different picture. He's constantly trying to make me corpse. For instance ..."

"Die, you mean?"

"No, laugh. Corpsing is when you laugh on stage when you're not supposed to. Once you get into a part, you know, the words come automatically, which leaves the mind free for all sorts of mischief – especially to an old hand like Laughton. You know the bit where he hands me a glass of cordial? Well, he laces that with something different every night – angostura bitters, peppermint that would skin your tongue, curry powder, garlic oil, half a ton of saccharin – eeurgh!" She shuddered. "Things like that. Were you in tonight? Did you notice he did the whole of our reconciliation scene standing on one foot?"

"He didn't!" Roger giggled and shook his head.

"He bloody well did! It doesn't sound like much but it was the way he did it. I mean, there am I, going through all those emotions, and there he is with that certain twinkle in his eye – like he's saying, *'Cherchez le tour* I'm playing a trick on you, little girl. See if you can find it!' And then there's that moment where I stand with my head downcast – and, of course, I see it at once. He's got this trick of hitching up one hip, the upstage one, naturally, so the audience can't see it. And he's standing there with his right foot two inches off the floor – all the way through the scene! Wherever he comes to rest ... up goes the upstage hip and those great twinkling eyes settle on me – and I'm supposed to act heartbreaking tragedy against all that!" She laughed. "It's something different every night."

Roger laughed, too. "Why d'you put up with it?" he asked. "Can't you complain?"

"And lose face? No, thank you! I regard it as training – all part of my education. If I can get through *this* performance without corpsing, I tell myself, I'll be all the stronger next time. But tell me about you! What are you doing with yourself these days?"

"As opposed to what I'm doing with Fifi up in Maida Vale, eh? Well, actually, there is no Fifi up in Maida Vale. No breathtaking butterfly in an open landau in Hyde Park each afternoon. It's amazing how quickly a fellow passes from memory. Most of those stage-door johnnies have hobnobbed with me at one time or another in Rotten Row – and how many recognized me now, less than a year on? One!"

"Oh dear, Roger – life has turned all serious, eh?"

" 'Fraid so, love. I wangled a post at the Foreign Office. I don't draw any salary, of course – so I may still hunt with the gentry."

"Foxes or actresses?"

"Why not both? Town affairs ... country matters."

"A very diplomatic reply!"

"Well ... I rather think I'm going to *be* a diplomat – to be sent to lie abroad for the good of my country and all that. 'Lie' is an interesting word, don't you think? A boat lies in harbour. A man lies with his mistress ..."

"And I lie upon the stage, night after night!"

"Yes," he said. "Let's talk about you, again. It's much more interesting. Tell me – have you been in touch with Louis Redmile-Smith lately?"

"If by 'lately' you mean yesterday, then yes, I have."

"He's doing rather well, so I hear."

"Do you?" She leaned forward with interest. "You hear more than me, then. He writes copiously about everything but his business. I don't know if it's misplaced gallantry, or if he thinks I'm not interested. And I've become afraid to ask in case it means he's not doing as well as he expected. How d'you get to hear about it? There are no quoted shares or anything."

He cleared his throat diffidently, "I got our commercial attaché in Washington to make a few discreet inquiries. Trenton Pils they call themselves ..."

"I know that. It's a Continental sort of beer."

"They're not ready for a public offering yet – according to my colleague, anyway. Your friend's partner has enough capital to be going on with and they'll make a bigger profit if they grow a little larger before floating. You seem surprised. D'you mean to say he doesn't tell you any of this?"

She shook her head.

"Extraordinary chap."

She reached out and patted his arm. "So are you," she said. "Extraordinarily kind. You made these inquiries on purpose, didn't you – before coming to see me tonight?"

He gave a diffident tilt to his head. "In a way. I rather hoped the news would be bleaker, if you must know."

She was astonished. "But why?"

"Can you not guess? It crossed my mind that an actress as dedicated to her profession as you would see some merit in a respectable ... what shall we call it? Coalition – yes, a good diplomat's word! I thought you might consider a respectable coalition with someone rich enough to fund any theatrical enterprise that you might fancy." His eyes said the rest for him.

"Oh, Roger!" She reached toward him again, this time to take his hand and hold it. "Oh, Roger!"

"The moment we parted company," he said, folding his other hand over hers, "I knew I'd made the biggest mistake of my life. Not in saying goodbye, though that was big enough, but in what happened earlier – the events that made old Roanoke chuck us out. I'd never ..."

"If you're thinking I regret ..." she began.

"No, hear me out first – please. I blame myself entirely for that, myself and my upbringing. Because of it, there were only two sorts of women for me – sisters, mine and other chaps', and the rest. One adored the first lot from afar and eventually picked one of them out and married her so as to continue the dynasty; and the rest ... well, you know. The rest were more fun to be with because one didn't have to pretend."

"Like me."

"Well ... I didn't know that then. It must have been intuition."

They both knew the real reason he had come to her bed that night but his eyes begged her not to speak of it. "Anyway," he continued, "the moment we parted I knew I'd just said goodbye to the third kind of woman. The unique kind. The woman one knows one would die for, give everything for, follow to the ends of the earth and beyond."

He smiled as he pulled the handkerchief from his pocket and dabbed at the tears that trembled on her eyelids.

"Of course, I told myself I was being a fool. I came straight up to London, found the prettiest little mistress in a milliner's shop in the Burlington Arcade, put her in the prettiest little villa in Maida Vale, and spent hours in her arms, trying to drown out your memory." He slumped. "Six weeks it lasted. Then I tried religion. Oh, you can laugh!"

"Sorry, I didn't mean to." She took his handkerchief again and blew her nose. "Just the thought of you in a dog-collar – unable to take your eyes off all the pretty ladies in the congregation."

"How well you know me! And now I'm trying the Foreign Office – with some success, you'll be pleased to hear. By the way, the offer to fund some theatrical enterprise of your choice is open even if you never do more than hold my hand from time to time and murmur my name in tones of sadness. I've got it bad, Lucille. Really I have."

The moment she had seen him standing out there in Angel Court a mischievous imp had urged her: 'Here's a man you could have a lot of fun with, because he's constitutionally incapable of taking a woman seriously. And you know that, while Louis lives, you're never going to take any other man seriously yourself. So go to it, girl – here's your chance!' She had nothing so specific in mind as *lying* with him, in one of the senses of the word, but she didn't rule it out, either.

Now, however, it was the last thing she could tell him – and certainly the last thing she ought to encourage between them. All the same – a man who was willing to be an angel to a production of her choice should not be brushed off like any old (or even young) lord. "I'm doing a show up north for the whole of next month," she told him. "I'm off there next week, in fact. But will you still be in London in September?"

He nodded.

"Let's meet again then," she said. "And see how things go, eh?" She gave his hand a final squeeze. "Love!" she exclaimed. "It just complicates *everything!*"

55

Sozzler met Rose off the train at Lancaster, where she would have had to change to the Morecambe line. He was trembling with excitement, like a filly under starter's orders. "Come on!" he cried before she'd even got her bags out of the luggage van, "we've got time before supper."

"Time for what?" she asked even as she insisted on making sure none of her luggage got left behind.

"A little touch of publicity. Have you ever been up in an aeroplane before."

Her eyes went wide with shock. "Me? Now?"

"This very minute – before you get time for cold feet. Come on – you're the cow's tail!"

"Cold feet? This weather?"

"Come on!" He fretted while she insisted on seeing her luggage aboard the cab he had hired to carry it. Then, throwing a duster and goggles at her, he shoved her into his Rolls-Royce and left her to put them on while he streaked down the road to Morecambe. Just before they reached the outskirts of the town he turned off up a farm lane and pulled into a field. And there in the corner, facing down a long, gentle slope, was the promised aeroplane, guarded by his chauffeur.

Rose had seen pictures of them, of course, and she had spotted the occasional one flying overhead; but she had never been close enough to touch the actual machine, like this. How fragile it seemed! Two sets of wings that looked as if you could poke a fist through them with ease; a tailpiece of the same flimsy construction; and to connect them, an open lattice of gas tubing and steel wire. It stood on four comic little pram wheels between which was slung a sort of ski on struts, presumably in case the wheels buckled or fell off. The sight of them was not reassuring.

"Yours?" she asked, hoping he'd say he'd just borrowed it, in which case she could beg off any flight until he'd cut his teeth properly at the controls.

"I've had her three months," he replied. "You're looking at an Avro 'D', my lady – designed by the great A. V. Roe, who made the first British aeroplane to fly. Put this helmet on and hop aboard! You're in front."

"Where are we going? Just round the town?" She imagined they'd tow a streamer saying *Sozzler's Follies* over the beaches and promenade ... something like that. The helmet smelled of sweaty leather but its earflaps would cut down the racket from the engine, which would be only thirty-odd inches in front of her face.

"Over *a* town, yes," he replied.

"What d'you mean – *a* town?"

"Blackpool." He winked.

She paused with one leg on the wing. "We're playing Morecambe and you're doing some sort of aerial publicity over Blackpool?"

"My sort of publicity, yes."

His chauffeur went to the propellor and stood ready to swing it.

Still she paused. "Is the engine safe?"

"As houses. You're casting nasturtiums on a thirty-five horse-power Gnome, I'll have you know. Very reliable. Come on – we're losing the light."

In fact, there were six hours of daylight left. If they were already 'losing it,' how long was this blessed flight going to last? Besides, they were due on stage in three hours.

"What if it conks out?" she asked.

"We'll glide down to ten feet," he replied.

"And then?"

He put his hands to her buttocks and gave her a push. "Are you telling me you can't jump ten feet? A big, buxom wench like you!"

The plane keeled slightly when he mounted, too.

Having secured her straps and plugged in the speaking tube, he went to his own cockpit behind her. His feet actually extended beneath her seat, because of the overriding importance of keeping the centre of gravity as far forward as possible. It did nothing to raise her confidence for, since the huge block of the motor prevented her from seeing anything dead ahead, how much could he see, being not only behind her but a good twelve inches lower into the bargain?

"You don't weigh more than ninety-five pounds, do you?" he asked, answering himself immediately with: "Too late now, anyway. Swing her, Jimmy!"

The chauffeur made a leap for the propellor. The engine coughed. Rose pulled the helmet strings tight to cover her ears. After three more coughs the engine fired. Control wires down to her left moved and the engine roar rose. For some inexplicable reason her fear lifted at that moment. Maybe it was just the comforting feeling of power behind that roar, or maybe her body had decided that they were committed now, so further resistance was fruitless. It was quite like going on stage – the panic and indecision before, and the what-was-all-the-fuss-about after.

The chauffeur was now down at the tail, doing his best to hold her back as the revs increased. She discovered one advantage of having the motor where it was – it diverted most of the slipstream from the propellor. She could feel it tugging at her hair, where it strayed out from underneath her helmet at the sides, but there was hardly a breeze on her face.

The moment came when the man could hold it back no longer. When he let go, the machine seemed to leap forward, like a slipped greyhound.

"Let's hope she takes off *this* time!" Sozzler cried out.

There was a deep rumbling sound – in fact, more of a sensation than a sound – beneath her feet. It grew louder and more violent the faster they went. It reminded her of a time when she went down Beacon Hill in Falmouth in a soap-box cart on pram wheels.

Then it stopped all of a sudden. She looked about them and realized they had left the ground.

"Whee!" she cried exultantly. "Up and away, boys!"

"She's never done that before," he shouted. "Let's see if she flies as well."

It amazed her to see how quickly the cows and fields and houses and things turned into toys. When you stood on the ground and looked at a house a few hundred yards off, it still looked like a full-size house; but when you looked down upon it from the same distance, it became a miniature. She could see washing in people's gardens. White specks that were geese. A woman sitting in an orchard with something in her lap – shelling peas, probably. A man repairing a rose pergola. A large dog running up and down a fence and a small dog running up and down the other side. Two children beating a carpet. Scenes from life that you'd hardly ever see from the highway were being played out before her, everywhere she looked. If you could be in a balloon and just drift over it, people would stop coming to the theatre – or playwrights would have to go back to writing grand histories – emperors and saints – or gruesome murders in country barns ... things you'd be very lucky to see from a balloon.

Funny. When she was in revue, like now, she thought of the legit theatre; and when she was in legit, she thought of revue. Oh Lord, please help me make my mind up, but not quite yet.

They were quite high, now, so that even the cows were little more than specks and the piers of Morecambe seemed no broader than a couple of matchsticks, jutting out into the water. One had a lighthouse, the other culminated in what could be a theatre. She focused on it and realized she would be performing there in – gulp! – two and a three-quarter hours.

Then she remembered the dark hints that Sozzler had dropped about getting his revenge against the Blackpool watch committee. Was this it? She began to laugh, slightly hysterically, for madness of that kind, allied to a notoriously lethal machine, is really only half funny.

"What are we going to do when we get there?" she shouted.

He pretended not to be able to make out her words.

Once again, since whatever was about to happen was now inevitable, she resigned herself to it and settled to enjoy every other aspect of the flight. If she stuck her head out sideways and peeped round the engine block, she could see Blackpool Tower in the distance – a half-pint Eiffel Tower. It looked dismayingly far away the first time she saw it, and no nearer on several subsequent peeps. She tried to work out how high up they were. The highest she'd been so far was up the Monument in London, which was about two hundred feet. This was certainly higher than that. Twice as high? More?

"How high are we?" she shouted.

He heard that, all right. "I'm five foot eleven," he replied. "You must be about five-six. What are you doing?"

"Looking for something to throw at you."

"Don't!" he shouted, with some urgency in his voice. "Save it for Blackpool! We must be about seven hundred feet up, if that's what you meant – and the word is 'altitude'!"

The sun was well down over the bay by the time they reached their target. "Now," he shouted, "feel under your seat."

Straining against her straps, she groped around beneath her seat and found something that felt like a heap of canvas. She twitched it forward and discovered it had a solid leather handle. She pulled it out and swung it up onto her lap. It was, indeed, a canvas bag and, when she undid its straps, she found it to contain a dozen rather meagre rolls of lavatory paper – the strong kind that children use for tracing paper and which, the makers promise on the wrapper, 'will not tear.'

"Got it?" he asked. "Read it." She could hear the giggle in his voice even over the engine's roar.

Each roll must have contained about eighty sheets, all of them covered with printing. In fact, they were numbered, as she saw by unrolling a strip of about eight. The odd-numbered sheets contained a list of names: ALDERMAN MULCAHY, ALDERMAN PRINGLE, COUNCILLOR DEEDES, COUNCILLOR POULTON, COUNCILLOR SIDEBOTHAM, COUNCILLOR FELLOWES. The even numbered sheets read:

ADMIT BEARER AT HALF PRICE
TO ANY PERFORMANCE OF
SOZZLER'S FOLLIES
NOW DELIGHTING THOUSANDS AT
THE WEST END PIER, MORECAMBE

And there was a tailpiece:

I hereby certify that I have used the other sheet of paper herewith for its due and proper purpose.
Signed . . . .
(NB! Concession Not Valid Unless Signed!)

"Sozzler!" she yelled, half laughing, half in despair. "You're an utter madman!"

The plane lurched violently. Her heart skipped a beat as she struggled to twist about and see what he was up to now. She noticed that the ground was considerably closer than it had been earlier. They were only a few dozen feet above the level of the top of the tower.

He was holding one of his rolls by the leading sheet and letting the rest pay out behind the plane. It reached the end almost immediately and jerked out of his grasp. "Like that!" he shouted to her. "I'll fly up and down the promenade until we've got shot of the lot."

She let one of her own pay out and then watched it drop, twisting and writhing like a snake in slow motion. She could see hundreds of faces turning up to watch – people on the beach, on the promenade, on the top decks of the trams. Soon they were running to pick up the streamers; the crowds, all converging on one location, looked like the tendrils of a multicoloured sea-anemone closing on some tasty morsel.

Three times they flew up and down the seafront, scattering the rolls of paper until their bags were empty. She wouldn't swear to it but she was almost certain she heard laughter wafting up from below.

The euphoria lasted only half way back to Morecambe. It had been a lovely stunt but what about the encore – their performance at the theatre in (*two* gulps!) forty-five minutes' time?

"You *are* a madman," she told him when they landed.

"Buy a ticket to the show," he replied, *"if you can!"*

They raced into town and reached the theatre with fifteen minutes to curtain up. The juices of fear had squirted into her veins so often over the past two hours that she was now past caring. So what if she hadn't more than the shadowiest notion of what they were going to do? So what if their last actual rehearsal had been a bit of impromptu larking about at London Zoo? Sozzler was a legend. Sozzler could read out that morning's fish-market prices and get a laugh out of it. They'd sort out something while the first few turns were on.

She wolfed a meat pie, washed down with a half of stout, while she dressed (in an old fashioned crinoline, of all things) and made herself up. The opening chorus was an old Sozzler favourite, *The Funny Things They Do Upon the Sly,* with five verses and two risqué belly laughs to each verse. Thus all ten members of the cast got in a solo, while the laugh-lines were punched out by all. Rose got the bit about the 'stiff old maid who likes to fume and boil. She's been *made* so long she's very like to spoil' and who, if she could get a man alone when no one was looking, would 'take away his breath' and 'squeeze that man to death!' CHORUS: *Some funny things are done upon the sly!*

Her gestures, miming precisely what sort of squeezing to death it would involve, brought the house down and the song to a temporary halt. So at least they were up and away.

But even then it didn't help that she and Sozzler managed to organize the skeleton of a sketch while the jugglers were on. Her opening words, 'Oh deah me! My husband dead and me with no water!' were just about all that was left of their plan by the time Sozzler had finished with his *ad-libidum* jokes. At one point he looked out of her (imaginary) window and shouted, "Gawd 'elp us, missiz. Some bleeder's nicked my 'oop!"

The rest, which Rose had to improvise, of course, ran:

ROSE: Your ooooop?
SOZZLER: Eoh, ay beg yaw pahdon, m'lady. Miy hhhooop.
ROSE: Your *hoop!*
SOZZLER: Yus! Moi 'oop. Some bleeder's gawn an' nicked it.
ROSE: What d'you need a hoop for, anyway? Plumbers don't need hoops.
SOZZLER: Oh, don't we just! 'Ow d'yer think I got 'ere, then? On *foot?*
ROSE: Well, how *did* you get here?
SOZZLER: By 'oop, of course!
ROSE: By oop? I mean, by hoop?
SOZZLER: Yerss! [*Runs once round the stage miming a boy bowling a hoop with a short stick.*] I bowled my 'oop all the way. [*Stops and stares at her aghast.*] 'Ow am I s'posed to get 'ome now, then? [*Grins craftily.*] I know! You'll 'ave to lend me the tram-fare!

ROSE: Lend you the tram-fare? I couldn't even afford to take the tram myself.
SOZZLER: That's all right then, ain't it – coz you're not comin' along, anyways!
ROSE: How far away do you live, for heaven's sake?
SOZZLER: 'Alf a mile.
ROSE: Well, that's no distance at all. Surely you can walk half a mile?
SOZZLER: It's not a question of whether I can or I can't. A gentleman in my position is expected to keep up certain standards – as I'm sure your ladyship can appreciate. Why, I should be the laughing stock of Morecambe if I was seen on foot when I should be travellin' by 'oop.

At this point Rose suddenly realized why Sozzler had insisted on her dressing in this ridiculous crinoline, something that hadn't been worn by ladies of her supposed class for thirty years. She saw him eyeing it now, and to the obvious delight of the house.

"You dare!" She wagged a finger at him. "Just you dare!"

There was a full minute of mime tableau while the laughter rang all around the theatre, dying here, leaping up again there, reigniting itself time and again. And when at last he lunged at her and dived under her skirts to steal one of the hoops, there were men begging them to stop and women crying for someone to loosen their stays.

They had two other turns before the final curtain and that same lunatic improvisation sustained them through both. Rose felt like a wet dishcloth, well wrung out, by the time they lined up for the final chorus.

"Not a bad start, eh?" Sozzler said as he swept her off for a supper celebration. "But we've gotta get a bit more life and pace in it for tomorrah!"

56

To appear on the same bill as Sozzler at any theatre in the land was a nerveracking experience. To appear in the same act and to be his 'straight,' as the butt of his jokes was called, was a torture infinitely greater, even if infinitely sweet. But Rose would not have missed it for the world, not even for the starring role in Mr G. B. Shaw's next play. In fact, although she was contracted to return to *Trelawny* on the sixth of September and would not be able to tour to America unless she did so, she was still tempted to break the contract and stay on with the Follies. It wasn't the camaraderie, though that helped; and it certainly wasn't the money, for she was getting only fifteen pounds a week for an 'and' billing – that is, a part announced as 'Charley Knox *and* Lucy Tremayne in ...' etc. on playbills and programmes. What tempted her was that magical rapport she could develop with a revue audience.

When Sozzler first told her about Morecambe – about playing the North in general – she had doubted he'd be able to duplicate his incredible popularity up there, the sort he enjoyed with London audiences. She'd seen northern comedians who'd been surprised at the lukewarm response they'd got at the Holborn Empire and she feared Sozzler would suffer the same in reverse, even though she knew he'd played up there for years. Now, after watching him woo the crowds into the palm of his hand, night after night, she not only realized how groundless her fears had been, she also thought she understood his secret.

You could say in a highfalutin way that his humour was universal, but what it boiled down to was that the fears he brought out into the open, the vanities he pricked, the innuendos he paraded with a wink ... were common to all working-class people, north and south. Even sublime bits of tomfoolery, like needing a hoop to bowl, so as to save his legs the chore of *walking* home and his pride the indignity of being caught hoopless, was an extended joke about working-class snobbery and insecurity. 'If the nibs and nobby persons can get all uppity about their phætons and their landaus,' he was hinting, 'then us common blokes can carry on the same about our 'oops!' And this from a bloke who, as every man and woman in the audience knew, went swanning about the place in a Rolls-Royce! To say nothing of his aeroplane – the toy of toys for all the rich.

As for the rest, it was all about coming home late, tiddly, and with blonde hairs stuck to his coat and being caught by the dragon-missiz with a rolling pin ... or (to redress the balance) what the missiz, a dragon no longer but allegedly a sweet, demure little angel, would get up to while her husband's back was turned ... or doing moonlight flits to avoid paying the rent ... or the awkwardness of being newly wed ... or the perils and pleasures of begetting children out of wedlock ... or putting over a fast one on the toffs, the gaffer, the 'pleece,' the beaks, the sergeant major, or anyone else in authority. North, south, east, or west – these small dramas were the very stuff of life and therefore of Sozzler's humour. Its highest intellectual achievement, in the verbal line, anyway, was the pun; and even then it was likely to be at the level of the 'ball' and 'cock' possibilities Sozzler saw in Rose's suggestion of a sketch about a plumber and a grand dame.

Even so, it was not the fascination of watching Sozzler at work, nor the pleasure of improvising comedy in a kind of knowing conspiracy with the audience that tempted her to stay. It was the joy of working that audience herself. Day by day, as she gained in confidence, so, too, did she add to her understanding of what would work and just how far she could push them. And, curiously enough, it almost always involved a decision about what *not* to say. The temptation was always to say too much, for fear they wouldn't get the point; and it was almost always fatal to give way to it.

Audiences came in wanting to laugh but they didn't want the jokes flayed and dissected for them.

For instance, when Sozzler merely cast a speculative but predatory glance at her crinoline dress in what came to be known as their 'oop sketch, it would have been fatal if she'd wagged at a finger at him and said something like, 'You're not having my hoops' or 'You leave these hoops alone' – as if they were afraid the audience hadn't twigged already. The simple 'Don't you *dare!*' was enough to copper-fasten the idea in everyone's mind. Mentally, they'd be under her skirts already – and that was always good for a laugh.

Comedy, she realized, is always about what to leave out. Once she had grasped the point, she wondered if the same wasn't true of high drama, as well. She had already cast off the kind of histrionics she'd learned with Lord Gordon Fitzroy's Players – beating the breast, clutching at the brow, declaiming at the gods with arms outstretched. Such sawing at the air had already been laughed off London's cosmopolitan stage, but the impulse survived in subtler mannerisms – a proud toss of the head here, a demonstrative turning of the back there, a falling upon the nearest table so as to heave with sobs ... She employed all three of these gestures in *Trelawny*.

What if, instead of hurling herself at the table in order to sob, she just stood there, rigid, head held high, facing the audience, light full upon her, and sobbed as if it were the last thing on earth she wanted anyone to see? Tears streaming down her face. Shoulders trembling so slightly you'd miss it if you blinked ... it could have a most powerful effect.

Then, to be sure, she could not wait to get back to the stage at the St James's and there put these new insights to work. She was not in *such* a hurry, however, as to welcome Sozzler's offer to fly her to London – not that it mattered, for he insisted upon it, anyway.

57

Trelawny reopened on the first Monday in September, and, from the start, played to capacity houses. De Witt's strategy of always leaving them wanting more was once again vindicated – though it didn't work in America, he said. Drop out of the public gaze for a month in New York and everyone forgot you; and even if they dimly recalled your play, they were already chasing after something newer, better, brighter. The trick over there was to build up a fury of expectations and then hit them with a big splash. They called it 'rooty-toot-toot.'

Rose soon put her new ideas about the portrayal of strong emotion into practice, though she was careful to introduce them gradually. In the scene where she had to fling herself down across the table and weep, for instance, she started by raising her head after the first few sobs so that the audience could see real tears pouring down her cheeks. It usually brought a gasp and filled the house with a new tension. Since she could not reliably produce tears to order, she had a chemist make up little gelatin capsules of extra-strong smelling salts, which usually did the trick. However, when Conrad Laughton copped on, he substituted a cod-liver-oil capsule one night. That was the night when panic taught her the trick of crying to order – all she needed to do was to imagine the stage manager bursting into her dressing room to announce that Louis had died.

She had decided to change her style gradually so as not to perturb the rest of the cast, especially Conrad Laughton, who had the most scenes with her. But after that little act of spite (disguised as a practical joke, of course) she felt that the gloves were off. The following night, which was about three weeks into the run, she switched completely to her new style. The reception from the stalls was rapturous but she could not help noticing that the dress circle and gallery were more subdued than usual when it came to her solo curtain calls. There were even a couple of catcalls. Laughton's smile was enough to tell her she had failed.

That night she spied Roger Deveril among the johnnies once again. And, once again, they went to The Old White Horse Cellar at Hackett's.

"You seem a bit subdued tonight, old thing," he said as they took their places in the same alcove as before.

"On stage or off?" she asked.

"Well, now that you mention it – both. What went wrong tonight? Bad news?"

"Where were you sitting? In the dress circle?"

He nodded.

She explained her theory – how the so-called Realism Movement in drama had been only half a revolution. Also what she'd learned in that most unlikely school – the end of Morecambe Pier – about the power of under- rather than over-statement.

"I obviously overdid the under tonight," she concluded glumly.

"Well, not as far as the pit was concerned," he pointed out. "They were as ecstatic as ever."

"Yes. If it weren't for that, I'd be down on the Embankment this very minute, looking for a brick and a rope. Oh, dear – they did warn me about this part. What am I going to do? I can't act at a permanent angle of forty-five degrees so that the upper tiers can see what's going on."

"You'll find it," he assured her. "Of course, I don't know anything about it but it seems to me that the sort of acting you're talking about would be more suitable for the motion pictures. In the theatre, on the other hand – from my point of view, a hundred yards away in the audience – I think you have to 'saw the air,' as you call it – just a bit, anyway. Otherwise give out free opera glasses all round, eh?"

She stared at him an uncomfortably long while and then said, "You wouldn't think of chucking the Foreign Office and taking up dramatic coaching, I suppose?"

"Sorry!" He pulled a face. "Teaching monkeys to hunt for fleas, was I?"

"No! What you've just said is so *right* – so obviously right – that I feel ashamed. I must try and *think* more. Instinct can obviously get me only so far."

"Actually ..." He hesitated. "I've seen you trying it out slowly, bit by bit. I think you had it just about ..."

"Wait a moment! What d'you mean, you've *seen* me?"

"Every single Thursday. I think you had it just about right this time last week."

"You came to see me every *week?*"

He smiled, but there was pain in his gaze as well – or, if not actual pain, a sense of vulnerability.

"Oh, Roger!" She reached across and squeezed his hand. "I'm sorry! Is it cruel of me to let you take me out like this?"

"Of course not!"

"It is. You must know there's very little hope."

His eyebrows shot up. "Very little? You mean there's *some?*"

"All right, none. I'll be going to America with *Trelawny* in the new year – in fact, we sail on Christmas Day. We're going on the *Olympic.* I'll get a second-class stateroom for only nine pounds! Noel says Lord Ismay owes H-d-W a favour or two."

He sighed. "And, of course, you'll see Redmile-Smith while you're there?"

"The very first thing. It's in my contract. We arrive in New York on New Year's Day. We open at the Castle Square Theatre in Boston on the fourth, so I'll spend New Year's Day in Trenton. D'you know, there are twenty-four theatres in Boston – only seven less than in central London. It must be quite a big city."

"Bigger than Trenton, anyway," he said. "And, by the sound of it, more exciting, too."

For a moment his point escaped her. Then she said, "Well – given present company – I didn't exactly want to dwell on Trenton. But, since you brought me back to it, have you heard any news?"

"He's still not telling you anything?"

She shook her head. "Have you?"

"I hear he's doing all right – Trenton Pils is, I mean. I've heard nothing about your man himself, though. Except ..." He hesitated.

"What?"

"It probably doesn't mean anything."

"What doesn't?"

"It could just be to keep his name out of it – you know – in case it frightened people off. Because the splash his bankruptcy made over here would have ..."

"If you don't tell me, I'll scream."

"Well ... his name isn't actually published among the list of directors. Nor is it among the beneficial owners in the share register. Of course, it could be that someone else is just a nominee for him."

While she absorbed this news, wondering how worrying it ought to be, he added, "As a matter of fact, there could be half a dozen very good reasons for not associating his name with the company."

"For instance?"

"Well ... English beer hardly has an inspiring reputation over there. Maybe a new American pilsner wouldn't sell too well if it were associated with the name of a prominent English brewer – especially one who went bankrupt in such a spectacular fashion."

"Smith's itself didn't go bust," she objected. "Only Redmile-Smith, the company that owned Smith's."

"Even so ..." His shrug implied it was the best he could do in the way of comforting explanations.

"You said there could be half a dozen reasons?"

"Well ... you know how odd our American cousins are about hard liquor. Half of them live by damning it while the other half can't live without it. Maybe they're touchy about foreign ownership of breweries? Your Louis may have to hide his light behind the nearest convenient bushel."

She nodded glumly, knowing he was scraping the bottom of the barrel. "Tell me about the Foreign Office," she said, forcing herself to cheer up.

"Not good there, either," he replied ruefully.

"Collapse of promising career?"

"Oh no, nothing personal. Just the state of the world. Germany is throwing her weight about, as usual. We'll be launching HMS *King George V* next month. That'll make 'em think twice! Russia's threatening Persia. Italy's mobilizing to take Tripoli and go to war with Turkey. The Froggies are grabbing Morocco and the Hun is conniving at it in exchange for large slices of the Congo. Poor old Belgium! And there's revolution in China. And the Suffragettes are spoiling for a fight at home ..."

"Is there going to be a war?"

He nodded grimly. "Beyond any shadow of a doubt. It's been on the cards so long we've almost stopped noticing it."

He glanced all around and then, leaning toward her and lowering his voice, added, "Keep this under your hat, old girl, but there's a strong opinion at the FO that Kaiser Bill is off his chump. I mean certifiably so. All this talk of Germany's 'place in the sun'! Honestly! They've been a nation for just fifty years and they expect to equal us after a thousand years! The arrogance of it! I tell you – if we don't clip the Teutonic eagle's wings pretty soon, the British lion will be losing *his* place in the sun."

"At least you'd be safe at home here."

He looked at her askance.

"I mean at the Foreign Office," she explained.

"But I'd resign that and join some regiment at once," he said.

"But you're not a soldier."

"Nor would most of the army be. Nor the German army, either. Anyway, I went through the Officers Training Corps at Eton."

"Bang-bang with blanks on the college cricket pitch." She laughed despairingly.

"Not a bit! The cricket pitch was sacred. No, I'd find a billet pretty quickly, I think. My father was in the Household Cavalry. Died at Pardeburg. They'd almost certainly find room for me." He frowned. "You wouldn't want to know anyone who was happy to be *safe,* would you?"

She had never thought of safety as degrading. And she didn't want to think of war at all, not just now.

"I suppose not," she said. "But it would be a pity."

"What would be?"

"You ... going." She didn't want to say the obvious.

He grinned. "You'd miss me?"

She nodded. "Of course I would. Just because I love Louis, it doesn't mean that I'm not as fond as fond can be of you."

END OF PART FOUR

Part Five

A Night to Remember

58 At the turn of 1911 the *Olympic* was the biggest liner afloat. *The Kaiser Wilhelm II* and the *Mauretania* were a shade faster – in fact, the *Mauretania* held the Blue Riband – but for stability and luxury nothing could compare with the *Olympic*. And when her sister-ship *Titanic* was completed in the April of 1912, the White Star Line would set a transatlantic standard hard to beat. Rose's secret ambition was for the American run of *Trelawny* to last until May at least; not only would that allow her plenty of Sundays with Louis but she could steam back home on *Titanic* – maybe first class – and boast for ever that she had travelled on the two most fabulous liners in the world.

When she first saw the *Olympic* at the Ocean Dock in Southampton she could not believe anything so massive could exist. It was Christmas Day, cold and overcast, and the top deck seemed almost lost in the clouds; certainly it was twice the height of a house, even of a big house like Nancemellin. And the funnels were as high again. For a long while she just stood on the quayside, imagining herself lost somewhere inside that vast floating town, which is what it was, really.

She already had a good picture of it in her mind, for Noel had given her the White Star Line's publicity booklet as a sort of going-away present. He knew that she always liked to know about a place before she visited it. He remembered she had bought that guide to London before she came up the line from Cornwall, and could reel off the complete list of London theatres before she even set eyes on one of them. And he had seen her send away for the municipal booklet about Morecambe before going up there, too. Even with individual theatres she liked to know how the audience was seated, so she had a little collection of those seating plans on which the box-offices mark off their sales.

The White Star booklet proudly described just about every rivet in both *Olympic* and the unfinished *Titanic*. Though their decoration was different, their plans were identical, so she knew exactly where the second class began and ended – shutting out the third class at the stern and being excluded, in turn, from the first class, which filled most of the front half, between the third funnel and the bridge. Actually – as the booklet itself pointed out – the terms first, second, and third were entirely relative. The first-class transatlantic passengers of the 1880s would look with envy upon even the third-class accommodation on *Olympic*.

The bustle all around her was intense, for they were due to cast off in less than two hours. Sometime during the previous night they must have refilled the coal bunkers, but there was no trace of dust or smuts about her now. Just think – a hundred and fifty-nine furnaces gobbling up more than a thousand tons of coal every day! It was a wonder they'd found room for it, what with all the other things they'd managed to pack in. Even a swimming pool, a turkish bath, and a racquets court – for the first class only, of course, but still ... And, talking of finding room for luxuries, someone was obviously taking a Daimler to America; it looked like a toy, dangling at the end of a hawser from the forward davit, turning gently in the icy breeze as it swung over the railing and came to a halt, presumably over the open cargo hatch. Crews at other davits were busy hauling up nets full of luggage, even to the topmost deck, where it was stored in the dummy fourth funnel.

Below the dangling Daimler was the third-class gangway, full of toiling emmets with carpet bags. Poor people! More than half of their accommodation was at the back but they had to enter at the front and make their serpentine way through the crew's quarters – past the bosun's mate, the quartermaster, the plate washers, waiters, stewards, engineers, one head chef, five first-class musicians, and the potato store before they reached their own cabins. However, if they looked at the plans, they would find it comforting to know that they were by no means the most cramped people aboard; one cabin, labelled '42 3RD CLASS STEWARDS,' was actually smaller than a single first-class stateroom.

"Aren't you going aboard?" asked a cheery voice.

Rose turned to greet Ellen Howe, who played the part of Sybil and who was to share the stateroom with her. (Her boast to Roger that she would have it to herself proved unfounded; the favour Lord Ismay owed H-d-W was not great enough for that.)

"Merry Christmas!" Rose replied.

"Merry Christmas!" Ellen, a well built natural blonde with the most enviably curly hair, looked the picture of health.

"I was just taking in the atmosphere. Isn't it exciting! Did you ever sail on a ship before?"

"A ferry to France. I didn't get seasick, though. You?"
"Only a big clipper – in harbour. Let's go aboard. Steward!"
Ellen still had her porter from the train; a second-class steward asked their names and stateroom number, which was E60.
"Middle deck," he said hefting Rose's two large suitcases. "Good."
The four of them set off up the gangway, which entered the boat at the same level as the third-class, symbolically one deck below the first class. There was yet another gangway, amidships, full of porters carrying sides of lamb and pork, crates of eggs, cases of wine, chests of tea and all the other things the two-thousand-odd humans aboard would gulp and guzzle over the next six days.
The interior was a shock, even to Rose, who had read the booklet so often she could quote whole paragraphs. The descriptions had been full of words like 'Jacobean ... oak-panelled ...' and so on – but it was all painted *white!* White Jacobean was a novelty, indeed. To the two actresses it looked like an undercoated stage set ready for painting. The deck on which they entered was, fortunately, also the deck on which their stateroom was located; in fact, it was just forty paces aft. Rose turned left as soon as they came to the first lengthwise corridor, even before the steward led the way.
"You've sailed on her before, miss?" he said.
"Only in my mind," she replied. "We're down the end, aren't we? Next to the purser's clerks and the second-class musicians?"
"Right again," he said. "Only I wouldn't let them hear you calling them that. 'Musicians for the second class' is what they prefer. How d'you know all this if you never sailed with us before?"
"She's one of those sickeningly efficient people who reads maps and guidebooks *before* visiting places," Ellen told him. "She turns up word-perfect to rehearsals, too. Don't you, darling!"
"Yes," Rose agreed, "but only because I like surprises."
"Actresses, are you?" the steward asked.
"How can it be a surprise if you know it all beforehand?" Ellen asked. "If you know we're next door to five musicians ..."
"Then the mere fact of it doesn't surprise me. Why should it? It's just a dull fact. And if I already know it, then I'm ready for the *real* surprise, which is to discover that one of them is a handsome Paganini. And I am talking to him about caprices while you are still muttering, 'Good heavens! I've just realized we're next to the musicians!' D'you see?"
They collapsed on each other, giggling, while the steward unlocked the door. "Actresses," he said, answering himself. "As a matter of fact, you're not too far from us stewards, either. I'm Hawkins, by the way."
"A good seafaring name," Ellen said as she tipped her porter.
The steward gave them their keys, pointed out the features of the room, and said, "I suppose you already know where the ablutions are, then, Miss Marteyne?"

"Diagonally aft, opposite the musicians. Do they use that bathroom, too?"

He shook his head. "And there's only six other ladies in this section of E-deck, so you won't have much waiting."

"How do you know my name?" Rose asked. "Are you interested in the theatre?"

"E-sixty ... Miss Lucille Marteyne, Miss Ellen Howe, both of Mister Hugo de Witt's party. You don't need to be an actor to have a memory, I hope?"

Rose, who had spoken to many a passenger-ship steward back home in Falmouth – though none from so great a vessel as this – gave him five shillings and said, "You look after us well, Hawkins, and there'll be as much again when we get to New York."

He beamed. "It's good to know where one stands, miss. I'll bid you both adieu." He gave an elaborate bow and left them.

"Cheeky chappie," Ellen said when they were alone. "*Are* their quarters very close to ours?"

"No," Rose replied scornfully. "They're on the port side, opposite us, and about four hundred foot nearer the bow."

"How long is the whole ship?"

"Eight hundred and eighty-two feet and nine inches."

Ellen pulled a face. "I'm going to discover six things about the ship each day and then test you on them. I'm determined to catch you out."

"All right." Rose squared up to the challenge. "Shall I tell you the first six things to test me on now?"

"Yes," Ellen replied without thinking. "No! Oh, you horrid thing! Come on – let's go and explore ... beginning with the ladies' whatsits. I need to plant a sweet pea."

Five minutes later, gloved, scarved, and coated against a wintry blast, they went back to the entrance hall and waited for the elevator. "We'll go all the way to the top," Rose suggested, "and explore our way down, deck by deck."

"Can't we walk up?" Ellen asked impatiently. The elevator seemed to be in constant use between the floors above them.

"Six decks?" Rose asked, pressing the button again and again. They waited.

When it arrived, the doors opened to disgorge, among others, Conrad Laughton, looking rather flustered. "Lost already!" he cried. "Where's F-fourteen?"

"Next floor down," Rose told him. "Through the watertight door. First left."

He gawped at her and then broke into a knowing grin as the elevator doors closed.

"Damn!" Rose cried. "Now he'll think I learned the way to his and Henry's cabin deliberately. Damn, damn, and double-double damn! And if you say anything about being hoist on my own petard, I'll strangle you."

Light flurries of snow were swirling round the boat deck as they emerged from the elevator; luckily for the porters, they had finished stacking baggage in the dummy funnel, which rose out of that small portion of the boat deck around which second-class passengers were permitted to promenade.

"Lifeboats." Ellen patted one of the davits and said, "Let's hope you fellows stay all tied up there, all the way to New York!"

Rose eyed her askance. "What a gruesome thought!"

"You should read this novel I'm reading! I'll bet it's one you'd never find in the library of any liner."

They sheltered in the lee of the dome over the first-class smoking lounge. "You'd never believe some of the things they say in the White Star booklet," Rose said. "We could get up a comic recitation party, reading bits of it aloud. For instance." She cleared her throat portentously and quoted from memory: "The third class smoke room! 'Here, under the soothing influence of the fragrant weed, many a thought will be given to the homeland and those left behind.' Or how's this for the third class general room: 'The friendly intercourse, mutual helpfulness and bonhomie of third class passengers is proverbial ...' I say, wouldn't it be great gas to do this as a comic turn actually in the third-class general room one night! The booklet actually says that if Sozzler Knox were on the *Olympic,* he would find conditions in the third class so favourable that his exceptional talents would hardly be required to make them jollier yet. I forgot to tell him that." She shivered. "What were we talking about? Let's go down to the bridge deck."

They had to walk down two flights, skipping the promenade deck because there was no exit for the second class there; it was exclusively first class. Looking out through the locked doors as they passed, Rose said, "We might also see if we can organize an evening of songs and declamations to entertain the first class."

Ellen looked at her despairingly. "Can't you stay away from audiences for just five days?"

Rose laughed and apologized; all the same, she intended to get into the first class by fair means or foul. She'd seen one of their menus in the London office and that was incentive enough.

"This book I'm reading," Ellen said as they went on down to the bridge deck. "It's called *Futility* and it's all about ..."

"Who's it by?"

Ellen had to think. "Someone Robertson or Robinson. Morgan Robertson! I'm pretty sure."

"Never heard of him."

"Nor had I. But David Dent, who was with me in *Hamlet* at the Haymarket, gave it me to read. He had a sort of twisted smile on his face but I didn't realize why at the time."

They gave the bridge deck a miss because it was snowing quite heavily by now. They arrived at the shelter deck, where they had a choice between the covered promenade or the second-class library.

"I expect they only have second-class authors in here," Rose said as she held the door for Ellen. "Like Ouida and Mrs Humphry Ward and Dickens."

"Dickens is second class?"

"Of course. He used to be first but now he looks at the third class with envy."

Their hunt for Morgan Robertson's *Futility* was vain.

"What's it all about, then?" Rose asked.

"There's this liner called the *Titan.* The biggest luxury liner in the world – at least it was twelve years ago, when the book came out. That's why I asked how long *Olympic* is, because *Titan* is eight hundred feet. What's our tonnage?"

"Sixty-six thousand, give or take a few lumps of coal."

"*Titan* was seventy thousand. God! It's uncomfortably close, what! How about top speed – twenty-four, twenty-five knots?"

"Spot on! Was it triple-screw?"

"D'you mean three propellors? Yes. And she carried three thousand people." She raised her eyebrows inquiringly.

Rose nodded. "Three thousand is the maximum for *Olympic.* What happens? I've got to know now!"

"Ssshh!" cried an angry fellow-passenger, engrossed in that day's edition of the ship's newspaper.

"Not yet cast off," Rose murmured as they went out on deck, "and already the library is crammed with people saying *shhh!*"

"What happens in the book," Ellen said, "is that *Titan* hits an iceberg and starts to sink. Up until then everyone has been calling it 'unsinkable.' And suddenly it dawns on the passengers that they've only got lifeboats for about a thousand people. They're all rich and snobbish and complacent and most of them drown – which is why it's called *Futility.*" After a pause she said, "I don't want to start a panic but I could only count eighteen lifeboats when we were up on the boat deck just now. How many people do they carry, each?"

Rose shrugged. "The booklet didn't say – only that they're thirty foot long."

"I was trying to imagine them filled with people. I reckoned no more than three dozen to each. Four dozen at the risk of sinking."

An officer came through from the first class, whose sheltered promenade was forrard. As he was making for the well deck, Rose stepped in his way. "Please, officer," she said, "could you tell us how many people each lifeboat can hold."

"Oh, plenty, miss," he replied cheerily. "More than enough."

"We were having a friendly argument. I say three dozen, my friend here thinks it's more like four."

"You're both about equally right. Forty would be a good average."

"And there are eighteen of them?"

"And collapsibles and rafts and floats – enough for nearly eighteen hundred souls, so you needn't worry your pretty little heads about such things, ladies." His eyes narrowed. "Have you been reading that pernicious book?"

"What pernicious book is that?" Ellen asked innocently.

"*Futility* it's called. Every voyage there's someone who's read it – spreading dismay and melancholy. We have wireless telegraphy these days, you know – which is something that clever Mister Robertson didn't even think about. And the north Atlantic is like Picadilly on a busy morning with ships going in all directions. Added to which, *Olympic* is unsinkable – literally unsinkable. So even if we were so foolish as to try a naval engagement with an iceberg, we'd just sit tight and wait for a tow. Now, if you'll excuse me – someone has to cut the piece of string that ties us to the jetty at the blunt end – and the happy duty has fallen to me."

"Well, I'm glad I asked," Rose said as they watched him go out on deck. "I think that's a fairly comprehensive answer to your Mister Robertson, don't you."

59

Even in the second class it was a luxury for the cast of *Trelawny* to be at the receiving end of whatever entertainment and cosseting was on offer. They enjoyed it morning, afternoon, and evening – especially in the evenings, when they would normally be providing the entertainment. Rose enjoyed it unashamedly for two whole days – one of which was spent on the leg to Queenstown, in Ireland, while the other took them out upon the great wide Atlantic. Hawkins, the steward, advised her and Ellen to eat well, to brave the open air as much as possible, and to keep their eyes on the horizon. First-class passengers, he said, were 'indisposed'; second-class passengers had *mal-de-mer;* the third class were just plain seasick.

Since it was Christmas and the menu was, accordingly, rich, the women were happy enough to follow his advice. They gorged on goose and plum pudding, mince pies and Cumberland butter, which is brown sugar, butter, and rum. And the trick seemed to work. At least, they felt only the slightest queasiness, and even that deserted them by the middle of the second day. However, it amused them to observe that Hawkins's remarks on class and seasickness were pretty accurate; there were, indeed, marked differences. From the back of the covered promenade on Deck C they could look down into the narrow well deck, which provided the only patch of open air available to the third class; it measured a mere ninety feet by fifty and fully one third of it was taken up by the coamings of two big cargo hatches, a winch, and two cranes. The passengers there ran to the railings – downwind, if they remembered in time. And there they 'laid a Persian carpet' on the waves, as Henry Lacy, Conrad's cabin companion, expressed it; the second class, on the other hand, tended to make for the boat deck and lay their carpet in a discreet corner; the first class, in contrast to both, pretended it wasn't happening at all. They pretended they were merely coughing elegantly into handkerchiefs, and they fixed each other with ghastly smiles that challenged the world to think otherwise. When the two young women realized they had beaten the scourge, they became insufferably superior beings, at least in the eyes of those who still despaired of ever feeling right again.

After two days, though, when they had 'done' the second-class restaurant, the second-class library, the second-class smoke room and bar, and the second-class dining room – and had braved the wintry Atlantic air on the boat deck for as long as they could bear it – they began to wish there was a second-class swimming pool, turkish bath, gymnasium, and racquets court, too. Then they might just about get through the six-day crossing without dying of tedium.

To be alone on any ocean, with nothing but an albatross for company, is an awesome experience; and the awe can persist, even for a day or two, but not for six. Awe-inspiring, too, were the boiling surges of white water at the stern. The huge propellors, though out of sight, seemed to cut the ocean into chunks, each about the size of an elephant, and to ram them backward with the speed of an express train so that they all piled together about twenty yards astern. There they broke one another to bits and came boiling to the surface in a sizzling, seething, foaming chaos.

"Wouldn't it be fantastic if that were warm seawater and one could take a bath in it!" Rose murmured as they watched it in fascination. "Think of all those myriads of bubbles tickling you all over and bursting all around you!"

"I'm not sure I should be listening to this," Ellen said in a tone of wholehearted agreement. Then, apropos nothing, she added, "I can understand how people have shipboard romances, can't you?"

"Oh?" Rose was wide-eyed. "Have you someone in your sights?"

"Never you mind! I asked a question – which you seem suspiciously reluctant to answer, miss. Don't you feel the urge to have a whirlwind romance with one of the officers? Or with that young Norwegian about four doors down from us – the one with about sixty pearly white teeth?"

"He is *exactly* four doors down from us."

"You've counted!"

"So have you."

"Well," Ellen complained, "I saw him first. Also I've found out what he does for a living and I'll bet you don't know."

"For a whirlwind romance does it matter?"

"He's an expert on managing forests – so there!"

"Well-well! With twenty miles of Atlantic visible in every direction – and not much else – it would be interesting to hear your conversational opening! Anyway, you're welcome. I've got my eye on the Italian-looking gentleman in the first class – the one who seems to hang around the dividing doors close to whatever deck you and I happen to be on. Hadn't you noticed?"

"Not ... particularly," Ellen replied, much too casually.
"I think he's got his eyes on *you,* actually. Not me, alas."
Ellen looked up sharply. "You're only saying that to distract me away from the Norwegian. You want my Norwegian, don't you!"
Adopting a melodramatic stance and tone, Rose said, "I only seek your happiness, my dearest child! You are all in the world to me." Then, businesslike again, "Shall we go and see if we can tempt him from C-Deck up to A-Deck – if he's there at all?"
He was there, all right, and this time he made so bold as to raise his hat to them through the glass door that defined their separate worlds. They dipped their heads gracefully in return and turned toward the elevator.
"You're walking verreh provocatively, deah!" Rose reprimanded Ellen in Lady Vane-Trumpington's voice.
"Seo are yooo," Ellen retorted in the same accent. "By the way, what is the pressure of the steam in the engine room?"
"To the piston engines or to the turbine?"
"Oh!" Ellen pulled a face. "He didn't say."
"Hard luck!" In fact, Rose knew the answer to either but she wasn't going to help Ellen out because sooner or later the dear girl was going to hit on at least one of the three million things she *didn't* know about the vessel.
"Here's another then: Where are the electric generators?"
They boarded the elevator. Ellen snatched a peep as the doors closed. "He's still watching. He's waiting to see if the pointer goes up or down," she said. "What about the generators?"
"I can tell you that. You know where the third-class have their little promenade space? Well, if you go down five decks from there, that's where they are – the main ones. Four of them. A hundred volts. One-point-six ..."
"All right! All right!"
"One-point-six megawatts. Also there's an emergency set by our dining room. It's only thirty kilowatts but it would be just about enough to light up your brain."
"You could play Polonius in *Hamlet,* you know. And I could play the prince. We could rehearse it now – with a real dagger."
Laughing, they emerged onto the boat deck, where they strolled forward, past the lifeboats on the port side, stopping near the gate that separated the first and second. The only people in sight were a lady, wrapped in what looked like three grizzly-bear skins, and a middle-aged gentleman with a pedometer strapped to his left ankle. The lady was pretending not to be indisposed; the gentleman, huffing and puffing like a grampus, seemed to be engaged in setting some kind of personal walking record.
The two women had plenty of time. The first-class elevator was well forrard, so their target gentleman would either have to walk along half the ship to reach it – and back again – or climb several flights of stairs, from the bridge-deck, where he had seen them,

past the exclusively first-class promenade deck, to the boat deck, where they now stood and gazed raptly out to sea as if it contained enough of interest to occupy them all the way to New York.

"Thar she blows!" Ellen murmured out of the side of her mouth, although the man was still a hundred paces away.

Without conferring they turned and walked away, round the back of the dome over the first-class smoking room.

"It's like passing one of those Oxford Street humidors," Rose said as they got downwind of it.

"They're dreadful places," Ellen said. "The cigars are just an excuse. You know what they're mainly used for?"

"I've heard. And ho-ho-ho – look who's suddenly found the starboard side more interesting, too!"

"Shall we put him out of his misery?"

"I think – in common humanity – it's our Christian duty."

Again they strolled forrard, as far as they could go, just as he strolled aft, to the same limit. All three developed a sudden, acute interest in the stencilling on the lifeboat davits and tarpaulins.

Suddenly Rose cried "Ouch!" and, bending almost double, clasped a hand to her left eye.

"What?" asked an anxious Ellen.

"A smut in my eye. It's huge. Could you? Use my handkerchief."

Ellen, with her back to the gentleman, grinned hugely and peered into her face. The grin soon vanished, however, and she murmured, "Is it genuine?"

"Of course not!" Rose muttered back.

"Well, your eye is watering like mad." She gave it several dabs and said aloud, "Hold still! I can't see it."

Behind her the gentleman cleared his throat.

"Oh, sir!" Ellen turned to him. "Would you be so kind?" She passed him the handkerchief even as she spoke. There was no need for any great subtlety here.

He had a smirk on his face as he prepared to give her eye a token dab or two; but when he saw how copiously it watered, he actually began to hunt for the offending bit of soot.

Even at six inches distance he remained handsome, which Rose knew was not always the case. His jet black hair was thick and sleek and wavy; his eyes, dark brown, curiously flecked with green, were deep-set beneath a noble brow; his nose was aquiline and elegant; his lips were finely drawn and yet sensuous beneath a neatly trimmed moustache with small, waxed points; and his chin was firm and deeply dimpled. Ellen was more than welcome to her Norwegian, no matter how much he knew about forests.

Rose took pity at last and, blinking her eye several times, said, "You clever man! You've cured it. I'm eternally in your debt."

He smiled shyly and murmured something inaudible as he handed her back the handkerchief.

Lord, didn't he know *anything?*

"How can I ever repay you?" she added, playing the last card.
"Er ... you could hear my lines?" he suggested timidly. "I'm Max Duggan, by the way."
"Lucille Marteyne. And this is my friend Ellen Howe."
"You're an actor, too?" Ellen asked.
"A baritone. I go under the name of Massimo Leone but I doubt if you've heard of me."
"Oh, but I have!" Rose remembered where she'd seen the name before – every day for a couple of months. "You sang Googly-whatsit in *Cosi fan tutti* at Covent Garden last spring."
"Guglielmo," he murmured, smiling.
"Googly-*whatsit!*" Ellen sneered.
"Well I don't know how all those eyetie words are pronounced, do I!" She turned to him. "Sorry."
He bowed. "Not at all, Miss Marteyne. And you, if I remember correctly, were in *Twin Sisters* at the Kingsway, just round the corner. I saw you, in fact. I thought you were amazing."
She curtsied. "Now I feel awful – because I didn't see you. Did you recognize me just now?"
"The moment you stepped aboard. Look – this is silly. Please allow me to invite you both to join me in the Palm Court. It's just down these steps." He opened the gate for them.
"Is it allowed?" Rose asked, stepping onto hallowed ground.
"I have discovered eight words that produce the most amazing results," he replied. "D'you want to hear them?"
"Yes!" the women cried as he closed the gate behind Ellen.
"'I never had this trouble on the *Lusitania'!* It's amazingly effective, especially if spoken by one who knows how to project the voice without increasing the volume."
Now that the ice was broken he had lost his bashfulness. Rose had thought it endearing, all the same. "Are you singing anywhere in America?" she asked as they started down the stairs.
"I'm engaged for the rest of the winter season at the Grand Opera in Boston."
Both women burst out laughing.
"You too?" he asked.
"We're in *Trelawny of the 'Wells'* at the Castle Square Theatre," Rose replied. "I think you're less than half a mile away."
"She reads maps," Ellen explained.
"Only to locate the theatres. What are you singing there?"
They emerged onto the promenade deck; plenty of people stared at them, men and women, but none had the look of those who suspected interlopers. The men were admiring, the women interested, for, second class passengers or not, the pair of them were fashionably dressed and knew how to carry themselves.
"*Don Giovanni* and *Figaro*. It alternates with Verdi, but I'm not in that. We're against *Siegfried* at the Turnhalle in Middlesex Street. D'you know where that is?"

Rose shook her head. "Sorry. I could tell you next time we meet, because I've got the *Baedeker* in our stateroom."

The Palm Court was a verandah bar at the very tail end of the promenade deck. In fact, the elevator in which Rose and Ellen had travelled ran up through the heart of it to the boat deck above. They ordered china tea and settled in a corner, where he took a sheaf of paper from his pocket and placed it on an empty chair at his side. *"Don Giovanni,"* he said.

They drank tea and talked theatre for well over half an hour before Rose, thinking he'd donated quite enough of his time to Ellen, looked at her watch and said, "Darling! Isn't it time for your Norwegian lesson?" She grinned and, turning to Mr Duggan, explained: "She's hoping for a part in a revival of *A Doll's House."*

"In Norwegian?" He was impressed.

"The play's in English translation," Rose said. "But a smattering of Norwegian helps her to see the wood from the trees."

"Will you come, too, love?" Ellen asked.

"Oh – one hardly needs a chaperon here." She turned to him. "What does Mister Duggan think?"

"Mister Duggan thinks that whatever is congenial to Miss Marteyne is highly gratifying to him."

He escorted Ellen all the way down to the door on the bridge deck, immediately below where they had been sitting. Rose, meanwhile, sat in her capacious wicker chair, flipping through the script for *Don Giovanni,* which was all in Italian, and promising herself that she would definitely return first class on *Titanic.*

60

When Max described the plot of *Don Giovanni,* Rose said, "Once upon a time I almost married a man like that."

"What became of him?" Max asked.

"He met his match – in both senses of the word, I think."

"He could hardly have matched Don Juan, though. His manservant, Leporello, lists his conquests as six hundred and forty in Italy, two hundred and thirty-one in Germany, a hundred in France, ninety-one in Turkey, and in Spain – hark – one thousand and three!"

Rose looked him up and down critically. "You are simply not old enough to play this part, signior Leone!"

He laughed. "This is opera, Miss Marteyne – where Juliet may outweigh a dozen Romeos and everyone is happily amnesiac or blind when the plot demands it. Could you hear me through scene nine? Would that be a terrible bore?"

"Not at all." She turned over the pages to the appropriate place. "Fire away. I'll just read Zerlina's lines, shall I?"

He began: *"Alfin siam liberate, Zerlinetta gentil …"*

She interrupted: "Aren't you going to sing the part?"

"Here?" He glanced around the Palm Court. "No. It's just to be sure of the words."

"D'you understand them or d'you just know them by heart?"
"I don't speak much Italian but I know more or less what's being said in each scene." He continued with his almost toneless recitation of words that meant nothing to Rose.
When he came to Number Seven, the famous duet between the Don and Zerlina, she recognized the words, *Là'ci darem la mano* ... as the favourite bathtime duet of Signor Vignelli and Madame Devigny in the bed-sitters in Bedford Street. So when it came to Zerlina's lines – *Vorrei, e non vorrei* ... – she sang them quietly.
"You know it!" he cried.
"I know this bit." She explained how it came about. "I have no idea what they're saying, mind."
"Perhaps that's just as well. And just as well that your two operatic neighbours are in separate bathrooms, too! It's the Don up to his old tricks – trying to add yet another female to Leporello's list – even though Zerlina is on her way to the church to marry a peasant called Masetto."
"The Don obviously enjoyed a challenge!"
"Don't we all!" After a pause he added, "Look – shall we sing it together, then? We could go back up to the boat deck and sing to the winds."
"I warn you I have no singing voice," Rose told him, but she was already half way toward the stairs. "You'll have to tell me what's happening, otherwise I shan't know what expression to give it."
He explained the scene as they went. "The Don is obviously keen to seduce Zerlina, so he has invited the whole wedding party to his villa for a prenuptial celebration, and he's told Leporello to distract Masetto, the groom. Zerlina is in love with Masetto but she's also smitten with the Don's charm, his good looks, his easy manners. He tells her she was born for better things than the life of a peasant – and he can offer her them. She knows what he really wants and she tells him she's afraid he'll desert her afterwards. He says that's nonsense – a nobleman's honour is written on his face – come on – time's a-wasting, and so forth. And then comes the duet. He opens it by pointing to his villa and saying 'take my hand – *darem la mano.*' She sings an aside, saying she'd like to but dares not. 'My heart is all a-flutter ... I know I'd be happy ... and yet he's such a deceiver!' He presses more ardently. *Vieni, mio bel diletto!* – Come, my dearest treasure!' She, still aside, sings that she's sorry for Masetto. *'Mi fa pietà Masetto!'* He says, 'I promise to change your destiny!' She: 'Quick then! I can resist you no longer!' And together they sing: 'Come! Come! O, my dearest! Together let us cure the pains of a chaste love.' And off they go, arm in arm, toward the villa."
"And to think it's as easy as that!" Rose said.
"It's the sublime music that does the trick," he replied. "The words are rubbish, chosen merely for their singable vowels – which is why it must be sung in Italian, of course."

By now they stood in the lee of the smoking-room dome, sandwiched between it and the aftermost lifeboat – alone, to all intents and purposes, in the vastness of the ocean.

"I don't have perfect pitch," he said after clearing his throat. "Do you?"

"I don't know. I've been taking singing lessons mainly to be able to project my voice to the back of the gods – and to preserve it when I sing in variety. But Madame Devigny sings it like this, I think." And she sang her first line, *"Vorrei e non vorrei ..."*

"That sounds close," he said. *"Bene* – ready? Here we go!"

They sang it right through, with Max la-la-ing the orchestral obbligatos. They finished by walking a little circle on the deck, arm-in-arm as the script required, before bursting out laughing. Rose felt so triumphant she wanted to hug him, but she was afraid it would be misunderstood; she sensed he was happy with their brief performance, too.

"D'you know," he said solemnly, "with only three or four years' more training you might be able to sing grand opera."

"Thank you *so* much!" She butted his shoulder with her forehead.

"Seriously," he assured her. "Your voice is sweet and pure – and you can certainly hit the notes and sing in key. But it's completely untrained at the moment ..."

"Completely?" she protested, thinking of the hours she'd spent in Shenstone Street, singing arpeggios until her tonsils ached.

"Well," he said condescendingly, "it's trained enough for the drawing room ..." His voice trailed off and a thoughtful look crept into his eyes.

"What?" she prompted.

He turned to her. His deep dark eyes seemed to gaze right into her. "Please feel absolutely free to say no to this, but it so happens that one of the American ladies who runs a charity for down-and-outs in Boston has asked me to give a recital tonight, in the reception room. For charity, of course – I'm not a ship's baritone, thank you very much! Would you consider singing this whole scene with me? She carries a lot of weight in Boston society."

Rose didn't care if the woman carried the weight of forty Juliets in Boston – not at that moment, anyway. Her heart leaped up at the prospect of singing this most sensuous of operatic duets with Mr Duggan; also she was beginning to feel so audience-starved that she had toyed with the idea of offering a free hour of song and comic monologue to the third class. "I only know the duet," she pointed out.

"That's no obstacle. We have several pianos. I can teach you the rest. It's all *recitativo,* which means you can sing in a monotone, almost. Are you a quick study?"

She took his arm and pointed him at the stairwell. "Try me!"

Within an hour she had the notes *and* the words – all thirty-two of the recitative, to add to the thirty-eight of the duet, which she already half-knew from eavesdropping on the aquatic duets in Bedford Street.

They sang it through twice. She would have welcomed a couple of times more but he was afraid of tiring her 'untrained' voice. She was somewhat chastened when he told her he didn't even consider his own voice fully trained as yet; he would happily sing Mozart and Handel, and some of the less-demanding roles in Verdi, but he wouldn't even *look* at Wagner for at least another couple of years. So Lord only knew where that put *her* along the scale between untrained and trained! All the same, she learned more about breathing and voice production during that rehearsal with Max than she had in six months of singing lessons in London.

"I must offer you a solo, too," he said – with slight reluctance, she thought. "It wouldn't be a very balanced programme if you just sang one duet. One of Moore's melodies – *The last rose of summer,* perhaps? Or *Plaisirs d'amour?"*

"I know both of those," she said brightly, remembering her weekend with Louis. If she sang them in his honour, it would make her feel less treacherous now.

"Oh!" he replied. "Well, er ... sing them both, by all means. Please do."

"And *Home sweet home?"* she suggested.

But this time her smile gave her away.

"Come to think of it, Miss Marteyne," he said, "I'm *glad* you're not considering a career in opera. I must have been mad to encourage you."

"Actually, signior Leone," she said, "to be quite serious a moment – do you know songs like that? *Home sweet home ... Dear old pals ... The road to Mandalay?"*

"Why d'you ask?" He eyed her suspiciously.

"And could you make up harmonies to them on the spot – without the notes in front of you, I mean?"

"I still want to know why."

"Because don't you think it would rather jolly if tomorrow – on the last night of the voyage – we gave the third class a bit of a free concert, too? I could do some comic monologues and we could sing duets and a few solos each. Does that enigmatic look mean yes or no?"

He smiled ruefully. "This enigmatic look means I'm recalling my agent's parting words to me. 'You've been overdoing things lately, Max,' he said. 'This week of enforced rest on the *Olympic* will do you more good than a month in Bognor.' Little did he know!"

Rose frowned. "But what was he thinking of? Bognor? Bognor's a theatrical *grave!* Everyone knows that."

Max sighed. "It's also a seaside resort – somewhere people go to *rest,* you know! Quite a few people know that, too."

"Oh yes. Oh! I see what he means now. Sorry."

61

Ellen tried to pretend she was being drawn away from her book only with the greatest reluctance; really, though, she could not wait to hear how the recital had gone. Rose was so full of excitement she could hardly get one sentence out before the next one cut across it, then the next, then the next …

"I never realized what a small, intimate audience can do … well, not all *that* small, actually … but by London-theatre standards … anyway, just about *everyone* was there because … it isn't actually very big – the lounge …"

"Stop!" Ellen cried. "The lounge. Begin with the lounge. Set the scene – properly now."

"Oh, well … um … light in colour … airy … about seventy feet wide and sixty long. It's amidships on the promenade deck. Louis Quinze decor – you know – fanciful cartouches, swags, and all that sort of thing. *Much* grander than ours. Decorations everywhere. And then, in the middle of the forrard wall is a shallow …"

"Bulkhead. Walls are called bulkheads."

"Good for them! Anyway, in the middle there's this shallow, curved recess for an *armoire-à-glace.* Floor-to-ceiling. Filled with books – most of them even more trivial than the ones in our library. I expect the third-class library is all Plato and Aristotle. So that's where Max placed the orchestra …"

"Max, is it? Already? I say!"

"We are colleagues. Sort of. We're going to do an entertainment in the third class tomorrow night."

"Finish with tonight first. Actually, come to think of it, you haven't even started yet."

"Give me a chance! So there's the orchestra – two violins, cello, bass, and piano – and Max and me in front. Me sitting demurely on a chair most of the time, because it's his recital, after all."

"Oh! So he did manage to wrest it back from you then!"

Rose stuck out her tongue and continued. "The place was packed, as I said. And talk about jewelry! Diamond tiaras and jeweled evening shoes and everything in between – brooches, pendants, earrings, bracelets, chokers. I was blinded. And some of the dresses must have cost four or five hundred pounds – honestly. Materials you'd never see outside Burlington Arcade or what's that place in Paris? Faubourg something."

"All right – it was like a first night in the presence of their majesties. Didn't you feel a frump in that old frock?"

Rose pulled a face. "I shan't tell you if you keep saying such things. Of course I didn't. I sparkled brighter than any of their gemstones. Anyway, I bought this in the Burlington Arcade. The funny thing is, to hear Max talk, you wouldn't think he had much of a singing voice. I mean, his everyday voice is pleasant enough, but the richness … the – what's the word? *Sonority!* The sonority he can put into it the moment he starts singing is just ..." She hunched her shoulders and shivered. "I just sat there – miserable – thinking what on earth am I doing here, singing on the same bill as this wonderful, glorious voice?"

"What did he sing?"

"A good mixture. Several songs by Handel ... *O Sleep! Why dost thou leave me?* A minute without drawing breath, I'd swear. Parry. Some Gilbert and Sullivan. *Drink to me only.* He claims his voice isn't ready for grand opera yet but he sang a number of solos from Verdi superbly. *Bada, di'l ver* and *Pari siamo* from *Rigoletto* and a drinking song from *Falstaff.* I'm sure he could do a full-length opera if he tried. All he needs is a bit more confidence."

"Oh, *do* give him some of yours, dear!" Ellen said. "I'm sure you can spare it."

"Mock on!" Rose said airily. "You don't get very far in our business without a surplus of it."

Ellen sighed. "Alas, 'tis true. What's your programme for tomorrow night in the third class?"

"Well, there's a lot of Irish emigrants down there, so I suggested some sentimental songs – *Danny Boy, Slievenamon,* and that one by Percy French, *Come back Paddy Riley to Ballyjamesduff,* to show his heart's in the right place. Then the arias from *Rigoletto* to show he doesn't scorn their culture and intelligence. And we can do the Mozart duet ..."

"Lucille?"

"What?"

"What has happened to you?"

"Nothing. I had a very successful evening in the ..."

"No! Not that. Don't you realize – you've described one recital in which you took part and now you're describing the plans for another – and so far you haven't mentioned your own part in either! Not once. It's all Max-Max-Max. It's so unlike the dear Lucille we all know and love." She grinned knowingly. "And now you're blushing!"

"I am *not!*"

"You are. Look at your ears in the mirror. If we had some bread we could make toast."

"Well ..." Rose, cornered, exclaimed. "He is rather ..." The right word eluded her.

"Alluring? Tempting?" Ellen offered.

"Isn't it rather bright in here?" Rose asked. She turned off the main cabin light and started to prepare for bed.

"Just about bright enough for reading," Ellen agreed; she was already in nightdress and dressing gown, ready for bed.

"Of course he's tempting," Rose said, unhitching her dress and stepping out of it. "A girl would need a heart of stone not to see that. The curious thing ..."

"Yes?"

"Can you unbutton me?" She presented her back to Ellen. It was easier to talk of certain things when you could hide your face. "The curious thing is that the moment I realized he was interested in one of us – I really thought it was you, actually – I thought *yes!* A brief flirtation which would inevitably be cut short when we dock in New York – that's just what I need. Especially if I'd be seeing Louis again within hours of landing. Where's the harm?"

"You mean to say it's no longer like that?" Ellen went on to unlace her stays.

"Wait! It's more complicated. Oh, bliss! Why do we wear these instruments of torture?" She went to the washbasin. Or set-bowl, as her mother would call it. *Oh, Mom! I wish you had the telephone because I'd squander a week's wages to talk to you from New York!*

"Complicated?" Ellen prompted her.

"Yes." She answered between bouts of soaping and swilling. "The moment he told us he'd be at the Grand Opera in Boston, I thought no! Absolutely not. Never. Have you looked it up? We're only four streets away from him."

Again, Ellen noticed, *he* was the reference point, not Lucille, who usually placed herself at the centre of any world she happened to occupy. "Therefore?" she said.

"Just so," Rose replied. "If a three-or four-day flirtation would be harmless, why not one lasting a mere three or four weeks? That was so-o-o tempting! Because, after all, Louis and I would be meeting in New York every Sunday."

"And he is very *taken* with you – signior Leone, I mean."

"I know. And I don't want to hurt him." She raised her hands to the vent, where warm air entered the cabin; it seemed to stick to her in eddies that ran pleasurably down her arms – though her fingers remained cool until they dried completely.

"Are you sure you would?" Ellen asked as she climbed the ladder to her bunk.

"What d'you mean?"

"Well ... obviously you'd hurt one of them but are you sure it would be Leone?"

Rose held up her nightdress and let it fall down over her. "When I think of Louis," she said, "remembering that wonderful weekend we were together ... remembering how *perfectly* suited we were – and are – then, of course, I'm sure it would be Max I'd have to disappoint. But when I'm with Max, when he's near me ... oh God! It's actually in my *flesh,* you know. When we're standing side-by-side, singing that duet from *Don Giovanni,* every bit of me that's nearest to him seems to glow ..."

"And that never happened with Louis?"

"Yes! It did, too! That's precisely why it's so hard to choose. I'm hopeless, aren't I!" She laughed bleakly. "That duet, you know ... it's very like our real-life situation, at least as far as I'm concerned. Max isn't remotely like the Don – except when he's singing the part. Then I think, 'Yes, this could be you!' But there's a point, when he has successfully persuaded Zerlina to go into his villa with him – for you-know-what! And she sings, *Mi fa pietà Masetto* – I pity Masetto, who is her would-be husband. And I can't help thinking *Mi fa pietà Louis!* Isn't that just awful?"

"Theatre people often marry each other because they have the same hours," Ellen said.

"I know. And I always planned to give up the stage when I married Louis. But now I don't know that I could. What does *Mister* Patrick Campbell do?"

"Tolerates *her* profession, mostly. D'you think Louis would?"

"It never arose, but he hasn't objected since. You see, the *only* thing that makes me hesitate about Louis is that he doesn't tell me anything about his business here – just that it's going well. Vague things like that. I tell him everything – except I haven't told him I'm coming to America. I want to see his face when he realizes it really is me."

"Why should his vagueness concern you? It doesn't even strike me as odd. Most men wouldn't bore their wives with talk about their business."

Rose's reply was punctuated with the brushing and swilling of her teeth. "It's just that ... oh dear, it sounds dreadful, but I just think he's being evasive. I suspect it's not going as well as he says – or gives the impression it is. Which, in turn, suggests he doesn't trust me – as if he thinks I'd jilt him, abandon him."

"And wouldn't you?"

"Not if he were straight with me – which I'm sure he is being." She climbed between her sheets and added, "I'm sure all these fears are groundless."

"And if they're not?" Ellen asked.

"The other thing is – am I deceiving *myself?* Am I deliberately keeping my love for Louis alive just because he's so far off and can't get in the way of my career. I mean, I daydream about him every night before I drop off to sleep ... and go through all the time-honoured emotions. But if I'm being brutally honest, I have to admit it's a-a-a-awful convenient having him three thousand miles away."

"A-a-awful convenient?" Ellen imitated her. "Do you switch to American once we're past the half-way line?"

"Sorry!" Rose laughed. "I was thinking of my mother just now. Anyway, I couldn't have done half the things I have done this past year if he'd always been around. So ... these feelings I have about Max – are they some kind of proof that Louis has become just a convenient love? Have my feelings found me out at last, and are they making me pay this price?"

"You'll know soon enough." Ellen did her best to stifle a yawn.

"Yes," Rose agreed. "Soon enough is true."

62

The Pennsylvania Railroad Depot was the grandest building Rose had ever seen, and certainly the grandest she had ever entered. Its vast façade on Seventh Avenue was like four British Museums, side-by-side. Even so, it gave no hint of the grandeur that lay within. A vestibule led to a lofty arcade which, in turn opened into a vast marbled space in which even the smallest semicircular arch was massive enough to dwarf a man. Two ranks of ornate lamp-posts, which would have seemed in scale with any street lighting outside, reached no more than a fifth of the way to the high vaulted ceiling. A thousand tall men could have stood there, swinging cats without hitting a neighbour. And even so, there was grander yet to come.

Sweeping marble steps led up to a vast concourse, the length of three city blocks. Suddenly the passenger on her way to her train was no longer in some epic vision of Ancient Rome, for here was a light and airy Crystal Palace of glass and steel. One Crystal Palace? No – eight! Seven running parallel, shoulder to shoulder down the tracks, and one laid at right angles, across the middle; and all supported on columns of steel latticework so slender that you'd wonder the pounding of the trains had not already shaken them to pieces. Though the platforms and concourse were swept as clean as any public space can be where thousands pass to and fro each day, the walls and roof were rather dirty; glass lights and coal-burning locomotives are not ideally made for each other. Still, Rose thought, it was no worse than any of London's main termini.

She was in good time for the train to Philadelphia, which would carry her as far as Trenton, some sixty miles down the track. It left at five-fifteen from from platform eight and, since New Year's Day was a holiday in America – unlike England – the place was hardly busy. The ticket inspector asked her if she was travelling alone and, on learning that she was, he passed her into the care of the conductor, a smiling black man with a face like burnished ebony; he was to warn her in plenty of time, so that she wouldn't miss the stop at 'Tren'n,' as he called it.

Rose thought back over all the uninvigilated journeys she had made since leaving Cornwall – to Paddington and back a couple of times, to Morecambe ... it was a wonder she had survived them without the vigilance of a man in uniform! And what about flying all the way back from Morecambe to London with Sozzler Knox? She sat in the train, waiting for it to leave, and recalled that dreadful, wonderful flight to Hendon airfield, north of London. Though it had been a nightmare at the time, it was quite amusing to look back on now. They'd had to keep a lookout for stubble fields where they could land and refill the petrol tank. About six times. And then there was the time when they flew into cloud and when they came out into the clear again, they'd lost the railway line they'd been following. And then they saw this city up ahead and Sozzler had shouted, very confidently, "Wolverhampton. We won't be home by dark." And Rose had shouted back, "It's got a hell of a lot of dreaming spires for Wolverhampton!" And he'd looked again and cried, "You're right! We'll be back in time for tea!" A laugh would have spoiled it. She missed Sozzler. They shared the same sense of humour and there weren't too many others who did. If he and she could do a musical comedy together, people would see that he could act as well as do his own, highly original variety turn. She could probably ask for quite a big rise in salary if this American tour went off well. Max's mention of his agent prompted her to think that she ought to get one for herself. However, she'd even take quite a cut in salary if that were the only way of working with Sozzler.

At that point her thoughts came crashing to a guilty halt. They were hardly the thoughts of a dedicated fiancée who was only working on the stage in order to help her beloved out of a financial hole – the very man she'd be taking by surprise in ... she checked her watch ... less than two hours from now!

As if responding to her thought the train began to ease its way out of the station. A last minute passenger, a tall, good-looking woman in her forties, came bustling into the car and settled herself with a flustered sigh, diagonally across from Rose. She grinned and raked the ceiling with her gaze. Rose, not in the mood for an hour of conversation with a stranger, smiled vaguely back and turned to stare out of the window.

They did not pick up speed until they were across the Hudson. They emerged from the tunnel into canyons of brick and concrete, already blackened with soot even though this stretch of the line had been opened less than two years. At Newark, ten miles down the line, she looked out for the breweries mentioned in her Baedeker, so that she'd have something to compare Louis' new premises with; she saw two, both dauntingly large. No wonder Louis was having an uphill struggle – if, indeed, that was the reason for his reticence.

The landscape between towns lay under a deep blanket of snow. It was certainly very flat. Any small slope was more likely to be a river valley than a hill. And for long stretches there was not a hill in sight. Here and there the wind had thinned the snow cover to a few inches, where clumps of sedge-like grass mottled the fields; it looked like a land of cold, wet soil.

On through Elizabeth and Rahway they sped, unimpeded by gradients. Rahway was a strange name. The conductor, when he came to check on her, said it derived from 'rocks away' because they hauled a whole mess of stone from there once; after he'd gone by, the woman sitting across from her said that was nonsense. It was originally Jahweh, like the God of the Hebrews. Rose said it was odd that in a country so young such things could be so soon forgotten and confused. "Shoot!" the woman replied. "Ain't it so even in your own life? It sure is in mine! You start in with one set of aims. You don't make it – you make something else instead. So you look back and tell yourself that's what you really meant all along. Me, I took center-aim at a deaconate and here I am, a fulltime campaigner for the female vote." She grinned. " 'Course, it's what I *really* wanted all along – so I tell me. You're English?"

"Cornish."

" 'Aint that England?"

"Only because we're so small. If we were bigger, we'd be the same as the Irish."

"Your time will come, honey. So will Ireland's. You'll be next. Where the big lead, the small will follow – America, Ireland, Cornwall. It's in the stars."

Rose thought she'd have made a good deaconess; she radiated confidence and certainty. "How is the suffrage movement going here?" she asked.

"We got Wyoming way back. This year we're looking to Arizona and Kansas and maybe Wisconsin. Then it'll be like bowling pins."

"We had riots in London last November. It's getting very bitter on both sides. They're force-feeding them in prison. Someone will die before too long. Then it'll be like a war."

"And are you an enlisted woman?"

Rose shifted uncomfortably. "I believe I can do more on the stage than in the streets. I do satires aimed against the ruling class. I'm Lucille Marteyne, by the way."

"Sophie Graham. Married and happily divorced." They shook hands and the woman moved to sit opposite. "I'm headed for Washington, else I'd catch your act in Trenton."

"Oh!" Rose laughed awkwardly. "It's not a *stage* act I'm heading for there. In fact, it's not an act at all – I don't know why I said that. The truth is – I'm going to surprise my fiancé. But the closer we get to Trenton, the more nervous I find myself becoming."

"How long has it been?"

"One year, six months, thirteen days."

"Someone's been counting! D'you reckon he has, too?"

"He writes pretty regularly – several times a week. Only ..." She hesitated.

"Uh hunh?" Mrs Graham arched her eyebrows.

Rose explained how Louis never said much about the progress of his business, and all the misgivings she had about it.

"Men were ever deceivers," the woman said.

"Women don't lag far behind," Rose countered.

"Speaking from personal experience?"

"Personal experience of daydreams – so far, anyway."

"Uh hunh. You wanna find out something about your beau before you spring this little surprise on him, right?"

"I guess so." Rose eyed her hopefully.

"Where are you staying in Trenton? I'd recommend the Windsor, at three dollars a night. Or one dollar if you just want the room. Oh!" She pointed out the window. "This is Menlo Park, by the way, former home of Thomas Edison. My sister says inventors like him will do more to liberate women than all the political campaigners in the world. She could be right. Look what the typewriter and telephone have done already. What was I saying? Oh yes! The clerk at the Windsor is called Elmer McKenna. He's a cousin to my brother-in-law, Tom McKenna, the husband of the sister I just told you about. So you can mention me and tell him it's okay for him to wise you up on everything he knows about your Mister Redmile-Smith. And if he knows nothing, then there ain't no Redmile-Smith in Trenton."

Rose suddenly felt as if a great weight had been lifted from her. Her biggest worry had been how to discover as much as possible about Louis and his venture before springing her surprise – just in case it wouldn't be all that happy.

"I know I ought to trust him when he says everything is going well," she sighed. "It's just the lack of detail."

"No, you're doing absolutely the right thing, honey," the woman assured her.

"Also, you know, men have such *fun* building up a business ... battling their way in the world ... making their own empires, big or small ... a long engagement isn't such a dreadful thing to them. I *know,* because I'm doing the same with my own life. But if I were pining away at home like most women, waiting for *him* to decide the time is ripe, I'd be a gibbering loony by now."

"Surely!" Mrs Graham agreed. "Also" – she eyed Rose uncertainly – "there's a whole passel o' females makes a living out of helping such men to postpone the day without feeling the burden too hard, if you know what I mean?"

"I don't even think of that," Rose told her. "There's no point."

"Mebbe you're wise," the woman conceded.

The conversation drifted away from those uncomfortable regions and for the next half-hour or so, from New Brunswick through Princeton Junction to Trenton, Rose told Mrs Graham how she'd gone from lady's maid to wardrobe mistress to strolling player to leading parts in London productions – with a handy little side career in vaudeville.

The woman was enthralled. "Hark now, honey," she said when the collector told her they were approaching Trenton. "You sniff a rat down here and you just turn tail and head straight back to New York. Or Boston. Wherever. You've got a great life ahead of you, without the help of any man."

Rose thanked her for all her help and advice though privately she resented the last installment. If she discovered Louis had been deceiving her, she'd probably turn around without seeing him; but now it would feel as if she were doing it at Mrs Graham's behest.

63 Rose left her overnight bags at the station, just in case Louis had a better idea; there might even be a room to spare at his lodgings in Lawrenceville Road. The Newton Hôtel was a short cab-ride away through streets banked with shovelled snowdrifts. Trenton, best known as the state capital, was also the centre of New Jersey's pottery industry; smoke and soot were its second atmosphere. The Newton looked as if it had once been a gentleman's country house, maybe even in colonial days. If so, it had stood through the siege in which George Washington and his band of farmers had defeated first the Hessian mercenaries and then Lord Cornwallis himself, backed by the mighty British army. Admittedly, Rose had been in the country less than twenty-four hours – and had gone directly from Pier 48 to the Penn Depot – but this was the first place that seemed to her to carry any real sense of history.

It ceased the moment she went into the foyer, which had obviously been completely remodelled – and recently at that – with heavy and over-elaborate furnishings and decoration.

"Mister McKenna? Mister Elmer McKenna?" She approached the clerk at the desk.

"At your service, lady." He checked her up and down and obviously decided she was respectable, despite her lack of luggage. "We got four rooms left at three dollars, and ..."

She interrupted. "A question first, if you please." Suddenly she was shivering like a leaf. "I travelled as far as Trenton with your sister-in-law – I mean your *cousin's* sister-in-law, Mrs Sophie ..."

"Sophie!" He laughed. "Off to pull a few more Washington beards, I guess."

"That seemed to be the idea. Anyway, she sends her regards and says to tell you it's okay to let me know everything *you* know about a man called Louis Redmile-Smith."

He became grave at once and, tilting his head judiciously, said, "Hardest working man this town ever saw – one of 'em, anyways."

Her heart leaped up at the words. Surely after such praise there could be little to his discredit?

He misread her nervous hesitation and added, "You don't believe me? Go look for yourself." He jerked a thumb toward a door to her right. "He's in the bar right now. *Serving!*"

Her spirits fell again at these words, which put his earlier praise – 'hardest working man' – in a new context. But the stress he laid on the word 'serving' puzzled her. Someone else approached him and started a conversation, leaving her no choice but to 'go look for herself,' as he had suggested. The door was of a kind she was to see in many establishments in America: a pair of half-doors, or what she would have called 'hepps doors' in Cornwall – on two-way spring hinges, designed to let a waiter see if anyone was coming before he backed between them with a full tray. One of them did so as she approached it, carrying down a tray full of empty bottles and glasses from upstairs. It gave her an intimidating glimpse of a room full of men – laughing, drinking, and smoking. She opened one of the doors, just a crack, to see if there was another woman anywhere inside. She opened the other and checked that side, too.

Not one.

Still not venturing within, she turned her attention to the bar. It was Louis all right – just his face visible every now and then as other heads passed to and fro between him and her. That dear face on whose memory she had lavished so many sighs and tears over the past eighteen months and thirteen days. There he was – smiling, laughing, listening, fitting his every mood to that of his present customer – and *serving drinks!* His brilliant new career, which was advancing so splendidly, was that of barkeep!

She drifted away from the door into a corner of the foyer. She glanced toward the clerk but he was still occupied with the same gentleman. She settled completely out of his sight, behind a shallow partition, and tried to think what to do next. Her instinct was to run to her lover at once and tell him it didn't matter that he'd been less successful than he'd hoped – she could more than make up for it. They could get married, go back to London, and he could be her agent! Didn't she say she needed one? Who better? It all fitted perfectly.

But then she began to ask herself if she thought it really didn't matter – all the obvious lies he'd been telling her in his letters? They didn't matter? And anyway, what would it do for his pride to live off her earnings? Would he ever believe that offering him the position of agent was anything other than mere window dressing to disguise his true status as a kept man?

She was at war with herself. Every particle of her body ached to be in his arms again – and devil take all those nice feelings and calculations. She loved him with all her heart, all her body, all her soul. Nothing could come between them, surely – certainly not such worldly calculations as those. Love conquers all! What had Mom said when she first mentioned Louis to her parents? 'Love is the most important thing in anybody's life, honey. It doesn't just laugh at locksmiths, you know – it laughs at everything that stands in its way, and that includes class and social convention. You see a gap – you go for it!' Something like that. Well ... here was the test, and she was failing it.

And yet, the more she thought about it, the angrier she grew that he could deceive her so cruelly. She had more or less forced this American tour on H-d-W, who, if he hadn't been afraid of losing her to rivals before the Frivoli opened this coming spring, would never have taken the risk. It was a risk for her, too – to be out of the West End for a couple of months when her career there was less than a year old. She had done all this so as to prepare a nice surprise to spring on Louis – and he had ruined it with his duplicity and lies.

She'd have to go away and think it over. Maybe she'd come back. She'd write to him. Or perhaps a period without any communication between them wouldn't be such a bad thing. He must already be wondering where all her letters for this week were. Soon he'd wonder why the ones that were piling up in Bedford Street weren't being answered, either. It was all too much. The best thing to do now, though, was to go away and try to think straight when this shock had died down.

Slowly she rose and went back to the clerk.

"Dja see him?" the man asked.

"Somebody must have given me the wrong name ..."

"They gave you Redmile-Smith as a wrong name? Wow! They were taking a risk. Everybody knows him round here."

I'll just bet they do, she thought. *My pal Louis – the friendliest barkeep in town!* She drew out a twenty-dollar bill and passed it to him. "I wasn't here today," she said. "You didn't see me. You don't know my name. And ..."

"Well, that at least is true," he pointed out.

"Good. You can't recall a single thing about me." Disconsolate, she drifted out into the dark, where, at last, the tears began to flow. "Oh, Louis!" she whispered to the indifferent lamp-posts and snowbanks. "Louis! Louis! My dearest darling! It could have been so wonderful if only you had been *honest!* Where shall I turn for comfort now?"

64

Ellen took one look at Rose's face and said, "Oh, dear!"

"I don't want to talk about it," Rose told her.

"There are half a dozen messages for you, down at the stage door. Most of them from signior Leone."

"Oh God! Throw them away. I'm through with men. Finished. From now on I shall live for my art. When is this rehearsal?"

"In half an hour. You cut it pretty fine, I must say. Full dress – straight through."

"Including make-up?"

"Well, darling, any actress *totally* dedicated to her art wouldn't even ask! What happened, anyway?"

They both started to prepare for this their first and last rehearsal on American soil. "I said I don't want to talk about it," Rose replied. "The *duplicity* of the man! All those letters telling me how well things were going! Why did I waste space bringing them?"

"Dear me! Can I borrow some of your ... thanks. Was he begging on the streets or what?"

"Something almost as bad. I don't even want to think about it. He was serving behind a bar – a *barkeep!* Pouring whiskies and chasers with a smile as wide as ... as the Delaware. I'd rather not say any more. I've forgotten the first Act – am I tragic or cheerful?"

"You start cheerful and end up miserable. Tragedy isn't until the third Act."

"That's my own biography, come to think of it! If only he'd had the honesty to admit ... aargh! I've finished with him so it doesn't matter now. Do I coil my hair this way? Or this? Lord – two weeks away and it's all gone out of my mind. I think *I* must be going out of my mind."

"It'll all come back the minute the curtain goes up – you'll see. And no matter what troubles you have beyond the stage door – parents dying, bailiffs hovering, stage-door johnnies jostling – they all cease to exist."

"The Grimaldi thing, eh? Tell me – why can't a man accept being kept by his wife? Wives have no difficulty with being kept by a husband. Why is 'breadwinner' thought to be an exclusively masculine noun?"

"You put it to him and he turned it down? D'you think I've overdone the powder?"

"It depends on the lighting. I shouldn't think so. Actually, I didn't even speak to him. I was so outraged."

Ellen was silent following this admission.

"Well?" Rose prompted.

"Well what?"

"Why can't we be the breadwinners?"

"You didn't even *speak* to him?" Ellen asked quietly.

"I told you. I was so angry ... and disappointed ... and bitter."

Ellen cleared her throat diffidently. "He could have been the owner of the bar, you know – standing in for someone who didn't turn up, or was at a funeral or something."

"It was a bar in an hôtel." Rose had a terrible sinking feeling now.

"Worse and worse! He could own the entire hôtel. His brewery or whatever could own it."

"No." Rose was regaining her confidence. "The clerk said something about Louis being the hardest worker they'd ever had – and he wasn't being facetious, the way a man would be if he were talking about his boss. I'd swear it. He meant *worker,* as in barkeep."

"If you say so, darling. What's Louis going to think when he hears you came and went without a word?"

"I took care of that – I hope. Anyway, as I said, it's something I'd rather not discuss, even with you."

"Well ..." Ellen shrugged. "I'm beginning to understand why!"

After a frosty silence Rose said, "What was that supposed to mean?"

"What I said. If I'd done the same as you – and left *undone* the same loose ends as you – I'd want to keep pretty quiet about it, too. Certainly until next Sunday."

"And then?"

"Then I'd be on the first train to New York and the first one out to Trenton – just to make sure I hadn't got the wrong end of every stick in the town."

"You weren't there," Rose told her. "If you had been, your intuition would have told you exactly the same as mine told me. It's over and done with and I'm not looking back."

65

It was a poor dress rehearsal, scrappy, full of false starts and bad timing. No one was very good but Rose was among the worst. Marcus Turpin, their London producer, who had come over with them to start them off in Boston, even gave up his sarcasm after a while – telling Rose she wasn't supposed to act this badly until much later in the play. When they were practising the order of their curtain calls he threw a bag of stale buns he'd found under one of the seats at them, one by one. Rose started to duck and run but Conrad Laughton caught her wrist and held her back. "We shall stand shoulder-to-shoulder until he runs out of ammunition!" he boomed.

Had he known what verbal ammunition was to follow, he might not have been so brave. Rose herself was mortified, of course, and full of apologies, and yet not terrified – as she would have been only six months earlier. She might sneer, in a mildly dismissive fashion, at 'the Grimaldi effect' – named after the famous clown of Regency days who kept all London in fits of laughter though he himself was eternally morose and depressed – but she knew its power, which was the power of an audience to make an artist forget his or her woes and entertain the customers instead. Its other name was, 'It'll be all right on the night.'

And so it proved. Their disastrous dress rehearsal had jolted the entire company, and especially Rose, on whom so many of the scenes depended. Their first-night nerves were tense to breaking point; their performance was therefore electric and the audience was enraptured; everyone backstage could feel it. The following day the *Boston Globe* noted that many English theatrical companies did not deserve the cachet accorded to them by an uncritical American public but the cast of *Trelawny* was 'an honorable exception.' They singled out Rose and Conrad Laughton for especial praise.

The *Herald* commented on the creakiness of the plot and its unpalatable assumption that a successful actress would be so eager to give up her career in order to marry a minor booby; but it urged its readers to flock to the Castle Square Theatre, where they would find their disbelief and distaste wonderfully suspended for a couple of hours.

"There's something about critics, isn't there," Rose remarked to Ellen as they read their reviews at the theatre the following morning. "They've always got to have a 'but' in there somewhere. I swear they'd rather own up to some disease not mentioned in polite society than to whole-hearted enjoyment of anything."

They left the theatre, intending to walk up Ferdinand and Columbus to Park Square where they could catch one of the Seeing Boston observation cars. Immediately outside the door they found Max Duggan waiting at the kerbside in a big, gleaming Daimler. He looked like a millionaire. Rose wondered if he was. His astrakhan collar was even wider than H-d-W's. "Allow me to show you off to the city of Boston, ladies!" he cried, leaping out upon the sidewalk. His chauffeur bent and gave the handle one turn, at which, of course, the well-bred machine started. Rose and Ellen exchanged glances. "How's your resolve *now?"* Ellen asked.

"The wheels fell off," Rose replied as she accepted Max's help. To him she said, "I saw them loading this at Southampton."

"I'm glad someone did," he replied, helping Ellen in after her. "For my part, I didn't dare look."

He himself sat in the front and turned half about to face them, saying, "Whither away, O damsels fair?"

"Bunker Hill," Rose replied at once.

He was surprised. "The site of one of our country's more ignoble defeats at the hands of colonial bumpkins?"

"It just happens to be the place from which you can see the whole city spread out ..."

"Like a *map!"* Ellen interrupted. "You and your maps!"

"Head north," Max told his chauffeur.

"I hate being lost," Rose explained. "I like to know where I am and what's round the next corner at all times. Actually, if you turn left up ahead, you'll get to Park Square and from there you can just follow the electric lines of the Seeing Boston cars."

The chauffeur looked at Max, who merely nodded. "You're no explorer, then?" he said to Rose.

"What is an explorer?" she replied.

"Marco Polo? Christopher Columbus?"

"Marco Polo's discoveries weren't news to several hundred million Chinese, were they! Nor were Columbus's to the American Indians. If there had been a good postal service in those days, they needn't have stirred an inch."

"It's no use arguing with her," Ellen warned Max. "She always has a ready answer. Oh look! What a pretty park!" Her attempted diversion was futile, though. What Ellen called argument was, to Max and Rose, a subtle continuation of the flirtation that had started during the duet from *Don Giovanni* – with the difference that Rose's heart was no longer promised away.

Max was quick to notice the change in her. Before they were half way to Bunker Hill, following the streetcar lines up Fremont and through Stoflay Square, he was asking her if acts of exploration could still exist, since she seemed to be claiming that all explorers were extinct. "Could a singer and an accompanist, for instance, *explore* different approaches to a ballad?" he asked. "Could an actor and actress *explore* a novel portrayal of lovemaking upon the stage?" Rose said she thought they might – and yet, if they got lost, who would play Stanley to their Livingstone and go in search of them?

"So?" he asked. "You will *permit* some forms of exploration?" And he was a while before adding, "To exist, I mean?"

"Anything that does not interfere with my career is permitted," she replied; she, too, paused before she added, "To exist, I mean."

He came back: "Then let me see if I read your intentions correctly. Two people must be involved in the activity – whatever it may be – and it must be possible for them to get lost in it? Such is the sort of cooperation you will permit? To exist, that is."

"What d'you think, Ellen?" Rose asked innocently. "As long as it doesn't interfere with takings at the box office, I say 'Explore away!' Don't you?"

"I take a more personal view," Ellen replied. "I say as long as it doesn't interfere with my figure – explore away!"

"And yet, Miss Marteyne, it seems to conflict with your need to know where you are at all times," Max pointed out.

Rose drew breath to reply but Ellen got in first. "Miss Marteyne is a bundle of contradictions, signior Leone. I think she would most love to be a world-famous hermit, or a millionairess living in a charcoal burner's cottage in some remote Cornish forest."

"There's no such thing!" Rose said, laughing.

"My point exactly," Ellen responded.

"And do these contradictions reveal themselves when she is upon the stage?" he asked. "I have seen her myself, of course, and have my own opinion – but I should welcome yours, Miss Howe."

"Par excellence, signior. One minute she is holding an audience at the Kingsway spellbound with the simultaneous portrayal of chalk and cheese. Ten minutes later, on the stage of the Holborn Empire, she has them in fits with the simultaneous portrayal of Lady Augusta Vane-Trumpington and her maid. In July she has the Saint James's audience in tears of tenderness at Rose Trelawny's predicament. In August she has the seaside crowds in Morecambe in tears of laughter at Lady Augusta's vanities." Turning to Rose, and still pretending that this was a light and frivolous conversation, she added, "And yet there is *no map* to connect these two territories – much less to describe the roads between them."

Max turned to Rose; his expression was solemn but his eyes sparkled with merriment. "Dear me, Miss Marteyne! For a young lady who insists on knowing exactly where she stands, you do seem to go out of your way to confound yourself!"

"Miss Howe's mistake," Rose replied calmly, directly to Ellen, "is to call them 'territories' when, as we all know, they are just people. People-here or people-there. To put it bluntly – they are backsides on benches. Without the steady clink of silver and gold, these so-called 'territories' would evaporate. And when even my dearest colleagues, for whom I have the greatest affection, try to tell me that my working in variety will harm my reputation as a tragic actress, my answer is the same as Sozzler Knox's when he refuses managements' requests to be more orthodox – 'Buy a ticket – *if you can!*' When the complimentaries for my shows begin to infiltrate the front stalls, *then* I'll mend my ways."

Ellen made a hopeless gesture. "What do you think, signior Leone? Could you sing in *Naughty Marietta* one season and *Il Seraglio* the next?"

Max looked from one to the other, several times, before saying, "This is the judgment of Solomon! All I can say is that, while my diary is full for the next two years, I feel no need to consider musical comedy – yet I cannot say I would turn down any serious proposal to appear in one." These last words he spoke directly to Rose, who said, "Nor would I."

"Bunker Hill, sir," said the chauffeur. "It's Shanks's pony from here on."

"Were the Americans on the heights and the English attacking – or the other way round?" Ellen asked as they walked up the hillside to the monument.

Nobody knew, but either way they didn't envy the attackers who fought their way up such a slope.

"Mesdemoiselles – je vous donne Boston!" Max turned and waved a theatrical arm over the panorama before them.

"It was worth fighting for," Ellen said.

"It will do to be going on with," Rose murmured. "And I'll bet that's what George Washington said of it, too."

"You're not falling for him, are you?" Ellen asked as they made up for that afternoon's matinée, back at the theatre.

"I'm not falling for anyone ever again," Rose replied. "Love and this kind of life cannot be mixed."

"You're just saying that because of the shock you got down in Trenton. I still think you've made a huge mistake there. Everything you've ever told me about Louis suggests he'd never ..."

"About *whom?*"

Ellen sighed and gave up that line of argument. "Plenty of people find that love and a life on the stage are perfectly compatible with ..."

"Love is for settled people, not for nomads like us. Actors and actresses who are *settled* on the stage – yes, all right, love is possible for them. But not for us. I think that even if I hadn't caught Louis out ..."

"Which you *haven't!*"

"Well, we've been over that a score of times. Let's just agree to differ. As I was about to say – even if I hadn't got that shock in Trenton, I'd almost certainly have broken it off with Louis during this American tour. I used to think how wonderful it would be to whiz down to New York each Sunday and spend the whole day with him, but even then, part of me dreaded the strains it was going to reveal. And then saying goodbye again. And another year in London, 'sighing my heart toward the Syrian tents'! Maybe two years. Getting deeper and deeper into a way of life he couldn't possibly understand – because you have to be honest here and admit that no one outside our profession can possibly understand its fascination and the power it exercises over our very souls."

"And meeting exciting men like Max Duggan!"

"I'm not denying it. All I'm saying is that I'm not going to fall in love with him."

Ellen stopped applying her make-up and turned to stare. "Are you saying you've found some magic way of making sure it never happens to you."

Rose continued making up, speaking through small clouds of powder. "It's not magic, darling. You just drift with the current until it starts feeling dangerous, and then you say stop."

"Just like that!"

"Just like that. It's a simple matter of willpower, that's all."

66

When a couple of weeks' worth of back letters from Louis arrived in Boston, toward the middle of *Trelawny's* three-week run, Rose finally plucked up the courage to write. Ever since Trenton she had known it was the least she owed him, but each day, as she squared herself to the task, she faltered and backed away from it. A bundle of nine unopened letters, however, was more than she could face without responding. She wrote:

Dearest Louis,
At least you will always be that to me, one of the dearest men I have ever known and am ever likely to know. There is no easy way to write this letter. My heart rebels at it and every emotional fibre of my being cries <u>No!</u> But still I must. When I embraced this vagabond life on the stage, it was with the sole object of earning enough not to be a drag upon your finances in the condition they then were. I had no idea what I was really letting myself in for. Your letters since then have spoken of steadily improving fortunes, which, through most of last year, gave me nothing but delight.

More recently, however, each optimistic phrase of yours has produced a parallel emotion. Beside my pleasure at hearing how well you are doing nowadays I have felt an increasing anxiety, mild at first but lately amounting to positive alarm. I was too busy to pay it much attention. Only the week-long respite while crossing the Atlantic gave me time to reflect, and then I realized that I was alarmed at the prospect that you would soon feel prosperous enough to 'take me away from all this.'

As I said before, I had no idea, when I first wheedled and machinated my way into the title role in *Leah,* what an all-consuming, all-demanding, all-satisfying taskmaster this theatre-life can be. Even more so than love itself. It would be so much easier to write this letter if some other man had entered my life and captured my heart; love is tender to its object and ruthless to all the world beside. But the stage, the play, the audience – that nameless, magical make-believe which unites all three – is more ruthless still. I know it now and am too deeply caught in it to struggle free.

I love you still. I think of your dear face and person every day. But I am in utter thrall to this business and cannot get free.

Can you see the irony of it all? You were not free to ask me to marry you (though I would have done so without a care in the world) until you had established yourself in a new business and could support me in a manner to which only my dreams were ever accustomed. And now our situation is practically reversed. I do not feel that freedom to forsake my new business, my career upon the stage, until I have established myself, too. And perhaps not even then, for that blissful state is many years away, and who can foretell her feelings over such a span of time?

In other words, I cannot in all conscience continue the implicit falsehood in every letter to pass between us (which once was the very truth), namely that I am only waiting for you to feel prosperous and secure enough before I say farewell to greasepaint and powder and wig. Much less can I expect you to wait until I tire of it. And there is no compromise, Louis darling. I could never be Mrs Louis Redmile-Smith, wife of the famous New Jersey brewer, who is also the leading lady in the Trenton Amateur Drama Guild and their twice-yearly productions.

You must be surprised to see this letter postmarked Boston. This American tour has been planned for weeks but I said nothing about it to you. I had intended riding down to Trenton one Sunday and taking you by surprise. But, having as I say thought things over during the voyage out here, I realized what dishonesty it would involve – unless I were heartless enough to make my surprise out of the things I say in this letter. So, though it breaks my heart to admit it, I have decided not to take that ride and not to risk overturning my decision to deny Lucinda-Ella Tremayne her dearest wish in favour of Lucille Marteyne's. The latter has the title role in *Trelawny, of the 'Wells',* which opens at the Belasco Theatre, Broadway and 42nd, on Tues. 27th Feb. The former will leave a ticket to a box in your name at the front of the house. If you are not utterly disgusted with her by then and wish to talk this over, she will be there for you.

With all the love I can ever hold for you or any man,

Rose

* * *

She read it over so many times she could have rattled it off by heart; and still she had her doubts. Eventually she showed it to Ellen, who read it through once and said, "Why don't you tell him the simple truth? You *did* go to Trenton. You saw him serving behind the bar. You concluded he must be a humble barman. You were too embarrassed by the contrast between your success and his failure – his *relative* failure – and so you crept away again."

By now Rose was regretting showing it to her at all. "What good would that do?" she snapped. "Rubbing his nose in it like that!"

Ellen continued calmly, "Then you could go on to say how much you regretted your hastiness ... that, rich or poor, you love him still ..." She paused. "Do I hear no denial?"

Rose sighed. "No denial. I realized when I sat down to write that I do love him still. Everything I tell him is true as far as that goes. But I also know it won't work."

"You're deciding that for him, are you?"

"For both of us. What you're *really* suggesting – what it boils down to – is that I should say to him, in effect, 'I know you haven't made much of a success of your new life but *I* have – swank-swank. So let me keep you as you would have kept me.' He wouldn't do it. And anyway, what sort of woman could admire a man who'd accept such a proposal?"

"He needn't be a parasite. He could become your agent."

So the same idea had occurred to Ellen, too.

"And if he were useless at it? That would be too much of a risk – to stake my heart *and* my career on a single man? I think not!"

"Are you resigned to the possibility that you'll *never* marry, then? Not *ever?*"

"Not at all. I might even marry quite soon – but not for love. I'd marry someone with an independent income – someone who wouldn't feel kept. In fact, he'd consider my income to be mere pin money for me ... the main thing is he'd be a good father for my children. And actually ..." A thoughtful look crept into her eye.

"What?" Ellen prompted.

"Oh ... nothing important," Rose assured her.

67

Once Rose had solved the 'problem' of Louis – to her own satisfaction at least – the remainder of *Trelawny's* Boston run simply flew by for her. She began to appreciate the advantages of touring. When a play moved into a city theatre for an indefinite run, it rarely played to full houses after the first week or two. People could put off going to see it for the most trivial reasons, confident they could catch it next week, or the next. On a tour, by contrast, they knew they had only a limited time, and there was no certainty they might catch it next week because it might be fully booked. In fact, if the reviews were good, the houses were almost always sold out.

It was especially so for a London company performing in America. Of all the surprises America sprang upon her, it was the greatest – that this brash, thrusting, self-confident country should hold the *English* theatre in such veneration. No self-respecting American actor would speak the great classical roles in his native accent; he would have been laughed off the stage if he had tried it. When Rose remarked upon it, people told her it was the same in what they called 'high society" – among the upper two thousand. "They think an English accent proves they came over on the *Mayflower,"* one fellow explained. Whether or not that was the reason, she noticed a marked lack of the drawl and the hard r-sounds among the dandies who were privileged to enter her dressing room and to take her out to dine.

Her most constant escort, however, was Max, who only had three nights a week in *Don Giovanni.* Tongues began to wag but she didn't care; she was now in absolute control of her own life and destiny. Make or break, she was the maker or the breaker.

"Ellen says people are talking," she told him one evening toward the end of their run. "We're seen too often together."

"She's welcome to join us," he offered.

They were dining in the German Café in the basement of the Hôtel Touraine, a favourite after-theatre resort.

Rose laughed. "That's not what she's fishing for. Isn't it strange – if I dine out with a different stage-door Johnny each evening, people assume that nothing could possibly be going on. We're like ambassadors whose hospitality, given or received, carries no personal meaning. But if one ambassador were seen dining out with a particular colleague several nights a week, people would soon say, 'Oh-oh! Something's up with those two.' That's us."

"And are they right?" he asked. "In our case, I mean." His tone was casual but his attitude was tense.

"You know it can't be, Max. You scooting off to Milan, Vienna, Berlin, New York ... Rio ... all the time. And me in London, America, anywhere in the empire. What sort of marriage would that be?"

"Marriage?" he asked in a shocked tone. "I wasn't actually thinking of *marriage."*

"Oh!" She pulled a face.

"More a question of gathering rosebuds while ye may. 'The grave's a fine and private place but none I think do there embrace' ... that sort of thing."

"*That* sort of thing," she echoed. "I'm still a little provincial servant girl at heart, aren't I!"

"You are whatever you feel you are. And you answer to no one but yourself – in private matters, anyway. That's my belief." He leaned forward and stared at her ardently; in the subfusc lighting his eyes were darkly intense. "Do you know the story of Selemnus?" he asked, and, without waiting for her reply, continued, "He was a shepherd of Achaea, in Ancient Greece, who had a love-affair with a sea-nymph called Argyra. But, as he grew older and less attractive, she tired of him and eventually came no more to his call. Alas, he could not forget her – not for one moment, day or night. He died of a broken heart. And even then he could not forget her. In fact, his lifeless corpse wept so many tears that the goddess Aphrodite took pity on him and turned him into a river, the River Selemnus – which flows in Greece to this very day. *Still* he could not forget her. And all who drank or bathed in the river waters were afflicted with the strange melancholy of an unrequited love. At last Aphrodite realized she had done only half a job, so she granted him the gift of total forgetfulness. And now all who are lovesick and who drink or bathe in the waters of Selemnus are miraculously cured."

After a pause Rose said, "It *would* take a miracle, I think."

"Like that, is it?"

She nodded.

After an emotional final night for *Trelawny* in Boston, they had two days free before opening at the Hyperion in New Haven. Since John Barrymore was giving his Hamlet at Wallack's Theater in New York, and since his Hamlet was reputed to be the best ever seen, many in the cast decided to spend the first free evening testing his reputation. He was then just into his thirties and at the height of his powers. All this was arranged days in advance. When Max heard that Rose was going, he joined the party.

It was not one of Barrymore's best evenings. Most of the public were probably unaware of it but the keener senses and long experience of the professionals told them that he had been liberally entertained somewhere in the city before going on stage that night. In the middle of the 'To be or not to be' soliloquy he walked – with the exquisite care of the controlled inebriate – to the prompt corner and hung upon the curtains, groaning and shaking.

"My God, he's planting a sweet pea!" Ellen whispered to Rose. "The audacity of the man!" Her tone was a curious mixture of outrage and admiration.

His final shiver was unequivocally the droplet shaker; however, all was decent again by the time he returned to his place and completed the soliloquy. Very few in the audience had twigged what they had just witnessed; for the most part they thought it a daring and brilliantly effective piece of acting. He received a standing ovation at the end. And Rose, even though she knew what had happened, found herself joining in as enthusiastically as any, for the man had an undeniable stage presence. He radiated some kind of hypnotic quality that held everyone spellbound.

Of course, none of the *Trelawny* cast would admit to it in the bar at the interval, but they had been enraptured, too. "He is quite dreadful," Conrad Laughton said. "I remember when poor Charley Frohman brought him to the Comedy, in London, back in oh-five, to play in *The Dictator* – does anyone know it? He played the part of the wireless operator who has to come on with a couple of pages of messages, which Willie Collier had to read out. It's the pivot-point of the whole plot. Without it the audience wouldn't make head nor tail of the action. So what does young Jack Barrymore do? He comes on with a teeny-tiny triangle of paper, about the size of those Cape of Good Hope stamps." He held finger and thumb about two inches apart. "And poor Willie is expected to speak about ten minutes of dialogue – reading off an alleged wireless message, this big!"

Jaws dropped all around him as fellow actors wondered what they would have done in the circumstances.

"How did he get out of it?" Rose asked.

"Well, of course, he sent Jack back to look for the proper message – which was a mistake, because Jack left him to stew alone on stage, desperately improvising a five-minute monologue. What he should have done is say to Jack, 'You stay here, you incompetent booby! *I'll* get the proper message' – and then left *him* to stew alone for five minutes. Anyway, back comes Jack – eventually – with the *same* little triangle of paper, saying, 'Sir, I have authenticated it and this is indeed the message – *the only one!'* Poor Willie! He had to cut his ten-minute exposition to shreds, pretending to read a message printed in brevier on that tiny scrap!"

An American actor, standing nearby, joined in to tell of a time when the great man had a fit of temper in mid-performance and simply stormed off the stage. "Locked himself in his dressing room for half an hour," he said. "The audience was ready to murder him. We could all feel it. We were sure that when he cooled down and returned to the stage, he'd be hissed and pelted. But no! The moment he reappeared ... cheers! He is just amazing."

Rose thought of the pranks Laughton had played on her during the first run of *Trelawny* and realized how lightly she had escaped. After the performance the rest went to pay homage backstage but she decided not to join them. She explained that she didn't want her memory of his Hamlet, which was, indeed, monumental, polluted by the memory of a drunk in a dressing room.

"Nobody believes you," Ellen murmured as she went off with the rest.

"I do," Max said, taking her arm. "Anyway, I have a table booked at Delmonico's, if you'd care to join me? The portions served there are too extravagant for a solo diner."

The theatre was on Broadway at 30th, near Madison Square; the restaurant was on Fifth Avenue at 44th, beside Grand Central. They considered walking it but the night was too cold. A hack got them there in no time. The moment she saw that the table he had booked was in a private room she knew what was going to happen. More – she realized that part of her had known it almost from the moment they met, back on the *Olympic*.

He helped her into her chair and, taking the bottle from the waiter's hand, said, "I hope you'll find this wine to your liking." And when he had filled her glass he held the label for her to read. *Eau de Selemnus,* it proclaimed. *'Mis en bouteille à Patrœ, Achaea, en particulier pour les malades d'amour.'* He must have had it especially printed.

Or, to look at it another way, he must have been especially certain of her tonight. Had Ellen somehow discovered about the private room when she said, 'No one believes you'?

Max's seduction of her was the smoothest, pleasantest thing, neither too hasty nor long drawn-out. The meal was not heavy and the *Eau de Selemnus* was just enough to fill her with a soporific drowsiness. It was a very different affair from the violent, passionate encounter with Napier Henry on the beach beneath the moon at St Ives. It was languorous, sensual, deliberate ... and beautiful – both there at the Delmonico and later in his suite at the Waldorf-Astoria, down on 34th Street.

She did not start to panic until she was on the steamer back to New Haven, some way into Long Island Sound – and her panic was not over the obvious, either, for he had been a perfect gentleman. She was panicking at the revelations of the previous night. That brief experience in St Ives had been pleasant enough but it had done nothing to prepare her for an entire night of passionate exploration with an obvious past-master like Max. She would never have believed that the capacity for such ecstasy had existed all these years, locked away inside her. And now she was panicking because she knew that the impulse to unlock that box – Pandora's box? – would never be far away, from this day on.

Naively she had supposed it was a box that only a true lover could unlock; now Max, for whom she felt affection but no deep emotions of any kind, had shown her it was not so. Already she suspected that any good-looking man who paid her the appropriate attention and set the scene amiably enough would be able to seduce her into unlocking it once again.

She said nothing of it for several days, not even to Ellen, with whom she was once again sharing a room, this time in downtown New Haven on Elm Street, near the Graduates' Club, a few blocks from the theatre. Then, late one night, when they were walking back across the Public Green, she could keep silent no longer. She confessed all to her friend.

"I knew it!" Ellen crowed. "I could tell."

"You mean everyone knew it," Rose said glumly.

"I don't think so. They gossip like that about lots of people – I'll bet you've done it yourself – but most of it is their own wishful thinking projected onto someone else."

"But not in *your* case!" Rose teased.

"Not this time, anyway." Ellen did not rise to it. "Did you do it on the ship?"

"No!"

"All right! No need to scream. I'm right here. You mean last week was the very first time?"

"The very first time I realized how tremendous it can be." She glanced shyly at Ellen, trying to read her face in the dim and distant street lighting. "I expect it's no news to you?"

"No-o-o ..." The response was drawn-out, guarded.

"I'm dreadfully afraid now, Ellen."

They were arm-in-arm so she felt the woman stiffen. "You don't mean he ..."

"No, no – he behaved perfectly in that way. No, I'm afraid of *me*. I'm afraid it's going to show."

"I don't follow."

"Well, when men know you're an innocent – like a virgin, even if technically you aren't – it must show in our behaviour. Or we must radiate some sort of virginal aura. I don't know. But I do know that men treat us with a sort of deference. The stage-door johnnies – we all know what they want, and what they probably get with some lady from the chorus ..."

"You mean they treat you with deference? My God! I have to fight them off sometimes. They make it perfectly clear to me what they want!"

"You see! That's exactly what I mean!"

Ellen gave a baffled laugh. "*Your* intentions, by contrast, are as clear as mud to me, dear."

"I mean, because you are, well, have had some experience, you must have a different aura. And now I'll have it, too. And what makes me particularly fearful is that if the man is young and good-looking – and plays his hand with sufficient skill and patience – I won't be able to fight him off. Because I'll remember how glorious it was with Max."

After a long moment's thought Ellen brightened suddenly. "You had the answer yourself – the other day."

"Did I? When?"

"When we were talking about being in love and getting married. Has Louis replied, by the way?"

"Leave him out of this discussion, please."

"I only asked."

"The answer is no. What did we say about love and marriage?"

"'I shall probably marry quite soon,' you said. You must have known something like this was going to happen."

"Must I? Why?"

"Because ... you know that preamble to the marriage service, where it says that matrimony is 'ordained for a remedy against sin and to avoid fornication; that such persons as have not the gift of continency might marry, and keep themselves undefiled members of Christ's body.'" She chuckled. "I expect you have someone in mind, eh? It would be very unlike you *not* to have."

68 Louis left his letter at the box office of the Belasco Theatre, on the third day of *Trelawny*'s three-week run in New York. Rose carried it around for several hours before she summoned the courage to open the envelope. It was written on Union League notepaper and it read:

My darling Lucinda,
For the first time I feel as if I am writing to a stranger. And not without cause, I think, for it was a stranger who wrote to me that 'final' letter, signed in your name. I did not take up your offer of a box at the first night performance. To be honest, I was too hurt and too angry. Also, to be practical, I wanted to see you on stage without your knowing I was in your audience at all. I did so tonight, and now I have come to my club to write this.

Goodness, how stilted my sentences are! Even my handwriting is awkward, suddenly. In all my previous letters I have been able to write as if you were beside me. I felt you were there and so writing was easy. But now I know you are no longer there, which is curious, because you are, at this moment, closer to me than you have been for the past twenty months. [*Twenty months and twenty days,* Rose thought.] I knew it the moment you stepped on the stage. There, in outward form, was the dear lady for whom I have pined since the day we parted. I almost stood in my seat and cried out your name. But, just in time, I realized I was deceived. The outward form may remain unchanged (and long may that continue!) but inwardly, in spirit, you are changed beyond recognition.

You must have heard of John Barrymore, who is at this moment appearing in Hamlet at Wallack's Theatre. First I should explain that I have become an assiduous theatre-goer since you took up the profession, so I speak now with some knowledge and authority. As an actor, Barrymore can vary between the sublime and the disappointing, but what he never loses is his utter command of the stage and the audience. He hardly needs to act at all. Whatever he does, he manages to persuade one that it is genuinely the way to do it, the perfect way. I say all this because, almost from the moment you walked on to the stage at the Belasco tonight, you radiated that same quality.

I know. I know! I am biased. Of course I am. But the same cannot be said of my neighbours, on either side and behind. During the interval we all agreed we had not ever seen an actress who could so dominate the stage, in whom one believed so implicitly. In short, I have no choice but to accept that you and the theatre are made for each other. I see now that I should have known it from the very beginning. When you 'brought me back from the dead' and we passed that magical weekend together, you were so convincing as a true daughter of Nancemellin House that to call it mere acting is a travesty. In any case, the idea that you might settle happily as the wife of an American brewer – even a prosperous one, as I shall shortly become – is absurd. Biased as I am, I can surely see that.

I grieve to write these words, but it is a personal grief and will one day fade away. As for you, you must go onward and upward, of course. It is your destiny. And you must do so free of the slightest tinge of obligations you assumed in altogether different circumstances. Insofar as you felt an obligation to me, I hereby cancel it, and I do so gladly (at least when I think of you). You will one day be ranked along with Fanny Burney, Sarah Siddons, and the Divine Sarah, I have no doubt of it. In my dotage I will boast of knowing you once and of commanding your affections for a few brief months, long ago. ...

Rose, blinded by her tears, could read no more. What a good, *good* man he was. And what a fool she, Lucinda-Ella Tremayne, was to reject him. But it was not Lucinda-Ella Tremayne who ruled the roost here; it was Lucille Marteyne – driven, hounded by her vocation to accept this noble and generous release.

There was a polite cough behind her. She turned to find Henry Lacy, one of the cast, offering her a clean, folded handkerchief; he was one of those actors who posed no danger to a girl's virtue – although, curiously enough, she had caught him looking at her with a sort of speculative light in his eye rather often of late. In fact, he was doing so now. "Bad news?" he asked as she took the proffered handkerchief and wiped her cheeks.

"I don't really know," she replied as she tucked the letter back in its envelope. "I don't know if I've let the most wonderful man in the world slip through my fingers or ..." She couldn't phrase the alternative so she just shrugged.

"A member of the Union League!" He squinted at the envelope.

"So it would seem. He's a barman – or barkeep, as they call them here. He must have joined a trade union and I suppose they have a club here in New York. You've heard of Smith's Ales, back in England?"

"Didn't they go smash?"

She nodded. "That was him. He came over here, to Trenton, New Jersey, to start afresh with a new brewing business. He keeps writing to say how well he's doing, but it's just ..." She hesitated.

"A lie?" he suggested.

"Not really. More like whistling to keep up his courage. I'm not blaming him for that. If you were born with a silver spoon in your mouth, it must be almost impossible to start again from nothing. Also you feel the disgrace more keenly, so it must be doubly hard to admit it to ... well, someone like me who took ten years to work up to eighteen shillings a week and then went on the stage and ... well, you know the rest."

"I do indeed!" he said with a peculiar emphasis. He pointed at the letter. "And you still love him?"

She nodded. "If some dictator seized power today and closed all theatres permanently, I'd be on the first train to Trenton. At least, Lucinda-Ella Tremayne would be – that's my real name – and she'd be singing, too. Isn't that awful!"

They drifted away from the foyer, back into the theatre. A pair of upholsterers were busy working on some seats in the front stalls – the 'orchestra' as the Americans perversely called those seats from which no musicians ever performed – otherwise they had the place to themselves.

"The really awful thing," she went on, "is that he's not begging me to give up all this." She waved a hand at the safety curtain. "Quite the opposite. He's telling me I belong here, not with him ... making all sorts of absurd comparisons ..."

"How absurd?"

"I'd be too embarrassed to say it." She took out Louis' letter and found the paragraph at which she had broken off, comparing her to Sarah Siddons and others. She folded the paper so that only that paragraph was visible and showed it to him.

"Ha!" he exclaimed after reading it. He shook his head as people do at the folly of those who know no better.

"You needn't be quite so brutal, you know," she told him, feeling slightly miffed.

He steered her into the back row of the stalls. "When an actor boasts, 'I have the theatre in my blood'," he said, "he actually means *this.*" He waved a hand vaguely about them.

"What?" she asked. "I can't see anything."

"Just so! It's dead. No lights. No music. No dialogue. No audience. Dead. What he means is that he's dead between last night's curtain-call and today's overture – like this place now."

"How bleak!" She sighed.

"Not really. Once you accept the truth of it, once you realize that your only chance of a life worth living is when that curtain rises, you throw everything you've got into it."

"But if that's true, it makes the life-in-between *not* worth living."

"Only if you want a *separate* life out there. Those actresses who marry into the aristocracy and come back for occasional performances – which, I presume, is the fate of your Rose Trelawny character – they have the most miserable life of all."

"The worst of both worlds."

"That's right." He laughed. "If you want a life-in-between, marry a man who owns a theatre – or a successful playwright – someone who'll want to get his moneysworth out of you!" His amusement faded and he eyed her nervously as he added, "Actually, Miss Marteyne, would you mind a bit of advice? Professional advice, I mean."

She cupped her hands to her ears.

"I don't think your friend Louis is right. You are never going to be an actress in the Sarah Siddons category – or a new Mrs Patrick Campbell. I know everyone thinks so at the moment, but I've been watching you over these months and I think you're absolutely *made* for quite a different kind of theatre."

"You do?"

He nodded. "Musical comedy."

"Really?" She knew she ought to feel affronted, that a minor member of the cast should tell her she would never gain the heights of their profession on the legitimate stage, and yet something within her responded eagerly to his words.

He continued: "I know it's considered a pretty lowly form at the moment, but I think you could do for it, for musical comedy, what Irving and Tree have done for drama – and Ibsen and Shaw, of course. And even old Pinero in his way. You could raise it to the status of an art."

"I don't have the voice," Rose protested.

"That's not what *I* heard."

"What have you heard?"

"The duet you sang with signior Leone on the ship? The ballads you belted out with Sozzler's Follies up north? Ours is a small, incestuous profession, you know. Word gets around."

"But I feel so happy in drama."

"And you felt happy in melodrama, too? Down West with Lord Gordon's Players?"

She looked at him askance. "Word *does* get around! Yes, I did, if you must know."

"And you could happily go back to it?"

She shook her head.

"That's how you'll feel about the drama one day – after your first season in a musical comedy. But you must be sure to get the right librettist – and the right composer. Don't let H-d-W cast you in something anæmic, something he needs to rescue – which is a favourite trick of his: to recover his costs at the expense of an artist's reputation."

"Maybe you should write the book," Rose said with a laugh.

"Maybe I will," he responded calmly. "You're not the only one who's cut out for something other than the drama." He drew a deep breath and added, "What would you say to the lead role in a musical comedy based upon your own life story?"

Rose threw back her head and roared.

"Seriously," he said as her laughter faded. "I only say 'based on' – not an actual biography. The English are utterly fascinated by the whole business of accent and class. A comedy based on the idea that a servant-girl could promote herself to the very top of the class ladder by teaching herself to speak like her alleged betters would be a sensation. They say Shaw is working on a similar idea – for a play, of course ... nothing so vulgar as a musical comedy for the great G. B. S! But in his case the girl is a mere pawn in the hands of some elocution teacher. A man, naturally – who takes all the glory. The idea that a girl could do it *all by herself* would be truly revolutionary, don't you think?"

By now the hair was bristling on Rose's neck; the idea had bitten. "You say it wouldn't *exactly* be my own life story?" she asked. "Not incident-for-incident?"

"Lord no! Just the general proposition – that accent equals class equals merit. A nobody becomes a somebody just by shifting a few vowels and consonants. I've even got a title!"

"Go on."

"Taking the cue from your part in *Trelawny* – *A Rose by Any Other Name*. There – how about that!"

She eyed him coolly. "You're not taking the cue from *Trelawny* at all," she said. "You've really been digging deep into my past, haven't you."

He grinned, unabashed. "Only because it's going to be so rewarding. We could work on it during the voyage home."

"On the *Titanic,* I hope," she said.

He raised his eyebrows.

"If we keep playing to these houses, they'll extend the run until mid-April. Next month. We have to be back by the end of the month because of the London commitment. And, it so happens, *Titanic* will dock at Pier Forty-eight on the sixteenth, after her maiden voyage. And she'll sail home the following day – perfect for our plans."

"But you'll be going first class, I suppose?"

She hesitated. "For such a venture as this ... maybe not. We'll just have to see."

As they rose to make their way back to the foyer, she felt Louis' letter, which she had only half-tucked into her pocket. "Well!" she said softly. "How swiftly we moved from tears to careers!"

69

ALL SAVED FROM TITANIC AFTER COLLISION screamed the banner headline in the New York *Evening Sun* for its final edition of Monday, April 15, 1912. Lesser headlines filled in the details. They said that the *Carpathia* and the *Parisian* had rescued all passengers and crew, that the great liner was being towed to Halifax after smashing into an iceberg, that she carried over 1,400 passengers, 'many of prominence,' and that the *Olympic,* five hundred miles from the incident, had sent the first word of the amazing rescue. The cast of *Trelawny* breathed a sigh of relief, not just for the lucky passengers and crew but for their own good fortune, too. A tragedy on that scale would have led to the closing of all public entertainments in New York – indeed, right across America and Europe. It was, in any case, the final week of *Trelawny* in America. The cast had been booked to return on *Titanic,* as Rose had hoped, that coming Thursday.

Even as the *Sun* hit the streets, however, alternative versions of the event were beginning to emerge at the White Star Line's offices at the bottom end of Broadway. All day long anxious relatives of the Astors, Guggenheims, Morgans, and other passengers of prominence had been sent away with reassurances that even in the worst case, the Titanic could float for days and that there were more than enough lifeboats to go round. Rumours said otherwise; and at 6:15 that evening a wireless message from the *Olympic* arrived at head office to confirm them. *Titanic* had gone down twenty hours earlier; *Carpathia* had picked up all the lifeboats and was returning to New York with the survivors.

Even then the news fluctuated for days. Captain Arthur Rostron of the *Carpathia* kept his wireless exclusively for official and personal messages, leaving the press free to speculate. No fantasy was too absurd to print. Passengers had been rescued clinging to the fatal iceberg, which still had smears of red paint from the collision; men had been shot dead 'like dogs' as they scrambled for places in the boats; the captain and first officer had committed suicide; the band drowned while playing 'Nearer my God to Thee'; the iceberg had been visible for an hour before the collision; one of the men rescued, a banker, had taken over the *Carpathia's* wireless and was hogging it for himself.

By the Thursday of that week, however, when *Carpathia* was due to dock back in New York, it was clear that even the most lurid fantasy was a mere embellishment of a history whose horror could not be exaggerated. Stores, motion-picture houses, and theatres all closed spontaneously; there was, in any case, little point in opening their doors. The Battery alone was crowded with ten thousand awed spectators, gathered to watch *Carpathia* steam past the Statue of Liberty. Her own thirteen lifeboats rested on her boat deck while a like number of *Titanic's* hung from her davits. A further thirty thousand – Rose, Ellen and other members of the cast among them – stood in the pouring rain along the waterfront to watch her pass, all the way up to her regular berth at Pier 54, by West 13th.

There was a silence you could put a shoulder to as they watched her lower the empty lifeboats, which were immediately rowed back downstream to White Star's Pier 48, at Bank Street.

"There won't be much left of them by dawn tomorrow," Henry Lacy murmured.

Rose was shocked. "Destroying evidence, d'you mean?"

He shook his head. "Vultures. Hunters after souvenirs. What d'you think any bit of the *Titanic* will fetch ten years from now? Twenty? Thirty? Don't look at *me* like that! I didn't create human beings the way they are."

Since the company was now stranded in New York for the next few days, along with everyone else who had booked on the *Titanic* for her return voyage, the Belasco Theatre reopened on the

Friday, offering two extra nights of *Trelawny,* with all proceeds going to the disaster fund. The cast was glad of it, too, for the awfulness of the real-life tragedy would have made any regular performance of a 'tragedy' about an actress's loss of nerve seem gross and offensive.

Rose was at first numbed by the losses, then outraged.

"Just look at this, would you!" she cried, throwing down that day's crop of newspapers.

Several of the cast had gathered in the green room to read them – as avidly as they would normally have scanned the first editions for their own notices.

"Acres of print about the Astors and Guggenheims – not a single word about the third class. You'd almost think a third-class ticket included the *right* to drown."

"Steady the buffs!" Conrad Laughton exclaimed. "Most of them would have been mere servant girls and labourers. You could hardly expect ..."

"Seventy-six third-class children?" She cut across him. "Only twenty-three saved! She had twenty lifeboats, capable of carrying nine hundred people – and how many were actually lowered in them? Six hundred and fifty-one! So there were two hundred and forty-nine empty seats. They could have saved every woman and child on board and *still* have had room for five dozen men."

"Even so there's no need to turn it into a matter of class," Laughton replied. "It's just a typical British muddle, if you ask me. *All* life is cheap to those in power. Ask the soldiers who fought in the Boer War. Aristocrat and hedgetrimmer fought and died side by side. And a fat lot those people in Westminster cared about *any* of them!"

"So!" Rose sneered. "I suppose it's just a simple everyday miracle that one third of all the men in the first class survived? I won't call them gentlemen."

"Four gentlemen in every five were drowned; four women in every five were saved – that's the figure which matters. If it's miracles you're after, the real miracle is that fifty survived at least two hours in that freezing sea."

Other cast members intervened to make this the last sally in an argument that could do no one any good and the esprit of the company a great deal of harm. But the horror of the tragedy rankled with Rose – especially the fact that fifty-three children in the third class had been allowed to drown, while only twenty-three were saved. Even worse was the fact that no newspaper or magazine thought it at all remarkable.

"You're not going to turn into some sort of radical campaigner, I hope," Henry Lacy said to her after the final performance that Saturday night. They had gone to the Dorlon oyster bar at Madison Square to wind down after the show – and, of course, to talk about his project for a musical comedy.

"Don't you think it's shocking?" she replied. "Here's the *Social Register* tying itself in knots over how to avoid saying that Mrs J. J. Astor arrived in New York on such a common little boat as the *Carpathia!*"

"Eh?"

"It's true. I'm not making it up. The boat you travel on is *desperately* important to New York's Upper Ten Thousand. To have them read that you arrived on some plodding little passenger ship would expose you to ridicule for months to come. Fortunately, they seem to have found a solution." She drew a press cutting from her handbag. "I'm keeping this to show my grandchildren, for I'm sure they'll never believe it else. See!"

She rested a glossy red fingernail against the line that read: 'Mrs J. J. Astor and Maid: Arrived *Titan-Carpath,* 18 April 1912.'

"Note the size of the hyphen," she said. "Small though it is, they've somehow managed to squeeze fifteen hundred dead into it. Including fifty-three children."

He shook his head. "I won't argue with you, Lucille," he said. "Because I can't say you're wrong. All I can say is that if you're intending to go back on stage with Sozzler Knox at the new Frivoli, you'd better spend the next few weeks getting this bitterness out of your system, because you're an instinctive sort of actress and it's bound to come out. And it won't suit his sort of show at all."

70

Everyone was on the lookout for ice, of course, though nobody mentioned it. To do so they would have needed to adopt the sort of joking manner people use when talking of hazards in an 'I don't mean to say it'll happen to *us,'* tone – which, in turn, might be taken as a tasteless joke about the two thousand-odd people to whom it most certainly did happen, and in these very waters. So people spent more time on deck than the weather and season would normally encourage; they scanned the waves, particularly the waves ahead, more than was customary; and when their eyes met, they smiled in guilty but silent complicity, as if caught in some furtive action.

Rose had decided not to travel 'first class' – words that had acquired inverted commas for her, following the behaviour of some 'gentlemen' of that description on the *Titanic.* In any case, the *Mauretania,* already six years old, did not boast the same opulence as the White Star liners. Speed was her strong point for she had been built specifically to wrest the Blue Riband from those impudent Germans.

Henry Lacy had a more sinister explanation. "She's strengthened there," he said, pointing to her foredeck, "and again on the afterdeck to take four- and six-inch-gun mountings. My father was a reporter for the *Daily Mail* at her launching. He says everyone thought they were in for the usual self-congratulatory speeches, full of the expected superlatives. Instead they got a rambling defence of all the money the government had sunk into the building of both *Mauretania* and *Lusitania.* In fact, we are presently sailing aboard the fastest merchant-cruiser in the world, disguised as a floating hôtel during this brief lull between the last European war and the one that will soon be upon us."

"D'you think so?" She felt a sudden chill, even though the day was sunny and warm for early May. At least, it was warm once you got out of the permanent breeze created by her speed.

"Dad says many people he knows, people in War Office circles, are surprised it hasn't already started. The Hun obviously wants to do a Napoleon on Europe – and we've obviously got to stop him. What are we waiting for? His navy grows stronger by the day."

She just stared out to sea.

"Today it's icebergs," he said. "Tomorrow you can bet it'll be German U-boats."

Still she said nothing, having nothing to contribute.

"Doesn't it worry you?" he asked.

She shrugged and leaned against the rail. "It's too big. I can't do anything to control it. The things that worry me are the things I *can* control." With a sigh she added, "Or fancy I can."

"Oh?" He joined her at the rail. "Such as?"

"D'you remember, that day back in New York, you said I was an *instinctive* actress?"

"So you are."

"What d'you mean by that? I don't understand."

"Whew!" He sighed as people do when facing some monumental task, quite beyond their powers.

"I don't want a long essay, now," she warned. "Just tell me what you meant by it."

"I meant there's been a lot of claptrap talked and written lately – ever since Ibsen and Shaw and other writers with intellectual pretensions burst upon the scene – claiming that acting is also an intellectual business. And I say balderdash. You know that bit in your Lady Augusta act where you consult some reference book your maid has fetched from the local library ...?"

She looked at him in surprise. "How d'you know that?"

"I've watched you," he replied with a grin. "Quite often, actually. Anyway you know that bit of silent business you do – the way you take the book from her as if it's a bomb, and you open it gingerly and look right and left and over your shoulder and then sniff at the page with distaste, also looking a little guilty ... all those small gestures that reveal your absolute horror of the common people who have handled this book before you? You know that bit?"

"Yes, of course. I don't do it every time, mind. It all rather depends on the audience."

"You make my point even more strongly. I think I was in the stalls at the Holborn Empire on the very first night you introduced it as a bit of business. Of course, I had no idea then that 'Lucy Tremayne' and 'Lucille Marteyne' were one and the same. Anyway, you only made it last about five seconds then. But when I saw you do it for the third-class passengers on *Olympic,* you kept them splitting their sides for a full minute. And the really extraordinary thing is you don't need to speak a word. Even those people in the topmost gallery know *exactly* what you're thinking."

"Dear Henry!" She squeezed his arm. "It *is* turning into an essay. However, as it's all about me, I'll find it in my heart to forgive you this once, even though I still can't see the point."

"Deutschland ahoy!" cried a man up ahead.

People hastened to join him, as if the view from his vantage would be any better.

"The point," Henry replied, "is that the original idea was pure inspiration. Before you did it, that first time, I'll bet you had never sat down and coldly worked out what someone like Lady Augusta would do on being forced to open a library book. You didn't need to. Something inside you was instinctively in touch with her character and just ... *did* it. Correct me if I'm wrong?"

"Something inside me instinctively resents being analyzed like this!" she replied darkly.

"That's the same point as the one I'm making!"

"And something inside me instinctively resents the way you write off all the *thought* that helped me stretch a five-second inspiration into a full minute's worth of business. I really sweated over each little extra bit that got added. If thought isn't intellectual, what is?"

"Ah, but you misunderstand me. I'm not saying the intellect has *no* place in our business. In fact, it has precisely the place you've just described. It's for taking an instinctive inspiration and helping to develop it. It's a handmaiden, not a mistress. But if an actor or actress lacks that original instinct which creates the inspiration in the first place, then even the most massive intellect in the world won't help. Otherwise we'd have to watch our backs for passing dons and professors!"

"Is that really the *Deutschland?"* she asked, peering up ahead.

He glanced at it briefly. "Who cares? Why did you ask about this instinct business anyway? You seemed to accept it at the time."

"D'you think one ought always to trust one's instinct, then?"

"Absolutely. Beyond any shadow of a doubt."

"Because, you see, Henry dear, my instinct is telling me more and more strongly each day that I have made the most stupid blunder of my life, back there in New York."

He chuckled. "If you did, no one else noticed."

"That's because they weren't standing in the right place."

"Where was that?"

She tapped her brow, right between her eyes. "Inside here. You remember that letter I showed you?"

"From your friend Smith of Smith's Ales – in the Union whatsit?"

She nodded. "I thought it released me from any obligation to him. And so it did, in a way. My *intellect* agrees with every word he wrote. But my *instinct* – the bit you advise me to trust absolutely – says I should take the next boat back and go to him and ..." She shrugged hopelessly.

"And what?"

"I don't know. Just *be* with him."

After a while he said, "Well, I don't know enough about it to say whether that's sensible or not."

"In a way, you see, I owe him everything. You know I was once a lady's maid?"

"To Noel Carclew's sister – he told me."

"Oh, he did, did he! Did he also tell you about the time when he and the rest of the family were away in the Holy Land and a young man was washed up near the house, half dead? And we servants on board wages were dressing up in our mistresses' clothes? And I happened to be wearing one of his sister's day dresses when the young man came round ..."

"And you spoke in your impeccable upper-class voice and he took you for the daughter of the house? Yes, he told me – in the end. That is, I badgered it out of him – because I already had the germ of the idea for *A Rose by Any Other Name.*"

"Did he tell you the name of that young man?"

"No."

She stared into his eyes, thinking he must be lying – but, apparently, he was not. Why on earth had Noel told him only half the story, then – and the least interesting half at that?

"Is it important?" he asked.

"The man's name was Louis Redmile-Smith – my 'friend in the Union whatsit'! Late of Smith's Ales. Are you sure Noel didn't mention him?"

"Not by name. Why should he? I was only interested in learning how Noel discovered you for H-d-W. He said he heard the tale and got you to put on his sister's clothes and repeat your bit of play-acting. He says your Lady Augusta is his mother to a tee."

"She was to start with. She's moved on a bit since then. Well ... bless him! He was avoiding telling the full story." And she went on to fill in the details Noel had omitted – from her magical weekend with Louis to the dinner party at Henry Roanoke's. "But it was Louis who said I should go on the stage – and who gave me the confidence to even think of it. Without that, I'd never have dared take the first step, you know."

"And so?"

It was the *Deutschland.* She was pouring on the coals in a desperate attempt not to be overhauled too swiftly. For three years she had been struggling vainly to take the Blue Riband back from *Mauretania,* but her best crossing time was five days and seventeen hours (as several knowledgeable passengers nearby informed the world at large), whereas *Mauretania's* was four days and five hours – give or take a few minutes; she was overhauling her rival at the pace of a brisk walker.

Rose and Henry yielded their places at the rail to those more interested in seeing Germany humiliated once again; they drifted over to the now-deserted starboard deck.

"So?" he repeated.

"So, at the very least, I ought to have met him. I ought not to have shirked a meeting like that. It's just that when I saw he was nothing more than the most popular barman in Trenton – and remembering all his letters describing how well his non-existent business was doing – and me being so successful and ... and ..."

"Happy?" he suggested.

She nodded. "I just got cold feet and crept away. That was scurvy, though. The least I owed him was a meeting."

"And for *that,* you'll get on the next boat back to New York?"

Her eyelids were prickling and she felt a lump in the throat. "No. I don't suppose I will. But I will miss him. I *do* miss him."

"Apart from the letters, you've only been in his company ... what? Two or three days?"

"A Friday to a Monday – and my love for him has burned with a hard, gemlike flame ever since. Unwavering. That must surely mean something?"

Henry had the sense to say nothing.

"Maybe if I throw myself into my work" she suggested. "You know ... body and soul ...?"

"You'd do that anyway."

"It's the feeling of emptiness. The feeling of no-one-there. When the curtain falls and they switch off the lights and you take off all the make-up and step outside the stage door ... that gauntlet of johnnies!" She shuddered. "It was fun for a few months but I don't want it to start all over again." She dropped her head and peered up at him. "Go on! Spit it out! I can feel you're dying to advise me."

He scratched diffidently behind his ear. "Love is greatly overrated, you know. Isn't there someone out there you could be just very *comfortable* with?"

"Live in sin, you mean?"

"God no! Not if you want a career in musical comedy. You might get away with it as a tragedienne, but not at the more popular end of the business. No, I'm talking about marriage – the best cure for night starvation *and* stage-door johnnies."

"Burn my boats, you mean?"

"Burn your transatlantic liners, anyway." He grinned. "Except for professional purposes, of course. Can we now turn to the much more rewarding topic of *A Rose by Any Other Name?*"

71

Everybody saw the shimmering white Silver Ghost waiting on the quayside at the Ocean Dock, Southampton; most noticed its proud owner; Rose alone recognized him – and guessed why he had given his chauffeur the day off. He was shielding his eyes against the sun while he scanned the first class promenade deck.

"Roger!" she called down to him. "Back here!"

He swivelled round, located her, and, with a baroque flourish, invited her to step into his car.

"You bet!" she yelled back.

She tipped her porter and told him to put her bags in that car. As she shuffled among the crowd toward the second-class gangway she noticed H-d-W and a throng of reporters beyond the gate to the first class. He beckoned to her. The gesture needed no baroque extravagances; his air of wealth and authority was sufficient. The seaman guarding the gate flung it open and bowed her through. Immediately the reporters surrounded her.

"How did you find America, Miss Marteyne?"

"Are American audiences as good as English ones?"

"How much did you raise for the *Titanic* disaster fund?"

"Did you visit any 'night clubs' over there?"

"Did you see the Niagara Falls?"

"What did you think of American food ... hôtels ... trains ... spitting habits ...?"

"Could you understand the way they speak?"

And, finally, from a stooping little fellow with the face of a travelling rat: "Who is the gentleman waiting for you with his Rolls-Royce down there?"

She replied, respectively, that America wasn't too hard to find; some kind officer of the White Star Line had placed it right at the end of the gangway. American *and* English audiences are only as good as the play and its players; personally she had no complaints. Forty-thousand dollars. No, too busy. No, still too busy. Palatable ... comfortable ... punctual ... as bad as those in England.

"Sho' thing, honey."

An old friend of her family.

"Might he be concealing a ring somewhere about his person?" asked ratface.

Rose turned wearily upon him. "If I were to say yes, you'll print it. If I were to say no, you'll hint it. So I shall say nothing." She looked around, catching the eye of each man briefly. "You know, you people have a lot to learn from your New York counterparts. There was a bishop on the *Olympic,* on the outward voyage. And the poor man was besieged, just like this, when we docked. And one of the questions they fired at him was, 'You gonna visit any nite clubs in Noo Yawk, bishop?' And he, sweet innocent gentleman that he was, asked in surprise, '*Are* there any night clubs in New

York?' You know what headline they gave him? 'Bishop's *first* question: Are there any night clubs in New York?'"

Amid their laughter de Witt led her away to be photographed on the boat deck. "Well done!" he said. "America has matured you. How right I was to insist on your tour there. Who *is* the gentleman with the Silver Ghost?"

"An old family friend – just as I said."

"That's all?"

"He has rescued me from many a stage-door johnny – which is enough. How are we getting on with the Frivoli?"

"Fair to middling. We should still be able to start rehearsals in mid-June and we should open in ..." He broke off and laughed. "You're incorrigible, Miss Marteyne."

"Am I?"

"Every other actress I've ever met on her return from America just bubbles over with her experiences there. It takes *days* to get her looking forward once again. But you – I think the past vanishes behind you at sunset each day."

"I hope so," she replied quietly. "Oh – with all my heart I hope that's true."

When she emerged into the sunshine on the boat deck she went directly to the railings to show Roger she hadn't forgotten him; but he was no longer there. His car stood alone in a circle of admirers, with one officious urchin standing guard. The porter was strapping her bags on the luggage rack, so that was all right.

It was no casual photograph that de Witt had arranged. Two assistants stood ready with large white boards to reflect the light into the shadowed side of her face. He placed her where a lifebelt would establish the name *Mauretania* at one edge of the picture; he arranged her right arm, holding a parasol, partly in front of it, so no one could crop the name without cutting off her arm; and he spent a good five minutes in placing the two reflector cards so as to model her features to his satisfaction. And all the while a make-up lady worked on strengthening the tone of her lips, darkening her eyebrows and eyelashes, and subtly exaggerating the modelling of her cheeks and dimples.

At some point, Roger must have arrived on the boat deck, too – and H-d-W must have intercepted him and kept him out of sight until the photographer was about to remove his lens cap for the exposure. For at that precise moment Roger walked into view. She had discipline enough to keep her head in pose but not enough to suppress the radiant smile she gave him.

"You beast!" she shouted at de Witt when the lens cap went back on again. "I'm perfectly capable of giving a genuine smile without resorting to such tricks. Roger, darling! How *wonderful* of you to come all this way to meet me!" She flung her arms around him and left a lot of the make-up lady's artistry smeared on both his cheeks – and lips.

"Oh, well," he said nonchalantly as he accepted a finger of cold cream and a wad of cotton wool. "I've just had her serviced at Hythe Road, so I thought I'd give her a spin ... give her cylinders a good long drink of oil, you know. And then I remembered you were due today. So I thought, why not? And so here I am."

"Print every word!" she called to ratface, the one remaining reporter, who was lurking behind a davit, trying to look like a first-class passenger in no hurry to disembark.

"What about my other question?" the man asked as he came out of hiding. "Do we perchance hear the chime of wedding bells, sir – be they never so distant?"

"You'll hear the chime of boot leather on trouser seat if you don't clear off, you dog," was all the answer he got.

Grinning, the fellow walked well out of range, scribbled in his notebook, saying loudly as he wrote: "No de-ni-al," and skipped away, delighted with himself.

"You won't be able to hold them off for ever, you two," de Witt warned as they left, arm in arm.

"I was sure you'd be returning first class," Roger said as they went back down the companionway.

"Isn't that typical H-d-W?" she said. "Why splash out on a first-class ticket for your leading lady when you can bribe a seaman to let her through from the second class, looking as if she was just coming back from a visit there?"

"You *look* first class, like a million dollars – is that the right expression? That's a gorgeous dress. *Very* first class."

"Well, thank you, kind sir." She dropped a curtsy. "I found it at Le Boutiller just before we left. But New York is expensive. They are *scum,* aren't they – theatrical impresarios. We should form an actors' cooperative and do without them." She squeezed his arm.

"What?" he asked.

"Nothing. Just ... it really is you!" She grinned.

He strode like a king through the quayside crowd, looking neither right nor left, keeping his eye fixed on his motor car. People drew aside to let them pass – the lord and his elegant lady. Rose wanted to shout at them not to be so silly. "He's only a mister and I'm only me!" However, she had to confess that she enjoyed the respectful deference. Also – surprisingly – it no longer felt like a masquerade.

Something had happened in America, but she had to come back to England to realize what it was. Over there she'd never had the feeling that people might laugh behind her back if they knew her true origins. She had once been a lady's maid? So what? She was *now* a leading lady in a pretty fine company – *that* was what counted. Over there, one's past really did – in H-d-W's phrase – vanish behind him or her each night. It would be good to work that idea into *A Rose by Any Other Name,* if possible. She should keep a little pocket notebook and write these things down.

"D'you like her?" Roger asked, placing one foot on the running board like a big-game hunter with his trophy. He flipped a sixpence to the urchin-guard.

"Give him another sixpence," Rose said. "He has the most beautiful eyes."

Laughing, Roger did as she asked, passing the sixpence to her. "I mean it sincerely – about your eyes," she told the lad as she handed it over. "You should try to get into the motion pictures. It doesn't matter how you speak. They're all silent, anyway. But you have the face for it. I mean it."

The youth stared at her, speechless, while she tied the travel duster round her hat.

"If this lady says such things, you should listen young fellow-my-lad," Roger said. "You know who she is?"

He shook his head, still not taking his eyes off Rose, who was now putting on her goggles.

"She's Miss Lucille Marteyne, a famous London actress. So she knows what she's talking about. D'you think you could crank the starting handle for that extra tanner?"

When they were on their way he chuckled and said, "I wonder if *you* started something back there?"

"I hope so," she replied. "I was talking to people over there. The movies are changing. Slapstick and burlesque romance are still the staple fare but pathos is beginning to come in, too. And that kid has just the right face for it. 'Famous London actress' is laying it a bit thick."

"I don't think so. The social columns have been following *Trelawny's* success in America pretty closely. Didn't that little reception back there take you by surprise?"

"I don't know. This is a splendid motor – even better than the Daimler, I think."

"Much better. What d'you mean, you don't know? You must know if you were surprised or not."

"Well ... I never expected to become wardrobe mistress to Lord Gordon's Players, nor to step into the lead in *Leah,* nor to be taken up by H-d-W, et cetera, et cetera. So, when *everything's* a surprise, *nothing* is." She peered out across the passing mudflats. "Southampton Corporation Baths?" she said. "Is this the London road?"

"I thought we'd stop for a bite of lunch at a little place I know in the New Forest – if that's all right with you."

"Have you a map?" she asked.

He laughed.

"I'm serious. I like to know where I'm going."

"But maps don't really do that. They only tell you where someone else has been."

She was about to laugh, as one does at a shallow witticism, when she realized it was not shallow at all. To enter an unknown part of the country with a map in your hand might, indeed, prevent you from making your own discoveries about it. She began to look around her as they went out through the suburb of Millbrook and the outlying villages of Redbridge and Totton, making her own mental map of their progress.

"I do have a map, as it happens," he said after a while. "If you feel such a desperate need."

"No, it's quite exciting," she replied. "Unknown country."

"I quite often come down here, in the hunting season."

The car surged forward down the winding country lanes, scattering hens and geese outside cottages and bringing barking sheepdogs from the farms. The forest oaks were all in new green leaf. The breeze winnowed through her hair. Sunlight dappled the road ahead and pushed shafts of gold through the dust they raised in their wake. She thought briefly of all those millions now hard at work, especially of housemaids and their drudgery, and was filled with wonder that she had escaped it all. To be young, vigorous, and healthy, to be applauded in 'work' that was itself the greatest pleasure, to be free, to be sitting beside a rich and handsome young man who adored you … heaven itself could hardly improve on such a moment as this, she thought.

"How long have you had this car?" she asked.

"I bought her the day you sailed for America – feeling in need of consolation, I suppose."

"You could have come over and joined us there. I'd have loved that." She thought of Max and wondered if that were true.

"I almost did," he replied. "Guess which ship!"

She stared at him. "Oh my God – no!" She reached out and clutched his arm.

"Steady!" He pulled the car back into line, just as it was about to peel off into the ditch.

Still she clung tight. "Oh, Roger, *darling!* I couldn't have *borne* that. You coming over to see me and … of course, you'd have done the gentlemanly thing – not like so many. And now you'd be … oh God, Roger. Isn't life so *precious!*"

"Not of itself," he replied. "Only for what we find – and make – within it. My life has changed completely since that evening I first met you. D'you realize it's two years ago, all but a few weeks?"

"The twenty-eighth of June, nineteen ten," she said. "My life hasn't exactly been dull since then, either."

"Little enough to do with me, though," he remarked. "Whereas the change in *my* life has …"

"I wouldn't say that. The night we got chucked out by old Roanoke, I thought, *That's it. That's the end. There's nowhere to go to next.* I'd gone from housemaid to lady's maid to small-town hostess – for one night – to … the street. And you made me an offer that …"

"Don't!" He almost steered off the road again. "I'm so ashamed of that now. The only thing I'd ever kill you for is if you ever breathe a word of it to another living soul. It wasn't me – or it was a different me. I don't know ..."

"You shouldn't be ashamed, Roger. You actually put a ... what's the word? What's the man in cricket who stands immediately behind the wicket?"

"The wicket keeper."

"And the one behind him who catches what he misses?"

"Long stop. Why are we talking about cricket all of a sudden?"

"No. What I'm saying is that your offer was like a long stop to me. Suddenly it wasn't true that I had *nowhere* else to go – don't you see? It relieved me of the need to panic, to take any job on offer. Actually ..." She hesitated. "I don't know if I ought to tell you this. I'll kill *you* if ever you breathe a word about it. I did have one other possibility then – pretty much in the same line."

"Do I really need to know?"

"I think so. It was an address of a house in Paris. A very particular sort of house ..."

"Sally Winnen!"

She frowned and said, "I beg your pardon? Who?"

He laughed. "Very convincing! You're a good pal to have. But you forget she's Ruby Penhallow's partner now. And dear Ruby got the truth out of her in under two minutes."

"And carried the tale directly to you!"

"Not directly. She didn't say a word about it until they wanted a couple of thou' more for working capital. She thought it only fair I should know. Quite right, too."

"Oh. Well, yes, I suppose so. Anyway, where were we?"

"A big-number house in Paris."

"Is that what they call them? No, don't tell me why, please. I think I can guess."

"You'd probably be wrong. It's nothing terribly subtle. The numbers over the doors on those particular houses are always at least eighteen inches high. So – it was whore, mistress, or actress! And you picked the topmost one and never looked back. What's next, I wonder?"

Their eyes dwelled briefly in each other's. "Lunch," she said.

They stopped at the Balmer Lawn Hôtel, near the southern edge of the forest.

"Roast beef!" Rose said. "I haven't had good roast beef in months. The Americans murder it."

Over lunch she asked him about hunting in this country. Was it for deer or foxes? Or hares? Did he keep a horse down here? And so on. He let drop the fact that he also had a cottage at Whitley Ridge, not too far away. She said she'd love to see it.

The moment they were through the door their hands reached for each other. They embraced, their lips met, their bodies trembled, their knees gave way. The floor was hard but the time they passed upon it was short. Then they were in bed for a longer, sweeter embrace. They awoke for the third time around seven that evening, ready to dress for dinner, this time at the Londesborough Arms in Lymington.

On the way there he said, "I suppose we'd better get married, then."

"Is that a proposal?" she asked.

"What d'you think of the idea?"

"I suppose we had," she said.

Then they decided to make a night of it back in his cottage.

"I don't have a map for this sort of thing," he told her as he held open the door.

"I think I owe another of my life's great turning points to you today," she replied. "The discovery that certain adventures are more exciting if one deliberately ignores the existing maps."

END OF PART FIVE

Part Six

A Rose by Any Other Name

72 The engagement was short enough to set shocked tongues wagging all over London. They announced it on the seventh of May, the day after *Mauretania* docked, and the wedding date was set for Friday the twenty-eighth of June – a date of huge significance to both of them, though Rose would, as she had said, kill him if he ever explained that significance to another living soul. They had wanted a quiet wedding, down in Cornwall, perhaps. But Hugo de Witt would hear none of it; they were to be married in St George's, Hanover Square – like all the best people – or he would scour her contract for some clause that would allow him to prevent it utterly.

The attendant publicity suited him well, too, for his 'fair-to-middling' report to Rose of progress on the Frivoli had, as usual, been pretty optimistic. They would be lucky to open in time for the autumn season. So a fine, sentimental excuse for a 'postponement' would only serve to whet the public curiosity and appetite.

"Stay away on your honeymoon – until I call you," he ordered.

"Why?" she asked.

"There's nothing the public likes better than to stare into the eyes of a blushing bride, newly returned from that great adventure – the passage from vestal innocence to carnal erudition."

She laughed. "And what do you see in my eyes now?" she asked.

"What they hope to see then – otherwise, believe me, I should not be talking to you like this!"

So much to do, and so little time to do it in! Arrangements to make for her parents to come up – and any old Falmouth friends who could get a few days off. And Mr Swindlehurst and the other Players ... if they could get away, too. And dear old Sozzler ... well, she already knew he couldn't come. He'd be up in Blackpool, where the watch committee had capitulated rather than risk another bombardment of insulting lavatory-paper rolls. And all the London theatre people. And not forgetting all Roger's family, relatives, and friends.

Including Sally Winnen and Ruby Penhallow?

Of course!

It intrigued them both that a high-class *courtisane* from Paris and a former mistress of the groom should attend under the guise of schoolfriends of the bride.

And there was a letter to write to Louis.

She dreaded having to do it but she could not bear the thought of letting him learn of her marriage through the social columns of the press. She wrote:

My darling Louis,
For you will always be that to me, I hope. Your favourite poet and mine once wrote, 'It is a characteristic of the human mind to hate the man one has injured.' In *Agricola* I think. Well, for once, he was fallible. I have injured you. I know it only too well. But hate you? Never! Though if you were to hate me, I should not be a whit surprised. Especially when I tell you that any day now you will read in the papers that I am to marry a Mr Roger Deveril, whose family used to live in Falmouth and who now lives in London. Believe me, I had not the faintest inkling, when I was in America, that this was about to happen, or I should have told you then.

He proposed to me in Falmouth two years ago, just ten days after our last meeting on the lawns at Nancemellin. I did not even consider it then, of course. But when he met me at Southampton on my return at the beginning of this week (Lord, was it only three days ago?) and offered to finance a musical comedy that is dear to my heart – one based very loosely on my own life, in fact, and showing up our English hypocrisy in judging the merits of people almost entirely by their accents – I could not help wondering what his true purpose might be. And, of course, I asked him directly.

He was candour itself ... still loves me ... isn't particularly downhearted at my inability to reciprocate (*yet,* he always adds) ... swears he has love enough to spare for both of us ... is sure I'll warm to him in time.

Well, I am warm enough to him already. You would despise me, I hope, if I could not truly say he is good company, kind, considerate, a gentleman in every way, and one of the best friends I could ever hope to have. Do I love him? No – and, as you will already have gathered, I have told him so. Will I love him in time? It is possible. Indeed, it is probable.

Oh Louis, my dearest, isn't love the most wonderful thing when all goes well with it! And isn't it the greatest torment when everything about it goes wrong! How different our lives would have been if I had simply stepped into that boat with you at Nancemellin on the 18th of June two years ago! Yet 'now I see the true old times are dead' ...

She paused and read over what she had written. And then, with a sigh, she tore it in three strips and dropped them in the basket.

Let him read it in the papers. Let it twist a knife in his heart. Let him see what a weak, shallow, self-serving creature she was.

And let him forget her all the sooner for it.

73

A wedding between an Eskimo and a South Sea islander could not have produced a stranger assortment of guests. The youngest, at twenty months, was George Tresidder, Frank and Ann's firstborn, present with his parents; the oldest, at sixty-two, was Mr Dudley Dennison, who still played Lorenz in Lord Gordon's productions of *Leah,* present with the rest of the cast. The fattest, at two and a quarter imperial hundredweights, was Mrs Jean Swift, Roger's widowed aunt; the skinniest, with a genuine, uncorseted eighteen-inch waist, was the child prodigy herself, Miss Petronella Fitzroy. The highest in precedence was Lord Justice Phillips, Roger's somewhat bemused godfather (only a life peer, but still ...); the lowest, juveniles excepted, was the theatrical agent Georg 'Gorgeous George' Zeligman – it was a cross that commoners whose names started near the end of the alphabet had to bear. The richest, apart from the groom himself, was almost certainly Hugo de Witt – though no one was vulgar enough to mention it; the poorest, juveniles again excepted, was without doubt Miss Titania Moore, who saved from Monday to Thursday and blew it all between Friday and Sunday – still. The least surprising were the bride's parents; the most surprising was signior Massimo Leone, also known as Max Duggan, who was resting his voice in London between engagements.

Rose's heart skipped several beats when the note from him arrived, the day before the ceremony, asking if he might at least join the breakfast for the toast to the bride and groom. It would be decidedly awkward, she felt, on the occasion of her marrying a man with whom she had (so far) passed one blissful night *in flagrante,* to entertain another with whom she had done the same. She kept the messenger waiting an hour or more while she wrestled with her conscience, and only then did it strike her that Roger was in precisely the same boat. She had asked Sally Winnen to be her chief bridesmaid, and Sal, seeing the chance to publicize their Falmouth Lady's Emporium by associating it with one of *the* fashionable weddings of 1912, had asked to include her partners, Ruby Penhallow and Jennifer Divett; they would have their own gowns made up, to Rose's specifications, of course, plus one more for Ellen Howe, whom Rose had picked to make up the quartette.

Thus one of her bridesmaids also happened to have been her new husband's mistress for the best part of a year; not that he gave it a second thought, and he certainly felt no embarrassment at it. What was one night of bliss compared with that! So she sent the messenger back with an invitation to Max for the whole event, wedding and breakfast.

Noel was Roger's best man, which surprised Rose for she had never thought of them as being particularly close. They claimed to have met socially, many times, when the Deverils had lived in Falmouth. She suspected their association was more recent – in fact, only since Roger had decided he could not face life without her and so had needed to keep in touch with H-d-W's plans for her. In any case, she supposed it was no more extraordinary than her own choice of Sally Winnen as her chief bridesmaid – what Mom called her 'matron of honor.' The idea of Sally as matron of *anything* was worth several fits of giggles between them – though not until the event was over.

On the run-up to it, by contrast, the giggles were as rare as June snowdrops. To Rose, her wedding was, naturally, a production – her own, this time – and so every little detail had to be perfect. From the precise shade of red in the roses that formed the core of her decorative theme to the matching red in the rose-bordered place cards at the breakfast banquet – not forgetting that of the petals which were to be strewn in place of vulgar confetti – she was dictator of all. The vicar eventually conceded to her that she and Roger would speak their vows directly rather than tamely parrot the words at his prompting. ("It would feel to me as if I were correcting your delivery," she explained – though to him the 'explanation' sounded more like a threat.) The order of the service was to be printed on handmade 'Three Trees' paper from Barcham and Green; no other paper would do. M. Henri de Pusy, the French *maître de cuisine* at Frascati's, roasted four trial joints of prime English beef before producing one to her satisfaction. The *chef de pâtisserie* denied that such a rose-pink sugar-icing was possible until she threatened to take off her gloves and mix it before his very eyes (and subordinates). Rolls-Royce, in Conduit Street, just round the corner from the church, could not possibly rustle up such a fleet at such short notice; however, as Frascati's was so close by, the guests would surely not mind being ferried there in shifts? They changed their tune when four of their best customers sent notes in their own hand, urging them to try harder. And as for her wedding dress ...

It was modelled on the one worn by Princess Maud at her marriage to Crown Prince Charles of Denmark, some sixteen years earlier – the one that had caused such a sensation with its huge puff sleeves and epaulettes. But 'modelled on' is a most elastic term, and Rose had variations in plenty. The rented diamond tiara needed to be an inch higher and it should curve more gently round to the sides; also the veil should be gathered more at the back when worn off the face, so as to show as much of her richly coloured hair as possible. The train could be cut more generously and in a lighter weight of silk, so that it could seem to cascade and froth behind her, rather than simply fall in one heavy swathe. And the hemline could be a little higher, couldn't it ... these days? No one saw any harm in a glimpse of ankle. And those jeweled silk court shoes from Devigny's deserved their day of glory. In short, by the time Rose had finished with it, not even Princess Maud herself would have recognized the original inspiration.

Rather late in the day Roger discovered the way to curb her more outré demands – not that he minded their financial impact, which was a flyspot to an elephant as far as he was concerned, but he feared for the sanity of those who bore the brunt of them. His first attempt – "You don't need to impress *my* side of the family, you know. We didn't get rich on extravagances" – failed abysmally. She wasn't insisting on perfection for *that* reason; the press would expect a parvenu like her to get something wrong and would pounce on every little gaffe. She was determined to cheat them of that satisfaction.

His next attempt hardly fared better. He recalled the shambles of several aristocratic weddings, starting with Queen Victoria's own, where everyone grew so fed up with the muddle that they stopped for refreshments while the warring parties sorted out the protocol. To Rose it merely proved that the upper classes had long ago had their day and should already have passed the baton gracefully to those who knew how to manage properly.

His third approach was more oblique: He put Noel up to it.

"You'll have to give up the Lady Augusta act, old thing," he said to her, about a week before the great day, when tensions were close to the snapping point. "Why?" she asked abstractedly, running her eye down the eighth but certainly not final list of seating arrangements at the restaurant.

"Because you're getting more like the mater every day. I hadn't realized it until now but this wedding-thing has brought it all to the surface." Nothing short of such a dreadful accusation could have attracted her eyes away from that sheaf of papers. "I don't believe you," she said.

"I didn't think you would." And now he pretended to an interest in her sketches of the seating plan, forcing her to snatch it out of his sight. "What d'you mean, anyway?" she asked. "I thought you no longer had any intercourse with Nancemellin."

"I don't, but one hears things, you know. Why can't I look at your seating plan?"

"Bugger the seating plan!" She stuffed it in her handbag. "What have you been hearing about your ma?"

"Oh ..." He stifled a yawn. "It's fuss, fuss, fuss all the time, I hear. Her precious footmen are now in their third sets of livery and still she's not satisfied. Fenella says it drives her mad. I say she should tell the mater she's turning into Lady Georgius Midas."

Sir Georgius and his lady were *Punch's* cartoon-caricatures of the ultimate *nouveaux riches*! – the very epitome of showy vulgarity and conspicuous extravagance.

After that, only those who had not previously experienced Rose's perfectionism thought her a holy terror; the old hands, or victims, all remarked on how mild she had grown as the wedding day approached. However, just to ward off any last-minute backsliding, Roger brought his elder sister, Mrs Gwendoline Ferris, to assist Rose over any finer points of detail concerning his side of the family. She had lately returned from a visit to Persia and she found occasion to remark to Rose on the habit of oriental craftsmen to leave a deliberate imperfection in their work, on the ground that to attempt perfection would be to mock God.

Rose dismissed the thought with a single barb. "That's why they've got camels and we've got Rolls-Royces," she said.

"Well, actually, I was thinking that the English upper classes discovered the same principle long ago – except in our case we don't need to make *deliberate* imperfections."

It was enough to keep the fires of perfectionism at least partially dampened until the morning of the great day dawned. But then, not long after that same dawn, Rose sat surveying herself in the looking glass and suddenly realized that the frame of dazzling white around her face served only to emphasize her freckles, which, in turn, had been brought upon her by the recent spell of brilliant sunshine. She had done her best to stay out of it, hiding away behind parasol *and* veil, but there was so much pale stucco in the West End these days that you'd need to be a bat or a mole to escape the dreaded rays completely.

"Fetch me my Leichner set," she commanded.

It added a nailbiting half hour to her preparations, cutting into the two hours she had allowed for unforeseen disasters, but the end result was the one she had always intended – a natural, healthy, country-girl's face without a trace of cosmetic assistance. She spared one freckle on her left cheek – on the Persian principle.

She had moved out of Bedford Street at the beginning of the week and was now staying at the Savoy. She and Roger would return there that evening, to the bridal suite, before leaving for Paris from nearby Charing Cross the following afternoon. Her Mom and Pop were in the next room, to which there was a communicating door, so Mom was in and out like a cuckoo in a clock all that morning. Although she had a republican's contempt for the aristocracy and its ways, she had no aversion to wealth *per se;* much less to the privileges it could buy. She, too, was dressed by the Falmouth Lady's Emporium; Pop was kitted out by Roger's tailor, Samuels of Savile Row. The clothes did for them what an impeccable upper-class accent had done for their daughter.

"It's going to be hard to go back to that little old italian warehouse, Pop," Rose said as he escorted her downstairs at last, in good time to arrive late at the church, which – since all distances in London are measured by the clock – was fifteen minutes away.

"I don't hardly think so, maid," he replied. "This-here lark is, to us, like what you do do on the stage. The wedding itself, that's serious, but the rest is like Johnny Meagor's geese – all show."

"You're not going to say things like that in your speech, I hope. What you call 'show' is the most serious business in my life."

"I do know what to say in my speech, right enough," he replied as the limousine drew out into the Strand. "Aren't you frighted?"

"About what? Being married to Roger?"

"No. About marrying into all they high-quarter folk."

"Am I frighted?" She considered it. "No. Excited, more like. Hurrisome. Like going on at a first night. Part of me fears it's going to go all wrong but the rest just knows it won't. Fear and confidence, we juggle with them all the time."

"You never *dreamed* you'd be wed like this, though."

They were entering Trafalgar Square. "That's true," she said, gazing up at Nelson. "And yet it doesn't seem strange to me any more. I've stopped pinching myself to see if it's all just a dream. Actually, I think that happened on the *Olympic*. Being taken for what I am in America has made me realize it's true. I *am* what I am. I don't even feel it's a privilege for which I ought to be grateful. Does that sound dreadful?"

"Never, you!"

By now they were going up Haymarket; Rose divided her attention between him and the two theatres there – His Majesty's and the Haymarket itself. "You know you and Mom could retire now," she said. "Buy a house up in Wodehouse Terrace. I could see you all right for ever now."

"And die of boredom? No thanks! We're so happy as two dorymice in velvet in Mister Watts's old place. Shopkeeping's in our blood just like what acting is in yourn. 'Sides, you done enough for us already. You acted in there, have you?" He nodded at the Haymarket Theatre.

"Not yet. Has any of my make-up come off on this veil?"

"What make-up?" He peered closely at her.

"That's all right then," she said. "I wish today were over already. In fact, I wish the whole honeymoon was over. I hate the thought of people looking at me and thinking … well, what people always think when they stare at new brides."

They entered Piccadilly Circus and made for the bottom end of Regent Street.

Pop cleared his throat awkwardly. "*Her* wedding, *his* honeymoon! You do know all about that old caper, I daresay? Honeymooning and that?" She stared at him and her jaw dropped. "No!" she exclaimed. "Why? Is there something I ought to know?"

He swallowed heavily.

Her laugh gave the game away. "Pop! Did you really imagine a girl could be two years on the stage and *not* know why she's fighting off men at the stage door after just about every performance?"

He grinned awkwardly. "I should ought to have thought. Still – knowing's one thing but experience is another."

"Well, you needn't worry any more. Mom did a good job with the basic truths and, if you must know, Roger and I jumped the starter's gun, as they say, about six weeks ago. Not that we've done anything like it since, mind," she added at the sight of his shocked expression. "And that's another reason why I'm looking forward to the end of the day – the daylight part of it, anyway! No fears there. Don't breathe a word of it to Mom, though."

She grabbed his arm and laughed as they turned into Conduit Street. "I never dreamed I'd be wed like this, and I'll bet *you* never dreamed you'd have such a conversation with me on the day, eh?"

He joined in her laughter. Lifting his silk topper to wipe his brow, he said, "Isn't that a fact!"

"There's the Rolls-Royce showrooms. They drummed up this car for us – and all the others. Money is a wonderful thing, you know. Two hundred guests ... fifteen thousand rose petals. Just like that."

"Your Mom says you counted every one."

"Pffft!"

The limousine made the turn into George Street, where the pavements were already lined with onlookers. A great cheer went up the moment they saw the car with its traditional pink bunting.

"Here we are at last!" She gestured toward the church. "Pop – I'm never going to be able to thank you and Mom for everything, but the wish is there. Hold on to that."

"Dam-me!" he complained, dabbing away a tear as he helped her out. "Now you made me baal like a babby."

As the car slid silently away again, to park in Hanover Square, she turned and acknowledged the cheers.

"Come-us on in where 'tis dark," Pop said, still dabbing his eyes.

But it was not dark inside, for St George's is a Georgian church, dedicated to a rational God of the Enlightenment; it has large windows and no dark, medieval corners where dubious spiritual mysteries might lurk.

Her heart was going like a water hammer, but not even Sally, standing with the other three bridesmaids just inside the church door, could have guessed it from the exuberant smile she gave them as they took up her train.

Everyone knew that Rose was an actress, and one who would be expected to make a spectacular appearance, but the gasp that propagated itself like a wave down the aisle, the moment she entered, showed by just how much she had overtopped even their wildest expectations.

And so the most dreaded moment was over – the equal to that instant when a first-night curtain rises and the whole of life hovers uncertainly between triumph and disaster. Here at St George's that united gasp had nudged her away from disaster, at least.

At first she had eyes only for Roger, up by the altar rail, grinning at her over his shoulder. Such a handsome man ... such good company ... so comfortable to be with ... she *was* doing the right thing. There could no longer be the slightest doubt about that. If there should be one of those absurdly melodramatic scenes in which Louis were to turn up and shout 'I can!' at that moment when the vicar asked about any man being able to 'shew any just cause' ... even then ... no. It was just too absurd to consider. As all faces turned toward her she could not help noticing the difference between those to her right – Roger's lot – and those to her left – hers. His were, in Caesar's phrase, 'sleek headed ... men who sleep o' nights.' They looked as if they had been reared on steak, kippered in smoke from Havana, and preserved in port-wine since birth ... faces that had hunted the shires and shot over heathered braes ever since the invention of double-entry bookkeeping.

Hers, on the other hand, had Cassius's 'lean and hungry look' – not the hunger of starvation but of ambition. Actor, impresario, producer, shopkeeper, ex-*courtisane,* ex-mistress – all were on a higher rung of that ladder on which their parents had first set their feet. How would these two sides mix down at Frascati's, she wondered? She must do what she could to make it all smooth.

She stood as close to Roger as possible throughout the ceremony, thrilling at every touch. It was like electricity, running up and down inside her. She *was* doing the right thing – absolutely; there could be no possible doubt about it now.

"... let him speak now or else hereafter for ever hold his peace," the vicar said.

The silence was electric, too.

She wished she had, after all, finished that letter and sent it to Louis. She had thought the same the day after she tore it up and threw it away – though, funnily enough, when she went back to the waste-paper basket, it wasn't there. All the other rubbish was, but not that letter. The remaining waste baskets *had* been emptied, so she assumed she must have dropped it in one of them, instead. Anyway, this was no time to let her thoughts wander down such pathways! She almost missed her cue for responding, "I will."

Then, unprompted, it was: "I, Lucinda-Ella Tremayne, take thee, Roger Wilbraham Teniers Deveril, to my wedded husband, to have and to hold from this day forward, for better for worse, for richer for poorer, in sickness and in health, to love, cherish, and to obey, till death us do part, according to God's holy ordinance; and thereto I give thee my troth." And then the moment of finality as Roger slid the ring down her finger, assuring her that he worshiped her with his body and endowed her with all his worldly goods.

Then: "Those whom God hath joined together let no man put asunder." And, finally: "I pronounce that they be Man and Wife together ..." after which everything else was mere decoration.

It was done! Final, irrevocable, indissoluble. The moving finger had writ and moved on. And it *was* the right thing. The organist played the Wedding March from *A Midsummer Night's Dream* at a pace more suited to the Dead March from *Saul,* but what did it matter now? The smiles from both sides of the aisle as she and Roger progressed arm in arm to the west door said all that needed to be said.

Outside, the crowd had more than doubled since her arrival. Roger, even though he must have been expecting something of the sort, was taken aback; the verger, pocketing his tip, said there were three times as many as there had been for the Marchioness of Dufferin, which, he implied, was some kind of benchmark. They moved on to their limousine in a deluge of rose petals that soon became a carpet underfoot.

Her meticulous preparations bore fruit at the wedding breakfast, which Lord Phillips declared to be the best he had ever attended. Rose, who knew the power of applause, brought the chefs out for their own minute of glory; before he returned to the kitchens, M. de Pusy leaned confidentially toward her and Roger to say that if ever they desired a dish that was not on that night's menu, they had only to mention it and he would personally attend to their wishes.

Pop made a speech in which he told many of his 'Zacky Polkinghorne' stories – slanting them to give some matrimonial reference; Rose gritted her teeth and decided she did not grudge him the laughter they won. Noel, though he rattled through the telegrams, still took twenty minutes to read the lot, before making the expected speech full of ambiguous praise for the bride and backhanded compliments for the groom. Roger responded with a short, embarrassed, touching speech promising her parents his utter and lifelong devotion to their daughter.

And then Rose stood up, provoking cries of "Oh? What now? Well, here's a thing!" and the like.

"Come, come!" she cried. "A *non*-speaking role for me on this of all days? Think again!" Amid laughter she continued, "Every marriage is special. Every husband is special to his wife ..."

"And every wife special to her husband!" Roger butted in.

"You took the words out of my mouth," she replied, pursing her lips at him in a pretend annoyance. "We are no different in that respect – and so you could say we are *not* special, in that respect. But there is one way in which no one could deny that this *is* a most special wedding, the start of an equally unusual marriage. I'll go further and say it is a very *English* marriage, because we English are a rather peculiar people. We like to suppose that we are ridden by snobbery and class distinctions – that we are, indeed, the Two Nations lamented by Benjamin Disraeli. Nothing could be further from the truth. We need only look across the Channel to discover nations that truly are divided, and into classes far more rigid than anything we have devised for ourselves here. And what has been the result? During the past five centuries they have been racked by one gory revolution after another, as stiff-necked pride bowed before Madame Guillotine or her like ..."

"Thank you, Miss Marteyne," a wag shouted from the back of the restaurant. "You have the part!"

She joined in the general laughter but continued: "Fortunately, gracious sir, it is a part I cannot shirk, not upon the stage but in life itself. For a thousand years we, the English, have avoided revolution on a continental scale precisely because of events like this. Tens of thousands, no, *hundreds* of thousands of them down the ages. Occasions on which the established wielders of power and influence open their ranks – and, I trust, their hearts – to those who clamour outside. To us. I speak not only of marriages but of alliances of all kinds – in business, government, charitable committees, parish councils, clubs, societies, sports ... in every sphere it is possible for prince and publican to work side-by-side for some common goal."

There was a silence now; even the waiters stood and listened.

"I did not marry Roger for any such reason – I hope that goes without saying. I have married him because I love him with all my heart, all my body, all my soul." She turned to him and added, "Without the smallest reservation, my darling."

He swallowed heavily and blinked several times.

To the audience again, she concluded, "But I cannot prevent our marriage from making one more contribution, minuscule but not trivial, to that great English game of perpetual revolution. These thoughts, incoherent and shallow as they are, occurred to me the moment I entered the church this morning and saw the Deveril party to my right and the Tremayne party to my left. To me, then, you were them-and-us. I would like to think that, by accepting the name of Deveril from this wonderful man and by promising to share the rest of my life with him, we – Roger and I – have abolished that division as far as we here today are all concerned. If we have – and here I'm sure I speak for him as well as for myself – then we ask you to rise and join in one final toast: To us! To *all* of us!"

74

The cast of *Trelawny* had got up a little skit – a few extra scenes tacked on to the play in which the heroine, having married the booby, returns from her honeymoon unable, yet again, to act. This time, however, the twist is that she regains her confidence through singing. Unfortunately, she sings at auditions for several quite inappropriate parts – Portia in *The Merchant*, Ophelia, Desdemona, and so on. Ellen Howe, playing the part of

Rose Trelawny, managed a devastatingly funny caricature of the new Mrs Roger Deveril in that same role. Through her laughter, Rose could see that H-d-W was sitting up and taking an interest; if she herself were still going back into that play, she would have been quite worried – and not at all pleased with her bridesmaid's behaviour. It frightened her, not for the first time, to realize that there was so much talent out there in the world, most of it latent, all of it desperate to shine.

Max took advantage of this skit to announce that he had written a further scene, to be tacked on to the end of it, a scene in which Rose Trelawny discovers her true vocation – as a singer. This linkage must have been a last-minute inspiration, for he had clearly planned it originally as a self-contained party piece to spring upon Rose by surprise; she realized it when the string quintet they had hired for the occasion struck up the introduction to the duet, *Là'ci darem la mano.* He sang his opening verse as he approached the top table and handed her the text just as she should come in with *Vorrei, e non vorrei* ... But they were words she would never forget; she laid the paper aside and, joining him, sang as if they were acting their parts upon the stage, walking down the aisle among the tables. They were not allowed to get away under two encores.

And this time Rose was pleased to see not only H-d-W but also Gorgeous George staring at *her* with a new, speculative light in the eye. After that, coffee and comfits were served and the tables broke up into informal groups among which people flitted as the whim took them. It was the newlyweds' chance to get round and have a word with everybody. They started out together but, finding that the conversations were either banal, being repetitive comments on the wedding, or exclusively about Rose, her performances, her prospects, and so forth, they soon parted and made their own ways about the room.

"The Deverils are a very *old* family, you realize," one of the aunts told Rose. "Originally de Verreuil, as Roger will have told you, I expect?"

Her husband cast a weary eye ceilingward.

"Yes," Rose replied, "from a village in Normandy that vanished during the Black Death."

"Well ... *we,* naturally, came over much earlier – in 1066, in fact. With the Conqueror."

"And you're still here!" she replied in delighted amazement. "I suppose that means you're quite fond of us natives. You, of course, fought those Anglo-Saxon interlopers. We Celts had a go at them five hundred years before you, but we lost. So well done you! And I hope it's not too late to say you're very welcome here?"

"Why ... no," was the bemused reply. "Thank you very much."

Rose's true reward was the confidential wink the husband gave her as she moved on.

"I'm glad you didn't *entirely* forget your old colleagues," said Mr Swindlehurst after an exchange of shallower civilities.

"Dear Mister S!" She gave his arm a squeeze. "Not a week has gone by but I have thought of my promise to dig a hole and pull you through, once I became established here in London. But I have also been aware that there are something like fourteen thousand people in this city with ambitions to tread the boards, where there is room for only twelve-hundred at most. What favour would I have done you had I secured you three months of glory followed by nine of fruitless searching? However, you can take your chance on it tomorrow, if you like. One word from me ...?" She raised an inquiring eyebrow. He thought it over and said, resignedly, "You're right, I suppose. All the same, I should like even three months of West End glory before I retire."

"Ah now that's an entirely different matter. I know I should not be where I am today – on the stage, at least – without the help you gave me at the start. And I never will forget you – not even twenty ... thirty years from now, when it will be time for you to think of retirement. If I still have any influence then, it will be at your command."

"Nineteen forty-two!" he said in his best hollow voice. "Another thirty years of strolling melodrama!"

Max said, "We were pretty good together just now, Lucille – at least that seems to be the general opinion. D'you think we might find time, next spring, say, to do a couple of charity concerts together? I have six days between Zurich and Vienna."

His eyes betrayed his real purpose, however. He was hoping that by then her ardour for Roger might have lost some of its edge and she wouldn't be above a little *affaire* on the side. Well ... she could take advantage of the professional engagement, especially with a singer of his international stature, without letting him take any more intimate advantage of her.

"Have a word with H-d-W," she replied. "Say 'Barkiss is willin'!' Or Marteyne in this case. I'd love nothing more."

Did she flutter her eyelashes a little *too* encouragingly? She hoped not. She hoped that people in opera were so used to overacting that you had to hit them with a hammer before they'd notice you.

"I've just been telling H-d-W what a lucky fellow he is," Gorgeous Gorge remarked to her. "There's his theatre, not finished to time, and here's his brightest star obliging him by getting married and going off on her honeymoon. How long will you be away?"

She turned to H-d-W. "When do we open – *really?*"

"See!" GG laughed. "Honeymoons tailored to order!"

"Luck has nothing to do with it," de Witt told him. "All you need is a bright young assistant with a private income and a discerning eye, in love with the theatre, and you send him out among the strollers and repertory players ... it's like panning for gold."

"Then how," GG asked, not taking his eyes off Rose, "does your gold miner come back with diamonds – especially a diamond like *this* – in his hand?"
"You're too kind, sir." Rose interrupted de Witt's intended response. "But we all know that the real value of any diamond lies in the skill of that man who cuts and polishes it." She dropped H-d-W a curtsy.
"That's very true," his rival continued, unabashed. "But once the cutting and polishing is done, the stone goes onto the open market – or so my friends in the diamond trade tell me."
"Every man should have friends in *some* trade," de Witt observed.
"Especially those with few in their own," countered the other.
Rose startled them both by frisking them, as a policeman might feel for weapons. "That's all right, then," she said, dusting her hands. "Carry on. It's just that they charge extra for blood on the carpets here."
"All's well as do end well, then," her cousin Frank said.
"Where's young George?" Rose asked Ann.
"Fast asleep under one of the tables over there."
Rose smiled at Frank. "Takes after his father then!"
He laughed. "Not any more. Them days is done, maid."
Rose glanced at Ann, who, she now suspected, was expecting again. "Spoken with a certain tinge of regret?" she said.
"Not in my hearing." She glared at Frank with jocular belligerence.
"How many are you milking now?" Rose asked.
"Three dozen," he said. "We got one Frisian doing fifteen hundred gallons. She'll be county champion up the Royal Cornwall next month."
"That's two dozen at Trefusis," Ann said, "and another dozen across the Fal."
"At your parents' place?"
She nodded. "We do only put the best milkers to a Frisian bull. We bought a good Hereford for the rest, so we do get the best beef off of they others."
"You must be one of the biggest farmers around the whole estuary now."
"We're *the* biggest," Ann said proudly. "'Cepting for the big estates' home farms. If we could buy Nancemellin home farm, we'd be the biggest of all."
"But that Lady Carclew, she won't sell, yo'," Frank added. "'Tis a terrible shame. Ditches clogged and fences all abroad. She won't spend a penny on 'n nor she won't sell, neither."
"Is there any point in speaking with Mister Noel, I wonder?" Ann asked. Rose shook her head. "He and his mother aren't even on speaking terms. Tell me, d'you see her ladyship out and about much these days?"
"Never!" they replied in unison.
"What do people say about her, locally?"

They glanced all around, checking to see if Noel was in earshot. Then Frank said, "They do say as she've gone a bit ... you know – like Sir Hector."

"Betwattled," Ann said bluntly.

"Daw-brained."

Rose nodded. "Noel says the same. There are some tales about her new footmen?"

Frank and Ann smirked at each other. "More'n just tales, I can tell 'ee," she said. "We went out and bought some gert telescope for to see the farm across the water. And the goings-on we seen over to Nancemellin ... I can tell 'ee. Well, I *can't* tell 'ee, is the long and short of it."

"We do call them the Four Musketeers," Frank added. " 'Cos they can *stand* and *drill* for hours!"

"Frank!" Ann blushed and nudged him with her elbow, even as she added to Rose, " 'Tis true, though."

Rose eyed them thoughtfully for a moment and then said, "Promise me one thing – if you notice or even hear of any marked change in her ladyship's condition, or fortunes, let me know at once. Promise?"

"How?" Frank asked, meaning 'why?'

"I have my reasons," was all she'd say. "It could be to your advantage, too."

She moved on toward a nearby table where a silvery haired woman of middling years sat alone, watching her closely. "Do forgive me," Rose said as she approached and sat down. "You must be on Roger's side of the family, but I don't ..."

"I'm Mrs Redmile-Smith," the woman said. "Louis' mother."

"Ah." Rose was on the point of adding that she didn't recall sending her an invitation when the other saved her the trouble. "That's right, my dear. I am the proverbial spectre at the feast – though I've only just arrived, in fact. I couldn't resist the temptation to see what Louis has been talking about these past two years."

"Two years and ten days, probably."

"Goodness me! You are very precise, Miss Marteyne. I'll leave if you wish."

Rose shook her head. "I don't know if your son has told you of our correspondence?"

"Ending your association? Yes. I do think you might have had the courage to tell him so in person. He was very hurt to be brushed off by the postman."

"It wasn't like that – I promise you."

"Wasn't it?"

Rose sighed and looked all about her. "Please don't ever tell him this," she said, drawing closer. "It would hurt him so much more. I went over there intending to surprise him – a pleasant surprise, I thought, naturally. In fact, on the very day of our arrival in New York, I went directly from the pier to the railway station and caught the first train to Trenton. And" – she swallowed hard – "I did, in fact, see Louis."

"He never said a word of this to me."

"I said I saw him. He didn't see me. He'd been writing me all these letters about how well the new business was going, and ..."

"And so it has. He writes to me as well, you know."

"Tell me, are you still living in South Audley Street?"

"I am, as it happens – not that it's any business of yours, mind."

Rose realized that the woman's aggressive attitude had almost provoked her into saying precisely what she had seen on that dreadful day. Just in time she realized she would be taking away the last prop of comfort in her life, her life in that grace-and-favour apartment in Mayfair. She couldn't do it. No matter at what cost to herself, she could not tell her the truth about Louis. "Let me just say that the moment I saw him – for the first time after almost a year and a half apart – I suddenly realized I was no longer in love with him. I was ..."

"Why?" she snapped. "He hasn't changed. He's sent me photographs of ..."

"It was nothing to do with physical appearances. He's as handsome as ever. It was nothing to do with him. It was *me.* The change was on my side. Roger Deveril had proposed to me before I left for America. And the moment I saw Louis – it was across a rather crowded room in a hotel there ..."

"The Windsor, probably," Mrs Redmile-Smith said. "The company owns it."

Rose had to bite her tongue to prevent herself from blurting out precisely what she had seen that day. "It was the Windsor, as it happens," she said, "but it has nothing to do with that, either. As I said, I simply realized I loved Roger instead. But how could I walk up to him and say, in effect, 'Hallo, Louis – I've come three thousand miles just to tell you I've fallen in love with another man!' It would be just too cruel. Perhaps what I did was cowardly, but it was a great deal kinder than that."

"One of your Falmouth friends?" Roger asked, catching up with her as she walked away. "Not a friendship I wish to maintain," she replied. When she saw the woman had left the restaurant she added, "It was Mrs Redmile-Smith, in fact – Louis' mother."

"The devil it was!" He glared angrily at the open doorway. "Where are those two fellows who looked at everyone's invitations?"

"I suppose they think no one's going to gatecrash now that all the scoff has gone. She waited for that moment, of course."

"What did she want?"

"Just to tell me how disappointed Louis is – can't blame her."

"I studiously haven't asked this before now, but ... did you, in fact, see him over there." She nodded. "I've just told her about it. Not the full truth, of course. I merely said that the moment I saw him I realized it was you I loved and really wanted to marry."

He hugged her and kissed the side of her brow. "And what truth did you withhold from the old dear?"

"That her son is just a barman."

"Really?" He frowned. "But ... No, go on."

"That's all. I went down there to tell him in person that it was over between us – that I'd met you ... fallen in love with you, and so forth. And then I saw that, contrary to all those glowing reports he'd been writing me, he was nothing more than a barman ... you know ... the humiliation of failing in America as well ... how could I add to it by telling him that? So I just went on to Boston and wrote him a letter. She thinks it was cowardly. Maybe it was. I don't really mind. It's all over with now, anyway. I'm safe. You're safe. That's all that matters."

He lowered his voice and murmured in her ear, "I wish we were safe in bed, this very minute."

"Me, too, my darling," she whispered fervently. "How soon can we get away?"

"Soon. It'll snap off if we don't do something about it."

"I'll ask Mom," she said.

She found her mother in the ladies' powder room. After checking that none of the stalls was engaged, she asked how soon she and Roger could slip away.

Mom thought that seven would be the earliest, even if they were going to dine in their suite. "About that, honey," she said. "You don't feel in need of any further advice?"

Rose took her into the passageway outside and, lowering her voice almost to a whisper, told her she knew it was going to be all right. "In fact," she added, "the night *Mauretania* docked at Southampton, Roger took me to a little hunting lodge he owns in the New Forest and we jumped the starter's gun. All night. We haven't done it since, so we're both pretty desperate by now. That's how I know it'll be all right. Don't breathe a word of that to Pop, by the way."

75

They overslept so late that they only just made it to Charing Cross in time for the cross-channel train, which left at five past two. Still exhausted, they slept further on the Folkestone – Boulogne ferry, where they took a state cabin on the main deck for an extra three pounds. To Rose the extravagance lay not so much in the money as in the fact that she ignored the romance of her first glimpse of the White Cliffs of Dover from the sea for that of lying in bed beside her marvellous new husband, doing nothing but cradling his exhausted body in her arms – and, to be sure, dreaming of the busy days or weeks ahead in Paris.

They arrived at the French port at twenty-five past five and departed it, nonstop for Paris, just under half an hour later, after a fairly casual passage through customs. They would probably have slept on the train, too, had there been a sleeper. Instead, there was a restaurant car – a *French* restaurant car – so most of the three-hour journey was passed not in their own reserved carriage but at the table. It had the heaviest damask tablecloth Rose's fingers had ever felt. The seats, upholstered in crimson velvet plush, sighed as you sank into them. And a small electric lamp with a low-wattage bulb in the centre of the table created all the ambience of a candle without the wax-tallow odour.

"The sea always gives me the most acute hunger," Roger said.

"You only saw the bit between the gangplank and the ship!"

"It was enough," he asserted.

Between them they had *foie gras truffé, caviar Beluga, salade d'ecrevisses des gastronomes, châteaubrand maître d'hôtel, mignons de veau Sainte-Alliance* with *haricots verts, fenouils à l'Italienne,* and *pommes duchesse,* rounded off with *crêpes Suzettes* and *oeufs à la neige à la pistache* ... all of which meant that when they arrived at the Hôtel Bristol at half past nine, they required no further *alimentation.* A small army of hopeful flunkeys escorted them to their suite – which comprised a sitting room, a dining room, a bathroom, a separate water closet, a double bedroom, and two dressing rooms, all at a cost of £4. 13*s.* 4*d.* a day, meals not included; a more frugal visitor could stay for four months at one of the Latin Quarter hôtels for that same amount. Rose wondered briefly if, two and a half months earlier, anyone on the *Titanic* had gone directly from this very suite to join the ship at Cherbourg; it was an effective antidote to any delusions of grandeur.

Roger, fully rested again, looked hopefully at the bed; but Rose directed one of the maids who went along with the suite to unpack their evening dress. "Tonight," she told him, "we go to the Folies Bergères." The maid pricked up her ears at that. *"Je m'excuse, madame,"* she said, "but it's not suitable for a lady. Fashionable, yes, but not suitable."

"What's your name?" Rose asked.

"Gabrielle, madame."

"Well, Gabrielle, my husband is a theatrical impresario. So a visit to any theatre is a professional matter for us."

"May God forgive you," Roger said once they were on their way to the rue Richer, a mile or so away to the northeast. "You lie supremely well."

"You could say that lying's my trade," she replied. "And, come to think of it, forgiveness is God's. So, anyway, tonight's just a bit of frivolity, eh? Before the serious stuff. Tomorrow – I mean Monday – we could see Bernhardt in *L'Aiglon.* They say it's quite magical. And then next Tuesday, if we can get tickets, we could go to the Châtelet to see this extraordinary Ballet Russes piece with Nijinsky, which has one half of Paris at the throats of the other half."

"I haven't heard of that."

"You must have. It was even in the London papers the day after we came back from the New Forest – Fokine taking umbrage because Diaghilev set Nijinsky to work in secret on the Debussy piece, *L'Après-midi d'une Faune,* which he dances – some say – like a clumsy half-animal, while others say it's the perfect marriage of Cubism and the ballet. Anyway, we'll go and see it and make up our own minds."

"*Our* own minds?" He chuckled.

"Of course! If you're going to be a proper impresario, darling, you'll have to be in touch with everything that's going on in art. Not just the theatre. There's a huge revolution going on in this city ... all around us. Right now. I'll bet van Dongen is throwing one of his great parties in Montmartre, this very evening, where great decisions are being argued over – things that will set all the arts off in amazing new directions. What's the difference between Futurism and Cubism, for instance?"

He threw up his hands. "How do I know? I didn't even know Celtic art was dead until I heard it was being revived. I mean, I never even knew it had been alive in the first place. What *is* the difference, then?"

"I don't know either. It's the sort of thing we must find out. We must return to London just sizzling with ideas so that people will see we're really in touch with all the very latest movements."

'Hunh!" He grunted. "There are some ancient but time-honoured *movements* I'd prefer to be in touch with at this moment."

"Yes, well, there'll be plenty of time for that, too." She snuggled against him and kissed the lobe of his ear. "But we can't waste all the other opportunities Paris offers, now can we."

"D'you think England's ready for ... I mean, it all sounds rather avant garde, don't you think?"

"What do I think? I think England's more ready for something new than even England believes. Look at what happened over Epstein's statue for Oscar Wilde's tomb, up in Père Lachaise cemetery. Ten years ago the papers wouldn't even dare print poor Oscar's name ..."

"Bloody right, too!"

She sighed. "That sort of talk just shows that silly old Roanoke still has the power to fret you. Anyway, the point is, the English took a keen interest in the progress of the Epstein sculpture – you saw the photos? A sort of winged male figure, vaguely Assyrian?"

"But not at all vaguely male!"

"No, well, that's the point. The English saw nothing wrong with it. But the French shrouded it under a tarpaulin and posted a gendarme to tell people it was banned. They don't visit cemeteries to be reminded about genital organs, they claim. The French! And now, so Noel told me, they've covered that offending organ up with a bronze plaque. So I think the English are ready to sweep away a few old cobwebs, too. Another thing we must do is go to Kahnweiler's gallery. He's got these two amazing Spanish painters, one called Juan Gris and the other ... something Picasso. Pablo Picasso. Henry Lacy says it's a new style of painting that's going to have a big influence on theatre design. It'll take it right away from all that romantic realism. Also there's the Gustave Moreau Museum, where there's this dreamy Russian called Chagall, who could also have quite a different influence on theatre design. So it'll be very interesting to compare them."

"Goodness, Lucille!" Roger exclaimed as the fiacre drew up in front of the Folies Bergères. "It seems we got married just in the nick of time. Another few weeks and we might have missed it all!"

76

If Roger had ever thought 'his' honeymoon would be the usual Parisian idyll of gastronomic and connubial delights, punctuated by visits to Longchamps, the Louvre, the Catacombs, the Eiffel Tower, and so forth, the schedule that Rose outlined inside their first few hours was enough to disabuse him. His mood passed from wary acceptance through stubborn resentment to weary acquiescence to, finally and surprisingly, a sort of bewildered enthusiasm. He himself was the most surprised of all; Rose, by contrast, was the least. He had to shake himself from time to time and ask, 'Is this really me?' She just said, "It is impossible to be here, in the midst of all this passion and fervour and *not* get caught up in the excitement of it all, even if you don't quite understand everything yet. Besides, darling, you've got more intelligence than half a dozen of them put together – you've just never used it much, that's all. In one single afternoon at Kahnweiler's you completely grasped what Cubism's all about. You certainly left *him* looking very thoughtful."

Roger privately thought that Kahnweiler's 'thoughtful' expression had more to do with the discovery that Mr and Mrs Deveril were occupying the royal suite at the Bristol, but he did not point it out. And, indeed, he was beginning to have a faint inkling of what these odd fellows – Gris, Bracque, Leger, Picasso etc were striving for; and it was mildly interesting; and, anyway, his darling Lucille was so passionate about it all ('even if she did not quite understand everything yet'), so how could he cavil?

In a way it helped that he was such a stolid, middle-of-the-road, middle-of-everything Englishman. His diffident judgment that something was 'pretty good on the whole' was worth ten of the more hysterical Gallic cries of *'magnifique ... du tonnerre ... au poile!'* and so forth. He came to be seen as something of a rock in the turbulent hither-and-thither of opinion. His comment that such-and-such an exhibition or performance was something he might just about summon the energy to cross the road to experience was taken as an endorsement worth several rave reviews from the likes of Roger Marx or Robert Brussel.

And so, since no man can withstand such all-round flattery without coming to believe that his lukewarm is another's red-hot and that his bewildered and imperfect comprehension of a topic is yet more valuable than another's doctoral thesis upon it, Roger found himself inexorably sucked into the vortex of Parisian culture. Indeed, his very bewilderment was turned into a serious critique; its targets did not say, 'This man is an ignoramus; we can ignore him' – rather they sighed, 'We have failed to make our point clearly; we must try harder'!

He himself did not fully grasp the situation until sometime toward the end of July, when Paris was beginning to empty for the August holidays, and they could at last spare the time to go as far afield as Versailles, all of eleven miles away; they went on a Sunday to be sure of seeing the great fountain display.

Most of the paintings on the walls were pretty second-rate stuff, as even the guide admitted – historical confections commissioned by this king or that to depict ancient scenes that no contemporary artist had thought fit to record. But the post-revolutionary rooms, filled with the works of more recent painters, like Gustave Doré, Vernet, and Gérôme were an exception. You didn't need any formal art training to feel the difference at once.

"I'll tell you one thing, darling," Roger said, having remarked on the sudden leap in quality. "Being surrounded by *real* painting and *real* art like this – good or bad, it doesn't matter – is a bit of an eye-opener."

"In what way?"

"Well – these Cubist fellows – you've just got to take their word for it that what they're churning out is art. A fellow shows you a portrait with one eye up here and another down there and the nose seen both side-on and from underneath at the same time ... and he tells you it's art – just because a lot of other fellows agree with him ..."

"Oh dear! You're not turning back into a philistine, I hope?"

"I don't know about that. What I *do* know is that if that's art, and everyone starts accepting it as such, then you open the floodgates to anything and everything. I mean you could lean a canvas against the wall and throw buckets full of colours at it and claim to have discovered Gravityism or something. Or take sculpture. Some of the stuff we've been looking at isn't all that different from driftwood, is it."

"But driftwood doesn't have any artistic *intention.*"

"Ha! You could soon give it that. Walk out along any seashore, pick up a bit that appeals to you ... straightaway you've got a bit of artistic *selection,* see? Then you decide where to cut it – top and bottom – before you mount it on a nice bit of polished wood with a little brass plaque saying *Dungeness Beach, 1912,* and abracadabra! Your own unique artistic sensibility has turned a bit of jetsam into a work of art. You could call it Discoveryism. Or, if you wanted a bit more class, Trouvéism." Rose thought it over and then said, "You don't sound as if you're criticizing it."

"I'm not!" He laughed. "I think it's marvellous. Because – you see – what's sauce for the artist-goose is sauce for the connoisseur-gander. If they can say any old thing can count as art, then so can I!" He looked at his watch. "Coming up to four-thirty. We'll miss the fountains."

As they descended the stairs again, down into the Hall of the Crusades (one half-good canvas by Vernet), Rose said, "A few cubist paintings might make quite a good investment. The things our parents' generation scoffed at are doing pretty well now. Twenty years ago you could have bought Cézannes for a few dozen francs, but look at them now! And we could get a handful of Picassos and Bracques for the cost of a week at the Ritz."

He was surprised. "You'd like that?"

"I don't know that *like* is quite the word. I'd like to hang them on our walls back in London and keep on looking at them until I could say I understood what they're striving after."

"And then?"

"Well then I'd be able to enjoy them wholeheartedly, of course."

"Right – consider it done! What of your dreamy Russian?"

"Chagall? He's almost *too* easy to like, don't you think?"

Roger pulled an incredulous face. "Is he?"

"Well then, you can make that *your* project – you keep looking at them until you can see what *he's* striving after."

The fountains sprang to life in a fabulous display. "One day," he murmured, "I'll learn when to keep my mouth shut."

77

After Paris there was Florence, Verona, Rome, Cap Ferrat ... On the Riviera, Roger found a piece of driftwood that, he felt sure, those who cooed over Epstein would adore. He agonized for almost half a minute about where to cut it and then, since it had cost him nothing, splashed out on an expensive block of lignum vitae on which to mount it.

"I think the contrast between the salt-etched frailty of the driftwood and the heart-of-darkness solidity of the mount is *so-o-o* poignant, don't you?" he said, making exquisite movements with his hands. "What shall we say we gave for it? Two and a half thousand francs? Or twenty-five thousand?"

Rose glowered at him and dug him with her elbow. Back in early August, at the end of their Paris visit, his growing scepticism had annoyed her. But then, recognizing that she herself was equally ignorant of 'modern art' in all its manifestations, she had come to welcome his 'infidel spirit,' as Soutine had called it; especially as it had not prevented his buying quite a few paintings for their new home in Hampstead – four Picassos, three Bracques, two Chagalls, and others by Duchamps, Delaunay (Sonia and Robert), Matisse, and Bonnard. He liked Matisse especially. "A no-nonsense man after my own heart," he said. "I asked him what his definition of art was and he said, 'It's a pick-me-up for tired businessmen.' That's something I can accept."

Privately Rose considered Matisse's paintings to be no more than sentimental lechery dressed up in sensual colours – "But what's one opinion against so many?" she would add.

Their new home was on the rural edge of Hampstead, overlooking the Vale of Health. From a mile or so off it looked classical but as you drew nearer you could see numerous little Arts & Crafts Movement details. Rose renamed the house Janus, after the two-faced Roman god. The Deverils were only the second owners; the original ones, Sir Charles and Lady Peguy, had commissioned its design from Sir Edwin Lutyens around the turn of the century.

The first thing the Deverils did on their return to London and 'real life' in early September was to hang their paintings.

"What means that enigmatic expression?" Rose asked when they had finished.

"I was just thinking – you see a daub like that leaning against a filthy old wall in an artist's garret and you think, 'My God! Ten quid for a dog's breakfast like that!' And then you see it hanging up here, in these surroundings, and you think, 'Tee-hee! I snapped that up for a mere tenner!' Funny old world, eh!"

Rose said nothing. She just stood there, lost in thought, delicately chewing her lip.

"Eh?" he prompted.

"I was thinking – what you've just said is actually the theme of *A Rose by Any Other Name.* We've decided to make Rose a girl from Whitechapel, by the way. With ..."

"We?"

"Henry Lacy and I. The man who wrote all those letters to me in Paris and Rome. Rose wiv an 'orrible cockney accent. The story now is that she applies for a place in the Mayfair household of Mrs Manners, an eccentric old widow, played (we hope) by Constance Craig. And ..."

"Is she expensive?"

"She's the best – that's all that matters. Anyway, I apply for this position and she turns me down because she 'can't grasp a dicky from me fish.' "

"What on earth is that?"

"Dicky-bird – word. Fish-and-chips – lips. She can't grasp a word from my lips."

He pulled a dubious face. "Does Rose have to be cockney?"

"Yes, because her dad is to be played by Sozzler Knox, and he can't do other accents. He turns up in the grand finale. If we get the timing right, he can do his usual turns in the music halls and come on to the Haymarket for the closing scene. See? Anyway, dear old Mrs Manners turns me down because she can't understand me. Then we sing 'We've all got a chain through the tongue,' and, as I leave, all despondent and dejected, I mutter in Yorkshire accent,

'Thou'd not turn uz off if I'd coom from York,' which, I should have explained, is the old woman's home town. So then she calls me back and discovers I can copy several other accents – including hers. So she gets me to shout an order down the speaking tube, in her voice, of course, to the kitchen, and then when the maid comes up the old woman says she didn't say a word and the maid swears black and blue she heard it. Then, as the maid turns to go, *I* say – again in the mistress's voice – 'You must learn to tell the truth, Millie.' And she bursts into tears and swears she did. So then Mrs Manners hatches this plot to dress me in all that finery and introduce me into high society as her ward. That's when we sing, 'Ain't the world peculiar!' And then there's all the learning stuff, where we poke lots of fun at quaint conventions and etiquette."

She broke off and sang a snatch: " 'We're all just a pack of cards, you know – calling cards, calling cards ...' That's the chorus, which is all the maids and footmen. And then, at a grand ball, the old lady and I sing this duet – 'All the world is here' and the chorus responds, ' 'Ceptin' them as ain't invited' – and I meet this absolutely gorgeous young lord, played by Gerald du Maurier, I hope. I hear he's grown tired of playing businessmen and posh policemen. And yes, before you ask, he *is* expensive – but he's also very good. His name will fill half the house. Mine will do the rest and Sozzler's will guarantee a waiting list. The only teeny problem is that they'll all want 'before the title' in their contracts."

"Du Maurier's also a terrible practical joker, they say."

She paused and stared at him. "You must stop mixing with theatrical people, you know."

"But it's true, isn't it? I heard he was in a play where one of the characters is tied up in a chair and has a long, serious dialogue with his captor and du Maurier paid one of the stage hands to go up into the flies and drip water on the poor chap's head – sort of Chinese water torture. Also, can he sing?"

"It doesn't matter. There's a technique where you sort-of half-talk, half-sing. It's quite effective in musical comedy – provided the man is handsome and languid and debonair, et cetera. So then in the third act, Lord Thing discovers ..."

"That's his name?"

"No. We can't decide. Henry wants 'Lord Bognor-Regis' because it's King George's favourite spa. I lean towards 'Lord Waverley' because he wavers so much. But neither of us is very happy."

"Lord Janus?" Roger suggested. "Looks forward ... looks back? Remembers the old ... surveys the new-mmmnh!"

She smothered his suggestion with a fervent kiss. "Brilliant!" she cried. "So in Act Three, Lord Janus discovers the truth about my origins in Whitechapel and calls the engagement off. Did I mention we were engaged? Never mind – he calls it off, singing, 'All that glitters surely is not gold.' And then there are some weepy bits where he mopes, 'I can't get over her,' and I sing, back in cockney,

'Gimme a gentle man and yer can keep all yer gentlemen.' And then Mrs Manners throws another grand ball, this time for all me cockney chinas (china-plates – mates, see?) and we do a reprise on 'All the world' changing the words to 'All the world is welcome here' and the chorus sings '*even* them as ain't invited.' And Lord Janus turns up in the middle of it and sings his reprise – 'I couldn't get over her' and our only problem then will be stopping Sozzler from making some innuendo out of that." She kissed him again. "And all for *your* investment of just ten thousand pounds!" She laughed. "Why, Roger, darling – you've turned quite pale!"

78

A Rose by Any Other Name was the theatrical sensation of the autumn season in 1912. The rumours that G. B. Shaw had been working on a drama with a similar theme proved true. When the curtain rose on *Pygmalion* the following year, with Herbert Beerbohm Tree as Professor Higgins and Mrs Patrick Campbell as Eliza Doolittle, it proved to be the better drama, too – especially as the action didn't have to keep pausing for a song. Rose and Henry Lacy kicked themselves that they had not made Sozzler Knox an *unmarried* father, like Doolittle in Shaw's play. They had, in fact, thought of it but had rejected the idea as one scandal too many in a story that was already shocking enough to bourgeois sensibilities – with a heroine who bamboozles her way into 'good' society by her own skill and cunning. Shaw got round the problem by making his heroine mere putty – almost uncomprehending putty – in the hands of an eccentric but respectable *gentleman;* 'her' achievement thus became his, which was something far more acceptable to a public already alarmed at the shrill demands of women at the gates of public life.

Be that as it may, the catchy music, the glittering cast (four names above the title!), and the fairy-tale ending, all ensured that *A Rose* did not lose ground to *Pygmalion.* Both played to crowded houses throughout their respective runs, and *A Rose* repaid Roger's investment twice over – and continued to do so even after Rose herself left the production to star in one that was even more important: her first baby.

Edward Roger Teniers Deveril weighed in upon the world at eight pounds seven ounces, at three-twenty in the small hours of Palm Sunday, April 5, 1914. Lord Moresby, who had been the first man to see each of more than two hundred heads that would one day be entitled to a coronet of some kind – and several others in line for a crown – was in attendance; but it was plain Mrs Treadwell, the midwife, who, when she saw his lordship reach for the foreceps, made the adjustments to the baby's position that ended Rose's suffering and brought happiness to the household. Mrs Treadwell was from Falmouth; in fact, it was she who had brought Rose into the world just over twenty-seven years earlier.

"There, my lover," she said, placing the washed and swaddled bundle into Rose's arms. "All's well as do end well – but you really shouldn't ought to of waited all these years to have your first. You'd have found it a lot easier ten year ago."

Ten years ago? April, nineteen-oh-four? She was then just starting in her second place – housemaid at Spernen Wyn Farm, Swanpool, at twenty-five pounds a year. She chuckled. "Somehow, I don't think so, Mrs Treadwell."

She glanced down at the wizened, hatchet-faced mite in her arms and was horrified to discover not the faintest shred of maternal feelings toward it. Or him. His movements were mere tics and his grimaces meaningless. "Shouldn't he be crying?" she asked.

Physician and midwife exchanged amused glances. "It *is* her first, sir," Mrs T said in extenuation.

"Did you love me from the moment they put me in your arms?" she asked her mother after Mrs Treadwell had left – just before they allowed Roger in to see her at last.

"Well, since you ask, honey ..." Mom lowered her voice and looked all about her. "I couldn't stand the sight of you. Everyone said you were the prettiest baby they ever clapped eyes on and I just couldn't see it. I'd gladly have given you away, except I felt sure they'd only have given you back."

"And when did you change?"

"Who says I did?" She laughed. "Seriously? I think I *began* to come round the first time I saw you smile and was sure it wasn't wind. Six weeks, maybe. And I guess I was won over completely that day you said 'Cutty Sark'."

It was a hoary legend in the family that Rose's first words had been 'Cutty Sark' – on being held up to watch the stately clipper sail into Falmouth Harbour. Flattering though it was, Rose herself never believed it.

Now she leaned down and kissed Edward's brow, which was damp and smelled of something not very edible, "Say 'Cutty Sark'," she urged.

He began to cry, just in time to greet his father, who was allowed in to see her at last. "My son!" he cried as he crossed the room. On catching her eye he said, *"Our* son! Edward – hallo Edward! Cheer up, little man, there's a bright day dawning." He kissed Rose fervently on the forehead. "Well done, old thing! Was it pretty bloody?"

"No and yes," she replied. "I mean it wasn't pretty and it was bloody. I should try to feed him, I suppose." She opened her pyjama jacket and, taking him back, helped him find a nipple.

Was this the moment when mother-love would mysteriously arrive? Seemingly not. She sighed and gazed down dispassionately at the little thing. Perhaps it was meant to be like this? If you were besotted with love, you maybe wouldn't notice any faults. She began to look for faults. The soft bit in the cranium she knew about. The fontanelle. If something had a name, it was usually normal. And the rough bits of skin. That had a name, too, but she couldn't recall it. And the hatchet face. The fingers were rather sweet, though; how could anything so small and delicate bend and grip like that?

She decided she could love the fingers, at least. She lifted his hand and kissed them. He fretted and grunted.

Why did he frown so much? It was like he was rejecting everything before he even tried it.

"That's it," Roger said, gazing fondly down at them. "Get him well filled up and contented. I'll bring the photographers in here in half a jiff."

"What?" Rose and her mother exclaimed in unison.

"Protecting our investment," he said. "You've been out of the public eye since last Christmas. I know it was in the best possible cause but we can't let a chance like this pass by. Every paper in London will want these pictures."

"Over my dead body!" Rose said stoutly.

"Don't say things like that. You know I'm talking sense ..."

"Roger! Have you any idea what I've just been through?"

"It was hardly fun for me, either, darling – pacing up and down out there, listening to your groans and cries. It was all I could do to stop myself from bursting in to comfort you."

"Well, I wish you had done. Then you'd understand that you're asking the impossible now." She smiled winsomely. "Send them away, there's a dear."

He shook his head. "If we do that, they'll only print some innuendo about things having gone wrong. Maybe they'll even suggest the baby's abnormal. You know what they're like. Go on – it'll only take a few minutes. Can the make-up girl start on you while he's suckling?"

Rose looked at her mother, who raised her hands as if fending off the unspoken request. "This is between you two, honey. You made Roger your impresario, I guess you can't grumble if he starts thinking and acting like one."

"I'll go and get the make-up girl," Roger said. "And my mother's christening shawl. The family heirloom. She'll kill me if the baby's pictured in anything else."

"Now just see what you've started!" Rose said to her baby, and, though she spoke with gentle mockery, he stopped suckling and began to bawl.

He bawled all the way through the five photographs the pressmen took; the air was thick with the smoke of the burned flash powder and they had to open the windows to let it escape – and let in the cold night air. Little Edward jumped at the first two flashes, causing Rose to hug him tightly; there was a little stirring of affection in her gesture, too. However, by the fifth flash he remained quite calm. "He's a publicity hound already," Rose murmured.

"I know how they'll caption this lot, Miss Marteyne," one of the photographers, well known to her, remarked.
"What's that, Bert?"
"'It may be gone midnight, but this Cinderella's not too late for the bawl!' Bawl spelled bee-hay-doubleyou-ell – geddit?"
"Very funny," she said wearily. "And if it doesn't strike them spontaneously, I'm sure you'll prompt them, anyway. The only trouble is, my name's not Cinderella."
He grinned. "Someone had the bright wheeze to nip across to Somerset House and look out your birth sustificate."
After he had gone she handed the now somnolent baby over to the night-nanny and said, "Roger?"
"Don't worry," he said, picking up the phone. His secretary, on the switchboard downstairs, answered at once; few were asleep in the house that night. "Get me Lord Northcliffe," Roger told him. "On his private line. Yes, of course I know what hour it is – I just want the man to understand how important *we* consider it to be."
When he put the phone down he said, "Well, he's not pleased but I think he got the point." He looked at his watch. "It's a bit early to ring Eton and get his name down, I suppose."
Mom's memory of gradually coming to terms with Rose turned into a self-fulfilling prophecy. At five weeks Edward broke into his first unequivocal smile, on seeing her enter the nursery, and she felt the first genuine stirrings of maternal interest in him. By then she, too, was climbing back out of the uncharacteristic depression that had settled on her almost from the moment of his birth. In her case it had been easy – she had simply returned to the stage, taking over from Margaret Asche in *All of a Sudden* at the Gaiety. Miss Asche, too, was expecting a baby that September and her physician had advised her to rest all through the third trimester.
"What's it like?" she asked Rose. "And don't palm me off with 'simply bliss-making' because it can't be. It's hell, isn't it."
"Not quite, darling," Rose replied. "Hell is supposed to be *utterly* unendurable. However, the worse you fear it'll be, the better it'll probably turn out. I'd trust a midwife before I'd trust a physician – though I'd make sure there's a physician handy, too."
"I knew I shouldn't have gone into a musical play called *All of a Sudden*. I hunted around for one called *All in Good Time* but it was playing Inverness."
"Well," Rose replied, "in my experience, the good time comes well before the all-of-a-sudden bit."
"Was yours sort of planned? I mean, were you using anything?"
"Lamb's bungs."
"Oh, I've heard of them. Are they any good? They don't *sound* very nice."
"We found them in Paris. They make them from a sort of blind alley in a lamb's intestines but you'd never guess it. They dry them out and sterilize them. There's no smell. You soak them for about

ten minutes before you need them. A man will complain it takes the spontaneity out of it but what I say is it forces him to warm up the house before the top act of the night goes on – and we thespians all know how important *that* is, don't we!"

She understudied for a week, taking the two matinées, and then stepped into the part. The takings jumped at once. Her darling public had not forgotten her.

But the world had grown more sombre, even in the six-odd months she had been away. America had invaded Haiti and was at war with Mexico. The suffragettes hacked holes in Velasquez's 'Rokeby' *Venus* in the National Gallery to persuade the House of Lords to pass a bill for women's enfranchisement; outraged, they threw it out instead. The Commons voted in favour of Irish Home Rule but Ulstermen formed a provisional government to resist it to the death – preferably not their own. And on Sunday, 28th of June – at the end of Rose's first week back on the stage – a Bosnian revolutionary student shot and killed Archduke Francis Ferdinand of Austria and his wife on a visit to Sarajevo. Big-bully Austria delivered an ultimatum to plucky little Serbia.

Anti-German feeling, which had been seething for most of the new century, boiled over in England. *We* were more powerful than *they* in every department, especially with France on our side. We had 25 dreadnoughts to their 13, 82 cruisers to their 7, 260 destroyers to their 163, and 119 submarines to their 38. True, they had mobilized over four million men while we had a mere three-quarters of a million regulars; but, again, with France's three and three-quarter million, we outmanned them, too. The Empire had twenty-one million tons of merchant shipping; the Germans little over five and a half million.

'What in God's name are we waiting for?' everyone was asking. 'Biff the Hun now – the minute the harvest is in – and, with superiority like that on our side, we will surely be able to hang the Kaiser among Berlin's Christmas decorations!'

"And even if it does last a *little* longer," Roger explained to Rose, "we have over three and a half thousand million pounds of foreign investments to draw on. Germany has little over one thousand million. We've got them boxed in from every angle."

It still sounded a great deal to Rose. You could buy hundreds of bullets for just one pound, so a thousand million could procure a great many deaths – even if every machine gunner in the German army were as blind as a bat.

"What'll you do?" she asked.

"I've already done it, actually," he replied. "My father was at Eton with Colonel Cook of the First Life Guards – they joined the Household Cavalry together."

"And he died at Paardeburg, I know."

"Well, they're forming a composite regiment of the First and Second and the Royal Horse Guards – under Cook's command."

She guessed what was coming and didn't wish to hear it – or to hear that it was irrevocable. "But we haven't even declared war yet. Can't you wait to decide when …"

"Germany's just declared war on Russia. It's coming. It has to come. France is mobilizing …"

"But you're not a *soldier,* Roger! You're an impresario now. You can do much more good by organizing entertainments for …"

He put a finger to her lips. "I am a soldier, darling. I was in the OTC five years at Eton. Summer manoeuvres with the Guards on Salisbury Plain and Aldershot. My father's uniform fits me – just take off a couple of pips." He whipped out his breast-pocket handkerchief and dabbed her eyes. "I'm sorry, darling, but a fellow has to do his duty."

"To his family?" she asked.

"To his king and country. In the long run it's the same thing. Besides, I'm afraid that if I delay, I'll miss the whole show."

79

Death never 'makes sense' but Roger's death, so early in the war, was incomprehensible. The telegram, stating baldly that he had been 'killed in action,' filled Rose with a grief not assuaged by understanding. She gave her usual performance in *All of a Sudden* that evening, and on every following day, because, as everyone said, 'we must all do our bit to keep the home fires burning.' An actress who withdrew from a show or a play 'merely' because her husband or son had been killed at the front was doing the Hun's work for him. Though the world itself may have ended, the show must go on.

A week later, the letter from Captain Hallows, Roger's company commander, shed a little further light. Roger, though not a professional soldier, had taken to regimental ways with commendable speed and dedication … had inspired great confidence among the members of his troop … led them gallantly in several actions … was mentioned in despatches … had died instantly and without suffering under shellfire at two o'clock on the afternoon of October 22nd … mourned sincerely by all who knew him, even for so brief a time. She might also like to know that Lt-Col. Cook and Capt. Astor were wounded in the same explosion … the colonel perhaps fatally. Three fine officers … dreadful loss to the regiment.

It was a comfort to know these things, of course, even if she didn't quite believe the would-be-comforting things the captain listed. She wrote at once to thank him, to say how much such a personal letter meant to her.

After that, she took to walking around the house at odd hours of the day or night, cradling baby Edward in her arms, singing gently to him, telling him what a wonderful man his father had been, and weeping for him that they would never meet this side of the grave. Now she was ashamed of her earlier indifference to his son. In fact, her love for the little mite was now so fierce, so deep, that she could not believe she had ever felt otherwise. It must have been there all the while, hiding beneath that inexplicable depression, just biding its time. And now he was the dearest, sweetest, most treasured little bundle in all the world. He was also all she had left of Roger.

She never turned a corner nor entered a room without remembering that Roger had been there once. Her memory conjured up his image and she prayed to God – or to any primitive deity that might also have the power – to suspend the laws of life and death and do whatever else was necessary to put his scattered parts together again and breathe the quickness back into him and let him be *there* – in that chair, by that window, at that table, leaning on that mantelpiece – when she opened her eyes.

In bed she hugged the bolster to her as she fell asleep, hoping that the cues of touch would summon him into her dreams. It worked for her once and once only. She came upon him in the moonlight beside a track near their cottage in the New Forest. His Silver Ghost had left the road and tumbled into a ditch. He was sitting on the bit where the canvas hood packed away, with his muddy feet on the back seat. He was facing away from her, staring into the pitch-dark among the trees, watching something that only he could see. She called his name but he would not turn and face her. And every time she took a hesitant step toward him, the ground shuddered under her feet and threatened to turn to water, and so she had to leap back onto the firm ground of the track.

The ringing of the telephone woke her from this dream. It was Hugo de Witt, distraught, frantic, telling her that Noel was 'missing in action, presumed dead.' She was beyond weeping by now. She invited him round and they passed the remainder of the night drinking oblivion without getting remotely drunk. Two days later Noel was confirmed dead.

Rose went at once to Welwyn North, to the home where Sir Hector was being cared for. 'Nanny' Constance said a telephone call would have saved her the journey, for the old boy had died eighteen months back. Hadn't Noel told her? Noel had never said a word to a soul, nor, as far as she could remember, had he worn anything black, not for a single day.

She came home and, recalling what a comfort Capt. Hallows's letter had been, wrote to Lady Carclew:

I know we have said bitter words to each other, and have never retracted a syllable, but that was long ago and, it now seems to me, in another world. After my late husband, Noel was my closest friend – and he was a true friend, too, which is something rare in the world of the theatre. I thought I had expended every last ounce of grief in the weeks after I learned of Lieutenant Deveril's death in action, but this new affliction has plumbed an even deeper reservoir and I am distraught all over again. Who is next, I wonder, and will it ever cease?

So, dear Lady Carclew, it is no easy conventional comfort that flows off this pen when I write that I know how you feel and what you must now be enduring. Your son, once he found his true vocation, was the greatest credit to you, his parents. In an insecure world, full of backbiting and meanness, he was genuinely popular and, by many, adored. Mister de Witt is beside himself with grief and quite unable to write, though I am sure he will when he is over the worst of it. He, too, held your son in the highest regard.

I'm sure that, like me, you will be getting a letter from his company commander; indeed, you may already have it. I do hope that, together with this from me (all past rancour forgotten), our words will sustain you through the darkness. If we, the women of England, who must watch our menfolk go into action and, some of them, vanish into that dateless night ... if we cannot draw together and sustain one another in our sorrow, it would seem to me like handing an uncontested victory to the enemy.

I am turning over a project to visit 'the front' – or, at least, the rear echelon of the front – around Christmas, with several other artistes, to boost the morale of our gallant men. Naturally I shall try to meet as many of my husband's comrades as I can, officers and men, and to learn all there is to know about his final days and hours. Naturally, too, I shall do the same in Noel's case and will share with you whatever I may glean. They have both done a great and noble thing and we owe it to them, I think, to see that their memory is not lost to the following generations.

She wrote in similar vein to Fenella, who replied by return, thanking her. Lady Carclew took ten days. She wrote:

Dear Miss Tremayne,
I thank you for your recent communication, which I'm sure was kindly intended. If you and my son were as intimate as you represent, you will know that there has been no communication between us since June, 1910, when he left home for the last time. I infer from the lack of condolence in your letter that you were not aware my husband died in May last year, in the devoted care, as it happens, of my son's old Nanny – not that he ever visited either of them.

This estrangement from my son has naturally tempered the sorrow that I, like any mother, must feel on the receipt of such news. This war, which is completely unnecessary in my view, has proved the greatest inconvenience in every department of life. Three of my four footmen have rushed to the colours for fear of missing what they seem to think will be a boy scout party and I must be served in my own drawing room by two ugly sisters from Flushing. I have written a letter of complaint to the War Office and have not even had the courtesy of a reply. It is all so unnecessary.

Yours sincerely,
Hygenia, Lady Carclew

God, I must show this to Noel! she thought – before she remembered. It was still happening, both with Noel and Roger. The spaces they had made in her life were still there, waiting for them. It just seemed impossible that she would never see them or speak to them again.

The following week, Roger's pigskin suitcase was delivered to the house. It still bore traces of an old LUGGAGE IN ADVANCE label, just to mock her. There was only his officer's cap inside; his father's old field uniform (with two pips removed) was missing – which told an ominous tale in itself. There was blood under the peak of the cap, or, rather, there had been blood there. His batman must have done his best to remove it, but Rose's old eye for stains and materials saw it nonetheless – saw and forgave that impulse to tell the comforting lie. But blood shed for one's country could never be a stain, so she stole down to the larder that night and replaced it with blood from an ox's heart. Only she would ever know. And those soldiers at the front should not believe they had a monopoly of valour; their women at home could be as stout of heart as they.

The suitcase also contained his writing set, his silver hipflask (with a chit from HM Customs permitting the remaining 4fl. oz. of brandy it still contained to enter free of duty), all her letters to him, done up in tape, and – the only real surprise – a school exercise book on which he had written: WAR DIARY – August 14, 1914 to . The blank was full of foreboding. She opened it and read:

Aug. 14: The Colonel to Buckingham Palace *pour prendre congé* of their majesties and lodge our standards there. I will keep this diary as a true account of the war, or my part in it. So far, nothing seems quite real. Here we are, sweltering in dear old London where everything seems so ancient and permanent – not least the Household Cavalry! – and tomorrow we are off to fight in Germany, living from hand-to-mouth, marauding through the woods and galloping with sabres drawn across the fields, as we did at Dettingen in 1740 and the Peninsula in 1808! Spirits are high and everyone eager to draw first blood.

Aug. 15: Departed with 1st Life Guards' Squadron, Hyde Park Barracks 9.40AM. Met with 2nd LG and RHG Squadrons at Southampton. Embarked SS *Thespis* 8PM from same quay as where I greeted my darling Lucille on May 6, 1912. More nervous then than now! Her refusal would have been worse than death. Horses all aboard by 2AM. We made a dog's breakfast of shipping the wagons by 5.

Aug 16: Under way 5.30AM. Smooth crossing. Arr. off Havre 3.30PM and were cheered into port like conquering heroes. Turnout magnificent. Everyone in awe. No dog's breakfast disembarking. Let's hope we are as quick to learn in the field. Marched 5 miles to rest camp, arr. midnight. Saw troop and horses settled before turning in. Capt. Astor's horse fell and hurt him but he refuses to be left behind.

Aug 17: Orders to leave by train, destination not stated, so it must be the front line. Everyone bucked at the thought of putting the kibosh on the Kaiser so soon. Prepared all day. I had thought that there could be no greater difference than that between the world of the theatre and the Life Guards, yet they are united in one most important respect. Lucille and I often remarked on the intensity of the friendships people form as members of a cast; at the time they feel like friendships-for-life even though we know they will break up the moment the curtain falls for the final time – and will resume again at all their former intensity the moment any two find themselves in the same cast once again. Well the friendships that form within the regiment, among both officers and men, and even across that divide, are no different. They are intense and moving but are not built to last. Or is that that we dare not let them?

Aug 18: Left by train 9.45AM. Crawled all day, with many unexplained stops and detours into sidings (while ammo trains went ahead of us to the front?), via Amiens and Busigny, arr. Hautmont at 2.30AM. Everyone weary.

Aug 19: Detrained immediately, 2.30AM and marched 6mi to Brigade HQ at Dimont. Good billets. Bath, change, and first real sleep in 5 days, 9PM to 7.30

Aug 20: More rest and sleep. Two keen subalterns suggested an exercise but old hands told them to save it, for it would be needed soon enough. More sleep but only until 4AM. We learn that Fritz marched into Brussels today, so we shall be fighting him in Belgium – gallant little Belgium – not on his home ground (yet!).

Aug 21: Leave at 5.30AM, marching through Aibes to the frontier at Jeumont. Our outriders met German patrols, too far off to charge. No skirmish. Billeted at Harveng, 8PM. The village is very crowded. Some say they are to advance, others claim to be in tactical withdrawal.

Aug 22: Left 11AM with heavy gunfire to our right. I think a stone-deaf man could 'hear' its vibrations in the very pit of his lungs. Pity the poor b–s at the receiving end! Were sent to support 2nd and 3rd Brigades at Halte. Stayed there until 7PM but were not called upon. Came under artillery fire 5PM, sporadic and inaccurate. One horse killed. Marched on to Basaire, arr. midnight. Gunfire all evening along the line of the canal. We hear the 16th Lancers killed several Uhlans and an officer of the Greys was wounded.

Aug 23: Were held in billets all day. Left at 5.40PM to Saultain. Capt. Bethel's troop took several German officers prisoner who say many of their men have died. They thought the war would be over inside a month (with them victorious); we still have a chance of finishing it by Christmas (with them defeated). Bethel was in

Brinton's at Eton. We were ordered to commence trenching before the village – not a cavalry accomplishment. Didn't finish in time and had to doss down in the streets.

Aug 24: Continued trenching in good company, with the 6th Dragoon Guards at Curgies and the 3rd Hussars just beyond them. With the Germans in such disarray some of us wonder why we're digging in instead of attacking, pressing home our advantage.

Aug 25: Completed the trenches just in time to face an overwhelming infantry attack. They came in like grey waves on Pendeen Sands, right and left as far as the eye could see. Too hot for us. We got out so fast we left certain things behind, entrenching tools, maps, etc. Came under heavy shellfire as we withdrew. Reached Viestry around 11PM but still too hot. Withdrew farther to Beaumont, 12.30AM.

Aug 26: Cambrai – the first big battle of this war but again we are denied a part in it. Instead are sent to Ligney, to stand as rearguard to Gen. Snow. We are stood to all night. No sleep. The Germans seem able to materialize men out of thin air. His disregard for human life is outrageous.

Aug 27: The war is two weeks old and, apart from a few skirmishes, all our actions are rearguard. Today we were rearguard to the whole army – ourselves, the 3rd Hussars and the 6th Dragoons, who lost six officers under heavy shelling. Retired on Lampire and then, overnight, to Ham, at 2AM, near the junction of the Somme and the Crozat canal.

Aug 28: Further orderly withdrawal, from Nesle to Cressy. (Is this Creçy of Edward III fame? If so, no repeat of victory for us, alas.) Then farther back to Moyencourt where six wonderful letters from my darling Lucille await me! Also the latest photographs of our darling Edward, who definitely has my brow and eyes, poor chap! I read them half a dozen times and forget the war for an hour.

Aug 29: If we keep ~~retreating~~ withdrawing, never finding time to prepare positions, where will it end? On the Place de la Concorde? We took up good defensive positions south of the canal but the rest of the army withdrew and we had to fall back with them. Met a German mounted patrol. Killed three horses and wounded their riders but all got away. Reached Dives at midnight. We have now withdrawn over 80mi in 4 days but the regimental spirit is still amazingly good.

Aug 30: Another 30mi of withdrawal. Someone is being harried mercilessly and pushed back but not us. We simply draw back with them – 30mi more today and not a shot fired. I know the men are puzzled. We came out here to fight. Bivouaced S of Compiegne. Got more letters and more photos of my two treasures. "All of a Sudden" is making me £200 richer each day, Lucille writes. I would gladly give a thousand times that amount, and daily, if it would end this war and bring me safely home to them. No one mentions survival but I'm sure we all think of it constantly.

Aug 31: A bit of action at last. Left Compiegne early, 5.30AM and scouted westward. 3rd Hussars were pressed hard so we formed a rearguard to their ~~retr~~ withdrawal – another 10mi back, to Verberie, at 8PM. A long, hot day. The Hussars had a few prisoners to pass back up the line, truculent Huns, already boasting of their release before Christmas.

And so the record continued – a depressing litany of rearguards and retreats, with the occasional skirmish, usually with three or four deaths on either side. By September 5th Roger noted that the Germans had advanced to within twenty-three miles of Paris, at which time the Lifeguards – and the rest of the British army under Sir John French – were lined up along a twenty-mile front well to the southeast of the city.

On September 7th the tide seemed to have turned and the Germans started retreating; he first wrote 'withdrawing' there and crossed it out. On the 9th they were among the first British – indeed, Allied – contingents to recross the River Marne, going northward and driving the Germans before them. On the 15th they came to a halt at Corberry north of the Aisne, having recovered all the ground lost since the end of August. From then on it was a further month of skirmishes, trenching, scouting, and rest days. Then:

Oct 17: Someone has realized that Fritz may have been pulling back in order to swoop across Normandy to take the Channel ports and cut us off! Their whole drive toward Paris may have been a feint to draw the Allies even farther south to oppose them. So today the regiment entrains for Amiens, thence to Boulogne, to Calais, to Hazebrouck, just behind the Belgian line. But I stay behind because my trivial encounter with barbed wire, not even mentioned at the time, has turned nasty and I must to a dressing station and follow on tomorrow.

The station is at 1st Army Corps, Blaine. I am lying on a palette, reading Lucille's letters once again, waiting to be seen, when I hear someone call, "Captain Redmile-Smith?" You could knock me down with the proverbial feather when an officer on a stretcher, two away from me, pipes up, "Yes!"

The orderly takes some details from him and goes away. Capt. R-S smiles at me and says, "It's only the fifth time I've told them!"

Consternation! What's to do?

I go and sit by his stretcher.

"Redmile-Smith," he says, offering his hand.

I don't take it – yet. "Deveril, sir," I say. "Roger Deveril. Here's a turn-up for the books!"

Wincing, he reaches out and grasps my hand, shakes it, clutching it between both of his. "Capital!" he says. "Funny thing. Had a premonition ever since landing in France. Felt sure we'd meet." (I paraphrase. He doesn't really speak so clipped.) "How's Lucinda-Ella?"

I give him all our latest news. He is particularly delighted to hear about Edward. More delighted to learn that she is coming out here for Christmas. Jokes that if he has to bribe Fritz to shoot him in the foot so as to get down the line to see her, he'll do it. Actually, he should find it easy enough, being in the Motor Transport division of the Service Corps. He's burned his leg where a motor-cycle exhaust lay on him while concussed. Very nasty. It will not be quick to heal, I fear – though, of course, I assure him it's the sort of thing they can mend in no-time these days.

They squirt jets of carbolic into my little scratch, which makes it feel like a six-inch gash. The Spanish Inquisition missed a trick there.

Later, before catching my train, I went back and showed Redmile-Smith the latest pictures of Lucille and Edward. He begged to keep one, which I reluctantly agreed to, but the poor fellow may not live. He is clearly still in love with Lucille – and who can blame him? Certainly not me!

Also gave him that letter. Often wondered why I really kept it, especially bringing it to France. To remind one never to take the dear girl for granted, I used to say. Now not so sure. There is a Destiny shapes our ends ...?

Following this rather enigmatic reference, the War Diary continued with a ragged tally of attacks and counter-attacks, patrols, rearguards, rest days, mail deliveries ... until:

Oct 22: Continued digging-in and fortifying all morning, ready for CO's inspection at 2. Trooper Martin said, "Now let Fritz do his worst, eh, sir?" just before the Colonel entered our section, with Capt. Astor immediately behind. Before he could say a word to me, we were hit by a shell and thrown into the open, where we had to lie until 7. Two troopers and a corporal of horse were killed while rescuing us. Someone else will have to write... 'popular with their comrades ... died gallantly ... almost instantaneous ... no pain ... mourned by us all.' The dead alone know the end of war – 'happy men that have the power to die,' as Tennyson said. Lucille quoted that to me once. I have lost much blood. Motor ambulance to Bailleul Hospital. Astor not bad. A staff officer drove the Colonel to Boulogne, for Blighty. They say I must stay until I can be moved. I will sleep now and then write to Lucille.

The record ended there. No letter had been found, just the War Diary and a much-thumbed photograph of his wife and baby son.

80

They toured *Aladdin* from the south of the BEF sector on the Somme to the north. Rose was in the title role, with Sozzler Knox as Widow Twankee, Ellen Howe as the princess, and Henry Lacy as the wicked Uncle Abanazer, wearing, of course, the insignia of a regimental sergeant major twice life-size on each arm. There were lots of anti-officer jokes (naming different officers at each new venue, of course), anti-general-staff jokes (ringing the changes between Snow, Haig, and French), and gentle anti-French (nation) jibes; there were also songs to stir the spirit and songs to bring tears to the eye. Sometimes German prisoners, who happened to be passing back down the line through whatever bivouac or billet the company visited, were allowed to sit at the back and watch; those with some command of English could not understand why the actors were not arrested and shot on the spot; and when they were told that generals Snow and French and Haig had almost died laughing at this or that performance where they were lampooned without mercy, they could only conclude that the Tommies were mad, with no idea of discipline, much less of how to fight and win a war.

The pantomime played in tents, bombed churches, village halls, barns, and even, one fine, starry night, in the open air. ("Scenery by God, alterations by Tommy, Fritz, and the Frogs," Sozzler said as he walked onto the stage.) They played twice or thrice a day, to a regiment, a company, a platoon. Near Bailleul, a captain in the Household Cavalry escorted her to the artillery lines, as close to the front as any civilian was allowed, and showed her, through a telescope, where Roger had been mortally wounded – an insignificant patch of hillside in a portion of nondescript country. The view explained nothing, carried no meaning. All she could think was that his death had enriched it.

No one could tell her where Noel had gone missing; it was, in any case, several miles behind the enemy's present front.

And, of course, everywhere they went, from Béthune to Poperinghe, Rose asked particularly after a certain Captain Louis Redmile-Smith of the Service Corps (Motor Transport) – always without success.

She had asked friends at the War Office to let her know his whereabouts as soon as she read Roger's account of him toward the end of his all-too-brief War Diary. They assured her that he was being treated for burns at Messines, but when she got there she learned that the hospital had been overrun by the enemy shortly afterward and, though it had since been recaptured, all records had vanished with them. They were still trying to piece individual histories together. They were almost certain he had not been taken prisoner, because his name would have turned up in the Red Cross lists by now. He must have been moved to rear echelon around the time that Messines was overrun, most likely on that very day. They would raise queries with all the likely rear units to see if his name was still to be found on their lists.

By the third week in January, 1915, Rose had just about given up all hope of finding Louis through official channels, when a Major Fullbright of the RAMC (Royal Army Medical Corps, but cynically redubbed Rob All My Comrades by Tommy Atkins) came to her tent. It was late one evening, after the show.

After the usual compliments about that night's performance, he said, "I believe you're trying to find a Captain Louis Redmile-Smith, Miss Marteyne?"

She almost fell upon him in her eagerness.

"Well," he continued, "these records are a little ancient by now – 'ancient,' by the way, means more than seven weeks old out here – but I believe I have been able to trace his movements back to Southampton, to a base hospital there. Um ..." He eyed her speculatively. "How close was he to you?"

"*Was?*" she cried. "Oh no! Don't say he, too ..."

"No, no! I'm sorry. I expressed it clumsily. It's just that I knew you were married to Lieutenant Deveril. It didn't seem ..."

"Yes, yes! I'm sorry I responded like that. It's just that ... lately ... you know, there have been too many ... Anyway, I take it he's *not* dead?"

The major bit his lip. "It's most unlikely. However ..."

"Yes?"

"I'm pretty certain they had to amputate a leg – I'm afraid. That's why I hesitated."

"Oh!" She closed her eyes and breathed out in one quick sigh. "Forgive me," she murmured. "The only thought in my mind is 'Thank God!' I suppose that sounds awful?"

"Not after such a loss as yours," he replied.

"Losses," she said. "My husband was not the only one."

"Of course."

The following week, after the very last of their performances, she was approached by a shy young sergeant wearing a Press flash. "You'll not remember me, Miss Marteyne," he said. "Norman Taylor. I was that lad who guarded Lieutenant Deveril's Rolls-Royce at Southampton, that day you ..."

"But of course I remember you!" she exclaimed. "I advised you to have a go at motion pictures. You still have those wonderful eyes, I see. Did it work? Are you busy? Will you let me buy you a drink? I see a Sally-Ann over there. It'll only be Horlick's, I fear, but I have a flask here with something stronger. We can tip it in when they're not looking."

In fact, he took her to an anteroom of the sergeants' mess, where ladies were allowed – and he bought her a drink, a good, stiff whisky, which he said he owed her for the favour she had done him that day.

"There was a film company in Southampton," he told her, "but I had no luck there – except one of the cameramen gave me an address in Wardour Street, in London, where he said I might try."

"And you were more successful there? You should have called on me. I was in the clouds that day but I certainly thought you had the right sort of face ..."

"No, I got work there, all right – as an extra, of course. Just doing things in the background. But I soon discovered that what really interested me was the camera-work. Cameras and lighting. So, to cut a long story short, that's what I switched to. And that's what I do now, and all. And as soon as war was declared I volunteered to join the army camera unit, making motion pictures of ... well, everything, really. From base depots in England to the front line out here. Beyond the front line at times."

"Gosh! I've seen the pictures. To walk out there into no-man's-land without a weapon, just a camera – not even facing toward the enemy most of the time – that must take incredible courage. Yet we never think about it."

He shook his head. "I've only done it half a dozen times. There are men who do it every day. Anyway, the thing I was going to say is that when I read of your husband's sad death, I remembered I'd taken some footage of him not two weeks earlier, when the Household Cavalry were crossing the Marne ..."

Rose sat up so abruptly that she spilled her drink, fortunately on the carpet. "What an incredible coincidence!" she cried.

"Oh, it was no coincidence, Miss Marteyne," he replied. "We get regimental lists before we shoot a thing like that – so's we can just tick off the names of who we film. I mean, you can't stop an officer in the middle of a battle and say 'Deveril? Is that one ell or two, sir?' can you!" They laughed. "But," he continued, "the minute I saw his name there I remembered it on the picnic basket in his car. A little silver whatsit with his name engraved ..."

"Yes, I know."

"Of course you do. Silly of me. Anyway, I searched him out and I took quite a lot of film of him crossing the Marne. In fact, he crossed it three times before I got it just right. I was going to get it all printed up and send it to him for Christmas, but ..." He raised his hands in a gesture of hopelessness.

"You've lost it?" she guessed. There was a dreadful sinking feeling in her stomach.

"Oh, no!" he replied. In fact ..." He got to his feet and crossed the room to the buffet. From one of its cupboards he drew out a packet, wrapped in plain brown paper but with crude holly leaves and bells scrawled all over it. "Dare I say 'Happy Christmas'?"

"You darling man!" she cried, kissing him ecstatically on the cheek – which brought ironic whoops from other sergeants and warrant officers nearby, all of them fascinated that the fabulous Lucille Marteyne should be gracing their humble mess.

"It was the least I could do," he said. "Those few words you spoke to me changed my life. I can never forget it."

"Well, Norman Taylor – is your name written down here, by the way?"

He blushed. "It's on a little card inside."

"When this wretched war is over – if you're spared and I'm spared – you call on me in London and I'll guarantee you the job of your dreams in films, no matter which side of the camera you may choose. I'm sure you could get it all by yourself, but it never hurts to take a short cut if you can, eh?"

The following day the rest of the cast returned to engagements in London via Boulogne–Folkestone; Rose returned, to a period of well-earned rest, via Havre–Southampton.

At the General Hospital they referred her to Highfield Hall, where Lady Emma Crichton, vice-president of the local Red Cross Society, said she recalled Mr Redmile-Smith very well. Yes, they did have to amputate his leg – just *below* the knee, fortunately, which makes a false leg so much easier to fit and use. No, he was no longer there. In fact, she seemed to remember his expressing a desire to convalesce in Cornwall, where he had connections of some kind. Used to sail down there, didn't he? Falmouth Harbour. Yes, the Red Cross had just opened a new convalescent home down there ... funny name ... just a mo' ... yes! Here it is – Nancemellin House. Did she know it, by any chance?

81

When Rose had gone up the drive to Highfield Hall, she had been filled with excitement at the thought of meeting Louis again – possibly even here, within the hour. But now that she knew of his true whereabouts, a curious reluctance to pursue her quest further overcame her. As she sat in the taxi on her way back to the station, she realized that the moment she stepped up to the ticket-office window she would have to make a decision: Truro-for-Falmouth ... or Waterloo – for Hampstead and home?

If only Louis had been somewhere else – *anywhere* else in the world but Nancemellin House! Meeting him again would be fraught enough; there would be so many different emotions to hold back, to explore but slowly, delicately – if at all. To meet him there of all places would be just asking for trouble.

Trouble?

No, that wasn't the right word. She couldn't think of the word she really wanted. It was too confusing. She had been through too much these past months. She needed to rest, to think. To forget?

Yes, there were things to forget as well. She had never really answered Ellen's accusation that she ought to have found the courage to meet Louis, that time in Trenton. He *could* have been the owner of the hotel. Improbable as it seemed at the time, from the way he was behaving and the way that clerk talked about him, he still could have been. She tried to remember the clerk's expression, his tone of voice. Miss Sophie Graham's nephew. Or was it brother-in-law? Did the women get the vote in Wisconsin that year?

She couldn't keep her mind on anything for longer than ten seconds. She must rest before deciding. Also, she must see Edward again. And take him to Cornwall, too. Some instinct, far deeper than thought, told her that when she and Louis met again, she must be holding Edward in her arms.

"First to Waterloo, please," she said to the clerk.

"Single, madam?"

"I beg your pardon? Oh! Yes – single."

Among the mail waiting for her in Hampstead was a personal one from Gorgeous George, congratulating her on what everyone said had been a wonderful, morale-boosting tour of the BEF front. In passing it also invited her to drop by at her convenience for a chat about several projects he had in mind.

There was one from Fenella, too. She and Rose had struck up quite a pen-friendship since exchanging letters of mutual condolence the previous autumn. This one, written shortly after Christmas, told her of the changes at Nancemellin House.

Mother has moved into the gatelodge for the duration of the war [she wrote]. Joan Perkins, who was assistant to Mrs Browning, you remember?, is her cook. Your friend Mary Hocken (Mary Hind when you saw her last) is still her lady's maid and her husband George is chauffeur-gardener-odd-job-man. He also does coast-guard duty part-time so, I suppose, will be spared conscription, which I see they're beginning to talk about now. The tweeny is a new girl, Sally Mitchell, a cousin to Mitchell, who was our footman in your time. He, by the by, is now at Ypres, serving with the DCLI. A corporal, I hear.

There was also one from Louis. She recognized the handwriting at once, and the Flushing postmark told her precisely where he had written it – or almost. Which actual room was his, she wondered? Sir Hector's bedroom – where she had wakened him with a kiss? Or would they have turned the old servants' rooms into small dormitories – and would he have wangled his way into the one that had been hers and Mary's? Mary was still there, so he could have found out from her.

She was on the point of opening the letter when she heard Edward crying in the nursery. He had been fast asleep when she arrived. She stuffed it in her pocket and ran to him.

"Bless you, ma'am, but he's only waking up," Mrs Riddington, the wet nurse said.

And, as if to prove it, the howling turned to giggles and the pruneface to smiles at the sight of her.

"Oh, Edward!" she exclaimed, picking him from his cot and hugging him to her. "Your smile does more for me than a standing ovation from a full house – you know that?" A moment later, however, she was passing him to Stella, the night nurse, for a change of nappies. When he was clean again they lay on the carpet and did 'Round and round the garden ...' and 'Here's the church, here's the steeple ...' and 'This little piggy ...' and named all his fingers, from Tommy Thumbkins to Little Quee-Quee-Quee. And then Rose turned her left hand into a deer and her right hand into a wolf and played out a little drama from natural history on the nursery rug. It was a magical sort of natural history in which all deer have the power to transform themselves into super-wolves when threatened and to send *ordinary* wolves howling away with their tails between their legs. Edward was especially fond of that.

Half an hour later the night-nurse found them curled up together, both fast asleep. "Well!" Stella exclaimed to Mrs Riddington as they lifted their slumbering mistress between them, "I'd have thought she'd be heavier than this – specially with all that army food out there." The wet-nurse shook her head ruefully. "She's not been eating properly for months, poor thing – not since you-know-when." She did not wake up, not even when they undressed her. "There's hardly a pick of flesh on her!" Stella said.

"And no one left to speak a bit of sense to her, neither."

The letter from Louis was on her bedside table when the maid brought her breakfast in the morning. The reluctance she had felt about such a momentous step as going directly to Nancemellin from Southampton now prevented her from even the trivial act of slitting the envelope. She put it aside until she had finished her porridge – a good, stiff overnight brew that would clasp a spoon upright. Her plate empty, she was once again on the point of opening the envelope when Mrs Blessington came into the bedroom with a second breakfast, saying, "I thought, seeing as you'd been asleep so long, ma'am, you'd not say no to a little extra."

Rose looked at the letter, then at the covered plate on the tray, and said, "Oh, very well. I mean, how kind!" The 'little extra' proved to be bacon, eggs, devilled kidneys, fried bread, and a slice of black pudding. Rose replaced the cover and said, *"Really,* Mrs Blessington!"

"Yes, really!" the woman replied. "You *really* ought to eat more. Stella and I agreed as much between ourselves last night when we watched little Master Edward pick you up, put you under his arm, and carry you here to bed."

Rose laughed. "I'd like to hear what little bedtime tales you've both been telling him while I've been away!"

"It's true, though, and *someone* should tell it to you. Call me impudent if you wish but Stella hit the nail on the head when we undressed you last night. 'Why, there's not a pick on the poor mite,' she said. And it's the truth."

Rose sighed, looked again at the still-sealed envelope, lifted the cover once more, smelled the kidneys and bacon, felt the floor of her mouth fill with sudden saliva, and said, "Why not!" Even before she had finished it, however, Stella arrived, bearing yet another tray, this time with Melba toast and lemon marmalade, shimmering with slivers of ginger. "The man at Fortnum and Mason's says it's your favourite, ma'am," she remarked.

"Listen – if I'd wanted force-feeding, I'd have chained myself to the railings outside Number Ten, Downing Street," Rose said. But she ate the toast – and with relish. It was so thin, after all – and dear Mr Gregory at Fortnum's hadn't lied. He knew her quite well as Miss Lucille Marteyne, a regular customer – but much more warmly as the daughter of his good friends, Mr and Mrs Tremayne of Falmouth, whose italian warehouse was practically an outpost of his grand London emporium.

Thoughts of her parents led her to pick up the telephone – something she ought to have done last night – if not, indeed, from Southampton. The house switchboard had been bypassed since Roger had enlisted; she was connected directly through to the exchange. She cranked the handle several times before there was an answer. Then it took another age to wake up 'Trunks,' who, in turn, took their time in reaching Bristol, Exeter, Plymouth, Truro ... *And Mom complains I don't ring more often!* Rose thought as she followed each patching of line into line. But at last she was through.

"Mom? It's me – Lucinda-Ella – back from France ... yesterday, but I couldn't get through." There were noises like ocean waves on the line. It was hard to make out Mom's words but it sounded like, "You'll never guess whose beer ..." Then a fade into inaudibility.

'Whose beer?' Smith's Ales? Were they selling Smith's Ales in their new off-licence department? What an eerie coincidence! "Did you say beer?" she shouted.

"Yes – *here!* You'll never guess who's here!"

Rose laughed almost hysterically. "I don't need to guess. I heard the news only yesterday. I arrived back in Southampton yesterday and the local Red Cross told me. Have you seen him? How is he?" The ocean waves faded and the line became a lot clearer.

"Fine! You know about ... well, about his operation?"

"Darling Mom – the soul of tact! Yes, I know all about it. Have they given him a new leg, yet?"

"They fitted it last week. He sailed over to Custom House Quay, all on his own, on Monday. Took us by surprise – a very pleasant one, I must say. He told us he saw you in *All of a Sudden* before he left for France ..." The line went dead abruptly. She hung up the earpiece and cranked the magneto to 'ring off.' She considered trying to reconnect but then, realizing that she'd simply have to go down to Falmouth now, she got back to the exchange and dictated a telegram, telling them she was on her way, bringing Edward, two nannies, and a wet-nurse with her.

She sprang from the bed, completed her morning ablutions, asked Mrs Wilkie, the housekeeper to book the requisite berths on the night sleeper to Truro, told the two nannies and Mrs Riddington of her plans, and then, at long last, opened Louis' letter.

82

Louis' letter was postmarked the previous Tuesday, the day after he had visited her parents. It began without an address or date:

Dear Lucinda-Ella,
I write to offer you my deepest sympathy over Roger's death, which, I'm appalled to admit, I heard of only yesterday, from your parents. (I hope my use of his Christian name does not offend you; I shall explain in a moment.) I know he died over three months ago and in any other circumstances it would be just too shameful to be writing now. The fact is, I have been lying, feeling shamefully sorry for myself, in various hospitals since early October last. My one desire now is to let you know how desperately sorry I am and how much I feel for you. I do not need to reach for phrases beginning 'he must have been ...' or 'I'm sure he was ...' because, I don't know whether he had time to tell you this, but he and I actually ran across each other at a field dressing station one Saturday last October – the Saturday before he died, I now learn. So I know at first hand what a sterling character he was. We talked about you a lot – naturally – and I know you were the whole universe to him. I caught sight of a bundle of letters from you, so I also know how deeply devoted you were to each other. "Closer is he than breathing, and nearer than hands and feet." If the sympathy of an old friend can assuage your grief, even by the smallest amount, you have an ocean of it to draw upon here.

Let us not lose touch again! The circle of our mutual friends is dwindling so fast. I also heard of Noel Carclew's death, again only very recently – when I came here ten days ago, in fact. I know he was a close friend of yours, too, so please accept my condolences on that account also.

Some more about my meeting with Roger: He was annoyed that day to have been left behind by his regiment, to have what he called "a little scratch" attended to. It was, in fact, a barbed-wire wound, not large, and only mildly septic, but in the worst possible place for a cavalryman. He had all his personal kit with him, ready for a quick dash to the station once he'd done. I was lying a couple of stretchers away, waiting for them to attend to a burn on my calf, where it had touched a motor-cycle exhaust. Some orderly called out my name and, when I answered, took down a few particulars. A moment later, Roger was at my side, introducing himself and offering his hand! But for that chance, we should have come that close together and then parted again without any of us ever knowing how close it had been! I never had a superstitious fibre in my being until this war; now I cannot believe our meeting each other, for the first and, sadly, the only time, was mere happenstance. Roger felt it, too. He even said as much to me as we parted, quoting Hamlet's, "There's a divinity shapes our ends, rough hew them how we will." In fact, he said "destiny" instead of "divinity," which I presume was deliberate?

At this point he had written vertically in the margin, obviously after reading the whole letter: 'I'm not hinting here that he had even the slightest premonition of his impending death – no more than any soldier has on the eve of battle. And every evening over there in Flanders is that.' The letter continued:

Unfortunately the burn on my leg went septic and then the entire foot went gangrenous. For a while everyone, including me, was sure my time was up. I thought a lot about you and Roger during those delirious days. Thought ... dreamed ... phantasized ... it was all a jumble, but the thread running throughout was the notion that I must not die – that when this lousy war is over, such a good new friend as Roger and such a dear old friend as you would be among the world's surviving treasures for me. (In the end, true friendship is life's <u>only</u> lasting treasure – don't you think?) I seemed at times to be traversing a long, long tube, narrow and dark, and you and he were at the end of it, calling out encouragement, willing me to struggle through.

Oh, I'm sorry! When I started to write, I didn't intend to go on like this. It's pure guilt at discovering this awful truth so late and writing to you in this vein at a time when – like my leg – you must be just starting to heal a little. He showed me photographs of you and little Edward, who must now be one of the bonniest and most strapping half-year-olds in the land. He, surely, must be your greatest comfort now. Roger even pressed one of the prints upon me, which I shall always treasure, not just for its subjects but also as a mark of his true greatness of spirit.

I have saved one surprise to the end – and it is an end that I did not even rough-hew. Lady Carclew has retired to live in her own gate lodge for the duration of the war and Nancemellin House has been turned into a convalescent home for officers – myself among them! Your mother tells me you are in France at the moment, doing a panto for the BEF. (Roger told me of your plans back in October and offered to get me a ticket, come hell, come high-water.) She says you'll be returning soon, maybe this week, and that you've written to her about taking a short holiday down here. If so, I do hope we can meet.

Yours most sincerely,
Louis

Nancemellin House – Tuesday, 2nd February, 1915
PS In Memoriam, xxvii!

Rose did not need to turn to her bookshelf to know what verse he intended:

I hold it true, whate'er befall; / I feel it when I sorrow most; / 'Tis better to have loved and lost / Than never to have loved at all.

The false rhyme between 'most' and 'lost' had always irked her. Until now.

83

Rose had telephoned the matron at Nancemellin and had learned that Capt. Redmile-Smith usually went sailing directly after lunch. The doctors had limited him to an hour and a half, on pain of withdrawing the privilege, so he was usually pretty prompt about returning to the jetty in good time – before half-past three.

At a quarter past the hour her taxi approached the ornate wrought-iron gates, now somewhat neglected. She ducked down out of sight as they passed the gatelodge; an encounter with Lady Carclew would have been one complication too many. Rose even asked the driver to go right past the house and into the stable yard, round not one but two corners from the lodge, before letting her down. The stables were oddly silent and cold as she edged her way among the stalls to the back door, taking care to guard Edward's head from accidental bumps. This was where young Graham Noy used to wheel out the muck each morning. There was still a heap of it to one side of the backyard, old and black by now. They should get the convalescents gardening – they'd be amazed what good manure like that would grow.

"Listen to your Mom!" she said wearily. "Not five minutes here and she's already working on Regimental Standing Orders! I just hope you've got some of my rebellious spirit, little man."

Beyond the backyard gate she was on open ground, though her view of the sea was cut off by the walled garden.

"See that little fruit orchard down the side there?" She turned his eyes toward it. "That's where I almost slit the throat of your Aunty Ann – and now I can't for the life of me remember what it was all about!" She cradled him in her arms again and turned toward the path that leads down to the jetty. "She's not your real aunt – just the wife of one of my cousins. You'll meet them soon, anyway." She laughed. "And *here* ...! Guess what happened here!"

She rubbed noses with him and he giggled, so she repeated it several times. "Have you guessed yet?" she went on. "I can see I'll have to tell you then. Here, on this very spot, a very silly woman called Hortensia, Lady Carclew, told me she'd see to it that I wouldn't last two weeks in any position for which I applied. And I told her that one day – I didn't know how and I didn't know when but I did know where – which was *here* – I told her I'd make her eat her words, also on this very spot! What a big, bold maid I was and no mistake! Oh yes I was! Oh yes I was!"

She was about to rub noses again when she caught sight of a small, red, triangular sail emerging from behind the pine trees.

"Dear God!" she murmured, no longer in a playful tone. "That's where he was when I last saw him. Or last saw him *here,* I mean. I don't want to think about the *other* last time I saw him – so don't you tell him anything about that! Understand? No? Good!"

He saw her the moment she set off again, down the path to the jetty. He waved and she waved back. The sun emerged from behind a large bank of cloud before she had gone a dozen paces. There were patches of blue – enough to make a sailor's shirt.

Though they were about equidistant from the jetty, the breeze was so light that she reached it well ahead of him. "Look! There's Falmouth," she told Edward. "There's Gran and Grampaw's house – where I was born ... Oh! I'm sorry. Is it as boring as all that?" She took out a handkerchief and wiped away the drool that had come out with his yawn. "Oh, don't drop off now you silly sausage! You're just about to meet Uncle Louis ..."

His eyes vanished up inside his skull just before the lids closed.

Louis was now a mere dozen yards away – and sculling with an oar, since the wind had died completely inshore. She tried to guess which of his legs was false.

"You've had a long wait!" he said, recalling her promise to be there every day. "Actually, but for the baby, I could feel I've suddenly slipped back four and a half years. You haven't aged a day, I'll swear!"

"Four years and seven months," she said, reaching out one free hand to grab the painter.

"*And* twenty-one days!" He gave a smug but self-deprecatory grin as he handed it to her and leaped ashore.

It was his right leg but you'd hardly know it. He took the painter back from her and, with a bit of abracadabra, coiled it round a little wooden bollard. "I'll come back," he said, glancing at the sky. "Should be safe enough. Stowing the sails is a bit tedious."

He offered his hand but she took it only to pull him down to where she could kiss his cheek. "Thanks for your letter," she murmured. "It meant more to me than *any* of the others I received."

"I'm glad. I was ... I mean, when I met Roger ..." He looked away, toward the horizon but did not really see it. "God, this *bloody* war! We started with such high spirits. We never for one moment dreamed ..." He looked at her and smiled wanly.

"It's all right," she told him. "I've seen the front, even the front line. The big brass tried to stop me but I saw it all the same."

"*They* tried to stop *you!* Ha!" He laughed grimly at such folly. Then he smiled down at Edward. "So this is the bonny boy – my God, he *is* bonny, too. Those are Roger's curls." He moved the shawl an inch or two aside. "And his chin. Your father was a splendid fellow, Edward. The salt of the earth." To Rose he said, "He won't get too cold?"

She laughed. "On a day like this? Would you like to hold him?"
He pulled a dare-I? face. "You'd trust me?"
She put the baby into his embrace. "Now I've gotcha!" she said, wrapping her right arm round his left. "There's no need to crush him. He'll lie quite comfortably if … that's better."
"Well!" he exclaimed as they set off along the private length of the foreshore. "Wasn't that a silly way to go and lose a leg!"
"Roger said you had a motor-bike crash?"
He laughed drily. "I fell asleep while riding one! I hadn't so much as closed my eyes for seventy-two hours and … well, I just fell asleep … slid down a bank … didn't wake up … just went on sleeping with the motor going phut-phut-phut and the exhaust slowly toasting me."
"Ouch!" She clutched his arm tight and winced.
"Just in time to get sent to Nancemellin!" he added with a chuckle. "I couldn't believe it."
"Did you get sent or did you wangle it?"
He cleared his throat. "A few brown ales and whisky chasers may have slipped down one or two influential throats."
"And which room are you in?"
She felt his arm muscles tighten briefly. "Up the stairs, turn right, first door on your left."
"That's the room you woke up in."
"Good heavens!" He looked up at the sky. "Is it really! Well, well! You live in Hampstead now, your mother says."
"Overlooking the Vale of Health. Have you thought about what you're going to do next? Will you go back to America?"
"God, no! No, I didn't mean it to sound like that. America was dam' good to me. I could see the war coming several months off so I sold out my interests in June last year. Made enough to pay off what I regarded as debts of honour back here and discharged my personal bankruptcy – repay some of Mother's debts – otherwise, of course, I'd never have been given a commission." She was amazed that the point had not occurred to her before now. "America's the place to learn about business though!" He had the bit between his teeth by now. "There's none of that boss and worker nonsense – well, I wouldn't say *none* but by English standards it's virtually none. If I were only interested in making money, I'd head straight back. Like a shot."
"And instead …?" she prompted.
"I don't know. Even after paying off everything, I've still got enough to live comfortably for quite a while. Modestly, of course. I want something where I meet people. The motor car is obviously going to be a thing of the future. You've got one of the original Silver Ghosts, Roger told me?"
She nodded. "It's with a blacksmith in the New Forest. Roger put it in, before he left, to have some bracket fitted in the boot. I haven't been down there since."

"Anyway, people are no longer going to be tied to the village or the suburb. One idea I'm turning over is to build a sort of cross between a hotel and a large pub – halfway between London and Brighton, say, or in the South Downs, or the Hog's Back. Somewhere scenic and within easy motoring distance of town, where people would get away for weekends."

"Dirty weekends!" Rose said.

"I won't ask for marriage lines. If Mister and Mrs John Smith sign the register, they'll be Mister and Mrs John Smith to me."

She leaned forward and peered up into his face. He hadn't aged much either. He had changed, subtly, but not aged; it was too late to tell him now, though. "Brewmaster turns publican?" she taunted. "Isn't that a bit of a come-down. Are you sure they'll let you back in at the Falmouth Yacht Club?"

He laughed. "That's what I mean about America. We, my fellow directors and I, built up a business the size of the old Smith's breweries here, you know? And we did it in two and a half years. And d'you know how? By never losing sight of the customer! Every director worked one evening a week serving drinks in one or other of the bars in Trenton – mainly serving up our competitors' muck – stuff from Milwaukee! Can you see the directors of an *English* brewery rolling up their sleeves and pitching in like that!"

Rose felt she had lost all contact with the ground she was walking on. And the scenery was shifting subtly all around her, too.

Could she tell him? *Dare* she tell him? Would it even be fair to tell him?

Whatever the rights and wrongs of the situation, she knew she'd never have the courage to admit it – not merely because it would betray such a lack of faith in him but because it would also be as good as admitting that she would never have said yes to Roger if only she had known the truth.

"You've gone quiet," he said.

"I was just wondering ... what was the Union League ... the notepaper you used?" It was the first thought that came into her head – a sort of holding-off-reality question.

"The Union League *is* – not was – just about the most exclusive capitalist club in New York – if not all America. Why? Oh – of course! I wrote you from there."

"Yes. Going back to your roadhouse – have you picked an actual site yet?"

"Not at all. It could also be out in the Chilterns ... Beaconsfield way. Or High Wycombe. Actually, halfway between London and Oxford might be even better than London and Brighton. Why d'you ask, anyway?"

"Nothing," she replied. "Idle curiosity." She dug in a heel and spun him around, facing back the way they had come. "I ... there's one thing ... he's not getting too heavy?"

"Ask me in an hour's time. What were you going to say?"

"Oh!" She sighed. "To ask, really – except that I think I already know the answer. That letter ..."

"Letter?" he echoed. But again she could tell from the sudden tension in his arm that he knew very well what it was about.

"The one Roger gave you. I won't beat about the bush. It was a letter from me to you, wasn't it. Unfinished and torn in two."

"In three, actually. Roger had pasted it all together again. He said you wrote it about a month before you and he got married."

"That's right. I can't remember a word of it. All I know is that it was the most difficult ... no, the most impossible thing to convey. Did he tell you *why* he was giving it to you? Did he even tell you why he rescued it and kept it?"

After a pause, Louis said, "Yes."

After another pause she said, "Yes ... what?"

"Yes, Lucinda-Ella?"

She pinched his arm.

"Ouch! He *did* tell me – and it was the same answer to both questions. I mean, he passed it on to me for the same reason that he rescued it and kept it in the first place."

"In his diary he wrote that he kept it to remind himself never to take me for granted – which he never did, anyway."

"And you're still asking *me* why?" Louis hesitated and then went on. "I think he never intended you to see that diary unless he died – not to see it *during* the war, anyway."

Rose thought this over and realized it was something she had suspected from the beginning, even if she had never articulated it in so many words.

"So he meant an entry like that to provoke you to think about it. From the way you phrased your question, I assume he didn't specify *what* letter he gave me?"

"No. He just underlined it. *That* letter."

"But he knew you'd have a pretty shrewd idea? D'you think he also suspected you'd just *have* to get in touch with me again – to find out if your guess was right?"

Now she had goosebumps all up and down the back of her neck. "Yes," she whispered. "Of course!"

"You could say he intended this meeting then? After his death, he intended us to meet and to talk about *that* letter."

"Oh, my God!" She looked up at the sky, then all about her, at the grass, at the water ... "Do you still have it?"

"Not on me. But I can tell you what it said. 'My darling Louis, for you will always be that to me, I hope. Your favourite poet and mine once wrote, "It is a characteristic of the human mind to hate the man one has injured." In *Agricola* I think. Well, for once, he was fallible. I have injured you. I know it only too well. But hate you? Never! Though if you were to hate me, I should not be a whit surprised. Especially when I tell you that any day now you will read in the papers that I am to marry a Mister Roger Deveril, whose family used to live in Falmouth and who now lives in London. Believe me, I had not the faintest inkling, when I was in America, that this was about to happen, or I should have told you then.' New paragraph. 'He proposed to me in Falmouth two years ago ...' "

"Stop!" Rose said. "I remember it now."

"And you remember why you tore it up? You got as far as, 'How different our lives would have been if I had simply stepped into that boat with you at Nancemellin on the 18th of June two years ago!' A few more words and then ..." He made a noise imitating the tearing of paper.

"I couldn't find the right words," she said.

"To express what?"

"It kept sounding as if I was saying I was still in love with you but I was going to marry Roger anyway. I couldn't find the words that would give a different impression."

"A true impression?"

She didn't answer. After a while she asked, "D'you think Roger saw that in it, too?"

"He didn't say as much, not to me, anyway."

"No, but do you *think* he did?"

"What I think, dear, is not half so important as what *you* think."

"Oh God!" She halted, closed her eyes, and bowed her head.

"Here!" He nudged Edward back into her arms.

She accepted him mechanically. "I was so confused," she said. "And disappointed ..."

"Disappointed? After such a successful run in ..."

"Not that." She stared beyond him, up the neglected parkland. A lady – and she was sure it was Lady Carclew herself, stood at the very top of the path, beside the house. "I can see I have to tell you, Louis. And now you're going to see what a shallow, unworthy ... utterly despicable person I am – but I have to tell you. You see, I *did* come to Trenton ..."

She studied his reaction closely to see if it were news to him. He was either a better actor than any she had ever met, or his shock was genuine. "I hopped straight off the boat and on to a train. I met a woman on the train who had a cousin or brother-in law – I forget – called Elmer McKenna, who ..."

"Elmer! The clerk at the Windsor! I know him! By God, if he played you some idiot jape, I'll ..."

"No! Nothing like that! He told me you were in the bar. So I practically *ran* across the foyer, because, you see, I expected to find you in there talking big deals with other businessmen and ... I can't say it!" She buried her face in the shawl around Edward's body and mumbled. "I can't go on!"

Edward woke up and started crying. Then they were both crying. Somewhere way above her she heard Louis speaking in a voice that sounded curiously flat. "You saw me serving behind the bar and you thought ... Dear God!"

She nodded, still hiding her face from him. "I thought the Union League was, you know, a sort of trade union." Only a thought so preposterous could have made him laugh at that moment. "Here!" His hands lifted the baby from her; she turned three quarters away from him and scuffled blindly for her handkerchief. He put a clean one into her hands, ironed and folded.

Edward stopped crying and started giggling between one split second and the next. She looked through stuck eyelashes and remnant tears and saw Louis making grimaces with his tongue and staring cross-eyed at Edward, only inches from his nose. Edward kept trying to catch his elusive tongue, and missing, and giggling.

Lady Carclew was coming down the path. Rose ran to the water's edge and dipped the handkerchief in it, wringing it out and pressing it to her eyes – desperately trying to make it look as if she had not been crying at all.

When her ladyship drew near *that* spot, Rose cried out, "Stop! Stay there! I'm coming up."

Holding tight to her hat, she ran up the path to where an astounded Lady Carclew stood waiting. Had she forgotten? Did she not know what was about to happen?

Actually, what *was* about to happen?

Revenge of some kind? Of some completely unspecified, unprepared, unplanned-for kind?

She drew level. Breathless, she said, "We were about to come up ... I didn't want you to ... come all the way down ... only to have to ... turn round at once. Good afternoon, Lady Carclew." She offered her hand.

"Good afternoon, Mrs Deveril." Her ladyship took it and smiled benignly. "D'you know, when you called out to me to stop here, I thought you had *quite* a different purpose in mind! But I see you've forgotten what words were exchanged at this very spot, the last time we met here. Eh?"

Rose, still slightly out of breath, swallowed heavily and prepared to answer.

But the other continued. "And a good thing, too! I can't say I intended it – quite the opposite, in fact – but I believe I did you a favour that day. And an even greater favour when I made it impossible for you to continue in service – or am I wrong?"

Rose felt bitterly disappointed. In her present emotional turmoil she realized she was just spoiling for a fight. She longed to fight with *someone,* and this woman had seemed such an ideal target. But how could she – in the face of such determined sweetness? And, dammit, the woman was right, too. Being denied the chance to go into service was the best thing that ever happened to her.

However, she didn't for one moment believe that Lady Carclew had changed her character, nor her true opinion of her daughter's former lady's maid; but the woman belonged to that class and generation whose very instinct is to hide their true feelings in every awkward social situation – a subtle and invisible armour that had preserved them down the years on ancestral acres they had won in suits of steel and chain mail. To think of tackling it head-on was … well, *un*thinkable.

She smiled back, having recovered her breath by now – and her wits along with it. "Revenge?" she said. "My dear Lady Carclew, if I have learned only one thing in the past four years, it is that to 'get one's own back' as the saying has it, is quite impossible. If you cannot do it at once, you cannot do it at all. For, by the time you're in a position to do it, you find that 'your own' no longer exists. It has moved on. It has *aged.* It has become … how may I put it? A thing of no consequence … quite beneath one's dignity to bother about it at all."

Her ladyship froze. Her countenance turned gray and cold. Without another word she spun on her heel and walked away, back up the path toward the house.

"What was that?" Louis asked, approaching her at last.

"I was just keeping a promise."

"To her? She's not worth it." He chuckled grimly. "In fact, she's not worth much in *any* sense of the word. D'you know what she asked me yesterday?"

"What?"

"Did I want to buy the house! She's down on her uppers."

Rose gave an excited little scream, then stuffed her fingers into her mouth. "Did she hear?" she asked him, semi-coherently.

He glanced over her shoulder. "If she did, she's giving absolutely no sign of it."

"Tell her yes! Say you've thought it over and you'll agree."

"What?"

"Just do it! What is she asking?"

"Five thousand. The house will need a lot of …"

"Offer her four and go up to four and a half. As my agent, of course, except don't tell her that. Oh, her *face* when she finds out!"

He narrowed his eyes and peered into hers. "You're serious!"

"Of course I am. My cousin Frank can take this land – look at it! It's desperate for a bit of good husbandry. And we'll have … I don't know – a summer retreat? A place to sail from? A place for Mom and Pop to retire to …"

"We?" he echoed.

"Well … me," she said awkwardly. "My family … No."

She gave up.

Her face softened, her whole body relaxed, she lifted her fingers and touched his face gently.

"We," she said.

THE END